D1460881

READER'S DIGEST
SELECT EDITIONS

READER'S DIGEST
SELECT EDITIONS

www.readersdigest.co.uk

The Reader's Digest Association Limited
11 Westferry Circus Canary Wharf London E14 4HE

For information as to ownership of copyright in the material of this book, and acknowledgments, see last page.

Printed in Germany
ISBN 978 0 276 44216 2

SELECTED AND CONDENSED
BY READER'S DIGEST

THE READER'S DIGEST ASSOCIATION LIMITED, LONDON

from the editors

Picking new books for Select Editions is about as tricky as trying to place a winning bet on the Grand National. There is always a dazzling array of talent in sight, and it's a tough job studying the contenders, trying to predict the stars destined to gallop ahead of the pack as well as spotting the interesting outsiders set to surprise and delight. Just like any keen race-goers, we're always looking at form: is the plot suspenseful enough? Have the author's previous books been popular? What's the competition like?

And there *are* always surprises. While finalising this collection, we were informed of a late entry from legendary jockey-turned-writer, Dick Francis. With an excellent mystery, Stephen Booth's *Scared to Live*, already in the line-up, we weren't on the lookout for more sleuthing. But how could we ignore a new book from one of Britain's best-loved storytellers? We took the decision to put *Under Orders* on a fast track to publication, in order to get it into the hands of Select Editions readers as soon as it appears in the bookshops. It's been a heck of a gallop, but we hope you'll agree it was worth it.

The latest field of four are under starters orders now, ready for your enjoyment. Why not email us at Select_Editions@readersdigest.co.uk, and let us know which of our choices you think is destined for the winner's enclosure?

CONTENTS

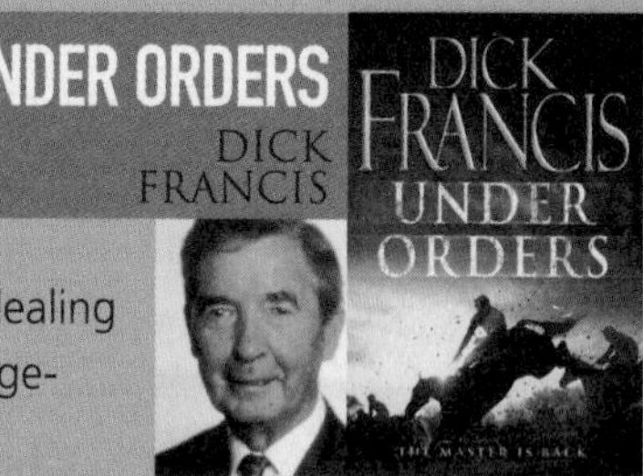

The nation's favourite storyteller is back with his first new novel in six years. Starring Sid Halley, the ex-champion jockey hero of Francis's early blockbusters, it's bang up-to-date in dealing with racing-related issues and combines page-turning excitement with warm romance.

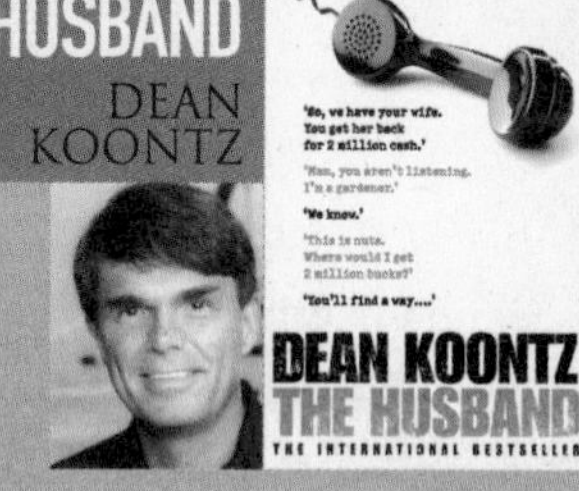

Imagine receiving a ransom demand and knowing you can't possibly pay—even though the life of the one person you love is on the line. That's the gripping premise of *The Husband*, which has shot up the charts in America and is being rated Dean Koontz's best book yet.

Shortlisted this year for a major award at the Harrogate Crime Writing Festival, *Scared to Live* is a double treat for crime fans: the setting is the stunning Peak District, rich in history and atmosphere; plus there's Booth's detective duo, Fry and Cooper, who are addictively likable.

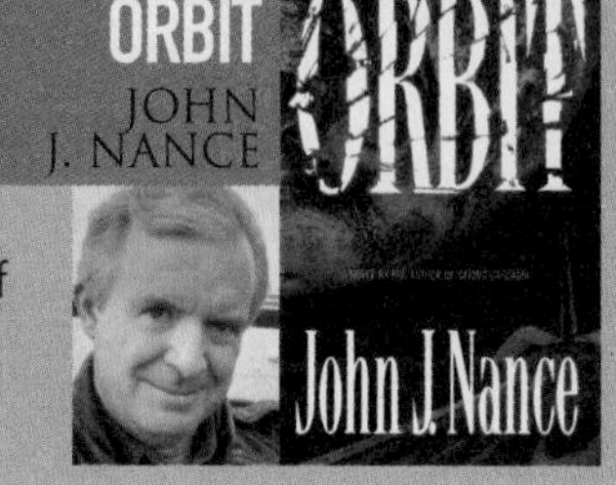

For Kip Dawson, winning a seat on a commercial space flight is a dream come true—until disaster strikes. Part rescue drama, part space adventure, *Orbit* tells the unusual story of a family man who becomes a hero when he's plunged into the worldwide media spotlight.

UNDER ORDERS

DICK FRANCIS

Steeplechase racing is a dangerous sport, as former champion jockey Sid Halley knows all too well, but in his heyday riders didn't usually end up with a round of bullets in the chest. However, that's precisely how he finds the winning jockey of the Triumph Hurdle at Cheltenham Races.

As Sid starts to investigate Huw Walker's death, he finds himself drawn into the murkier side of the high-stakes racing world.

CHAPTER 1

Sadly, death at the races is not uncommon.

However, three in a single afternoon was sufficiently unusual to raise more than an eyebrow. That only one of the deaths was of a horse was more than enough to bring the local constabulary hotfoot to the track.

CHELTENHAM GOLD CUP day had dawned bright and sunny with a fine dusting of a March frost showing white between the grass. The forecast for the day was dreadful, with heavy rain due to drive in from the west, but as I stood in my ex-father-in-law's kitchen looking through the window at the westerly sky, there was no sign yet of the warm front that was promised.

'There you are, Sid,' said Charles, coming into the kitchen in his dressing gown. Rear Admiral Charles Rowland, Royal Navy (retired), my ex-father-in-law, my confidant, my mentor and, without doubt, my best friend.

I still introduced him to strangers as my father-in-law, although it was now some ten years since his daughter, Jenny, my wife, had seen the need to give me an ultimatum: give up my job or she would give me up. Like any man at the top of his profession, I had assumed she didn't really mean it and continued to work day in and day out. And so Jenny left with acrimony and spite.

The fact that a crippling injury put paid to my chosen profession just a few months later, was one of those little ironies from which there is no escape. Jenny and I had divorced and she had remarried, to a title and serious wealth. Nowadays, we were civil to each other and I had real hope that an arm's-length affection might be the end game of our tempestuous relationship.

'Morning, Charles,' I said. 'It's a good one, too.'

'Bloody forecasters,' he replied, 'never have the slightest idea.' He looked out at the weather vane on the garage roof. 'Southwesterly,' he remarked. 'That front has still to arrive. Better take an umbrella with us.'

We went to the races in his Mercedes, with raincoats and umbrellas stacked on the back seat. As we drove from his home in the Oxfordshire village of Aynsford towards Cheltenham, the sun began to hide behind high cirrus clouds. It had disappeared altogether by the time we arrived at the racecourse, and there were spots of rain on the windscreen as we parked.

I had ridden so often round this course that I felt I knew each blade of grass as an old friend. In my dreams I still rode here, surging down the hill towards the home straight. It had been a racing fall that had ended my riding career. My young mount, stumbling while landing over the second fence in a novice chase, went down slowly to our right. I moved with the falling animal and rolled away from his flailing hooves. It was just unfortunate that a following horse, having nowhere else to go, had landed with all its weight on the outstretched palm of my left hand. But it was more criminal than unfortunate that the horse had been wearing an old racing shoe, sharpened by use into a jagged knife-edge, which had sliced through muscle, sinew, bone and tendon, leaving my hand useless and my life in ruins.

But I shouldn't complain. I had been Champion Jockey for four consecutive years, having won more jump races than anyone else, and by now, at thirty-eight, would probably have had to retire anyway.

'Sid,' Charles said, snapping me back to reality. 'Remember, I'm the guest of Lord Enstone today and he asked me whether you'd be coming up to his box for a drink later.'

'Maybe,' I said, still half thinking about what might have been.

'He seemed quite insistent that you should.'

Charles was pressing the point, and I knew him well enough to know that this was his way of saying that it was important to him.

'I'll be there.' I owed Charles a lot, and paybacks such as this were cheap. At least, that is what I thought at the time.

We joined the throng pouring into the racecourse from the car parks.

'Hello, Mr Halley,' said the gateman. 'What do you fancy for the big race?'

'Hello, Tom,' I replied, reading the name on his badge. 'Oven Cleaner must have a good chance, but don't quote me.'

He waved me through without properly checking my jockey's metal badge. Like me, it was getting a bit old and worn. I had not returned it when forced to retire and I had been using it ever since. No one seemed to mind.

Charles disappeared with a wave to make his way to the private luncheon boxes high in the grandstand while I walked unchallenged to the terrace in front of the weighing room next to the parade ring.

'Sid Halley!'

I turned with a smile.

'How's the sleuthing business?' Bill Burton, ex-jockey and now a mid-rank racecourse trainer whose waistline was getting bigger rather more quickly than his bank balance.

'Fine, Bill.' We shook hands warmly. 'Keeping me in mischief.'

'Good, as long as you keep your nose out of my business.' He said it with a smile that didn't quite reach his eyes.

We had ridden against each other regularly over many seasons, and I knew that he had never been averse to a little extra cash for ensuring that his horse didn't get to the line first. He would argue that he would only 'stop' those who had no chance anyway—what crime was there in that? I thought that he had probably not changed his ways. Bill was not a real villain, but rumours were beginning to circulate that he was not fully honest, either.

'Do you have any runners today?' I asked.

'Candlestick in the first and Leaded Light in the fifth. But I wouldn't risk your shirt on either of them.'

I wasn't sure whether he was warning me that they might not be trying their best. My doubts saddened me. I liked Bill a lot.

He turned away. 'Sorry, Sid,' he said. 'Got to go and find my jockey.'

I watched him disappear through the door to the weighing room, then I looked up in the paper who his jockey was. Huw Walker. One of the sport's popular journeymen. He had never yet made it to number one but had been consistently in the top ten over the past eight or nine years, with numerous rides and plenty of winners. Son of a Welsh farmer with, it was said, a fondness for fast women and fast cars, in that order.

In one of those strange, almost supernatural moments, I looked up to find Huw Walker coming towards me.

'Hello, Huw,' I said.

'Hi Sid. Did you get my message?' He looked far from his usual cheery self.

'No,' I replied. 'Where did you leave it?'

'On your answering machine. Last night.'

'Sorry, I'm staying with my father-in-law for the Festival.'

'It doesn't matter. I can't talk here. I'll call you again later.'

'Use my mobile,' I said, and gave him the number.

He rushed off, disappearing into the weighing room.

EVEN THOUGH it was still well over an hour to the first race, it was beginning to be rather crowded on the weighing room terrace. There was the usual mix of officialdom and press, bloodstock agents and the media, trainers and their jockeys, present and past. Here the gossip of the week was swapped, juicy rumours spread like Asian flu—who was sleeping with whom, and who had been caught doing so by a spouse. I wandered through the throng with my ears open, catching up on events in racingland.

'Useless jockey, flogged my horse half to death just to get a third place.' A large, duffle-coated trainer, Andrew Woodward, was in full flow in front of a small group. 'Damn idiot got himself banned for four days. I'll give him excessive use of the whip on *his* bloody arse if he does that again.'

His fan club chuckled, but I believed him. Having once found his teenage daughter canoodling with a jockey in the feed store, he had held the hapless young man down over a hay bale and thrashed him with a riding whip.

He was a good trainer but he had a well-deserved reputation as a hater of jockeys. I had ridden for him a few times and more than once had received the lash of his tongue when results did not pan out as expected. He was not on my Christmas card list.

I drifted over nearer to the steps down to the parade ring, where I had spotted someone I *did* want to talk to.

'Sid, my old mucker!' Paddy O'Fitch was a fellow ex-jockey and a walking encyclopedia on racing. He spoke with a Belfast accent and revelled in all things Irish, but the truth was that he had been born in Liverpool and christened Harold. The surname on his passport was just Fitch.

'Hello, Paddy,' I said, smiling.

We shook hands, the camaraderie between us as ex-jockeys being far greater than that between us when we were competing day by day.

After retiring from the saddle six years before, Paddy had turned his knowledge into a business. He wrote brief but wonderfully entertaining histories of racecourses and races, of racing characters and great horses, then sold them as slim booklets in racecourse car parks around the country. The booklets were soon selling so fast that Paddy had employed staff to sell while he busied himself with the writing.

'What chance do you think Candlestick has in the first?' I asked him.

'Could win. It depends . . .' He stopped.

'On what?' I prompted.

'Whether it's trying.' He paused. 'Why do you ask?'

'I thought I might have a bet.' I tried to make it sound normal.

'Bejesus! Now did ya hear dat!' He addressed no one in particular. 'Sid Halley's having a bet. And pigs may fly, I s'pose.' He laughed. 'Now don't be telling lies, Sid. Why *did* ya ask about Candlestick?'

'What makes you think it may not be trying?' I asked instead of answering.

'I didn't say dat,' he said. 'I merely said dat it could win *if* it was trying.'

'But you must think it may not be, else why say it?'

'Rumours, rumours, that's all,' he said. 'The grapevine says dat Burton's horses are not always doing their best.'

It was at this point that the first of the day's deaths occurred.

At Cheltenham, one end of the parade ring doubles as the winner's unsaddling enclosure. A semicircular stepped viewing area rises up from the rail round the ring. This early on a wet afternoon it was almost empty, with a few hardy folk under umbrellas watching the comings and goings at the weighing room and waiting for the sports to begin.

'Help! Help! Somebody help me!'

A middle-aged woman was screaming from the bottom of the stepped area. All eyes swivelled in her direction.

She continued to scream. 'For God's sake, someone help me!'

Paddy and I ran over to the rail on the inside of the parade ring, where we immediately could see that it was not the woman but the man she was with who was in trouble. He was lying at her feet, up against the four-foot high chain-link wire fence that kept the crowd away from the horses.

The racecourse doctor, more used to treating injured jockeys, ran from the weighing room, speaking rapidly into his walkie-talkie. Two green-clad paramedics came hurrying into the parade ring, carrying large red back-packs. The chain-link fence was in their way, so an enterprising group of bystanders lifted the poor man over the top of it. He was laid on the closely mown grass, exactly where the afternoon's winners would later be.

The doctor and the paramedics set to work, but it soon became clear that they were fighting a losing battle. They took it in turns to force air into the lungs or compress the chest. Almost half an hour had passed before they began to show signs of giving up. By then an ambulance had driven into the parade ring. The man was lifted onto a stretcher, but it was clearly all over for him. Another heart attack fatality, just one more statistic.

With the departure of the victim, accompanied by his grieving wife, the crowds drifted away to the bars to get out of the rain, tut-tutting about the shame of it and the need to look after our bodies. Sales of crackling at the hog roast stall didn't seem to be affected.

I WATCHED the first race from the Owners and Trainers Stand. The Triumph Hurdle is the blue riband event for four-year novice hurdlers over a distance of two miles and a furlong. The start was impressive as the twenty-five runners spread right across the course, resembling a cavalry charge to the first flight of hurdles. The climb to the highest point of the course began to sort them out, and there were only half a dozen or so in with a chance as they swung left-handed and down the hill. Huw Walker on Candlestick was third going to the second last, where the leader got too close to the hurdle, hit the top and fell in a flurry of legs. Huw pulled left to avoid the carnage and kicked Candlestick hard in the ribs.

It was one of those finishes that gives racing a good name. Four horses jumped the final flight abreast and the jockeys almost disappeared in a whirl of arms and whips as they strove to get the final effort from their mounts. There was no question that, this time, Candlestick was trying his best, with Huw Walker driving hard for the line. His labours were well rewarded as they flashed past the post to win by a head.

Pleased, I walked back to the paddock to see the horse come back in, only to find that the trainer Bill Burton was looking like thunder. It seemed that a win was not in his game plan. If he's not careful, I thought, he will confirm to all those watching that the rumours are true.

I leaned on the rail and watched Bill Burton and Huw Walker unsaddle the sweating horse. They seemed oblivious of the thousands around them as they shouted insults at each other. The confrontation appeared to be heading towards violence when an official stepped in and pulled Bill Burton away.

Huw looked in my direction, saw me, shrugged his shoulders, winked and then smiled broadly as he went past me to be weighed.

I was standing there wondering what to make of all that when I was slapped hard on my back. Chris Beecher, mid-forties, balding and overweight. A journalist and a pain in the neck—and the back.

'How's that fancy hook of yours?'

He didn't seem to realise that it was one of those questions one shouldn't ask. Rather like enquiring if that strawberry birthmark on your face goes brown in the sun. Some things were best left alone. But Chris Beecher made his living hurting other people's feelings. He was responsible for the Diary page in *The Pump*, a daily and Sunday newspaper that I'd been at odds with some year ago. Half of what he wrote was pure fiction, but there was enough truth in the rest so that many believed it all.

My fancy hook, as he called it, was an expensive myoelectric false left hand. What the jagged horseshoe had started had been well and truly finished by a sadistic villain, and I was now the proud owner of a state-of-the-art hook. In truth, I had learned to do most things one-handed but I wore the false limb as a cosmetic defence against people's stares.

'Ready for action,' I said, turning and offering my left hand for a shake.

'Not bloody likely! You'll crush my fingers with that thing. I've heard stories of you hitting people with that and, by all accounts, they stay hit.'

It was true, I'd broken a couple of jaws. No point in fighting clean when I had a ready-made club firmly attached below my left elbow.

'What do you make of that little exchange between trainer and jockey then?' he asked, with apparent innocence.

'Don't know what you mean.'

'Ah, come off it,' he said. 'Everyone must have seen that tiff.'

'What's the story, then?' I asked, equally innocently.

'Obvious, Walker won when he wasn't meant to. No stable money on the nose. I'll be surprised if the stewards don't have them in. Fancy a beer?'

'Some other time. I promised my father-in-law I'd have a drink with him.'

'Ex-father-in-law,' he corrected.

'No secrets on the racecourse, not from you, anyway.'

'Now you're really joking. I couldn't beat a secret out of you if you didn't want to tell. I've heard that on the grapevine.'

He had heard too much, I thought.

'How's your love life?' he asked abruptly.

'None of your business.'

'See what I mean.' He tapped me on the chest. 'Who's Sid Halley screwing now? The best-kept secret in racing.'

He went off in search of easier prey. I watched him go and wondered how he got to sleep at night. Who Sid Halley was presently 'screwing' was indeed one of the facts I tried to keep from the racecourse. Apart from keeping my work and my pleasure separate, I knew from experience that I was vulnerable to threats being made against those I loved. Much safer for me, and for them, if their existence was unknown.

LORD ENSTONE'S BOX was bursting at the seams. As I forced my way in, a waitress offered me a glass of champagne. As a general rule, I held drinks in my real right hand, but it made shaking hands so complicated, and I felt that I should use my left more to justify the large amount of money I had spent to acquire it. So I carefully sent the correct impulses and the thumb of my left hand closed just enough round the stem of the glass. I had shattered even best crystal by not knowing how hard to grip with my unfeeling digits to prevent a glass from falling out. It could be humiliating.

Charles had spotted me across the throng and made his way to my side. 'Got a drink, good,' he said. 'Come and see Jonny.'

We squeezed our way out onto the balcony that ran the length of the grandstand in front of the glass-fronted boxes. The view from here across the racecourse and beyond to the hills was magnificent, even on a dull day.

Three men were standing close together at the far end of the balcony. One of them was Jonny. Jonny was our host, Lord Enstone. Another was Jonny's son, Peter. The third I knew only by reputation. I had never actually met George Lochs. He was in his thirties and already a big player in the Internet gambling business. His company, make-a-wager.com, was expanding rapidly and, with it, so was young George's fortune.

I had once been commissioned by the Jockey Club to do a background check on him, a routine procedure for those applying for bookmaking licences. He was the second son of a bookie's runner from north London. He'd won a free scholarship to Harrow, where apparently the other boys had laughed at his funny accent and the way he held his knife. But George had learned fast, conformed and flourished. Except that he hadn't been called George then. He had been born Clarence Lochstein, named by his mother after the Duke of Clarence pub at the end of her road in Islington.

There were rumours that Clarence/George had been asked to leave Harrow for taking bets on the horses from the other boys and, it was said, from some of the staff. However, he still won a place at the London School of Economics. Clarence Lochstein/George Lochs was a bright chap.

'Can I introduce Sid Halley?' said Charles.

George Lochs jumped. While his reputation had reached me, mine had also clearly reached him. It was a reaction I was quite used to. It's a bit like when a police car stops behind you at traffic lights. A strange feeling of guilt inevitably comes over you, even when you've done nothing wrong.

'Sid. Good. Glad you could come.' Lord Enstone smiled broadly. 'Have you met George Lochs? George, Sid.'

We shook hands and looked into each other's eyes. His gave nothing away.

'And you know my son, Peter,' he said.

I had met him once or twice on racecourses. We nodded in recognition. Peter was an averagely competent amateur jockey in his early thirties who had for some years enjoyed limited success, mostly in amateur races.

'Do you have a ride in the Foxhunters later?' I asked him.

'I wish,' he said. 'Couldn't convince an owner to put me up.'

'What about your father's horses?' I asked, giving his father a wink.

'No bloody chance,' said Peter with a halfhearted smile. 'Mean old bastard won't let me ride them.'

'If the boy wants to break his neck riding in races, that's his business, but I don't want to aid and abet him,' said Jonny, ruffling his son's blond hair. 'I'd never forgive myself.'

Peter pulled his head away from his father's hand with irritation and stomped off through the doorway. It was clearly a much discussed topic.

'Charles, take young George here inside and find him a glass of fizz,' said Lord Enstone. 'I want to have a word with Sid in private.'

A few years previously, I had done a check on Enstone for a horse-owning syndicate that he had wanted to join. Jonny Enstone was a builder. He had left school in Newcastle at sixteen to become an apprentice bricklayer with J. W. Best Ltd, a small local building company. Within two years he was running the business, and soon after he bought out the owner. Expansion was rapid and, under the banner 'The J. W. Best built house you'll ever buy', Best Houses marched north, south and west, covering the country with smart little three- and four-bedroomed boxes from Glasgow to Plymouth. Jonny Enstone had become Sir John, then Lord Enstone, but he still had his hands on his business.

'Now, Sid,' Enstone said as Charles and George walked off. 'I need you to find out something for me.'

'I'll try,' I said.

'I want you to find out why my horses aren't winning when they should be.'

It was something I was regularly asked to do. I inwardly sighed. Most owners think their horses should be winning more often than they do.

'I think,' he went on, 'my jockey and trainer are stopping them.'

That was what they all thought.

'Move them to another trainer.' I was doing myself out of a commission.

'It's not as simple as that. I tell you, my horses are not just not winning when they should, they're running to orders that aren't mine. I feel I'm being used and I don't like it.' I could suddenly see the real Jonny Enstone beneath the Savile Row exterior: powerful, determined, even dangerous.

'I'm in racing because I like to *win*. It's not the money that's important, it's the *winning*.'

'Who trains your horses?' I asked. 'And who rides them?'

'Bill Burton and Huw Walker.'

I STAYED TO WATCH the Gold Cup from Lord Enstone's box. The balcony was heaving with bodies pressed up against the front rail as everyone strove to get a view of the supreme challenge for a steeplechaser, three and a quarter miles over twenty-two fences, all horses carrying the same weight. The winner of the Cheltenham Gold Cup was a true champion.

I had ridden eight times in this race and I knew all too well the nervous anticipation being experienced by the jockeys as they paraded in front of the packed grandstands. This was one of only two or three really big jump races in the year that put the winning horse and jockey into the history books. For a horse to win this race more than once was the stuff of dreams. Winning it three times put the animal into the legend category.

Oven Cleaner, in spite of his name, was aiming to join the legends.

As I watched the big grey canter down to the start with the others, I wondered if I would ever stop envying those doing what I still longed to do.

I hadn't sat on a horse until I was sixteen, when my widowed mother, dying of kidney cancer, had taken me to be apprenticed to a Newmarket trainer simply because I was very small for my age and I would soon be an orphan. But I had taken to riding like the proverbial duck to water. I found the bond between horse and rider exhilarating, especially when I realised that I could read their minds. When I discovered that they could also read mine, I knew I was part of a winning combination.

And so it had been until it all fell apart. A jockey feels a horse through his hands on the reins connecting like power cables to the horse's mouth, transmitting commands and data in both directions. With only one hand, it was like a battery with only one end. Useless—no circuit, no transmission, no data, no go. At least, no go fast, which is what racehorses are supposed to do.

I watched the best steeplechasers in the world gallop past the stands on the first circuit and positively ached to be among them. It had been ten years since I'd ridden in a race, but it felt like only yesterday.

Oven Cleaner cleaned up. In his trademark manner, he looked to all to have left his run too late but, to a deafening roar from his tens of thousands of faithful supporters, he charged up the hill to win by a whisker.

The crowd went wild, cheering and shouting and even throwing their soggy hats into the air. The big grey nodded his head in approval as he took the applause on the walk to the winner's unsaddling enclosure. He was a hero and he knew it.

The cheering rose to a new height as the legend was led into the enclosure by his euphoric lady owner.

Then the legend died.

Tears of joy turned to tears of despair as the much loved champion suddenly stumbled and collapsed onto the grass, pulling down his owner and pinning her leg under his half-ton bulk. The crowd fell silent.

Oven Cleaner had given his all. His heart, so strong in carrying him up the Cheltenham hill to victory, had failed him in his moment of triumph.

Willing hands managed to free the poor owner, but she refused to leave for medical treatment on her broken ankle, cradling the horse's head in her lap and crying the inconsolable tears of the bereaved.

I watched a vet examine the animal. He placed a stethoscope to the grey-haired chest and listened for a few seconds. He stood up, pursed his lips and shook his head.

DEEP GLOOM descended on the racecourse. The fourth race on Gold Cup day is the Foxhunter Steeple Chase. The favourite won but returned to almost silent grandstands. The will to cheer had gone out of the crowd, which politely applauded the winner's return.

'Where's that bloody jockey of mine?' Bill Burton was asking anyone and everyone outside the weighing room.

'Huw Walker?' I asked, as Bill hurried towards me.

'Bloody unreliable bastard, that's what he is. He's due to ride Leaded Light in the next but he's gone bloody AWOL. Have you seen him, Sid?'

I shook my head.

'I'll have to declare another jockey.' He went back inside.

Leaded Light was beaten into second place in a close finish that should have had the crowd on their feet shouting. Such was the mood that the jockey on the winner didn't even look happy at having won. I decided I'd had enough. I opted to wait for Charles at his car.

I was making my way past the rows of outside broadcast TV vans when a wide-eyed young woman came stumbling towards me. She was unable to speak but she pointed down the gap between two of the vans.

She had found Huw Walker.

He sat leaning against the wheel of one of the vans, looking at me with an expression of surprise. Except his eyes could not see and never would again.

He was still wearing his riding clothes and a blue anorak to keep out the rain. It hung open so that I could clearly see the three closely grouped bullet wounds in the middle of his chest showing red against his white shirt. There seemed little doubt as to the cause of death.

CHAPTER 2

Charles and I didn't arrive back at Aynsford until after midnight.

The police cancelled the last race of the day and closed the racecourse, refusing to let anyone leave. Totally ill-equipped to interview nearly 60,000 people, they relented in the end and allowed the wet, angry and frustrated multitude to make its way to the car parks and home.

I didn't get away quite so easily as I was a material witness, and I reluctantly agreed to go to their hastily established incident room to give a statement. I pointed out that I hadn't actually been the first to find poor Huw. However, the young woman who had was so shocked that she had been sedated by a doctor. She was unable to speak to the police. Lucky her.

It was clear that they had received reports of the shouting match between Bill Burton and Huw Walker after Candlestick's victory in the first. The trainer, it appeared, was already their prime suspect.

I pointed out to Detective Chief Inspector Carlisle of Gloucestershire CID that Huw had obviously been killed by an expert assassin, who must have brought a gun with him to the races for the purpose, and that Bill Burton couldn't have magically produced a shooter out of thin air.

'Ah,' he said, 'maybe that's what we are meant to think while, meantime, Burton had planned it all along.'

I promised to contact them again if I thought of anything else which might be important. I remembered the message on my London answerphone and decided not to mention it. I wanted to listen to it first, and the remote access system on my machine was broken.

THE FOLLOW MORNING, all the national dailies ran the ecstasy and agony of Oven Cleaner on their front pages. *The Times* ran the story over the first three pages with graphic photographs of his victory and the subsequent disaster.

Only on page seven was there a report of the discovery of the body of jockey Huw Walker by Sid Halley, ex-champion jockey and now private detective. Even this item referred to the sad demise of the equine hero. There was no mention of the three bullet wounds in Huw's chest.

The *Racing Post* went even further, with an eight-page spread of Oven Cleaner's career and an obituary to rival that of a prime minister.

'It was only a bloody horse,' declared Charles over breakfast. 'Like that memorial in London for the animals in war. Ridiculous sentimental rubbish.'

'Come on, Charles,' I said. 'I've seen you almost in tears over your dogs when they die. Same thing.'

'Poppycock!' But he knew it was true. 'When are you off?' he asked, changing the subject.

'After breakfast. I have some reports to write.'

'Come again. Come as often as you like. I like having you here and I miss you when you're gone.'

I was surprised, but pleased. Charles was not one to show his emotions openly. He had initially detested his daughter marrying a jockey. Not a suitable match, he'd thought, for the daughter of an admiral. A game of chess, which I had won, had been the catalyst to an enduring friendship that had survived the break-up of my marriage.

'Thank you,' I said. 'I enjoy being here and I will come again soon.'

We both knew that I tended to come to Aynsford only when I was in trouble or depressed, or both. Anysford had become my sanctuary and my therapy. It was my rock in the turbulent waters I had chosen as my home.

I LEFT PROMPTLY after breakfast and drove home to London along a relatively empty M40. The rain beat relentlessly on the roof of my Audi as I made my way round Hyde Park Corner and into Belgravia. I lived in a fourth-floor flat in Ebury Street and, after five years, it was beginning to feel like home. Not least because I did not live there on my own.

Who Sid Halley was presently 'screwing', the secret I kept from Chris Beecher, was Marina van der Meer, a Dutch blonde beauty, and a member of a team of chemists at the Cancer Research UK laboratories in Lincoln's Inn Fields searching for the Holy Grail—a simple blood test to find cancers long before any symptoms appear.

When I arrived back at noon, she was sitting in our large bed wearing a fluffy pink towelling robe and reading the Saturday papers.

'Well, well, quite the little Sherlock Holmes!' She pointed to a picture of me in the *Telegraph*. 'It says here that you discovered the body. I bet Colonel Mustard did it in the conservatory with the lead piping.' Her English was perfect with a faint hint of accent. Music to my ears.

'Well, he might have done, but he must have melted the lead piping into bullets first.'

She looked surprised. 'It doesn't say he was shot.'

'The police kept that gem to themselves and I didn't tell the press either.'

'Wow!'

'What are you still doing in bed, anyway?' I asked lying down beside her on the duvet. 'It's nearly lunchtime.'

'I'm not hungry.'

'Fancy working up an appetite?' I grinned.

'I thought you'd never ask.' She giggled and shrugged the robe off her slender shoulders.

Chris Beecher, eat your heart out.

We lay in bed for much of the afternoon, watching the racing on the television while I should have been writing up reports for clients. We decided against a walk to St James's Park because of the rain, but eventually we did huddle under an umbrella and make our way to Santini, the Italian restaurant on the corner. Marina had chicken while I chose Dover sole, off the bone.

We contentedly shared a bottle of Chablis and caught up on the week.

'Tell me more about the jockey who was killed?' Marina asked.

'He was nice enough. In fact, I spoke with him earlier.' I remembered Huw's message still sitting unheard on my machine. 'He won the first race,' I said. But I wondered if he should have. Had he been told to lose? Was that why he'd died?

The rain had stopped by the time we walked back to the flat hand in hand—her left, my right—dodging the puddles and laughing out loud. This was why I never took Marina to the races. This was a different world, one in which I could relax, one in which I was increasingly happy and near to the point where I would seek to make it permanent. We stopped and kissed at least four times during the short fifty-yard stroll and went straight back to bed.

I had always preferred lovemaking to be gentle and sensual and it was clearly Marina's pleasure, too. After the violence of the previous day, I found solace in her tender embrace. Afterwards we lay in the dark, touching occasionally, close to sleep.

I gently eased myself out of bed and went into the bathroom to remove my arm. The five or so inches remaining of my left forearm fitted snugly into the open end of a hard fibreglass cylinder. The steel myoelectric hand was attached to the bottom end of the cylinder. A tight-fitting rubber cosmetic glove covered the hand and wrist, and shapes had been moulded into the rubber to represent fingernails and tendons, with bluish lines for veins. The fingers were permanently slightly bent, and the hand was able to grip between forefinger and thumb by means of an electric motor that moved the thumb in and out. The motor was powered by a rechargeable battery that clipped into a recessed holder above the wrist.

Electrodes inside the arm-cylinder were held close to my skin near to where my real arm ceased. I had had to learn how to open and close the hand using impulses I had previously used for bending my wrist. Try to move back the real hand that wasn't there and the false hand opened. Move it forward and the hand closed. Unfortunately there was a slight delay between impulse and action and, consequently, I had broken eggs and almost everything else I gripped. Nowadays, the thought processes were second nature, but I still tended not to stop the impulses soon enough and breakages were common. Hence I had learned to live a mostly one-handed life.

The open end of the arm cylinder fitted over my elbow, a plastic cuff gripping tightly round the ends of what was left of my ulna and radius bones, the bumps on each side of the elbow. I was impressed by the strength of the join, and had recently discovered that, if I locked my elbow straight and stressed my biceps, I could use the arm to hang my whole body weight.

I bent my elbow as far as it would go, eased the plastic away from my skin and placed it on the shelf over the washbasin. As I padded along the hallway to the kitchen to get some water, I noticed the flashing light on the answering machine in my office. I pushed the button and the mechanical voice answered: 'You have six messages.'

The second was from Huw Walker.

'Hi, Sid,' he said in his usual jovial manner. 'I wish you were there. I need to talk to you.' The laughter had faded from his voice. 'I'm in a bit of trouble and I . . .' He paused. 'I know this sounds daft but I'm frightened.'

There was another brief pause. 'Actually, Sid, no kidding, I'm really frightened. Someone called me on the phone and threatened to kill me. I thought they were bloody joking so I told them to eff off and put the phone down. But they rang back and it's given me the willies. I thought it was all a bit of a lark but now I find that it ain't. I need your bloody help this time, mate, and no mistake. Call me back. Please call me back.'

There was another long pause then there was a click and the next message played. It was from my financial adviser, reminding me to buy an ISA before the end of the tax year. Message four was also from Huw.

'Where are you when I need you, you bugger?' His voice was slurred and he had obviously been drinking in the time between messages. 'Come on, pick up the bloody phone, you bastard! Can't you tell when a mate's in trouble.' There was a pause in which I could hear him swallow. 'Just a few losers, they says, for a few hundred in readies, they says. OK, I says, but make it a few grand.' He sighed loudly. 'Do as we tell you, they says, or the only grand you'll see is the drop from the top of the effing grandstand.' He was now crying. 'Should have bloody listened, shouldn't I?'

The message ended abruptly.

I stood in the dark and thought of him as I had last seen him; three closely grouped deadly holes in his heart.

Yes, he should have bloody listened.

ARCHIE KIRK called me at eleven o'clock on Sunday morning as Marina and I were still sitting in bed in our robes, surrounded by the newspapers.

'Thought you were meant to be a *private* detective,' he said. 'Not very private to be splashed across the front pages.'

I assumed Archie was referring to the front-page banner headline in *The Pump* that read SID HALLEY IN CHELTENHAM MURDER MYSTERY above a three-column photograph of me looking extremely furtive. Someone in their newsroom clearly had a source in the Cheltenham police who had reported that 'Sid Halley, ex-champion steeplechase jockey, is helping the police with their enquiries into the murder of jockey Huw Walker at Cheltenham races on Friday. No arrest has been made at this time.'

'Ridiculous,' I said. 'They're fishing.'

'Nevertheless,' said Archie, 'enough people will believe it.'

Archie was some sort of civil servant, but he didn't belong to any specific department. Nominally, he answered to the Cabinet Office, but he appeared to work in his own way with little contact with, or regard for, his superiors. He was the chairman of a small group tasked with attempting to foretell the future. Its remit was to try to work out the consequences of proposed legislation, to try to ensure that it would do what was intended without any unpleasant side effects that had been overlooked. Officially it was called the Standing Cabinet Subcommittee on Legislative Outcomes, but was referred to by the few who knew of its existence as the Crystal Ball Club.

I respected Archie and had grown to like him more and more as, over the past four years, I had become his very private ears and eyes.

'Well, what are you going to do about *The Pump*?' Archie asked.

'Oh.' I paused to think. 'Nothing. Their lawyers will have made sure they haven't libelled me. It's just absurd speculation.'

Laced with loathing, I assumed, but I didn't like them much either.

'Why don't you rant and rave like any normal man?' Archie asked.

'You wouldn't,' I replied. Archie was one of the most even-tempered men I had ever met. 'What good would it do? *The Pump* seems to have it in for me again, and complaining will only make it worse.'

I had once shown *The Pump* to be completely wrong about someone who they claimed to be a saint but who turned out to be a bigger sinner than even I had realised. The press doesn't like to be shown to be foolish.

'It's so unfair.' I rarely heard such anger in Archie's voice.

'Look, Archie,' I said, 'this is not worth getting upset about. Let it blow over.' Let the police find the killer, I thought.

'Can you come and see me at the office tomorrow?' Archie asked, changing the subject.

'Ten?' I suggested.

'Fine.'

I didn't ask him what it was about. Archie was a secretive man, and on the telephone he habitually gave an excellent impression of a Trappist monk. He didn't trust telephones and, as an ex-member of MI5, he should know. Today he had been unusually effusive and was probably regretting it already.

MARINA AND I DECIDED to walk to the Goring Hotel for a glass of wine and a light lunch. We took the lift down and stepped out into the marble-floored lobby. I had chosen this apartment building partly because of the twenty-four-hour manned desk facing the entrance, with its bank of CCTV monitors. I had been attacked outside my previous home, so I valued the peace of mind provided by the team of porters/security men.

'Morning, Derek,' I said.

'Afternoon, Mr Halley,' he corrected.

An eclectic band of individuals, reassuring, reliable and discreet, no one set foot in the building without their knowledge and say-so.

Half an hour later, sustained by a shared smoked salmon sandwich and a glass of wine, we hurried back to the flat in watery March sunshine.

'Ah, Mr Halley,' said Derek as we walked in, 'guest for you.'

My 'guest' was sitting in the lobby. He was in his mid-sixties and was wearing dirty brown corduroy trousers and an old green sweater with a hole in the front. A shock of grey hair protruded from under a well-worn cap.

In his right hand he held a copy of *The Pump*.

'Sid Halley!' he said, getting up and taking two quick steps towards me.

Oh no, not again. I looked around for reinforcement from Derek, but he had decided to stay in relative safety behind his desk.

Instead of trying to hit me, however, the man thrust the newspaper in my face. 'Did you kill my son?' he demanded at maximum decibels.

I nearly laughed but thought better of it. 'No, I did not.'

'No, I didn't really think so,' he said, speaking in a strong Welsh accent, and his shoulders slumped. 'But *The Pump* seemed so . . . so believable.' He sat down heavily on the arm of the chair. 'I've driven all the way here from Brecon.' He gulped and his eyes filled with tears. 'I set out to kill you. In revenge. But the more I drove, the more stupid that seemed. It wouldn't bring Huw back, and by the time I'd gone halfway I realised you wouldn't have done it. Huw always says'—he faltered—'said . . . that you, look, are on the side of the bloody angels. God, what am I doing here?' He began to cry, his shoulders jerking up and down with great sobs.

Marina squatted next to him. 'Mr Walker.' Her melodic tone brought his chin up a fraction. 'Let's go upstairs and get you a cup of tea.'

She stood and pulled him to his feet and guided him towards the lift.

In the flat, she fussed around Mr Walker like a mother hen, and soon had him sitting on the sofa sipping sweet tea from a blue-and-white striped mug.

'What's your name?' she asked while stroking his hand.

He smiled at her. 'Evan,' he said.

'Well, Evan,' she smiled back, 'have you had anything to eat for lunch?'

'To tell you the truth,' he said, 'I haven't had anything to eat since Friday night. Since when the police came to tell . . .' He tailed off, the memory still too raw to describe. 'I don't feel like eating.'

Nevertheless, Marina disappeared into the kitchen.

'How did you know where I lived?' I asked.

'I didn't,' he said. 'The man from *The Pump* told me.'

'You just phoned them up and they gave you my address?'

'No, I didn't phone *them*.' He looked slightly disturbed. 'A man from *The Pump* phoned *me* at six o'clock in the morning. He read the whole thing out to me over the phone. I was bloody mad, I can tell you. "Sid Halley murdered your son," he said, and he said you'd probably get away with it because you'd done a deal with the police. Then he gave me your address and asked me what I was going to do about it.'

'Was it a man called Chris Beecher?' I asked.

'I don't know, I didn't ask his name.' He paused again and shook his head. 'Right bloody idiot I've been. See that now, but at the time I was so bloody angry.' He dropped his eyes from mine. 'I'm glad that bloody drive was long and complicated enough for me to come to my senses.'

So was I.

He sighed, 'I suppose you'll call the police now?'

'How were you going to kill me?' I asked, ignoring his question.

'With my shotgun. It's still in the car.'

'Where?' I asked.

'Outside on the road.'

'I'll get it,' I said. 'What type of car and where are the keys?'

'Old grey Ford.' He patted his flat pockets. 'Keys must be in it.'

I went down and it was still there with the keys in the ignition, unstolen. Amazingly, the shotgun was still there, lying in plain view on the back seat.

I picked it up, locked the car and turned to go back upstairs.

I am not sure why I noticed the young man in a car on the far side of the road take aim at me. I strode straight across to him and lifted the business end of the shotgun I was holding in his general direction.

He had aimed not a gun but a camera, which he now lowered to his lap. An experienced paparazzo would have gone on snapping, I thought.

'What are you after?' I shouted at him through the closed car window. 'Put the window down.'

He pushed a button and the window opened a couple of inches.

'Who sent you?' I asked through the crack.

He didn't reply.

'Tell Chris Beecher he shouldn't tell tall stories to Welsh farmers,' I said.

He looked at me, then nodded slightly. I lowered the shotgun. Deciding that retreat was the best plan, the young man ground his gears and was gone.

I strode back through the lobby, grinning broadly, with the gun slung over my shoulder. Derek, who had watched the whole episode through the glass, stared at me with an open mouth.

I winked at him as the lift closed.

EVAN WALKER stayed for another hour before remembering that he had cattle to feed. In the meantime, he managed to consume four slices of toast with lashings of strawberry jam, and two more mugs of tea.

He talked about Huw and how proud he was of him.

'Glynis, that's my wife, and me, we were so pleased when he won the Welsh National at Chepstow. Best thing that happened to us for ages. Glynis passed away last October, see. Cancer it was.' He was again close to tears. 'Stomach. Poor lass couldn't eat. Starved to death, really.'

'Do you have any other children?' I asked.

'Did have,' he said. 'Another boy, Brynn. Two year older than Huw. Knocked off his bike, he was. On his way to school. On his fifteenth birthday.'

Life is full of buggers.

'Glynis never got over it,' he went on. 'Buried next to him she is.' There was a long pause as he stared down at the floor. 'Suppose I should put Huw with them.' Another longer pause. 'Just me left now.'

He stood up. 'It says in that damn rag that you're a private detective. I remember you as a jockey. I often wondered what Huw would do when he gave up riding . . . Doesn't matter now . . . Anyway, what I meant to say was, will you find out for me who killed my son.'

'The police will do that,' I said.

'The police are fools,' said Evan forcefully. 'They never found out who killed our Brynn. Hit-and-run, you see. Never really tried, if you ask me.'

I noticed that Marina's eyes had filled with tears. Just how much pain could a single man take?

'I'll pay for your time,' he told me. 'Please . . . find out who killed my Huw.'

I thought of the desperate messages Huw had left on my answering machine. How could I say no?

'I'll do my best,' I said.

I LAY AWAKE for much of the night thinking nasty thoughts about what I would like to do to Chris Beecher and his young snapper. Sure enough, the Monday edition of *The Pump* had, on its Diary page, a photograph of Marina and me walking hand in hand along Ebury Street with the headline, WHO'S SID HALLEY'S NEW GIRLFRIEND? The picture seemed to accentuate the fact that Marina was some four inches taller than I am, and the brief paragraph underneath was hardly flattering, with the words 'divorced', 'diminutive' and 'crippled' all making an appearance alongside 'murder suspect'. At least the photo wasn't one of me pointing a double-barrelled shotgun at the camera with the line WHO'S SID HALLEY'S NEW VICTIM?

So much for keeping my relationship away from the press and a secret from those persons who might look for 'pressure points'.

I had created a reputation among the racing villainy that I would not be put off by a bit of violence. Such a reputation takes a while to establish and, unfortunately, quite a few had already tried the direct route. One such incident had resulted in the loss of my left hand. It had, by then, been useless for some time but I was still attached to it both literally and metaphorically. Its loss to a poker-wielding psychopath had been a really bad day at the office.

These days there were those who would stoop to different methods to discourage me from investigating their affairs. Consequently, I had tried to keep Marina's existence a secret and I was frustrated that I had been so glaringly unsuccessful. Marina, meanwhile, seemed more concerned that the photographer had captured her with her mouth open and her eyes shut.

'At least they haven't got my name,' she said.

'They'll get it. And your life story. Just take care,' I warned.

'You work for the Civil Service,' she said. 'How dangerous can that be?'

There was nothing 'civil' about some of those I had separated from their liberty or from their ill-gotten gains. But that had been before I had encountered my Dutch beauty at a friend's party and invited her first to share my bed, then my life. I would have to admit that nowadays most of my time was filled with regular safe jobs provided by Archie Kirk. Boring but profitable.

Finding Huw Walker's killer might prove to be a little more dangerous.

MARINA AND I slipped out of the building through the garage, in case there were more telephoto lenses awaiting us. She took the tube to work while I walked along Victoria Street to Archie's office in Whitehall.

'*The Pump* have really got it in for you, haven't they?' he said by way of a greeting, the newspaper on his desk open at the Diary page.

'Ignore them,' I replied. 'Then they might go away.'

I sat down on a simple wooden upright chair. Archie clearly didn't want his visitors to become too comfortable. Although I had been in this office several times, we normally met elsewhere, usually in the open air.

He cleared his throat. 'Have you heard about the Gambling Bill that's making its way through Parliament?' he asked, getting to the point.

'Of course,' I said. 'All the talk on the racecourse.'

The proposals in the Bill were, it seemed to me, designed to make it easier to separate a fool from his money, to provide easier access to casinos and to allow more Internet gambling sites into every home. The racing fraternity was concerned about the impact the Bill might have on their industry.

Twenty years before, racing had had almost a monopoly on gambling. Casinos existed but they were 'members clubs' and out of the aspiration of the general public. Then came betting on football and on every other sport. Next the National Lottery took a slice. Now the supercasinos planned for every town might prove the death knell for some of the smaller racecourses.

'Well,' he went on, 'my committee and I are looking at the influences that organised crime may have on the way licences are issued to new gambling centres. As you might know, until recently, the issuing of licences for serving alcohol was under the remit of a magistrate. Now that duty has been transferred to the local councils. It is our expectation that gambling licences will be issued in the same manner under the control of a new Gaming Board.'

He sounded very formal, as though addressing a public meeting, but I was used to it.

'There are over three thousand bookmaking permits issued in this country and nearly nine thousand betting shop licences,' Archie continued. 'There's already lots of scope for corruption and we feel this will only increase. And that doesn't include the Internet sites, which are breaking out like a rash. Online poker seems to be the latest craze but racing is still the biggest market. Many of the new sites are based overseas and it will prove very difficult if not impossible to license and regulate them.'

He paused and seemed to have run out of steam.

'What do you want me to do?' I asked.

'I don't really know. Get your antennae working and listen. Ask the right questions. What you usually do.'

'How long do I have and how many days do you want to pay for?' I asked.

'Give it a month. Usual terms, OK?'

'Fine,' I said. We had an arrangement that worked well. In the month I might spend about half my time on Archie's work and I would charge him for twelve days plus expenses.

Archie stood and offered his hand. My audience was over.

Work-wise, the last few weeks had been rather thin, but now, like the buses in Whitehall, three jobs had come along at once. Since Friday morning I had agreed to look into the running of Jonny Enstone's horses, find Huw Walker's murderer, and now the minor matter of determining if a change in the system might lead to major corruption in the issuing of betting permits and licences. Piece of cake, I thought, but where the hell do I start?

I decided I could get going on the first two jobs at the same time and, I thought, maybe the third one, too. I went to see Bill Burton.

I COLLECTED my Audi from the garage under my flat and drove the sixty or so miles west along the M4 to Lambourn.

I had phoned Bill to make sure he would be in. 'Come if you like,' he had said. 'Can't think that it'll do any good.' He had sounded tired and lifeless.

It was nearly two in the afternoon when I pulled up the driveway and parked behind the house near the back door. I could see through into his stable yard from here and all was quiet. A few inquisitive equine heads appeared over the stable doors to inspect the new arrival.

I knocked, then, as is always the way in the racing world, I opened the door and walked straight into the kitchen.

'Hello! Hello, Bill, Kate,' I called out.

An elderly black labrador raised its head from its bed, took a look at me and decided not to bother to get up. The house seemed very quiet. Dirty dishes were stacked in the sink and an opened milk carton sat on the kitchen table.

I called out again. 'Bill, Kate, it's Sid, Sid Halley.'

No reply. I went through into the hallway and then into the den, where I knew Bill spent many an afternoon watching the racing on the television.

He was there, lying on a leather sofa. He was fast asleep.

I shook him gently and he sat up.

'Sorry,' he said. 'Didn't sleep too well last night.' He struggled to his feet. 'Fancy a coffee?'

'Love one,' I replied.

We went into the kitchen and he put the kettle on the Aga. He took a couple of mugs from the stack in the sink, rinsed them briefly under the tap, and measured instant granules into them with a dirty teaspoon.

'Sorry,' he said again. 'Kate's not here. Left with the children on Friday.'

'How long will she be away?' I asked.

'Don't rightly know.' He sighed. 'We had a row . . . another row, but this was a big one. This time, maybe, she won't be coming back.'

'Where's she gone?'

'Not sure. To her mother's, I expect, or her sister's.'

The kettle started to boil, but Bill didn't seem to notice. I took the kettle off the heat, closing the lid on the Aga. I poured the boiling liquid into the mugs.

'Haven't you tried to call her?' I asked. I sniffed the milk. It was off.

'I did call her mother's number,' he replied. 'I've never got on with my mother-in-law and she predictably put the phone down on me. I haven't bothered to try again. Kate knows where I am if she wants me.'

I put a steaming mug down beside him on the table. 'It'll have to be black; the milk's off,' I said, taking my own mug and sitting down on a chair.

'It hasn't been very good for a while,' he said, 'not since Alice was born, that's my youngest. Three she is now.' He paused briefly and smiled. 'We've been married twelve years. Bloody marvellous it was at first. We were so in love, and we both wanted masses of children. She got pregnant as soon as we tried. She came off the pill on our honeymoon and "bingo" first time.'

I knew—I'd heard this story numerous times before.

'That was young William. Then there was James and Michael, and finally we had Alice.' He smiled at the thought of his lovely little daughter. 'But since then, things have been going wrong. When I was riding it was easy. I went to the races, rode what the guv'nor told me to, never had to bring work home. But this training lark is much tougher. Always kowtowing to the bloody owners. Then there are the entries, the orders and the staff. You wouldn't believe how unreliable staff can be.' He took a gulp of coffee.

'Anyway, what with all the problems and the lack of money, Kate and I started to row. Usually it was about nothing, or something so small I can't even remember now. We would laugh about how silly we were and then go to bed and make it up. But recently things have been worse.' He stopped and looked at me. 'Why am I telling you all this?'

'You don't have to,' I replied. 'But carry on if it makes you feel better. I won't tell anyone.' Especially not Chris Beecher.

'I've heard that you can keep a secret,' he said, looking at my false hand.

Far too many people, I thought, had heard that story.

'It all came to a head on Thursday night.' He seemed relieved to be able to tell someone. 'For some time now Kate has been coming to bed late, really late, one or two in the morning. Well, I have to be up at five thirty for the horses so I'm usually in bed by ten, ten thirty at the latest.'

He finished his coffee. 'Well, that doesn't do much for your love life, I can tell you. So about ten o'clock on Thursday I said to her that I wanted her to come to bed now. She said something about wanting to watch some programme on the telly. So I said to her, "Why are you so frigid these days? You used to love sex. Is there anything wrong?"'

He paused and looked out of the window. The memory obviously hurt.

'I thought she might have a medical problem or something. Then she said something I'll never forget.' His eyes filled with tears and he swallowed hard. 'She said that Huw Walker didn't think she was frigid.'

'Oh.'

'I thought she must be joking,' he said, 'but she started to goad me. Said that he was a much better lover than me. I still didn't believe it so I went to bed. But I couldn't sleep. She never did come to bed that night. She packed some things for her and the children and left while I was out with the first lot. I came back to find the house empty.'

He stood up and leant against the sink, looking out at the stables beyond.

'It isn't the first time she's left,' he went on. 'Third time since Christmas but before it was only for one night each time. I wish she'd come home.'

'Is that why you were so angry with Huw on Friday?' I asked.

He turned round and wiped his eyes with his shirt sleeve. 'I tried to be as normal as possible, so I went to the races—it was Cheltenham, after all. I hoped Kate would come home while I was out. And I still didn't really believe her about Huw Walker. I thought she had just said it to upset me.'

'What changed your mind?' I asked quietly.

'I was about to give him a leg-up onto Candlestick in the first when he turned to me and said, "Kate called me. Sorry, mate." I was stunned. I just stood there. Juliet, you know, Juliet Burns my assistant, she had to do everything. I stood in the paddock for the whole race.' He laughed sardonically. 'My first winner at the Festival and I never saw it.' His laughter died. 'I was still there when Candlestick returned to the winner's enclosure. I hadn't moved an inch. Juliet came and fetched me. Sort of woke me up. Then I lost it. God, I was so mad with that bastard! I could have killed him.'

The enormity of what he'd said hung in the silence.

He looked down at his hands. 'When I heard he was dead, I was glad. But now, well, you know, I don't really want that.'

But he is, I thought.

'Who would want him dead?' I asked.

'Don't know. I thought everyone loved him.'

'Did he win or lose to order?' I asked.

Bill's head came up fast. 'My horses are always trying to win,' he said, but he didn't sound totally convincing.

'Come on, Bill,' I said. 'Tell me the truth. Did Huw and you ever fix races?'

'Candlestick was sent out to do his best and to win if he could.'

It wasn't what I had asked.

'The stewards had me in after the race. They were furious that I had been shouting at Huw in the unsaddling enclosure.' He laughed. 'Bringing the sport into disrepute, they said. Stupid old farts. Anyway, they accused me of being angry with Huw for winning on Candlestick. I told them it wasn't anything to do with that, it was a personal matter, but they insisted that I must not have wanted the horse to win. I told them that that wasn't true and I'd had a big bet on him. Luckily I was able to prove it there and then.'

'How?' I asked.

'On their computer. I logged on to my online betting account and was able to show them the record of my big bet on Candlestick to win.'

'How did they know that you hadn't had another bet on him to lose?'

He grinned. 'They didn't.'

'So had you?'

'Only a small one to cover my stake.'

'Explain,' I said.

'Well, I have an account with make-a-wager.com,' he said.

I remembered my meeting with George Lochs at Cheltenham.

'The site allows you to make bets or to lay—take bets from other people. They're known as the exchanges as they allow punters to exchange wagers.' He was clearly excited. 'So I can place a bet on a horse to win. Or I can stand a bet from someone else who wants to bet on the horse to win, which means I effectively bet on it to lose. The Triumph Hurdle—Candlestick's race last Friday—is a race that you can gamble on ante-post, which means you can bet on the race for weeks or months ahead. The odds are usually better, because you lose your money if the horse doesn't run. Prices are even better before the entries close because you're also gambling that the horse will be entered for the race in the first place.' He briefly drew breath. 'The entries for the Triumph Hurdle close in January, but I put a monkey on Candlestick to win at thirty-to-one way back in November.'

'So if he won, you'd win fifteen thousand,' I said. A monkey is gambling slang for five hundred.

'Right,' he said, 'but if he didn't win, I'd lose my five hundred. So on Thursday morning, I bet on him to lose to cover my stake.'

'How exactly?' I asked.

'I took a bet of a monkey at sevens. So if the horse wins I would win fifteen thousand minus the three and a half thousand I would have to pay on the other bet, and if he didn't win I was even. I would have lost my win stake but made it back on the lay bet. Understand?'

'Sure,' I replied. 'You stood to win eleven and a half thousand against a zero stake.' And win he had.

'Money for old rope.' He laughed. 'But you lose badly if the horse doesn't run, so I only do it if I'm sure my horse will run and it has a reasonable chance, which means the starting price will be a lot shorter than the ante-post price. On Friday, Candlestick's starting price was down to six-to-one.'

'Do you ever make money if the horse loses?' I asked.

'Well . . .' He paused, then said, 'I suppose I do sometimes, when I know a horse isn't too well or hasn't been working very well. Occasionally I will run a horse I really shouldn't—say if it's got a cold or a bit of a leg.'

'A bit of a leg' was a euphemism for heat in a tendon, a sure sign of a slight strain. To run a horse in such a condition was quite likely to cause the horse to 'break down', that is, to pull or tear the tendon completely, requiring many months of treatment and, at worst, the end of a racing career.

Bill would know, as I did, that the powers-that-be in racing, while allowing trainers to bet on their horses to win, forbid them to bet on them to lose.

'So the stewards only saw the win bet on your account?' I asked.

'Bloody right,' he said.

'So how did you take the lose bet on Thursday?'

'There are ways.' He grinned again.

I wondered how big a step it was from running an under-the-weather horse that was likely to lose, to running a horse that was fit and well that would also lose because the jockey wasn't trying. I was getting round to asking such a pivotal question when we were interrupted by the arrival of vehicles in the driveway, the gravel scrunching under their tyres.

'Who the hell can that be at this time?' said Bill, moving to the window.

It was the police.

In particular, it was Detective Chief Inspector Carlisle of Gloucestershire CID, together with several other policemen, four of them in uniform.

Bill went to meet them at the back door.

'William George Burton?' asked the Chief Inspector.

'That's me,' said Bill.

'I arrest you on suspicion of the murder of Huw Walker.'

CHAPTER 3

'You must be having a joke,' said Bill. But they weren't.

Carlisle continued, 'You do not have to say anything, but it may harm your defence if you do not mention when questioned something you later rely on in court. Anything you do say may be given in evidence.'

Bill didn't say anything but just stood there with his mouth open.

They weren't finished. One of the policemen came up and arrested him again, this time on suspicion of race-fixing. Same rights. Bill wasn't listening. He went very pale and looked as thought he might topple over. He was stopped from doing so by two of the uniformed officers, who stood each side and held him by the arms as they led him to one of the cars.

Bill looked back over his shoulder at me standing in the doorway. 'Tell Juliet to feed the horses,' he said. A policeman wrote it down.

'I'll stay here until she comes,' I said.

'She lives down the road. Look after things, will you?'

'OK.'

He was bundled into the car and driven away. Seven policemen remained.

'You again, Mr Halley.' Detective Chief Inspector Carlisle made it sound like an accusation.

'You again, Chief Inspector,' I replied in the same tone.

'What brings you here?' he asked.

'Visiting my friend,' I replied.

More policemen started to come in through the door.

'What do you think you are doing?' I asked.

'We're going to search this house,' said Carlisle. 'As Mr Burton has been arrested, we have a right of search of his premises. We would be most grateful if you would vacate the property now, Mr Halley.'

I bet you would, I thought. 'I believe that Mr Burton has the right to have a friend present during any such search and, as he told me to look after things, I intend to remain.'

'As you wish,' said Carlisle. 'But please keep out of our way.'

Instead, I fetched my digital camera from my car and took shots of the policemen as they worked their way through the house. My presence was clearly an irritation to Carlisle, who tut-tutted every time my camera flashed.

'Is that really necessary?' he finally asked.

'I thought you had to make a detailed record of the search,' I replied. 'I'm just helping out. I'll email you a complete set of the pictures.'

'Do you know if Mr Burton owned a gun?' he asked. 'In particular, a .38 inch revolver.'

'No, but I think it most unlikely.'

I knew Bill would never give his children toy guns for Christmas or birthdays as he thought it would teach them to be violent. I couldn't imagine that he would own a real one.

By the time Juliet Burns and the other stable staff arrived at four thirty for evening stables, the police had removed all of Bill's computer equipment from his desk and loaded it into one of their vehicles. They were bagging up his business record books when Juliet walked into the office.

'Hello, Sid—what the bloody hell's going on?' she demanded.

'And who are you, madam?' asked Carlisle.

'Juliet Burns, assistant trainer, and who the hell are you?'

'I'm Detective Chief Inspector Carlisle, Gloucestershire CID. We are searching these premises in the course of our investigation.'

'Investigation into what?' she demanded. 'And where's Mr Burton?'

'He is helping us with our enquiries.'

'Into what?' she asked again.

'Into a suspicious death at Cheltenham last Friday.'

'And you think Bill did it? Ha!' She laughed. 'Bill wouldn't hurt a fly. You've got the wrong man.'

'We have every reason to believe that Mr Burton had a powerful motive for killing Mr Walker,' said Carlisle.

'What motive?' I asked. Their heads turned towards me.

Carlisle seemed to realise that he had given away too much information. 'Er, none of your business, sir.'

'Have you been speaking to Mrs Burton?' I asked him.

'That's none of your business, either,' he replied. But I could see that he had. He had known that Kate and the children were not in the house when he had arrived. There had been no female police officers in his party.

So I assumed Carlisle's 'powerful motive' was that Kate had told him that she was having an affair with Huw and that Bill had found out about it on Thursday evening. On Friday Huw had turned up dead, and Kate must have thought Bill was responsible. Not an unreasonable conclusion. No wonder she'd not come home. She believed her husband was a murderer.

Juliet stood with her hands on her hips. I hadn't seen her since she was a child but I'd known her family for years. Her mother had died bringing her into the world and she'd been raised by her blacksmith father and four elder brothers. Now about twenty-five, Juliet was in her first job as an assistant trainer after doing her time as a stable groom in and around Lambourn.

'Hey, you can't take that. It's the entries record,' she shouted at a policeman who was busy placing a large blue-bound ledger into a polythene bag.

'We can take whatever we like,' said Carlisle.

'Bill was arrested on suspicion of race-fixing,' I said, 'as well as murder.'

'Bloody hell!' She turned to Carlisle. 'You'd better take all the bloody horses as well, then. They'll be accessories.'

Carlisle was not amused and politely asked us both if we would leave his men to their task.

Juliet and I went out to the stable yard, where the lads were busy with the horses. The daylight was fading fast and bright yellow rectangles from the stable lights extended out through the box doors. Steel buckets clanged as they were filled with water from the taps in the corners of the yard and figures carrying sacks of straw or hay scurried about the shadows. Life in the yard, at least, was continuing as normal.

'Evening, Miss Juliet,' said one lad coming up to us. 'I think old Leaded has a bit of heat in his near fore. Evening, Mr Halley. Nice to see you.'

I smiled and nodded at him. Fred Manley had been Bill Burton's head lad since Bill had started training. He had a wizened face from a life spent mostly outdoors with far too many early cold mornings on the gallops. He was in his late forties but looked at least ten years older.

'OK, Fred,' said Juliet, 'I'll take a look.'

She and Fred walked to a box midway down the left-hand bank. They went in and I followed. Leaded Light turned and looked at the three of us.

Juliet moved over to the left hand side of the docile animal, bent down and ran her hand slowly down the back of his lower leg. She straightened. 'Mmm. There's a touch of heat there but nothing too bad. Thanks, Fred. We'll give him light work for a day or two.'

'OK, Miss,' Fred replied. 'Is the guv'nor not here?'

'I'm afraid he's a bit tied up this evening,' said Juliet.

I hoped not and nearly laughed. Unlike in the United States where handcuffs were de rigueur, Bill had been driven away without restraint.

'I'll be doing the round tonight,' Juliet went on. 'Measure out the feed as usual, Fred.'

He nodded and slipped away into the darkness.

She turned to me. 'Would you like to come with me?'

'Yes, I would,' I said.

So we went round the whole yard, all fifty-two horses, with Fred fussing over each one like a loving uncle. Candlestick was there and looking none the worse for his exertions of the previous week. Then Fred went off to reprimand one of the lads he'd caught smoking near the wooden stables.

'Fire is such a nightmare for trainers,' said Juliet. 'Horses panic near flames and will often refuse to come out of their boxes. We have signs everywhere to remind the lads not to smoke in the yard and stacks of fire-fighting equipment just in case.' She pointed at the bright red extinguishers and sand-filled fire buckets in each corner of the yard. 'But there are always those who ignore the warnings and some silly buggers have even been known to steal a quick fag in the hay house. I ask you. Stupid or what?'

I was only half listening. I was wondering if Bill Burton could have fixed races without the knowledge of his staff. I casually asked Juliet whether it was a surprise to her that Bill had been arrested for race-fixing.

'What do you think?' she replied. 'I'm astounded.'

She didn't sound very astounded.

'Can you remember rather too many short-priced losers?' I asked. It was the classic sign of malpractice.

'No,' she replied almost too quickly. 'Lots of favourites don't win, you know that. If they all did, then the bookies would be out of business.'

'OK,' I said. 'Not just short-priced losers but horses that occasionally didn't run as well as expected and lost when they should have won.'

'That happens all the time. Doesn't mean the race was fixed. Horses aren't machines, you know.' She was getting quite stirred up, 'Look, what do you want me to say: "Bill and I worked out which horse would win and which would lose?" Don't be bloody daft, Bill's as straight as an arrow.'

I wondered if she believed it. I didn't.

IT WAS PAST SIX by the time I left. I drove up the M4 towards London against the rush-hour traffic, the never-ending stream of headlamps giving me a headache. So what next? I wondered.

Jonny Enstone had asked me to investigate the running of his horses. The obvious place to start was to interview his jockey and trainer. But now one of them had been murdered and the other had been locked up on suspicion of having done it, and all before I could question them.

I decided to go and see Lord Enstone himself.

'Delighted, Sid,' he said, when I called him using my natty new voice-recognition dialling system in the car. With only one hand, it was prudent to keep it firmly on the steering wheel.

'Come to lunch tomorrow,' Enstone said. 'Meet me at the Peers' Entrance of the House of Lords at one.'

'Fine,' I said. 'Tomorrow, one o'clock.'

MARINA WAS BUSY in the kitchen when I got home, and I was firmly told to 'go away' when I tried to nibble her ear.

'I'm experimenting,' she said. 'Go and get me a glass of wine.'

I chose a Châteauneuf-du-Pape and opened it with my favourite cork remover. It consisted of a sharp spike that one drove through the cork. Then a pump forced air down the spike and the increased pressure forced the cork out of the bottle. Easy, even with only one hand.

I poured two generous glasses and handed one to Marina.

'It's not going well,' she said. 'Do you fancy beans on toast?'

'I just want you,' I said, kissing her on the neck.

'Not now,' she screamed. 'Can't you see that my soufflé needs folding? Go away. Dinner will be ready in about half an hour, if you're lucky.'

'I'll be in my office,' I said, pinching a slice of avocado.

The flat had three bedrooms but I had turned one end of the smallest into an office the previous year. I sat at my desk and switched on my computer. Over the years I had become quite good at typing one-handed and I could churn out client reports at a reasonable pace.

The computer slowly came to life, and I typed www.make-a-wager.com into the machine and entered an alien world. I had never felt the need to wager my hard-earned cash on the horses or on anything else. The rules of racing were meant to prohibit professional jockeys from having a bet, but it wasn't the rules that stopped me, it was the lack of desire.

As I explored the make-a-wager.com website, I was amazed at how many different ways there were to lose one's money. Without moving from my seat I could back horses racing in South Africa or Hong Kong, in Australia or America; I could have a flutter on football matches in Argentina or Japan, and I could bet that a single snowflake, or more, would fall on the London Weather Centre on Christmas Day. I could put my money on Tipperary to win the 'All-Ireland' hurling in the Gaelic Games, or on the Swedish team Vetlanda to win at bandy, whatever that might be.

The choice was almost overwhelming, and that didn't include the online bingo and poker. I could bet to win or I could bet to lose. I could be both the punter and the bookmaker.

Was my computer the door to Aladdin's Cave or to Pandora's Box?

The website was an 'exchange'. Rather than simply being a method of placing a bet with a bookmaker, an exchange was a site that matched people who wanted to have a wager between themselves. Like a couple of mates in a pub discussing a football match where one might say, 'I'll bet you a fiver that United win.' If the other thinks they won't then they have a wager between them. The barman might hold the stake, a fiver from each, and give both fivers to the winner after the game.

The make-a-wager.com website was like a very big pub where you could usually find two people with opposite opinions to make a bet between them. The company that ran the site, George Lochs's company, acted like the barman and held the stakes until the event was over and the result known.

George Lochs made his money by simply creaming off a five per cent commission from the winner of each wager. A nice little earner, I thought.

Marina came in and cuddled my back. 'It's ready,' she said. 'I hope you like it. It doesn't quite look like it does in my cookbook.'

'What is it?' I replied.

'Beef medallions with marsala and crème fraîche sauce, accompanied by a cheese soufflé and avocado salad. I think the soufflé was a mistake and it will be a complete disaster if you don't come and eat it *now*!'

We ate it on trays on our knees and it was delicious. Marina had prepared the medallions so that they were single-mouthful size and they were tender and juicy. She kept apologising about the soufflé, which, in truth, was not quite cooked through and didn't really go with the beef, but it didn't matter. This was the first time that she had cooked a 'special' meal here and it was, I hoped, a sort of 'marking out of territory'. We finished the bottle of wine with a homemade chocolate mouse, and coffee and then went straight to bed.

Marina was poles apart from my ex-wife.

When I had first met Jenny, we had almost bounced around the room with happiness. We had married quickly and without her father's blessing. We hadn't cared, we had each other and that was all we'd needed.

It was difficult to say exactly when things had begun to go wrong, but love had gradually drained away to nothing, at least on her part. Worse still, where no love remained, bitterness and hatred had made a home. More recently, the loathing and disgust had lessened and those, in time, might also fade away to nothing. We might then again be able to meet as normal human beings without the urge to damage and to hurt.

For a long time after Jenny, I had been afraid of starting any relationship. I'd enjoyed a few fleeting encounters but I had always been looking for a way out, a return to the solitary male condition I imagined was my lot.

With Marina, it was different. Sure, I had fancied her at our first meeting, a dinner party at a mutual friend's house. Who wouldn't? She was tall, fair and beautiful. But my first attempts to ask her out fell on stony ground. She confided in the friend that she wasn't sure about going out with a man so much shorter than she, and one with only one hand to boot.

Fortunately for me, the friend convinced Marina that a single date wasn't going to be the end of the world so, reluctantly, she agreed. I decided on jazz downstairs at the Pizza on the Park.

'I hate jazz,' she said as we arrived. Not a great start.

'OK,' I said. 'You choose.'

She opted for a quiet pizza and a bottle of wine upstairs. We sat in increasingly warm companionship for three hours and a second bottle before she took a taxi home, alone.

She telephoned me in the morning to thank me for dinner and we chatted for an hour. Eventually she asked if I would like to meet for lunch, 'a lovely place' she knew, 'super food'. Sure, I said, why not.

She arrived before me and was waiting on a bench outside the cafe in Regent's park. We sampled the 'super food': I chose an over-cooked hamburger while she selected a hot dog with congealed onions. We strolled through the park to the lake and fed the last bit of our lunches to the ducks. By the time we walked back to my car, we were holding hands and making plans for the evening.

It was more than a month later that she first came willingly and eagerly to my bed. We slipped delightedly into each other's arms between the sheets. It was an adventure, a voyage of discovery, and it was hugely satisfying to both of us. We drifted contentedly to sleep still entwined.

I woke early as I always did, trained by a life of rising before dawn to ride. I lay in the dark thinking not how I was to escape this encounter but how to make it permanent. Very scary.

And here we were, some eighteen months later. I loved her more and more each day, a situation that was wonderfully reciprocated. To love someone is a delight; to be loved back as well is a joy beyond measure.

I snuggled up to her back. 'I love you,' I whispered into her ear.

'You're only saying that because you want a bit of nookie,' she replied.

'No, I mean it.'

But we had a bit of nookie nevertheless.

WITH JONNY ENSTONE'S reputation for promptness in mind, I arrived at the Peers' Entrance at one o'clock exactly. The tones of Big Ben were ringing in my ears as I stepped into the revolving door, a time-warp portal rotating me from the hustle and bustle of twenty-first-century London on the outside to the sedate world of nineteenth-century formality on the inside.

The staff still wore knee breeches and silk stockings, their tailcoats and starched collars looking incongruous next to machine-gun-toting police in flak jackets, such are the necessities in our fear-of-terrorist-atrocity society.

Lord Enstone was already there, and he glanced at his watch as I arrived. He seemed to nod with approval, then came forward to shake my hand.

'Sid, glad you could make it,' he said. 'Let's go and find a drink.'

He waited as I went to pass through the security checkpoint. What to do? I had learned from multiple experiences at airports that to remove the pound and a half of steel from the end of my left arm usually caused more problems than leaving it where it was.

I stepped through the detector and, predictably, it went into palpitations.

'Sorry, sir,' said the security man. 'Please stand with your legs apart and arms out to your side.'

He waved a black wand up and down my legs and round my waist without success, and was about to wave me on through when the wand went berserk at my left wrist. The poor chap was quite startled when he discovered the hard fibreglass shell that constituted my lower arm.

Lord Enstone had been watching with amusement and now burst into laughter. 'Why didn't you tell him?' he asked.

'He would ask me to take it off and it's such a bore. It's easier this way.'

The guard regained his composure and, with an embarrassed chuckle, he allowed me to pass.

Jonny Enstone was in his element, and clearly loved being a member of what has often been described as the best gentlemen's club in London (women were not admitted until 1958, and then reluctantly). We strolled along bookcase-flanked corridors to the peers' bar overlooking the Thames.

'Afternoon, my lord,' said the barman.

'Afternoon, Eric. G & T for me, please. You, Sid?'

'G & T would be fine, thank you.'

We took our drinks over to a small table by the window and sat and discussed the state of the weather.

'Now, Sid,' said His Lordship at last, 'how can I help?'

'Well, sir,' I started, opting for formality. 'After our little chat at Cheltenham I was hoping you might be able to give me some more details of why you think that Bill Burton and Huw Walker were fixing races.'

'Did you hear that Burton's been arrested for killing Walker?' he replied.

'I was there when it happened,' I said.

'Were you indeed!' He made it sound like an accusation.

'I went to ask him about your horses but never got the chance.'

'Well, it doesn't really matter now, Sid. Took your advice and moved the lot this morning. New trainer, new start. No good crying over spilt milk.'

'Who's your new trainer?' I asked.

'Another Lambourn man. Chap called Andrew Woodward,' he replied. 'Fine fellow, won't stand any nonsense. My type of man.'

He of the riding-whip reputation. He was, indeed, Enstone's type of man.

'Sorry, Sid,' he went on, 'won't be needing your services any more. Send me the bill for your time—not that I've taken up much of it.' It was his way of telling me that my bill had better not be too big.

'Shall we go through to lunch?' he said, closing the matter.

There are two dining rooms in the House of Lords. One for peers alone, to discuss in private the affairs of state, and one for peers and their guests, where such discussion was frowned upon, if not exactly forbidden. Needless to say, we were in the second one, an L-shaped room with heavy oak panelling. The dining chairs were covered in red leather and the carpet was predominately red, and so were the curtains. Everything in the Lords' end of the Palace of Westminster was red. The commoners' end was green.

Jonny Enstone worked the room, stopping and speaking to almost every group as we made our way to what was obviously his 'usual' table. It was like walking into the pages of *Who's Who*. Lord Enstone almost purred, he was so enjoying being part of 'the club', and all the more for having me in tow.

I decided on the soup and the mushroom risotto for one-handed eating while Lord Enstone chose the pâté and the rack of lamb. We talked racing for a while and I asked what hopes he had for his horses.

'Well,' he said, 'I hope that Extra Point might be ready for the big handicap at Sandown next month. He's not fully fit—at least that's what Burton told me last week. I'll reserve judgment until Woodward has seen what he can do.'

'When did you start to question what Bill Burton told you?'

'I didn't really, not until last week.'

'What happened last week specifically?' I asked.

'It was something I heard on Tuesday, after the Champion Hurdle. I was in the Royal Box having a drink with Larry—you know, Larry Wallingford.'

Larry Wallingford, or rather Lawrence, Duke of Wallingford, was a major owner of racehorses and a stalwart of the Jockey Club.

'Did the Duke tell you something specific?'

'No, no. It was a lady who was sitting with him. I didn't get her name. She said something about having been told by a friend that Burton's horses didn't seem to be always doing their best.'

'That doesn't sound much like evidence to me.'

'No, nor to me. But it was enough to make me ask around and to look at the results of my horses.' He stopped to take a sip of an excellent merlot, the 'House' red. 'I have seven horses at present. I keep a detailed account of all their races, and on Tuesday evening I went right through my records for the past two years. I had ninety-two runners over that time. Fourteen winners but not one of them won when they started with odds of less than five to one. Sixteen started favourite and only one of those won, and that was when the leading pair both fell at the last.' He took another drink. 'So I began to be suspicious and asked your father-in-law to get you to my box last week. I didn't want to go to the Jockey Club. Discreet enquiries were what I wanted. And now I've moved the horses so that's that. End of story.'

'But it's not the end,' I said. 'Huw Walker's been murdered. Maybe he was shot because he was fixing races. Or perhaps for not fixing them when he had been paid to do so.'

'Maybe, but I don't want to get involved.'

'You may not have that luxury,' I said.

'I won't thank you for getting me involved with this business and it will be to your advantage not to.' He moved closer to me. 'Leave it alone, Halley. Let the police do their job. Do you understand me?' It was said with venom and there was little doubt that I was being warned off.

'Sure,' I said, 'but the police are still likely to talk to you because you have seven horses in Bill Burton's yard.'

He smiled, leaned back in his chair and spread his hands. 'I know nothing.'

Lord Enstone and I finished our lunch mostly in silence, and I was content to pass again through the revolving time-portal and back to the present.

ON MY WAY BACK to the flat, I called into an office equipment store to buy a new telephone answering machine. My old one had served me well, but I decided on a fancy replacement with a vast digital memory, one that could also tell me the dates and times when my messages were received.

I connected it to the telephone in my office, recorded a greeting and tested it by calling it from my mobile. Then I threw the old machine in the bin, after extracting the cassette tape with Huw Walker's messages recorded on it.

I was hiding all the wiring beneath my desk when the phone rang.

I clambered up and lifted the receiver. 'Hello,' I said.

'Sid! Great. It's Bill. I need your help.'

'Bill! I wasn't expecting to hear from you. But where are you?' I asked.

'At home, where do you think, Dartmoor?' He laughed but it was a hollow laugh, the worry very close to the surface.

'They let you go?'

'Yup, insufficient evidence to charge me, I'm out on police bail. I'm not allowed to leave the country and I'm not allowed on a racecourse.'

'That's crazy,' I said. 'How can you earn your living if you can't go racing?'

'Doesn't matter. The bloody owners are queuing up at the gate to remove their horses.' The forced cheerfulness had gone out of his voice. 'That bastard Enstone was the first off the mark. Had two horseboxes here at seven this morning to collect them. Taken them to that other bastard, Woodward. His lordship still owes me two months' training fees, which I probably won't get now. Three other owners came later, but Juliet was wiser by then and wouldn't let the horses go until their bills had been paid. She didn't get it all because she didn't have the details—the police had taken so much away.'

'How did they all know so quickly about you?' I asked. 'Your name hasn't been on the news.'

'That bastard Chris Beecher wrote a piece in today's *Pump*. You don't have to be a bloody rocket scientist to work out who he was writing about. And he had a copy of the paper couriered to each of my owners with the article marked in red. Couriered! You didn't tell him, did you, Sid?'

'I wouldn't tell Chris Beecher if his trousers were on fire,' I assured him.

'No, I didn't really think it was you.'

'Did you get any sleep last night?' I asked him.

'None to speak of. I mostly sat in a room at the police station. They asked me a few questions about where I was last Friday. Bloody stupid. I was on the television at Cheltenham races, for God's sake!' He yawned loudly down the receiver.

'Bill,' I said, 'you're exhausted. Go to bed and sleep.'

'I can't,' he said. 'I've too many things to deal with here. And I want to go and find Kate. I tried calling her mother twice but she puts the phone down on me. I'm going round to her place in a minute. Sid, I love Kate and the children and I want them back. And I didn't kill Huw Walker.'

'I know that,' I said.

'Thank God someone believes me.' He paused. 'Anyway, Sid, I called you because I need your help.'

'I'll help if I can,' I said.

'I know the murder thing is the more serious but I didn't do it and I can't think that a murder rap will stick. There were far too many people who saw me all afternoon for me to have had the chance of getting a gun and doing a bit of target practice on Huw's chest. But this race-fixing stuff really worries me.'

'What do you want me to do?' I said.

'You're an investigator. I want you to bloody investigate.'

'Bloody investigate what?'

'Why my horses look like they've been running to order.'

'And have they?' I asked.

'Now look, Sid, don't you start. I promise you that as far as I was concerned all my runners were doing their best. I'll admit there were a few that I reckoned had no chance due to illness or injury but even those weren't sent out with orders to lose.'

'Bill, I'll not even think of helping you unless you level with me.'

'I am bloody levelling with you,' he said. 'I've heard the rumours, too, that my horses are not always trying, but it's not true, or if it is, it's nothing to do with me. I promise you, on my mother's grave.'

'But your mother's not dead.'

'Details, details. It's true, though. I never tried to fix a race by telling the jockey to lose, or any other way either. Absolutely never.'

I wasn't sure if I believed him.

'Why do you think that it looks like you were?' I asked.

'The cops showed me a list,' he said. 'All Lord Enstone's horses. They won at long odds and lost at short ones. I told them it must be coincidence. But they said I could go to the slammer on coincidence and wouldn't it be better to come clean? Then I sat in a cell for a couple of hours and did some thinking. Was someone else fixing my horses? Was Huw losing on purpose?'

'And what conclusions did you come to?'

'None,' he said. 'That's when I thought to ask you.'

'Was the list of Lord Enstone's horses for the last two years?' I asked.

'I think it probably was. Why?'

'I think the police may have been given the list by the good lord himself.'

'Bastard!' he said with feeling. 'Anyway, Sid, I need your help to get me out of this hole. I'm not guilty of either thing and I intend to prove it. Come over and let's talk it through.'

'I can't just come over, I live in London,' I said.

'Oh yeah, I forgot. Well, come tomorrow,' he said. 'I know, come and ride out for me in the morning.'

'Do you mean it?' I asked. Invitations to ride out were rare.

'Of course I mean it. A one-handed Sid Halley is streaks better than most of my lads.'

'OK,' I said, 'I'd love to.'

'First lot goes out at seven thirty. Come at seven, or six thirty if you want a cup of coffee first.'

'Right,' I said, 'I'll be there at six thirty.'

I WOKE AT four thirty the next morning, took extra care attaching my arm and was on the road by a quarter past five. I had brought the answering machine tape with me to listen to in the car, but I could glean nothing more from Huw's messages. I also had a copy of the previous day's *Pump* on the seat beside me, opened at Chris Beecher's column.

> It has now been four days since the murder of top jump jockey Huw Walker at Cheltenham last week and *The Pump* can reveal that the police have someone in custody. But who? I can disclose that it's a racing man, a trainer, and he has also been arrested for race-fixing. I can further assist any amateur sleuth in identifying this chief suspect. Try using a Candlestick to give you Leaded Light to show you the way.

As Bill had said, it didn't take a rocket scientist to work out those clues.

I made good time to Lambourn and pulled into Bill's gateway at twenty-five past six. I was really excited by the prospect of being back in the saddle on a thoroughbred, travelling at speed with the wind in my hair.

So I was rather disappointed to find that I wasn't Bill's first visitor of the day. There was a police car in the driveway, with its blue light flashing.

I climbed out of the car and was met by a wide-eyed Juliet Burns.

'Bill's killed himself,' she said.

CHAPTER 4

I stared at Juliet in disbelief. 'He can't have,' I said stupidly.

'Well, he has,' said Juliet. 'He's blown his brains out.'

'*What? When?*'

'I don't know,' she said. 'I found him in the den about half an hour ago and called the police. He usually comes into the yard to see me at a quarter to six. When he failed to turn up, I thought he might have overslept. I went up to his room but he wasn't there and the bed was still made. So I looked for him in the office and then in the den.' She shook her head. 'I could see straight away that he was dead. The back of his head is missing.'

Her matter-of-fact description made me feel quite queasy, but Juliet seemed perfectly fine. Shock affects people in different ways and I suspected that Juliet was currently shutting out the trauma.

I took her arm and sat her down in the passenger seat of my car. Then I went to the back door of the house. A young uniformed policeman politely informed me that no one was allowed in. He said that his superiors were on their way, together with the Scene of Crime Officer.

I returned to my car and sat down in the driver's seat. 'Juliet,' I asked, 'is Bill still in the den?'

'Yes, I suppose so. That policeman was here pretty quickly but no one else has arrived. I mean, there's been no ambulance or anything.'

'I expect the policeman will have called one.'

'Suppose so.' She was staring straight ahead, hardly listening.

'Juliet!' I called loudly to her and she slowly turned her head. 'Stay here in the car and I'll be back in a minute and take you home.'

She nodded. I picked up my camera from the glove box and jumped out of the car. Avoiding the policeman by the back door, I made my way round the house to one of the windows of the den and looked in.

Bill was indeed still there, although I couldn't see him very well as he was sitting in an armchair with its back towards the corner of the room between the two windows. I could, however, see his right hand hanging limply down. In the hand was a black revolver. I took some pictures.

I shifted round to the next window, but it didn't give me a much better view of Bill. However, it did allow me to see and photograph a large red stain on the wall above and behind the chair. I could see that the stain was dry. Bill had killed himself some time ago.

But why? Why would he kill himself after all that he had said to me yesterday? He had seemed so positive and determined. Had he been rejected by Kate? And where did he get the gun?

I went right round the outside of the house, looking in all the ground-floor windows. Nothing seemed to be unusual or different than I remembered.

I stopped by the policeman standing guard over the back door and told him that I was taking Juliet Burns home and that they could find her there.

'Don't know about that, sir,' he said rather hesitantly. 'I think she should stay here until the others arrive.'

'Well, I don't,' I said. 'She's going into shock and needs a hot drink and a warmer place than sitting in my car.'

'All right, sir,' he said at last. 'But I need your name and a telephone number where Miss Burns can be reached.'

I gave him my name and my mobile number and drove away. Just in time, too. As we went down the road, a convoy of police cars passed us going the other way. Violent death had roused a posse from their beds.

Juliet's home was one of four identical little cottages standing in a line right up against the Baydon road on the southwestern edge of Lambourn.

'Number 2,' she mumbled.

'Give me your key,' I said.

'It's under a stone in the window box,' she said. 'No pockets in my jodhpurs so I leave it there when I go to work.'

'You should put it on a string round your neck,' I said.

'Tried that but I still lost it. String broke.'

Use stronger string, dear Liza, dear Liza. But I didn't say so.

I helped her out of the car, found the key and took her in.

Juliet went upstairs to lie down while I made her a strong sweet cup of tea. I took it up and sat on the edge of her bed as she drank it.

'Why would he *do* such a thing?' she asked. 'Now I suppose I'll need a new job. Oh my God, the job!' She sat up and started to get off the bed.

'Juliet,' I said, 'lie down. You don't have to be at work today. I'm sure Fred will feed and water the horses. They'll survive without you for a while. You are staying here and that's an order.'

I picked up her jacket from where she had dropped it on the floor and went to hang it in the wardrobe.

'That's OK,' she said. 'Leave it on the bed, I'll do it.'

'It's no problem.'

I opened the wardrobe and found some space for the jacket. Juliet always gave such an impression of being an out-and-out tom-boy that I was surprised to find that she had a row of dresses hanging there, many in their designer-named plastic covers. There was also a line of fancy shoes with colours to match the dresses. I closed the door without comment.

'Juliet,' I said, 'I'll go back to the yard and sort out any problems that Fred has with the horses. I think you should rest here as long as you can. The police will be down to see you soon enough.'

'Thanks, Sid.'

I drove back to Bill's place and parked at the far end of the stables. I went into the yard to find Fred. He was there, looking slightly agitated.

'Fred, hello,' I called to him.

'Oh, Mr Halley, good morning,' he said. 'I'm sorry but Mr Burton and Miss Juliet aren't here yet. I can't understand it—they should have been here about half an hour ago, at least.'

'They won't be coming, Fred,' I replied. 'There's been a bit of a disaster.

Death in the family. The police are in the house with Mr Burton. Just tell the lads that the horses aren't going out this morning. No need to tell them why.'

They would know soon enough. It wasn't only Juliet who would need to find a new job.

'Right,' he said.

I left him to it and went back to my car. There was a task I had to perform before I went into the house to see the police, and it was something I was not looking forward to.

I drove out of Lambourn on the Wantage road and turned into the drive of Kate's parents' house. They had moved here five years ago when Kate's father had retired and Bill had taken over the stables. But Arthur Rogers had enjoyed his retirement for only a few weeks before being diagnosed with pancreatic cancer. He had survived for barely two months after that. Daphne, his widow, was one of the grande dames of the racing world.

I stopped in front of the house and wondered if anyone would be up yet. I pushed the bell and heard a reassuring faint ringing somewhere deep inside. Daphne was up but still in her dressing gown as she opened the door.

'Good morning, Sid,' she said, smiling. 'What brings you here this early?'

'Morning, Daphne,' I said. 'Is Kate here? I have to see her.'

The smile disappeared. 'Did Bill send you?' she asked. 'I always said that Kate shouldn't have married that man. He's brought disgrace on this family. Race-fixing, indeed!'

Murder, it seemed, was acceptable.

'Is she here?' I asked again in a more forceful tone.

'She's asleep. In the spare room.'

'Are the children with her?' I asked.

'No. They're in the attic rooms,' she said. 'Shall I go and wake them?'

'No,' I said, 'leave the children. Let me go and wake Kate.'

She looked at me quizzically, but made no objection as I went past her into the house and up the stairs.

'It's the room at the front,' she called after me, 'over the front door.'

I knocked gently on the door and opened it a little.

'Is that you, Mum?' said Kate sleepily. 'Who was that at the door?'

'Kate,' I said, speaking through the crack. 'It's Sid Halley. Can I come in?'

'Sid! What are you doing here? Did Bill send you?'

'Can I come in?'

'Just a minute.' I heard her get up and open the wardrobe door. 'OK,' she said. 'Come in.'

She was wearing a tweed overcoat and pink slippers. 'Sorry,' she said with a laugh, 'I haven't got a dressing gown with me. Where's Bill?'

'At home.'

'What are you doing here, then? I told Bill I'd be back by ten.'

'When did you tell him?'

'Last night. Look, Sid, what's all this about? Is Bill all right?'

'No, Kate,' I said. 'I'm afraid he's not.'

'Oh my God! What's happened? Where is he?'

'Kate, I'm afraid Bill's dead.' There was no easy way.

'*Dead?* He *can't* be. He was here last night.'

'I'm so, so sorry.'

She sat down heavily on the bed. 'He *can't* be dead,' she whispered. 'Everything was all right last night. He came round about eight o'clock and we talked for a couple of hours. He wanted me to go home with him then but the children were asleep so I said that I'd be home this morning.'

She looked at me. 'Was it a car accident?'

I nodded. Better, I thought, to have only one shock at a time.

A tear rolled down her cheek and fell onto her coat. A second followed and soon she was sobbing uncontrollably. She lay down on the bed and I put a pillow under her head and covered her with the duvet.

'I'll go and get you a cup of tea,' I said, and went downstairs to find that Daphne was still where I had left her.

'Is Bill dead?' she asked.

'Yes.'

'Thought so. Why else would you be so determined to see Kate. How?'

'Let's get some tea.'

She led the way to the kitchen and put the kettle on.

'How?' she asked again.

'I'm not really sure. He was shot.'

'Shot! I thought it must have been an accident.'

'No, I'm afraid not. He was shot in the head. It looks like suicide—but I'm not so sure it was.'

'You mean it might be murder? It can't be. He was here last night.'

'How did he seem?' I asked.

'Oh, the usual . . . bloody minded. He came round here and begged Kate to go back to him. I thought she was better off without him and I told her so.'

'Grannie, why is Mummy crying?' Eleven-year-old William was standing in the kitchen doorway. His carefree, little-boy days had ended.

I made the tea for us all and took one up to the spare room.

Kate was lying on her side, curled up like a foetus. She wasn't crying now. She was staring with unseeing eyes at the pillow next to her head.

I sat down beside her and laid my feeling, right hand on her shoulder. 'Kate, I'm so sorry.' It seemed to be an inadequate starting point.

She rolled onto her back and looked at me. 'Where was the crash?' she asked. 'Was it last night? I must go and see him.' She started to get up.

I held up my hand. 'Kate, you mustn't go and see him. You must remember him as he was and not as he is now.'

'Oh God!' she wailed, and the tears flowed again.

She clung to me, her head on my shoulder. I could feel the wet warmth of her tears on my neck. And I cried with her. I cried in grief for my lost friend.

'Please tell me what happened,' she said, when at last the sobs eased.

'Kate, my love, I'm afraid Bill didn't die in a car crash. It seems that he may have shot himself.' I tried not to make it sound as dreadful as it was.

'You mean—he committed suicide?' She leaned back to look at my face.

'It appears that he might have.'

'Oh, my darling. Why?' her voice was aquiver as a fresh round of sobbing sent a shudder through her body.

'Here, drink your tea.'

She drank the hot, sweet liquid. 'Why?' she said again. 'Why would he? It's my fault. I should have gone with him last night. Oh God, why didn't I go?'

'Kate, you mustn't blame yourself.' But I could see that she would. 'You need to be strong for the children.'

'Oh my God, how will I tell the children?'

'You'll find a way,' I said.

There was a gentle knock at the door and Daphne came in with all four of them, little three-year-old Alice in her arms.

I told Daphne to contact me on my mobile if she needed anything and left them to it. This was a family-only task.

I let myself out of the front door and was walking over to the Audi just as a police car swept up the drive.

The same young policeman as before climbed out. 'Ah, Mr Halley,' he said, 'we've been wondering where you'd got to.'

'You only had to call,' I said, holding up my phone.

'I have to inform the next-of-kin of Mr Burton's death. Is his wife here?'

'Yes, she is. But I've saved you the trouble. I told her myself, gently.'

'Oh,' he seemed relieved.

'She's telling her children now. So don't interrupt her.'

'Right,' he said rather indecisively. 'I'll just wait here for a while. I'm expecting a female officer any minute. Please will you go back to Mr Burton's house to see Inspector Johnson right now.'

'OK,' I said, and drove away.

THE POSSE had made themselves at home in Bill's kitchen. Four men sat at the table. One of them stood up as I walked in through the back door.

'Yes, sir,' he said, 'can I help you?'

'I'm Sid Halley,' I replied.

'I'm Inspector Johnson, Thames Valley Police,' he said. 'Where is Miss Juliet Burns?'

'At home in bed.'

At their request, I gave them Juliet's address and my own. They said I was free to go but I should expect to be contacted in due course by the coroner.

'Don't you want to interview me?' I asked.

'Why should I?' said Inspector Johnson. 'Looks like a pretty straightforward suicide. Couldn't bear the thought of going to prison for murder. Saved us all the time and money.'

'Are you sure it's suicide?'

'Forensics will find out. We're waiting for them now.'

'Just make sure they check that he did fire the gun,' I said. 'Residue on the hands and all that.'

'Everyone's a bloody detective these days,' he said. 'You've been watching too much television, sir.'

'Ask them to check all the same.'

'I'm sure they will.'

He had made up his mind that Bill had killed himself and I wasn't going to convince him otherwise. I hoped forensics might do so in due course.

I WENT TO SEE Chief Inspector Carlisle in Cheltenham. I had phoned first to see if he would be there and he met me in the police station reception.

'Morning, Mr Halley.' It felt like afternoon but my watched showed that it was still only nine thirty.

'Morning, Chief Inspector,' I replied. 'Can I borrow some of your time?'

'As long as it's not a waste.' He smiled. 'Wasting police time is an offence, you know. Shall we go through to an interview room?'

'I'd rather go out for a coffee,' I said. 'I've haven't had breakfast yet.'

He agreed to let me drive us the short distance down to the Queen's Hotel in my car. We found a quiet corner of the restaurant and ordered not only coffee, but toast and marmalade as well.

'Now, what do you want to see me about?'

'You are aware, I presume, that Bill Burton was found dead this morning.'

'Yes,' he said, 'Thames Valley rang me. But how did *you* know?'

'I arrived at the house just after he had been discovered by Juliet Burns.'

'You're making a bit of a habit of being around at critical moments.'

'Coincidence,' I said, and remembered that Bill had been told he could go down for coincidence. 'Do you think Bill Burton killed himself?'

'Why do you ask?' he said.

'Because I don't.'

We waited as a waiter put the coffee and toast down on the table.

'Tell me why you don't believe he killed himself.'

'He had no reason to do so. When I spoke to him last night he was positive and determined. He was hardly likely to ask me to come and ride out this morning if he was contemplating doing himself in.'

'Maybe something happened overnight,' he said.

'It did. His wife agreed to return home.'

'How do you know?'

'I've spoken to her. I went to tell her that Bill was dead. I thought it was better coming from a friend. I told her mother, too. They can both confirm that Kate was going home this morning. So he had every reason to live.'

'You're telling me he was murdered?'

'Yes.'

'Who by?'

'Almost certainly the same person who murdered Huw Walker.'

'But why? What's the motive?'

'To stop the hunt for the real killer. If the police's prime suspect is found with his head blown off, with the gun that was used for the first murder still in his hand, the obvious conclusion is that he had been overcome with guilt for his actions and done the honourable thing.'

'Seems a reasonable conclusion to me,' he said.

'Bit too convenient, don't you think? And where was the gun? You failed to find it when you searched his house.' I was guessing, but it had to be so.

'True,' he said, 'but we didn't take the whole place apart brick by brick.'

'Nevertheless, I'm convinced he didn't kill himself. If he had, he wouldn't do it in the house for his wife to find—or his children, for heaven's sake.'

'He might have done if he wanted his revenge on her for talking to the police about Huw Walker.'

The waiter came over and politely asked if we minded moving to the lounge so he could set up for lunch.

'I have something for you to listen to,' I said. 'Can we go out to my car?'

We went and sat in my car in the hotel car park.

I slotted the answering-machine tape into the cassette player and played it to the end of Huw's second message.

'You should have given this to me sooner,' Carlisle said.

'I only found it this morning.'

Carlisle looked at me in disbelief. Then he pushed the rewind button and listened to the tape again.

'When did he leave these messages?' he asked.

'I'm not absolutely sure.'

'Didn't your answerphone tell you?'

'No, it came out of the ark,' I said, 'but, as you heard, there was another message between the two from Huw. I found out from that caller that he telephoned just before eight in the evening the day before Huw died. So one of Huw's calls was before eight p.m. and the other after.'

'So you didn't just find them this morning,' he said.

'Well, no,' I admitted.

Carlisle ejected the tape. 'I'll take this, if you don't mind,' he said, putting it in his pocket. I was sure he'd have taken it even if I had minded.

I drove back to the police station and pulled up in front of the entrance.

'Will you do me a favour?' I asked.

'Maybe,' he said.

'I asked the inspector this morning to make sure his forensic team checks if Bill actually fired the gun—you know, residue on the hands. He seems convinced it was suicide and . . . well, could you check that the test is done?'

He nodded. 'Standard practice but I will ask.'

'And will you tell me the result?'

'Don't push your luck, Mr Halley.'

THE FOLLOWING DAY I went to Sandown races and spent a tedious time asking anyone and everyone why they thought Huw Walker had become a murder victim. Some suggested race-fixing as a possible reason. No one could come up with any names other than Bill Burton as the likely murderer, many easily believing that, by killing himself, Bill had as good as confessed. I spent the afternoon sowing seeds of doubt to this theory and spreading the word that I believed that Bill had been murdered, too.

By the next morning there was still no word from Carlisle about the results of the forensics. Frustrated, I sat in the office in my flat playing with the make-a-wager.com website.

Come on, I thought, how could this be a big earner for organised crime?

The surest way for a fraudulent bookmaker to separate honest men from their money has always been to fix the result. Not such an easy task in a race with plenty of runners, not unless nearly every jockey is in on the fix, which is very doubtful since the penalties for such behaviour are harsh. To be 'warned off Newmarket Heath' means to lose one's livelihood and to be banned not only from Newmarket Heath but from all racecourses and all racing stables. It is quite a deterrent. Fixing races has to be subtle, but just a slight manipulation of the odds can pay huge dividends in the long run.

If you knew that a well-fancied horse was definitely not going to win because you had paid the jockey to make sure it didn't, then you could offer considerably longer odds on that horse than its form would justify. You could even offer slightly better odds on the other runners to encourage people to bet with you rather than someone else. Your extra losses on the winner would be far outweighed by the extra gains from the sure loser.

But make-a-wager.com was not a normal bookmaker. As an 'exchange', it didn't stand to lose if the punters won. As long as individuals were prepared to match bets, there would always be commissions to collect. Unless it was the site itself that was matching the bets, betting to win and betting to lose, laying the sure-fire loser with long odds to attract the market.

The Internet sites all claim, of course, that they are squeaky clean, and that their detailed computer credit-card records make the system secure and foolproof. But organised crime is no fool. It's true that the system would show up any unusual pattern of gambling by individual groups, but the computer records themselves are under the control of the websites.

With the right results and a creative approach to the digital paperwork, make-a-wager.com could become make-a-fortune.com.

So it came back to fixing the races.

I knew that Huw had been involved in race-fixing, his voice from beyond death had said so. *Do as we tell you, they says.* Who were 'they'? He hadn't specified that they were Internet sites. I was simply putting that into the mix because of Archie. 'They' could have been a bookmaking firm, or even a gambling syndicate determined to improve the odds in their favour.

I looked up make-a-wager.com on the Companies House website and downloaded all the information I could find, including the annual accounts for the previous year. Make A Wager Ltd was doing very nicely, thank you, with a turnover in excess of £100 million and a hefty operating profit of £15 million. There was big money to be had in this business.

George Lochs was not listed as one of the five directors of the company but Clarence Lochstein was. So George/Clarence had never officially changed his name. But it was one of the non-executive directors listed that really caught my eye—John William Enstone.

I did another search and found that Jonny Enstone was quite a busy chap, with no less than fourteen different companies listed of which he was, or had been, a director. J. W. Best Ltd, his construction company, was there as expected, as was Make A Wager Ltd. I hadn't heard of the others, but I downloaded the list nevertheless and saved it on my computer.

Marina called my mobile and said that she would be home a little late that evening. A colleague, she explained, was leaving to work in America, and she and others were giving her a farewell drink.

'Fine,' I said, 'I'll be here.'

After a quick lunch of scrambled eggs, I spent the afternoon doing reference checks on four short-listed candidates for the post of manager of a smallish educational charity. Such checks were the bread and butter of my one-man business. I had a reputation for sorting the wheat from the chaff.

It was almost eight o'clock by the time I printed out my report for the charity and shut down the computer. I thought about food and decided that as soon as Marina arrived home we'd go out for a local Chinese. Meanwhile, I opened a bottle of red wine and flicked on the television.

I was gently snoozing in front of some magnificent images of wildlife on the Nile when the buzzer from the front desk woke me.

'Yes,' I said, picking up the intercom phone.

'You had better come down here, Mr Halley, at once,' said Derek.

There was something about the tone of his voice that made me drop the phone, rush to my door and charge down four flights of concrete stairs.

A very pale-looking Marina was half sitting, half lying on the sofa in the lobby, bleeding. She was wearing the light fawn suede coat I had given her for Christmas and it was never going to be the same again. The front was covered in red splodges.

'Derek,' I said, 'go up to my flat—the door's open—and fetch me a large bath towel from one of the bathrooms. Wet it first.'

As he went up in the lift, I sat down next to Marina. She was staring at me with wide eyes.

'Fine mess you've got yourself into,' I said with a smile.

'Just the usual for a Friday night.' She smiled back and I knew that she was fine on the inside. She was tough as well as smart. But blood was flowing from two places on her face. One was a deep cut over her right eye and the other was a nasty split lower lip. Head wounds nearly always look worse than they are due to their profuse bleeding, but I could see that these two were bad enough for stitches and I hoped they wouldn't leave scars.

Derek returned with not just one towel but with a whole armful. I took one of them and applied pressure with it to the deep cut in Marina's eyebrow. It must have hurt like hell but she didn't flinch or complain one bit. She took another of the towels and held it to her lip.

'Darling,' I said, 'I think you are going to need some stitches in these cuts. We're going to have to go and find a doctor.' I had one in mind.

'Don't you want to know what happened?' she mumbled.

'You got mugged,' I said. 'What did they take?'

'Nothing.'

'You were lucky,' I said.

'You call this lucky!' She almost laughed. 'But I wasn't being robbed. I was being given a message.'

'What? What message?'

She removed the towel from her mouth and said, '"Tell your boyfriend to leave things be. Tell him to leave it well alone. Savvy?"'

Wow, I thought, I really must have touched a nerve at Sandown yesterday.

Derek asked if he should telephone for the police or for an ambulance.

'No ambulance,' I said. An ambulance meant casualty department and a long wait to be stitched by the duty nurse. 'Did you see him?' I asked Marina.

'No,' she said. 'He grabbed me from behind. Anyway, he was wearing a scarf or a balaclava.'

'No police.' I told Derek. Police would mean masses of time and endless interviews with no real chance of catching the non-mugger. I picked up the towels and turned back to Marina. 'Come on, my darling, let's get you cleaned up and into the car. Time to go and see my doctor.'

'No, not yet. I want to go upstairs first.'

I went to take her left hand to help her up. She pulled it away.

'Are you all right?' I asked, concerned that she might have other injuries.

'Fine.' She smiled rather crookedly at me. 'You'll see.'

I thanked Derek, who appeared to have taken this fresh incident in his stride. Never a dull moment when you lived with the Halleys.

We went up in the lift. The cuts were now merely oozing rather than gushing and some colour had returned to Marina's cheeks. Crisis over.

Marina went straight into our bedroom and picked up some nail scissors from her dressing table.

'Can you fetch me a clean plastic bag from the kitchen?' she asked.

I found some small polythene sandwich bags and took one back to her. 'What are you doing?' I asked.

'I scratched his neck.' She smiled at me with her lopsided mouth. 'Maybe I have some of his skin under my fingernails.'

'Good girl. Perhaps we should involve the police after all?'

'No,' she said. 'I want you to get this bugger for Huw's murder, not just for punching me.'

She used the scissors to cut the elegantly long finger nails on her left hand, and placed the clippings in the plastic bag. She then scraped the ends of her fingers and placed the resulting material and the scissors in the bag.

'I can extract the DNA at the lab, but we should go and do it now before it dries out too much. There might not be anything to find but it's worth a try.'

'After the doctor,' I said.

'No, before. This won't take long.'

'Are you sure you don't want me to call the police?' I said. 'They could run a check against the National DNA database?'

'No police, Sid. I'm sure. We can give them the DNA results later, if there are any. I don't want to spend hours at a police station being poked about by some police doctor.' She picked up the plastic bag. 'Come on, let's go.'

IN THE WORLD of racing, especially among jockeys, the need for medical services are frequent and crucial. A jockey with a broken bone needs immediate treatment for the injury, obviously, but he also needs to get back in the saddle in the shortest time. A jockey not riding is a jockey not earning.

Hospitals accident and emergency centres will lavish plaster of Paris on the injured and tell them it must stay on for six weeks minimum. A whole industry has grown up that will get jockeys back in the saddle in half that time. Ballet dancers, footballers and athletes have the same needs.

My doctor, Geoffrey Kennedy, had managed to get me back in the saddle after injury in record time on many occasions. He had trained as a GP but had become a sports injury specialist after his brother, an international rugby player, had complained to him about the lack of understanding of sports injuries at the local hospital. Geoffrey had opened a specialist clinic and soon a line of A-list sportsmen and women were queuing up at his door. He was now semiretired, and the Kennedy Sports Clinic was thriving in the hands of a younger man, but we old lags preferred to deal with the master.

Since my riding days ended, Geoffrey had continued to patch up the damage caused by two-legged rather than four-legged opponents, sometimes willing to turn a blind eye where others might have called in the police.

I rang him while Marina changed out of her bloody clothes. Sure, he'd said, no problem. He would pack his sewing kit and meet us at the Cancer Research UK London Institute in Lincoln's Inn Fields.

As I drove, Marina told me what had happened.

'I was almost home, passing those bushes outside Belgravia Court, when I was grabbed from behind. He dragged me to the path between the bushes and I thought I was going to be raped.' She paused. 'I was very frightened. He held me from behind and spoke into my ear. I reached over my head and felt the wool on his face. So I pulled it up from his neck and dug my nails in.' She laughed. 'He groaned. Serves him right. He spun me round and punched me hard in the face. He had gloves on with shiny bits on them.'

Gloved fists with brass knuckle-dusters, I thought. That fitted; there was too much damage for fists alone.

'I went down on my knees and he ran off. It was quite a while before I could stand up and make the twenty yards home.'

Geoffrey beat us to the Institute from his home in Highgate, but Marina kept him waiting as she electronically signed in to the building.

'Some experiments need constant monitoring,' she said, 'so the labs are always open. Some of the staff almost live here at times.'

'My, my,' Geoffrey said, seeing Marina in the light. 'That's quite a face. Is this a police job, Sid?'

'No,' both Marina and I said together.

'Walked into a door, did you?' Geoffrey said sarcastically. 'Correction. Two doors. Very careless.'

He tut-tutted under his breath as we went up in the lift. We walked down endless corridors with blue vinyl flooring, then Marina punched numbers into another electronic lock. With a beep, it gave us entry to her domain.

She flicked on the stark overhead fluorescent lamps and went to one of the laboratory benches, where she carefully removed the plastic bag from her pocket. Then she put it in a fridge.

'That will keep it fresh for a while,' she said. 'OK, Doc, do your worst.'

Geoffrey worked for nearly half an hour, cleaning the wounds, injecting some local anaesthetic, and finally closing the gaps with two rows of minute blue nylon stitches. I had brought my camera up from the car and took a series of shots as her wounds were transformed from an ugly bleeding mess to two neat lines, one horizontal in her eyebrow and the other vertical through her lower lip. With a rapidly blackening eye, she looked like one of those advertisements for wearing seat belts.

'There,' he said at last. 'I'll have to take them out again in about five or six days, but you won't be able to spot the scars in a few weeks.'

'Thank you,' said Marina. 'Can I get back to work now?'

'Sure,' said the doctor. 'What do you do here?' he asked. 'Reminds me of medical school.'

'This is a haematology lab,' she said. 'We look at blood to try and find a marker for various types of cancer. We take blood cells and cut the proteins into amino acid chains using the enzyme trypsin.'

Geoffrey seemed to understand and he was nodding furiously as he moved around, inspecting the mass spectrometer from every angle.

Marina took the plastic bag out of the fridge. 'Now from this little lot,' she said, 'what I want is a DNA profile. DNA is the code for making cells. It's the minute differences in the codes that produce our distinctive characteristics and give us a unique DNA profile. I can use restriction enzymes to cut the DNA strands in this sample into polynucleotides. Then I'll put them in an agarose gel matrix for electrophoresis. The polynucleotides are charged, so they'll migrate in the electric field. The bigger the polynucleotide, the less distance it will migrate. So in the gel matrix you get separation of polynucleotides into different bands. Then you bake the matrix onto a sheet of nitrocellulose paper to get a permanent pattern of lines where the bands are.'

Geoffrey was still nodding. I was out of my depth.

'Everyone has a different DNA, so everyone has a different pattern. Apart from identical twins, of course. However, what I'm doing now wouldn't be acceptable as evidence in court. The law requires much stricter systems for producing the profile to prevent cross contamination. This one will be contaminated with my DNA for a start. I'll have to do another pattern of just my DNA so I can subtract my lines to leave those of our friend alone.'

'Our friend?' asked Geoffrey.

'The door Marina walked into,' I said. 'Twice.'

'Ah.' The penny dropped. 'Yes, the door, our friend. Good. Well done.'

Geoffrey seemed happy to wander around the lab while Marina worked away with the fingernails. She then scraped some cells from the inside of her cheek to do a profile of her own DNA alone.

'It will take several hours for the polynucleotides to migrate in the gel matrix,' she said. 'We'll have the results next week.'

'What will they give us?' I asked.

'Nothing on their own, but if we get more samples and one of them matches, then bingo, we have our man.'

'So all I have to do is go around asking everyone for a DNA sample.'

'You don't *have* to ask,' said Marina. 'Just pluck out a hair. As long as the root follicle is attached, there'll be enough cells to get a profile.'

'Is that legal?' I asked.

'No,' she admitted. 'The Human Tissue Act makes it illegal to hold a sample for the purpose of DNA profiling without the donor's consent.' She waved her hand at her work. 'All this is technically illegal but I'm not telling.'

'Me neither,' said Geoffrey flamboyantly. 'Doctor/patient confidentiality, don't you know.'

MARINA AND I went back to Ebury Street while Geoffrey returned home to Highgate.

'See you next week to take the stitches out,' he said as he got into his Volvo. 'Take care with that girl of yours. I'll send you my bill.'

He hadn't sent me a bill for years.

We arrived home at ten thirty, far too late to go out to eat as I'd planned.

'Package for you, Mr Halley,' said the night porter as we walked in. Derek had gone off duty.

The package was, in fact, a brown manila envelope about seven by ten inches. It had the words *SID HALLEY—BY HAND* written on the front.

'When did this arrive?' I asked the porter.

'About five minutes ago,' he said. 'It came by taxi. The driver said that he'd been paid to deliver the package and that you were expecting it.'

'Well, I wasn't.'

I opened the envelope. There was a single piece of paper inside. It was a newspaper cutting from Monday's *Pump*. It was the picture of Marina and me walking down the road, hand in hand. This copy had some additions.

Listen to the message. Someone could get badly hurt, was written across the bottom of the picture in thick red felt tip.

And a big red X had been drawn across Marina's face.

CHAPTER 5

When in trouble, seek sanctuary. I decided we should go to Aynsford. Marina had become very agitated on seeing the newspaper cutting. She was sure that we were being watched, and I agreed with her. She packed a few clothes while I rang Charles.

'What, now?' he asked. Charles's telephone was on a table in the hallway and I could imagine him glancing at his long-case grandfather clock. It would have told him that it was after ten thirty, almost his bedtime.

'Yes, Charles. Now, please.'

'I suppose it's all right,' he said, without conviction.

'Look, Charles, we won't come. Sorry to have bothered you.'

'No,' he said, sounding more determined. 'Come. I'm looking forward to it. How long will you be staying?'

'Only for the weekend, I expect.'

'Jenny and Anthony are coming on Sunday.'

Ah, now I understood, Jenny, my ex, had always put her father in a spin.

'What time on Sunday?' I asked.

'Oh, for dinner, I think. Mrs Cross has the details.'

Mrs Cross was his housekeeper.

'We'll be gone by then.'

'Oh, right. Good.' Charles could see that it was an encounter best avoided.

'We'll be there in an hour and a half,' I said. 'Leave the back door open and I'll lock it when we get in. No need for you to stay up.'

'Of course I'll be up. Drive carefully.'

As if I wouldn't.

We left the lights on in the flat and went down through the building to the garage. Marina lay down on the back seat of the car as I drove out onto Ebury Street. Anyone watching would have thought I was on my own and assumed that Marina was alone upstairs.

I jumped two sets of red lights and went round Hyde Park Corner three times before I was satisfied that we weren't being followed.

I drove, very carefully, along the M40 to Oxford, then cross-country to Aynsford, arriving there soon after midnight. Charles was not only still up but he was still dressed, and in a dark blue blazer and tie.

He came out to meet us as I pulled up in front of the house, and fussed over Marina. He was shocked by her swollen lip and two blackening eyes.

'It's outrageous,' he said. 'Only a coward would hit a woman.'

He found some painkillers and a sleeping pill for Marina and she was soon tucked up in bed. Charles and I retired to his sitting room for a whisky.

'I hope I'm not keeping you up,' I said.

'You are,' he replied, 'but I'm happy to be kept up. What's this all about?'

'Do you remember Gold Cup day at Cheltenham?' I asked.

'Difficult to forget.'

'Huw Walker was murdered over something to do with race-fixing. He left two messages on my London answering machine the night before he died and as good as said he was caught up in it. He was frightened that someone might kill him for not doing as he was told.'

'I thought Bill Burton had killed him for playing around with his wife.'

I raised my eyebrows, both at the fact that Charles had heard the rumour and at the way he expressed it.

'So someone told me,' he added.

'Look,' I said, 'I think Huw's murder was premeditated. Bill Burton didn't believe that Huw was playing around with his wife until just before the first race. Bill couldn't have suddenly magicked a gun out of thin air. And Huw left the message on my machine hours before Bill had any hint that there was an affair going on between him and Kate. Huw wasn't frightened of Bill killing him. So I think we can discount the tidy solution that Bill did it.'

'But Burton was bloody angry with Walker for winning on Candlestick. I saw it myself.'

'No, he wasn't. He was bloody angry because he had just found out it was true that Kate and Huw had been at it.'

'Oh.' Charles went over to the drinks tray and poured two more large single malts. It was going to be a long night.

'Bill Burton was murdered as well,' I said. 'I'm sure of that, too. It was made to look like a suicide but it wasn't.'

'The police seem to think it was, or so everyone says on the racecourse.'

'I've been doing my best to cast doubts about the accuracy of that theory. That's why Marina got beaten up. It came with a message to me to stop sticking my nose into Huw's death and allow Bill to carry the can.'

'So that the case will be closed and the guilty party will still be free?'

'Exactly,' I said.

'So are you going to stop sticking your nose into Huw's death?'

'I don't know.'

I swallowed a mouthful of Glenmorangie's best ten-year-old. I realised that I had eaten hardly anything all day and that drinking on an empty stomach was a sure fire way to a hangover. But who cared?

'No one has been able to stop you in the past,' said Charles.

'I know,' I said. 'But this is different. Hurting Marina is out of order.'

'Hurting you is all right, I suppose?'

'Well . . . yes. I know how much I can take. I'm somehow in control, even when I'm not. Nothing, short of actually killing me, would stop me if I thought it was right.'

'Didn't a man once threaten to cut off your right hand if you didn't stop trying to nail him for something?'

'Yes,' I paused. I remembered the paralysing fear, the absolute dread of losing a second hand. I remembered the utter collapse it had caused in me. I remembered the struggle it had taken to rebuild my life, the will-power required to face another day. I remembered it all too well.

'That didn't stop you, either.'

No, I thought, not in the end, although it had for a while.

'You're surely not going to be stopped by a couple of punches to the face.'

'But it's not *my* face that's being punched. It's not *me* that's being hurt. I make the decision and someone I love takes the pain. I can't do that.'

'The shooting of hostages never stopped the French Resistance killing Germans,' he said profoundly.

'It would have done if it had been their families.'

We went up to bed at past two o'clock. By then, we'd polished off the bottle and I'd more than made up for the lack of calories in my missed dinner.

I slipped in next to Marina and kissed her sleeping head. How could I knowingly put this precious human being into danger? But how could I not? Suddenly, for the first time since I had started this caper, I was vulnerable to the 'We'll not get you, we'll get your girl' threat. How could I operate if I were forever fearful of what 'they' might do to Marina?

I tossed this dilemma round in my whisky-fuzzed brain, found no acceptable solution, and finally drifted into an uneasy sleep.

SURE ENOUGH, I woke with a headache. My own fault.

Marina had a headache too, not hers. Her face looked worse than it had last night. And it was nothing to do with the daylight.

The skin round her eyes was not only going black, it was going yellow and purple, too. Her left eye was bloodshot and the plaster over her eyebrow gave her a sinister appearance. She looked like a refugee from a horror film.

She sat up in bed and looked at herself in the mirror on the wardrobe door, which was cruelly at just the right angle.

'How do you feel?' I asked.

'About as good as I look.' She turned and gave me a lopsided smile.

That's my girl, I thought, and gave her a gentle kiss on the cheek.

We beat Charles to breakfast and found Mrs Cross busy in the kitchen.

'Good morning, Mr Halley.' I had never managed to get her to call me Sid.

'Morning, Mrs Cross,' I replied. 'Can I introduce Marina van der Meer.'

'Oh, my dear, your poor face!'

Marina smiled at her 'It's fine, getting better every day. Car accident.'

'Oh,' said Mrs Cross again. 'I'll get you some tea.'

'Thank you, that would be lovely.'

I had coffee and dear Mrs Cross provided me, as always, with ready buttered and marmaladed toast.

Charles came in wearing his dressing gown and slippers and sat down at the long kitchen table. He rubbed his forehead and his eyes.

'Good morning, Charles,' I said.

'Good morning to you, too,' he replied. 'Why did I allow you to keep me up half the night boozing?' He turned to Marina. 'Good morning, my dear, and how do you feel today?'

'Better than you two, I expect,' she said, smiling.

'Morning, Mrs Cross,' said Charles. 'Black coffee and wholemeal toast for breakfast, please.'

We sat and ate our breakfast for a while in silence, Charles poring over the Saturday papers.

'It says here,' he said, pointing at the page, 'that the English are turning into a race of gamblers. It claims that more than nine million people in this country regularly gamble on the Internet. Unbelievable.' He drank some coffee. 'It also says that online poker is the fastest expanding form of gambling. What's online poker when it's at home?'

'Playing poker on your computer,' I said. 'You join a poker table with others on their computers.'

'On their computers? Can't you see their faces?'

'No, just their nicknames. You have no idea who you're playing against.'

'That's crazy,' said Charles. 'The whole point of poker is being able to see the eyes of the other players. How can you bluff if you can't see who you're playing against? And how do you know that the players aren't cheating if you can't actually see the cards being dealt?'

'The cards are "dealt" by a computer, so the players can't be cheating.'

But what if the computer is cheating, I thought. What if the player only thinks he is playing against others who, like him, log on to the game from their own computers? What if the website has a seat or two at each table for itself to play against the visitors? What if it's able to fix the 'deal'? Just enough to make the new players win. Just until they're hooked. It's a tried and tested formula: give away the cocaine just long enough to turn the users into addicts, then charge them through the nose.

I had read that there were thought to be more than a quarter of a million gambling addicts in Britain. Gambling compulsion may be different to those of alcohol or drugs in the immediate damage it does to health, but in the long run, as with all untreated addictions, it destroys sure enough.

'Is it OK with you if I go to Newbury races?' I asked Marina.

'Yes, fine,' said Marina, 'but be careful. I'll stay here and rest. Is that all right with you, Charles?'

'Oh, yes, fine by me. I'll stay here, too, and we can watch the racing on the telly together.'

I suspected that 'watching the racing on the telly' wasn't in Marina's plans, but she would be too polite to say so.

AFTER BREAKFAST I called the Cheltenham police and managed to get through to Chief Inspector Carlisle.

'I meant to call you yesterday,' he said. 'Forensics came back with the results. It was the gun that killed Walker, and Burton definitely fired it on the day he died. There was gunpowder residue on his hands and his sleeve.'

Oh, I thought. Oh, shit.

'So you believe that it was suicide?' I asked.

'That is the consensus of opinion in the Thames Valley force, but it will be up to the coroner to decide.'

'Don't you think it was odd that he still had the gun in his hand?'

'It is not the unusual for a suicide to grip the gun so tightly that it stays there. Like a reflex. The hand closes tightly at death and stays that way.'

'Are you still investigating Huw Walker's death?' I asked.

'We're waiting for the inquest now.'

I took that to mean no. 'How about if Bill Burton was already dead when he fired the gun?'

'What do you mean? How could he fire the gun if he was already dead?'

'Suppose you wanted to make murder look like suicide. First you shoot Bill through the mouth. Then you put the gun in his dead hand and pull the trigger again with his finger. Bingo—residue all over his hand and suicide it is.'

'But there was only one shot fired from the revolver.'

'How do you know?' I asked him.

'According to Johnson, there was only one spent cartridge in the cylinder.'

'The murderer could have replaced an empty cartridge with a new one.'

'Then why wasn't a second bullet found?' Carlisle asked.

'Perhaps Inspector Johnson wasn't really looking for one.'

I WENT TO NEWBURY races still turning over in my head whether I should ask around about Huw Walker and Bill Burton again. To continue to sow seeds of doubt over the guilt-driven suicide theory here at the races might be ill-advised after the previous evening's little message to Marina.

I parked in the trainers' and jockeys' car park, as usual. A large Jaguar pulled up alongside my car and Andrew Woodward climbed out.

'Hello, Sid,' he said. 'How are things?'

'Fine, thank you, Mr Woodward.' I'd never called him Andrew.

'Good.' He didn't really sound like he meant it. 'I'm told that I should consult you about a reference. I'm appointing a second assistant at my yard. I've too many horses for just one now.'

I remembered that Jonny Enstone had transferred his allegiance and there were probably others too.

'What can I do for you?'

'Everyone tells me I should get the applicants checked out by Halley.' His tone implied that he didn't agree. 'I reckon I'm a good judge of character and I've think I've made up my mind but, as you're here, will you give me an opinion of my chosen candidate?'

'I'll give you one for free if I know anything about him.'

'Her, actually. Girl called Juliet Burns. Used to work for Burton.'

'I know her,' I said, 'but not very well. I was a friend of her father and I knew her as a child. I've met her at Burton's place a couple of times recently.' I recalled the evening she did the stable round. 'She seems to get on with the horses all right. I could do a more detailed check if you'd like.'

'I knew it would be a waste of time to ask you. Anyone could have told me that,' he sneered. 'I don't know what people see in you—you're just an ex-jockey.' He turned to walk away.

'I know that two of your lady owners pay you no training fees and that you only use their names to market your yard.'

He turned back slowly. 'That's rubbish,' he said.

'You own the horses yourself.'

There was nothing illegal in it but it was a minor deceit of the betting public that was not approved of by the Jockey Club. I decided not to mention that I also knew he was having an affair with one of the ladies in question.

'How do you know?' he said.

'I just know.' I didn't tell him that the other lady owner had supplied me with both bits of information because she was jealous.

'Who else knows this?' he demanded.

'No one,' I said. 'Not yet.'

'Keep your bloody mouth shut, do you hear, or you'll regret it.' He turned and strode away towards the racecourse entrance.

Damn, I thought. Why did I rise to that little insult? That was stupid.

I spent a depressing afternoon avoiding Andrew Woodward and not mentioning Huw Walker or Bill Burton to anyone.

Woodward won the big race and stood beaming in the rain as he received the trophy on behalf of one of his non-paying owners. Beaming, that is, until he saw me watching him. His expression of thunder showed that his antipathy towards me had deepened.

I'd actually been daydreaming about how I might pluck out one of his hairs to check on his DNA. He had very few remaining on the top of his head and kept those out of sight beneath a brown trilby. It wasn't going to be as easy as Marina had suggested to acquire the necessary follicles from him.

I retreated out of his eye line and found myself standing on the weighing-room steps next to Peter Enstone, who was dressed in breeches and boots.

'Hello, Peter,' I said. 'What are you riding?'

'Hi, Sid. I'm on a no-hoper called Roadtrain in the last.'

'Good luck.'

'Thanks.' He turned to go inside, into the warm.

'Oh, Peter,' I called after him, 'do you know how long your father has been a director of Make a Wager Ltd?'

I already knew the answer to my question from the Companies House website but I wanted to see if Peter knew of the connection.

'Oh, for years,' he said. 'Dad helped George set up the company. He's been a director right from the start. Nonexecutive.'

'Did he know George before the company was formed?'

'Absolutely. We've known George for ever. Sorry, Sid, must dash.'

So Jonny Enstone and George Lochs/Clarence Lochstein go back a long way. How did they meet? I wondered.

I sought out Paddy O'Fitch. If anyone knew the answer it would be him.

'Hi, Paddy.' I found him in the bar under the Berkshire Stand.

'Hello, Sid, me old mucker. D'ya fancy a Guinness?'

'No, Paddy, but I expect you do.'

I ordered a pint for him and a diet Coke for me. It was an unwritten rule that if I were seeking information it would cost me a drink, at least.

He took a long draught, finally appearing for breath with a creamy-white moustache, which he wiped away on his sleeve.

'Now, Sid,' he grinned, 'what is it ya'd be after?'

'Jonny Enstone.'

'Ah,' he said, 'the good lord. What's he done to ya?'

'Nothing. I had lunch with him recently. We were discussing business.'

'What business?'

'His, not yours,' I said with a smile. 'How about George Lochs?'

'Ah,' he said again, 'young Lochs. A calculator on legs, he is. Real whiz kid.'

'What might connect George Lochs and Jonny Enstone?' I asked.

'Come off it, Sid. Ask me another. Dat one's far too easy.'

'What's the answer, then?'

'It's make-a-wager.com.' He smiled broadly. He knew I was impressed.

'I was wondering how they met,' I said.

'Enstone helped Lochs set up his business. Years ago now. Must be seven or eight at least. Apparently, he put up some money to help start the company and so he became a director. Still is, I think.'

I nodded. 'But how did George Lochs know him to ask for the help in the first place?'

Paddy downed his pint. 'Rumour has it that Peter Enstone knew Lochs first and introduced him to his father. I don't know how Peter met him.'

'Oh, interesting.' I made it sound like it wasn't that interesting. I finished my Coke. 'Thanks, Paddy. Will I see you at Aintree?'

'Absolutely. Wouldn't miss the National.'

'See you there, then. Bye.' I turned to go.

'Is dat all ya want?' he said. 'Was dat really worth a pint?'

'Not everyone measures things so precisely,' I said. 'Maybe I just wanted to buy a mate a drink. For old time's sake.'

'Don't be bloody daft,' he said and laughed.

I HUNG AROUND for the rest of the afternoon, managing not to run into Andrew Woodward. Roadtrain, Peter Enstone's mount, the no-hoper, won the last race by ten lengths at a canter. I glanced at the Tote pay-out information. Roadtrain had started at odds of ten to one in a five-horse race. If that didn't ring some alarm bells in the stewards' room, nothing would.

I decided not to wait around to find out and made my way with the throng to the exits, coming up behind an unsteady Paddy O'Fitch.

'Hello again, Paddy,' I said. 'Are you all right?'

'To be sure I am,' he said with a slur. 'But I tink I've had a bit too much.' He wobbled and grabbed hold of an iron fence.

'Are you sure you'll be OK?' I asked again.

'I'll be fine just as soon as me bloody lift arrives.'

'Who's giving you a lift?' I asked.

'Chris Beecher. We're neighbours.'

Are you indeed? I thought.

'I'll leave you here, then.' I had no wish to see Chris Beecher today.

'Right.' He sagged against the fence. I left him there, scanning approaching faces with unfocused eyes. He'd be fine.

MARINA WAS FEELING much better when I returned to Aynsford. She and Charles were in the little sitting room and had already started drinking.

'Sun's over the yardarm, I see,' I said, giving Marina a kiss.

'Just a small sharpener before I change for dinner,' said Charles. He waved at the drinks cupboard. 'Help yourself.'

I poured myself a small Scotch with plenty of water. I was determined to take it easier that evening.

'Have you had a good day?' Marina asked.

'No, not really,' I said. 'I had a row with a trainer I should have kept as a friend, and I was cold and miserable all afternoon. Did you?'

'Yes, as a matter of fact we did.' She smiled across at Charles, who smiled back at her.

'You two look as thick as thieves,' I said.

'We've been talking about last night,' said Charles.

'And about your fears for me,' said Marina.

I glanced at Charles but he didn't seem to notice.

Mrs Cross had left us smoked salmon and cream cheese cornets as a starter and a beef casserole in the Aga for our main course. We ate formally at the dining-room table with silver cutlery and cut-glass crystal.

'I'm sorry if I broke a confidence,' said Charles, 'but I told Marina of our little discussion about what it takes to stop you investigating.'

'As I understand it,' said Marina, 'you have a reputation. Villains know that beating you up won't stop you investigating them. In fact, quite the reverse. The more they hurt you, the more determined you become to continue.'

'Something like that.' It sounded implausible but I knew it was true.

'So the only way you protect yourself from violence is to not give up even if you are assaulted. Any potential attacker doesn't bother trying because it won't stop you anyway, and will make things worse for them.'

'That's about it,' I said. 'But it has taken a few bad beatings for them to find it out. Times I would rather not remember.'

'But someone beating *me* up has now made you question whether you should go on asking questions about the murders. Is that right?'

'Yes.'

'So what makes you think that I don't want the same protection? If you stop now because some vicious thug punches me in the face, then every time anyone wants you to quit it will be "punch Marina" time.'

'She's right, you know,' said Charles. 'The same goes for me. If it's not "punch Marina" it may be "punch Charles". Neither of us wants that burden. Neither of us want our love for you, yes, our love for you, to be a cause for us loving you less. Does that make sense?'

I couldn't speak.

'So no more of this nonsense about not asking questions about the deaths of your friends,' Charles ordered. 'Their families need you. So get on with it.'

'And,' added Marina, 'if I get beaten up again then all the more reason for carrying on. Let me have the reputation too.'

'And me,' said Charles. 'Come on, let's have a toast.' He raised his glass of claret. 'Fuck the lot of them!'

I laughed. We all laughed. I'd never heard Charles use such 'below decks' language and certainly never in front of a lady.

'Fuck the lot of them,' we echoed.

'So WHAT WILL you do now?' Charles asked after dinner, with his nose deep in a brandy glass.

'What do you two suggest?' I asked with a grin.

'Well,' Marina said, 'I suggest that you get yourself a bell, go and stand on street corners and shout about the deaths. No point in doing things by halves. Go out there and make a fuss. Show the bastards who's the boss.'

'Good idea,' Charles agreed.

'I'll sleep on it,' I said.

So I did. I slept the sleep of the reprieved. Deep, dreamless, refreshing sleep. I leapt out of bed the next morning with renewed vigour. The sun had even come back to echo my mood of optimism, and I stood by the window looking out at the rolling west Oxfordshire countryside.

Marina was still sound asleep and I decided to leave her that way. I dressed quietly, attached my arm, and slipped out and down the stairs. I wanted some time to think, and a wander through the village was just what I needed to energise my brain cells.

Aynsford was a peaceful village, with stone cottages nestling round the Norman church and a large and imposing old vicarage. It took me only five minutes to walk to the far end of the village, so I continued on down the lane between the high hedgerows to the little humpback bridge over the canal. I sat on the parapet and threw stones into the brown water.

Where do I go from here? I thought. Would I be able to live with myself if anything dreadful were to happen to Marina, or to Charles, as a result of my investigations? Conversely, would I be able to live with myself if I did nothing and stood idly by?

I knew as well as I knew anything that Bill had not killed Huw. So if I did nothing more, then the real killer of Huw, and of Bill, would literally get away with murder, and the name of Bill Burton would forever be unfairly tarnished. Was I really considering leaving Bill's family that legacy?

In my heart, I knew that I would continue to search for the truth, but I didn't want to be too hasty. I needed to be comfortable with the decision, at ease, if not exactly relaxed, about the possible consequences. I promised myself that I would be less reckless in the future. That is, if I remembered.

BY THE TIME I made my way back to the house, both Marina and Charles were in the kitchen, munching on toast and marmalade.

'Where have you been?' Marina asked.

'For a walk,' I said. 'I went down to the bridge over the canal.'

Mrs Cross had made me a breakfast of scrambled eggs on an array of inch squares of toast and I gratefully wolfed down the lot.

'My,' said Marina, 'that walk has given you quite an appetite.'

It certainly had, and not just for food. I was now itching to get back on the trail of a killer.

After breakfast, Marina and I went up to pack our bags, which we put in the car ready for our quick get-away after lunch. Then we joined Charles for a pre-lunch drink in his expansive drawing room with its large open fireplace. He had lit the fire and was standing in front of it, warming his back.

'Ah, there you are,' he said. 'Have a glass of bubbles.' He gave us one each from a tray. 'To you two,' he said, raising his glass.

'To all of us,' I said, raising mine.

'Now, when are you two going to get married?' asked Charles.

Marina nearly choked on her champagne.

'We haven't discussed it,' I said.

'You haven't discussed the date?' he persisted.

'We haven't discussed whether.'

'Oh, sorry. I'm a bit premature, then.'

'You could say that.'

I am sure that Charles had been a great sailor, but as a diplomat he still needed lessons. We all smiled at one another, lost for words.

Then, into this domestic tableau, where we had been discussing whether Marina might become the second Mrs Sid Halley, walked the first.

CHAPTER 6

'Hello, Sid,' said Jenny. 'I wasn't expecting *you* to be here.'

You neither, I thought. Surely she wasn't due until much later?

'Ah, hell, Jenny,' said Charles, all of a fluster. 'I thought you were coming for dinner.'

'We are, but also for lunch. I spoke to Mrs Cross about it yesterday.'

'Anyway, you're here now,' said Charles. 'Lovely to see you. Where's Anthony?'

'Getting our things out of the car.'

He went over and gave her a peck on the cheek. Charles and Jenny had never really enjoyed an intimate relationship. He had been away at sea for long periods during her early childhood and even the untimely death of Jenny's mother had not brought them close.

Jenny was looking at Marina.

'Oh, so sorry,' said Charles. 'Jenny, can I introduce Marina van der Meer—Jenny Wingham, my daughter. Marina is Sid's friend,' he added.

Jenny's eyebrows lifted a notch.

While Charles and I had become somewhat used to the state of Marina's damaged face, to Jenny, on first seeing the ugly black eyes and the still swollen lip, it must have appeared shocking.

'I hope Sid didn't do that,' she said.

'Oh, no,' said Marina with a nervous little laugh. 'Car accident.'

'Who was driving?' asked Jenny.

Unfortunately both Marina and I said 'I was' at the same instant into the sudden small silence.

'Really?' said Jenny sarcastically. 'Collided with each other, did we?'

Thankfully, Anthony arrived at that moment and the matter was dropped.

Sir Anthony Wingham, Baronet, was something in the city. I never had been sure what, nor cared. He had inherited pots of cash, which is why, I thought cynically, he had proved so attractive to my ex-wife.

Introductions were made and, as usual, Anthony was distinctly cold towards me. I couldn't think why. Jenny and I had been separated for many years before she met Anthony, so I found his attitude odd. I certainly did not reciprocate it, and shook his offered hand with a smile.

The coldness he showed me was more than made up for by the warmth and concern he showered on Marina.

'My dear girl,' he said in a most caring tone, 'what dreadful bad luck.'

Jenny glared at him.

It transpired that they had always been coming to lunch, but Charles had forgotten. Mrs Cross, habitually one step ahead of her employer in domestic matters, had laid the table for five and I found myself seated next to Jenny, opposite Anthony.

It was an uncomfortable occasion with forced conversation. True sentiments were not spoken but were communicated, nevertheless. Only Marina had no previous form in this family, so the discussion focused on her.

'Where did you study?' Anthony asked her.

'I was at high school in Harlingen in the Netherlands. That's my home town in the Friesland province, in the north, near the sea. Then I went to university in Amsterdam. I did my doctorate at Cambridge. And you?'

'I went to Harrow and Oxford,' replied Anthony. It rolled off his tongue, a much-repeated couplet.

'I know someone who was at Harrow,' I said. 'But he's younger, so he'd have been there after you.'

'I keep in touch with the old place,' Anthony said. 'What's his name?'

'George Lochs,' I said. 'But at Harrow he was called Clarence Lochstein.'

Anthony thought. 'Sorry,' he said. 'Neither name rings a bell.'

'How would I find out about his time at school?' I asked.

'You could always contact the old boys' association,' he said. 'They have a resident secretary at the school, chap called Frank Snow. There's nothing worth knowing about Harrow that he doesn't know.'

'Thanks,' I said. 'I'll give him a call.'

Anthony suddenly looked irritated with himself, something to do with collaborating with the enemy, no doubt.

Finally, after soup, roast beef and then apple crumble, the lunch was over. Jenny had not failed to notice that Mrs Cross had cut my roast beef into strips that I could eat in single mouthful portions. She had said nothing, just rolled her eyes and smiled. But the smile did not quite reach her eyes.

MARINA AND I made our escape soon after lunch, as we had planned.

Jenny came out to my car as I was loading our last few things.

'Are you happy?' I asked her.

She hesitated. 'Mostly. Are you?'

'Yes,' I said. 'Very.'

'Good, I'm glad. Life with Anthony is more predictable than with you.'

'Less exciting?'

'Yes, that too. If you call spending nights on hospital sofas exciting.'

We laughed. Something we hadn't done together for a long time.

Marina, Charles and Anthony came out of the house.

'Take care of yourself,' Jenny said. She stroked my arm, the real one.

'Take care of yourself, too.' I gave her a kiss on the cheek and, just for a moment, there were tears in her eyes.

Marina gave Charles a hug, which seemed to embarrass him somewhat.

'Thank you so much,' she said. 'This was just what I needed. I can go back now and face the world.'

'It was nothing,' said Charles. 'Come whenever you want.'

'Thank you, I will.'

Anthony gave her a peck on the cheek and Jenny didn't seem to mind one bit. I shook hands with them both.

'Thank you again, Charles,' I said.

He waved a hand.

I drove away. In the end, I was thankful that we hadn't avoided Jenny and Anthony.

I DECIDED TO GO and see Kate Burton and the children on the way back to London. They had gone back home the day before.

We drove into the familiar driveway and pulled up outside the back door. Immediately the children came running out to greet us. Life seemed to be back to normal, deceptively normal.

The children dragged us both into the kitchen, where Kate was waiting. She looked worse than when I had seen her last. Her eyes showed the signs of a great deal of crying and she looked thinner, almost gaunt.

'Sid, how lovely to see you.' She gave me a kiss.

'Kate, this is Marina—Marina, Kate.'

'You poor thing, what happened to your face?'

'A car accident,' said Marina.

'Bad luck,' said Kate. 'Come and have a coffee.'

The children went out to play in the garden while the three of us sat in the same kitchen at the same table where, just a week previously, a mere seven days ago, I had sat with Bill. It seemed like a lifetime since. It was.

'I thought you might still be with your mother,' I said.

'I wanted to come back here as soon as possible. The police wouldn't let me in until Saturday. They were doing tests or something.'

And clearing up, I thought. 'How about the horses?' I asked.

'All gone,' she said, tears welling up in her eyes. 'The last ones went yesterday. Nothing else for it.'

I took her hand. 'How's the house?'

'Oh, fine. Have to sell it now, I suppose. I don't really want to stay here any more, not after what's happened. I wanted to come back to feel closer to Bill, but I haven't been into the den, and I don't want to. Just in case . . .' There was a long pause, then she said, 'How *could* he have done this to the children? I'm so bloody angry with him that I'd shoot him myself if he was still here.'

She started crying, so I put my arms round her and held her close.

'Kate,' I said, 'I am absolutely certain that Bill didn't kill himself. And I'm sure he didn't kill Huw Walker either. And I intend to prove it.'

She pulled away from me and looked into my eyes. 'Do you really mean that or are you saying it to make me feel better?'

'I really mean it. I am sure that Bill was murdered.'

Marina touched Kate's arm. 'I'm sure Sid will find out who did it,' she said.

Kate smiled. 'I do so hope you're right. At first, I couldn't think why Bill would have killed himself. I was sure he'd never leave the children in that way. But the police have kept telling me that he did it because he couldn't stand the guilt for having killed Huw.' She hung her head in her hands. 'How I so wish that I hadn't got involved with Huw.'

'Would it be all right, Kate,' I said, 'if I were to have a look in the den?'

'What for?' she asked, raising her head.

'I want to go and look for something. Something that might show that Bill didn't kill himself.'

'Oh,' she said. 'I suppose it's all right. I mean, the police haven't said we can't go in.' She got up and took a key from the top shelf of the Welsh dresser and gave it to me. 'But I'm staying here.'

'And I'll stay with you,' said Marina.

I left them making themselves another cup of coffee and went through into the hallway, then into the den.

It was much the way I remembered it. Along the wall next to the door was a leather sofa, and the far end of the room was filled with floor-to-ceiling bookcases. A large flat-screen television sat in one corner with video and DVD players beneath. There was only one armchair where there used to be two. The other, I suspected, had been removed for forensic testing. There was a paisley-patterned rug on the wooden floor and a few occasional tables.

I looked at the wall where I had seen the blood last Wednesday morning. Someone had done their best to get rid of the redness from the cream paint, but thorough redecoration would be needed to remove all the remaining brown deposit. Near the top of the stain, I could see where the police must have dug the bullet from the plaster. It had passed right through Bill's skull and embedded itself in the wall.

If Bill had not shot himself, then the gunpowder residue must have got on his hands because there was a second shot. The murderer put the gun into Bill's hand and used his dead finger to fire it. So where was the second bullet? I searched the bookcases, lifted the rug, looked under the sofa and the tables, examined every nook and cranny in that room. I missed nothing.

In the end, I had a few coins and a ball-point pen from down the back of the sofa, a piece of a jigsaw puzzle and some fine, gritty, sandlike material from the paisley rug. No bullet. No cartridge case. Nothing. Not a thing to indicate that a second shot had been fired.

I sat down in the chair, exhausted and fed up. Was I wrong? I had been so sure that a second bullet existed. But now what? I looked out at the garden. Had the second bullet been fired out through an open window?

I went back into the hall and let myself out through the front door. I spent some time looking but could find nothing. It was a hopeless task, I thought.

If the bullet had been fired out here, it could have gone anywhere.

Discouraged, I went back inside. In the kitchen, Kate and Marina had been joined by the children who were sitting at the table ready for lunch.

'Any luck?' asked Marina quietly.

I shook my head.

'Would you like some lunch?' asked Kate. 'There's plenty.'

'Please stay,' said William.

'Yes, stay, pleeeeeeeease,' chorused the others.

'OK,' I said laughing. Kids were a great tonic for the soul.

We stayed, squeezed round the kitchen table, and ate fish fingers, baked beans and mashed potato, with chocolate ice cream to follow. Wonderful.

After lunch, the children took Marina up to their bedrooms to show her their toys, and I went for a walk round the stable yard. I had happy memories of many hours spent here. I had ridden here first for Kate's father when I was about nineteen, and had done so on and off until I had been forced to retire. But my memories were of a place buzzing with activity. Now it stood empty and quiet like a Wild West ghost town.

I made my way back to the house. Beside the gate from the yard sat a red fire extinguisher and a red metal bucket filled with sand. Some of the stable staff had put out cigarettes in the sand and left the stubs standing upright.

I went through the gate, then stopped. *Fine, gritty, sandlike material.*

I walked back to the bucket and tipped the whole thing out onto the concrete path. I went through it with my fingers and there it was, a lump of lead, slightly misshapen but still identifiable as a .38 bullet.

'YOU'VE FOUND another *what?*' said Detective Chief Inspector Carlisle.

'Another bullet,' I said. 'At Bill Burton's place. Look, can I come and see you to explain?'

He sighed. 'Oh, all right. I can give you half an hour, no more.'

Marina stayed with Kate and the children while I drove to Cheltenham.

I made it to the police station in forty-five minutes flat but Carlisle kept me waiting for fifteen more before he hurried into the reception area. This time I accepted his invitation to join him in one of the interview rooms.

'Now, what is all this about another bullet?' he asked. 'Where is this bullet? Where did you find it?'

'All in good time,' I said. 'Look, if Bill didn't shoot himself, someone else must have murdered him. But there was gunpowder residue on Bill's hand and sleeve, so he did fire a gun, probably the gun that killed him. Now, he could have shot the gun before he was murdered or his dead hand could have been used afterwards so that the residue would appear on his hand. Yes? Either way, there had to be a second bullet.'

'And you found it?'

'Yes, I did.'

'Where?' he asked.

I took the misshapen lump out of my pocket and put it on the table in front of him. 'It was in a sand-filled bucket in the stable yard.'

Carlisle bent forward to look at the lump of lead, then glanced up at me. 'What on earth made you look there?' he said. He rolled the bullet between his fingers. 'Perhaps Burton had a practice shot into the fire bucket outside in the yard first to make sure the gun was working.'

'I thought of that, too,' I replied, 'but a number of things don't add up. First, you've proved it was the same gun that killed both Bill and Huw. Since it had fired perfectly well the week before, why did it need testing? Second, why would Bill replace the empty case in the gun with a fresh bullet so that there was only one fired cylinder? And third, there was a trace of sand on the rug in the den, which tells us that the bucket had been brought here from the yard. Why would he bother to take it back outside?'

'Hmm,' said Carlisle. 'He might have tested the gun before he went to Cheltenham races. There's nothing to say that bullet was fired the day he died.'

'True,' I said, 'but what about the sand on the rug? Kate Burton told me they have a cleaner who comes in every Monday. Also, Bill would *never* have fired a gun close to the horses. If he'd wanted to test a weapon, he'd have walked off into the fields and fired it into the ground.'

'So what do you want me to do about it?' asked Carlisle.

'Reopen the case,' I said. 'You're a detective, so detect.'

'The case isn't shut.'

'All but. Order Inspector Johnson to start believing that Bill Burton didn't kill himself and that he was murdered.'

'I can't order him to do anything. He's in a different police force. But I will speak with him about this.' He looked at his watch. 'Now, I must get on.'

We shook hands warmly. He wasn't a bad chap, for a copper.

I PICKED UP MARINA from Lambourn and we drove back to London against the rush-hour traffic.

'What did the policeman say?' she asked as soon as we had driven away.

'I think it's safe to say he wasn't wholly convinced by my argument,' I replied. 'He'll probably speak to the man from Thames Valley police, but I don't hold out much hope that they'll put a team back on the case.'

'You'll just have to do it yourself, then,' said Marina.

'How was Kate?' I asked, changing the subject.

'Poor girl. She blames herself. We had a good long chat while the children watched television. She thinks everyone will blame her for Bill's death.'

'I expect they will,' I said, 'but I doubt they'll do it to her face.'

'She said that she was seduced by Huw Walker, that she made no moves to get him.'

'You two really did have a good chat.'

'Yes, I like her. She also told me that recently Huw had been really worried about something. He wouldn't tell her what exactly but he said that it was all about power and not about money. Does that make sense?'

'Perhaps,' I said, as we turned into Beauchamp Place. 'Maybe Huw was fixing races not because he enjoyed the financial rewards but because he felt it gave him even more power over Bill—screw his wife *and* his business.'

'So what are you going to do now?' asked Marina.

'Take a bell, and go and stand on street corners and shout.'

'Good boy.'

'It's dangerous.'

'Then we'll take precautions. You take me to work and collect me and I'll be very careful not to talk to strangers.' She laughed.

'It's not a laughing matter.'

'Yes, it is. If you can't laugh, you'd go mad.'

We carefully checked every dark shadow in the garage and chuckled nervously at each other as we continually looked around like secret service agents. However, I was right. It was definitely not a laughing matter.

We made it safely to our flat and locked ourselves in for the night.

In the morning I drove Marina to work. She had woken feeling much better, and the ugly bruises to her face were, at last, beginning to recede.

I parked outside the London Research Institute in Lincoln's Inn Fields and we went up to Marina's lab to see the results of her DNA work.

'I have to bake the gel matrix onto the nitrocellulose paper to see the results. I'll need some help. Rosie, probably. She spends all her time doing DNA profiles but mostly of fruit flies.'

We went to find Rosie, who was deeply disturbed by Marina's two black eyes. She stared at me and was clearly asking herself if I were the guilty party, but Marina introduced me in glowing terms and trotted out the car accident story again. I wasn't sure if Rosie was much reassured.

'Rosie, can you help me with a DNA profile?' asked Marina.

'Sure. Do you have the sample?'

'I've already done the electrophoresis.' Marina gave her the square of gel.

'Right,' said Rosie, turning to the bench behind her and fitting the gel matrix into a machine. 'Ready in a few minutes.'

At last the machines behind her emitted a small beep and Rosie removed what looked like an early Polaroid photograph from a small door in its side.

'Looks human to me,' she said. 'Anyone I know?'

'I hope not,' said Marina.

'So it wasn't a road accident,' said Rosie.

Rosie was a smart cookie, I thought.

'I'm going to have to go,' I said, 'or I'll get a parking ticket on the car. Be careful, my love.' I gave Marina a kiss.

'I'll look after her,' said Rosie.

I went down and retrieved my car from under the gaze of a traffic warden with just one minute remaining on my time. He didn't look happy.

I drove round the corner and stopped to ring Frank Snow at Harrow.

'Yes,' he said, 'I'll be in the office on Thursday morning and you are welcome to come and see me. What is it about?'

'A former pupil,' I said.

'We don't discuss former pupils with the media,' he told me.

'I'm not media,' I said.

'Who are you then?'

'I'll tell you on Thursday. See you about nine?'

'Make it ten.' He sounded unsure. 'Come for coffee, if you must.'

'Right,' I said. 'Coffee at ten on Thursday. Thanks. Bye.'

INSTEAD OF GOING back to the flat, I went to the races. I needed a street corner to ring my bell and shout from.

Towcaster racecourse is set in the beautiful surroundings of the Easton Neston Estate to the west of Northampton. My spirits were high, as was the sun, as I turned into the car park. I chose my parking space carefully, then went in search of my prey. As always, he was in the bar nearest to the weighing room in the ground floor of the Empress grandstand.

'Hello, Paddy,' I said.

'Hello, Sid, what brings you all the way to Northamptonshire?'

'Nothing much. How come you're here?'

'Oh, I live just down the road. This is me local course.'

I knew. That's why I had come. I was pretty sure he'd be here.

'Now what can I do for ya, Sid?' he asked.

'Nothing, Paddy.'

'Are ya going to by me a drink?'

'Why would I want to do that?' I replied. 'It's time you bought me one.'

We stood for some time in silence and I could tell that I would die of thirst before Paddy put his hand in his pocket, so I ordered myself a diet Coke.

'Well, why are ya here then?' asked Paddy.

'I'm meeting someone,' I replied.

'Who?'

'Never you mind.'

Paddy's antennae were almost quivering and he could hardly contain himself. He absolutely hated not being 'in the know' about everything.

Charles came through the door at the far end. I had called him on the drive north, had very briefly explained to him my little game and he had eagerly agreed to help. He had brought with him a distinguished-looking white-haired gentleman in a tweed suit and a dark blue bow tie.

'Ah,' I said, and walked over to greet them, leaving Paddy at the bar.

'Hello, Charles,' I said. 'Thanks so much for coming.'

'Sid,' he said, 'meet Rodney Humphries.'

We sat down at a table. I checked to see that we were still in Paddy's view, then we spoke with our heads bowed close together.

'Rodney lives near me,' said Charles. 'He was keen as mustard to come.'

'Any excuse not to do the gardening,' said Rodney with a smile.

'Well, Rodney, if anyone asks you, which they probably won't, you can give a fictitious name and say that you're a retired professor of ballistics.'

'Professor of ballistics, eh? I like that. Retired from anywhere special?'

'Anywhere obscure that no one could check up on.'

He thought for a moment. 'Professor Reginald Culpepper from the University of Bulawayo, in Rhodesia. In the days of UDI, which is when I was out there. No one will be able to check on that now that it's Zimbabwe.'

'Perfect,' I said, 'but I hope you won't need it.'

I watched Paddy out of the corner of my eye. He was a good sort and I felt a little guilty treating him in this way, but it was important.

'Why don't you just tell Paddy O'Fitch what you what him to know?' Charles asked.

'Because I want him to tell a journalist called Chris Beecher what he knows and, unless Paddy thinks it's a secret, he might not do that. The more secret a thing is, the more likely he is to tell someone.'

I could see Paddy moving over towards us. He couldn't resist any longer.

'So, Professor,' I said loudly, 'what is your expert opinion?'

Before Rodney/Reginald could say anything, I made great play of putting my finger to my lips.

'Good afternoon, Admiral,' Paddy said, arriving at our table. He knew who Charles was, but then Paddy knew everything. Well, almost everything.

'Good afternoon,' Charles replied, getting up.

Neither Charles nor I made any move to introduce Rodney. Charles sat down again, and the three of us waited in silence.

Paddy eventually got the message. 'See you later then, Sid,' he said. He went to the door, but couldn't resist a backward glance as he went through it.

'But I still don't understand,' said Charles. 'Why do you need him to tell this journalist? Why don't you tell the journalist yourself?'

'If I told Chris Beecher something directly, he probably wouldn't believe me in the first place, and even if he did he wouldn't write it in the newspaper because he would think that I only told him because I wanted him to. This way, if Paddy extracts the secret from me, which I'll let him do eventually, he's bound to go and blabber it to Beecher, who'll put it in his newspaper solely because he thinks I don't want it there.'

'And what is this great secret?' asked Rodney. 'Or can't I know?'

'Sorry,' I said, 'of course you can know. It's not actually a secret at all. It just has to appear to be a secret to Paddy, and also to Chris Beecher. It's simply that I found a second bullet at Bill Burton's place and also that I *know* he didn't kill himself and the police are now looking for his murderer.'

'And are they?' asked Charles.

'Well, not exactly, but Chris Beecher won't know that.'

'I'm none the wiser,' said Rodney.

'It's a long story. Charles will fill you in. I want to go now so that Paddy can begin to needle me. If he asks you, say I asked you to look at a second bullet. Enjoy your day at the races.'

'I will. Do you have any tips?' Rodney asked.

'He'll tell you to keep your money in your pocket,' said Charles.

I laughed. He knew me too well.

I went out to the parade ring. As expected, Paddy came up to me as I watched the runners for the first.

'Who's the professor then?' he asked.

I looked suitably appalled. 'None of your business.'

'Come on, Sid. What's he doing here?'

'I just wanted some advice. Nothing important.'

I hoped he didn't believe me. I moved onto the stands to watch the race and he followed, as I knew he would. He was now on a mission.

'So what advice could he give ya that I couldn't?'

'You don't know anything about ballistics.'

He was about to ask again when thankfully he was cut off by the public address system. 'They're under starter's order . . . they're off.'

I had always enjoyed riding here and I enviously watched others doing what I longed to do. Towcaster is a 'park' racecourse set among rolling green hills. The fences are inviting and fair but the real challenge for a horse is the last mile to the finish, which is all uphill.

On the far side of the course, one jockey kicked his mount hard in the ribs and they started to move away from the others in their bid for victory. Much too soon, I thought. At the second last, the leader was still in front but by a much-reduced margin, which was diminishing with every tired stride. By the last fence he had been caught by the others, and would not have won even if he had not come to grief in a bone-crunching fall.

A close finish was fought out between two of the country's leading riders, who had bided their time and made their runs late. A job well done.

'Now, what do ya want to know about bullets for?' Paddy asked, when the cheers of the crowd had died down.

'It's none of your business.'

'So which bullets are ya interested in?' he persisted. 'Is it the one dat killed Huw Walker or the one dat killed Bill Burton?'

'Neither,' I replied, watching with relief as the horse and jockey who had fallen both rose to their feet and walked away, bruised but not broken.

'So what other bullets are there, then?' asked Paddy.

'I'm not saying another word,' I said.

'Aw, come on, Sid, me old mate, are there other bullets?'

'One other bullet.'

'Great!' said Paddy. 'Who was shot with it?'

'No one.'

He looked disappointed. 'Well, why is it important, then?'

'Did I say it was important?' I asked.

'Stands to reason,' he said. 'Why else would ya get a professor?'

'Look, I found another bullet and I wanted some advice about it, OK?'

'Where did ya find it?'

'Come on, Paddy, what is this? Leave it alone, will you?'

'Bejesus, dat's not me nature.' He grinned at me.

'I found a bullet in a sand bucket at Bill Burton's stable yard, OK?' I said. 'I wanted it checked by a ballistics expert.'

'But why?' asked Paddy. 'What did ya want him to check about it?'

I sighed. 'If it was fired from the same gun that killed Bill Burton.'

He looked confused. 'So, what if it had?'

Eventually, I told him everything. I told him I was certain that Bill Burton had been murdered. I told him about the gunpowder residue on Bill's hand and sleeve and why there must have been a second shot fired. I told him about finding the bullet. I made up a bit about having it checked by my professor and his confirming that it came from the same gun. I also told him that the police were now investigating Bill's death as murder. I hoped I was right. I told Paddy everything twice, then I told him not to tell anyone else.

'Ya can trust me,' he said.

I hoped I could do just that.

CHAPTER 7

There was nothing about any second bullet or the Sid Halley theories on the Chris Beecher page of *The Pump* on Wednesday morning. I had bought a copy on my way back to the flat after taking Marina to work. Rosie had been waiting for her at the front door, and Marina had rolled her eyes at me as she climbed out of the car. I had laughed.

I parked the car in the garage under the building, went upstairs and searched the paper from start to finish. Nothing. I was beginning to doubt my assessment of Paddy's character when Charles telephoned me.

'I've just had a call from someone who said that you had said that they could check with me the name of the ballistics professor you had consulted.'

'Really?' I said. 'And did you give them his name?'

'I couldn't remember it.' He laughed. 'So I made another one up. Rodney is now Professor Aubrey Winterton, retired from the University of Bulawayo—I could remember that bit.'

'And did this individual have an Irish accent?' I asked.

'No,' said Charles, 'he did not.'

'I wonder who he was.'

'I dialled 1471 to get his number and then I phoned back,' said Charles. 'The number was for *The Pump*. I got through to the switchboard.'

'Thank you, Charles.' I was impressed. 'If you need a job, you can be my new assistant.'

'No, thanks,' said Charles. 'I like to give orders, not take them.'

'Be my boss then.'

He laughed and disconnected.

Good old Paddy, I thought. I knew he wouldn't be able to resist telling.

Bejesus, dat was his nature.

I ARRIVED to pick up Marina from Lincoln's Inn Fields at half past five.

I'd spent the morning writing a preliminary report for Archie and the afternoon doing chores around the flat. I had called Detective Chief Inspector Carlisle but he was unavailable, so I left him a message asking him to call me on my mobile. I wanted to find out if he'd taken any notice of what I'd said on Monday. He rang me back while I was waiting outside the London Research Institute for Marina to appear.

'I did have a word with Inspector Johnson,' he said. 'He took a little convincing but at least he's considering that Burton may have been murdered. Although he's still pretty convinced that Burton killed himself.'

'Oh,' I said. 'And are you?'

'I don't get paid to think about other coppers' cases. But, if I were a betting man, which I'm not, I'd bet on your instinct over his.'

It was quite a compliment and I thanked him for it.

'Any news on the bullet I gave you?' I asked.

'Same gun,' he said. 'Forensics came back with the confirmation this afternoon. No real surprise.'

'No,' I agreed, but I was relieved nevertheless.

MARINA AND I spent a quiet evening at home in front of the television eating ready-made and microwaved shepherd's pie off trays on our laps.

'You know those street corners I was going to ring my bell on?' I said.

'Yes.'

'Well, tomorrow's *Pump* may have a certain ding-dong about it.'

'Are you saying that I should be extra careful tomorrow?'

'Yes,' I said. 'And always.'

'Rosie hardly leaves my side.'

'I think I'll go and get *The Pump* now,' I said. 'Tomorrow's papers are always on sale at Victoria Station about eleven at night.'

'You be careful, too,' said Marina.

I was. I avoided dark corners and kept a keen eye on my back. I made it safely to the newsstand, then back to Ebury Street without incident.

There was no need to search this paper. You would have had to be blind to miss it. They must have been short of news.

Under a 'Pump Exclusive' banner on the front page was the headline MURDER OR SUICIDE? with the subheadline HALLEY ORCHESTRATES THE INVESTIGATION. The article beneath described in detail everything I had revealed to Paddy. They 'quoted' Professor Aubrey Winterton as saying that the bullet definitely came from the same gun that had been used to kill Bill Burton. They even managed to state that Sid Halley was confident that an arrest was imminent. I put that down to Paddy's tendency for exaggeration.

'That's what I call shouting from a street corner,' said Marina. 'Is it true?'

'Not about the arrest. And some of the rest is guesswork.'

No one could be in any doubt that I had blatantly ignored the message that Marina had received the evening she was beaten up. Even I had not expected my game to work so well that it would make the front page. This much coverage made me very nervous, but it was too late now; *The Pump* printed more than half a million copies a day.

I double-checked the locks, removed my arm and went to bed.

IN THE MORNING I dropped Marina at work, though not before taking a few detours to see if we were being followed. Rosie, the petite bodyguard, was waiting for Marina in the Institute foyer. She waved at me as I drove away.

I pointed the Audi towards northwest London and went to see Frank Snow. Harrow School is actually in Harrow-on-the-Hill, a neat little village, perched, as its name suggests, on a hill surrounded by suburban London.

I eventually found the right office near the school chapel and Frank Snow was there, seated at a central table sticking labels on a stack of envelopes.

'For the old boys' newsletters,' he said in explanation.

He was a tall man with a full head of white hair. He wore a tweed jacket with leather patches on the elbows and looked every inch the schoolmaster.

'Would you like a coffee?' he asked.

'Love one, thank you.'

He busied himself with an electric kettle in the corner while I wandered around looking at the rows of framed photographs of boys on the walls.

'Milk and sugar?'

'Just a little milk, please,' I said.

He placed two steaming mugs down on the end of the table.

'Now, how can I help you, Mr Halley?'

I decided against telling him I was a private detective. 'I'm assisting the Standing Cabinet Subcommittee on Legislative Outcomes in their consideration of Internet gambling as part of the new Gambling and Gaming Act,' I said. 'And I need some background information on one of your old boys.'

If you can't blind them with science, I thought, baffle them with bullshit.

'I see,' he said. He didn't appear to.

'Yes. One of your old boys runs an Internet gambling website and I was hoping you might be able to tell me about his time at Harrow.'

'I'm not sure that I can. Our records are confidential, you know.'

'Don't worry about the Data Protection Act,' I said. 'This is an official inquiry.' It wasn't, but he wouldn't know that.

'Who exactly are you asking about?'

'George Lochs,' I said. 'At least, that's what he calls himself now. When he was at Harrow he was—'

'Clarence Lochstein,' Frank Snow interrupted.

'Exactly. You remember him, then?'

'I do,' he said. 'Has he been up to no good?'

'Why do you ask?'

'No reason. What do you want to know about him?'

'I heard that he was expelled for taking bets from the other boys.'

'That's not exactly true,' he said. 'He was sacked for striking his housemaster. Lochstein and another boy were indeed caught taking bets from the other boys and, it was rumoured, from some of the younger staff. It was in the latter days of corporal punishment and the headmaster instructed the boys' housemasters to give each of them a sound beating. Six of the best.'

'So?'

'Lochstein took one stroke of the cane on his backside and then stood up and broke his housemaster's jaw with his fist.' Snow stroked his chin absentmindedly.

'You were his housemaster, weren't you?'

'Yes, I was. The little swine broke my jaw in three places. I spent the next six years with my head in a metal brace.'

'So Lochstein was expelled,' I said. 'What happened to the other boy?'

'He took his beating from his own housemaster.'

'And the boy was allowed to stay?'

'Yes,' said Mr Snow. 'His father subsequently gave a large donation to the school appeal, which was said by some to be conscience money.'

'Do you remember the boy's name?'

'I can't recall his first name but his surname was Enstone.'

'Peter Enstone?' I asked.

'Yes, I think that's it. His father was a builder.'

Well, well, I thought. No wonder the Enstones had known George Lochs for ever. And, I thought, Lochs has a history of punching people in the face.

Frank Snow had little else of interest to give me. Harrow had done its best to keep the whole matter out of the press and had closed ranks. Lochstein was not even in the official list of old boys that Frank showed me.

I thanked him for his time and for the coffee and he walked me towards the door. We shook hands,

'If you need anything further, Mr Halley, don't be afraid to ask.' He smiled. 'I still owe Lochstein a beating—five strokes, to be precise.'

ON MY WAY BACK to central London, I made a detour to Wembley Park to look at the Make A Wager Ltd office building. Their address had been on the Companies House website. I parked round the corner and walked back.

The building was pretty nondescript. It was a simple rectangular red-brick structure of five floors with a small unmanned entrance lobby at one end. There were security cameras pointing in every direction. A notice next to the entrance intercom stated that visitors should press the button and wait. Visitors, it seemed, were not encouraged.

I pressed the button and waited.

Eventually a female voice said, 'Yes?' from the speaker next to the button.

'Sid Halley here to see George Lochs,' I said back.

'Just a minute,' said the voice.

After at least a minute, the voice said, 'Do you have an appointment?'

'No,' I replied. 'I was passing and I thought I would drop in to see George. I know him.'

'Just a minute,' said the voice again.

I waited. And waited.

'Take the lift to the fourth floor,' said the voice and a buzzer sounded.

I pushed the door open and did as I was told.

George/Clarence was waiting for me when the lift opened. He was lean, almost athletic, with blond hair brushed back showing a certain receding over the temples. But he was not wearing his suit today. Instead he sported a dark roll-neck sweater and jeans. He hadn't been expecting guests.

'Sid Halley,' he said holding out a hand. 'Good to see you again. What brings you to this godforsaken part of north London?'

Was there a hint of anxiety in his voice? Or maybe it was irritation?

'I was passing and I thought I'd come and see what your offices looked like.' I don't think he believed me, but it was true.

'There's not much to show,' he said.

He slid a green plastic card through a reader on the wall, which unlocked the door to the offices on the fourth floor. He stood aside to allow me in.

There were thirty or so staff sitting at open-plan desks along the windows, each with a computer screen shining brightly in front of them.

'On this floor we have our market managers,' said George in a hushed tone. 'Have you seen our website?'

'Yes,' I said, equally hushed.

'You know, then, that you can gamble on just about anything, as long as you can find someone to match your bet. The staff here look at the incoming bets and try to match them, if the computer doesn't do it automatically.'

'Do you do online gaming as well as exchange wagering?'

'Yes, but not from this office. We have a Gibraltar-based operation for that. More cost-effective. Why the interest?' he asked.

'No real reason,' I said. 'I'm just naturally inquisitive.' And nosey.

I wandered a little further down the office.

'Is this all the staff you have?' I asked.

'Nooo,' he said, amused. 'There are lots more. The accounts department is on the floor below here and there must be fifty personnel there. Then we have the technical staff, who live among the computers on the first and second floors. The ground floor has the company security staff, and a canteen.'

'Quite a set-up,' I said, sounding impressed. And I was.

'Yes. We operate here twenty-four hours a day, every day of the year. Now is there anything else you want, Sid? I'm very busy.'

His irritation was beginning to show through more sharply.

'No,' I said. 'Sorry. Many thanks for showing me around.'

And, oh yes, by the way, could I have a hair, please?

I followed him to the door, and could see no convenient blond hairs lying on his dark sweater. This wasn't easy as Marina had suggested.

We stopped in the doorway.

'I see you're on the front page of *The Pump* today,' he said.

'So I saw,' I replied trying to keep my voice as normal as possible.

'Are you having any luck with your investigation?' he said.

'I'm making steady progress,' I lied.

'Well, I hope you get to the bottom of it. I liked Huw Walker.'

'How well did you know him?' I asked.

'Not very well. We spoke a few times.'

'What about?' I asked.

'Nothing much. About his chances, you know, in passing.'

'Is that sensible for a man in your position?' I asked. 'Is the Jockey Club aware that you ask jockeys about their chances in races?'

'Now look here, Halley, what are you accusing me of?'

'Nothing,' I said. 'It was *you* who told me that you had talked to Huw Walker about his chances.'

'I think you ought to go now,' he said.

He didn't hold out his hand. I looked into his eyes and could see no further than his retinas. Whatever he was thinking, he was keeping it to himself.

I wanted to ask him what he had been doing last Friday evening. I wanted to know if he had scratch marks on his neck beneath the high roll collar of his sweater. And I wanted to know if he had ever owned a .38 revolver.

Instead, I rode the lift down and went away.

BACK AT EBURY STREET, I parked the car in the garage. Instead of going straight up to my flat, I walked to the sandwich bar on the corner to get myself a late lunch of smoked salmon on brown bread with a salad.

I was paying across the counter when my mobile rang.

'Hello,' I said, trying to juggle my lunch, the change and the telephone in my one real hand.

A breathless voice at the other end of the line said, 'Is that you, Sid?'

'Yes,' I replied, then with rising foreboding, 'Rosie? What is it?'

'Oh God,' she said, 'Marina's been shot.'

'What?' I said numbly, dropping my change.

'Marina's been shot,' Rosie repeated.

I went cold and stopped feeling my legs. 'Where?'

'Here, on the pavement outside the Institute.'

'No,' I said. 'Where on her body?'

'In her leg.'

Thank God, I thought. She's going to be all right.

'Where is she now?' I asked.

'Here, by the ambulance,' said Rosie, 'They're desperately working on her on the pavement. Oh God, there's so much blood. It's everywhere.'

Maybe my relief was premature. My skin felt clammy.

'Rosie,' I said urgently, 'go and ask the ambulancemen which hospital they'll be taking her to.'

I could hear her asking.

'St Thomas' Hospital,' she said.

'Go with her. I'm on my way there.'

She hung up. I looked at my phone in disbelief. This can't be happening, I thought. But it was.

I stumbled out of the shop and fairly sprinted back to my car. I drove as quickly as I could to St Thomas', which is on the other side of the Thames from the Houses of Parliament. In spite of two jumped traffic lights and numerous near misses, I made it unscathed to the hospital's casualty entrance. I pulled the car onto the pavement and got out.

'You can't leave it there,' said a well-meaning soul walking past.

'It's an emergency.' I wasn't going to waste time finding a parking meter.

Oh God, please let Marina be all right.

I ran into the Accident and Emergency Department and found a line of six people at the reception desk.

I grabbed a passing nurse. 'Please,' I said, 'where's Marina van der Meer?'

'Is she a patient?' asked the nurse in an eastern European accent.

'Yes,' I said. 'She was on her way here by ambulance.'

'Ambulance cases come in over there,' she said, pointing over her shoulder.

'Thanks.' I ran in the direction she had indicated, towards some closed double doors. I pushed one open and looked through.

A trolley surrounded by medical staff was being wheeled quickly by from right to left. I only had a glimpse of the person on it and I couldn't tell if it was Marina. Then a dazed-looking Rosie came into view.

'Rosie,' I shouted.

She turned. 'Oh, Sid, thank God you're here!' She was crying and seemed to be in a state of near collapse.

'Where's Marina?' I asked urgently.

'In there,' she said, looking at some doors on the right.

There was a glass circular window and, with trepidation, I looked through.

Marina lay very still on a trolley with about six people rushing around her. There were two bags of blood on poles with plastic pipes running to needles on the backs of each of her hands.

'What are you two doing here?' asked a voice.

I turned to see a stern-looking nurse in a blue uniform.

'You'll have to go back to the waiting room,' she said.

'But that's Marina in there,' I said turning back to the window. One of the staff was putting a tube down her throat. Her face looked horribly grey.

'I don't care if it's the Queen of Sheba,' said the nurse. 'You can't stay here. You'll be in the way.' She mellowed. 'Come on, I'll show you where you can wait. You'll be told what's happening as soon as we know.'

Rosie and I allowed ourselves to be led down the corridor. We were shown into a room with FAMILY WAITING ROOM painted on the door.

'Now stay here and someone will be along to see you.'

I mumbled, 'Thank you,' and sat down heavily on one of the chairs. All I could think about was whether Marina was going to be all right.

Rosie sat with her head in her hands.

'What happened?' I finally asked her.

She looked up at me. Her eyes were red from crying. 'I'm so sorry, Sid,' she said. 'We only went outside for a bit of air.'

'It's all right, Rosie. It wasn't your fault. Tell me what happened.'

'It was all so fast,' she said. 'We had gone only a few yards when a motorcyclist drew up and sat there on his machine looking at a map. He beckoned us over to him, pointing at the map. Marina went over to him and he just shot her. I think the gun was under the map.'

'Could you describe the motorcyclist?' I asked her.

'No, I don't think so,' she said, slowly. 'He was wearing a crash helmet.'

'How about the motorbike?' I asked.

'It was just . . . just a motorbike,' she said. 'I don't know what type.'

She paused and I could tell she was replaying the scene in her mind.

'At first I didn't realise she'd been shot. I mean, I didn't hear a gunshot or anything. Marina doubled up and grabbed her knee and the motorcycle roared away. Then there was all the blood. It spurted out of her leg all over the place. I screamed for help. The Institute's security men called the ambulance but it took ages to arrive. She lost so much blood. I held her leg in both my hands and squeezed hard to stop the blood, but it oozed between my fingers and ran all over the pavement. It was horrible.' She shuddered.

I looked at her dark clothes and saw that they were covered in blood.

'You did brilliantly, Rosie. Without you, she would have probably died there on the pavement. At least here she has a chance.' I hoped so anyway.

The door opened and a uniformed policeman came in.

'Good afternoon,' he said, showing us his warrant card. 'Do either of you know the name of the young lady who was shot?'

'Marina van der Meer,' I said. 'Do you know how she's doing?'

'The doctors are still working on her, sir,' he said. 'I'm afraid I don't know anything further.' He took a notebook out of his pocket. 'How do you spell her name?' he asked.

I told him and he wrote it down.

'And what is your name?' he asked me.

I told him that as well. Come on, I thought, where's the bloody doctor?

'And you, madam?'

Rosie's name went into the notebook.

'Are either of you related to the young lady?'

'I am,' I said. 'I'm her . . .' What am I? I'm too old to be a boyfriend. I hate the term 'partner'. Significant other? No. 'I'm her fiancé,' I said.

'Are you therefore her next of kin?'

I didn't like the sound of that. 'Next of kin' always seemed to go with 'inform' and 'death'.

'Her parents live in the Netherlands,' I said. 'I have their address somewhere at home. She also has a brother. He lives in the States.'

'And you, madam?' said the policeman turning to Rosie.

'I work with Marina at the London Research Institute. I was there when she was shot.'

His eyes opened wider. 'Were you? My superiors will want to take a statement.' He turned away and spoke quietly into his personal radio.

One of the medical staff came into the room. 'You're here with the girl who was shot?' he asked.

'Yes,' I said. 'She's my fiancée. How is she doing?'

'Not good, I'm afraid. She's gone to theatre so I've handed her over to a surgeon. Sorry, I should introduce myself, I'm Dr Osborne; I'm the duty Accident and Emergency Consultant.'

'Sid Halley,' I said. He didn't offer his hand. Germs and all that.

'Ah,' he said nodding, 'the jockey. I thought I recognised you. Well, your girlfriend has lost an awful lot of blood. In fact, I'm amazed she was still alive when she arrived here. There was no measurable blood pressure.'

'But she will be all right, won't she?' I was desperate.

'I'm afraid I don't know yet. The bullet missed the knee itself but it tore open the femoral artery, hence the blood loss. She was very unlucky.'

'But have you stopped the bleeding?' I asked frantically.

'I have for the time being, but I'm worried about further bleeding into her internal organs. We had to give her a great deal of blood and other fluids to replace that which was lost, to fill the pipes up again, as it were. Such a large transfusion reduces the ability of the blood to coagulate. The next few hours are critical. If she survives that, then her chances are reasonable.'

'How long will she be in theatre?'

'Not long,' he said. 'She's gone to have a better repair of the artery.'

'When can I see her?' I asked.

'After theatre she will be taken to intensive care. You'll be able to see her there but she'll be sedated and asleep. We'll try and keep her blood pressure as low as possible for a while. Look, I'm sorry, but I must go now.'

'Thank you,' I said. It was insufficient.

He went out, leaving Rosie, me and the policeman.

'She's in the best hands,' said the policeman kindly.

I nodded. I felt so helpless.

'I left my car on the pavement outside the hospital,' I said. 'I'd better go and move it.'

'Sorry, sir,' said the policeman. 'You're not to leave until you've given a statement to my super.'

His super turned out to be Detective Superintendent Aldridge of the Metropolitan Police, who arrived with another plain-clothes officer in tow. They showed me their warrant cards.

'Thank you, constable,' said the Super, dismissing our uniformed friend.

'I'll go and check on your car, sir,' he said to me. 'What's the registration?'

I gave him the registration and the keys.

The Superintendent wanted a blow-by-blow account of everything either Rosie or I had done all day. It was tedious and my mind was elsewhere.

'I'm going to see Marina,' I said finally with exasperation.

'All in good time, Mr Halley,' said the Super.

'No, now,' I said, standing up and walking to the door. 'I'm going to see my fiancée.' The term was beginning to grow on me.

I SAT ON ONE of the chairs outside the door to the Intensive Care Unit, opposite the lifts. A plain-clothes policeman sat alongside me and time passed very slowly. I looked at my watch. Unbelievably it had been only fifty-five minutes since Rosie had rung me in the sandwich bar. It felt like hours.

I thought about Marina's parents. I had only met them a few times. They had stayed with us in London last year at Easter, and we had been over to stay with them in Holland during August so Marina could show me where she was brought up. I should give them a call. But it would have to wait. I didn't have their number with me and I wasn't leaving to get it.

Who else should I call? Perhaps I should tell Charles. I'd welcome his support. Charles! For God's sake! If they, whoever 'they' might be, were trying to pressurise me into stopping my investigation by shooting Marina, they might try and shoot Charles, too.

'I've got to make a phone call,' I said to the policeman. 'It's urgent!'

There was a big NO MOBILE PHONES sign on the door to the unit. Too bad, I thought. This is an emergency. I moved to the window at the end of the corridor, switched on my mobile and dialled Charles's number. Thankfully he answered at the fourth ring.

'Charles,' I said, 'it's Sid. Marina's been shot and I'm frightened you might be next. Get out of the house. Take Mrs Cross with you, then call me.'

'Right, on our way,' he said. 'Call you in five minutes.'

Thank goodness for military training. But it was not the first time I'd had to do that, and on the previous occasion I had been right to warn him. I remembered and, apparently, so had Charles.

I waited near the window, and the five minutes seemed to be an eternity.

At last he called back. 'We're safely in the car and well away from the house,' he said. 'Is Marina . . .?' He couldn't finish.

'I'm at St Thomas' Hospital,' I said. 'It's touch and go. She's in theatre but it's not too good.'

'I'll drop Mrs Cross and then come on.'

'Thanks, I'd like that,' I said. 'I'm in the Intensive Care Unit waiting for Marina to come out of the operating theatre.'

'I'll find it,' said Charles, and I was sure he would.

I went back to sitting with my shadow. One of the lifts opened. I jumped up but it wasn't Marina. It was Superintendent Aldridge and Rosie. The poor girl looked about half her normal tiny self and absolutely exhausted.

The plain-clothes policeman had stood up on the arrival of his boss, and Aldridge sat down next to me on one side with Rosie on the other.

'Now, Mr Halley, I know all about you.'

I looked at him quizzically.

'There's not a copper alive who doesn't, not a detective anyway.'

I wasn't sure whether it was flattery or not. 'So?' I said.

'Was this shooting anything to do with your investigations?'

I was saved from the immediate need to answer by the appearance through the door of another medic. 'Mr Halley?' he asked.

I stood up. My heart was thumping in my chest.

'My name's Mr Pandita,' he said. 'I've been operating on the lady with the bullet wound in her leg. She's been transferred here.' He cocked his thumb towards the double doors behind him.

'How is she?' I asked.

'The operation went well. Now it's a matter of time.'

'What chances are we looking at?' asked the Superintendent.

'Reasonable,' said Mr Pandita. 'She's a fit young girl and obviously a fighter. I give her a better than fifty-fifty chance.'

'Can I see her?' I asked.

'Not just yet,' he said. 'The nursing staff are with her, setting up all the monitoring equipment. Soon. But she'll be asleep. We've given her a sedative to keep her blood pressure low. I'll tell the staff you're here and they'll come and get you when they're ready.'

I nodded. 'Thank you.'

He disappeared back through the door and I sat down.

'Now, where were we?' said Superintendent Aldridge. 'Ah, yes, did this shooting have anything to do with your investigations?

'What do you mean?' I asked.

'I presume this wasn't a random shooting,' he said, 'and that Miss Meer was specifically targeted by the gunman.'

'But he'd have had to wait there for ages,' I said. 'It was only by chance that Marina came out when she did.'

'Assassins can wait for days or weeks to get an opportunity if they're determined enough,' he said. 'So, do you think this has anything to do with your investigations?'

'I don't know,' I replied. 'If you mean do I know who did this, then the answer's no. If I did, I'd tell you, you can be sure of that.'

'Do you have any suspicions?'

'I always have suspicions,' I said, 'but they're not based on anything solid.'

'Anything you say might be useful.'

'Do you remember the jockey who was murdered at Cheltenham races two weeks ago?'

'I remember that horse, Oven Cleaner, died,' he said. 'That was a shame.'

'Yes, well, a jockey was murdered on the same day. Then a racehorse trainer appeared to kill himself. Everyone, and especially the police, seem to think he committed suicide because he'd murdered the jockey.'

'So?' he said.

'I believe the trainer was in fact murdered by the same man who killed the jockey and that it was made to look like suicide so that the police file on the jockey's death would be conveniently closed. And I've been saying so loudly and often for the last ten days to anyone who'll listen.'

'What has any of this to do with Miss Meer being shot?' he said.

'Last Friday, I was warned that, if I didn't keep my mouth shut, someone would get badly hurt. And now they have.'

CHAPTER 8

They finally allowed me in to see Marina around four.

First I had to don the regulation outfit of blue smock with matching cap. And I had to wear a mask over my mouth and nose. I wondered how she would know who I was, but I needn't have worried; she was asleep.

She looked so defenceless lying there, connected to the machines, with the tube still in her mouth. Her breathing was being assisted by a ventilator and the rhythmic purr as the bellows rose and fell was the only sound.

I sat to one side and held her hand. I told her how much I loved her and how dreadfully sorry I was to have brought all this on her. I told her to fight, to live, and to get better. And I told her that I'd get the man who'd done this. And then we'd see. Maybe I'd take up gardening as a career, though one-handed gardening might be a problem. And I asked her to marry me.

She didn't reply. I told myself she was thinking it over.

A nurse came to tell me that there were some people to see me outside. Not more police, I thought. But it was Charles, and he had brought Jenny.

'Hello, Sid,' she said. She gave me a peck on the cheek. 'How is she?'

Charles and I shook hands.

'She's doing OK—at least, I think so. The nurses seem optimistic, but I suppose they would. Certainly her colour is much better than earlier.'

'Jenny picked me up from Paddington,' said Charles. 'I called her on the way up on the train and she wanted to come. You know, to give support.'

'I'm glad you're here,' I said. 'Both of you.'

I looked past Charles and was astonished to see Rosie still sitting on one of the chairs opposite the lifts.

'Rosie,' I said, 'why don't you go home?'

She turned and looked at me with sunken eyes. She was clearly in no state to leave the hospital on her own.

'Charles, Jenny, this is Rosie.'

Jenny sat down next to Rosie and put her arm round her shoulder. The human contact was too much and Rosie burst into tears, hanging on to Jenny as though her life depended on it.

'We'll look after her,' said Charles. 'You go back to Marina. We'll be here when you need us.'

He ushered me back to the unit door and almost pushed me through.

I stayed with Marina for what seemed like a long time. Every few minutes, a nurse would come and check on her and twice Mr Pandita, the surgeon, came in too.

'She's doing fine,' he said on his second visit. 'I'm more hopeful. We will leave her sedated overnight and attempt to bring her out of the induced coma in the morning. Only then will we really know.'

We stood at the foot of the bed, looking down at the unconscious figure.

'I think I'll go and get something to eat,' I said. It was a while since I'd left my uneaten lunch on the floor of the sandwich bar, and even longer since dinner the previous night. 'Then I'll come back, if that's all right?'

'There are no visiting times on this ward. We run a twenty-four-hour service here.' He smiled. At least I think he smiled. Because of his mask I couldn't see his mouth, but there was a smile in his eyes.

CHARLES, JENNY AND ROSIE were still there when I came out.

They had made themselves at home and were surrounded by the remains of bacon rolls and chicken sandwiches. Empty polystyrene coffee beakers stood in a row on the bottom of an upturned waste bin that had doubled as a table.

Rosie looked much better for having had something to eat and other people to take her mind off the horrors of earlier.

'Hello,' said Charles, looking up from a newspaper. 'How's she doing?'

'The official bulletin is "more hopeful".'

'That's great,' said Jenny.

'A young policeman came and gave me these,' said Charles, holding out my car keys. 'He said to tell you that your car is in the hospital administrator's car space to the left of the front door.'

'Fantastic,' I said.

'He also told me to ask you to move it as soon as possible.'

'I'll drive it home now and put it in the garage,' I said. 'We could get something to eat there, and I could put on a clean shirt.'

'The policeman didn't really want to give me the car keys but I told him I was your father-in-law.'

'And I told him I was your wife,' said Jenny.

That must have confused him.

MY CAR WAS WHERE it was promised and I drove the four of us back to Ebury Street. Rosie didn't want to go home on her own, and Jenny and Charles were happy to have her stay with us.

'Hello, Mr Halley,' said Derek at the desk. 'Delivery for you.'

He held out an envelope to me. I just looked at it and he put it down on the marble top.

'Did it come by taxi?' I asked him.

'Yes,' he said. 'About an hour ago.'

'You didn't get the number of the taxi, I don't suppose?' I asked.

'No, sorry.'

'Could you identify the taxi driver?'

'I doubt it,' he said.

'Do you have security film?' I asked, pointing at the bank of monitors.

'Yes, but we only have cameras on the garages and round the back. There are none in reception.'

Dead end. I looked at the envelope. It was white, about four inches wide by nine long with *SID HALLEY—BY HAND* written on the front, as before.

'This is the same as I received last time,' I said to Charles. 'After Marina was attacked.'

'You ought to give it to the police,' he said. 'Don't touch it.'

'The envelope's been handled by the taxi driver and by Derek,' I said.

I used Derek's pencil to turn the envelope over. It was stuck shut.

'I'll open it,' I said.

I used another sheet of paper to hold the envelope down on the desk and used the pencil to slit it open. Only touching the sides I withdrew the contents. It was a card with the words 'Get Well Soon' on the front, along with a painting of some flowers. I used the pencil to open it.

There was some writing inside: *NEXT TIME SHE'LL LOSE A HAND. THEN SHE'LL BE A CRIPPLE, JUST LIKE YOU.*

Charles drew in his breath sharply. 'Not much doubt about that, then.'

'What does it say?' said Jenny coming closer and reading it. 'Oh.'

'Don't let anyone touch this. I'm going to get something to put it into for the police,' I said.

'Can you get fingerprints off paper?' Charles asked.

'I'm sure you can,' I said.

'You can also get DNA from saliva,' said Rosie. 'If someone licked that envelope to stick it shut then they will have left their DNA on it.'

I stared at her. 'But won't it have dried out by now?'

'The DNA will still be there.'

'Could you get a profile from it?' I asked.

'I can get a profile from a single fruit fly you can hardly see,' she said, smiling. 'This would be a piece of cake.'

'Shouldn't you leave that to the police?' asked Jenny.

'There's plenty of stick for both of us,' said Rosie. 'I would only need a tiny bit of the envelope. And I really want to do it.' She looked at me.

'So do I,' I said. 'I'll fetch some scissors and two bags.'

We went up to my flat and I made a plateful of ham and mustard sandwiches and found some bananas lurking in the fruit bowl. The others kindly let me have first go, but then they tucked in with relish.

I went into my office to try to call Marina's parents but there was no answer. I wrote down their address to give to the police, just in case.

I went back into the sitting room. Rosie was on a mission. She wanted to go off to Lincoln's Inn Fields straight away with her bag containing a piece of the envelope.

'What's the hurry?' I asked. 'It takes hours for the stuff to move in that gel, anyway.'

'Not with my machine in my lab,' said Rosie. 'I can get results quicker than Marina could. The whole thing would take me less than an hour.'

I knew that Rosie was desperate to do something that, in her eyes, would compensate for what she saw as her failure to keep Marina from harm, and I wasn't going to stop her.

'Do whatever you like,' I said. 'I'm going to change and then I'm going back to the hospital. I'll call the Superintendent after I've gone and tell him to collect the card from reception.'

'I don't mind going with Rosie to her lab,' said Charles. 'We'll come on to the hospital after.'

'And I'll go with Sid,' said Jenny.

I LEFT THE CAR in the garage and we took two taxis. It was a long time since I'd been in a taxi alone with Jenny.

'Just like old times,' I said.

'I was thinking the same. Funny old world.'

'What do you mean?' I asked.

'Here I am, going with you to see the woman who's taken my place and I am desperate that she should be all right.'

'Are you?' I asked.

'Of course. I liked her last Sunday. You two go well together. I do want you to be happy, you know. I know we're divorced but it doesn't mean I don't care for you. I just couldn't live with you. And . . .' She tailed off.

'Yes?' I said. 'And what?'

She didn't answer. We'd arrived at the entrance to St Thomas' and I started to get out of the cab. She put her hand on my arm, the real one.

'I'm not sure how to put this,' she said. 'And obviously it's not the reason I want her to get better but,' she paused, 'Marina . . . takes away my guilt.'

I sat back in the seat and looked at her. My dear Jenny. The girl I had once loved and ached for. The girl I thought I knew.

'Are you getting out, guv'nor?' asked the driver, breaking the trance.

'Sorry,' I said.

Jenny and I climbed out of the taxi, paid, and went into the hospital.

DR OSBORNE in Casualty had said that the first few hours would be critical, but he had said that over four hours ago and Marina had survived so far. Every passing minute must surely improve her chances.

When we arrived at Intensive Care, Jenny said she would wait on the same chairs outside by the lifts, and read.

I put on the regulation blue uniform and went in to be met by the police guard that had belatedly appeared in the unit. Yes, a nurse agreed, she could vouch for Mr Halley; he's Miss Meer's fiancé. Pass, friend.

Marina looked the same as when I'd left her. I sat down as before and held her hand. It seemed natural to talk to her, so I did, albeit softly. I stroked her arm, then sat there for a while in silence.

Mr Pandita, the surgeon, came into the cubicle.

I nodded at Marina. 'How's she doing?'

'Fine,' he said. 'I think I would refer to her condition now as serious but stable. It's no longer critical. I do believe your girl is going to live.'

I could feel the welling in my eyes. I cried the tears of relief and of joy.

'Provided we can bring her out of unconsciousness safely tomorrow, she should make a complete recovery. But we'll keep her sedated for the night just to be on the safe side.'

'What time in the morning?' I asked.

'We'll stop giving her the sedative in the drip around seven. We'll remove the ventilator, and then we'll see. If I were a betting man'—he smiled again—'I'd say she should be awake by noon at the latest.'

'Should I stay here the night?' I asked.

'You're welcome to if you want,' he said, 'but it's not necessary. She's over the danger time. There shouldn't be much change overnight and we can always call you if there is. The best thing you can do is to go home and get a good night's sleep and be here for her tomorrow.'

'Thank you,' I said. 'You saved her life.'

He waved a hand. 'All in a day's work. Bye now.' He moved on.

I went back out to Jenny. Charles and Rosie appeared out of the lift at the same moment as I came through the door.

'Great news,' I said. 'The official bulletin is now that Marina is no longer critical and she is expected to make a full recovery.'

'Thank God,' said Charles.

Rosie clasped her hands to her face but it did nothing to stem the rush of tears down her cheeks. The release of tension was tangible for us all.

'That's all right, then,' said Jenny.

Yes, indeed, it was very much all right.

WE WENT STRAIGHT DOWN to the street and set off back to my flat in a cab.

'Well?' I said to Rosie.

'No match,' she said.

'Oh,' I said. 'We're looking for two people then.'

'Yes,' said Rosie. 'And this one's a woman.'

'Are you sure?'

'Absolutely. Men and women have different chromosomes and different DNA. It's easy to tell from the two profiles that it was a man who punched Marina last week, and a woman who licked the envelope tonight.'

'So what are we going to do now?' asked Charles.

'No idea,' I said. 'And there's one thing that really bothers me. Is race-fixing sufficient motive for murder?'

'Money is always a motive for murder,' said Jenny.

'But we're not talking big money here,' I said. 'Huw Walker was offered a few hundred a time to fix a race. He told me that himself. If really big money was involved, then you'd be likely to offer the jockey a bit more than a few hundred. That's not much more than his riding fee.'

We arrived back at my flat, piled out of the taxi and went inside.

'So what could be the motive for the murder?' said Rosie, when we were all settled and I had provided more ham sandwiches and a bottle of wine.

'That's the million dollar question,' I said. 'Kate Burton, that's Bill's wife, told Marina that Huw Walker had said to her that the whole race-fixing thing was more about power than money.'

'But money gives you power,' said Jenny.

'Indeed it does,' I said, 'but if you have enough money, there may be the urge to have power merely for its own sake.'

'So what's the order of the day tomorrow?' Jenny asked.

'I'll go to the hospital early,' I said. 'They're taking Marina off the sedative at seven and I want to be there when she wakes. As far as I'm concerned, you can all come—so long as you don't mind more sitting around in the hospital corridor. I'll need to get some food in before I go, though. Marina will want more than ham sandwiches when she gets home.'

'I suspect she'll need lots of rest, too,' said Charles.

'Nonsense,' said Jenny. 'What she'll need is shopping. Trust me, I'm a woman. Things get better with shopping. Retail therapy and all that.'

'You're right,' I said. 'She's been nagging at me for ages to take her to Bond Street to buy her some designer dresses. Armani, I think she wants.'

'Blimey,' said Jenny. 'You never treated me to anything so extravagant. I hope you've got your gold card ready.'

'They can't be that expensive,' I said.

'Don't you believe it,' said Jenny. 'You won't get any change from a couple of grand for each dress.'

'Really,' I said. But I wasn't paying attention. My mind was replaying the image of a long line of designer dresses with matching shoes that I had seen in Juliet Burns's wardrobe.

'WHAT TIME IS IT?' Marina said softly into the silence.

Her condition had steadily improved during the night and she had been moved to a new room with a view of the Thames. I was standing looking out of the window, and I hadn't noticed her open her eyes.

I glanced at Big Ben across the river. 'Twenty past ten.' I turned and smiled at her.

'What day?' she said.

'Friday. Welcome back to the land of the living.'

'What happened?'

'You got shot. In your leg.' I sat down on the chair by the bed and held Marina's hand. I leaned forward and kissed her. 'You had us all worried for a while,' I said.

'All?' she asked.

'Charles and Rosie are outside, and Jenny too.'

She raised her eyebrows. 'And will I survive?'

'Yes, my dear, indeed you shall.'

'What damage is there?' she said.

'None that will be permanent,' I asked. 'But you emptied most of your life-blood onto the pavement outside the Institute. If it hadn't been for Rosie's attempts at stopping the bleeding, you wouldn't be here.'

'Which leg?' she asked.

'Can't you tell?'

'Both of them hurt.'

'They had to take a piece of vein out of your left leg to repair the artery in your right, which was damaged by the bullet.'

'Clever stuff,' she said smiling.

I marvelled at how a human being can be at death's door one day and then seemingly fine and dandy the next.

'I'll go and get the others,' I said.

'What am I wearing?' asked Marina, trying to sit up a little to look down at the off-white regulation-issue hospital nightgown.

'They're not going to worry about what your wearing,' I said.

'Well, I do,' she said. 'And what's my hair like?'

'It's fine,' I said. 'You're beautiful.'

In truth, she appeared washed out, with the two lines of stitches from last week still prominent in her face. But all things considered, she looked great.

I fetched Rosie, Charles and Jenny. They came in and gathered round the bed, fussing over Marina and astonished at how quickly she was mending.

I stood back by the window and watched, frightened by how close I had come to losing Marina. Fear, relief, desperate fear and overwhelming relief—the emotional rollercoaster of the last twenty hours had drained me.

But now the feeling of joy at finding that Marina would fully recover was slowly ebbing away and being replaced by a growing anger towards the person, or persons, responsible for this.

I LEFT MARINA to rest for a couple of hours. Rosie went back to work, and I urged Charles to stay with Jenny in London for a few days.

'But why?' he asked.

'Where you live is common knowledge,' I replied. 'And I don't want you to get any visits from a gun-toting motorcyclist.'

'Oh!' he said. 'Well, perhaps for a day or two. Or I could stay at my club.'

I laughed inwardly at his dilemma. The Army & Navy club had much more attraction for Charles. It had a decent bar for a start. Jenny was always complaining about the amount of whisky he drank, so he was unlikely to get much of it at her place. They decided to discuss it over some lunch.

I walked back to Ebury Street and busied myself clearing up.

SO HOW COULD Juliet Burns afford to have a wardrobe full of designer clothes with shoes to match?

I was mulling over this little teaser when my mobile phone rang.

'Mr Halley?' said a voice.

'Yes.'

'Superintendent Aldridge here,' said the voice.

'How can I help you?' I asked.

'Glad to hear that Miss Meer is making steady progress,' he said.

'Yes,' I said. 'Miss *van der* Meer is awake and doing fine this morning.'

There was a moment's pause. 'Exactly,' he said. 'Excellent news.'

'Are you still providing her with a guard?' I asked him.

'We are, but I don't really think it's necessary.'

'How so?' I said.

'The gunman clearly didn't mean to kill her in the first place as he shot her in the leg. He was obviously trying only to wound her. So I don't really believe that she is in any danger in the hospital. I'm afraid the guard will be withdrawn this afternoon at the change of shift.'

Reluctantly, I agreed with his assessment.

'Did you get any fingerprints off the card?'

'It's still with forensics but they weren't very hopeful. The card appears clean but they are still testing the envelope.'

'So what do you do now?' I said. 'How are you going to find this gunman?'

'This wasn't a murder,' he said, 'and I have limited resources.'

'But it was a shooting in broad daylight in a London street.'

'Mr Halley, every day in London streets there's about one shooting that results in injury or death. And there's a gun crime somewhere in London on average every five or six hours.' He paused for effect. 'I'm sorry,' he said, 'If Miss van der Meer had died, I might have had a few officers in a team to help find the gunman. Thankfully, she didn't, so I don't get the resources. We're too busy trying to catch some other poor sod's killer.'

'But it may be the same person who killed Huw Walker,' I said.

'Who?'

'The jockey at Cheltenham.'

'Oh, yes,' he said. 'Perhaps I'll give Gloucestershire police a call.'

'Ask for Chief Inspector Carlisle,' I said.

'Right,' he said, and disconnected.

I'd better investigate this myself, then.

MARINA WAS SITTING up in bed, looking much better, when I returned to see her at four thirty. I had brought with me a suitcase of things for her but I needn't have bothered. She was already wearing a pretty pink nightdress and a matching cotton dressing gown. She had applied some make-up and the stitches had been removed from her eyebrow and lip.

'You look wonderful,' I said. 'Where did you get the nightie?'

'Rosie had it sent over from Rigby and Peller. Isn't she fantastic?'

'Absolutely,' I agreed, sitting down on the chair beside the bed.

'A policeman did come to see me this morning,' said Marina. 'He asked me if I could describe the man who shot me.'

'And can you?' I asked.

'No, not really. It all happened so fast. I remember him looking at a map and beckoning me over to him. He was wearing black leathers and a black helmet—you know, one of those ones with a full front with a dark visor. That's why I couldn't see his face. That's about it.'

'Are you sure it was a man?'

'You think it might have been a woman?'

'It's possible,' I said.

She paused. 'No, it was a man. I could spot a woman, even in leathers.'

'What else did the policeman say?'

'He asked if I'd recognise the motorbike.' She laughed. 'I told him it had two wheels but that didn't seem to help. I don't know what type it was. I wouldn't know if I'd had all day to examine it.'

'But it was blue,' I said. I didn't know.

'No, it wasn't,' she said. She stopped with her mouth open. She closed it. 'It was red. How funny, I didn't remember before.' She paused for quite a while. 'It also had a big red fuel tank with yellow flashes down the side. And the rider had more yellow bits on his trousers, along his thighs.'

'Could you draw the shape of the yellow flashes?' I asked.

'Absolutely,' she said. 'They were like lightning bolts.'

'Good girl,' I said. 'I'll get you some paper and a pencil.'

I managed to borrow a pad and pen from the nursing station. Marina set to work and had soon produced some drawings of the lightning-type flashes on the fuel tank and on the motorcyclist's leather trousers.

Just as she finished, a nurse came in and told me it was time to go.

'See you tomorrow, my love,' I said to Marina, giving her a kiss.

WHEN I WAS RIDING, Saturday morning had always been a 'work day' in Andrew Woodward's yard, and I assumed that nothing would have changed. On a 'work day', a large string of horses would be out on the exercise grounds early, galloping hard to increase their stamina and speed.

First lot in the Woodward stable had always gone out at half past seven sharp. There was much to do for the trainer and his assistants prior to the 'mount up' order, and at ten past seven they would be busy with the horses and the stable staff. Which is why, on Saturday morning at ten past seven precisely, I let myself in through the front door of Juliet Burns's tiny cottage.

Lambourn is set in a hollow of the Berkshire Downs, appropriately close to the Bronze Age white horse figure carved into a chalk hill at Uffington. Locally the area is known as the Valley of the Racehorse. At about 2,000, there are almost as many racehorses living in the village as there are people.

Thankfully, Juliet's front door key was under the stone in the window box, just as before. I turned the lock, put the key back under the stone, and stepped into the cottage.

I stood listening in the hallway for a moment, then closed the door and padded silently up the stairs. It would be just my luck if she was still here, ill in bed. I risked a peep into her bedroom. The bed was empty and unmade. I put my right hand down on the sheet; it was cold.

I reckoned I had at least twenty minutes before Juliet could possibly come home. I wasn't worried about fingerprints. I'd been in this house only last week. My right hand dabs must have already been everywhere. I went across to her wardrobe and opened the door.

Altogether, I counted a dozen outfits hanging there, many of them in designer-named plastic covers. It was an impressive list, with four Giorgio Armanis, two each from Versace and Gucci, and a scattering of others, all of them from well-known designers that even I had heard of. There were rows of shoes from Jimmy Choo and a shelf of handbags from Fendi. It was a veritable treasure trove. I did a simple mental calculation using some information about prices that I had obtained from Jenny.

Good assistant trainers could command quite high salaries, I knew, but I wondered how Juliet Burns would have the means to have clothes and accessories worth nearly £30,000 in her wardrobe.

I took my camera out of my pocket and took some shots through the open wardrobe door. I didn't want to disturb things more than I needed to. Then I closed the wardrobe door and looked round the rest of the bedroom. I looked in the drawers in her dressing table but there was nothing unusual. There were bedside cabinets on either side of the double bed. In one I found a pair of men's boxer shorts and a rolled up pair of men's socks.

In the bathroom, two toothbrushes stood in a beaker on a glass shelf, but otherwise there was nothing of interest. I made a last check of the bedroom and noticed Juliet's hairbrush on her dressing table. Among its mass of black bristles were some hairs that had conveniently been pulled out with the follicles still attached. I took a photograph of it.

Very carefully, I removed at least a dozen of the hairs and placed them in a plastic bag. I put the brush back where I had found it and went downstairs. I glanced at my watch. I had already used up ten minutes, half my time.

I searched the kitchen but there was nothing of interest there, either. The waste bin under the sink was empty and I didn't dare go outside to rummage through the dustbin. There were too many eyes that might have been watching. Such a shame. I had discovered all sorts of secrets in dustbins.

In the small sitting room, a laptop sat on the floor next to the sofa. I opened the lid. It was on but in 'hibernation' mode. I woke it up and I was busy sifting through the recent document list in Word when there was a noise from the front door. I froze.

The noise came again. A metallic clink. I moved behind the sitting-room door and looked through the crack by the hinges into the hall. A letter came through the letterbox in the front door and joined some magazines already on the mat. The cover closed with a metallic clink. I heard the postman move away. I chanced a look out of the window and saw him going next door.

I started breathing again and my heart rate began to return to normal.

I looked at my watch. My time was up.

I went back to Juliet's computer. I put back into hibernation and returned it to its original spot on the floor.

After checking that I had my camera and the bag containing the hairs, I opened the front door and took a quick look each way down the road. The postman was a good hundred yards away by now and moving further away with every step. There was no one else visible, so I quickly pulled the door closed behind me and walked steadily to my car. I had parked on the grass verge fifty yards away. I climbed in and sat in the driver's seat. My hand was shaking. I was getting too old for this cloak and dagger stuff.

BY THE TIME I got back, I was tired. At six that morning, the journey from my flat to Lambourn had only taken about an hour, but the return had been a nightmare. Three hours of stop-start in heavy traffic due to major road works on the approach to London.

I changed out of my housebreaking clothes of black jeans, dark sweater and loafers into grey trousers, blue collared shirt and black leather slip-on shoes. I snapped a recharged battery into my arm and made myself a cup of strong coffee to recharge the rest of me.

Marina phoned. 'Please come and get me out of here,' she said. 'I can't stand daytime TV.'

'I'll be in later,' I said, 'and I'll bring you a book.'

'I want to come home.'

I told her to stay put for the moment and I would see what could be done.

At lunchtime I took the tube to Lincoln's Inn Fields with my precious parcel to give to Rosie. I had phoned her at home and she had agreed to give up some of her Saturday afternoon to analyse the hairs.

While she went up to her laboratory, I took my camera to a photographic shop. They had one of those machines that convert digital images into prints while you wait. I made two sets of all the pictures stored on the camera memory card, including six images of a wardrobe full of designer gear.

There was no sign of Rosie when I returned, so I sat in the reception area and read leaflets about why early diagnosis of cancer is so important. By the time Rosie reappeared, I was examining my body for lumps and bumps.

'Jackpot!' she called, as she emerged from the lift. She was almost jumping up and down with excitement. 'In fact, double jackpot.'

'Why double?' I asked.

'I tested all the hairs in the bag separately,' she said. 'They're from two different people. Most of them are from the woman who licked the envelope.'

'And?' I said.

'One of them is from the man who attacked Marina.'

CHAPTER 9

'You're a bastard,' said Chris Beecher. 'You used me.'

He was right, on both counts. My window-cleaner father had fallen off a ladder to his death only three days before he had been due to marry my pregnant mother.

It was Saturday afternoon and I had telephoned him while I watched the racing from Kempton on the television.

'You didn't have to run the piece,' I said.

'Wish now we hadn't. Wasn't so much of a scoop after all, was it?'

'How do you know?' I said.

'Worked it out, didn't I?' He was a bright chap. 'No bloody police reaction, was there? Bloody Paddy O'Fitch. Why do I ever listen to him?'

'Can I come and see you?' I asked. 'I may have a real scoop for you after all.'

I despised the creep, but he was the best man for what I had in mind.

'On the level?' he said.

'On the level. But not on the telephone. And not until tomorrow.'

'It may have disappeared by then or some other bloody paper may have it.'

'Rest easy,' I said. 'This will be your exclusive, but all in good time.'

In the end we agreed to meet in the Ebury Street Wine Bar at seven the following evening. I needed to do some thinking before I talked to him, and also I wanted to have the day free to bring Marina home.

I WENT TO St Thomas' at about four. I could sense that all was not well in Marina's world. I stood by the window looking out across the Thames.

'At least you've got a nice view,' I said, trying to lighten the mood.

'I can't see it,' said Marina. 'The bed is too low. All I can see is the sky. And the nurses won't let me get up.'

'Calm down, my darling,' I said. 'You shouldn't be pushing your blood pressure up at the moment. Give the artery in your leg a chance to heal.'

She took a few deep breaths. 'OK, I'm calm. And what have you been up to that has kept you from me until four in the afternoon.'

'I've been with another woman,' I said.

'Oh,' she said, pausing for a moment. 'That's all right, then. I thought you might have been working.'

We giggled.

'I went to Lambourn this morning,' I said. 'To Juliet Burns's cottage.'

'What on earth for?' she asked.

I pulled out the pictures of Juliet's wardrobe. 'Look at these,' I said.

She studied the six photographs. 'So?'

'They're pictures of Juliet Burns's wardrobe, in her bedroom.'

'So what's so special about Juliet Burns's wardrobe?' she asked.

'It contains at least thirty thousand pounds' worth of designer dresses, Jimmy Choo shoes and Fendi handbags.'

'Wow!' she said. She took another look at the pictures. 'I take it you don't think she obtained them through hard work and careful saving.'

'I do not.'

'But how did you know they were there?' Marina asked.

'I saw them when I took Juliet home the morning she found Bill dead.' I suddenly wondered whether she had, in fact, 'found' him dead.

'How come?'

'I hung her jacket up in that wardrobe. But I didn't realise what I was looking at until Jenny told me yesterday how much designer clothes cost.'

'It doesn't make her a murderer,' said Marina.

'There's more.' I told her about the hairbrush and the hairs and about Rosie's DNA test on them. And I told her about the card that had been waiting at Ebury Street for me and also about its handwritten message.

She went very quiet.

'Well,' I went on, 'whoever licked the envelope on Friday is the person who left the hairs on the hairbrush, and that has to be Juliet Burns herself.'

'So what now?' she asked. 'Shouldn't you tell the police about it?'

'As far as I can see, the police aren't even investigating your shooting. I was told they don't have the resources.'

'Another policeman came to see me this morning,' said Marina. 'He wanted to know if I had remembered anything else.'

'And have you?'

'Not really. I told him about the flashes on the motorbike fuel tank and gave him the drawings. He didn't think it helps much. Apparently masses of bikes have flashes on their fuel tanks. Oh yes, and another thing.'

'What?'

'The policeman told me that you'd told him I was your fiancée.'

'It was the only way they'd let me in to see you,' I said.

'Oh. You didn't mean it then.'

'I did ask you to marry me, on Thursday night. But you didn't answer.'

'That's not fair. I was unconscious.'

'Excuses, excuses.'

'If you really meant it, then ask me again.'

I looked deeply into her eyes. 'Do you want me to kneel?' I asked her.

'Absolutely,' she said. 'Get down to my level.'

I knelt on one knee beside the bed and took her left hand in my right. 'Marina van der Meer,' I said, smiling at her, 'will you marry me?'

She looked away from my face. 'I'll think about it,' she said.

I SPENT ALL OF Saturday evening researching the running of horses from Bill Burton's yard. The Raceform data base, with its almost instant access to a whole mass of statistics, proved invaluable as I delved into the running of all Bill's horses over the last five years.

I was not so much looking for a needle in a haystack, as looking for a piece of hay in a haystack that was slightly shorter than it should have been. Even if I found it, I might still not be sure it was what I was looking for.

The classic telltale signs of race-fixing have always been short-priced losers followed by long-priced winners. A horse is prevented from winning until the betting price lengthens, then a big gamble is landed at long odds when the horse is really trying. But the ability to use the exchanges to bet on a horse to lose has changed all that. The classic signs no longer exist. Indeed, I asked myself, what signs might exist?

Raceform Interactive allows the user to look for hitherto unseen patterns in performance, to ask his own questions and use the huge data available to answer them. Could the system, I wondered, be used to look for dodgy dealing in Bill Burton's yard?

My computer refused to serve up the hoped-for answers. Either there was no pattern to find, or the pattern was so long established that variations to it didn't show up over the past five years. And there had been no dramatic change to Bill Burton's results when Juliet Burns had arrived in his yard three years ago. Another dead end.

I went into the kitchen to make myself some coffee.

So what *did* I know about the race-fixing allegations? I knew that Jonny Enstone believed his horses had been running to someone else's orders. He had told me so himself over lunch at the House of Lords.

I went back to my computer. Now I asked it to look only at the running of Lord Enstone's horses. I spent ages giving every Enstone runner a user rating, depending on whether it had run better or worse than its official rating would suggest. I then asked my machine if there was anything suspicious. Give me your answer, do. Sadly, it was not into suspicion.

However, the Raceform software did throw up a pattern of sorts. According to the data, Enstone's horses tended to run fractionally above their form at the northern tracks, say north of Haydock or Doncaster.

I brought Huw Walker into the equation. I thought that he might not have ridden them in the north, but that wasn't the case. Every time in the past year that an Enstone horse had run north of Haydock Park, it had been ridden by Huw. Which is more than could be said for races further south. Huw had been sidelined with injury for five weeks the previous September, and eight of Lord Enstone's horses had run in the south during that time. They didn't appear to have run better for having had a different pilot.

What made running in the north so special?

My eyes were growing tired from staring at on-screen figures. I looked at my watch. It was past midnight. Time for bed.

EARLY ON SUNDAY morning, I called Neil Pedder, another trainer in Lambourn, whose yard was down the road from Bill's. 'What's special about the racecourses north of Doncaster or Haydock?' I asked him.

'I wouldn't know,' he said. 'I hardly ever send runners up there.'

'Why not?' I asked. There are eighteen racecourses north of Haydock and Doncaster out of a total of fifty-nine in Great Britain.

'Because it means the horses having to be away overnight,' he said. 'Doncaster is as far from Lambourn as you can send a horse on the morning of the race and still expect it to perform. So I won't send my horses north of there unless the owner pays for an overnight stay. Most of them won't.'

Why, I wondered, did Jonny Enstone's horses run slightly better whenever they had to stay away overnight?

'Who goes away with the horses when they have to stay away?' I asked.

'It varies,' said Neil. 'If I absolutely have to send a horse away overnight, I usually send at least two, sometimes three of my staff with it.'

'Don't you go as well, on the race day?' I asked.

'That depends on whether the owner will be there, or if the race is televised, or if I have other runners somewhere else. I won't go if I can help it. It's a bloody long way up there, you know.'

'How about your assistant trainer? Would he go?'

'Maybe, but it's doubtful.'

'But there doesn't seem to be any standard practice?' I said.

'No, everyone does things differently.'

Next I called Kate Burton.

'Oh, Sid,' she said, 'how lovely of you to call.'

'How are things?' I asked.

'Pretty bloody,' she said. 'I can't even organise Bill's funeral because the police won't release his body.'

That was interesting, I thought. Perhaps after all the police are taking more notice of my murder theory than they were letting on.

'And Mummy is being absolutely horrid. She keeps going on and on about the disgrace Bill's brought on the family. I tell you, I'm fed up with it.' She paused. 'Why is suicide so shameful?'

'Kate,' I said, 'listen to me. I am certain that Bill didn't kill himself. He was murdered. And I'm becoming equally convinced that he was not involved with any race-fixing.' Raceform didn't show it.

'Oh God.' She was crying. 'I do so hope you're right.'

'Believe it,' I said. 'It's true.'

We talked for a while longer about the children and the future of the house. I managed to steer the conversation round to the stable staff.

'What has happened to them all?' I asked her.

'Gone off to other jobs. Mostly in Lambourn,' she said.

'What about Juliet Burns?' I said.

'She's with Andrew Woodward now,' said Kate. 'It's a good job, and she's done really well to get it. I'm so pleased for her. I like Juliet.'

'How about Fred Manley?' I asked. Fred had been Bill's head lad.

'I'm not sure. He may have retired.'

'I doubt it,' I said. 'Fred is a lot younger than he looks. He's not yet fifty.'

'I don't believe it!' said Kate. She laughed. It was a start.

'Do you know where he lives?' I asked.

'In one of those cottages on the Baydon road. Next door to Juliet, I think.'

'Do you have his phone number?'

'Yes.' There was a pause while she went to get it. She gave me the number.

'One more thing,' I said. 'Could you do me a favour?'

'Of course. What do you want?'

I explained what I needed without giving away the whole truth.

'It sounds a bit strange,' she said after I told her, 'but if that's what you want, I suppose it's no problem.'

'Thanks,' I said. 'It will probably be tomorrow afternoon. I'll call you.'

I ARRIVED at St Thomas' at noon to find Marina dressed and sitting in a chair.

'They've cleared me for release,' she said. She made it sound like the parole board.

'Great,' I said.

A hospital porter arrived with a wheelchair and he pushed Marina along the corridors and down in the lift to the patient discharge desk near the main entrance. I retrieved the car from where I had parked it, and we were soon a distant memory at the hospital. Today's dramas had taken over.

'Stop fussing,' Marina said, as I shepherded her into the Ebury Street building. 'I'm fine.'

I knew she was fine. I was fussing because I was worried about her security.

At one o'clock, with Marina settled on the sofa with the Sunday papers, I telephoned Fred Manley, and spoke to him for nearly an hour.

He told me all about the system that Bill had used, and about who went away with horses that needed to stay overnight at the northern tracks. In the end he told me more than I could have hoped for.

'Thanks, Fred,' I said. 'That's very helpful.'

'What's it for?' he asked.

'Oh, just some research I'm doing about training methods. I was about to ask Bill about it when he died.'

'Damn shame that was. Mr Burton was a good man and a fine employer. I knew where I stood with him.'

I ARRIVED AT THE Ebury Street Wine Bar at a quarter to seven to be sure to be there before Chris Beecher. I had left Marina on the sofa and had double-locked the flat on my way out. I didn't expect to be away for long.

The wine bar was very quiet when I arrived, so I chose a table where I could sit with my back to the wall with a good view of the door.

Beecher arrived at ten to seven and was surprised to see that I was there ahead of him. 'Hiya, Sid,' he said. 'What are you drinking?'

I hadn't yet ordered. 'Are you buying?' I asked.

'Depends,' he said. 'Is it a good story?'

'The best,' I assured him.

'All right, I'm buying.'

I had a large glass of the wine of the month while he had a pint of bitter.

'So what's the angle?' he asked, after having a good sip.

'All in good time. I need you to set something up for me first.' I explained in detail what I wanted him to do and when.

'Why?' he asked.

'You'll find out. That will be the story. Are you on?'

'Yes, I'm on.'

'Good. You can make the call now.' I gave him the number.

He spoke into his mobile phone for quite a time before hanging up.

Then he smiled at me. He was enjoying the conspiracy. 'All set,' he said. 'Tomorrow at one o'clock. Where you said. We'll meet in the kitchen.'

'Great. I'll be there by twelve. You arrive by twelve thirty at the latest.'

'Right. Now don't talk to any other papers in the meantime.'

'I won't,' I said. 'And you keep mum, too.'

'You bet.'

ON MONDAY MORNING, Marina's leg was sore, so she stayed in bed while I spent some productive time calling Bond Street boutiques.

Charles rang at nine thirty to tell me that after two nights at Jenny's he was leaving for his club, and that I should call him there if I needed him.

'Thanks for telling me,' I said, 'but could you come round to Ebury Street first, to sit with Marina for a few hours?'

I could sense the hesitation in him.

'I've got an excellent bottle of Glenfiddich that could stand some damage,' I said. 'And a side of smoked salmon in the fridge for lunch.'

'I'll be there in thirty-five minutes,' he said.

'Perfect.'

I spent the thirty-five minutes telling Marina what I was going to be doing this afternoon.

'Darling, please be careful,' she said. 'I don't want to find myself a widow before we even get married.'

'I thought you were still thinking about it.'

'I am, I am. All the time. That's why I don't want to lose you before I decide. Then all this thinking would be a waste.'

'Oh, thanks.'

'No, I mean it, my darling, please be careful.'

I promised I would. I hoped I could keep the promise.

Charles arrived and took up his post as guardian of Marina.

'I don't need anyone,' Marina had protested when I told her he was coming.

'I'd prefer it,' I'd said. And, I thought, it would give Charles a purpose in life. To say he was bored with his time in London was an understatement.

'Now rest that leg and I'll be back later,' I said, and left them.

I ARRIVED IN Lambourn at ten to twelve, drove round the back of Bill Burton's now empty stables and parked the car.

I'd called Kate earlier that morning to tell her that it was definitely this afternoon that I needed the favour. Fine, she'd said, see you later.

I removed a large hold-all from the boot of my car and carried it through the lifeless stable yard to the house. Kate was in the kitchen giving some early lunch to Alice, her youngest, Bill's much-wanted daughter.

'Hello, Kate,' I said, giving her a kiss.

'Hi, Sid. How nice to see you. Do you want some lunch?'

'Just coffee would be lovely,' I said. 'Do you mind if I go and set up?'

'Help yourself—though I'm not really sure what you're doing.'

I had purposely not told her everything. It would have been too distressing.

'My visitor is coming at one o'clock,' I said.

OK,' she said. 'I'll be going to do some shopping in Wantage, and will have Alice with me. I have to pick the other children up from school there at three, so I won't be back until three thirty at the earliest. Is that OK?'

'Better make it four,' I said. 'Or even four thirty, if that's not too late.' I wasn't sure how long my little plan would take.

'OK. I'll take the children to see Mummy for tea. Black or white coffee?'

'White, please.'

'I'll bring it through.'

Setting up took me about twenty minutes and, just as I finished, Chris Beecher arrived. I heard his car on the drive.

'Your visitor is here early,' said Kate as I went back into the kitchen. 'We're off now, and we may see you later. If you finish early, put the key through the letterbox when you go. I've another one to get in with.'

'Right,' I said. I gave her a kiss. 'And thank you.'

Chris and Kate passed each other at the kitchen door and briefly paused to shake hands. I watched Kate strap Alice into her car seat and drive away.

I went through everything again with Chris to be sure we had the sequence right.

'And once you start talking,' he said, 'you don't want me to say anything, is that right?'

'Yes,' I said. 'Please try not to say or ask *anything*, however keen you might be. But don't stop listening.'

'No chance of that.'

I went into the sitting room to wait, and Chris went back to the kitchen. I couldn't hear a car on the drive from where I was, but at one o'clock I detected voices in the kitchen. Our real visitor had arrived, and then I could hear Chris laying on the charm as he guided our visitor through the house.

I waited. When I was sure that they'd be in the right place, I left the sitting room and walked into the hall. The house had old-fashioned locks with big black keys on all the internal doors. I went silently through one of the doors on the other side of the hall, then closed and locked it behind me. I put the key in my pocket. Our visitor was facing the window, sitting in the big armchair.

We were in Bill Burton's den. The scene of his death.

I walked round until I was in front of the chair.

'Hello, Juliet,' I said.

CHAPTER 10

Juliet looked at me, then at Chris and back to me again.

'Hello, Sid,' she said. 'What are you doing here?' She looked uneasy.

'I arranged it,' I said.

'But, I thought . . .' She turned to look at Chris again. 'I thought you said you wanted to interview me for the newspaper.'

'He did,' I said, 'because I asked him to.'

Chris had called her from the wine bar to ask if he could write an article for *The Pump* about her as a rising assistant trainer. He had told her he wanted to meet her at the place where she had started her career, at Bill Burton's. I had assumed that her vanity would overcome any reluctance, and I had been right. Juliet had been keen and had readily agreed.

I hoped that she was feeling a little uncomfortable to be back in the room where Bill had died. I was.

'Why?' she said.

'I wanted to have a little chat,' I said.

'What about?' She was keeping her cool but her eyes betrayed her anxiety. 'And what's that for?' she asked, pointing at the video camera on a tripod that I had set up facing her.

'To make sure we have a full record of what we say in our little chat,' I said.

'I don't want a little chat with you,' she said, and stood up. 'I think I'll leave now.' She walked over to the door and tried to open it. 'Unlock this immediately,' she demanded.

'I could,' I said slowly, 'but then I would have to give these to the police.' I took the photographs of the contents of her wardrobe from my pocket.

'What are those?' There was a slight concern in her voice.

'Photographs,' I said. 'Sit down and I'll show you.'

She stood for a moment, looking first at me and then at Chris. 'All right, I will, but I'm not going to answer any questions.' She moved back to the chair and sat down. 'Show me the photographs,' she said.

I handed them to her.

She looked through all six prints, taking her time. 'So?' she said.

'They are photographs of the inside of your wardrobe, which is full of designer clothes, shoes and handbags.'

'So? I like smart things. What's wrong with that?'

'They're very expensive,' I said.

'I'm an expensive girl,' she replied, smiling.

'Where did you get them?'

'That's none of your bloody business,' she said, growing in confidence.

'I think it is,' I said. 'Because assistant trainers don't usually make enough to buy upwards of thirty thousand pounds' worth of clothes,' I said. 'Not unless they're up to no good.'

'They were given to me by a rich admirer,' she said.

'Oh, you mean George Lochs.'

That shook her. She sat forward in the chair, but then recovered her composure and leaned back again. 'Now what makes you think that?' she said.

'I called the Jimmy Choo boutique in New Bond Street and said I was phoning on behalf of Miss Juliet Burns, who was abroad and had lost a buckle off a shoe and wanted to have a replacement sent out to her. They told me they had no record of a Juliet Burns having bought shoes from them.'

I walked round behind the chair and bent down close to Juliet's ear.

'I told them that maybe that was because I had bought them for her myself. And who was I, they had asked. George Lochs, I'd said. Well, of course, Mr Lochs, they said, how nice to hear from you again. Now, which pair was it? So I described the turquoise pair you can see in the photographs and they knew it straight away.'

I didn't tell her that I had also called Gucci and Armani, saying I was George Lochs. They, too, had all been so pleased to hear from me again.

'So what if he did buy them for me,' she said. 'There's no crime in that.'

'Were they payment for services?' I said.

'I don't know what you mean.'

'Was he buying sex?'

'Don't be ridiculous,' she said, offended. 'Do you think I'm a prostitute?'

No. I thought she might be a murderer but I didn't say so. Not yet.

I changed direction. 'Did you know I found a second bullet?' I asked.

'I read it in the paper,' she said. 'But I don't know what you're talking about anyway.'

'I'm talking about the fact that Bill Burton was murdered and you know more about it than you're telling.'

'That's nonsense,' she said. 'I've had enough of this. I'm not saying another thing until I see a lawyer.'

'A lawyer?' I said. 'Why do you need a lawyer? You're not under arrest and I'm not the police.'

'Am I free to go them?' she asked.

'Absolutely,' I said. 'Any time you like. But then I'll have to tell the police about the DNA evidence. *Your* DNA.'

'You're bluffing,' she said.

'Can you be sure?' I asked. 'Take a look at this.' I handed her the photograph of her hairbrush.

'How did you get these photographs?'

'I visited your house,' I said, 'while you were at work.'

'Is that legal?' she asked.

'I doubt it,' I replied. 'Have a close look and tell me what you see.'

'A hairbrush,' she said.

'Not just any hairbrush, it's your hairbrush,' I said. 'Did you know that you can obtain a DNA profile from a single hair follicle?'

She didn't say anything.

'Well, you can.' I again went round behind her so that both our faces would be in the video recording. 'And I bet you don't know that it was also possible to get your DNA from the saliva you used to lick the envelope of the "get well" card you left for me last Thursday.'

It was a bombshell. She jumped up. Her mouth opened and closed but no sound came out. She looked for a place to run and went over again to the door and wrestled with the knob. The door didn't budge.

'If you run away,' I said, 'I'll hand the whole lot over to the police.'

Her gaze swung round to my face. 'And if I don't?'

'Then we'll see. But I make no promises.'

'I didn't shoot your girlfriend,' she said, still standing by the door.

'I know that,' I said. 'But you know who did, don't you, Juliet?'

There was no reply.

'Come and sit down again.' I went over and took her arm and led her back to the chair. 'That's better,' I said as she sat down.

I sat down on a stool facing her, but not in the way of the camera.

'And the same man murdered Huw Walker, didn't he?' I said.

She sat very still, looking at me. She said nothing.

'And Bill Burton. In this very room. And you were here at the time.'

'No,' she whispered. 'That's not true. I wasn't here.'

'But you didn't find Bill in the morning like you said, did you?'

'No.' She began to cry and buried her head in her hands.

'There have been lots of tears,' I said. 'The time has come, Juliet, to stop the crying and tell the truth. The time to put an end to this madness.'

'I never thought he would kill Huw Walker, or Bill,' she said.

'Who was it?' I asked.

Still she didn't reply.

'Look, Juliet, I know you've been sleeping with someone. I found some of his clothes in a drawer beside your bed and his hair was also in the hair-brush. So I have his DNA and it matches that of the man who attacked Marina the first time, in Ebury Street. You won't be able to protect George Lochs, even if you won't tell us he's the murderer.'

'George?' she said. 'George is gay. He'd never sleep with me.'

It was my turn to stand with my mouth open. 'Why, then, did he buy you the clothes?' I asked.

'As thankyou presents.'

'For what?'

She didn't answer.

I stood up and walked round behind her. 'Did George give you something every time you told him a horse wasn't going to win?'

'What do you mean?' she asked.

'I mean that it was you who was fixing the races, wasn't it? It never was Bill. And George Lochs would have loved to have had the information so that he could adjust the odds on his website.'

'But how could I?' she said.

'Because you were responsible for helping the lads prepare the horses for running. Fred Manley told me that you wanted that particular job and had badgered Bill until he gave it to you. Fred said that you also insisted on "putting them to bed" the night before they ran. And you insisted on helping to groom each runner early in the morning of the race. You plaited their manes and polished their hooves. You took a pride in their presentation.'

She nodded. 'We won lots of "best turned out" awards.'

'But it also gave you the opportunity to keep the horses thirsty. You threw away their water the night before a race and again in the morning. You only then had to ensure that the horses had a good drink just before the race. If the water in their bellies didn't slow them down, then the lack of water for nearly twenty-four hours beforehand would have done so.'

She hung her head again.

'And when horses ran at the northern tracks, you didn't go with them, did you? So you paid Huw Walker to make sure they didn't win. But they still ran slightly better in the north because Huw was only trying to stop them win—second was fine—but your little water trick slowed them right down. Some of them in the south finished last.'

Chris was now the one with an open mouth. He was almost rubbing his hands with glee at the scoop he would have.

'But why,' I asked, 'did you only stop Lord Enstone's horses? And then not every time they ran? Did you really do it for a few dresses?'

'I don't even like the dresses. I never wear them. They were George's idea. He loves designer wear and thinks everyone else does too. He bought me something whenever he made a good profit from a race where one was stopped. He could make an absolute fortune out of some races, sometimes more than a hundred thousand, especially if we stopped the favourite.'

'We?' I asked. 'Who are we?'

She didn't answer.

'Juliet,' I said, 'I need to know his name or I'll call the police and I won't tell them you've helped me. They'll find out who it is anyway. We have his DNA, and his fingerprints must be all over your cottage. It will only be a matter of time before he's caught, and it will be your fault if he harms anyone else in the meantime.'

'Will . . . will I go prison?' she asked in a faltering voice.

I don't think she had been listening to me. 'Probably,' I said. 'I'll do my best to keep you out of prison if you tell us everything, but I can't promise. At the very least, I'll try to ensure you don't get charged with murder.'

Her head came up fast, 'But I didn't kill anyone.'

'So who did?' I asked.

'Peter did,' she said it so softly, I hardly heard her.

'Peter?' I said. 'Peter Enstone?'

'Yes.'

SUDDENLY EVERYTHING came out. Chris sat in the corner, listening intensely and scribbling furiously in his notebook as Juliet spoke.

She started at the beginning with her first meeting with Peter Enstone, when she had been working at Bill's for only a few weeks. It was clear that she had fallen head over heels for Peter, and soon they were lovers.

'He said that no one must know, especially his father,' she said. 'It was all very exciting.' She smiled.

Peter's father, Lord Enstone, was a social climber par excellence. I expect that the daughter of a blacksmith was not what he would have had in mind as a suitable match. No wonder Peter had wanted the affair kept quiet.

'Peter said wouldn't it be funny if we were able to influence the running of his father's horses just by wanting to. We used to sit in bed some afternoons watching the racing holding the television remote and pretending that we were using it to control the horses like robots. Silly, really.'

She took a deep breath. 'I remember saying to Peter that there was a way to control the horses for real. But I only said it as a joke. I recalled my father telling me of a betting coup at the local point-to-point where a horse was stopped by giving it a big drink just before the start. He always said that water didn't show up on any dope test. Peter was excited by the idea. He doesn't like his father. He hates the way he still tells him what to do even though Peter is over thirty. And he didn't have a happy childhood.'

'So when did you start to fix the races?' I asked.

'A few months after I met Peter,' she said. 'God, I was nervous the first time. But it was really easy. I'd send the lads off to do something while I poured the water away. I'd then feed the horses. It was dead easy.' She smiled again. It was not a new trick but she was undoubtedly pleased with herself for having managed to do it without being detected—until now.

It seemed like more unnecessary mental and physical cruelty to me. I could feel the anger rising in me again. Anger at the callous nature of this person, who had been trusted to look after the horses but had been the cause of great distress for them instead.

'But soon it stopped being a game,' she said. 'Peter became obsessed with being in control of his father's horses. It gave him such power to know when they would do well and when they would not.'

Huw had told Kate it was more about power than money.

'Lord Enstone liked his horses to run at Newcastle or Kelso or the other northern tracks when he was up there at home for the weekends. I couldn't go up with them, but Peter was specially keen that the horses should be stopped when he knew his father was going to be at the races with all his mates—so he'd be shown up when the horse lost. So he paid Huw Walker to stop some. I told him it was stupid to get someone else involved, but he was determined. He said he needed Huw to get at the horses in the north.'

I wondered how long it would take Juliet to work out that Peter had probably only bedded her to get at the horses in the south.

'Then it all started to go wrong,' she said. 'Huw Walker said that wanted out, but Peter told him that if he didn't do as he was told then he'd fix him good and proper, so much so he'd get warned off by the Jockey Club.'

'But surely that would have been the same for Peter?' I said.

'As you know, professional jockeys are not allowed to bet, but Peter placed bets on the other horses in the races that Huw was going to fix and used an account that could be traced back to Huw. Peter had it as a hold over him. Unless Huw did as he was told, Peter said he would anonymously tell the Jockey Club where to look to see Huw's name on the account.'

'Why didn't Huw report Peter to the Jockey Club himself?' I asked.

'When Huw threatened just that, Peter said that no one would believe him, that they would just see it as attempt to shift the blame.'

'How many races did Huw fix?' I asked.

'Only a few,' she said. 'Maybe eight or ten, all in the north. He'd wanted out after only two. Then Huw said he'd tell Peter's father what we were doing if we didn't stop. Peter went mad and threatened to kill him. I didn't think he meant it, but . . .' She stopped.

'Peter shot Huw at Cheltenham,' I said.

She nodded. 'I didn't know anything about it at the time, I swear, but Peter told me later that it was during the Gold Cup when everyone was watching the race. He said no one noticed him and Huw going off for a chat.'

'I suppose the crowd noise at the end of the race would have drowned out the noise of the shots,' I said, 'but it was still a hell of a chance.' Perhaps he'd used a silencer, I thought.

'I know,' she said, 'but Peter was desperate. He's terrified that his father would find out about the race-fixing and go and change his will just before he drops off the perch.'

'Is he likely to drop off the perch?' I asked.

'He's got prostate cancer,' she said. 'He's had some treatment but it isn't working. Peter doesn't think he'll last much longer, a year maybe.'

So it *was* about money, after all. It usually was.

'And how about Bill?' I said.

'Peter started a rumour some time ago that Bill Burton was involved in race-fixing. He said it would keep the heat away from us if anyone started asking too many questions.'

Seemed to me like waving a red flag, bringing needless attention.

'Peter was so excited when Bill got arrested,' she went on. 'He reckoned that the only thing better than getting away with something was to have someone else convicted for it. He was annoyed when the police released Bill. He said that it meant that they didn't really think he'd done it.'

'But why did Peter kill Bill?' I asked. 'He'd done nothing to deserve that.'

'He wanted to get the police to think that Bill had killed himself after killing Huw. So they'd stop looking for Huw's murderer.' She looked at me. 'And it would have worked, too, if you hadn't stuck your damn nose in.'

'Did you see him do it?' I asked her.

'No, absolutely not,' she cried, 'I didn't know that he was going to kill him. I'm not a murderer.'

I still wasn't sure about that.

'So what happened that night?' I asked her.

'Peter rang to tell me he had to talk to Bill,' she said. 'He said he was going to help Bill get his father's horses back from Andrew Woodward's yard. I tried to get Bill on the phone but he'd gone out.'

To see Kate, I thought, at Daphne Rogers's place.

'Peter picked me up from home,' she continued, 'and we waited in the driveway for Bill to come back, which he finally did at about half past ten.'

'Then what did you do?' I asked.

'Bill was a bit surprised to see us, I can tell you. He asked us in for a drink so we went into the den. Bill poured himself a Scotch and Peter asked me to go and make him a coffee in the kitchen, as he was driving.'

To get her out of the way, I thought.

'I was in the kitchen waiting for the kettle to boil,' she said, 'and there was a loud bang and the next thing I know Peter comes out to the kitchen all frantic. He said that would sort out the police. I asked him what he'd done.'

She began to breathe more quickly with the memory.

'He didn't reply,' she went on. 'He just stood there laughing and saying that would show them. So I went into the den and saw Bill.' She glanced up at the faint stain on the wall. 'I couldn't believe he'd killed him.' She held her head in her hands. 'I was bloody mad with Peter. I didn't want Bill dead and I had nothing to do with it. I'm not taking the bloody blame for it.'

'Why didn't you go to the police?' I asked her.

'I wanted to,' she said. 'I told Peter I was going to call the police right then, but he said the same thing would happen to me if I did. I thought he was joking but I didn't do it. I was really frightened of him that night.'

With good reason, I thought. I also wondered if that was the first ounce of truth she had actually said for a while. I wasn't at all sure that I believed her account of how Bill died.

'Did Peter say how he managed to shoot Bill in the mouth?' I asked.

'Peter said that when he pulled out the gun Bill was absolutely terrified of him,' she said. 'He was pleased about that. Apparently Bill just sat there shaking with his mouth open, so Peter just shot him through it.'

'So what happened next?' I prompted.

'I was in a panic but Peter was dead calm,' she said. 'He kept saying he wanted to fire another shot so that it looked like Bill had killed himself but there had to be no second bullet found. I suggested firing it into one of the fire buckets, so I went to get one from the yard.' She looked up at me with pleading eyes. 'I know I shouldn't have done that. I am really sorry . . .' She began to cry. 'I didn't mean for Bill to get killed, I promise.'

Did I believe her? Did it matter? It was a jury who would ultimately decide if she were telling the truth or not.

'So what did you do then?' I asked.

'Peter drove himself home and I just sat here in the kitchen all night. I didn't know what to do. I kept thinking I should call the police but I was worried they'd want to know why I'd been at the house in the middle of the night, so I waited until the time I usually came to work, then I phoned them.'

'But why did you target Marina?'

'Peter said that you wouldn't be put off by a bit of violence. I said that perhaps he should kill you.'

Thanks, I thought. For that I wouldn't try too hard to keep her out of prison.

'Why didn't he?' I asked.

'Peter said that would defeat the object. Then the police would know Bill's death wasn't suicide. He said the way to you was through your girlfriend.'

It nearly was.

'Peter is not very bright,' I said. 'If he was, he'd have killed you before you had the chance to tell me what you have.'

'But he loves me,' said Juliet. 'He wouldn't harm me.'

She wasn't very bright either.

'As you like.' I said, 'but if I were you, I'd watch your back. You can't testify against him if you're dead.'

She sat there looking at me. I had sown a seed of doubt.

I jerked my head at Chris to come out with me into the hall. I unlocked the door. Juliet remained sitting in the chair looking at her hands. I took the video camera and the tapes out into the hall with me.

'I simply can't believe that!' exclaimed Chris as I shut the door of the den behind us. 'How the hell did you work it all out? And what now?'

'First you had better get on and write your piece,' I said. 'If Juliet is charged, you won't be able to publish. It will be *sub judice*.'

'Blimey,' said Chris, 'you're so right. What will you do with her now?'

'I'd like to strangle the little bitch,' I said.

'You can't,' he said. 'You've only got one hand.'

I smiled at him. It had broken the tension.

'I suppose I'll give these to the police,' I said indicating the tapes. 'Then I'll let them get on with it.'

'What's on those tapes will surely be inadmissible in a court.'

'Probably, but I reckon the police will be able to get the same information from Juliet as I have done.'

'Well, don't give it to them until my piece has appeared in print.'

'Your article might prejudice a court case.'

'I don't care,' he said. 'I want to expose Peter Enstone as the bastard he is. And I also want to make his father squirm with front page headlines.'

I wanted it, too.

CHAPTER 11

In the end, Juliet accepted an invitation from Chris Beecher to be put up in a swish hotel for a night or two. He made out that it was for her own safety, but it was really to allow time for him to write his piece and get it published before the police or the courts put a stop on the story.

I went back to London to relieve Charles from his guard duties in Ebury Street and found him snoring on the sofa.

'Right little Cerberus, aren't we?' I said to him, shaking his foot. I was not best pleased. 'I thought I left you on guard and you're bloody asleep.'

'What?' he said, rubbing his eyes.

'Never mind.'

All appeared well, however, and there was no point in making a fuss. And I had offered him my bottle of malt for lunch, so what did I expect?

Marina was in the bedroom, resting her leg as instructed and watching an afternoon game show on the television.

'How do you feel?' I asked.

'Bored, but mending,' she said. 'Did your plan work well?'

'Yes,' I said, and told her all about my little chat with Juliet.

'So, Peter Enstone shot me,' Marina said finally.

'Yes, I think he did. Unless he organised someone else to do it.'

'And where exactly is the little swine now?' she asked.

'According to the *Racing Post*, he's in Scotland, riding at Kelso races. That's why I was so keen to talk to Juliet today, while he was out of the way. I don't know where he will go from there. I think he lives in London.'

Marina shivered. 'I don't want him coming here.'

'He won't get past Security downstairs, even if he does,' I said. 'And I'm not having you left alone anyway.'

'Sid,' Charles called from the hallway. He put his head round the door. 'I think I'll go back to my club now, if that's all right.'

'Of course, Charles,' I said, feeling guilty about my earlier outburst. 'And thank you so much for coming over and spending the time with Marina.'

'Humph,' he muttered. He was not greatly soothed. 'See you, then.' His head disappeared for a moment, then came back round the door. 'I forgot,' he said. 'Jenny asked me to ask you, Marina, if you'd be up to going out for lunch with her tomorrow. If yes, she'll pick you up here at twelve thirty.'

'I don't know,' I said. I was worried about what reaction the next day's edition of *The Pump* might produce.

'I'd love to,' said Marina. 'I'll be fine. Don't fuss.'

'OK,' I said, 'but I'll organise a security guard to go with you. He'll sit quietly in the corner of the restaurant and not disturb you, but I'd be happier.'

'Fine,' said Marina. 'Charles, tell Jenny that would be lovely and I'll see her tomorrow at twelve thirty.'

'Right,' he said, and his head disappeared again.

I went out to see him off and make my peace. 'I'm sorry,' I said. 'I didn't mean to sound so cross when I found you asleep.'

'No, it's all right,' he said. 'It is me who should be sorry.'

We shook hands warmly and I walked him to the lift.

'I'll pop round tomorrow after lunch,' said Charles, 'to see the girls when they get back from lunch.'

'That would be great,' I said. 'But take care. Mount Vesuvius has nothing on the eruption that's going to occur tomorrow mourning when *The Pump* comes out. Don't get in the way of the molten lava. It might be dangerous.'

'I'll be careful,' he said.

I decided that, much as I loved him, I should no longer place Marina's security in the hands of a septuagenarian retired admiral with a penchant for single malt whisky. So I called a fellow private sleuth who worked for a firm that had a bodyguard department, and asked for their help.

Certainly, Mr Halley, they said, they would happily provide a bodyguard for Miss Marina van der Meer, starting at eight o'clock the next morning.

I spent much of the evening making duplicates of the videotape from my little chat with Juliet. I'd made one copy at Kate's using her video recorder. Chris had taken it with him, as he was pretty certain that, without it, *The Pump*'s lawyers weren't going to let him write anything about the Enstones.

Now I made six further copies onto VHS tapes between performing my nursing and domestic duties. I steamed some salmon fillets in the microwave for dinner and we ate them in front of the television with trays on our laps.

Marina watched the tape with growing fascination. 'I really don't think I want to meet this Peter,' she said.

'You already have. He was wearing motorcycle leathers.'

'Oh, yes. So he was.' She rubbed her knee.

My phone rang. It was Chris Beecher.

'It's all in,' he said excitedly. 'Front page! They allowed me to do the lot.'

'Good,' I said, 'you've done well.' It was under seven hours since we had left Lambourn. 'Where's Juliet?' I asked him.

'Bricking herself in the Donnington Valley Hotel,' he said. 'She has tried to call me on my mobile at least fifteen times but I won't answer. She leaves messages saying she doesn't want to be named. Bit late now!' He laughed.

'Will she stay there?' I asked.

'What would you do? I don't reckon she'll go back to her place. I think we can safely say that young Mr Peter is not going to be best pleased with her in the morning. If I were in her shoes, I'd stay put in the hotel.'

In her Jimmy Choo shoes, I thought. Young Mr George is not going to be too pleased with her, either.

'Right, then,' I said. 'Now that I know that the story will definitely be in the paper tomorrow, I'll get these other tapes off to their new homes.'

'Yes,' Chris said, 'and . . . thanks, Sid. Guess I owe you one.'

'More than one, you bugger.'

He laughed and hung up. He wasn't a bad soul, but I still wouldn't be sharing any of my secrets with him in the future. Not unless I wanted to read them in the paper.

I spent some time packing the six videotapes into large padded envelopes, then went round to Victoria Station to await the papers. I double-locked the door and told Marina not to open it under any circumstances.

At ten minutes past eleven, I watched a bale of *Pumps* being thrown out of a delivery van. The paper's headline was clearly visible. MURDERER, it read across the whole width, above a smiling photograph of Peter Enstone.

The news vendor cut the strings and stacked the papers on a shelf. I felt very vulnerable as I picked up seven copies and stood there, in the open, paying for them. I could feel the hairs rising on the back of my neck.

I turned round and looked behind me but there was no one there. Just some late-night revellers making their unsteady way to their trains home.

With the papers safely tucked under my arm, I went swiftly back to the flat to find that all was well. I let myself in and locked the door behind me. Marina and I sat at either end of the sofa and read a copy of *The Pump* each.

Chris Beecher had done a great job. Everything was there. Juliet's story was largely quoted word for word, and there were pictures of Huw Walker and Bill Burton, and one each of Jonny Enstone and George Lochs. I was pleased to note that my usual *Pump* mug shot was not included. Indeed, there was no mention of me by name, just as the partner of the girl who had been shot in London.

It was a true hatchet job, with the comment section of the paper getting in on the act to criticise Enstone senior for having produced such a monster.

I was still packing the relevant pages of *The Pump* into the padded envelopes at a quarter to midnight when the buzzer of the internal phone sounded outside the kitchen door. The porter/security downstairs informed me that my preordered late-night courier service had arrived.

I took five of the envelopes downstairs with me in the lift. I was slightly taken aback to find a motorcyclist in reception dressed in black leathers and wearing a full-face helmet, but the courier took the packages and assured me they would be delivered during the night.

'The first three can arrive any time you like,' I said. 'The fourth must arrive after five o'clock when you'll probably find him feeding his cattle. And the fifth should be delivered last, on your way back.'

'Right.' He stuffed the packages in a bag and swung it onto his back.

'Don't go to sleep and fall off your bike,' I said.

'I won't,' he mumbled into his helmet, and left.

What would be his route, I wondered. New Scotland Yard first, I expected, for Detective Superintendent Aldridge, then on to Thames Valley police headquarters in Oxfordshire to drop off the one for Inspector Johnson. Then down to Cheltenham to deliver the one for my friend Chief Inspector Carlisle. Next to South Wales, to Brecon, to find Evan Walker's farm for package four. Finally, on his way back, the motorcyclist's last stop was to be at the House of Lords. Package five was for his Lordship. The videotape was in case he didn't believe what he read in newspapers.

THE BODYGUARD I had arranged for Marina arrived promptly at eight and turned out to be a six-foot-two ex-Marine with biceps bigger than my thighs. The biceps, along with an impressive pair of pecs and assorted other bulging muscles that I didn't even know existed, were squeezed into a bottle-green T-shirt that looked to be at least two sizes too small.

He dismissed my suggestion that he should sit in reception and wait for Marina to come down when she went out to lunch. No good, he said. He wanted to have 'the target' in sight at all times.

I said I would rather he did not refer to Marina as 'the target' and he couldn't have her in sight at all times as she was still in her dressing gown and was about to have a shower. He covered his disappointment well.

In the end, he settled for a chair outside the flat door, opposite the lift.

It was a great relief to see him there when I left for Archie Kirk's office at nine to deliver the last of the videotape packages. In the interests of my own security, I had telephoned for a taxi, which was waiting for me at the front of the building with its engine running for a quick getaway.

'Well, you have caused a bit of a stir,' Archie said as I arrived.

I needn't have bothered to bring the pages of *The Pump*, as he already had a copy open on his desk.

'Is it all true?' he asked.

'Perfectly,' I said. 'And the full interview with the girl is on this tape.' I handed the sixth package to him.

'Thank you,' he said, taking it.

'I'll leave it to you to decide who gets the information on the Internet gambling and gaming,' I said. 'I realise it's not really what you wanted, but it's a start, and I will do a bit more digging before you get my final report.'

'What do you think will happen?' he asked.

'About the murders, or the gambling?'

'Both.'

'I hope the police pick up Peter Enstone pretty quickly. With luck, there'll be enough evidence to remand him in custody, and then to convict.'

'And make-a-wager.com?'

'I think it will be far more difficult to prove anything against George Lochs. He's a very sharp cookie indeed and he will have covered his tracks carefully. However, punters like to have confidence when they gamble and all this is going to severely shake their trust in his website.'

'And I'm sure you could help to further undermine that trust,' he said.

'Indeed I could,' I said with a smile. 'And I just might. Especially the trust required for online gaming. If I can show that he has been involved with some dodgy dealings with race-fixing, it is only a small step for people to believe that he has also been fixing the games on his website. I think the value of Make a Wager Ltd is about to take a major dip in the market.'

'George made a wager, and lost,' said Archie.

I left him still chuckling at his little joke and took another taxi back to Ebury Street. My Charles Atlas lookalike was still on guard outside the door. I wondered if he ever went to the lavatory.

JENNY ARRIVED on the dot of twelve thirty as promised. In spite of being announced from downstairs and being met by me at the lift, she was still keenly scrutinised by the bodyguard, who insisted on looking in her handbag before he would allow her into the flat.

'But I know this person,' I said. All too well.

'Sir,' he said, 'most people are murdered by someone they know.'

I decided against mentioning that Indira Gandhi, the former Indian prime minister, had been murdered by her bodyguards.

After an inspection of the bag had revealed nothing more lethal than half a packet of menthol cigarettes, Jenny was allowed to proceed.

'What's that all about?' she asked.

'The man who shot Marina is still on the loose,' I said. 'And I don't want him having another go.'

'Oh,' she said. 'Was going out to lunch such a good idea after all?'

'Absolutely. We can't hide away for ever. And I've arranged for Muscles out there to go with you.' She opened her mouth. 'It's all right,' I said. 'He won't sit at the same table. You can tie his lead to a lamppost.'

Marina was ready and itching to get out of our cramped home, if only for a couple of hours.

'Take care,' I said, as they squeezed into the lift with the muscles.

They were both giggling as the doors closed. Would I have ever thought that Jenny, my ex-wife, and Marina, my future one, would be giggling together? Not in a thousand years.

I was just sitting down at my computer to answer a couple of emails when my phone rang. It was Chief Inspector Carlisle.

'Did you get the tape?' I asked him.

'Yes,' he said. 'Very interesting. But you should leave that sort of questioning to the police. You may have damaged the case by locking her in the room.'

'But the police weren't interested,' I said. 'If I hadn't questioned her, no one would have. Anyway, have you caught Peter Enstone yet?'

'Not yet, but we are now officially looking for him. An alert has been put out jointly by the Met, Thames Valley and us to other police forces, immigration services, customs and so on. It should prevent him leaving the country.'

'If he hasn't already done so,' I said. 'When did this alert get put out?'

'Only about an hour ago, I'm afraid. The Met went to his home at nine this morning but he wasn't there. His neighbour told the officers that Enstone had just popped out for a newspaper and would soon be back. So the officers waited for him for an hour, but he didn't come back.'

God help me, I thought. Of course he didn't come back. He would have arrived at the newsagents to find his smiling face on the front of *The Pump* and he would have done a runner.

'Where else are you looking for Enstone?' I asked.

'Where do you suggest?'

'How about Juliet Burns's house?'

'Ah, Juliet Burns,' he repeated slowly. 'And where is she exactly?'

'Last I heard she was at the Donnington Valley Hotel in Newbury,' I said, 'but that was last night. I expect she may be in need of your protection.'

'I'm sure we can find a secure cell for her somewhere.'

'Don't be too hard on her,' I said. 'She did help me in the end.'

The buzzer sounded on the internal telephone, so I went into the hallway to answer it, still holding my mobile.

'Just a moment,' I said to Carlisle.

'Yes,' I said into the internal system.

'Charles Rowland down here for you, Mr Halley,' said one of the porters.

'Fine,' I said. 'Send him up.' He was early, no doubt eager to have another go at my whisky.

I replaced the internal phone and spoke again to Carlisle. 'I must go, my father-in-law has arrived. You will call me if you catch Enstone, won't you?'

'Certainly will,' he said, and we hung up.

I went out to the lift to meet Charles, but it wasn't Charles in the lift.

It was the smiling man from the front page of *The Pump*. Only he wasn't smiling now. He held a black revolver very steadily in his right hand and he was pointing it right between my eyes.

Damn, I thought. That was bloody careless.

CHAPTER 12

'I've come here to kill you,' Peter said.

I didn't doubt it.

'Inside,' he said.

We were standing outside my front door near the lift and, typically, there was no sign of my neighbours. We went in through the door and he locked it behind us. Peter took the key out of the lock and put it in his pocket.

'In there,' he said, waving the gun towards the sitting room. He seemed to be looking for something.

'She's not here,' I said, assuming it was Marina he was after.

He ignored me. 'This way,' he said, again waving with the gun, this time directing me back into the hallway.

We proceeded to go all round the flat until he seemed satisfied that we were alone. I could see the clock in the bedroom. It was only ten to one; it would be at least an hour before Marina and Jenny came back.

'Go in there,' he said, pointing at the bathroom.

I went in. He turned on the light, and the extractor fan began to whine. I wished it could extract me from this situation.

The bathroom was a small room about six foot six square. It was in the interior of the building and had no windows. A bath stood against the wall on the right with a lavatory next to it, and there was a washbasin opposite the entrance. But Peter was most interested in what was behind the door, attached to the left-hand wall—a shiny chrome three-bar heated towel rail about three feet long. Three yellow towels were neatly hanging on it.

'Catch,' he said and threw me a pair of sturdy-looking metal handcuffs that he had brought with him in his pocket.

I caught them.

'Put one on your right wrist and the other round the bracket of the towel rail where it's attached to the wall. Shut them tight.'

I managed it with some difficulty. My real hand was now firmly attached to the heating system. Not a great improvement.

'Now put your left hand out towards me,' he said.

I wondered if and when I would not do as he said.

He seemed to sense the thought in me and raised his gun higher, taking deliberate aim at my head. I could see right down the barrel. I speculated about whether I would have time to see the bullet coming before it tore into my brain. I decided that I didn't want to find out. I put my left hand forward.

He lifted the sleeve of my shirt and removed the battery from my false arm and put it in his pocket. 'Now take that thing off,' he said, stepping back.

'I can't,' I said.

He held the gun in his left hand and grasped my left wrist with his right. He pulled. I pulled back. I stressed my arm to prevent the false bit from coming off. He pulled harder. The arm didn't shift.

'You won't remove it, it stays on permanently,' I said. 'You see those little rivets on either side? They're the ends of the pins that go right through what's left of my real arm to hold it in place.'

I wasn't really sure why I told him the lie. The rivets were actually holding the sensors in place on the inside, the sensors that sat against my skin to pick up the nerve impulses that made the hand work. It was only a small act of defiance, but it was something.

He gave the arm one last violent tug but I was ready for him, and the fibreglass shell didn't budge.

He stood back and looked at me. Then he said, 'Put the arm out again.'

I did so. He took the battery out of his pocket and clipped it back into place. I moved my thumb in and out.

'Grab hold of the towel rail,' he said. 'There.' He pointed.

I placed my unfeeling fingers round the hot rail and closed the thumb. He leaned forward and removed the battery, dropping it onto the floor. Without the battery the thumb wouldn't move. The hand and arm were locked in place. Now both my hands were firmly attached to the towel rail.

Peter Enstone seemed to relax a little. He had been as frightened of me as I was of him.

'What does it take to stop you?' he asked.

'Honesty,' I said.

'Don't be so bloody self-righteous. You have ruined my life.'

'You ruined it yourself,' I said.

He ignored me. 'Do you know what it's like to hate your own father? And to spend your life trying to please someone only for them to despite the very ground you walk on?'

'No,' I said. I had never even known my own father.

'It becomes your whole existence. Looking for things he will like but only finding things he hates. And all the time he thinks you're an idiot, an imbecile, a helpless child, with no feelings.'

I stood there looking at the monster. This man was no helpless child.

'Then I found a way of breaking out of the cage,' he said. 'I found a way to control his emotions. To make him happy, to make him sad, and especially to make him angry with someone else for a change. And now you have taken all that away, and he'll know that it was me who was controlling him. He's going to be so angry with me again.'

He's not going to be the only one, I thought. He sounded like a petulant schoolboy caught with his hand in the biscuit tin.

'I spent my whole childhood being frightened of him. He'd beat me for being naughty, and the harder I tried to be good, the more he saw me as naughty. "Hold out your hand, Peter," he'd say. Then he'd hit me with a wooden bat.' He stared off into space. 'He used to hit my mother as well. He drove her away. At first, she used to protect me from him, but then she left. She deserted me.' He paused. 'He as good as killed her. She was desperate to get away from him and she agreed to everything he said so long as he'd leave her alone. He saw to it that she left with nothing, no money, no home and no chance of ever seeing me again. I was twelve.'

She'd obviously not had a good solicitor, I thought. Times had changed.

'He never spoke about her. It was as if she'd never existed. I found out much later that she'd been destitute. When she tried to take him to court to get access to me, his lawyers blocked her. They tore to shreds the hardly qualified Legal Aid lawyer that my mother had to resort to. She walked straight out of her lawyer's office and under a number fifteen bus.'

He sat down on the edge of the bath. The longer he talked, the greater the chance that Muscles would come back and save my skin, but I would probably need to survive for another hour if the cavalry were to arrive in time.

'The inquest said it was an accident, but I reckon she did it on purpose. My father killed her as sure as if he'd been driving the bus himself.' He had tears in his eyes. 'When I got older and bigger, he stopped hitting me. I told him that if he hit me again I'd hit him back. So he changed his tactics from physical to mental abuse. He puts me down at every opportunity. He belittles everything I do. I hate him. I hate him.'

Why then, I thought, don't you go and shoot him instead of me?

'And when I find I am good at something, you go and wreck it. At last I discovered that it's me that has the power, it's me people are frightened of.' He looked at my face. 'Everyone except you. You're not even frightened now.'

I was. But I didn't say so. I stood there in silence and watched him.

I began to sweat. In spite of the insulating effect of the towels against which I was leaning, I was getting very hot. I was worried that he should think that my skin was damp due to fear. But did it matter? Yes. It did to me.

'You should be frightened,' he said. 'I am going to kill you. I've got nothing to lose now. I'll get done for the other two murders so why not for three? Three life sentences are just as long as two. And in all those years ahead, I will have the satisfaction of knowing that it was me that beat Sid Halley. I might be in jail but you'll be pushing up the daisies. Then one day I'll be out, but there'll be no bringing you back from the dead.'

He smiled. I began to be more than frightened. I became angry. Why should this little worm use his father as his excuse for his actions? Yes, his father was an ogre and a bully, but Peter was thirty-two years old and there are limits to how much and for how long you can blame the parents.

The rage rose inside me as it had done in the hospital. I raged, also, at my predicament. Damn it, I didn't want to die. I wanted to live. I wanted to marry Marina. I especially didn't want to die like this, trussed up and at the hands of Peter Enstone.

'I think I've talked enough,' he said suddenly, standing up. 'I get fed up with all those silly films where the gunman spends so long telling his victim why he's going to kill him that someone finally arrives to stop it. That's not going to happen here because I'm going to kill you now, then I'm going to wait and kill your girlfriend when she gets home.'

He laughed. He leaned forward until his face was just six inches away from mine. 'Bye, Sid,' he said. 'Now be a good boy and open your mouth.'

Instead, I hit him.

I hit him with all the pent-up anger and frustration of the last three weeks. I hit him with the stump of my left arm.

The look on his face was more of surprise than hurt. But I had put every ounce of my considerable strength into that blow and he went backwards fast. The edge of the bath caught him behind the knees and he went over it.

There was a satisfyingly loud thud as the back of his head hit the far rim of the cast-iron bath, near the taps. He lay face up in the bath, half turned, with his chin pushed into his chest. He groaned a little but he was unconscious. But for how long? Now what?

My left forearm hurt. I had been gradually easing it out of its case for some time, and the seal round the elbow had finally separated as I had cautiously flexed it back and forth without his noticing. Now I looked at the end of my stump. It was sore and bleeding, such had been the force of the blow.

The task now was to get out of the bathroom before Peter came round.

I tugged at the handcuffs on my right hand. I twisted and pulled, jerked and heaved, but made no impression whatsoever on the metal, I simply tore and chaffed my wrist until I was bleeding on both sides.

I trod on my arm battery, which was lying on the floor. I kicked off my shoes and used my left big toe to pull the sock off my right foot. I tried to pick up the battery in my toes but it was too big to grasp.

Peter groaned again. I was getting desperate now. I refused to be still attached to this bloody towel rail when he came round.

I went down on my knees and tried to get my mouth down to the battery, but it was too far. I used my toes to pull the battery closer, and between my right foot and left stump I managed to upend it so that it sat vertically on the floor. I hung down with most of my weight on my sore handcuffed right wrist, but I didn't care. I stretched my body down and forward as far as I could reach and put my mouth over the end of the battery.

Peter groaned again, this time more loudly. I looked at him in alarm. He was being sick. I hoped he'd choke on it.

I knelt on the floor again and tried to use my mouth to push the battery into its holder in the fibreglass shell, which stuck out rigidly sideways from the mechanical hand that was firmly gripping the towel rail. Eventually, I positioned the battery at the correct angle under the lugs and used my nose and forehead to push the other end in. It snapped into place. Hallelujah.

Now I had to get my bruised and bloody stump back into the fibreglass shell before it swelled up too much to fit. I stood up, and managed to ease it in after a fashion, although the elbow seal was far from perfect.

I sent the impulses but the thumb refused to budge. Bugger. Maybe there was blood between my skin and the electrodes. I tried again and then again.

The thumb moved a fraction but still refused to swing open fully.

I kept sending the necessary signals and slowly, little by little, the thumb moved enough to allow my hand to unclasp the towel rail.

But I was still firmly attached on my right-hand side.

My normally strong mechanical left hand was letting me down. Nevertheless, I used it to attack the handcuffs—without success. I wondered if I should shout for help. But wouldn't it rouse Peter? And would anyone be in their flats to hear me at one thirty on a Tuesday afternoon?

I looked closely at the handcuffs. The cuff round my wrist was too tight for me to slip my hand through, I'd tried that. The other cuff round the rail bracket was not so tight. I put the thumb of my false hand through the ring and tried to use the arm as a lever to break the lock.

I couldn't move it far enough, so I eased my forearm once more out of the shell and used my left elbow to push the prosthetic arm down. I'm sure that the boffins at the Roehampton artificial limb centre would have loved to know that I was using their expensive pride and joy as a crowbar.

But it worked. The thumb on the hand was stronger than the lock, which resisted for a while but finally gave way with a crack. My false arm fell to the floor, but it had done its job. I was free from the towel rail, although I still had the handcuffs dangling round my right wrist.

I wasted no time. I leaned over Peter in the bath and took his gun. I held it in my right hand and pointed it at him. Should I shoot him? I had never been one to shy away from a bit of violence if it were necessary, but shooting someone who was unconscious seemed at bit extreme.

I wasn't sure that I could bring myself to shoot Peter even if he woke up. If I wasn't going to use the gun, then no one else was, either. I removed the bullets from the cylinder and put them in my pocket.

I left Peter where he was and went into the sitting room to call for reinforcements. I put the gun down on the table and dialled 999.

'Emergency, what service?' asked a female voice.

'Police,' I said.

I could hear the voice give my telephone number to the police operator who then came on the line.

'Police emergency,' he said.

'I need help and fast,' I said. 'I have a gunman in my flat.'

He asked for the address. I gave it. He asked if I was in danger. Yes, I said, I was. He said they were on their way.

'Tell Superintendent Aldridge that the gunman is Peter Enstone.'

'Right,' said the police operator, but I wondered if he would.

I walked into the hallway and used the internal telephone to call down to the reception desk.

'Yes, Mr Halley?' said a voice. It wasn't Derek. It was one of the new staff.

'Some policemen will be arriving soon. Please send them straight up.'

'Certainly, sir,' he said, somewhat uncertainly. 'Is everything all right?'

'Yes,' I said. 'Everything's fine.'

I went back to check on my unwanted guest in the bath, but it was empty.

Oh my God! Everything was far from fine.

I should have shot him while I'd had the chance. Where was he? I went back to the kitchen door, picked up the internal telephone to push the buzzer to summon help from Security downstairs. I never got the chance.

Peter came charging out of one of the bedrooms straight at me. His lips were drawn back, and there was murder in his eyes. He was in a frenzy and a rage. That made two of us.

He dived at me as I tried to sidestep into the kitchen, and he used my own false arm as a club to aim a swing at my head.

That's a bit cheeky, I thought. That was usually my game plan.

I dodged, and he caught me only a glancing blow on my shoulder. I shoved him and sent him spinning across the hall on his knees. He was quickly back up on his feet and bunching for a fresh attack. I dropped the internal telephone, retreated into the kitchen and tried to close the door.

He stuck his foot in the gap and pushed hard. I leaned on the door to keep him out but he had the strength of the demented, as well as two good hands.

I looked around for a weapon. I had a pocket full of bullets but no gun. Too late to discover that I could have gladly shot him dead.

There was a pine block full of kitchen knives on the worktop on the far side of the room, but it would mean leaving the door to reach them.

I was asking myself if I had a choice when he heaved at the door and sent me sprawling across the floor.

I jumped up and went for the knife block.

He tore at my collar and tossed me away from it. He stretched for it himself. I grabbed at him, put my right arm round his neck and pulled him backwards. But I was losing this fight. Hand-to-hand combat is somewhat tricky when your opponent has twice as many hands and no scruples about using his nails and teeth as well.

He dug his nails into my wrist and used the dangling handcuffs to pull my hand up to his mouth, where he bit it. But I refused to let go and went on hauling him away from the knives. He bit me again, this time sinking his teeth into my thumb. I thought he would bite it off completely.

I gave up my neck lock, and tore my hand free of him.

He went for the knives.

I picked up the only thing I could see. My trusty one-handed cork remover. The spike sat ready for action on a shelf next to the wineglasses.

I tried to stab it into his back but I couldn't get it through his coat.

He chose a long, wide carving knife from the block and turned around. I knew the edge was sharp. I had honed it myself.

He stepped forward and I stepped back. In two strides I was flat against the wall. As he lunged, I stabbed him with the cork remover, driving the spike deep into the soft tissue between the thumb and first finger of his right hand.

He screamed and dropped the knife. The spike had gone right through. The sharp point was sticking out of his palm. He clutched at it.

I pushed past him. The front door to my left was no good; it was locked and the key was in Peter's pocket. I went right and fairly sprinted down the hallway to the bathroom. I locked myself in.

A moment later, I could hear him walking about.

'Sid,' he said. He sounded quite calm and also very close. 'I have my gun back now and I'm going to come in there and kill you.'

Not if I could help it. Where were the bloody police?

I heard the gun go click. Then click again, and again.

'Oh, very funny,' he said.

I hoped to God he hadn't brought more ammunition with him.

'Well, Sid, what shall we do now?' he said through the door. 'Perhaps I'll wait here until your girlfriend comes home. Then you'll come out.'

I WASN'T SURE whether it dawned on me or Peter first that Marina was not coming home.

I had been in the bathroom for well over an hour. I wasn't coming out and Peter hadn't been able to get in. He'd tried a few times. At first, he had attempted to kick the door down. I had leaned against it and I could feel the blows through the wood. Thankfully, the corridor outside was so narrow that he couldn't get a run at it, and the lock had held easily. Next, he had tried to hack his way through with the carving knife. I knew because he'd told me so, but wood doesn't cut very easily with a knife, even a sharp knife, and I reckoned it would take him all night to get through that way.

The phone had rung several times. I could hear my new answering machine picking up each time after seven rings, just as I'd told it to.

I worked out that the police had to be somewhere outside and it was probably them on the phone. They would have stopped Marina from coming back. By now they must have also intercepted the real Charles Rowland.

I wondered how long they would wait.

A long time. They would have no desire to walk in on a loaded gun.

The phone rang again.

'Answer the phone, Peter,' I called to him through the door.

There was no sound. He had been quiet for a long time now.

'Peter,' I shouted, 'answer the bloody phone.'

But the machine did it for him, again.

I wished I had my mobile. It was on its charging cradle in the sitting room and I had heard it ringing, too.

I sat on the edge of the bath in darkness. The light switch was outside in the corridor and Peter had turned it out long ago. The only light came from the narrow gap under the door. I had several times lain down and tried to look under, but without much success. Occasionally I had seen a shadow as Peter had walked past or stood outside the door. But not for a while now.

What was he doing? Was he still there?

I stood up and put my ear to the door. Nothing.

The floor was wet. I could feel it on my right foot, the one without the sock. What was he up to? Was he pouring something flammable under the door? Was he going to burn me out?

I went down quickly on my knees and put a finger in the liquid. I put it to my nose. It didn't smell of petrol. I tasted it.

I knew that taste—blood. I found I was paddling in the stuff and it was coming under the door. It had to be Peter's, but the wound I had inflicted on his hand would not have produced so much.

Gingerly I opened the bathroom door and peered out. Peter was seated on the floor a little to the left, leaning up against the magnolia-painted wall.

His eyes swivelled round and looked at me.

I was surprised he was still conscious. His blood was all down the wooden-floored corridor and there were splashes of it on the paintwork where surges of it had landed.

He had used the carving knife with its finely honed edge.

He had sliced through his left wrist so deeply I could see the bones. I had seen something like that before.

I stepped towards him and used my foot to pull the knife away, just to be on the safe side. He was trying to say something. I went down and put my ear close to his mouth. His voice was so weak I could barely hear him.

'Go back in the bathroom,' he whispered. 'Let me die.'

EPILOGUE

Three weeks later, Marina and I went to Huw Walker's funeral outside a rainy Brecon. The service took place in a small grey stone chapel with a grey slate roof, and every seat was filled. Evan Walker was there in a starched white shirt and stiff collar under his best Sunday suit. Chief Inspector Carlisle was there, representing the police.

Jonny Enstone had sensibly stayed away. The turbulent relationship between father and son had been much reported and dissected by the media, with little credit falling at his feet. I wondered if he still worked the dining room at the House of Lords.

However, it was the turn-out from the rest of the racing world that would have pleased Huw most. Chris Beecher had unashamedly been using his column in *The Pump* to restore Huw's reputation and to cast him as another victim of the Enstone conspiracy. It was the least he could do.

I wasn't entirely sure whether so many had made the long journey to south Wales out of genuine fondness for the man or, like Chris, because of their guilty feelings for having initially condemned him so easily as a villain. It didn't matter. In his father's eyes, it was a vindication of his son.

We stood under umbrellas in the muddy graveyard as Huw's simple oak coffin was lowered into the ground next to his mother and his brother, and then we retired to the pub across the road for a drink and to warm up.

'What news?' I asked Carlisle.

'Juliet Burns has been charged with aiding and abetting a felon, and with being an accessory after the fact.'

'And what does that mean?' I asked.

'About eighteen months, I suspect,' he said. 'Less if she plays her cards right. It will be up to Thames Valley and the Crown Prosecution Service.'

'I thought that plea bargains didn't happen in this country,' I said.

'Oh, yeah,' he said. 'Like euthanasia? It's just called something different. How about you?' He pointed at my left arm, which I had in a sling.

'I split the end of my ulna when I punched Peter Enstone,' I said. 'I haven't been able to wear my false arm since. But it's mending.'

In truth, I had been much more comfortable with my left arm these last three weeks than I had for ten years, since my racing disaster. I was aware that, in spite of its truncation, it was a part of me as a whole. It had saved my life. It was my friend again.

'And your girlfriend?' he asked, nodding towards Marina, who was talking to Evan Walker.

'My wife,' I said smiling, 'is just fine, thank you.'

Marina had found that she had thought about an engagement for long enough while she had waited outside the flat with the police. She had told both Charles and Jenny that if I came out alive she would marry me at once. 'At once' had actually been two weeks, because her parents had been away on a safari through the African bush. They had remained blissfully unaware of their daughter's fight for life until after the drama was over. We had waited for them to return and then had done the deed in the West Oxfordshire registry office, followed by a small reception at Aynsford. Jenny had been there all in smiles, her guilt forever purged.

'Congratulations,' said Carlisle. 'So what's next for you?'

'I'm still working on the Internet gambling investigation,' I said.

As I'd predicted, make-a-wager.com had taken a nose-dive. The Jockey Club had initiated an inquiry into the running of the exchange, which Chris Beecher had publicised at full volume in the paper. George Lochs had so far avoided being charged with a crime, but had been declared *persona non grata* on any racecourse. It was rumoured that all his assets had been held in his company's name and he was now going down the tubes quicker than Enron.

Frank Snow at Harrow would be pleased.

Marina came over to me with Evan Walker in tow.

'Mr Halley,' he said, 'thank you for what you've done for my Huw. I will expect to receive your bill in due course.'

'There will be no bill,' I said. 'There's nothing to pay.'

'I can afford it, you know,' he said, somewhat stiffly. 'I don't need charity.'

'Mr Walker,' I said, 'I wasn't offering you charity. The costs of the investigation have been covered by *The Pump*.'

'Conscience money.' He chortled. 'OK, I'll take that.' He went off to talk to a group near the buffet.

'Are you going back to Cheltenham tonight?' I asked Carlisle.

'No, I'm taking the train to London,' he said. 'It looks like Peter Enstone will survive after all, thanks to you. I have to go and formally arrest him at St Thomas' for the murder of Huw Walker.'

I'd heard that he had lost the use of his left hand.

He was crippled, just like me.

DICK FRANCIS

Born: Wales, October 31, 1920
Career: National Hunt jockey, novelist
Honours: OBE and CBE

RD: Who or what was it that persuaded you to pick up your pen again?

DF: My late wife, Mary, used to help me a lot with the research when I was writing my books, and in August 2000 we decided that *Shattered*, my twenty-ninth novel, would be our swan song. Then, can you believe, just one month after that Mary had a heart attack. As we had made that decision, I said, 'Right, I'm not going to do any more.' But, about eighteen months ago, my son Felix said, 'Come on, I know Mother would like you to keep this going.' So I decided to write again. I just hope that up there in the heavens Mary is approving what I've done.

RD: Online gambling is a theme in the book. What sparked your interest in it?

DF: Everywhere you go in the UK there are billboards for online gambling, especially online poker, and I decided it would make a good background for my novel. The internet has been my way of keeping up with the racing scene in the UK since I moved to Grand Cayman, but I'm not an online gambler. I've only ever placed one bet on a horse and it came unstuck at the first fence, so I gave up betting!

RD: How did you do the research on gambling?

DF: Felix did most of the research. He spoke to several MPs about the new gambling and gaming act in the UK. He wanted to find out about the effect it will have on the sport. Of course, a lot of what I write about in *Under Orders* is pure imagination.

RD: Do you think crime in the racing world is more prevalent these days?

DF: There's more crime in my novels than there is in racing, I think. But whenever there are large sums of money to be won and lost there will always be some people out to make a gain from it, probably unfairly and illegally. I was only asked once to throw a race for money and I told the man to go to hell. But it is a temptation to youngsters just coming into the sport, who might be looking to make a bit of quick money.

RD: Is the lovely Marina van der Meer based on anyone in particular?

DF: Both my sons' partners are very similar to her and I am very fond of them both.

RD: Sid Halley returns in *Under Orders*. Is there a lot of you in him?

DF: I've always got on very well with Sid Halley. I'm very fond of him. Of course he's aged a bit between *Come to Grief* and *Under Orders*. People do say to me, 'He's like you, isn't he?' but I'm not as tough as Sid. And, unlike him, I'm eight-five, you know.

RD: What makes you happy? Is it the writing?

DF: I've always found writing hard work. Riding came much more easily to me. But I'm happy when people stop me and say how much they enjoy the stories. And I'm really happy living in Grand Cayman. Life here is lovely. I walk along the beach in the mornings, have a dip in the warm sea. I've enjoyed all my life, right from the time I was a kid.

RD: Do you manage to get to the races in the UK sometimes?

DF: Oh, yes. In late July I come over and stay in a hotel in Devon with all my family. We've been going there for fifty-four years now and I feel I own at least a wing of the place! I enjoy going to Ascot on the last Saturday in July, and to the races at Newton Abbot. And I always fly over for the Grand National earlier in the year.

RD: It's been said that the Queen Mother was a great fan of your books.

DF: Yes, she was. She had the first copy of the first book I wrote, *The Sport of Queens*, and fully approved of the title. I would give her an advance copy of my current book every year on the last Saturday in July at Ascot. On one occasion, the Queen said, 'How about me?' I didn't have another book with me but I did send one to her the next day, and for the last eleven or so books I wrote, I made sure Her Majesty had a copy.

THE SPORT OF QUEENS

For half a century, Queen Elizabeth the Queen Mother (pictured here on Gold Cup day at the Cheltenham Festival in the year of her 100th birthday) was the first lady of National Hunt racing. She was also a huge fan of Dick Francis and kept all his novels displayed on a shelf at Clarence House in London, alongside photographs of her grandchildren. In her lifetime, she had more than 400 winners, although never at the Grand National. Dick Francis, riding *Devon Loch* in the Queen Mother's colours in 1956, came closest, but tragically the horse collapsed fifty yards from the winning post. Francis was devastated, but says the incident launched him on his second career as a writer.

DEAN KOONTZ

the husband

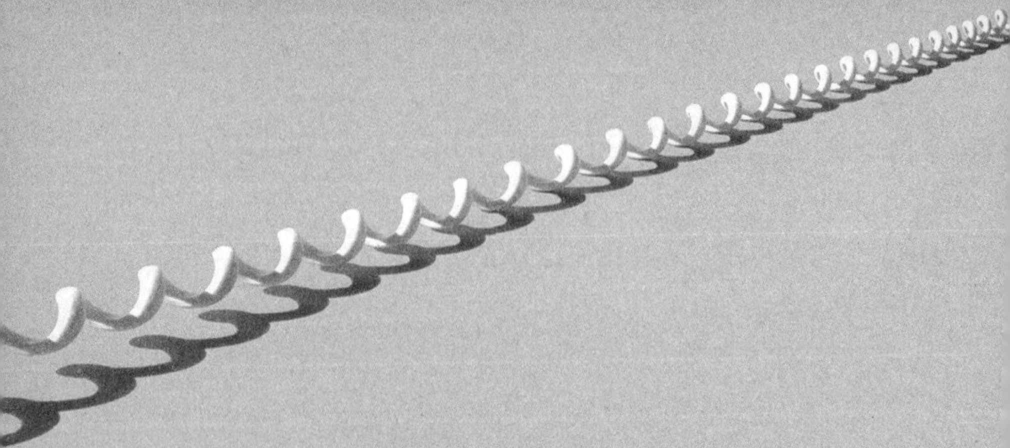

'To honour and protect,
until death us do part . . .'

The vows he made at his wedding have never hung so heavily on Mitch Rafferty's mind as on the day he gets the phone call that turns his world upside down.

Suddenly, Mitch, a self-employed landscape gardener and all-round down-to-earth guy, is the target of a kidnapping.

And a demand for $2 million.

1

A man begins dying at the moment of his birth. Most people live in denial of Death's patient courtship until, late in life, they become aware of him sitting bedside.

Eventually, Mitchell Rafferty would be able to cite the minute that he began to recognise the inevitability of his death: Monday, May 14, 11:43 in the morning—three weeks short of his twenty-eighth birthday. Until then, he had rarely thought of dying. A born optimist, charmed by nature's beauty and amused by humanity, he had had no cause to wonder when and how his mortality would be proven.

When the call came, Mitch was on his knees. Thirty flats of red and purple impatiens remained to be planted. The flowers produced no fragrance, but the fertile smell of the soil pleased him.

His clients, these particular homeowners, liked saturated colours: red, purple, deep yellow, hot pink. Raised poor, they had built successful businesses by working hard and taking risks. To them, life was intense, and saturated colours reflected the truth of nature's vehemence.

On this apparently ordinary but in fact momentous morning, the California sun was a buttery ball. The sky had a basted sheen.

Pleasantly warm, not searing, the day nevertheless left a greasy sweat on Iggy Barnes. His brow glistened. At work in the same bed of flowers, ten feet from Mitch, he looked boiled. From May until July, his skin responded to the sun not with melanin but with a fierce blush before he finally tanned.

Iggy did not possess an understanding of symmetry and harmony in landscape design, and he couldn't be trusted to trim roses properly. He was a hard worker, however, and good, if not intellectually bracing company.

'You hear what happened to Ralph Gandhi?' Iggy asked.

'Who's Ralph Gandhi?'

'Mickey's brother.'

'Mickey Gandhi? I don't know him, either.'

'Sure you do,' Iggy said. 'He hangs out sometimes at Rolling Thunder.'

Rolling Thunder was a surfers' bar.

'I haven't been there in years,' Mitch said.

'I thought you still dropped in sometimes.'

'So I've really been missed, huh?'

'I'll admit, nobody's named a bar stool after you. What—did you find someplace better than Rolling Thunder?'

'Remember coming to my wedding three years ago?' Mitch asked.

'Sure. You had great seafood tacos, but the band was woofy.'

'They weren't woofy.'

'Man, they had *tambourines*.'

'We were on a budget. At least they didn't have an accordion or finger bells.' Mitch trowelled a cavity in the loose soil. 'I don't do bars any more. I do marriage.'

'Yeah, but can't you do marriage *and* Rolling Thunder?'

'I'd just rather be home than anywhere else.'

'Oh, boss, that's sad,' said Iggy.

'It's not sad. It's the best.'

'If you put a lion in a zoo three years, six years, he never forgets what freedom was like.'

Planting purple impatiens, Mitch said, 'How would you know? You ever asked a lion?'

'I don't have to ask one. I *am* a lion.'

'You're a hopeless boardhead.'

'And proud of it. I'm glad you found Holly. She's a great lady. But *I've* got my freedom.'

'Good for you, Iggy. And what do you do with it?'

'Anything I want. Like, if I want sausage pizza for dinner, I don't have to ask anyone what *she* wants. If I want to go to Rolling Thunder for a few beers, there's nobody to bitch at me. I can get beer-slammed every night if I want, and nobody's gonna be calling to ask when am I coming home.'

Mitch began to whistle *Born Free*.

'Some wahine comes on to me,' Iggy went on, 'I'm free to rock and roll.'

'So what happened to Ralph?' Mitch said.

'Ralph who?'

'Mickey Gandhi's brother.'

'Oh, yeah. An iguana bit off his nose.'

'Nasty.'

'Some ten-footers were breaking, so Ralph and some guys went night-riding at the Wedge.'

The Wedge was a famous surfing spot at the end of the Balboa Peninsula, in California's Newport Beach.

'They packed coolers full of submarine sandwiches and beer, and one of them brought Ming,' Iggy went on.

'Ming?'

'That's the iguana. He'd always been sweet before but some wannabe tag-along—not even a surfer—slipped Ming a quarter-dose of meth in a piece of salami.'

'Reptiles on speed,' Mitch said, 'is a bad idea.'

'Meth Ming was a whole different animal from clean-and-sober Ming.'

Putting down his trowel, sitting back on his heels, Mitch said, 'So now Ralph Gandhi is noseless?'

'Ming didn't eat the nose. He just bit it off and spit it out. They put the nose in the cooler and rushed Ralph to the hospital. They said it was kinda blue when they fished it out of the iced water, but a plastic surgeon sewed it back on, and now it's not blue any more.'

'What happened to Ming?'

'He crashed. He was totally amped-out for a day. Now he's his old self.'

'That's good. It's probably hard to find a clinic that'll do iguana rehab.'

Mitch got to his feet, retrieved three dozen empty plastic plant pots and carried them to his extended-bed pick-up.

The truck stood at the kerb, in the shade of an Indian laurel. Although the neighbourhood had been landscaped only five years earlier, the big tree had already lifted the sidewalk. Eventually the insistent roots would invade the sewer system. The developer's decision to save a hundred dollars by not installing a root barrier would produce tens of thousands in repair work for plumbers and landscapers.

Mitch didn't need to make future work for himself, though. Green growing Nature would keep him busy.

The street lay silent, without traffic. Not the barest breath of a breeze stirred the trees. From a block away, on the farther side of the street, a man and a dog approached. The dog, a retriever, spent less time walking than it did sniffing messages left by others of its kind.

The stillness pooled so deep that Mitch almost believed he could hear the panting of the distant canine.

Golden: the sun and the dog, the air and the promise of the day, the beautiful houses behind deep lawns. He could not afford a home in this neighbourhood; he was satisfied just to be able to work here. You could love great art but have no desire to live in a museum.

Mitch noticed a damaged sprinkler head where lawn met sidewalk, got his tools from the truck and knelt on the grass, taking a break from the impatiens.

His cellphone rang. He unclipped it from his belt, flipped it open. The time was displayed—11:43—but no caller's number showed on the screen.

'Big Green,' he said, which was the name he'd given his two-man business nine years ago, though he no longer remembered why.

'Mitch, I love you,' Holly said.

'Hey, sweetie.'

'Whatever happens, I love you.'

She cried out in pain. A clatter and crash suggested a struggle.

Alarmed, Mitch rose to his feet. 'Holly?'

Some guy said something, some guy who now had the phone.

Holly squealed. He'd never heard such a sound from her, such fear.

'*Sonofabitch*,' she said, and was silenced by a sharp crack, as though she'd been slapped.

The stranger on the phone said, 'You hear me, Rafferty?'

'Holly? Where's Holly?'

Now the guy was talking away from the phone, not to Mitch: 'Don't be stupid. Stay on the floor.'

Another man spoke in the background, his words unclear.

She was with two men. One of them had hit her. *Hit* her. Mitch couldn't get his mind around the situation. A meth-crazed iguana was more real than this.

Near the house, Iggy planted impatiens. Sweating, red from the sun, as solid as ever.

Mitch couldn't draw breath. A great weight pressed on his lungs. He tried to speak but couldn't find his voice.

'We have your wife,' said the guy on the phone.

Mitch heard himself ask, 'Why?'

'Why do you think?'

Mitch didn't want to know why. He didn't want to reason through to an answer because every possible answer would be a horror.

'I'm planting flowers.'

'What's wrong with you, Rafferty? Are you buzzed or something?'

'That's what I do. Plant flowers. I'm just a gardener.'

'So we have your wife. You get her back for two million cash.'

Mitch knew it wasn't a joke. If it were a joke, Holly would have to be in on it, but her sense of humour was not cruel.

'You've made a mistake.'

'You hear what I said? Two million.'

'Man, you aren't listening. I'm a *gardener*. I have eleven thousand bucks in the bank.'

'We know.'

Brimming with fear and confusion, Mitch had no room for anger. He said, 'I just run a little two-man operation.'

'You've got until midnight Wednesday. Sixty hours. We'll be in touch about the details.'

Mitch was sweating. 'This is nuts. Where would I get two million bucks?'

'You'll find a way.' The stranger's voice was hard, implacable.

'It isn't possible,' Mitch said.

'You want to hear her scream again?'

'No. Don't.'

'Do you love her?'

'She's everything to me.'

How peculiar, that he should be sweating yet feel so cold.

'If she's everything to you,' said the stranger, 'then you'll find a way.'

'There *isn't* a way.'

'If you go to the cops, we'll cut her fingers off one by one. We'll cut her tongue out. Then we'll leave her to die.'

The stranger spoke without menace, as if he were merely explaining the details of his business model.

Mitchell Rafferty could not speak because suddenly it seemed that he might so easily, unwittingly say the wrong thing and ensure Holly's death sooner rather than later.

The kidnapper said, 'Just so you'll know we're serious . . . See that guy across the street?'

Mitch turned and saw a single pedestrian, the man walking the slow dog. They had progressed half a block.

Rifle fire shattered the stillness, and the dogwalker went down, shot in the head.

'Midnight Wednesday,' said the man on the phone. 'We're serious.'

STARTLED BY its master's collapse, the golden retriever halted midstep, frozen with one forepaw raised, tail extended, nose lifted to seek a scent. It had not spotted the shooter.

Directly across the street, Mitch likewise stood paralysed by confusion. The kidnapper terminated the call, but Mitch still held the cellphone to his ear. Superstition promised that as long as neither he nor the dog moved, time might be rewound, the bullet recalled to the barrel.

Reason trumped magical thinking. He crossed the street, first haltingly, then at a run. If the fallen man was wounded, something might be done to save him. As Mitch approached, the dog favoured him with a single wag of its tail.

A glance at the victim dispelled any hope that first aid might sustain him until paramedics arrived. A significant portion of his skull was gone.

Mitch was rendered impotent by this horror, immobilised by shock.

He sensed that he was in the company of someone other than the dog, and felt watched, more than watched. Studied. Attended. *Pursued*.

Lying on the sidewalk near its master, the golden retriever trembled, whimpered. Mitch's heart was a thundering herd, hoofs on stone. He surveyed the street but saw no gunman. The rifle could have been fired from any house, from any rooftop or window, or from behind a parked car.

Hardly more than half a minute had passed since the dogwalker had been killed. The crack of the rifle had not brought anyone out of any of the beautiful houses. In this neighbourhood, a gunshot would be dismissed as a slammed door.

Across the street, Iggy Barnes had risen to his feet. He didn't appear to be alarmed, merely puzzled, as if he, too, had heard a door and didn't understand the meaning of the fallen man, the grieving dog.

Midnight Wednesday. Sixty hours. Time on fire, Mitch couldn't afford to let hours turn to ashes while he was tied up with a police investigation.

He turned from the corpse, stepped off the kerb, halted. He and Iggy couldn't just load the unplanted impatiens into the truck and drive away either. Their indifference to the victim would suggest guilt, certainly to the police. The cellphone, folded shut, remained in Mitch's hand. He looked upon it with dread.

If you go to the cops, we'll cut her fingers off one by one . . .

The kidnappers would expect him to summon the authorities or wait for someone else to do so. Forbidden, however, was any mention of Holly or of kidnapping, or of the fact that the dogwalker had been murdered. His unknown adversaries might have put him in this predicament specifically to test his ability to keep his mouth shut at the very moment when he was in the most severe state of shock and most likely to lose his self-control.

He opened the phone, keyed in 9 and 1, hesitated, then entered the final digit.

Iggy dropped his trowel, moved towards the street.

Only when the police operator answered on the second ring did Mitch realise that from the moment he'd seen the dead man's shattered head, his breathing had been desperate, ragged, raw. For a moment, words wouldn't come, and then they blew out of him in a voice he barely recognised.

'A man's been shot. I'm dead. I mean, he's dead. He's been shot, and he's dead.'

2

Police had cordoned off both ends of the block. Squad cars, CSI vans, and a morgue wagon were scattered along the street. Under the unblinking gaze of the sun, windshields blazed and chrome gleamed. The light was merciless.

The cops wore sunglasses. Behind the dark lenses, perhaps they glanced suspiciously at Mitchell Rafferty, or perhaps they were indifferent to him.

In front of his client's house, Mitch sat on the lawn, his back against the bole of a Phoenix palm. The feathery shadows of the fronds provided him with no sense of diminished visibility. He felt as if he were on a stage.

Twice in two hours, he had been questioned. Two plainclothes detectives had interviewed him the first time, only one on the second occasion. They had not yet told him that he could go.

Thus far, Iggy had been interviewed only once. He had nothing to hide. Besides, he had less talent for deception than the average six-year-old.

More than an hour ago, he had returned to the flowerbed. He had nearly completed the installation of the impatiens.

Mitch would have preferred to stay busy with the planting. This inactivity made him keenly aware of the passage of time: two of his sixty hours were gone.

The detectives had firmly suggested that Iggy and Mitch should remain separated because, even if they were innocent, if they talked together about the crime, they might unintentionally start to conform their memories, resulting in the loss of an important detail in one or the other's testimony.

Sitting under the palm tree, Mitch had made three phone calls, the first to his home number. An answering machine had picked up.

After the usual beep, he said, 'Holly, are you there? If you're there, please pick up.'

Her abductors would not be holding her in her own home, but he was in denial of that fact because the situation made no sense. Kidnappers don't target the wives of men who have to worry about the price of gasoline and groceries.

Man, you aren't listening. I'm a gardener. I have eleven thousand bucks in the bank.

We know.

They must be insane. Delusional. Their scheme was based on some mad fantasy that no rational person could understand.

After getting no answer when he phoned home, he had tried Holly's cellphone but hadn't been able to reach her at that number. He had also called the realtor's office where she worked as a secretary while she studied for her real-estate licence. Another secretary, Nancy Farasand, had answered, 'She called in sick, Mitch. Didn't you know?'

'When I left home this morning, she was a little queasy,' he lied, 'but she thought it would pass.'

'It didn't pass. She said it's like a summer flu. She was so disappointed.'

'I better call her at home,' he said, but of course he had already tried to reach her there.

That was ninety minutes ago. Passing minutes unwind a watch spring; but they had wound Mitch tight. He felt as though something inside his head was going to pop.

Across the street, towards the end of the block, two women and a man were standing on a front lawn, watching the police: neighbours gathered for the drama. Not long ago, one of them had gone into a house and had returned with a tray on which stood glasses of what might have been iced tea. The glasses sparkled in the sunlight.

Now the three stood chatting, as if unconcerned that a sniper had cut down someone who had been walking in their community. They appeared to be enjoying this interlude, as though it presented a welcome break from their usual routine.

None of the three used the services of Big Green, although they would have seen him in the neighbourhood because he took care of four properties on this street. He had never met these tea drinkers, did not know their names, but he viewed them with an almost bitter aversion because their lives were still in order, because they did not live under the threat of imminent violence against someone they loved.

Although irrational, his animosity had a certain value. It distracted him from his fear for Holly. If he allowed his mind to turn entirely to worry about his wife, he would go to pieces. Each time her face rose before him he had to banish it because his eyes grew hot, his vision blurred. His heart fell into an ominous heavy rhythm.

An emotional display, so out of proportion even to the shock of seeing a man shot, would require an explanation. He dared not reveal the truth, and he didn't trust himself to invent a convincing explanation.

One of the homicide detectives—Mortonson—wore dress shoes, black slacks and a pale blue shirt. He was tall, solid, and all business. The other—Lieutenant Taggart—wore white sneakers, chinos and a red and tan Hawaiian shirt. He was less physically intimidating than Mortonson, less formal in his style.

Yet Mitch's wariness of Taggart exceeded his concern about the more imposing Mortonson. The lieutenant's precisely trimmed hair, his glass-smooth shave, his perfectly veneered teeth, his spotless white sneakers suggested that he adopted casual dress and a relaxed demeanour to mislead and put at ease suspects under his scrutiny.

The detectives first interviewed Mitch in tandem. Later, Taggart had returned alone, supposedly to have Mitch 'refine' something he had said earlier. In fact, the lieutenant repeated every question he and Mortonson had asked before, perhaps anticipating contradictions in Mitch's answers.

Ostensibly, Mitch was a witness. To a cop, however, when no killer had been identified, every witness also counted as a suspect. And Taggart's instinct told him that Mitch was concealing something.

Now here he came yet again, his sneakers so white that they appeared radiant. As the lieutenant approached, Mitch rose to his feet, wary and sick with worry, but trying to appear merely impatient.

'I'm sorry for all this inconvenience, Mr Rafferty. But I have just a couple more questions, and then you're free to go.' By contrast with his bronze face, Taggart's teeth were as white as an arctic landscape.

Mitch could have replied with a shrug, a nod. But he thought that silence might seem peculiar, that a man with nothing to hide would be forthcoming. 'I'm not complaining, Lieutenant. It could just as easily have been me who was shot. I'm thankful to be alive.'

The detective might strive for a casual demeanour, but he had eyes like those of a predatory bird, hawk-sharp and eagle-bold. 'Why do you say that?'

'Well, if it was a random shooting . . .'

'We don't know that it was,' said Taggart. 'In fact, the evidence points to cold calculation. One shot, perfectly placed.'

'Can't a crazy with a gun be a skilled shooter?'

'Absolutely. But crazies usually want to rack up as big a score as possible. This guy knew exactly who he wanted to shoot.'

Irrationally, Mitch felt some responsibility for the death. This murder had been committed to ensure that he would take the kidnapper seriously and would not seek police assistance. Glancing towards the cadaver across the street, around which the CSI team were working, he said, 'Who's the victim?'

'We don't know yet. No ID on him. No wallet.'

'How will you identify him?'

'There's no licence on the dog's collar. But that's almost a show-quality golden, so she might have a microchip ID implant. As soon as we get a scanner, we'll check.'

Having been moved to this side of the street, tied to a mailbox post, the golden retriever rested in shade, graciously receiving the attention of a steady procession of admirers.

Taggart smiled. 'Goldens are the best. Had one as a kid.' His attention returned to Mitch. His smile remained in place, but the quality of it changed. 'Were you in the military, Mr Rafferty?'

'Military? No. I was a mower jockey for another company, took some horticulture classes, and set up my own business a year out of high school.'

'I figured you might be ex-military, the way gunfire didn't faze you.'

'Oh, it fazed me,' Mitch assured him.

Taggart's direct gaze was intended to intimidate. Mitch felt compelled to avoid the detective's stare, but sensed that he dared not do so.

'You hear a rifle,' Taggart said, 'see a man shot, yet you hurry across the street, into the line of fire.'

'I didn't know he was dead. There might've been something I could do for him.'

'That's commendable. Most people would scramble for cover.'

'Hey, I'm no hero. My instincts just shoved aside my common sense.' Mitch dared to look away from Taggart, hoping that his evasion, in this context, would be interpreted as humility. 'I was stupid, Lieutenant, not brave. I didn't stop to think I might be in danger.'

'What—you thought he'd been shot accidentally?'

'No. Maybe. I didn't think, I just reacted.'

'But you really didn't feel like you were in danger?'

'No.'

'You didn't realise it even when you saw his head wound?'

'Maybe a little. Mostly I was sickened.'

The questions came too fast. Mitch felt off balance.

'You saw the head wound,' Taggart continued, 'but you still didn't scramble for cover.'

'No. I guess I figured if somebody hadn't shot me by then, they weren't going to shoot me.'

Flipping open his small spiral-bound notebook, Taggart said, 'You told the 911 operator that you were dead.'

Surprised, Mitch met the detective's eyes again. 'That *I* was dead?'

Taggart quoted from the notebook: '"A man's been shot. I'm dead. I mean, he's dead. He's been shot, and he's dead."'

'Is that what I said?'

'I've heard the recording. You sounded flat-out terrified.'

Mitch had forgotten that 911 calls were recorded. 'I guess I was more scared than I remember.'

'Evidently, you *did* recognise a danger to yourself, but still you didn't take cover.' Taggart's eyes remained a warm but enigmatic blue. '"*I'm dead*,"' he quoted again.

'A slip of the tongue. In the confusion, the panic.'

Taggart looked at the dog again, and smiled. In a softer voice he said, 'Anything more I should have asked you? Anything you would like to say?'

In his mind, Mitch heard Holly's cry of pain.

Kidnappers always threaten to kill their hostage if the cops are brought in, he thought. To win, you don't have to play the game by their rules . . .

Because he had no way to raise two million, if he told the police his story, they would at first doubt him. When the kidnapper called again, however, Taggart and Mortonsen would be convinced. What if the second call didn't come? What if, knowing that he had gone to the police, the kidnapper fulfilled his threat, killed Holly, and never called again? The police might think that Mitch had concocted the kidnapping to cover the fact that Holly was already dead, that he himself had killed her. The husband is always the primary suspect . . .

If he lost her, nothing else would ever matter. Nothing ever. No power could heal the wound, the gap that she would leave in his life. And to be suspected of harming her—that would be hot shrapnel in the wound, ever burning, forever lacerating.

Closing the notebook and returning it to a hip pocket, shifting his attention from the dog to Mitch, Taggart asked again, 'Anything, Mr Rafferty?'

If he kept the secret of Holly's abduction, he would stand alone against her kidnappers . . . He was no good alone. He had been raised with three sisters and a brother, all born within a seven-year period. They had been one another's confidants, confessors, counsellors and defenders. A year after high school, he moved out of his parents' house into a shared apartment. Later, he had got his own place, where he had felt isolated and had worked sixty hours a week just to avoid being alone in his rooms.

He had felt complete, fulfilled, connected, only when Holly had come into his world.

Lieutenant Taggart's eyes seemed less forbidding than they had been heretofore.

Mitch said, 'Well . . .'

Only paranoia allowed the twisted thought that a homicide detective might be allied with Holly's abductors, that this private moment between witness and investigator might in fact be the ultimate test of Mitch's willingness to follow the kidnapper's instructions. As earlier, when he'd been standing over the dead man, Mitch felt watched, not just by Taggart and the tea-drinking neighbours, but by some presence unseen. Watched, analysed.

'No, Lieutenant,' he said. 'There's nothing more.'

The detective retrieved a pair of sunglasses from his shirt pocket and put them on. In the mirrored lenses, Mitch almost didn't recognise the twin reflections of his face.

'I gave you my card,' Taggart reminded him.

'Yes, sir. I have it.'

'Call me if you remember anything that seems important.'

The smooth, characterless sheen of the sunglasses was like the gaze of an insect, emotionless.

'You seem nervous, Mr Rafferty.'

Raising his hands to reveal how they trembled, Mitch said, 'Not nervous, Lieutenant. Shaken. I've never seen a man murdered before.'

'You don't get used to it,' the detective said.

Lowering his hands, Mitch said, 'I guess not.'

'It's worse when it's a woman or a child.'

Mitch did not know what to make of that statement. 'I wouldn't want your job.'

'No. You wouldn't.' Turning away, the detective said, 'I'll be seeing you, Mr Rafferty.'

'Seeing me?'

Glancing back, Taggart said, 'You and I—we'll both be witnesses in a courtroom someday.'

'Seems like a tough case to solve.'

'"Blood crieth unto me from the ground," Mr Rafferty,' said the detective, apparently quoting someone, then walked away.

THE DASHBOARD CLOCK was digital, as was Mitch's wristwatch, but he could hear time ticking nonetheless, as rapid as the *click-click-click* of the pointer snapping against the marker pegs on a spinning wheel of fortune.

He wanted to race directly home from the crime scene—they might have left a message for him, further instructions. But, as usual, he had begun the day by picking up Iggy at his apartment in Santa Ana. Now he had to run him home.

As Mitch drove north from the fabled and wealthy Orange County coastal neighbourhoods, where he and Iggy worked, towards their humbler communities, Iggy wanted to talk about the murder and the police. Mitch had to pretend to be as naively excited by the novelty of the experience as Iggy was, when in fact his mind remained preoccupied with thoughts of Holly and what might come next.

Fortunately, as usual, Iggy's conversation soon began to loop and turn and tangle like a ball of yarn unravelled by a kitten.

'My cousin Louis had a friend named Booger,' Iggy said. 'The same thing happened to him, shot while walking a dog, except it wasn't a rifle and it wasn't a dog.'

'Booger?' Mitch wondered.

'Booker,' Iggy corrected. 'B-o-o-k-e-r. He had a cat he called Hairball. He was walking Hairball and he got shot.'

'People walk cats?'

'That's the way it was—Hairball was cosy in a travel cage and Booker was carrying him to a vet's office.'

Mitch repeatedly checked the rearview and side mirrors. A black Cadillac SUV had departed the freeway in their wake. Block after block, it remained behind them.

'So Booker wasn't actually *walking* the cat,' he said.

'He was walking *with* the cat, and this like twelve-year-old brat shot Booker with a paint-ball gun. Booker was totally blue.'

'Blue?'

'Blue hair, blue face. He was pissed. Booker was gonna break the little dismo's hand off, but the kid shot him in the crotch and ran.'

The Cadillac SUV remained reliably two or three vehicles behind them. Perhaps the driver hoped Mitch wouldn't notice him.

'Hey, Mitch, did you know there's a town in Pennsylvania named Blue Balls? It's in Amish country.'

Mitch accelerated to cross an intersection before the traffic light phased to red. Behind him, the black SUV changed lanes, sped up, and made it through on the yellow.

'Did you ever eat an Amish shoofly pie?' Iggy asked.

'No. Never did.'

'It's full-on rich, sweet. Like eating molasses.'

The Cadillac dropped back, returned to Mitch's lane. Three vehicles separated them once more.

'Earl Potter lost a leg eating shoofly pie.'

'Earl Potter?'

'Tim Potter's dad. He was diabetic, but he didn't know it, and he totally destroyed like a bucket of sweets every day. One day his foot's numb, he can't walk right. Turns out he's got almost no circulation down there 'cause of radical diabetes. They sawed his left leg off above the knee.'

By way of Hairball, Blue Balls and shoofly pie, they arrived at Iggy's apartment building.

Mitch stopped at the kerb and the black SUV went by without slowing.

The side windows were tinted, so he couldn't see the driver or passengers.

Opening his door, Iggy said, 'You OK, boss?'

'I'm OK.'

'You look stomped.'

'I saw a guy shot to death,' Mitch reminded him.

'Yeah. Wasn't that radical? I guess I know who's gonna rule the bar at Rolling Thunder tonight. Maybe you should stop in.'

'Don't save a stool for me.'

The Cadillac SUV dwindled westwards. It shimmered in the afternoon sun and seemed to vanish into it.

Iggy got out of the truck, looked back in at Mitch, and pulled a sad face. 'Ball and chain.'

'Wind beneath my wings.'

'Whoa. That's goob talk.'

'Go waste yourself.'

'I do intend to get mildly polluted,' Iggy assured him. 'Tell Mrs Mitch I think she's an uber wahine.'

He slammed the door and walked away, big and loyal and clueless.

With hands that were suddenly shaky on the wheel, Mitch steered the truck into the street once more. From time to time, his eyes were drawn to the rearview mirror, but no longer with the expectation of seeing anything suspicious. Evidently he had imagined the tail.

Coming north, he had been impatient to be rid of Iggy and to get home. Now his stomach turned when he considered what might wait for him there.

3

Mitch and Holly's house was in an older neighbourhood of Orange, one of the oldest cities in the county. When he turned into their street, except for the vintage of the cars, a curtain in time might have parted, welcoming him to 1945.

The bungalow—pale yellow clapboard, white trim, a cedar-shingle roof—stood behind a picket fence on which roses twined. Some nicer houses occupied the block, but none boasted better landscaping.

He parked in the driveway beside the house, under a massive old

California pepper tree, and stepped out into a breathless afternoon. He looked around. Sidewalks and yards were deserted. In this neighbourhood, most families relied on two incomes; everyone was at work. At 3.04, no latchkey kids were yet home from school. No maids, no window washers, no gardening services busy with leaf blowers. These homeowners swept their own carpets, mowed their own yards.

Mitch opened a side gate in the picket fence and crossed the lawn to the front steps. The porch was deep and cool. White wicker chairs with green cushions stood beside small wicker tables with glass tops. On Sunday afternoons, he and Holly often sat there, talking, reading the newspaper, watching hummingbirds flit from one crimson bloom to another on the trumpet vines that flourished on the porch posts.

They didn't spend much on entertainment. No skiing vacations, no weekends in Baja. They seldom went out to a movie. Being together on the front porch offered as much pleasure as being together in Paris.

They were saving money for things that mattered: to allow her to risk a career change from secretary to real-estate agent, to enable him to do some advertising, buy a second truck and expand the business.

Kids, too. They were going to have kids. Two or three. They didn't want the world, didn't want to change it. They wanted their little corner of it and the chance to fill it with family and laughter.

He tried the front door. Unlocked. He pushed it inwards and stepped inside. He stood for a moment, letting his eyes adjust. The living room was illuminated only by what tree-filtered sunlight pierced the windows.

Everything appeared to be in order. He could not detect any signs of struggle. Mitch closed the door behind him. For a moment he needed to lean against it. If Holly had been at home, there would have been music. She liked big-band stuff. Miller, Goodman, Ellington, Shaw.

An archway connected the living room to the small dining room. Nothing in this second room was out of place. On the table lay a large dead moth. It was a night-flyer, grey with black details along its scalloped wings. It must have got in the previous evening. They had spent some time on the porch, and the door had been open. Maybe it was alive, sleeping . . .

He hesitated, reluctant to touch it, for fear that no flutter was left in it. He wanted to believe that it was alive.

The connecting door between the dining room and the kitchen stood ajar. Light glowed beyond and the smell of burnt toast lingered. It grew stronger when he pushed through the door into the kitchen.

Here, one of the dinette chairs had been overturned. Broken dishes littered the floor. Two slices of blackened bread stood in the toaster. Butter left out on the counter had softened as the day grew warmer.

The intruders must have come in from the front of the house, surprising her as she was making toast.

The cabinets were glossy white. Blood spattered a door and two drawer fronts. For a moment, Mitch closed his eyes. In his mind, he saw the moth flutter and fly up from the table. Something fluttered in his chest, too, and he wanted to believe that it was hope.

On the white refrigerator, a woman's bloody hand print. Another full hand print and a smeared partial print darkened two upper cabinets. Blood spotted the terracotta tiles on the floor. It seemed to be a lot of blood. It seemed to be an ocean.

The phone rang.

MITCH PICKED UP the handset on the third ring, and heard his haunted voice say, 'Yeah?'

'It's me, baby. They're listening.'

'Holly. What've they done to you?'

'I'm all right,' she said, and she sounded strong, but she did not sound all right.

'I'm in the kitchen,' he said. 'The blood—'

'I know. Don't think about that now. Mitch, they said we have one minute to talk, just one minute.'

His legs would not support him. Turning a chair away from the dinette table, collapsing onto it, he said, 'I'm so damn sorry.'

'It's not your fault. Don't beat yourself up.'

'Who are these freaks, are they deranged, what?'

'They're vicious, but they're not crazy. They seem . . . professional. I don't know. But I want your promise. If anything happens to me—'

'Nothing's going to happen to you.'

'If anything happens to me,' she insisted, 'promise you'll keep it together. You keep it together and have a life.'

'You're my life.'

'You keep it together, mower jockey, or I'm going to be way pissed.'

'I'll do what they want. I'll get you back.'

'If you don't keep it together, I'll haunt you, Rafferty.'

'God, I love you,' he said.

'I know. I love you. I want to hold you.'

'I love you so much.'

She didn't reply.

'Holly?'

The silence brought him up from the chair. 'Holly? You hear me?'

'I hear you,' said the kidnapper to whom he had spoken previously.

'You sonofabitch.'

'I understand your anger—but I don't have much patience for it.'

'If you hurt her—' An acute awareness of his helplessness brought Mitch crashing down from anger to humility. 'Please. Don't hurt her again.'

'Chill, Rafferty. You just chill while I explain a few things.'

'OK. All right. I need things explained. I'm lost here.'

Again Mitch's legs felt weak. Instead of sitting on the chair, he brushed a broken dish aside with one foot and knelt on the floor.

'About the blood,' the kidnapper said. 'I slapped her down when she tried to fight back, but I didn't cut her. We put a tourniquet on her arm until a vein popped up, stuck a needle in it, and drew four vials just like your doctor does when you get a physical.'

Mitch leaned his forehead against the oven door.

'We smeared blood on her hands and made those prints. Spattered some on the counters, cabinets. Dripped it on the floor so it looks like she was murdered there. If you go to the cops, they'll see that kitchen and think you did it.'

'I didn't tell them anything.'

'I know. There's a butcher's knife missing from the rack in your kitchen, too,' the kidnapper said. 'We wrapped it in one of your T-shirts and a pair of your jeans. The clothes are also stained with Holly's blood.'

They were professional, all right, just like she had said.

'That package is hidden on your property,' the kidnapper continued. 'You couldn't easily find it, but police dogs will.'

'I get the picture. What now? Make sense of this whole thing for me.'

'Not yet. Right now you're very emotional, Mitch. When you're not in control of your emotions, you're likely to make a mistake. So I want you to chill, like I said. When you've got your head straight, then we'll discuss the situation. I'll call you at six o'clock.'

Still on his knees, Mitch opened his eyes, checked his watch. 'That's over two and a half hours.'

'You're still in your work clothes. You're dirty. Take a nice hot shower.

Then leave the house, go somewhere, anywhere. Just be sure your cell-phone is fully charged.'

'I'd rather wait here.'

'That's no good, Mitch. The house is filled with memories of Holly, everywhere you look. Your nerves will be rubbed raw. I need you to be less emotional.'

'Yeah. All right.'

'One more thing. I want you to listen to this . . .'

Mitch thought they were going to twist a scream of pain from Holly again, to emphasise how powerless he was to protect her. He said, 'Don't.'

But instead of Holly, he heard two taped voices, clear against a faint background hiss. The first voice was his own:

'I've never seen a man murdered before.'

'You don't get used to it.'

'I guess not.'

'It's worse when it's a woman or a child.'

The second voice belonged to Detective Taggart.

The kidnapper said, 'If you had spilled your guts to him, Mitch, Holly would be dead now.'

In the dark smoky glass of the oven door, Mitch saw the reflection of a face that seemed to be looking out at him from Hell.

'Taggart's one of you.'

'Maybe he is. Maybe not. You should just assume that everybody is one of us, Mitch. That'll be safer for you, and a lot safer for Holly.'

They had built a box around him. Now they were putting on the lid.

'Mitch, I don't want to leave you on such a dark note. I want to put you at ease about something. I want you to know that we won't touch her. We aren't rapists, Mitch. Obviously, I'm handling you, manipulating, finessing. And obviously there is a lot of stuff I won't tell you—'

'You're killers, but not rapists?' Mitch wanted to kill him. Never before had he felt an urge to do serious violence to another human being, but he wanted to destroy this man. He was clutching the phone so fiercely that his hand ached. He was not able to relax his grip.

'You're an instrument to me, Mitch, a valuable tool. In the interest of getting the best performance out of you, I want you to know we'll treat Holly with respect. If you do everything we want, then she'll come back to you alive . . . and untouched.'

Holly's captor might have raised the issue of rape with the intention of putting some of Mitch's fears to rest. But it was also a warning.

'Why should I believe you?'

'Because you have to, Mitch. Otherwise, you might as well consider her dead right now.'

The kidnapper terminated the call.

For a while, Mitch's sense of his own powerlessness kept him on his knees. He put the phone on the floor and rested his forehead against the oven door once more. Images of Holly tormented him, sweet memories fragmented and spinning, perhaps all he would ever have of her. Fear and anger. Regret and sorrow. He had never known loss. His life had not prepared him for loss.

He strove to clear his mind because he sensed that if only he could quiet his fear and be calm and *think*, he didn't have to wait for orders from her kidnappers. He could surely do something for Holly now. He could take action on her behalf.

Humbled against the hard terracotta tiles, his knees began to ache, and this physical discomfort gradually cleared his mind. Thoughts drifted as fallen leaves drift on a placid river.

He could do something for Holly, and the awareness of the thing he could do was right below the surface, floating just beneath his questing reflection. *Something.* He got to his feet, returned the telephone handset to its cradle.

He would have to wait for the next call.

THE APPROACHING NIGHT pulled every shadow towards the east, away from the westbound sun. Queen-palm shadows yearned across the deep yard.

To Mitch, standing on the back porch, this place, which had previously been an island of peace, now seemed as fraught with tension as the webwork of cables supporting a suspension bridge.

On the phone, he had told Holly that he was in the kitchen, and she had said *I know*. She could have known only because her captors had known. They would expect him to go home, so instead of tailing him they would have staked out his house. They were watching now.

At the end of the yard, beyond a board fence, lay an alleyway. On the farther side were other yards and other houses. Perhaps a sentinel at one of those first-floor windows observed him now with high-powered binoculars.

His suspicion settled on the detached garage at the rear of his property, which provided parking for Mitch's truck and Holly's Honda and which had windows on the ground floor and in the storage loft. It could be accessed either from the alley or from the driveway that ran alongside the house. None of the windows revealed a ghostly face or telltale movement, but if someone was watching from the garage they would not be careless. From the roses, from the Corabells, slanting sunlight struck luminous colour like flaring shards in stained-glass windows.

The butcher's knife, wrapped in bloody clothes, had probably been buried in a flowerbed. By finding that bundle, retrieving it, and cleaning up the blood in the kitchen, he would regain some control.

If he was being watched, however, the kidnappers would not view his actions with equanimity. To punish him, they would hurt Holly.

They dared not kill her. To continue controlling Mitch, they had to let him speak to her from time to time. But they could cut, disfigure . . .

The dark windows of the garage mocked him. The porch furniture, arranged in expectation of the enjoyment of lazy summer evenings, mocked him. The lush and sculpted landscaping, on which he had spent so many hours, mocked him as well. All the beauty born from his work seemed now to be superficial, and its superficiality made it ugly to him.

He turned back into the house and closed the back door. He did not bother locking it. The worst that could have invaded his home had already been and gone.

He crossed the kitchen and entered a short hall that served two rooms, the first of which was a den containing a sofa, two chairs and a large-screen television.

At the end of the hallway was the master bedroom. He went inside and withdrew clean underwear and socks from a chest of drawers. The day had been warm, but a night in the middle of May was likely to be cool. At the closet he slipped a fresh pair of jeans and a flannel shirt from hangers and put them on the bed.

He found himself standing at Holly's small dressing table, where she sat on a stool to brush her hair and apply her make-up. Unconsciously, he picked up her hand mirror. He looked into it, as if hoping, by some grace, to see her smiling face. His own countenance did not bear contemplation.

He shaved, showered, and dressed for the ordeal ahead. As he sat on the edge of the bed, tying his shoes, the doorbell rang.

The kidnapper had said he would *call* at six, not come calling. Besides, the bedside clock read 4:15.

Leaving the door unanswered was not an option. He needed to be responsive regardless of how Holly's captors chose to contact him.

If the visitor had nothing to do with her abduction, Mitch was nevertheless obliged to answer the door in order to maintain an air of normalcy.

He left the bedroom, walked down the hall, and crossed the living room before the visitor had time to ring the bell twice.

He opened the front door and found Detective Taggart on the porch.

4

The praying-mantis stare of the mirrored lenses skewered Mitch and pinned his voice in his throat.

'I love these old neighbourhoods,' Taggart said, surveying the porch. 'This was how southern California looked in its great years, before they cut down all the orange groves and built a wasteland of tract houses.'

Mitch found a voice that sounded almost like his own, though thinner: 'You live around here, Lieutenant?'

'No. I live in one of the wastelands. It's more convenient. But I happened to be in your neighbourhood.'

Taggart was not a man who *just happened* to be anywhere.

'Something's come up, Mr Rafferty. Can you spare a few minutes?'

If Taggart was not one of the kidnappers, if his conversation with Mitch had been taped without his knowledge, allowing him into this house with its incriminating evidence would be reckless.

'Sure,' Mitch said. 'But my wife came home with a migraine. She's lying down. Why don't we sit here on the porch.'

'You've got it fixed up real nice.'

Mitch pulled the door shut behind him, and they settled into the white wicker chairs.

Taggart had brought a nine-by-twelve white envelope. He put it on his lap, unopened. 'We had a porch like this when I was a kid,' he said.

He removed his sunglasses and tucked them in his shirt pocket. His gaze was as direct as a power drill. 'Does Mrs Rafferty use Ergotamine?'

'Use what?'

'Ergotamine. For the migraines.'

Mitch had no idea whether Ergotamine was an actual medication or a word the detective had invented. 'No. She toughs it out with aspirin.'

'How often does she get one?'

'Two or three times a year,' Mitch lied. Holly had never had a migraine. She rarely suffered headaches of any kind.

'I have ocular migraines,' Taggart said. 'They're entirely visual. I get the glimmering light and the temporary blind spot for like twenty minutes, but there's no pain. A doctor probably wouldn't prescribe Ergotamine until she was having a migraine a month.'

'It's just twice a year. Three times,' Mitch said.

He wished that he had resorted to a different lie. Taggart having personal knowledge of migraines was rotten luck. The small talk unnerved Mitch. To his own ear, he sounded wary, tense. He had been avoiding the detective's stare. With an effort, he made eye contact again.

'We did find an American Veterinary Identification Device on the dog,' Taggart said. A microchip ID.'

'Oh. Right.'

'They inject it into the muscle between the dog's shoulders. We scanned the retriever, got her number. She's from a house one block east, two blocks north of the shooting. Owner's name is Okadan.'

'Bobby Okadan? I do his gardening.'

'Yes, I know.'

'The guy who was killed—that wasn't Mr Okadan.'

'No.'

'Who was he? A family member, a friend?'

Avoiding the question, Taggart said, 'I'm surprised you didn't recognise the dog.'

'One golden looks like another. Mr Okadan's dog's name is Mishiki,' Mitch remembered. 'We do that property on Tuesdays, and the housekeeper makes sure Mishiki stays inside while we're there. Mostly I've seen the dog through a patio door.'

'Evidently, Mishiki was stolen from the Okadans' back yard this morning, probably around eleven thirty. The leash and collar on her don't belong to the Okadans.'

'You mean . . . the dog was stolen by the guy who was shot?'

'So it appears.'

This revelation reversed Mitch's problem with eye contact. Now he couldn't look away from the detective. He knew Taggart hadn't come here just to share a puzzling bit of case news.

From inside the house came the muffled ringing of the telephone.

The kidnappers weren't supposed to call until six o'clock. But if they called earlier and couldn't reach him, they might be angry.

As Mitch started to rise from his chair, Taggart said, 'I'd rather you didn't answer that. It's probably Mr Barnes.'

'Iggy?'

'He and I spoke half an hour ago. I asked him not to call here until I had a chance to speak with you. He's probably been wrestling with his conscience ever since, and finally his conscience won. Or lost, depending on your point of view.'

Remaining in his chair, Mitch said, 'What's this about?'

Ignoring the question, returning to his subject, Taggart said, 'How often do you think dogs are stolen, Mr Rafferty?'

'I never thought about them being stolen at all.'

'It happens. They aren't taken as frequently as cars but purebred dogs can be worth thousands. As often as not, the thief doesn't intend to sell the animal. He just wants a fancy dog for himself.'

Though Taggart paused, Mitch didn't say anything. He was anxious to know the point.

'Certain breeds are stolen more than others because they're known to be friendly, unlikely to resist the thief. Golden retrievers are one of the most sociable, least aggressive of all the popular breeds.' The detective lowered his head, sat pensively for a moment. 'Dogs are mostly stolen out of parked cars,' he continued. 'People leave the dog alone, the doors unlocked. When they come back, Fido's gone, and someone's renamed him Duke.'

Realising that he was gripping the arms of the wicker chair as if strapped into the hot seat and waiting for the executioner to throw the switch, Mitch made an effort to appear relaxed.

With his head still bowed, Lieutenant Taggart said, 'It's rare, Mr Rafferty, for a dog to be stolen out of its owner's back yard on a bright spring morning. Anything rare, anything unusual makes me curious. Any outright *weirdness* really gets under my skin.'

Mitch raised one hand to the back of his neck and massaged the muscles there because that seemed like something a relaxed man might do.

'It's strange for a thief to enter a neighbourhood like that on foot and walk away with a stolen pet. It's strange that he carries no ID. It's more than strange, it's remarkable, that he gets shot to death three blocks later. And it's weird, Mr Rafferty, that you, the primary witness, knew him.'

'But I didn't know him.'

'At one time,' Taggart insisted, 'you knew him quite well.'

White ceiling, white railings, white floorboards, white wicker chairs. Everything about the porch was open and airy, yet it seemed dark now to Mitch, and strange.

Taggart said, 'One of the officers on the scene eventually got a closer look at the victim and recognised him. Said he arrested the guy on a drug-possession charge after stopping him for a traffic violation about two years ago. The guy never served time, but his prints were in our system, so we were able to make a quick match. Mr Barnes says you and he went to high school with the victim. His name was Jason Osteen.'

Mitch wished that the cop would meet his eyes. As perceptive as he was, Taggart would recognise genuine surprise when he saw it.

'I didn't just go to school with him,' Mitch said. 'Jason and I were roommates for a year.'

At last re-establishing eye contact, Taggart said, 'I know.'

Eager to be forthcoming, Mitch said, 'After high school, I lived with my folks for a year, while I took some classes—'

'Horticulture.'

'That's right. Then I got a job with a landscaping company, and I moved out. Jason and I split apartment rent for a year.'

The detective bowed his head again, in that contemplative pose.

'That wasn't Jason dead on the sidewalk,' Mitch said.

Opening the white envelope that had been on his lap, Taggart said, 'In addition to the identification by an officer and the print match, I have Mr Barnes's positive ID based on this.' He withdrew an eight-by-ten colour photo from the envelope and handed it to Mitch.

The features of the face had been subtly deformed by the entrance, transit, and post-temple exit of the high-velocity shot. The left eye was shut, the right open wide in a startled cyclopean stare.

'It could be Jason,' Mitch said.

'It is.'

'At the scene, I only saw one side of his face. The right profile, the worst side, with the exit wound. Once I saw he had to be dead, I didn't want to look too close.' Mitch couldn't take his eyes from the photo. 'This *is* Jason. I haven't seen him in eight years, maybe nine.'

'You roomed with him when you were—what?—eighteen?'

'Eighteen, nineteen. Just for a year.'

Jason had always affected a cool demeanour. He was so mellow he seemed to have surfwaxed his brain, but at the same time he seemed to know the secrets of the universe. Other boardheads called him Breezer, and admired him, even envied him.

'You went to school together, you roomed together. Why didn't you stay in touch?'

While Mitch had been riveted by the photo, Taggart had been watching him intently with his sharp stare.

'We had different ideas about things,' Mitch said. 'Jason wanted to get everything the easy way. I thought he was headed for big trouble, and I didn't want any part of it.'

'You're a straight shooter, you walk the line,' Taggart said.

'I'm no better than anyone else, but I don't steal.'

'We haven't learned much about him yet, but we know he rented a house in Huntington Harbor for seven thousand a month. And so far it looks like he didn't have a job.'

'Jason thought work was strictly for inlanders, smog monsters.' Mitch saw that an explanation was required. 'Surfer lingo for those who don't live for the beach.'

'Was there a time when *you* lived for the beach, Mitch?'

'Towards the end of high school, for a while after. But it wasn't enough.'

'What was it lacking?'

'The satisfaction of work. Stability. Family.'

'You've got all that now. Life is perfect, huh?'

'It's good. Very good. So good it makes me nervous sometimes.'

Mitch realised that he was responding to Taggart less guardedly than he had previously. He reminded himself that he was no match for this guy.

'Aside from the drug-possession charge,' Taggart said, 'Jason seems to have stayed clean all these years.'

'He always was lucky.'

Indicating the photo, Taggart said, 'Not always.'

Mitch didn't want to look at it any more. He returned the photo to the detective.

'Your hands are shaking,' Taggart said.

'I guess they are. Jason was a friend once. We had a lot of laughs.'

'When you saw him walking the dog, before he was killed, you didn't think—*Hey, don't I know that guy*?'

'He was across the street. I only glanced at him, then the shot.'

'And you were on the phone, distracted. Mr Barnes says you were on the phone when the shot was fired.'

'That's right. I just glanced at him.'

'Mr Barnes strikes me as being incapable of guile. If he lied, I expect his nose might light up.'

Mitch wasn't sure if he was meant to infer, by contrast to Iggy, that he himself was enigmatic. He smiled and said, 'Iggy's a good man.'

'Who were you on the phone with?'

'Holly. My wife.'

'Calling to let you know she had a migraine?'

'Yeah. To let me know she was going home early with a migraine.'

Glancing at the house behind them, Taggart said, 'I hope she's feeling better.'

'Sometimes they can last all day.'

'So the guy who's shot turns out to be your old room-mate. You see why it's weird to me?'

'It is weird,' Mitch agreed. 'It freaks me out a little.'

'You hadn't seen him or spoken to him in eight or nine years.'

'He was hanging with new friends, a different crowd.'

'Sometimes coincidences are just coincidences.' Taggart rose from his chair and moved towards the porch steps.

Relieved, blotting his palms on his jeans, Mitch got up from his chair.

Pausing beside the steps, Taggart said, 'We've only begun a search of Jason's house, but we've found one odd thing already.'

Afternoon light from the slowly sinking sun penetrated the branches of the pepper tree. A dappled orange glare made Mitch squint.

Taggart, in shadow, said, 'In his kitchen there was a drawer where he kept loose change, receipts, spare keys. . . . We found only one business card. It was yours.'

'Mine?'

'"Big Green,"' Taggart quoted. '"Landscape design, installation, and maintenance. Mitchell Rafferty."'

So this was what had brought the detective north from the coast. He had gone to Iggy, guileless Iggy, from whom he'd learned that a connection did indeed exist between Mitch and Jason.

'You didn't give him the card?' Taggart asked.

'No, not that I remember. What colour was the card stock?'

'White.'

'I've only used white for the past four years. Before that, the stock was pale green.'

'So although you lost track of Jason, it seems like Jason kept track of you. Any idea why?'

'No. None.'

After a silence, Taggart said, 'You've got trouble here.'

'There must be a thousand ways he could've got my business card, Lieutenant. It doesn't mean he was keeping track of me.'

The detective pointed to the porch railing. 'I'm talking about this.'

On the white handrail, a pair of winged insects squirmed together.

'Termites,' Taggart said.

'They might just be winged ants.'

'Isn't this the time of year when termites swarm? You'd better have the place inspected. A house can appear to be fine, solid and safe, even while it's being hollowed out right under your feet.'

At last the detective looked up and met Mitch's eyes. 'Is there anything else you want to tell me, Mitch?'

'Not that I can think of.'

'Take a moment. Be sure.'

Had Taggart been allied with the kidnappers, Mitch thought, he would have played this differently. He wouldn't have been so persistent or so thorough. There would have been a sense that it was a charade.

If you had spilled your guts to him, Mitch, Holly would be dead now.

Taggart surveyed the street. 'I'm not your enemy, Mitch.'

'I never thought you were,' he lied.

'Everyone thinks I am.'

'I guess in your work, everything looks black and white.'

'Under all the shades of grey, everything *is* black and white, Mitch.'

'I wasn't raised to think that way.'

Taggart took his sunglasses from his shirt pocket and put them on. From the same pocket, he withdrew one of his business cards.

'You already gave me a card,' Mitch said. 'It's in my wallet.'

'That one just has the homicide-division number. I've written my cell-phone on the back of this one. You can reach me twenty-four/seven.'

Accepting the card, Mitch said, 'I've told you everything I know, Lieutenant. Jason being caught up in this just . . . mystifies me.'

Taggart stared at him from behind twin mirrors that portrayed his face in shades of grey.

Mitch knew Taggart had caught everything he had told him, every word and every inflection, every emphasis and hesitation, every facial expression and twitch of body language.

He put the card in his shirt pocket.

Taggart descended the porch steps, followed the front walkway towards the street, stepped through the front gate and closed it behind him.

The sun lost its view through the gap in the branches of the pepper tree, and Mitch was left alone in the shade.

IN THE DEN, the answering machine stood on a corner desk. The only message was from Iggy: 'Sorry, bro. I should've called as soon as he left here. But, Taggart . . . he scares you off the board and makes you want to sit quiet on the beach and just watch the monsters break.'

Mitch sat at the desk and opened the drawer in which Holly kept their chequebook and bank statements.

In his conversation with the kidnapper, he had overestimated their current account balance, which was $10,346.54. The most recent statement showed an additional savings account balance of $27,311.40. Their monthly mortgage payment was automatically deducted from their current account. The bank statement listed the remaining loan balance as $286,770.

Recently, Holly had estimated that the house was worth $425,000, a crazy amount for a small bungalow, but though old, the neighbourhood was desirable, and the greater part of the value lay in the large lot.

Added to their cash on hand, the equity in the house made a total of approximately $175,000. That was far short of £2 million.

Anyway, the equity in the house couldn't be converted to cash unless they took a new loan or sold it. Because the house was jointly owned, he needed Holly's signature in either scenario. They wouldn't have had the house if Holly hadn't inherited it from her grandmother, Dorothy, who had raised her. So the amount available for ransom was approximately $37,000.

Until now, Mitch had not thought of himself as a failure but as a young man responsibly building a life. Now, although Holly was the centre of his existence, and priceless, when forced to put a price on her, he could pay only $37,000.

Bitterness overcame him and that was not good. Bitterness could turn to self-pity, and if he surrendered to it, he would *make* a failure of himself. And Holly would die.

Even if the house had been without a mortgage, even if they had half a million in cash and were wildly successful, he would not have had the funds to ransom her. That truth brought him to the realisation that money would not be what saved Holly, if she could be saved. It would be his perseverance, his wits, his courage, his love.

He went to the kitchen and found Holly's car keys on the pegboard by the back door. She drove a four-year-old white Honda. After retrieving his cellphone from the charger beside the oven, he went outside and moved his truck to the garage at the back of the property.

The Honda stood in the garage in the second bay, sparkling because Holly had washed it on Sunday afternoon. He parked beside the car, got out of the truck and stood between the vehicles, sweeping the space with his gaze. If anyone had been here, they would have heard and seen the truck approaching and would have fled.

He stared at the low ceiling, the floor of the loft that covered two-thirds of the garage. Windows in the higher space faced the house, providing an excellent vantage point.

An observer had known when Mitch had come home earlier, had known precisely when he had entered the kitchen. The phone had rung, with Holly on the line, moments after he had found the broken dishes and the blood.

A board creaked overhead. In a building of this vintage, the creak might have been just the settling of old joints.

Mitch walked around to the driver's door of the Honda and opened it. He hesitated, but got in behind the steering wheel, leaving the door open.

For the purpose of distraction, he started the engine. The garage door stood open, eliminating any danger of carbon-monoxide poisoning.

He got out of the car and slammed the door. Anyone listening would assume he had pulled it shut from inside.

On the side walls were racked his many gardening tools. The various clippers and pruning shears all seemed too unwieldy. He selected a combination lug wrench and prise bar.

Mitch was aware that a kind of madness, bred of desperation, had come over him, but he could bear no more inaction. Why Jason Osteen had stolen the dog and why he, of all people, had been shot dead as an example to Mitch were mysteries. But intuition told him that the kidnappers were weaving a web of evidence that would force Mitch to trial for Holly's murder if they killed her.

With the long-handled lug wrench clutched in his right hand, he moved to the back of the garage where steep open stairs in the north corner led in a single straight flight to the loft. He climbed them warily, the steel bar held by the prise end, the socket end ready as a club.

Walled on three sides, the loft was open at the back. A wooden railing extended from the top of the stairs across the width of the garage. Windows in the three walls admitted afternoon light. Visible beyond the balusters at the top of the stairs were stacks of cardboard boxes arranged in rows, as low as four feet in some places, as high as seven in others. Because the boxes were not all the same size and were not always stacked neatly, gaps existed here and there in the rows, offering places large enough for a man to hide.

More than half the stuff in the loft had belonged to Holly's grandmother, who had collected ornaments and other decorative items for every major holiday. At Christmas, she used to unpack fifty or sixty ceramic snowmen of various sizes. She also had more than a hundred Santa Clauses, reindeer, Christmas trees, wreaths and sleighs. The bungalow couldn't accommodate Dorothy's full collection for any holiday. She'd unpack and set out as much as would fit: Valentine's Day lovers, Easter bunnies, Halloween ghosts and black cats . . .

Mitch stood at the head of the first aisle, between the rows. No one crouched there.

The second aisle proved darker than the first, but the light from windows in the west wall would have silhouetted anyone standing in the space.

The third aisle was brighter for having a window directly at the end of it. He checked out the fourth, then the fifth and final aisle which lay along the longest wall at the front of the building in the light of two dusty windows. He found no one.

The passageway that paralleled the west wall, into which all the east-west aisles terminated, was the only length of the loft that he had not seen in its entirety. Raising the lug wrench higher, he eased all the way along the aisle at the front of the loft.

He found that the entire area at the far end of the aisles was deserted. On the floor, however, against the end of a row of boxes, stood some electronic equipment that should not have been there.

It included a receiver and a recorder, but Mitch couldn't identify the other three items. They were plugged into a board of sockets, which was itself plugged into a nearby wall outlet. Indicator lights and LED readouts revealed the equipment to be switched on.

They had indeed been maintaining surveillance of the house. Its rooms and phones were probably bugged.

Having seen no one in the loft, Mitch assumed that the equipment was not being monitored, that it must be set to automatic operation. Perhaps they could even access and download recordings from a distance.

Just then, the array of indicator lights changed, and at least one of the LED displays began to keep a running count.

He heard a hissing and then the voice of Detective Taggart. *'I love these old neighbourhoods. This was how southern California looked in its great years . . .'*

Not just the house but the front porch, too, had been bugged.

He knew that he had been outmanoeuvred only an instant before he felt the muzzle of a gun against the back of his neck.

ALTHOUGH HE FLINCHED, Mitch did not attempt to swing the lug wrench towards the gunman. During the past five hours, he had become acutely aware of his limitations. He might be the architect of his life, but he could no longer believe that he was the master of his fate.

Behind him, the gunman said, 'Drop the lug wrench. Just drop it.'

The voice was not that of the man on the phone. This one sounded younger.

Mitch dropped the wrench.

'. . . more convenient. But I happened to be in your neighbourhood.'

Using a remote control, the gunman switched off the recorder. He said to Mitch, 'Maybe we made a mistake, choosing you. Maybe you'd be happy to be rid of her.'

'No.'

'A large life-insurance policy. Another woman. You could have reasons.' Every word matter-of-fact, emotionless.

'There's nothing like that.'

'Perhaps you'd do a better job for us if we promised to kill her.'

'No. I love her. I do.'

'You pull another stunt like this, she's dead. Let's go back the way you came.'

Mitch turned, and the gunman also turned, staying behind him.

As he began to retrace his steps along the final aisle, past the two dusty windows at the front of the building, Mitch heard the lug wrench scrape against the boards as the gunman scooped it off the floor.

'Get in the Honda,' he said. 'Go for a ride. Wait for the call at six o'clock.'

'All right. I will.'

As they neared the back of the loft and the top of the stairs, something like luck intervened.

A tower of cardboard boxes collapsed. Some tumbled into the aisle, and one or two almost knocked the gunman off his feet sending him stumbling.

Mitch dodged one box and raised an arm to deflect another.

The falling first stack destabilised a second. Mitch almost instinctively reached towards the gunman to steady him. But then he realised that any offer of support might be misinterpreted as an attack. To avoid being misunderstood—and shot—he stepped out of his enemy's way.

The old wooden railing at the back of the loft proved too weak to endure the impact of the stumbling man. Balusters cracked, nails shrieked loose of their holes, and he cried out in alarm as the handrail broke and fell away from him.

He fell to the floor of the garage. The distance was not great, approximately eight feet, yet he landed with a terrible sound. And the gun went off.

Mitch stood in stunned disbelief, before the silence shocked him from paralysis. He hurried to the stairs and descended to ground level. He passed the truck and the idling Honda, to where the gunman lay face down, head and shoulders under an overturned wheelbarrow. He must have slammed into one edge of it, flipping it over and on top of himself.

Mitch righted the wheelbarrow and shoved it aside. He crouched beside the gunman and detected the bitter pungency of gunfire and the sweetness of blood. He turned the body over and saw the face clearly for the first time. The stranger was in his middle twenties with a clear complexion and jade-green eyes. He did not look like a man who could talk coldly about mutilating and murdering a woman.

He had landed with his throat across the rolled metal edge of the wheelbarrow. The impact appeared to have crushed his larynx and collapsed his trachea. His right forearm was broken, and his right hand, trapped under him, had reflexively fired the pistol. The index finger remained hooked through the trigger guard. The bullet had penetrated just below his sternum, angled up and to the left. Minimal bleeding suggested a heart wound, instant death. If the shot hadn't killed him instantly, the collapsed airway would have done so very soon.

The number of Mitch's enemies had been reduced by one. But he was at once aware that this death complicated his situation. When this man did not report back to his associates, they might come looking for him. If they found him dead, they would assume that Mitch had killed him, and soon thereafter Holly's fingers would be taken off one by one.

Mitch hurried to the Honda and switched off the engine. He used the remote control to shut the garage door.

As shadows closed in, he switched on the lights.

The single shot might not have been heard. If it had been heard, he felt sure that it would not have been recognised for what it was.

Mitch returned to the body and stood looking down at it. For a moment, he was not able to proceed. He knew what needed to be done, but he could not act. He had lived for almost twenty-eight years without witnessing a death. Now he'd seen two men shot in the same day.

Necessity brought him to his knees beside the corpse. He removed the pistol from a hand that was still warm and put the weapon in the nearby wheelbarrow.

If the right leg of the dead man's khakis had not been hitched up in the course of the fall, Mitch wouldn't have seen the second weapon. The gunman carried a snub-nosed revolver in an ankle holster. Mitch undid the Velcro closures, put the holster and revolver with the pistol.

Then he dug through the gunman's pockets and discovered a set of keys—one for a car, three others—which he also added to the wheelbarrow.

He found nothing more of interest other than a wallet and a cellphone. The former would contain identification; the latter might be programmed to speed-dial the dead man's collaborators. He switched it off. They would be suspicious when they got voicemail, but they would not act precipitously on mere suspicion.

Restraining his curiosity, Mitch set the wallet and phone aside in the wheelbarrow. Other, more urgent tasks awaited.

From the back of the truck, he fetched a thick canvas tarp that he used for bundling rosebush clippings. Although not waterproof, it remained fairly water-resistant. He didn't know how long he would have to keep the body in the trunk. Mitch spread the tarp and rolled the gunman onto it. A wave of revulsion washed through him, but he closed his eyes and took several slow, deep breaths. Worry was a clock ticking, an hourglass draining, and he feared an interruption of one kind or another before this tidy-up could be completed.

After rolling the body in the tarp, he dragged the corpse to the back of the Honda and loaded it into the trunk of the car. The gunman weighed less than Mitch, but he was a dead weight. If Mitch had not been strong, if his business had not kept him in good physical condition, the job might have defeated him. Sweat glazed him by the time he slammed shut the trunk lid and locked it.

A careful inspection revealed no blood on the wheelbarrow. None on the floor, either.

He gathered the broken balusters and the fallen handrail, took them out of the garage and concealed them in a stack of firewood.

Inside once more, he climbed the stairs to the loft and returned to the fateful spot at the end of the aisle. The cause of the accident soon revealed itself. Many of the stacked boxes were sealed with tape, but others were tied shut with cord. The lug wrench was still caught in a loop of a knot. Carrying the wrench at his side, the gunman must have snared it. He had pulled the boxes down on himself. Mitch stacked most of them as they had been. If the gunman's pals came searching, they might never notice the damage.

Although he would have liked to vent some anger by smashing the electronic eavesdropping equipment Mitch left it untouched. When he picked up the long lug wrench, it felt heavier than he remembered. He took it downstairs and hung it on the tool rack where it belonged.

From the wheelbarrow, he retrieved the phone, the wallet, the keys, the two guns and the ankle holster. He put everything on the front passenger seat of the Honda. Then he drove out of the garage, parked beside the house, and went inside to get a jacket.

When he came out again he expected to find Taggart waiting by the Honda, but the detective didn't show.

In the car once more, he placed the lightweight sports jacket on the passenger seat, concealing the items that he had taken from the corpse.

The dashboard clock agreed with his wristwatch—5:11.

He drove out onto the street and turned right, with a dead man in the trunk of the car and worse horrors loose in his mind.

TWO BLOCKS from his house, Mitch parked at the kerb. He left the engine running, kept the windows closed and the doors locked.

He glanced at the rearview mirror, suddenly afraid that the trunk lock had not engaged, that the lid had popped open, presenting the swaddled cadaver for viewing . . . But the trunk remained closed.

In the dead man's wallet were credit cards and a California driver's licence in the name of John Knox. For the photo, the youthful gunman had flashed a smile as winsome as that of a boy-band idol.

Knox had been carrying $585, including five $100 bills. Nothing in his wallet revealed a single fact about his profession, personal interests or associations. No business card, library card or health insurance. No photos of loved ones. According to the licence, Knox lived in Laguna Beach. Something useful might be learned by a search of his residence, but Mitch needed time to consider the risks of going there. Besides, there was someone else he needed to visit before the scheduled six-o'clock call.

He put the wallet, the dead man's cellphone and the set of keys in the glove box. He tucked the revolver and the ankle holster under the driver's seat. The pistol remained on the adjacent seat, under his jacket.

Zigzagging through residential streets, ignoring the speed limits and even a couple of stop signs, Mitch arrived at his parents' place in east Orange at 5:35. He parked in the driveway of their handsome house and locked the Honda.

A languid breeze had uncoiled from the east. With their silvery-green tongues, the tall eucalyptus trees whispered to one another.

Mitch's father, Daniel, answered the doorbell. At sixty-one, he remained a strikingly good-looking man, still in possession of all his hair, though it had turned white. Perhaps because his features were so pleasingly bold—the perfect features of a stage actor—his teeth seemed too small. They were natural because he was a stickler for dental hygiene. Laser-whitened, they dazzled, like rows of white-corn kernels on a cob.

Blinking with surprise that was a degree too theatrical, he said, 'Mitch. Katherine never told me you called.'

Katherine was Mitch's mother.

'I didn't,' Mitch admitted. 'I hoped it would be all right if I just stopped by on this occasion.'

'More often than not, I'd be occupied with one damn obligation or another, and you'd be out of luck. But tonight I'm free.'

'Good.'

'Though I did expect to do a few hours of reading.'

'I can't stay long,' Mitch assured him.

The children of Daniel and Katherine Rafferty, all now adults, understood that, out of respect for their parents' privacy, they were to schedule their visits and avoid impromptu drop-ins.

Stepping back from the door, his father said, 'Come in, then.'

In the hall, with its white marble floor, Mitch looked left and right at an infinity of Mitches, reflected in two large facing mirrors with stainless-steel frames. He asked, 'Is Kathy here?'

'Girls' night out,' his father said closing the door. 'She and Donna Watson and that Robinson woman are off to a show or something. They chatter at each other all evening, and when they pull into the driveway, they're still chattering. The Robinson woman is annoying,' his father said. 'I don't understand why Katherine enjoys her company. She's a mathematician.'

'I didn't know mathematicians annoyed you.'

'This one does.'

Mitch's parents were both doctors of behavioural psychology, tenured professors at the University of California. Those in their social circle were mostly from what academic types had recently begun to call the human sciences, largely to avoid the term 'soft sciences'. In that crowd, a mathematician might annoy like a stone in a shoe.

'I just fixed a Scotch and soda,' his father said. 'Would you like some?'

'No, thank you, sir.'

'Did you just "sir" me?'

'I'm sorry, Daniel.'

'Mere biological relationship—'

'—should not confer social status,' Mitch finished.

The five Rafferty children, on their thirteenth birthdays, had been expected to stop calling their parents Mom and Dad, and to begin using first names. Mitch's mother, Katherine, preferred to be called Kathy, but his father would not abide Danny instead of Daniel.

As a young man, Daniel had held strong views about child-rearing. Kathy had no firm opinions on the subject, but she had been curious to see if Daniel's unconventional theories would prove successful.

For a moment, Mitch and Daniel stood in the hall, and Daniel seemed unsure how to proceed. Then he said, 'Come and see what I just bought.'

They crossed a large living room furnished with stainless-steel-and-glass tables, grey leather sofas and black chairs. The art works were black and white, some with a single line or block of colour.

Daniel Rafferty's shoes struck hard sounds from the mahogany floor. Mitch followed as quietly as a haunting spirit.

In the study, pointing to an object on the desk, Daniel said, 'This is the nicest piece of shit in my collection.'

The study decor matched the living room, with illuminated display shelves that presented a collection of polished stone spheres.

Alone on the desk, cupped in an ornamental bronze stand, was a sphere with a diameter just greater than a baseball. Scarlet veins speckled with yellow swirled through its rich coppery brown surface. To the uninformed it might have appeared to be a piece of polished granite. In fact it was dinosaur dung, which time and pressure had petrified into stone.

'Mineral analysis confirms that it came from a carnivore,' said Mitch's father.

'Tyrannosaurus?'

'The size suggests something smaller than a *T. Rex*. It was found in Colorado, Upper Jurassic, so it's probably a ceratosaurus dropping.'

As his father picked up a glass of Scotch and soda from the desk, Mitch went to the display shelves.

He said, 'I gave Connie a call a few nights ago.'

Connie was his oldest sister, thirty-one. She lived in Chicago.

'Is she still drudging away in that bakery?' his father asked.

'Yes, but she owns it now.'

'Are you serious? Yes, of course. It's typical. If she puts one foot in a tar pit, she'll never back up, just flail forward.'

Connie had earned a master's degree in political science before she had plunged into entrepreneurship. Some were mystified by the sea change, but Mitch understood it.

The collection of polished dinosaur-dung spheres had grown since he had last seen it. 'How many do you have now, Daniel?'

'Seventy-three. I've got leads on four brilliant specimens.'

Some spheres were only two inches in diameter. The largest were as big as bowling balls. The colours tended towards browns, golds and coppers, however, every hue, even blue, lustred under the display lights.

Brontosaurus, diplodocus, brachiosaurus, iguanodon, moschops, and other droppings were labelled by engraving on their bronze stands.

'I talked to Megan the same evening,' Mitch said.

He had also recently spoken to his youngest sister, Portia, but he did not mention her because he didn't want to start an argument.

Megan, twenty-nine, had the highest IQ in a family of high IQs. Each of the Rafferty kids had been tested three times, in the week of their ninth, thirteenth, and seventeenth birthdays.

After her sophomore year, Megan had dropped out of college. She lived in Atlanta and operated a thriving dog-grooming business.

'She called at Easter, asked how many eggs we dyed,' Mitch's father said. 'I assume she thought that was funny. Katherine and I were just relieved that she didn't announce she was pregnant.'

Megan had married a stonemason with hands the size of dinner plates. Daniel and Kathy felt that she had settled for a husband who was beneath her intellectually. They expected that she would realise her error and divorce him—if children didn't arrive first to complicate the situation.

Mitch liked the guy. He had a sweet nature, an infectious laugh, and a tattoo of Tweety Bird on his right bicep.

Freshening his Scotch and soda at the bar, Daniel spoke again. 'Anson had us to dinner two nights ago.'

Anson, Mitch's only brother and, at thirty-three, the oldest of the siblings, was the most dutiful to Daniel and Kathy. He had long been his parents' favourite. But then it was easier to be a dutiful child when your enthusiasms were not analysed for signs of psychological maladjustment and your questions not met with gimlet-eyed suspicion or impatience.

In fairness, Anson had earned his status by fulfilling his parents' expectations. He had proved, as had none of the others, that Daniel's child-rearing theories could bear fruit.

Top of his class in high school, star quarterback, he declined football scholarships. Instead he accepted those offered only in respect of the excellence of his mind. He earned his bachelor's degree in two years, a master's in one, and had a PhD at the age of twenty-three. Anson was neither resented by his siblings nor alienated from them. His good heart and natural grace had allowed him to please his parents without becoming like them. This achievement seemed no less impressive than if nineteenth-century scientists, with nothing but steam power, had sent astronauts to the moon.

'Anson just signed a consulting contract with China,' Daniel said. 'He'll be working with the minister of trade, *and* with the minister of education.'

Anson's success had long been used to goad Mitch to consider a career more ambitious than his current work, but the jabs never pierced his psyche. He admired Anson but didn't envy him.

As Daniel prodded with another of Anson's achievements, Mitch checked his wristwatch, certain that he would shortly have to leave to take the kidnapper's call in privacy. But the time was only 5:42. He felt as if he had been in the house at least twenty minutes, but it had only been seven.

'Do you have an engagement?' Daniel asked.

Mitch detected a hopeful note in his father's voice, but he did not resent it. Daniel now inspired in him only indifference and impatience.

Author of thirteen ponderous books, Daniel believed himself to be a giant of psychology, a rock in the river of contemporary American intellectualism, around which lesser minds washed to obscurity. Mitch knew beyond doubt that his old man was no such thing.

Throughout their childhood, Anson had counselled Mitch and his sisters against anger, urging patience, teaching the value of humour as defence against their father's inhumanity.

'Yes,' he said, 'I have an engagement. I should be going.'

Regarding his son with a keen interest that twenty years ago would have intimidated Mitch, Daniel said, 'What was this all about?'

Whatever Holly's kidnappers intended for Mitch, his chances of surviving it might not be high. The thought had crossed his mind that this might be the last chance he had to see his parents.

Unable to reveal his plight, he said, 'I came to see Kathy. Maybe I'll come back tomorrow.'

'Came to see her about what?'

For all her academic achievements, Kathy was clueless about the needs of children and the bonds of motherhood. She believed in the perfectibility of humanity and felt that children should be raised according to a system from which one did not deviate and which would ensure they became civilised. She might not have become a mother if she hadn't met a man with firm theories of child development and a system with which to apply them. But Kathy's cluelessness did not encompass malice, and therefore she inspired a tenderness in Mitch—not quite love, or even affection, more a sad regard for her congenital incapacity for sentiment.

'It's nothing important,' Mitch said. 'It'll keep.'

'I can give her a message,' Daniel said, following Mitch across the living room.

'No message. I was nearby, so I just dropped in to say hello.'

Daniel remained unconvinced. 'Something's on your mind.'

Mitch wanted to say *Maybe a week of sensory deprivation in the learning room will squeeze it out of me.* Instead he smiled and said, 'I'm fine. Everything's fine.'

'If it's money problems, you know our position on that.'

'I didn't come for a loan,' Mitch assured him.

'In every species of animal, the primary obligation of parents is to teach their offspring self-sufficiency. The prey must learn evasion, and the predator must learn to hunt.'

Opening the door, Mitch said, 'I'm a self-sufficient predator, Daniel.'

'Good. I'm glad to hear that.' He favoured Mitch with a smile in which his small white teeth appeared to have been sharpened since last he revealed them. 'Parasitism, isn't natural to *Homo sapiens* or to any mammal.'

Stepping out of the house, Mitch said, 'Tell Kathy I said hi.'

He pulled the door shut. Several steps from the house, he stopped, turned, and studied the place, perhaps for the last time.

He had not only lived here but had also been home-schooled here from first grade through twelfth. As always, his gaze drifted to the first-floor window that was boarded over on the inside. The learning room. When he was eight years old, he had spent twenty consecutive days there. Sensory deprivation focuses thought, clears the mind. That was the theory behind the dark, silent, empty room.

Because the front walk curved away from the house instead of leading straight to the street, when Mitch lowered his attention from the first floor, he faced not the door but the sidelight. Through the French windows, he saw his father. Daniel, at one of the big steel-framed hall mirrors, smoothing his white hair with one hand, then pinching his cheeks between thumb and forefinger as if to tweak some colour into them.

Mitch suspected that his visit had already more than half faded from his father's mind, now that the threat of a loan request had been lifted.

In the hall, Daniel turned sideways to the mirror, as though taking pride in the depth of his chest, the slimness of his waist.

How easy to imagine that between the facing mirrors, his father did not cast an infinity of echo reflections, as Mitch had done, and that the single likeness of him possessed so little substance that, to any eye but his own, it would appear as transparent as the image of a ghost.

AT 5:50, only fifteen minutes after he had arrived at Daniel and Kathy's house, Mitch drove away.

Perhaps two hours of daylight remained. He could easily detect a tail if one pursued him. He pulled the Honda into the empty parking lot of a church a block and a half away. A forbidding brick façade, with fractured eyes of multicoloured glass, rose to a steeple that gouged the sky and cast a hard shadow across the tarmac.

His father's fear had been unfounded. Mitch had not intended to ask for money. His parents could no doubt contribute $100,000 to the cause without being in the least pinched. But even if they gave him twice that sum, he would still have little more than ten per cent of the ransom.

Besides, he would not have asked because he knew they would have declined, ostensibly on the basis of their theories of parenting.

Furthermore, he suspected that the kidnappers were seeking more than money. Snatching the wife of a gardener who earned a five-figure income made no sense unless they wanted something that only he could provide.

From under the driver's seat, he retrieved the snub-nosed revolver and the ankle holster and examined the weapon with caution. All he knew about guns was what he had learned from books and movies. As far as he could tell, this one did not have a safety. When he broke out the cylinder, he discovered that it held five rounds.

The Velcro closure on the holster allowed him to strap the compact handgun far enough above his ankle to avoid exposing it if his trousers hiked up when he sat down.

He shrugged into the sports jacket. Before he got out of the car, he would tuck the pistol under his belt, in the small of his back, where the coat would conceal it. He looked at the gun. Again, he failed to locate a safety. With some fumbling, he ejected the magazine. It contained eight cartridges. When he pulled the slide back, he saw a ninth gleaming in the breach. After reinserting the magazine and making sure that it clicked securely into place, he put the pistol on the passenger's seat.

His cellphone rang. The car clock read 5:59.

The kidnapper said, 'Did you enjoy your visit with Mom and Dad?'

He had not been followed to his parents' house or away from it, and yet they knew where he had been.

He said at once, 'I didn't tell them anything.'

'What were you after—milk and cookies?'

'If you're thinking I could get the money from them, you're wrong. They're not that rich.'

'We know, Mitch. We know.'

'Let me talk to Holly.'

'Not this time. I'll put her on the next call. Is that the church you and your parents attended?'

His was the only car in the parking lot, and none were passing at the moment. Across the street from the church, the only vehicles were those in driveways, none at the kerb. Although he was in the car with the doors locked, he felt as exposed as a mouse in an open field with the vibrato of hawk wings above it.

'Were you an altar boy, Mitch?'

'No.'

'For a man who was never an altar boy, Mitch, you are so like one.'

When he didn't at first respond, the kidnapper waited in silence.

Mitch said at last, 'I don't know what that means.'

'Well, I don't mean you're pious. And I don't mean you're reliably truthful. With Detective Taggart, you've proved to be a cunning liar.'

In their two previous conversations, the man on the phone had been professional, chillingly so. This petty jeering seemed out of sync. The taunts must have a purpose, though it eluded Mitch. Perhaps the kidnapper just wanted to get inside his head and mess with him.

'Mitch, no offence, because it's actually kind of sweet—but you're as *naive* as an altar boy.'

'If you say so.'

'I do. I say so. Your eyes are wide open, Mitch, but you don't see.'

This statement unnerved him more than anything else that the kidnapper had said. Not an hour ago, in the loft of his garage, that very thought, couched in similar words, had occurred to him.

Having packed John Knox in the trunk of the car, he had returned to the loft to puzzle out how the accident had occurred. Having seen the neck of the lug wrench snared in the loop of cord, he had settled the mystery. But then he had been overcome by an instinctive sense that a greater truth waited in that loft to be discovered, that it hid from him in plain sight.

Now the mocking man on the telephone: *Your eyes are wide open, Mitch, but you don't see.*

He felt that the kidnappers could not only watch him and listen to him anywhere, but also that they could trawl through his thoughts.

He reached for the pistol on the passenger's seat. No immediate threat loomed, but he felt safer holding the gun.

'Are you with me, Mitch?'

'I'm listening.'

'I'll call you again at seven thirty—'

'More waiting? *Why?*' Impatience gnawed at him, and he could not cage it. *'Let's get on with this.'*

'Easy, Mitch. I was about to tell you what to do next when you interrupted. A good altar boy doesn't interrupt. A good altar boy knows the ritual. If you interrupt again, I'll make you wait until *eight* thirty.'

Mitch took a deep breath and said, 'I understand.'

'Good. So when I hang up, you'll drive to Newport Beach, to your brother's house.'

Surprised, he said, 'To Anson's place?'

'You'll wait with him for the seven-thirty call.'

'Why does my brother have to be involved in this?'

'You can't do alone what has to be done,' said the kidnapper.

'But what has to be done? You haven't told me.'

'We will. Soon.'

'I don't want Anson dragged into this.'

'Think about it, Mitch. Your brother loves you, right? He won't want your wife to be cut to pieces like a pig in a slaughterhouse.'

Throughout their beleaguered childhood, Anson had been the reliable one, the rope that kept Mitch tethered to reality. Always it was Anson who raised the sails of hope when there seemed to be no wind to fill them.

To his brother, he owed the peace of mind and the happiness that he had eventually found when he was at last free of his parents. The lightness of spirit that had made it possible for him to win Holly as a wife.

'You've set me up,' Mitch said. 'If whatever you want me to do goes wrong, you've set me up to make it look as if I killed my wife.'

'The noose is even tighter than you realise, Mitch.'

'My point,' Mitch said, 'is that you'll do the same to Anson. You'll wrap him in chains of incriminating evidence to keep him cooperative. It's how you work.'

'None of that will matter if the two of you do what we want, and you get her back.'

'But it isn't fair,' Mitch protested, and realised that he must in fact sound as ingenuous and credulous as an altar boy.

The kidnapper laughed. 'And you feel we've dealt fairly with *you*?'

Clenched around the pistol, Mitch's hand had grown cold and moist.

'Would you rather we spared your brother and partnered you with Iggy Barnes?'

'Yes,' Mitch said, and was at once embarrassed to have been so quick to sacrifice an innocent friend to save a loved one.

'And that would be fair to Mr Barnes?'

Mitch felt his face turn warm with shame.

'Mr Barnes,' the kidnapper said, 'is not the sharpest knife in the drawer. If for no other reason, your friend would therefore not be an acceptable substitute. Now go to Anson's house and wait for our call.'

Resigned to this development but sick with despair that his brother must be imperilled, Mitch said, 'What should I tell him?'

'Absolutely nothing. I'm *requiring* you to tell him nothing. When I call, I'll let him hear Holly scream, and then explain the facts.'

Alarmed, Mitch said, 'You promised not to hurt her.'

'I promised not to rape her, Mitch. Nothing you say to your brother will be as convincing as her scream. I know better than you how to do this.'

Mitch's hand began to shake. He put the weapon on the passenger's seat once more. 'What if Anson isn't home?'

'He's home. Get moving, Mitch. It's rush hour. You don't want to be late.'

The kidnapper terminated the call.

5

Famous for its yacht harbour and its mansions, Newport Beach was not home exclusively to the fabulously wealthy. Anson lived in the Corona del Mar district, in the front half of a two-unit condo. Shaded by a massive magnolia, approached by a used-brick path, the New England-style house did not impress, but it charmed.

The door chimes played a few bars of Beethoven's 'Ode to Joy'.

Anson arrived before Mitch pressed the bell a second time.

Although as fit as an athlete, he was a different physical type from Mitch: bearish, barrel-chested, bull-necked. That he had been a star quarterback in high school testified to his quickness and agility.

His handsome, broad, open face seemed always to be anticipating a reason to smile. At the sight of Mitch, he grinned.

'*Fratello mio!*' he exclaimed, embracing his brother and drawing him into the house. '*Entrino! Entrino!*'

The air was redolent of garlic, onions, bacon.

'Cooking Italian?' Mitch asked.

'*Bravissimo, fratello piccolo!* From a mere aroma and my bad Italian, you make a brilliant deduction. Let me hang up your coat.'

Mitch had not wanted to leave the pistol in the car. The gun was tucked under his belt, in the small of his back.

'No,' he said. 'I'm fine. I'll keep it.'

'Come into the kitchen. I was in a funk at the prospect of another dinner alone.'

The house featured a masculine but stylish decor, featuring nautical items and paintings of sailing ships.

From childhood, Anson had believed that perfect freedom could never be found on land, only at sea, under sail. He'd been a fan of pirate yarns, naval battles, and tales of adventure on the *Bounty*. He'd read many of them aloud to Mitch, who had sat enthralled for hours.

In the cosy, fragrant kitchen, Anson pointed to a pot steaming on the stove. '*Zuppa massaia*.'

'What kind of soup is *massaia*?'

'Classic housewife's soup. Lacking a wife, I have to get in touch with my feminine side when I want to make it.'

Sometimes Mitch found it hard to believe that a pair as leaden as their parents could have produced a son as buoyant as Anson.

The kitchen clock read 7:24.

On the table stood a bottle of Chianti Classico and a half-full glass. Anson opened a cabinet, plucked another glass from a shelf, and, as he poured the Chianti, he did a fair imitation of their father's voice. 'Yes, I'm pleased to see you, Mitch, though I didn't notice your name on the visiting-progeny schedule, and I had planned to spend this evening tormenting guinea pigs in an electrified maze.'

Accepting the wine, Mitch said, 'I just came from there.'

'That explains your subdued manner and your grey complexion.' Anson raised his glass in a toast. '*La dolce vita*.'

'To your new deal with China,' Mitch said. 'Sounds like a big opportunity.'

'The China thing? Daniel must've hyped what I told him. They aren't dissolving the Communist Party and giving me the emperor's throne.'

Anson's consulting work was so arcane that Mitch had never been able to understand it. He had earned a doctorate in linguistics, but he also had a background in computer languages and digitalisation theory.

'Every time I leave their place,' Mitch said, 'I feel the need to dig in the dirt, work with my hands, *something*.'

'They make you want to flee to something real.'

'That's it exactly. This wine's good.'

'After the soup, we're having roast loin of pork with chestnuts. There's plenty. The recipe serves six.'

'Sounds good, but I don't want dinner.'

Mitch glanced at the windows. Good—the blinds were shut. From the counter near the kitchen phone, he picked up a pen and a notepad. 'Have you got any sailing in lately?'

Anson dreamed of one day owning a yacht. Large enough not to seem claustrophobic but small enough to be managed with one mate. He used the word 'mate' to mean a fellow sailor but also a companion in bed. Anson was a romantic not just about the sea but also about women. He drew them to him as the gravity of the moon pulls the tides.

Yet he was no Don Juan. With charm, he turned away most of his pursuers. And each one that he hoped might be his ideal woman always seemed to break his heart.

The boat—an eighteen-foot American Sail—that he currently had moored at a buoy in the harbour was by no measure a yacht. But, given his luck at love, he might one day own the vessel of his dreams long before he found someone with whom to sail it.

In answer to Mitch's question, he said, 'I haven't had time to do more than bob the harbour like a duck, tacking the channels.'

Sitting at the kitchen table, printing in block letters on the notepad, Mitch said, 'I should have a hobby. You've got sailing, and the old man has dinosaur crap.' He tore off the top sheet of the pad and pushed it across the table so that Anson, still standing, could read it: YOUR HOUSE IS PROBABLY BUGGED.

To cover Anson's stunned silence and look of astonishment Mitch said, 'He just bought a new specimen, a ceratosaurus dropping. From Colorado, the Upper Jurassic.'

He presented another sheet of paper on which he had printed: THEY'RE SERIOUS. I SAW THEM KILL A MAN.

While Anson read, Mitch withdrew his cellphone from an inside coat pocket and placed it on the table. 'Given our family history, it'll be so appropriate—inheriting a collection of polished shit.'

As Anson pulled out a chair and sat at the table. He assisted in the pretense of an ordinary conversation: 'How many does he have now?'

'He told me. I don't remember. You could say the den's become a sewer.'

'Some of the spheres *are* pretty things.'

'Very pretty,' Mitch agreed as he printed: THEY'LL CALL AT 7:30.

Mystified, Anson mouthed the questions: *Who? What?*

Mitch shook his head. He indicated the wall clock—7:27.

They conducted a self-conscious and inane conversation until the phone rang promptly on the half-hour. The ring came not from Mitch's cell but from the kitchen phone.

Anson looked to Mitch for guidance.

Mitch indicated that his brother should answer it.

Anson picked up on the third ring and brightened when he heard the caller's voice. 'Holly!'

Mitch closed his eyes, bent his head, covered his face with his hands. From Anson's reaction, he knew exactly when Holly screamed.

MITCH EXPECTED to be brought into the call, but the kidnapper spoke only to Anson, and for longer than three minutes.

The substance of the first part of the conversation was obvious, and could be deduced from hearing his brother's half of it. The last couple of minutes proved less easy to follow, in part because Anson's responses grew shorter even as his tone of voice became more grim.

When Anson hung up, Mitch said, 'What do they want us to do?'

Instead of answering, Anson came to the table and picked up the bottle of Chianti. He topped up his glass and refilled Mitch's in spite of Mitch's protest. Anson said, 'If your heart's in the same gear as mine, you'll burn off two glasses of this stuff even as you're swallowing it.'

Mitch's hands were trembling.

'And Mickey?' Anson said, using the affectionate nickname that Anson had called his younger brother during a particularly difficult period of their childhood, 'Nothing will happen to her. I promise you. I swear nothing will happen to Holly. Nothing.'

Mitch looked up from his unsteady hands. 'But what do they want us to do? Is it even possible, is it something that *can* be done?'

Instead of replying, Anson sat down. Leaning forward, shoulders hunched, the wineglass all but concealed by his beefy arms and large hands, he was an imposing presence. Mitch knew this particular set to Anson's jaw, the flare of his nostrils, the emerald hardness in the eyes, and it heartened him. This was Anson rising to meet injustice. Mitch took comfort from the fact that his brother had joined the fight; he was no longer alone.

'I'm sorry about this. Man, I never anticipated you'd be dragged into it.'

'You don't have anything to be sorry about. Nada, zip, zero.'

'If I'd have done something different . . .'

'What you've done so far is the right thing or Holly would now be dead.'

Mitch nodded. 'What do they want us to do?' he asked again.

'First, Mickey, I want to hear everything that's happened. What the sonofabitch on the phone told me isn't a fraction of it. I need to hear it from the beginning.'

Surveying the room, Mitch wondered where an eavesdropping device might be hidden.

'Maybe they're listening to us right now, maybe they're not,' Anson said. 'It doesn't matter, Mickey. They already know everything you're going to tell me because *they did it to you.*'

Mitch nodded. He fortified himself with some Chianti. Then he gave Anson an account of this hellish day. In case they were being monitored, he withheld only the story of his encounter with John Knox in the garage loft.

Anson listened intently and interrupted only a few times. When Mitch had finished, he sat with eyes closed, ruminating.

Then, getting up from his chair, he said, 'Sit tight, Mickey. I'll be right back,' and left the kitchen.

Mitch glanced at the clock—7:48. He had been given sixty hours to raise the money, and fifty-two were left.

Anson returned, wearing a sports coat. 'We have places to go. I'll tell you everything in the car. I'd rather you drove.'

'Give me a second to finish this wine,' Mitch said, but instead on the notepad, he printed one more message: THEY CAN TRACK MY CAR.

Although no one had tailed him on his way to his parents' house, the kidnappers had known that he'd gone there. And later, when he had parked in the church lot they had known his precise location. If they had attached tracking devices to his truck and to the Honda, they had been able to follow him at a distance, out of sight, monitoring his whereabouts.

In response to the warning in the latest note, Anson switched off the flame under the pot of soup, and produced the keys to his SUV. 'Let's take my Expedition. You drive.'

Mitch caught the keys when they were tossed to him, then quickly gathered the notes that he had printed, and threw them in the trash.

He and his brother left by the kitchen door.

Softened by ferns and dwarf nandina, a brick courtyard separated the front and rear condos. The smaller back unit was above a pair of garages which contained. Anson's Expedition and a 1947 Buick Super Woody Wagon which he had restored.

Mitch got behind the wheel of the SUV. 'What if they have tracking devices on your cars, too?'

As he pulled shut the passenger's door, Anson said, 'Doesn't matter. I'm going to do exactly what they want.'

'So what do they want? What have we got to do? Hit me with it.' Mitch said backing out of the garage and turning into the alley that led to the street.

Anson pressed the remote to close the garage door. 'They want two million bucks transferred to a numbered account in the Grand Cayman Islands.'

'Yeah, but whose money do we have to rip off?'

The violent light of a red sunset flooded the alleyway.

'We don't have to rip off anybody. It's my money, Mickey. They want my money, and for this they can have it.'

FLUSHED WITH THE FIERY reflection of the smouldering sun, Anson's face seemed fierce, but his voice was tender. 'Everything I have is yours, Mickey.'

Mitch sat for a moment in bewildered silence, and then said, 'You have two million dollars? Where did you get two million dollars?'

'I'm good at what I do, and I've worked hard.'

'I'm sure you're good at what you do—you're good at everything you do—but you don't live like a rich man.'

'Don't want to. Flash and status don't interest me. Ideas do,' Anson said, 'and getting real freedom someday.'

Mitch was lost in this new reality. 'You mean you really have two million in the bank?'

'I'll have to liquidate investments. It can be done by phone, by computer, once the exchanges open tomorrow. Three hours tops.'

Dry seeds of hope swelled with this astonishing news.

'How . . . how much do you have? I mean, altogether.'

'This will almost wipe out my liquidity,' Anson said, 'but I'll still have the equity in the condo.'

'Wipe you out . . . I can't let that happen.'

'What I do with my money is my business, Mickey. And what I want to do with it is get Holly home safe.'

Through the streaming crimson light, through soft dusky shadows fast hardening towards night, a ginger cat stepped along the alley.

Caught in cross-tides of emotion, Mitch did not trust himself to speak, so he watched the cat and drew slow deep breaths.

Anson said, 'Because I'm not married, don't have kids, these scum came after Holly and you as a way to get at me.'

The revelation of Anson's wealth had so surprised Mitch that he had not at once grasped this obvious explanation of the abduction.

'If there'd been someone closer to me,' Anson continued, 'if I had been more vulnerable that way, then my wife or child would have been snatched, and Holly would've been spared.'

The ginger cat stopped in front of the Expedition, peered up at Mitch.

'The way you live, so modestly, how did they know?' Mitch wondered.

'Someone working in a bank, a stock brokerage? I haven't had time to think about it, Mickey. Ask me tomorrow.'

Sneaking forward, the ginger cat passed close by the SUV, vanishing from sight.

Facing his brother again, Mitch said, 'I couldn't see a way to go to the cops. But everything's changed now. You have that option.'

Anson shook his head. 'They shot a guy to death right in front of you to make a point. Unless they get what they want, they'll kill without compunction, and pin it on you or on both of us. We get Holly back, and *then* we go to the cops.'

'Two million dollars.'

'It's only money,' Anson said. 'It doesn't matter, Mickey.'

'Sure it matters. With that much money, you're close to having the yacht and a life without chains.'

It was Anson's turn to look for a distraction in the shadows. 'It's a child's dream anyway, Mickey. Pirate yarns and naval battles.'

'When did you plan to retire, to go for it?' Mitch asked.

'In two years. When I turned thirty-five. So it'll be a few years later. And I might make it back quicker than I think. My business is growing fast. I'm good at what I do.'

'No way I'd turn you down,' Mitch said. 'I'd die for Holly, so I'm sure as hell willing to let you go broke for her. But I won't let you minimise the sacrifice.'

Anson reached out, put a hand round the back of Mitch's neck, pulled him close, gently pressed forehead to forehead. 'Tell you something, bro. Normally I'd never mention this. But so you don't chew out your own liver with guilt . . . you should know you aren't the only one who's needed help. How do you think Connie bought her bakery?'

'*You*?'

'I structured a loan so a portion converts into a tax-free gift each year. I don't want to be repaid. And Megan's dog-grooming business, I saw what they needed. I've been trying to think what you need, but you've always seemed . . . so damned self-reliant.'

'This is way different from a loan to buy a bakery.'

'No shit, Sherlock. Growing up in Daniel's rat maze,' Anson said, 'the only thing any of us had was one another. The only thing that mattered. That's still the way it is, *fratello piccolo*.'

'I'll never forget this,' Mitch said.

'Damn right. You owe me for ever. Now let's roll.'

ONLY THE THINNEST WOUND of the fallen day bled along the far horizon. The sky and the sea were dark, and the moon had not yet risen to silver the deserted beaches.

Anson had said he needed to think. He thought most clearly in a car in motion, so he suggested Mitch drive south.

At that hour, only light traffic plied the Pacific Coast Highway, and Mitch stayed in the right-hand lane, in no hurry.

'They'll call the house tomorrow at noon,' Anson said, 'to see what progress I've made with the financials.'

'I don't like this wire transfer to the Cayman Islands.'

'Neither do I. Then they have the money *and* Holly.'

'Better we have a face-to-face,' Mitch said. 'They bring Holly, we bring a couple suitcases of cash.'

'That's also iffy. They take the money, shoot all of us.'

'Not if we make it a condition that we can be armed.'

Anson was dubious. 'Where do we get guns?'

'We buy them at a gun shop, wherever. I don't see the kidnappers letting us set conditions. Whoever has the power makes the rules.'

Mitch and Anson travelled in silence, the eastern hills speckled with the lights of houses, the black sea and sky merging into one great void. They worried their way southwards. The graceful highway curved, rose, and descended into downtown Laguna Beach.

In mid-May the tourist season had begun. People strolled the sidewalks, going to and from dinner, peering in the windows of the closed shops and galleries.

When his brother suggested that they grab something to eat, Mitch said he wasn't hungry. 'You have to eat,' Anson pressed.

Resisting, Mitch said, 'What're we going to talk about over dinner? Sports? We don't want to be overheard talking about *this*.'

'So we'll eat in the car.'

Mitch parked in front of a Chinese restaurant. Painted on the windows, a dragon rampant tossed its mane of scaly flagella.

While Anson waited in the SUV, Mitch went inside. The girl at the take-out counter promised to have his order ready in ten minutes.

The animated conversation of the diners at the tables grated on him. He resented their carefree laughter. While Holly remained in the hands of murderers, ordering Chinese takeout, eating, attending to *any* tasks of ordinary life seemed like betrayals of her. If Holly had heard the threats made to Mitch on the phone then her fear must be unbearable. When he imagined her state of mind, his face grew hot, and his throat so swollen with rage he could not swallow. His life had fallen into chaos and he was filled with the urge to tear down the colourful paper lanterns and shred the rice-paper screens.

Presenting two white bags containing his order, the counter girl sensed the pending storm in him, and she tensed.

The realisation that he might be frightening her reeled Mitch back from fury to passive misery. Leaving the restaurant and stepping into the spring night, he saw that his brother, in the Expedition, was on his cellphone.

As Mitch got behind the steering wheel, Anson concluded the call and asked Mitch, 'Was it them?'

'No. There's this guy I think we should talk to.'

Giving Anson the larger bag of takeout, Mitch said, 'What guy?'

'We're in deep water with sharks, and we need advice from someone who can keep us from being eaten alive.'

'They'll kill her if we tell anyone.'

'They said no cops. We aren't going to the police. Mickey. If we don't try to sway the odds in our favour, we're screwed anyway.'

Tired of feeling powerless, convinced that docile obedience to the kidnappers would be repaid with contempt and cruelty, Mitch said, 'OK. But what if they're listening to us right now?'

'They're not. To bug a car and listen in real time, they'd have to plant more than a microphone; they'd have to package it with a microwave transmitter and a power source.'

With chopsticks, Anson ate Szechuan beef from one container, rice with mushrooms from another.

'What about directional microphones?'

'I've seen the same movies you have,' Anson said. 'Directional mikes work best when the air is still. Look at the trees. We have a breeze tonight.

Besides, directional mikes don't work between one moving vehicle and another.'

Mitch ate the food unenthusiastically with a plastic fork. 'Then let's not talk about it till we're moving.'

'Mickey, there's a very thin line between sensible caution and paranoia.'

'I passed that line several hours ago,' Mitch said, 'and for me there's no going back.'

6

The Chinese takeout left an aftertaste that Mitch tried unsuccessfully to wash away with Pepsi as he drove south on the Coast Highway.

Sipping from a tall paper cup of lemon tea, Anson said, 'His name is Campbell. He's ex-FBI. He was shot, and shot bad, when he was twenty-eight. Other guys would have lived on disability, but he built his own little business empire.'

'What if they've got a tracking device on the Expedition, and they figure out we're going to go pow-wowing with an ex-FBI agent?'

'They won't know that he was. If they know anything at all about him, they might know I did a large piece of business with him a few years ago. It'll just look like I'm putting together the ransom.'

'I know what soil bougainvillea needs, what sunlight loropetalum requires,' Mitch said. 'But this stuff is another universe to me.'

'Me too, Mickey. Which is why we need help. No one has more real-world knowledge, more street smarts than Julian Campbell.'

Mitch had begun to feel that every yes–no decision was a switch on a bomb detonator, that one wrong choice would atomise his wife. But inaction would not save Holly. Indecision would be the death of her.

'All right,' he relented. 'Where does this Campbell live?'

'Get to the interstate. We're going south to Rancho Santa Fe.'

East-northeast of San Diego, Rancho Santa Fe was a community of four-star resorts, golf courses, and multimillion-dollar estates.

'Jam it,' Anson said, 'and we'll be there in ninety minutes.'

When together, they were comfortable with silences, perhaps because each of them, as a kid, had spent much time alone in the learning room.

That chamber was better soundproofed than a radio-station studio. No noise penetrated from the outside world.

They had been on I-5 for twenty minutes when Anson said, 'Do you sometimes feel we were held for ransom our entire childhood?'

'If it weren't for you,' Mitch said, 'I'd hate them.'

'I *do* hate them sometimes,' Anson said. 'Intensely but briefly. But they're too pathetic to hate for more than a moment.'

'Remember when I got caught with the copy of *Charlotte's Web*?'

'You were almost nine. You spent twenty days in the learning room.' Anson quoted Daniel: '"Fantasy is a doorway to superstition, the first step in a life of unreason and irrational beliefs."'

Mitch said, 'It would have been better if they hit us.'

'Much better. Bruises, broken bones—that's the kind of thing that gets the attention of Child Protective Services.'

After another silence, Mitch said, 'Connie in Chicago, Megan in Atlanta, Portia in Birmingham. Why are you and I still here?'

'Maybe we feel we have unfinished business.' Anson said.

That resonated with Mitch. He had often thought about what he would say to his parents if the opportunity arose to question their cruelty.

When he left the interstate and drove inland, desert moths swirled as white as snowflakes in the headlights and burst against the windshield.

JULIAN CAMPBELL lived behind stone walls, behind an imposing iron gate framed by a massive limestone frieze featuring rich carvings of leafy vines.

'This gate,' Mitch said, 'must've cost as much as my house.'

'Twice as much,' Anson assured him.

To the left of the main gate, the estate wall incorporated a guardhouse. As the Expedition drifted to a stop, the door opened and a tall young man in a black suit appeared.

'Good evening, sir.' He looked past Mitch to Anson. 'Pleased to see you, Mr Rafferty.'

With no sound that Mitch could detect, the ornate iron gates swung inward. Beyond lay a driveway paved with quartzite cobblestones, flanked by majestic Phoenix palms, each lit at its base, the great crowns forming a canopy. The driveway was a quarter of a mile long. Vast, magically illuminated lawns and gardens receded into mystery on both sides.

'Sixteen manicured acres,' Anson said.

'There must be a dozen on the landscape staff alone.'

The Italianate house with its red tiled roofs, limestone walls, mullioned windows, columns and terraces should have been intimidating. Instead it looked welcoming. At its end, the driveway encircled a reflecting pond with a central fountain. Mitch parked beside it.

'Does this guy have a licence to print money?'

'He's in entertainment. Movies, casinos, you name it.'

A silver-haired man, with the demeanour of a butler, greeted them on the terrace, said his name was Winslow, and escorted them inside. They followed him across an immense white-marble entrance hall. After passing through a living room measuring at least sixty by eighty feet, they came, finally, into a mahogany-panelled library.

In response to Mitch's question, Winslow revealed that the book collection numbered over 60,000 volumes. 'Mr Campbell will be with you momentarily,' he said, and departed.

The library offered half a dozen seating areas with sofas and chairs. They settled into armchairs, facing each other across a coffee table, and Anson sighed. 'This is the right thing. Julian is the real deal.'

'He must think a lot of you to meet at such short notice, past ten p.m.'

Anson smiled ruefully. 'What would Daniel and Kathy say if I turned away your compliment with a few words of modesty?'

'"Modesty is related to diffidence,"' Mitch quoted. '"Diffidence is a synonym for timidity. Timidity is a characteristic of the meek. The meek do *not* inherit the earth, they serve those who are self-confident and self-assertive."'

'I love you, little brother. You're amazing. You were raised in that rat maze and yet you're maybe the most balanced and modest guy I know.'

'I've got issues,' Mitch assured him. 'Plenty of them.'

'See? Your response to being called modest is self-criticism.'

Mitch smiled. 'Guess I didn't learn much in the learning room.'

Anson laughed softly, a warm and bearish laugh. 'Damn if we're getting him anything for Father's Day.'

'Not even cologne?' Mitch asked.

This was a jokey routine from childhood.

'Not even a pot to piss in,' Anson said. 'I'm proud of you, Mickey. You beat 'em. It didn't work with you the way it worked with me.'

'The way what worked?'

'They broke me, Mitch. I have no shame, no capacity for guilt.' From under his jacket, Anson withdrew a pistol.

MITCH HELD HIS SMILE in anticipation of the punch line, as if the pistol would prove to be a novelty-store item that shot bubbles.

If the salty sea could freeze and keep its colour, it would have been the shade of Anson's eyes. They were as clear, as direct as always, but they were coloured by a quality that Mitch had never seen before.

'Two *million*. Truth is,' Anson said almost sadly. 'I wouldn't pay two million to ransom *you,* so Holly was dead the moment she was snatched.'

Mitch's face set marble-hard, and his throat seemed to be full of broken stones that weighed down speech. His head was filled with a roar of lifelong perceptions collapsing like termite-eaten timbers.

'Some people I've done consulting work for—sometimes they come across an opportunity that is crumbs to them but meat to me. Not my usual work, but things that are more directly criminal,' Anson said. 'The people who kidnapped Holly are the team I put together for one of those jobs. They made a bundle from it, but they found out my take was bigger than I told them, and now they're greedy.'

So, Mitch thought, struggling to focus his attention, Holly had been kidnapped not solely because Anson had enough money to ransom her, but also because—primarily because—he had cheated her abductors.

'They're afraid to come directly after me. I'm a valuable resource to some serious people who'd pop anyone who popped me. On the phone,' Anson revealed, 'they said if I don't ransom Holly, they'll kill her and then shoot you in the street one day, like they shot Jason Osteen. The poor dumb babies. They think they know me, but they don't know what I really am. Nobody does. Jason was one of them, by the way. Sweet brainless Breezer. He thought his pals were going to shoot the dog to make their point. By shooting him instead, they made a sharper point *and* improved the split.'

Evidently, Anson had remained in touch with Jason long after Mitch had lost track of his former room-mate.

'Is there something you want to say to me, Mitch?'

Perhaps another man in his position would have had a thousand angry questions, but Mitch sat frozen, having just experienced an emotional polar shift. This was not the brother he had known, but a stranger.

Anson seemed to take Mitch's silence as a challenge. Leaning forward in his chair, he spoke in the brotherly voice that he had always used before. 'Just so you won't feel that you mean less to me than Megan, Connie and Portia, I should clarify something. I didn't give them money to start businesses. That was bullshit, bro.'

Because a response was clearly wanted, Mitch did not give one.

'Two million wouldn't wipe me out. The truth is . . . I've got closer to eight. I bought the yacht in March,' Anson said. 'Come September, I'll run my consulting service at sea, with a satellite link. Freedom. I've earned it, and no one's gonna bleed me for two cents of it.'

The library door closed. Someone had arrived. A tall man, iron-grey eyes bright with curiosity, his nose raised as if seeking an elusive scent. Clearly, he wanted privacy for whatever was about to come next.

Rising from his chair, pistol ready, Anson tried once more to sting a reaction from Mitch. 'You can take some comfort from the fact that this will be over for Holly quicker now than midnight Wednesday. When I'm not home to take their call tomorrow at noon, and when they can't get you on your cellphone, they'll know my buttons can't be pushed. They'll whack her, dump her, and run.'

The tall man wore tasselled loafers, black silk trousers, and a grey silk shirt the shade of his eyes. A gold Rolex brightened his left wrist, and his manicured fingernails were buffed to a shine.

Two solid men now stepped out from the shadows at the edge of the room and flanked Mitch's chair. Both had pistols fitted with silencers,.

'He's carrying a piece in the small of his back,' Anson told them. To Mitch, he said, 'I felt it when I hugged you, bro.'

In retrospect, Mitch wondered why he hadn't mentioned the pistol to Anson. Perhaps in the deepest catacombs of his mind had been interred a distrust of his brother that he had not been able to acknowledge.

One of the gunmen had a face pitted with acne. He told Mitch to stand, and the other gunman lifted the back of Mitch's sports jacket and took the pistol from him.

When told to sit down, Mitch obeyed.

At last he spoke to Anson, but only to say, 'I pity you,' which was true, though it was a wretched kind of pity, transfused with revulsion.

At Mitch's declaration of pity, disdain narrowed Anson's eyes, and his contempt brought a harder edge of brutality to his features.

As if he sensed that Anson was sufficiently offended to do something rash, the man in silk raised one hand, Rolex glittering, to stay a gunshot. 'Not here.'

Hesitating, Anson returned his pistol to the shoulder holster under his jacket. For an instant, he and his associates were as motionless as figures in a painting, the library hushed, the night air still. Then Anson walked out of the room, the two gunmen retreated a few steps, remaining alert, and the man in silk perched on the arm of the chair in which Anson had sat.

'Mitch,' he said, 'you've been quite a disappointment to your brother.'

JULIAN CAMPBELL had a smooth face that, for a man in his fifties, suggested a plastic surgeon on retainer, and his skin had a golden glow that could only have been achieved by a tanning machine. The wound that had ended his FBI career was not evident, nor was any sign of disability. His triumph over his physical injuries evidently equalled his economic success.

'Mitch, I'm curious.'

'About what?'

Instead of answering, Campbell said, 'I'm a practical man. In my business I do what I need to do, and I don't get acid indigestion over it. I know a lot of men who do what needs to be done. Practical men. But this is the first time I've seen a man drop the dime on his own brother just to prove he's the hardest hardcase around. Anson could have asked me to teach these pussies a lesson. They aren't as tough as they think. In twelve hours, we could find members of *their* families and have them begging to pay us to take your wife back unharmed.'

Campbell was as matter-of-fact as if he had been explaining the terms of a real-estate deal.

The two gunmen never took their eyes off Mitch.

'But, Anson,' Campbell continued, 'he wants to make a statement so nobody ever underestimates him again. Indirectly, the statement's also for my benefit. And I gotta say . . . I'm impressed.'

Mitch knew he must appear to be fearful—more than fearful, despairing. A man in the grip of despair, is not a man with the will to fight.

'I'm curious,' Campbell repeated. 'For your brother to be able to do this to you . . . what did *you* do?'

'Loved him,' Mitch said.

Campbell regarded Mitch as a wading heron regards a swimming fish, and then smiled. 'Yes, that would do it. What if one day he found himself reciprocating?'

'He's always wanted to go far, and to get there fast.'

'Sentiment is an encumbrance,' Campbell said. From the coffee table where one of the gunmen had put it, he picked up the pistol that had been taken from Mitch. 'Have you ever fired this?'

Mitch almost said that he had not, but then realised that the magazine lacked one bullet, the round with which Knox accidentally shot himself. 'Once. I fired it once. To see what it felt like.'

Amused, Campbell said, 'Your brother says you're not a man for guns.'

'He knows me better than I know him.'

'So where did you get this?'

'My wife thought we should keep one in the house. It's been in a night-stand drawer since the day we bought it,' Mitch lied.

Campbell rose to his feet. With his right arm extended full length, he pointed the pistol at Mitch's face. 'Stand up.'

Meeting the blind stare of the pistol, Mitch rose from the armchair.

'Take off your coat and put it on the table,' Campbell said.

Mitch did as he was told, and then followed another instruction to turn out the pockets of his jeans. He put his ring of keys, his wallet, and a few other items on the coffee table.

One of the gunman picked up Mitch's jacket, searched the pockets, and found only the cellphone.

To his watchful host, Mitch said, 'How did you go from being an FBI hero to this?'

Campbell's puzzlement was brief. 'Is that the yarn Anson spun to get you here? Julian Campbell—FBI hero?'

Although the gunmen had seemed humourless, the one with smooth skin laughed and the other one smiled.

'You probably didn't make your money in entertainment, either,' Mitch said.

'Entertainment? That could be true enough,' Campbell said, 'if you have an elastic definition of "entertainment".'

The acne-scarred gunman had produced a folded plastic bag from a hip pocket. He shook it open and filled it with the jacket, cellphone and other items that they had taken off Mitch. Before throwing away the wallet, he stripped out the forty odd dollars that were in it and gave it to Campbell, who folded the money, with hands as dexterous as those of a magician, into his own wallet.

Mitch remained on his feet, waiting. The three men were more relaxed with him now. He was Anson's brother but only by blood. He was an evader, not a hunter. He would obey.

One of the gunmen now produced a pair of handcuffs and, before Mitch had to be asked to extend his hands, he offered them.

The cuffs were snapped round Mitch's wrists.

'You seem very tired,' Campbell said, and his voice had an almost tender quality. 'You might even fall asleep on the way.'

'Where are we going?'

'I knew a guy who fell asleep one night, on a drive like the one you're taking. It was almost a shame to wake him when we got there.'

'Are you coming?' Mitch asked.

'Oh, I haven't in years. These gentlemen will be taking you to the car pavilion across the gardens. Goodbye, Mitch. It's not long now.'

Flanking Mitch, each holding him by one arm, the gunmen walked him across the library to the French doors. The man with the pitted face, on Mitch's right, pressed the muzzle of a pistol into his side.

Just before stepping across the threshold, Mitch glanced back and saw Campbell reviewing the titles on a shelf of books. He stood with the loose-hipped grace of a loitering ballet dancer, apparently choosing a book.

From the library terrace, they descended steps to another terrace. From there, the gunmen conveyed Mitch along garden pathways where hidden toads sang, across a broad lawn and through a copse of tall, silver trees, and by a roundabout route, they came to a large, elegant building encircled by a romantically lit loggia. Night-blooming jasmine twined round its columns and festooned the eaves. The heavy fragrance was so sweet as to be almost narcoleptic.

The pavilion contained exquisitely restored cars from the 1930s and 1940s—Buicks, Lincolns, Packards, Cadillacs, Pontiacs, Fords, Chevrolets, Studebakers. They were displayed like jewels under precisely focused pin lights.

The gunman with the pitted face fished a set of keys from his pocket and opened the trunk of a midnight-blue Chrysler Windsor from the late 1940s. 'Get in.'

The trunk was roomier than those of contemporary cars. Mitch lay on his side, in a foetal position.

'You can't unlock it from the inside,' the scarred man said. 'They had no child-safety awareness in those days.'

His partner said, 'We'll be on back roads where no one will hear you. So if you make a lot of noise, it won't do you any good. It'll just piss us off. Then we'll be harder on you at the other end than we have to be.'

'I don't want that.'

'No. You don't want that.'

They slammed the lid, and the darkness was absolute.

7

Holly lies in darkness, praying that Mitch will live. She fears less for herself than for him.

Her captors wear ski masks in her presence, and she assumes they would not bother to conceal their faces if they intended to kill her.

Always an optimist, having believed since childhood that every life has meaning and that hers will not pass before she finds its purpose, Holly envisions herself released, unharmed. She believes that picturing the future helps shape it, although hard work, not wishes, builds careers. Her goal is to be a real estate agent.

Free again, she will eat marzipan and chocolate peanut-butter ice cream and potato chips. Free, she will celebrate by going to Baby Style, that store in the mall, and buying the huge stuffed bear she saw in their window when she passed by recently. It was fluffy and white and so cute.

Free, she will make love to Mitch. She prays that her beautiful husband will live through this terror. He is physically beautiful, but the most beautiful thing about him is his gentle heart. Holly loves him for it, for his sweetness, but she worries that certain aspects of his gentleness, such as his tendency towards passive acceptance, will get him killed.

He possesses a deep and quiet strength, too, and has a spine of steel, which is revealed in subtle ways. Without that, he would have been broken by his freak-show parents. So she prays for him to stay strong, to stay alive. And during her ruminations she works steadily at a nail in the floorboard. It has a large flat head and the size of the head suggests that it may be large enough to qualify as a spike.

In a crisis, a spike might serve as a weapon.

The flat head of the nail is raised maybe a sixteenth of an inch above the rough, wooden floor. This gap gives her a little leverage with which to work the nail back and forth.

One of Holly's virtues is perseverance. She will keep working at the nail, and she will *envision* it loose, and eventually she will extract it.

An ankle cuff and a length of chain shackle her right leg to a ringbolt in the floor. This leaves both her hands free to work on the nail. The kidnappers have made some provision for her comfort: an air mattress, a six-pack of bottled water and a bedpan. Earlier they gave her half a pizza.

This is not to suggest that they are nice people. They are not nice people. When they needed her to scream for Mitch, they hit her. When they needed her to scream for Anson, they pulled her hair, suddenly, sharply, and so hard that she thought her scalp was coming off.

They are evil, and they have a business goal, so to speak, on which they remain focused.

One of them is evil *and* crazy. He's the one who worries her.

Holly vaguely understands that they are imprisoning her in order to use Mitch to manipulate Anson. She doesn't know why or how they think Anson can tap into a fortune to ransom her, but she is not surprised that he stands at the centre of the whirlwind. She has long felt that Anson is not what he pretends to be.

Now and then she has caught him staring at her in a way that the loving brother of a husband should never stare. When he realises he has been caught, the predatory lust in Anson's eyes vanishes under his usual charm.

Sometimes when he laughs, his mirth sounds manufactured to her. She seems to be alone in this perception. Everyone else finds Anson's laugh infectious. She has never shared her doubts about him. Her hope has always been to enrich Mitch's life, not to subtract anything from it.

She can put her life in Mitch's strong hands and fall at once into a dreamless sleep. In a sense, that is what marriage—a good marriage—is about. A total trusting with your heart, your mind, your life.

She worries, worries, worries the nail until her fingers ache.

As the minutes pass, Holly tries not to brood about how a day that began with such joy could spiral into these desperate circumstances. After Mitch had gone to work and before the masked men had burst into her kitchen, she had used the kit that she'd bought the previous day. Her period is nine days overdue, and according to the pregnancy test, she is going to have a baby. For a year, she and Mitch have been hoping for this. Now the kidnappers are unaware that *two* lives are at their mercy, and Mitch is unaware that it's not only his wife but also his child who depend on his cunning and his courage. Holly's knowledge is at once a joy and an anguish.

She envisions a child of three—sometimes a girl, sometimes a boy—at play in their back yard. She focuses on this child more vividly than she has focused on anything before, in the hope that she can make it come to pass. She tells herself that she will be strong, that she will not cry, but sometimes tears come. To shut off their flow, she works harder at the nail.

In the late 1940s, if you owned a car like a Chrysler Windsor, you knew the engine was big because it made a big sound. It had the throb of a bull's heart, a low fierce snort and a heavy stamp of hoofs.

The car's dark trunk reverberated with engine noise transferred along the drive shaft, through the body and the frame. Mitch could smell the rubbery scent of the mat on which he lay and the acidity of his own fear.

He remembered his father saying we should conduct ourselves not according to any code, only according to self-interest. Rationality is always in a man's self-interest, Daniel says. Therefore, any act that is rational is right and good and admirable. Evil does not exist in Daniel's philosophy. Stealing, rape, murder are merely irrational because they put he who commits them in jeopardy of his freedom.

Mitch had been steeped in his father's fanaticism so long that some of what he'd been told had stayed with him. This day, this night, Mitch had come face-to-face with evil. It was real, and although an irrational man should be met with compassion, an evil man was owed nothing more or less than resistance and retribution, the fury of a righteous justice.

In Julian Campbell's library, when the gunman had produced the handcuffs, Mitch had willingly held out his hands. If he had not appeared worn down, meek and resigned to his fate, they might have cuffed his hands behind him. Reaching the revolver in his ankle holster would have been more difficult; using it with accuracy would have been impossible.

Campbell had even commented on Mitch's weariness. They thought they knew the kind of man he was, and maybe they did. But they didn't know the kind of man he could become when the life of his wife was in the balance. Amused by his lack of familiarity with the pistol that they had confiscated, they had not imagined he would have a second weapon.

Mitch pulled up the leg of his jeans and retrieved the revolver.

Five rounds in five chambers. When the trunk lid went up, he would have to score two hits out of five. Direct hits. Perhaps just one of the gunmen would open the trunk. It would be better if the two men were there, giving him the advantage of surprise.

Perhaps both would have their weapons drawn—or only one. If one, Mitch must be quick enough to target his armed adversary first . . .

According to his luminous watch, they travelled for more than half an hour. Then, the car slowed and the surface seemed to change from tarmac to a dirt road. Small stones rattled against the undercarriage. Mitch smelt dust and licked the alkaline taste of it from his lips.

After twelve minutes on the dirt road, the car came to a stop. The engine idled for half a minute, and then the driver switched it off. The silence was like a sudden deafness.

One door opened, then the other. They were coming.

Facing the back of the car, Mitch splayed his legs, bracing his feet in opposite corners of the space. He could not sit erect until the lid was raised, but he waited with his back partly off the floor of the trunk, as if in the middle of doing a series of stomach crunches at the gym.

The cuffs required that he hold the revolver in a two-hand grip, which was probably better anyway.

He didn't hear footsteps, just the gallop of his heart. Then he heard the key in the trunk lock.

As the lid lifted, Mitch sat up, thrusting the revolver forward. The full-pitcher moon spilt its milk, backlighting the two gunmen. He didn't consciously squeeze off the first shot, but felt the hard recoil and saw the muzzle flash and heard the crash, and then he was aware of squeezing the trigger the second time.

Two point-blank rounds knocked down one silhouette. The second backed away from the car, and Mitch sat all the way up, squeezing off one, two, three more rounds. The hammer clicked, and there was just the quiet of the moon. *Only five, only five!* he reminded himself.

With no ammunition, he was a fish in a barrel. He had to get out of the trunk. His left foot came down on solid ground, but he planted his right on the twice-shot man. The body shifted under him and he fell.

He rolled away from the gunman, to the verge of the road. He was stopped by a wild hedge of mesquite, which he identified by its oily smell.

He had lost the revolver. It didn't matter. No ammunition left.

Around him lay a parched, moon-silvered landscape: desert scrub, boulders. Sleek and with its lustrous chrome features, the Chrysler Windsor seemed strangely futuristic in this primitive land. The driver had switched off the headlights when he killed the engine.

Lying face down and flat, head cautiously raised, Mitch could see a significant distance along the sandy soil of the roadbed as it dwindled through the gnarled scrub in the direction from which they had come. No second body lay on the road.

If the guy was only wounded, surely he would have charged, firing, as Mitch clambered out of the Chrysler? On the opposite side of the road, several blinds of scraggly vegetation offered concealment, as did low, weathered rocks. The man might have hobbled or crawled into the scrub or behind a stone. He could be anywhere out there, reviewing his options.

Mitch was afraid of the man hiding in the night. He also feared the one lying on the road at the back of the Chrysler. He might be dead, but Mitch didn't want to go near him.

He had discovered that he was capable of violence, at least in self-defence. Now, he had to do what he didn't want to do, because whether the man was a carcass or unconscious, he possessed a weapon. Mitch needed a weapon. And quick.

As far as he could tell, all was still.

Acutely aware that his own movement made him a target and, hampered by the handcuffs, Mitch wriggled on his belly to the man behind the car.

Wincing at the faint jingle produced by the short chain between his handcuffs, he patted down the corpse—and pressed his fingers in a wetness. Sickened, shuddering, he wiped his hand on the dead man's clothes.

He was about to conclude that this guy had no weapon, when he discovered the grip of the pistol protruding from under his body. He pulled the gun free.

The sound of a shot cracked in the night. The dead man's body jerked as it took a round that had been meant for Mitch.

He flung himself towards the Chrysler and heard a second bullet ricochet off the car. With the vehicle between himself and the shooter, he felt safer, but then, almost at once, not safe at all.

The gunman could come round the Chrysler at either the front end or the back. He had the advantage of choosing his approach. Meanwhile, Mitch was forced to keep a watch in both directions. An impossible task.

He thrust up from the ground and away from the car, running in a crouch, off the road, through the hedge of mesquite. The land sloped down from the road, which was good. If it had sloped up, he would have been visible, his broad back an easy target the moment the gunman rounded the Chrysler.

The moon mapped his route as he wove round clumps of brush instead of thrashing through them, mindful that keeping his balance would be more difficult with his hands cuffed in front of him.

At the bottom of the slope, he turned right. Based on the position of the moon, he believed that he was heading almost due west.

Something like a cricket sang. Something stranger clicked and shrilled.

A colony of pampas-grass clumps with scores of tall, feathery panicles drew his attention. They glowed white in the moonlight and reminded him of the plumed tails of proud horses. Mitch was able to pass among them and, in the heart of the colony, he felt safely screened. Through gaps between the plumes, he peered back the way that he had come and surveyed the edge of the roadway at the top of the slope.

He did not intend to hide for long. He had fled his vulnerable position at the car only to gain a couple of minutes to think. He wasn't boiling over with macho enthusiasm for a confrontation with this second professional killer, but he understood too well the consequences of avoiding it altogether. If the remaining gunman lived and reported back to Campbell, Anson would know, sooner rather than later, that his little brother was alive and free. Mitch would lose the advantage of surprise.

Most likely, however, Campbell wouldn't expect a report from his pair of executioners until morning. Perhaps he would not even seek them out until the following afternoon. Campbell might well miss the Chrysler Windsor before he missed the men.

Mitch needed to be able to catch Anson by surprise, and he needed to be in his brother's house at noon to take the call from the kidnappers. He could not hide, and his enemy would not. For predator and prey this had to be a fight to the death.

Small stones rattled like tumbling dice.

The sound seemed to have come from somewhere west of him. He turned in that direction. With caution, he parted the pampas panicles.

Fifty feet away, the gunman crouched like a hunchback troll, waiting for any repercussions of the noise he had made.

Mitch hesitated. The advantage still seemed to be his. He could fire from cover while the gunman stood in the open. He had not yet squeezed off a shot with this pistol, while his adversary had expended two.

Still crouching, the trollish figure took two tentative steps forward. He paused again.

Inspiration came to Mitch, a reckless idea, but his best chance. He let the panicles ease into their natural positions and slipped out of the pampas, moving away from the gunman.

He hurried eastwards, along the route that he had taken earlier, passing the point at which he had descended the embankment.

About sixty feet further on, he arrived at a wide shallow depression in the otherwise uniform face of the slope. Chaparral thrived in it and spilled up over the edges.

In need of his cuffed hands to climb, Mitch jammed the pistol under his belt. Always conscious that quiet was as important as swift progress, he insinuated himself upwards through the chaparral.

He thought of snakes, and then he refused to think of them.

When he reached the top without drawing gunfire, he wriggled out onto the shoulder of the dirt road. He crawled to the centre of it then stood.

The vintage Chrysler stood sixty feet west of Mitch, the trunk lid still half raised. He hurried to the car, lifted the lid higher, then climbed into the trunk and pulled the lid partway shut again.

After a little experimentation, he figured out that a sound suppressor was threaded to the barrel of the pistol. He unscrewed it and set it aside.

Sooner rather than later, when he failed to find Mitch, the gunman would come back to the Chrysler. He would expect his prey to return to the car in the hope that the keys might be in the ignition. But he might not expect that a cornered animal, once it had broken free, would return voluntarily to the trap that it had escaped.

If the gunman established a surveillance point behind the car, he might cross the road in the moonlight. He would be cautious and quick, but a clear target. Or he might undertake a general exploration of the area and cross Mitch's sights.

Only seven or eight minutes had passed since the pair had opened the trunk to a greeting of gunfire. Eventually, if his searches were not fruitful, the surviving man would consider packing up and getting out of here, regardless of how much he might fear reporting failure to his boss.

At that time, if not before, he would come to the back of the car to deal with the corpse. He would want to load it into the trunk.

Now Mitch half sat, half lay, swaddled in darkness, his head raised just enough to see across the sill of the trunk.

Under the moon's mesmerising stare, the desert seemed to be asleep and dreaming, rendered in the silver and black palette of most dreams, every shadow as hard as iron, every object as insubstantial as smoke.

Mitch had killed a man. He intended to kill another. The pistol felt heavy in his hand. He smoothed his trembling fingers along its contours, as he stared at the lonely moon-glazed road and understood that the innocence of which he had just been robbed was gradually being replaced by a capacity for awe, a deeper sense of the mystery of all things.

Some stone formations contained chips of mica that sparkled in the moonlight, and, where the rock rose in silhouette against the sky, the stars appeared to have salted themselves upon the earth. Out of the north, southbound on its feathered sails, a great horned owl, as pale as it was immense, silently swooped low across the road, then rowed itself higher into the night, much higher and away.

8

So stealthily did the killer return that Mitch was unaware of his presence until he heard one of the car doors click open and swing wide with the faintest creak.

The man had approached from the front of the Chrysler. Risking exposure in the brief glow of the car's interior lights, he got in and pulled the door shut as softly as it could be closed.

If he had got behind the wheel, he must intend to leave the scene.

No. He wouldn't drive away with the trunk lid open. And surely he wouldn't leave the corpse.

Mitch waited in silence.

The gunman was silent, too.

The desert remained breathless.

In these circumstances, the car would be as sensitive to motion as a boat on water. If Mitch moved, the killer would be alerted to his presence.

A minute passed. Another.

Mitch pictured the smooth-faced gunman sitting there in the car, in the gloom, at least thirty years old, maybe thirty-five. He tried to imagine what he was planning.

After a long stillness, the gunman shifted positions, and the movement proved to be a revelation. The unnerving intimacy of the sound indicated that the man wasn't behind the wheel—he was in the back seat.

He must have been sitting forward, watchful, since getting into the car. When at last he leaned back, the upholstery made a sound like leather or vinyl does when stressed, and the seat springs quietly complained.

The back seat of the car formed the back wall of the trunk. He and Mitch were within a couple feet of each other.

A car of this vintage would not feature a fire wall or a crash panel between the trunk and the passenger compartment, Mitch thought. The back of the rear seat might have been finished with a quarter-inch fibreboard panel or even just with cloth. It wouldn't be bulletproof.

Mitch was half lying and half sitting on his left side, facing the night through the raised trunk lid. He would need to roll onto his right side in order to bring the pistol to bear on the back wall of the trunk.

He weighed a hundred and seventy pounds. No degree in physics was required to figure out that the car would respond to that much weight shifting position.

Turn fast, open fire—and maybe he would discover that he was wrong about the partition between trunk and passenger compartment. If there was a metal panel, he might not only be nailed by the ricochet but also fail to hit his target. Then he would be wounded and out of ammunition, and the gunman would know where to find him.

A bead of sweat slipped along the side of his nose to the corner of his mouth. An urge to act pulled his nerves as taut as bowstrings.

As Mitch lay in indecision, hearing Holly's scream in his memory and the sharp *slap* of her being hit, a real sound refocused his attention on the present: his enemy, in the passenger compartment, stifling a series of coughs. Maybe the gunman's cough related to a wound.

When the guy coughed again, Mitch would seize the opportunity to change positions.

Beyond the partially open trunk, moonlight frosted the phosphorescent wings of swarming moths that whirled across the road.

Mitch's cuffed hands gripped the pistol so fiercely that his knuckles began to ache. His teeth were clenched. He heard himself inhale, exhale. He opened his mouth to breathe more quietly.

Seconds passed, then an empty minute, another, and another—and then the man's next bout of stifled coughing gave Mitch cover to roll from his left side to his right. The manoeuvre complete, he lay with his back to the open end of the trunk, very still.

The gunman's silence seemed to have a quality of heightened vigilance.

What angle of fire would be required? The man with the smooth face would not be sitting upright. He would slump to take full advantage of the darkness in the back seat. He might sit in the centre, the better to cover both front doors.

Keeping the cuff chain taut, Mitch quietly put down the pistol. He dared not risk knocking the weapon against something during the exploration he needed to perform. Then, blindly reaching forward with both hands, he found the back wall of the trunk. Although firm under his fingertips, the surface had a cloth covering. His hands crept left to right across the surface, testing. He pressed gently, and then a little harder.

Beneath his questing fingertips, the surface flexed slightly. Quarter-inch fibreboard, covered in cloth, might flex that way. It didn't have the feel of metal. The panel accepted his pressure in silence, but when he relaxed his hands, it returned to form with a subtle buckling noise.

From the passenger compartment came another protest of stressed upholstery. The gunman had most likely adjusted his position for comfort—though he might have turned to listen more intently. Mitch felt the floor, seeking the pistol, and rested his hands on it. Lying on his side, knees drawn up, he went through it in his mind once more, to be sure that he had not overlooked anything. The smallest miscalculation could mean death. He raised the pistol as best he could. He would shoot left to right, then right to left, a double spray, five rounds in each arc.

When he squeezed the trigger, nothing happened. Just a faint but crisp metallic *snick.*

His heart was both hammer and anvil, and he had to hear through that roar, but he was pretty sure that the gunman had not moved again, had not heard the small sound of the stubborn pistol.

Earlier he had explored the weapon and hadn't found a safety catch.

He eased off the trigger, hesitated, squeezed again.

Snick.

Before panic could seize him, he pulled the trigger again. A stop was incorporated into the trigger—maybe *that* was the safety—through which you had to pull to fire—a double action. He pulled harder than before, and the pistol boomed.

The recoil, exacerbated by his position, rocked him, and he was surprised by a blowback of debris—bits of singed cloth and flecks of fibreboard spraying his face—but he clenched his eyes shut and kept firing, left to right. He had thought he would be able to count the rounds, but he lost track after two, and then the magazine was depleted.

IF THE GUNMAN wasn't dead, even if wounded, he could return fire through the backrest. The car trunk was still a potential deathtrap.

Abandoning the useless pistol, Mitch scrambled out of it and dropped to his hands and knees in the road, then ran in a crouch for ten yards, fifteen, before stopping to look back.

The gunman hadn't got out of the Chrysler.

Mitch waited, sweat dripping off the tip of his nose, off his chin. When the air, as dry as salt, began to sear his throat, he stopped breathing through his mouth. He asked himself how long he should wait before assuming that the man was dead.

He needed the car. In his current condition, dirty and rumpled and no doubt wild-eyed, no one would give him a ride.

Finally he approached the Chrysler.

He circled the vehicle, staying back from the sides of it, alert for a smooth ghostly face peering from the shadows within. After arriving without incident at the trunk from which he had twice escaped, he paused.

If the kidnappers tried to reach Mitch, they wouldn't have any luck because his cellphone was in that white plastic bag back at Campbell's estate. The noon call to Anson's house would be his only chance to reconnect with them.

Without further hesitation, he went to the back door on the driver's side and opened it. Lying on the back seat, eyes open, bloody but still alive, was the smooth-faced man, with his pistol aimed at the door. The muzzle looked like an eyeless socket, and the gunman looked triumphant when he said, 'Die.'

He tried to pull the trigger, but the pistol wobbled in his hand, and then he lost his grip. The weapon fell to the floor of the car and the gunman's hand dropped into his lap. His one-word threat had been a prediction of his own fate.

Leaving the door open, Mitch walked to the side of the road and sat on a boulder until he could be certain that he was not going to vomit.

When this was finished, if it ever was finished, maybe the best thing would be to go to the police, tell his story of desperate self-defence, and present them with the two dead gunmen in the trunk of the Chrysler.

But Julian Campbell would deny that he had employed them or at least that he had directed them to kill Mitch. He would ensure there were no records that might betray the existence of his dark empire to the authorities. To all appearances, he was one of California's most upstanding citizens.

Mitch, on the other hand, was a humble gardener already set up to take the fall for his wife's murder in the event that he failed to ransom her. And in Corona del Mar, on the street in front of Anson's house, the trunk of his Honda contained the body of John Knox. He didn't for a minute believe that crime-scene investigation was as meticulous as portrayed on TV. The more evidence there was that suggested his guilt, the more they would find to support their suspicion, and the easier it would be to ignore the details that might exonerate him.

Anyway, the most important thing right now was to remain free and mobile until he ransomed Holly. He *would* ransom her. Or die trying.

The most urgent task before him was the disposal of a pair of dead men.

Mitch knelt beside the scarred gunman and searched his pockets, quickly finding the two things he wanted: the handcuff key and the keys to the Chrysler Windsor.

Having freed himself of the cuffs, he threw them in the open trunk of the car and rubbed his chafed wrists, then he dragged the body of the gunman to the shoulder of the road, south through the screening brush. Getting the second body out of the back seat was unpleasant, but in two minutes the dead pair were lying side by side, face up to the stars.

At the car once more, Mitch found a flashlight on the front seat. He'd figured there would be one because they must have intended to bury him nearby and would have needed a light to guide them. Mitch examined the back of the car with the flashlight and counted eight holes in the backrest, rounds that had punched through from the trunk. The other two had evidently been deflected or stopped by the structure of the seat.

He returned to the bodies and relieved them of their wallets to make identification more difficult, then decided to drag the dead men further away from the road and inter them in a tight grove of waist-high manzanita, where shrouds of leathery leaves would conceal them. Within an hour, the first carrion eaters would be drawn to the double treat. In the morning, the desert heat would begin to do its work as well. If ever they were found, their names might never be known.

He returned to the car and closed the trunk lid.

Having got the best of two experienced killers, perhaps he should have felt empowered. Instead, he had been humbled.

To spare himself the stench of blood, he rolled down the windows in all four doors of the Chrysler. The engine started at once: a full-throated song of power. He switched on the headlights and was relieved to see that the fuel gauge indicated the tank was nearly full. He turned the car round and drove to the end of the dirt road and turned right. He recalled that they had taken a left turn on the way here. The hard-top roads were well marked, and he was soon back on the interstate.

Seldom do dead men return to haunt the living in such style.

MITCH ARRIVED IN THE CITY of Orange at 2:20 a.m., and parked on a street that was a block away from the one on which his house stood. He rolled up the four windows, picked up the flashlight and locked the Chrysler. He now carried the second gunman's pistol under his belt, concealed beneath his shirt-tails. It contained eight cartridges.

He had parked under an old jacaranda tree in full flower, and when he moved into the light from the street lamp, he saw that he was walking on a carpet of purple petals.

Warily, he approached his property along the alleyway to the rear of the house and proceeded to his garage. The gate at the corner of the building was never locked. He passed through it into the back yard.

His house keys, with his wallet and other personal items, had been confiscated in Campbell's library, but he kept a spare key, which opened both house and garage, in a small safe padlocked to a ringbolt low on the garage wall, concealed behind a row of azaleas. Risking the flashlight but hooding it with his fingers, Mitch parted the azaleas. He dialled in the combination, disengaged the lock, plucked the key from the safe and switched off the light.

Making no sound, he let himself into the garage, which was keyed to match the house. He stood in the dark, listening, then turned on the garage lights. His truck was where he had left it. The Honda's space was empty.

He climbed the stairs to the loft. The boxes were still stacked to disguise the gap in the railing. At the front he discovered that the recorder and electronic surveillance gear were gone. One of the kidnappers must have come to collect the equipment.

He wondered what they thought had happened to John Knox. He worried that Knox's disappearance had already had consequences for Holly, but he forced his mind away from that dark speculation. Their lives had meaning, they had been brought together by destiny for a purpose, and they would fulfill their purpose. He had to believe that was true.

Leaving the garage dark, he entered the house through the back door, confident that the place was no longer watched.

The staged murder scene in the kitchen remained as he had last seen it. The spattered blood, dry now. Handprints on the cabinets. In the adjacent laundry room, he took off his shoes and examined them in the fluorescent light. He was surprised to find no blood. His socks were not stained, either, but he stripped them off anyway and threw them in the washing machine.

He found small smears on his shirt and jeans. In the shirt pocket, he found Detective Taggart's card. He saved it, tossed the clothes in the machine, added soap and started the wash cycle.

Standing at the laundry sink, he scrubbed his hands and forearms with soap and a soft-bristle brush. With a wet cloth, he wiped his face and neck. His weariness was profound. He needed rest, but he had no time for sleep. In shoes and underwear, carrying the pistol, he returned to the kitchen. From the refrigerator, he chose a can of high-caffeine Red Bull and swigged it. As he lowered the can, he saw Holly's bag open on the adjoining counter. It had been there earlier in the day, but he had not noticed the bits and pieces scattered beside it. A wadded cellophane wrapper. A small box, the top torn open. A pamphlet of instructions.

It seemed that Holly had bought a home pregnancy-test kit. She had opened it and evidently used it, sometime between when he had left for work and when the kidnappers had taken her.

As a child in the learning room, when you had spoken to no one for a long time, nor heard a voice other than your own, and when you have been denied food—though never water—for as much as three days, you reached a point where, in the silence and the darkness, in the horror of that extreme claustrophobia, you told yourself that you could not endure another minute. But you did, you endured another hour, a day . . . you endured, and then the door opened, the banishment ended, and there was light. There is always, eventually, light.

Holly had not revealed that her period was overdue. False hopes had been raised twice before. She had wanted to be sure before telling him.

Mitch had not believed in destiny; now he did. And if a man believes in destiny, he must believe in one that is golden, one that shines.

Carrying the pistol, he hurried to the bedroom. The switch by the door turned on one of two bedside lamps. With single-minded purpose, he went to the closet. The door stood open. Two pairs of jeans had slipped from their hangers and lay on the closet floor. He didn't remember having left them in this condition, but he snatched a pair and pulled them on.

Shrugging into a dark blue, long-sleeved cotton shirt, he turned from the closet and for the first time saw the clothes strewn on the bed. They were his clothes. He recognised them. They were mottled with dark blood. More planted evidence.

He retrieved the pistol from the closet shelf where he had put it while dressing.

The door to the dark bathroom stood open.

Crossing the threshold, he flipped the light switch and with bated breath stepped into the bathroom's brightness.

He expected to find something grotesque, but all was normal.

Returning to the bedroom, he noticed something out of place on the nightstand with the extinguished lamp. He clicked the switch.

Two colourful polished spheres of dinosaur dung from his father's house stood there on small bronze stands. They made him think of crystal balls, predicting dire fates.

'Anson,' Mitch whispered. 'My God. Oh, God.'

9

The hard winds that came out of the eastern mountains were usually born with the rising or setting of the sun. Now, many hours after sunset, a strong spring wind blew suddenly down upon the lowlands as if it had burst through a great door.

Along the alleyway where wind whistled, to the Chrysler, Mitch hurried but with the hesitant heart of a man making the journey from his cell on death row to the execution chamber.

He didn't take time to roll down all the windows. As he drove, he opened only the one in the driver's door. A gruff wind huffed at him, pawed his hair, its breath warm and insistent. Queen palms thrashed like madwomen tossing their hair, and bottle-brush trees shed millions of scarlet needles that were the petals of their exotic flowers. In the wind were scraps of paper, leaves and a large transparent plastic bag billowing along like a jellyfish.

Mitch's parents' house was the only one on the block with lights in the windows. He parked in the driveway, put the window up, left the pistol in the car, took the flashlight. The wind lashed the walkway with tree shadows.

He did not ring the doorbell. He had no false hope, only an awful need to know. As he had thought it might be, the house was unlocked. He stepped into the hall and closed the door behind him.

To his left, to his right, an uncountable number of Mitches receded from him in a mirror world. The house was not silent, for the wind gibbered at windows, groaned in the eaves, and eucalyptus trailers scourged the walls.

In Daniel's study, shattered glass display shelves glittered on the floor, and scattered everywhere were the colourful polished spheres, as if a poltergeist had played billiards with them.

Room by room, Mitch searched the ground floor, turning on lights where they were off. In truth, he expected to find nothing more on this level. He told himself that he was just being thorough. But he knew that he was delaying his ascent to the first floor.

As he climbed the stairs, nature's long exhale grew more fierce. Windows thrummed. Roof beams creaked.

Upstairs, on the landing, a black object lay on the polished wood floor. One end featured two gleaming metal pegs with a four-inch-wide gap between them. He hesitated, then picked it up. On the side of the thing was a switch. When he pressed it, a jagged white arc of electricity snapped between the pegs. It was a Taser, a self-defence gun. Chances were that Daniel and Kathy had not used it to defend themselves. More likely, Anson had brought it with him and had assaulted them with it. A jolt from a Taser can disable a man for minutes, muscles spasming as his nerves misfire.

Although Mitch wanted to delay the terrible moment, he went into the master bedroom. The lights were on except for a nightstand lamp that had been knocked to the floor in a struggle, the bulb broken. The sheets were tangled. The sleepers had been literally shocked awake.

Glancing through other doors but not taking the time to inspect the spaces beyond, Mitch moved more purposefully to the room at the end of the shorter of the two upstairs corridors. Here the door was like all the others, but when he opened it another one faced him, heavily padded and covered with a black fabric.

Shaking badly, Mitch hesitated. He had expected never to return here, never to cross this threshold again.

The inner door could be opened only from the hall, not from within. He turned the latch release. The channels of an interlocking rubber seal parted with a sucking sound as he pushed the door.

He switched on the flashlight.

Inside, there were no lamps, no ceiling fixture. The black material that upholstered every surface, densely woven and without sheen, soaked up the beam of the flashlight. Modified sensory deprivation. They had said it was a tool for discipline, a method to focus the mind inwards towards self-discovery—a technique, not a torture. Numerous studies had been published about the wonders of sensory deprivation.

Daniel and Kathy lay side by side: she in her pyjamas, he in his underwear. Their hands and ankles had been bound. The knots were cruelly tight, biting the flesh. They had not been gagged. Perhaps Anson had wanted to have a conversation with them. And screams could not escape the learning room.

Although Mitch stopped just inside the door, the aggressive silence pulled at him like quicksand. He could not hear the windstorm any more, but he was sure that it continued.

Looking at Kathy was harder than looking at Daniel, but not as hard as Mitch had expected. If he could have prevented this, he would have stood between them and his brother. But now that it was done . . . it was done.

Daniel's face, eyes open, was wrenched by terror, but there was puzzlement in it as well. At the penultimate moment, he must have wondered how Anson, his one success, could be the death of him.

Tasered and tied, Daniel and Kathy had then been stabbed. The weapons were a pair of gardening shears and a hand trowel. And Mitch recognised them as having come from the rack of tools in his garage.

MITCH CLOSED THE BODIES in the learning room, and sat at the top of the stairs to think. He could have wept if he had dared to allow himself tears, but he would not have known for whom he was crying.

He had never seen Daniel or Kathy cry. They believed in applying reason in place of easy emotion. So how could you cry for those who never cried for themselves, who talked and talked themselves through their disappointments, their misadventures and even their bereavements?

No one who knew the truth of this family would fault him if he cried for himself, but he had not cried for himself since he was five because he had not wanted them to have the satisfaction of his tears.

He would not cry for his brother. The brother he thought he knew and loved, had in fact never existed. Mitch had loved a sociopath, a phantom.

Anson had seized the moment to take vengeance on Daniel and Kathy, pinning the crimes on his brother, who he thought would never be found.

He had probably salted other evidence, too. Finding it would take time, and Mitch had none to spare. His wristwatch read 3:06 a.m. In less than nine hours, the kidnappers would call Anson with further instructions. Forty-five of the original sixty hours remained until the midnight-Wednesday deadline.

This would be over long before then. New developments required new rules, and Mitch was going to set them.

After turning off the upstairs lights, he went downstairs and left the house by the front door.

Brooms of fallen palm fronds swept the street, and in their wake came a rolling trash can spewing its contents. The eucalyptuses gave the wind a thousand hissing voices, and it seemed as if the moon would be blown down and the stars snuffed out like candles.

In the Chrysler, Mitch set out in search of Anson.

HOLLY WORKS AT THE NAIL even though she makes no progress with it, because if she doesn't work at the nail, she will go mad.

Suddenly the nail begins to wiggle, and that's exciting.

Her excitement wanes during the next half-hour, as she manages to extract only about a quarter of an inch of the nail from the floor plank. Then it won't budge further.

Nevertheless, a quarter of an inch is better than nothing. The spike might be—what?—three inches long. Cumulatively—discounting the breaks she took for the pizza—she has spent perhaps seven hours on the nail. If she can tease it out at the rate of an inch a day, by the Wednesday-midnight deadline she will have only an inch to go.

People have always called her sunny and cheerful. Annoyed by her unflagging positive outlook, a sourpuss once asked her if she was the love child of Mickey Mouse and Tinkerbell.

She could have been mean and told him the truth, that her father died in a traffic accident and her mother in childbirth, that she had been raised by a loving grandmother. Instead, she told him *Yes, but because Tink doesn't have the hips for childbirth, I was carried to term by Daisy Duck.*

At the moment, uncharacteristically, she finds it difficult to keep her spirits up. Being kidnapped fractures your funny bone. She has two broken fingernails, and the pads of her fingers are sore. But in the scheme of things, these injuries are insignificant. If her captors start cutting off her fingers like they promised Mitch, *that* will be something to bitch about.

She takes a break from her work, and lies back on the air mattress in the dark. Although she is exhausted, she does not expect to sleep. But soon she is dreaming about walking in a lightless place, carrying a bundle in her arms. The bundle grows heavy. Her arms ache. She doesn't know what she carries, but something terrible will happen if she puts it down.

A dim glow draws her. She arrives in a chamber brightened by a single candle. Mitch is here. She's so happy to see him. Her father and mother, whom she has never known except from photographs, are here, too.

The bundle in her arms is a sleeping baby. Her sleeping baby.

Smiling, her mother comes forward to take the baby. Holly's arms ache, but she holds fast to the precious bundle. Her parents are dead, and so is Mitch, and when she lets go of the infant, it will not just be sleeping.

She refuses to give her son to them—and then somehow it is in her mother's arms. Her father blows out the candle . . .

Holly is woken by the howling of the wind as it hammers the walls, shaking dust from the roof beams. A soft glow, not a candle but a small flashlight, reveals the knitted black ski mask, the chapped lips and the beryl-blue eyes of one of her keepers kneeling before her—the one who worries her.

'I've brought you candy,' he says. He holds out to her a Mr Goodbar.

His fingers are long and white. His nails are bitten.

Holly dislikes touching anything that he has touched. Hiding her distaste, she accepts the candy bar.

'They're asleep. This is my shift.' He puts on the floor in front of her a can of cola beaded with icy sweat. 'You like Pepsi?'

'Yes. Thank you.'

'Do you know Chamisal, New Mexico?' he asks.

He has a soft, musical voice, almost a woman's voice.

'Chamisal?' she says. 'No. I've never been there.'

'I've had experiences there,' he says. 'My life was changed.'

Wind booms and something rattles on the roof, and she uses the noise as an excuse to look up, hoping to see a memorable detail of her prison for later testimony.

She was brought here in a blindfold. She thinks she might be in an attic.

'Have you been to Rio Lucio, New Mexico?' he asks.

'No. Not there, either.'

'In Rio Lucio, there is a small stucco house painted blue with yellow trim. Why don't you eat your chocolate?'

'I'm saving it for later.'

'Who knows how much time any of us has?' he asks. 'Enjoy it now.'

Reluctantly, she peels the wrapper off the chocolate bar.

'A saintly woman named Ermina Lavato lives in the blue and yellow stucco house in Rio Lucio. She is seventy-two, very poor. The house is small but very beautiful. Each room is painted a different soothing colour. And her bedroom walls hold forty-two images of the Holy Mother.'

As he stares at her, she returns the scrutiny, to the extent his mask allows. His teeth are yellow, the incisors sharp.

'In Ermina Lavato's back yard, I buried a treasure.'

'As a gift for her?' Holly asks.

'No. She would not approve of what I buried. Drink your Pepsi.'

She does not want to drink from a can he handled. She opens it anyway, and takes a sip.

'Do you know Penasco, New Mexico?'

'I haven't travelled much in New Mexico.'

He is silent for a moment. Then, 'My life changed in Penasco.'

'I thought that was in Chamisal.'

'My life has changed often in New Mexico. It's a place of change and great mystery.'

Having thought of a use for the Pepsi can, Holly sets it aside with the hope he will allow her to keep it when he leaves.

'You would enjoy Chamisal, Penasco, Rodarte, so many beautiful and mysterious places.'

'Let's hope I live to see them.'

He meets her stare directly. His eyes are the blue of a sombre sky that suggests an impending storm. In a voice still softer than usual, he says, 'May I speak to you in confidence?'

If he touches her, she will scream until she wakes the others.

Interpreting her expression as consent, he says, 'There were five of us, and now just three.'

This is not what she has expected. She holds his gaze.

'To improve the split from five ways to four, we killed Jason.'

She cringes inwardly at the revelation of a name.

'Now Johnny Knox has disappeared,' he says. 'Johnny was running surveillance, but he hasn't called in.'

Mitch, she thinks at once.

Outside, the tenor of the wind changes. Ceasing to shriek, it rushes with a great shush, counselling Holly in the wisdom of silence.

'The other two were out on errands yesterday,' he continues, 'separately, at different times. Either could have killed Johnny. Maybe they decided on a two-way split. Or one of them may want to have it all.'

Not wishing to appear to sow discord, she says, 'They wouldn't do that.'

'They might,' he says. 'You should see Las Trampas, New Mexico, in the snow. A scattering of humble buildings, white fields, low hills dark with chaparral, and the sky as white as the fields.'

'You're something of a poet,' she says, and half means it.

His white, hairless hands come together, not in contemplation, certainly not in prayer, but as if they are pleased by the feel of each other.

'In Rio Lucio, Eloisa Sandoval has a shrine to St Anthony in her small adobe-walled kitchen. Twelve ceramic figures arranged in tiers, one for each child and grandchild. Candles every evening in the vespers hour.'

She hopes that he will make new revelations about his partners, but she knows that she must appear discreetly intrigued by everything he says. The chocolate has begun to cloy in Holly's mouth, to stick in her throat, but she takes another bite of it.

'Ancient spirits have dwelt in New Mexico, since before the existence of humanity. Are you a seeker?'

If she encourages him too much, he will read her as insincere. 'I don't think so. But sometimes we all feel . . . something is missing.'

'I see a seeker in you, Holly Rafferty. A tiny seed of spirit waiting to bloom.' His eyes are as clear as a limpid stream.

Lowering her gaze, she says demurely, 'I'm afraid you see too much in me. I'm not a deep thinker.'

'The secret is not to think. The secret is to feel.'

'See, to you that's a simple concept, but even that's too deep for me.' She laughs softly at herself. 'My biggest dream is to be in real estate.'

'You underestimate yourself,' he assures her. 'Within you are . . . enormous possibilities.'

WITH HOBGOBLINS of wind threatening at the open window in the driver's door, Mitch cruised past Anson's house in Corona del Mar.

Large creamy-white flowers had been shaken from the big magnolia tree and had blown in a drift against the front door, revealed in the light of a lamp that remained on all night. Otherwise, the house was dark.

He did not believe that Anson had come home, washed up, and gone happily to sleep almost at once after killing their parents. He must be out somewhere—and up to something.

Mitch's Honda no longer stood at the kerb where he had left it when he had first come here at the direction of the kidnappers.

At the next block he parked, rolled up the window, and locked the Chrysler. Unfortunately, it drew attention to itself among the surrounding contemporary vehicles.

Mitch walked to the alleyway that gave access to Anson's garage. Lights blazed throughout the lower floor of the rear condominium above the pair of two-car garages. Some people might have work that kept them busy just past three thirty in the morning. Or insomnia. Mitch studied the high, curtained windows. He saw things more clearly now.

If Anson had $8 million and a fully paid-off yacht, he probably owned both condos, not just one, as he had claimed. He lived in the front unit and used the back condo for the office in which he applied linguistic theory to software design, or whatever the hell he did to get rich.

The toiler in the night, behind those curtained windows, was not a neighbour. Anson himself sat up there, bent to a computer. Perhaps he was plotting a course, by yacht, to a haven beyond all law.

A service gate opened onto a narrow walkway beside the garage. Mitch followed it into the brick courtyard that separated the two condos. The courtyard lights were off. Bordering the brick patio were beds lush with nandina and a variety of ferns, plus bromeliads and anthuriums to provide a punctuation of red blooms. Mitch slipped under the arching fronds of a Tasmanian tree fern and crouched there, peering out at the patio.

In the condo above the garages, the lights went out. Perhaps assisted by the windstorm, a door slammed shut. Heavy hurried footsteps descended exterior stairs to the courtyard.

Between the fronds, Mitch glimpsed a bearish figure crossing the patio.

Anson was not aware of his brother approaching behind him, and let out a strangled cry when the Taser short-circuited his nervous system.

When he staggered forward, trying to stay on his feet, Mitch remained close. The Taser delivered another 50,000-volt kiss and Anson fell and rolled onto his back, his burly body twitching.

HOLLY HAS FINISHED THE CHOCOLATE. She feels sick. Her mouth tastes like blood. She uses Pepsi as a mouthwash.

Still the gentle voice regales her: 'In El Valle, New Mexico, there is a graveyard. Some graves are surrounded by small picket fences crafted from the slats of old fruit and vegetable crates. Loved ones paint them in pastels—robin's-egg blue, pale green, the yellow of faded sunflowers. Under a quarter-moon, only hours after a new grave was closed, we did some spade work and opened the coffin of a child.'

'The yellow of faded sunflowers,' Holly repeats, trying to fill her mind with that colour as defence against the image of a child in a coffin.

'She was eight, taken by cancer. They buried her with a St Christopher medal folded in her left hand, a figurine of Cinderella in her right because she loved that story.'

The sunflowers will not sustain, and in her mind's eye, Holly sees the small hands holding tight to the protection of the saint and to the promise of the poor girl who became a princess.

'By virtue of some hours in the grave of an innocent, those objects acquired great power. They were death-washed and spirit-polished.' One white hand vanishes into a pocket of his black jacket. When it reappears, it holds a St Christopher medal by a silver chain. 'Here. Take it.'

There is a subtext that Holly does not understand, but she senses that to reject the medal for any reason will have terrible consequences. She holds out her right hand, and he drops the medal into it.

'Do you know Espanola, New Mexico?'

Folding her hand, she says, 'It's another place I've missed.'

'My life will be changed there,' he reveals as he picks up the flashlight and rises to his feet.

He leaves her in pitch black with the half-full can of Pepsi. Her intention is—or had been—to squash the can and to create from it a bar with which to work on the stubborn nail.

The St Christopher medal will do a better job. Cast in brass and plated with silver or nickel, it is much harder than the can.

Her keeper's visit has changed the quality of this lightless space. It had been a lonely darkness. Now Holly imagines it inhabited by rats and legions of crawling things.

10

Like a creature accustomed to filtering its oxygen from water and now helpless on a beach, Anson twitched, spasmed. He gawped at Mitch, moving his mouth as if trying to speak, or maybe he was trying to scream in pain. All that came out was a thin squeal.

Mitch tried the door. Unlocked. He pushed it open and stepped into the kitchen. Not sure how long the effects of the shock would last, he put the Taser on a counter and returned to the open door.

Warily, he grabbed Anson by the ankles and dragged him into the house.

Closing the door, he turned on the lights. The blinds were shut, as they had been when he and Anson received the phone call from the kidnappers. The pot of *zuppa massaia* remained on the stove, cold but still fragrant.

Adjacent to the kitchen lay a laundry room. He checked it and found it to be as he remembered: small, no windows.

At the kitchen table, the four dinette chairs were retro-chic stainless steel and red vinyl. He moved one of them to the laundry room.

On the floor, hugging himself, Anson made the pitiable sounds of a dog in pain. The agony might be real. It might be a performance.

Mitch retrieved the Taser. Reaching to the small of his back, he withdrew the pistol that he had tucked under his belt.

'Anson, I want you to roll over, face down.'

His brother's head lolled from side to side, perhaps involuntarily.

Anticipation of revenge had been in its way a different kind of sugar rush. In reality, nothing about it tasted sweet.

'Listen to me. I want you to roll over and crawl to the laundry room.'

Drool escaped a corner of Anson's mouth. His chin glistened.

'I'm giving you a chance to do it the easy way.'

Anson continued to appear disorientated. Mitch wondered if two Taser shots in quick succession could have done permanent damage. Anson seemed to be worse than stunned.

'Damn it, Anson, if I have to, I can give you a third shock and drag you in there while you're helpless.'

The back door rattled, distracting Mitch. But it was only the wind testing the latch as a strong gust swept into the sheltered courtyard. When he looked at Anson again, Mitch saw a sly calculation in his brother's eyes, which then vanished in a glaze of disorientation.

Mitch waited half a minute. Then he moved quickly towards his brother.

Anson sensed him coming, thought he was going to use the Taser, and sat up to block it, grab it. Instead Mitch squeezed off a gunshot, intentionally missing his brother, but not by much. At the report of the pistol, Anson flinched back in surprise and Mitch slammed the gun against the side of his head, hard enough to knock him unconscious.

He ain't heavy, he's my brother. Bullshit. He was Mitch's brother and he *was* heavy. Dragging him across the polished wood floor of the kitchen and into the laundry room proved harder than Mitch expected. Hoisting him into the chair was one door away from impossible, but Mitch got it done.

The upholstered panel on the back of the chair was set between two steel verticals. Between each side of the panel and the frame was an open space. He pulled Anson's hands through those gaps. With the handcuffs that he had worn earlier, he shackled his brother's wrists behind the chair.

Among the items in a utility drawer was a thick orange electrical extension cord about forty feet long. After weaving it through the chair's legs and stretcher bars, Mitch tied it around the washing machine. Although Anson might be able to rise into a half-crouch, he would have to lift the chair with him. Anchored to the washer, he could not go anywhere.

The blow with the pistol had cut his ear. He was bleeding but not heavily. His pulse was slow but steady. He might come round quickly.

Mitch searched the kitchen drawers until he found where Anson kept keys. He plucked out a spare house key. He also took the keys for three different cars, including his Honda, and left the house by the back door.

He doubted that the neighbours could have heard the shot above the boom and cry of the wind. Nevertheless, he was relieved to see no lights in the houses to either side. He climbed the stairs to the condo above the garages and tried the door. It was locked. As he'd expected, the key to Anson's house also opened this place.

Inside, he found Anson's home office occupying space that would more often be a living and dining area. Four computer workstations were served by a single, wheeled office chair. Their size, much larger than anything usually seen in a home, suggested that his work required rapid multitiered computation and massive data storage.

Mitch wasn't a computer maven. He had no illusions that he could boot up these machines and discover the nature of the work that had made his brother rich. Besides, Anson would have layers of security to keep out even serious hackers. So Mitch left, locked the door, and went down to the first of the garages. Here were the Expedition that he had driven to Campbell's estate in Rancho Santa Fe and the 1947 Buick Super Woody Wagon.

In the other two-car garage were an empty stall and Mitch's Honda, which he had left on the street. Perhaps Anson had stored it here after driving it to Orange and taking two of Mitch's garden tools as well as some of his clothes to Daniel and Kathy's place to murder them, and then to Mitch's again to plant the incriminating evidence.

Mitch opened the trunk. John Knox's body remained wrapped in the weathered canvas tarp.

The accident in the loft seemed to have happened a long-ago time, in another life.

He returned to the first garage, started the Expedition, and moved it to the empty stall in the second garage. Then he moved his Honda, parked it beside the Buick wagon and closed the big roll-up door to that garage.

Grimly, he wrestled the body from the trunk of the Honda. While it lay on the garage floor, he rolled the corpse out of the tarp.

Serious putrescence had not set in yet. The dead man had a sinister sweet-and-sour smell, however, that Mitch was eager to get away from. He loaded Knox into the Buick wagon and closed the tailgate, then folded the tarp and put it in the trunk of the Honda. Eventually he would dispose of it in a Dumpster.

He couldn't recall ever having been this exhausted: physically, mentally, emotionally. His eyes felt singed, his joints half-melted. Fear had fuelled him all along. But what most kept his wheels turning was the thought of Holly in the hands of monsters.

Till death us do part was the stated commitment in their vows. For Mitch, however, the loss of her would not release him. The commitment would endure. The rest of his life would pass in patient waiting.

After he'd met Holly and fallen almost instantly in love, he had realised that he'd previously been only half alive. She had opened the emotional casket in which his parents had left him, and he had risen and flourished. He had thought himself fully alive, at last, when they married.

Now, he walked the alleyway to the street, returned to the Chrysler Windsor and drove it back to the second garage. He parked it beside the Expedition and closed the door.

He consulted his wristwatch—4:09 a.m.

He returned to the house and found Anson awake in the laundry room, and in a mood. The cut on his left ear had crusted shut, and body heat was quickly drying the blood that had trickled down his cheek and neck. Jaws clenched, eyes molten with rage, he sat in seething silence.

Mitch said, 'You're going to help me get Holly back alive.'

That statement elicited neither agreement nor refusal, only a glower.

'They'll be calling in a little more than seven and a half hours with wiring instructions,' Mitch said.

In Mitch's absence, Anson had tried determinedly to wrench the chair free of the washing machine. The steel legs of the chair had scraped the tile floor, leaving scars that revealed the intensity of his futile effort.

'You said you could put it together by phone, by computer,' Mitch reminded him. 'You said three hours tops.'

Anson spat on the floor between them.

'If you've got eight million, you can spare two for Holly. When it's done, you get to go back to the sewer of a life you've made for yourself.'

As long as Anson believed that Mitch didn't yet know about the murders of Daniel and Kathy, he would probably cooperate with him, hoping that Mitch would eventually make a mistake.

'Campbell didn't just let you go,' Anson said.

'No.'

'So . . . how?'

'Killed those two. Now I've got to live with that.'

'You popped Vosky and Creed?'

'I don't know their names.'

'Those were their names, all right. But Vosky and Creed? It just doesn't compute.'

'Then Campbell must have let me go.'

'Campbell would never let you go.'

'So believe what you want.'

Anson studied him with sour eyes. 'Where did you get it—the Taser?'

'Vosky and Creed,' Mitch lied.

'You just took it away from them, huh?'

'Like I told you—I took everything away from them. Now I'm giving you a few hours to think about things.'

'You can have the money.'

'That's not what I want you to think about. I need you to think about—who I am now. No more *fratello piccolo.* Huh? You understand?'

'But you *are* my little brother.'

'If you think of me that way, you'll pull some dumb move I would have fallen for then, but won't fall for now.'

'If we can make a deal, I'm not pulling any moves.'

'We've already made the deal.'

'How can any deal work without at least a little trust?'

'You just sit here and think about how fast you could be dead.'

Mitch switched off the lights and stepped through the doorway.

In the dark, windowless laundry room, Anson said, 'What're you doing?'

'Providing the best learning environment,' Mitch said, and pulled the door shut.

'Mickey?' Anson called. 'Mickey, don't do this.'

Mickey. After all this, *Mickey.*

At the kitchen sink, Mitch scrubbed his hands, using a lot of soap and hot water, trying to wash away the memory of John Knox's body.

From the refrigerator, he got a package of cheddar-cheese slices and a squeeze bottle of mustard. He found a loaf of bread and made a sandwich.

'I hear you out there,' Anson called from the laundry room. 'What are you doing, Mickey?'

Mitch put the sandwich on a plate. He added a dill pickle. From the refrigerator he got a bottle of beer.

'What's the point of this, Mickey? We've already got a deal.'

Mitch tilted another kitchen chair under the knob of the laundry-room door, bracing it. He switched off the kitchen lights and went upstairs to Anson's bedroom.

After putting the pistol and the Taser on the nightstand, he sat on the bed, his back against the padded headboard. He didn't take off his shoes.

After eating the sandwich and the pickle, and drinking the beer, he set the clock radio for 8:30 a.m.

He wanted Anson to have time to think, but he was taking this four-hour break primarily because his own thinking had been slowed by exhaustion, and he needed a clear head for what was coming.

The drapes were shut, and when he switched off the lamp, a coverlet of darkness fell over him. He didn't use either of Anson's night-lights.

Holly's lovely face rose into his mind, and he said aloud, 'God, please give me the strength and the wisdom to help her.'

This was the first time in his life that he had spoken to God.

With the most important day of his life soon to dawn, he didn't think that he could sleep, but he slept.

HOLLY SITS IN THE DARK, listening to the wind, fingering the St Christopher medal in her left hand. Her right hand drops to her belly. Her waist is narrow, her stomach flat. The child grows in her, a secret, as private as a dream. She moves her hand over it in slow circles. Of course, the baby is only a ball of cells at this stage. But even now, its full potential is there, a tiny person like a pearl steadily accreting in the shell of her body, and everything she does will affect her little passenger.

St Christopher, the protector of children, has brought her to a reconsideration of the nail as she blindly traces his image with her fingertips.

They say that if you listen to classical music while pregnant, your child will have a higher IQ. He or she will cry less and be more content.

This may be true. Life is complex and mysterious.

She's probably being irrational, taking this babies-learn-in-the-womb business too far. Yet it seems that if, while pregnant, she thrusts a nail into some guy's carotid artery, the incident will surely have an effect on the baby. For if too much caffeine in the blood can put the unborn child at risk, torrents of killer-mommy enzyme can't be desirable.

So, Holly broods about the nail. Prudence also plays a role in her thinking of the nail scheme. You better not strike out against people like these unless you are certain that you can carry through with the assault successfully, she tells herself. Otherwise, you are going to have a very angry psychopath on your case. Not good.

She is still fingering the St Christopher medal, pondering the pros and cons of fighting vicious men with a three-inch nail, when the representative of the New Mexico Tourist Board returns.

He comes with a flashlight, as before, and still has the hands of a pianist from hell. He kneels in front of her and puts the flashlight on the floor.

'You like the medallion,' he says, sounding pleased to see her smoothing it between her fingers as if it is a worry bead.

Instinct encourages her to play to his weirdness. 'It has an interesting . . . feel.'

'The girl in the coffin wore a simple white dress. She looked so peaceful. She wore white gardenias in her hair. When we opened the lid, the pent-up perfume of the gardenias was intense. We took the medallion and the figurine of Cinderella to a place near Angel Fire, New Mexico, where there's a vortex.'

Evidently he thought she knew what he meant by 'vortex'.

His gentle voice becomes gentler still, and almost sad, when he adds, 'I killed them both in their sleep.'

For a moment, she thinks this statement relates to the vortex in New Mexico, and she tries to make sense of it in that context. Then she realises what he means.

'They pretended they didn't know what happened to John Knox, but at least one of them had to know, all right, and probably both.'

In a room nearby are two dead men. She didn't hear gunfire. Maybe he slit their throats. She can picture his pale hairless hands wielding a straight razor with the grace of a magician rolling coins across his knuckles.

He says, 'I would have been next, and they would have done a two-way split.'

Five people had planned her kidnapping. Only one remains.

If he touches her, there is no one to respond to her scream.

'What happens now?' she asks, and at once wishes that she hadn't.

'I'll speak to your husband at noon, as scheduled. Anson will have fronted him the money. Then it's up to you.'

'What do you mean?'

Instead of answering her question, he says, 'As part of a church festival, a small carnival comes to Penasco, New Mexico, in August.'

She has the crazy feeling that if she snatches off his knitted ski mask, there will be no features to his face other than the beryl-blue eyes and the mouth with yellow teeth. No eyebrows, no nose, no ears, the skin as smooth and featureless as white vinyl.

'Just a Ferris wheel and a few games—and last year a fortuneteller. She calls herself Madame Tiresias, but of course that is not her real name.'

Holly is squeezing the medallion so tightly in one hand that her knuckles ache.

'Madame Tiresias is a fraud, but the funny thing is, she has powers of which she's unaware.' He pauses between each statement as if what he has said is so profound that he wants her to have time to absorb it. 'She would not *have* to be a fraud if she could recognise what she really is, and I intend to show her this year.'

Speaking without a tremor in her voice requires self-control. 'What did you mean, "then it's up to you"?'

When he smiles, part of his mouth disappears from the horizontal slit in the mask. This makes his smile seem sly and knowing.

'You know what I mean,' he says. 'You're not Madame Tiresias. You have full knowledge of yourself. You've been living behind a curtain, and now you know there's not just a window, but a whole new world beyond.'

She senses that if she denies his assertion, she will test his patience and perhaps make him angry. His soft voice and his gentle manner are sheep's clothing, and Holly does not want to poke the wolf beneath the fleece.

'You've given me so much to think about.'

He rises to his feet. 'You have some hours yet to decide. Do you need anything?'

A shotgun, she thinks, but she says, 'No.'

'I know what your decision will be, but you need to reach it on your own. Have you ever been to Guadalupita, New Mexico?'

'No.'

His smile curves up behind the slit in the black mask. 'You will go there, and you will be amazed.'

He follows his flashlight, leaving her alone in darkness.

Holly feels her heart shaking the cage of ribs against which it pounds. The baby, a tiny ball of cells, is now bathed in the fight-or-flight chemicals that her brain has ordered to be released into her blood. Maybe that isn't so bad. Maybe being marinated in that flood will make Baby Rafferty, him or her, tougher than would otherwise be the case.

This is a world that increasingly requires toughness of good people.

With the St Christopher medal, Holly sets to work diligently on the stubborn nail.

THE ALARM WOKE MITCH at eight thirty, and the wind that had worried his dreams still churned the real world.

He sat on the edge of the bed for a minute, yawning, looking at the backs of his hands, at the palms. After what those hands had done the previous night, they ought to have looked different from the way they had always looked before, but he could discern no change.

In the bathroom, searching drawers, he found several unopened toothbrushes. He unwrapped one and used it, then shaved with Anson's electric razor.

Carrying the pistol and the Taser, he went downstairs to the kitchen.

The chair was still braced under the laundry-room doorknob. No sound came from in there.

He cracked three eggs, spiced them with Tabasco sauce, scrambled them, and ate them with two slices of buttered toast. He washed it all down with a glass of orange juice. By habit, he began to gather the dishes to wash them, but then realised the absurdity of being a thoughtful guest under these circumstances.

When he opened the laundry and switched on the lights, he found Anson cuffed as before, soaked in sweat. The room wasn't unusually warm.

'Have you thought about who I am?' Mitch asked.

Anson slumped in the chair and hung his burly head. He did not look physically smaller, but in some way he had been diminished.

When his brother didn't answer, Mitch repeated the question: 'Have you thought about who I am?'

Anson raised his head. His eyes were bloodshot, but his lips were pale. Jewels of sweat glittered in his beard stubble.

'I'm in a bad way here,' he complained in a voice that he had never used before, one with a whine.

'One more time. Have you thought about who I am?'

'You're Mitch, but you're not the Mitch I know. There's some part of you now . . . I don't know what you are.'

'I'm a husband. I cultivate. Preserve.'

'I've got to go to the bathroom.'

'Go ahead. You won't offend me.'

'You mean *here*? Don't do this to me, bro.'

'Don't call me bro.'

Anson said, 'You're still my brother.'

'Biologically.'

He had struggled so fiercely to free the chair from the washer that the legs of the chair had scraped a lot more glaze off the floor tiles.

'Where do you keep the cash?' Mitch asked.

'I wouldn't take *your* dignity like this.'

'You handed me over to killers.'

'I didn't humiliate you first.'

'Where do you keep the cash, Anson?'

'I've got, I don't know, a few hundred in my wallet.' Anson's voice cracked. 'My arms. My shoulders are on fire. Let me change position. Cuff my hands in front of me. This is torture.'

Almost pouting, Anson looked like a big little boy. A boy with a coldly calculating, reptilian brain.

'Let's talk about the cash first,' Mitch said.

'You think there's cash, like a lot of cash? There's not.'

'If I wire-transfer the money, I'll never see Holly again. It has to be a cash trade in person.'

'Then it's not going to happen.'

'You've got cash somewhere,' Mitch insisted.

'Money earns interest, dividends. I don't put it in a mattress.' Grimacing as if in pain, Anson said, 'Please, man, let me go to the bathroom. I'm having bladder spasms.'

'The money you make consulting—yeah, it goes in the bank. But the money from jobs that are—how did you put it?—"more directly criminal", like whatever job you did with these guys and then cheated them on the split, *that* doesn't go in the bank. You don't pay taxes on it.'

Anson said nothing.

'I'm not going to march you over to your office and watch while you use the computer to move funds around, arrange a wire transfer. You're in that chair till this is done.'

Accusatorily, Anson said, 'I was always there for you when we were kids.'

'Actually,' Mitch said, 'we were there for each other.'

'We were. That's right. We can get back to that,' Anson assured him.

'Yeah? How do we get back to that?'

'I'm not saying it'll be easy. Maybe we start with some honesty. I screwed up, Mitch. I was doing drugs, and they messed with my head.'

'You weren't doing any drugs. Don't blame it on that. Where's the cash?'

'Bro, I swear to you, the dirty money ends up in the bank, too.'

'I don't believe it.'

'You can grind me, but it doesn't change what's true.'

'Why don't you think about it some more?' Mitch advised. He switched off the light.

'Hey, no,' Anson said plaintively.

Stepping across the threshold, pulling the door shut behind him, Mitch closed his brother in the dark.

MITCH STARTED IN THE ATTIC. A trap door in the ceiling of the walk-in closet off the master bedroom gave access. A ladder folded down from it.

Two bare light bulbs inadequately illuminated the high, empty space, revealing cobwebs in the angles of the rafters. Ducking to avoid the lowest of these, Mitch walked back and forth, listening to his hollow footsteps on the plywood floor. An odd feeling seized him, a sense that he was on the brink of a discovery.

His attention was drawn to a nail.

The other nails in the floor were pounded flat, but one was raised about a quarter of an inch. He knelt in front of it to examine it. The head was wide and flat. Judging by the size of it and the thickness of the quarter-inch of shank revealed, it was at least three inches long.

When he pinched the nail between thumb and forefinger and tried to wiggle it, he found that it was firmly lodged.

An extraordinary feeling overcame him. He felt so close to Holly that he looked over his shoulder, half expecting her to be there. The feeling did not fade, but swelled, until a chill nubbed the flesh on the nape of his neck.

He left the attic and went down to the kitchen. In the drawer where he had found the car keys was a small collection of the most commonly used tools. He selected a screwdriver and a claw hammer.

In the attic once more, he applied the claw end of the hammer and pulled up the nail. Using the screwdriver as a wedge, tapping the handle with the hammer, he levered the next nail a quarter-inch out of the plywood and then used the claw to extract it, too.

The chill on the back of his neck intensified nail by nail. When the last was extracted, he lifted aside the sheet of plywood eagerly. But he found only floor joists and blankets of fibreglass insulation. He lifted out the fibreglass. No strongbox or bundles of currency were concealed beneath.

The prophetic feeling had passed, as had the sense that somehow he had been close to Holly. He sat, mystified. *What the hell was* that *all about?*

In the master closet, after putting up the folding ladder and the trap door, he continued his search. He looked behind the hanging clothes, checked drawers for false bottoms. In the bedroom, he peered behind paintings in hope of finding a wall safe, although he doubted that Anson would be that obvious. He even rolled the king-sized bed out of place, but he found no loose square of carpet concealing a floor vault.

Mitch worked through two bathrooms, a hall closet and two spare bedrooms that had not been furnished. Nothing.

Downstairs, he began in the mahogany-panelled, book-lined study. He had only half finished with the room when he glanced at his watch and saw it was 11:33. The kidnappers would call in twenty-seven minutes.

In the kitchen, he picked up the pistol and went to the laundry room. When he opened the door, the stink of urine met him.

He switched on the light and found Anson in misery.

Most of the flood had been soaked up by his trousers, his socks, his shoes, but a small yellow puddle had formed on the tiles at the feet of the chair. His tan could not conceal an ashen undertone. His face appeared spongy. The bloodshot eyes were filmy pools of torment.

'Look what you've done to me,' he said.

'You did it to yourself.'

'This is sick, man.'

'It's way sick,' Mitch agreed. 'I hate this.'

'If you hate this, where's your shame now?'

'We're running out of time, Anson. I want the cash.'

'What do I get? What's in it for me?'

Arm extended full length, assuming the posture that Campbell had taken with Mitch himself, he pointed the gun at his brother's face. 'You give me the money and I'll let you live.'

'What kind of life would I have?'

No doubt Anson was thinking about Daniel and Kathy. He would have been able to pin their parents' deaths on Mitch with ease if Mitch had been dead and buried in a desert grave beyond discovery. Not so easy now.

'You keep everything else you've got. I pay the ransom, take care of this without the police ever knowing there was a kidnapping. You go on like before,' Mitch lied, 'make whatever life you want.'

'I give you the money,' Anson said, 'you set me loose.'

'That's right. Before I leave to make the trade, I Taser you again, and then I take off the cuffs. I leave while you're still twitching.'

Anson met his eyes.

Mitch didn't look away. 'I'll do it.'

'You're just like me,' Anson said at last.

'If that's what you want to think.'

Anson's gaze didn't waver. He was shackled to a chair, staring down the muzzle of a gun. Yet his eyes were full of calculation. 'There's a floor safe in the kitchen,' he said. 'It holds a million four hundred thousand in cash.'

11

The lower cabinet to the left of the sink featured two roll-out shelves containing pots and pans.

Mitch unloaded the shelves and detached them from the tracks in which they rolled, exposing the floor of the cabinet. In the four corners were what appeared to be small wooden angle braces. They were in fact pins holding the otherwise unsecured floor panel in place.

He removed them, lifted the floor out of the cabinet and exposed the concrete slab on which the house had been built. Sunk in the concrete was a floor safe, a fireproof box approximately two feet long, eighteen inches wide and one foot deep.

The combination that Anson had given him worked on the first try. The heavy lid hinged away from him. Inside were thick packets of $100 bills in plastic wrap sealed with clear tape.

The safe also contained a manila envelope. According to Anson, it held bonds issued by a Swiss bank. They were almost as liquid as the $100 bills but easier to transport across borders.

Mitch transferred the treasure to the kitchen table and checked the contents of the envelope. He counted six bonds denominated in US dollars, 100,000 each, payable to the bearer. Just the previous day, he would never have expected to be in possession of so much money. Yet he experienced not even the briefest delight at the sight of such wealth. This was Holly's ransom and he was grateful to have it. This money was also the reason she had been kidnapped and for that reason he regarded it with such antipathy that he was loath to touch it.

The kitchen clock read 11:54. Six minutes until the call.

He returned to the laundry.

'Six hundred thousand in bonds. How much in cash?'

'The rest of it,' Anson said.

'So there's a million four hundred thousand in cash?'

'That's what I said, didn't I?'

'I'm going to count it. If it's not all there, the deal is off. I don't turn you loose when I leave.'

In frustration, Anson rattled his handcuffs against the chair. 'What're you trying to do to me?'

'For me to keep the deal, you have to keep the deal. I'll start counting now.' Mitch turned away from the door, towards the kitchen table. Anson said, 'There's eight hundred thousand in cash.'

'Not a million four?'

'The whole bundle, cash and bonds, is a million four. I got confused.'

'Yeah. Confused. I need six hundred thousand more.'

'That's all there is. I don't have any more.'

Inspiration struck Mitch, and he said, 'The yacht. You bought yourself a yacht. How much do you have stashed aboard it?'

'Nothing. I've got nothing on the boat. Haven't had time to fit it out with a safe.'

'If they kill Holly, I'll go through your records here,' Mitch said. 'I'll get the name of the boat, find out where it's moored. I'll rip it up bow to stern, and when I find the money and know you lied to me, I'll come back here and tape your mouth shut so you can't lie to me any more.'

'I'm telling you the truth.'

'I'll close you here in the dark, to die of dehydration in your own filth.'

Mitch didn't believe that he could kill anyone in such a cruel fashion, but to his own ear he sounded convincing. If he lost Holly, maybe anything was possible.

Anson seemed to follow that same chain of reasoning, for he said, 'All right. Four hundred thousand. In the boat. I'll tell you where to find it.'

'We're still two hundred thousand dollars short.'

'There's no more. Not cash. I'd have to liquidate some stock.'

Mitch turned to look at the kitchen clock—11:56.

'Four minutes. No time left for lies, Anson.'

'Would you for once believe me? There's no more in easy cash.'

'I already have to change the conditions of the trade. No wire transfer. Now I have to bargain down two hundred thousand.'

'They'll take it,' Anson assured him. 'I know these pigs. Are they gonna turn down a million eight? No way.'

'You better be right.' Mitch had already turned away from him. He didn't switch off the laundry-room light, and he didn't close the door.

At the table, he stared at the bearer bonds and the cash. He picked up the pen and the notepad and went to the phone.

He could not bear the sight of it. Phones had not brought him good news lately.

He closed his eyes.

Three years ago, he and Holly had been married with no family in attendance. Dorothy, the grandmother who had raised Holly, had passed away five months previously; Mitch couldn't invite his brother and three sisters without extending an invitation to his parents, and he didn't want Daniel and Kathy to be there. He wasn't motivated by bitterness. He didn't exclude them in anger or as punishment. He'd been *afraid* of having them present. The marriage was his second chance at family. If it failed, he wouldn't have the nerve to try a third time.

He told his family they weren't going to have a wedding of any kind, but actually they'd had a small ceremony and reception at the house for a limited number of friends. Iggy was right: the band had been woofy.

After everyone had gone, Mitch and Holly had danced alone, to a radio, on the portable dance floor that had been set up in the back yard for the event. She had been so lovely in the moonlight, almost otherworldly, that he unconsciously held her too tight, as if she might fade like a phantom. She said, 'I'm breakable, you know,' and he relaxed as she put her head on his shoulder. Around them was the lush landscaping that was the consequence of his patient labour, and above them shone the stars that he had never offered her because he wasn't a man given to poetic declarations.

The phone rang.

He answered on the second ring and said, 'This is Mitch.'

'Hello, Mitch. Are you feeling hopeful?'

This mellow voice was not the same as on the previous calls, and the change made Mitch uneasy.

'Yes. I'm hopeful,' he said.

'Good. Nothing can be achieved without hope.'

On consideration, the change didn't disturb Mitch so much as the nature of the voice. The man spoke with a gentleness that was just one station up the dial from spooky.

'I want to talk to Holly.'

'Of course you do. She is the woman of the hour—and acquitting herself very well. This lady is a solid spirit.'

Holly came on the line. 'Are you OK, Mitch?'

'I'm all right. I'm going crazy, but I'm all right. I love you.'

'I'm OK, too. I haven't been hurt. Not really.'

'I'm not going to let you down.' he assured her.

'I never thought you would. Never. He wants the phone back,' she said, and returned it to her captor.

She had sounded constrained. He'd told her that he loved her, but she had not responded in kind. Something was wrong.

The gentle voice returned: 'There's been one change in the plan, Mitch, one important change. Instead of a wire transfer, cash is king.'

Mitch had worried that he would not be able to talk them out of having the ransom sent by wire. He should have been relieved by this development. Instead it troubled him. It was another indication that something had happened to put the kidnappers off their game.

'Are you with me, Mitch?'

'Yeah. It's just, you've thrown me a curve here. Listen, right now I can guarantee eight hundred thousand in cash and six hundred thousand in bearer bonds.'

Before Mitch could mention the four hundred thousand that was supposedly aboard Anson's boat, the kidnapper said, 'That's a disappointment. That other six hundred thousand would buy a lot of time to seek.'

Mitch didn't catch the last word. 'To what?'

'Do you seek, Mitch?'

'Seek what?'

'If we knew the answer, there'd be no need to seek. A million four will be all right. I'll think of it as a discount for paying cash.'

Surprised by the ease with which the lower figure had been accepted, Mitch said, 'You can speak for everyone, your partners?'

'Yes. If I don't speak for them, who will?'

'Then . . . what's next?'

'You come alone. Unarmed.'

'All right.'

'Pack the money and bonds in a plastic trash bag. Don't tie the top shut. Are you familiar with the Turnbridge house?'

'Everyone in the county knows the Turnbridge house.'

'Come there at three o'clock. Don't get cute and think you can come early and lie in wait. All you'll get for that is a dead wife.'

'I'll be there at three. Not a minute earlier. How do I get in?'

'The gate will be chained, but the chain will be loose. After you drive onto the site, replace the chain. What will you be driving?'

'My Honda.'

'Stop directly in front of the house. You'll see an SUV. Park well away from it. Park with the back of the Honda towards the house and open the trunk. I want to see no one's in the trunk. At that point, I'll phone you on your cell with instructions.'

'Wait. My cell. It's dead.' Actually it was somewhere in Rancho Santa Fe. 'Can I use Anson's?'

'What's that number?'

Anson's cellphone lay on the kitchen table, beside the money and the bonds. Mitch picked it up. 'I don't know the number. I have to switch it on and look. Give me a minute.'

As Mitch waited for the phone company logo to leave the screen, the man with the gentle voice said, 'Tell me, is Anson alive?'

Surprised by the question, Mitch said only, 'Yes.'

Amused, the caller said, 'The simple answer tells me so much.'

'What does it tell you?'

'He underestimated you.'

'You're reading too much into one word. Here's the cell number.'

After Mitch read the number and repeated it, the man on the phone said,

'We want a smooth simple trade, Mitch. Everyone walks away a winner.'

Mitch considered that this was the first time the man with the gentle voice had said *we* instead of *I*.

'Three o'clock,' the caller reminded him, and hung up.

REEKING, restless, rocking side to side on the red chair in the laundry room, Anson was resigned to cooperation. 'Yeah, there's one of them talks like that. Name's Jimmy Null. If he's on the phone with you, the others are dead. Something went wrong and he's decided to bag the whole payoff.'

'So you think there's just one of them now?'

'That makes it harder for you, not easier. Once he's wasted the others, his tendency will be to clean up totally behind himself.'

'Killing Holly and me?'

'Only when he's got the money.' In his misery, Anson gave a ghastly smile. 'You want to know about the money, bro? You want to know what I do for a living?'

Anson would be offering this information only if he believed that the knowledge would do his brother harm. But curiosity outweighed Mitch's caution.

Before either of them could speak, the telephone rang again.

Mitch returned to the kitchen, briefly considered not answering, but worried that it might be Jimmy Null calling with additional instructions.

'Hello?'

'Anson?'

'He's not here.'

'Who's this?' The voice didn't belong to Jimmy Null.

'I'm a friend of Anson's,' Mitch said.

Now that he'd taken the call, the best thing was to carry through with it as if all were normal here.

'When will he be back?' the caller asked.

'Tomorrow.'

'Should I try his cell?'

The voice teased Mitch's memory. Picking up Anson's cellphone from the counter, he said, 'He forgot to take it with him.'

'Can you give him a message?'

'Sure. Go ahead.'

'Tell him that Julian Campbell called.'

The glimmer of the grey eyes, the glitter of the gold Rolex.

'Anything else?' Mitch asked.

'That's everything. Although I do have one concern, friend of Anson.'

Mitch said nothing.

'Friend of Anson, are you there?'

'Yes.'

'I hope you're taking good care of my Chrysler Windsor. I love that car. See you later.'

MITCH LOCATED the kitchen drawer in which Anson kept two boxes of white plastic trash bags. He took a bag and put the blocks of cash and the envelope of bonds in it, then twisted the top but didn't tie a knot.

When Mitch returned to the laundry room, Anson said, 'Who called?'

'He was selling something.'

Anson's eyes were sea-green and bloodshot. 'It didn't sound like sales.'

'You were going to tell me what you do for a living.'

Malicious glee appeared on Anson's face. He wanted to share his triumph because it was knowledge that would wound Mitch.

'Imagine you send data to a customer over the Internet, and it appears to be innocent material—say photos and a history of Ireland. It's not encrypted data; it seems clear, unremarkable. But when you process it with special software, the photos and text combine and re-form into completely different material, into the hidden truth.'

'What is the truth?'

'Wait. First . . . your customer downloads the software. If police search his computer and try to copy or analyse the software, the program self-destructs. Likewise documents stored on the computer in either original or converted form.'

Mitch wasn't sure that he saw the most useful applications of this, but one occurred to him. 'So terrorists could communicate over the Internet, and anyone sampling their transmissions would find them sharing only a history of Ireland.'

'Terrorists aren't a stable, profitable market.'

'Who is?'

'There are many. But I want you to know especially about the work I did for Julian Campbell.'

'The entertainment entrepreneur,' Mitch said.

'It's true he owns casinos in several countries. Partly he uses them to launder money from other activities. One half of one per cent of men are paedophiles,' Anson continued. 'In the US—one and a half million. And millions of others worldwide. They are eager consumers of child pornography. Though it might destroy them, they risk everything to get it. If they can get their need filled safely, their appetite becomes insatiable.'

In this bright white room, Mitch felt on the threshold of a chilling darkness. He was glad now he had left the pistol on the kitchen table. Perhaps, subconsciously, he had not trusted himself with the weapon.

'Campbell has two hundred thousand customers. In two years, he expects a million worldwide, and revenues of five billion dollars. Profit on gross sales is sixty percent. And I've got a little piece of Julian's business. I told you I have eight million, but it's three times that much. Bro, I just wanted you to understand how filthy the money is that's going to buy Holly. The rest of your life, you're going to think about that.'

Chained helpless to the chair, Anson raised his head defiantly and his eyes shone with triumph, as though having facilitated Campbell's vile enterprise was payment enough, that having had the opportunity to serve the appetite of the depraved at the expense of the innocent was all the reward he would need to sustain him through his current humiliation.

Some might call this madness, but Mitch knew its real name.

'I'm leaving,' he announced, for there was nothing else to be said.

'Taser me,' Anson demanded, as if to assert that Mitch did not have the power to hurt him in any lasting way.

'The deal we made?' Mitch said. 'Screw it.'

He switched out the lights and pulled the door shut, wedging it with a chair. He might have nailed it shut, as well, if he'd had time.

He wondered if he would ever feel clean again.

At the sink, he splashed cold water in his face.

The doorbell rang and the chimes played a few bars of 'Ode to Joy'.

Only minutes had passed since Julian Campbell had terminated their phone call. Five billion a year in revenues was a treasure that he would do anything to protect, but surely he couldn't have got a fresh pair of gunmen to Anson's place this quickly.

Mitch turned off the water at the sink and, face dripping, tried to think if there was any reason he should risk checking on the identity of the visitor through the living-room window. He couldn't. Grabbing the trash bag that held the ransom, he plucked the pistol and his brother's cellphone off the table, and headed for the back door.

Time to get out of here.

The Taser. He had left it on a counter by the oven. He returned for it.

Again the unknown visitor rang the bell. Mitch ignored the summons.

'Who's that?' Anson asked from the laundry room.

'The postman. Now shut up,' Mitch called.

After retrieving the Taser, he turned in a circle, surveying the kitchen. As far as he could tell, he had forgotten nothing else.

He turned off the lights, stepped out of the back of the house and locked the door.

The inexhaustible wind played among the ferns and bamboo. Leathery banyan leaves, blown in from another property, scrabbled across the patio, scratching at the bricks. Mitch went to the first of the two garages, entering by the courtyard door. Here his Honda waited, and John Knox ripened in the back of the Buick Super Woody Wagon.

He'd had a vague plan for hanging Knox's death round Anson's neck but none of that mattered. When Holly was safe, John Knox and the bodies in the learning room and Anson handcuffed to the chair would matter again. For now, they were incidental.

More than two and a half hours remained before he could swap the money for Holly. He opened the trunk of the Honda and tucked the bag into the wheel well.

In the front seat of the Woody, he found a garage-door remote. He clipped it to the Honda's sun visor, so he could close the roll-up door from the alleyway. He put the pistol and the Taser in the storage pocket of the driver's door. They were easier to reach there than they would have been under the seat.

Triggering the remote control, he watched in the rearview mirror as the big door rolled up.

Backing out of the garage, he glanced to his right, saw the alleyway was clear—and stamped on the brakes in surprise as someone rapped on the driver's-door window. Snapping his head to the left, he discovered that he was face-to-face with Detective Taggart.

MUFFLED BY GLASS: 'Hello there, Mr Rafferty.'

Mitch stared at the detective too long before putting down the car window. He must have looked shocked, fearful.

Warm wind tossed Taggart's sports coat and flapped the collar of his yellow and tan Hawaiian shirt as he leaned close to the window. 'Do you have time for me?'

'Well, I do have a doctor's appointment,' Mitch said.

'Good. I won't keep you too long. Should we talk in the garage, out of this wind?'

'Sit with me in the car,' Mitch said, and he put up the window as he finished backing out of the garage. He remoted the big door and parked parallel to it, out of the centre of the alley, as it rolled down.

Getting into the passenger's seat, Taggart said, 'Have you called an exterminator about those termites?'

'Not yet.'

'Don't put it off too long.'

'I won't.'

Mitch sat facing forward, staring at the alley, determined to glance at Taggart only from time to time, because he remembered the penetrating power of the cop's stare.

'I guess you've been too busy to think about termites.'

An innocent man might wonder what this was about and might be impatient to get on with his day, so Mitch risked asking, 'Why are you here, Lieutenant?'

'I came to see your brother, but he didn't answer the door.'

'He's away in Vegas until tomorrow.'

'Didn't you hear the doorbell?' Taggart asked.

'I must have left before it rang. I had a few things to do in the garage.'

'Looking after the place for your brother while he's away?'

'That's right. Why do you want to talk to him?'

The detective turned sideways in his seat, facing Mitch directly. 'Your brother's phone numbers were in Jason Osteen's address book.'

Glad to have something truthful to say, Mitch reported: 'They met when Jason and I were room-mates.'

'You didn't stay in touch with Jason, but your brother did?'

'I don't know. Maybe. They got along well.'

Taggart said, 'Jason was hooked up with this girl named Leelee Morheim. You know her?'

'No.'

'Leelee says Jason hated your brother. Says your brother cheated Jason in some deal.'

'What deal?'

'Leelee doesn't know that. But one thing's pretty clear: Jason didn't do honest work.'

That statement required Mitch to frown with convincing puzzlement. 'Are you saying Anson was involved in something illegal?'

'Do you think that's possible?'

'He's got a PhD in linguistics and he's a computer geek.'

'I knew a minister who murdered a child.'

Considering recent events, Mitch no longer believed that the detective might be one of the kidnappers. This did not mean, however, that Mitch could turn to Taggart for help. John Knox, laid out in the Woody Wagon, would require some explaining. And Daniel and Kathy. And when Anson was discovered in such a miserable condition in the laundry room, he would appear to be a victim. Given his talent for deception, he would play innocent with conviction, to the confusion of the authorities.

Only two and a half hours remained before the hostage swap. Mitch dreaded the thought of having to sit helplessly as the minutes ticked away and the police, even if well meaning, tried to get their minds round the current situation and the events that had led to it.

Taggart said, 'How is Mrs Rafferty? Did she get some relief from her migraine?'

'Oh. Yeah.' Mitch could almost not conceal his relief that the source of Taggart's interest was the mythical migraine. 'She's better.'

'Not entirely well, though? Aspirin isn't ideal for a migraine.'

Mitch sensed that a trap had been laid before him. 'Well, aspirin is what she's comfortable with.'

'But now she's missed a second day of work,' Taggart said.

The detective could have learned Holly's place of employment from Iggy Barnes. His knowledge didn't surprise Mitch, but that he had followed up on the migraine-headache story was alarming.

'Nancy Farasand says it's unusual for Mrs Rafferty to take a sick day.'

Nancy Farasand, another secretary at the realtor's office where Holly was employed, was the person Mitch had spoken to the previous afternoon.

'Do you know Ms Farasand, Mitch?'

'Yes.'

'She strikes me as a very efficient person. She says it's not at all like your wife to fail to report in when she's going to miss work.'

This morning Mitch should have called in sick for Holly. He had forgotten. He'd also forgotten to phone Iggy to cancel the day's schedule. Having triumphed over two professional killers, he had been tripped up by inattention to a mundane task or two.

'Yesterday,' Detective Taggart said, 'you told me that when you saw Jason Osteen shot, you were on the phone with your wife.'

The car had become stuffy. Mitch wanted to open the window to the wind.

'Is that still what you remember, Mitch?'

In fact, he had been on the phone with the kidnapper. What had seemed a safe and easy lie at the time might now be a noose into which he was being invited to place his neck.

'Yeah. I was on the phone with Holly.'

'You said she called to tell you that she was leaving work early because of a migraine.'

'That's right.'

'So you *were* on the phone with her when Osteen was shot.'

'Yes.'

'That was at eleven forty-three a.m. You said it was eleven forty-three.'

'I checked my watch right after the shot.'

'But Nancy Farasand tells me that Mrs Rafferty called in sick *early* yesterday, that she wasn't in the office at all.'

Mitch did not reply. He could feel the hammer coming down.

'And Ms Farasand says that you called her between twelve fifteen and twelve thirty yesterday afternoon and asked to speak to your wife.'

The interior of the Honda felt like a tighter space than the trunk of the Chrysler Windsor.

Taggart said, 'You were still at the crime scene at that time, waiting for me to ask a series of follow-up questions. Your helper, Mr Barnes, continued planting flowers. Do you remember?'

'Sure. Of course.'

'What I can't understand,' Taggart said, 'is why you would call the realtor's office and ask to speak to your wife as much as forty-five minutes after your wife had already called *you* to say that she was leaving there with a terrible migraine.'

As Mitch lowered his gaze, a helpless sinking of the heart overcame him.

'Mitch?'

'Yeah.'

'Look at me.'

Reluctantly, he met the detective's gaze.

Those hawk's eyes didn't pierce Mitch now. Instead, worse, they were sympathetic and invited trust.

'Mitch . . . where is your wife?'

12

Mitch remembered the alley as it had been the previous evening, flooded with the crimson light of sunset, and the ginger cat stalking shadows.

He had allowed himself hope then. The hope had been Anson, and the hope had been a lie. Now the sky was hard and wind-polished and a frigid blue. The ginger cat was gone, and nothing moved.

'Where is your wife?' Taggart asked again.

The money was in the car trunk. The time and place of the swap were set. The clock was ticking down to the moment. He had come so far, endured so much, got so close.

He had discovered Evil with an uppercase 'E', but he had also come to see new meaning. If things happened for a purpose, then perhaps there was a purpose he must not ignore in this encounter with the persistent detective. *For richer or poorer. In sickness and in health. To love, honour and cherish. Until death us do part.*

The vows were his. Nobody else had made them to Holly. He was the husband. No one else would be so quick to kill for her, to die for her. To cherish means to hold dear, to support and comfort and *protect* . . .

Perhaps the purpose of him being here with Taggart was to warn him that he had reached the limits of his ability to protect Holly, to encourage him to realise that he could not go any further alone.

'Mitch, where is your wife? You've changed. You're all steel springs and ticking clocks.'

'You've only known me one day.'

'And you've changed.'

'I'm not a bad man. I guess all bad men say that.'

'Not so directly.'

In the sky, a sun-silvered jet caught his eye as it sailed north. The world seemed shrunken now to this car, to this moment of peril.

'Before I tell you where Holly is, I want a promise.'

'I'm just a cop. I can't make plea bargains.'

'We don't have much time. The promise I want is that when you hear the essence of it, you'll act fast, and not waste time picking at details.'

'The devil's in the details, Mitch.'

'When you hear this, you'll know where the devil is. But with so little time, I don't want to screw with police bureaucracies.'

'I'm one cop. All I can promise is—I'll do my best for you.'

Mitch took a deep breath. 'Holly has been kidnapped. She's being held for ransom. They want two million dollars or they'll kill her.'

Taggart stared at him. 'Am I missing something? You're a gardener. Where would you get two million bucks?'

'They said I'd find a way. Then they shot Jason Osteen, who was one of them, to impress on me how serious they are.'

The detective's eyes were too sharp to read.

'Jason thought they were going to shoot the dog. By killing him, they scared obedience into me and at the same time cut the eventual split from five ways to four.'

'Go on,' Taggart said.

'Once I got home and saw the scene they had staged for me there, once they had me in knots, they sent me to my brother for the money.'

'For real? He's got that much?'

'Anson once pulled some criminal operation with Jason Osteen, John Knox, Jimmy Null, and two others whose names I've never heard. Anson cheated them on the split, and they only found out what the real take was a lot later.'

'Why snatch your wife?' Taggart asked. 'Why not go after *him*?'

'He's untouchable. He's too valuable to some very important and very hard people. So they went after him through his little brother. Me. They figured he wouldn't want to see me lose my wife.'

'But he wouldn't give you the money.'

'Worse. He turned me over to some people. To be killed.'

'Your brother did?'

'My brother.'

'Why didn't they kill you?'

Mitch maintained eye contact. He could not hold back too much and expect cooperation. He said, 'Some things went wrong for them. So I came back to see my brother.'

'Must've been some reunion.'

'No champagne, but he had second thoughts about helping me.'

'He gave you the money?'

'He did.'

'Where is your brother now?'

'Alive but restrained. The swap is at three o'clock, and I've got reason to believe one of the kidnappers popped the others. Jimmy Null. Now it's just him holding Holly.'

'How much have you left out?'

'Most of it,' Mitch said truthfully.

The detective stared through the windshield at the alley. From a pocket, he withdrew a roll of hard-caramel candies. He peeled the end of the roll, extracted a candy. He held the sweet between his teeth while he folded shut the roll.

'So?' Mitch said. 'You believe me?'

'I've got a bullshit detector even bigger than my prostate,' said Taggart. 'And it isn't ringing.'

Mitch didn't know whether to be relieved or not. 'Now what?' he asked.

'Mitch, kidnapping is a federal offence. We have to notify the FBI.'

'I'm afraid of the complication.'

'They're good. Nobody's more experienced with this kind of crime. Anyway, because we have only two hours, they won't be able to get a special team in place. They'll probably want us to take the lead. We have an experienced hostage negotiator.'

'So many people,' Mitch worried.

'I'll be running this. You think I'm trigger-happy?'

'No.'

'OK. So we'll get your wife back.' The detective reached across the console and plucked the car key from the ignition.

Startled, Mitch said, 'Why'd you do that?'

'I don't want you having second thoughts, bolting off on your own, after all. That isn't what's best for her, Mitch.'

'I've made the decision. You can trust me with the keys.'

'In a little while. I'm only looking out for you here, for you and Holly. I've got a wife I love, too, and two daughters, so I know where you are right now, in your head. Trust me.'

The keys disappeared into a jacket pocket. From another pocket, the detective withdrew a cellphone.

Mitch watched the detective speed-dial a number. A part of him felt that with the contact of that finger to that button, Holly's fate had been sealed.

As Taggart spoke police code to a dispatcher and gave Anson's address, Mitch looked for another sun-silvered jet high above. The sky was empty.

Terminating the call, pocketing the phone, Taggart said, 'So your brother's back there in the house?'

Mitch could no longer pretend Anson was in Vegas. 'Yeah.'

'Where?'

'In the laundry room.'

'Let's go talk to him. He pulled some sort of job with this Jimmy Null, so he must know him well. If we're going to get Holly out of Null's hands smooth and easy, we need to know every possible thing about him.'

When Taggart opened the passenger's door to get out, a clear wind blasted into the Honda, bringing neither dust nor litter, but the promise of chaos. For better or worse, the situation was spinning out of Mitch's control. He didn't think it would be for the better.

As Taggart slammed the door and walked away, Mitch sat behind the wheel for a moment, his thoughts spinning, tumbling. Then he got out into the whipping wind.

MITCH LED THE DETECTIVE to the painted wooden service gate. The wind tore it from his hand as he slipped the latch, and banged it against the garage wall. Following the narrow brick walkway to the courtyard, he was aware of Taggart close behind him and he felt crowded, claustrophobic.

He could already hear Anson's voice in his mind: *He told me that he killed our mom and dad. He stabbed them with garden tools.*

At the back door, Mitch's hands were shaking so much that he had trouble fitting the key in the lock.

Taggart knew that Anson was bent. Nevertheless, when Anson told a story conflicting with Mitch's, Taggart would consider it. Cops were always presented with competing stories. Finding the truth would take time, and time was a coiled spring, a rat gnawing at Mitch's nerves.

The key turned. The deadbolt clicked open.

Standing on the threshold, Mitch at once saw on the floor a long blood smear. When Anson had been clubbed on the side of his head, his ear had torn. As he'd been dragged to the laundry room, he'd left a trail. The smears suggested something worse than a bleeding ear. By such misleading evidence were doubts raised and suspicions sharpened.

Mitch entered the kitchen, slipped open a button on his shirt, reached inside, and withdrew the Taser that was tucked under his belt. As he'd delayed getting out of the Honda, he had retrieved the weapon from the storage pocket in the driver's door.

'The laundry room is this way,' he said, leading Taggart a few steps forward before turning suddenly with the Taser.

The detective wasn't following as close as Mitch had thought. He was a prudent two steps back. Mitch had to get in close, get in fast.

As Mitch thrust with his right arm, Taggart blocked with his left. The Taser was almost knocked out of Mitch's hand.

Retreating, the detective reached under his sports jacket, with his right hand, surely going for a weapon in a shoulder holster.

Mitch feinted left, thrust right, and as the gun hand came from under the jacket he got the detective in the throat with the Taser.

Eyes rolling back in his head, jaw sagging, Taggart fired one round, his knees folded, and he dropped.

The shot seemed unusually loud, and shook the room.

MITCH THOUGHT ABOUT John Knox self-shot in the fall from the garage loft, and he knelt worriedly beside the detective.

Taggart shuddered as if chilled to the marrow, his hands clawed at the floor tiles, and bubbles of spit sputtered on his lips. Faint, thin, pungent, a ribbon of smoke unravelled from the pistol. Mitch shoved it out of reach. He pulled back the detective's jacket, looking for a wound. He didn't find one, but the relief he felt did not much buoy him. He was still guilty of assaulting a police officer and this was the first time he had hurt an innocent person. Remorse had a taste: a bitterness rising at the back of the throat.

Pawing at Mitch's arm, the detective tried to say something.

Mitch wanted to avoid having to Taser him a second time. He said, 'I'm sorry. I love her too much to trust anyone else with this,' and set to work searching Taggart's jacket. He found the car key in the second pocket.

In the laundry room, Anson began shouting. Mitch ignored him.

Taking Taggart by the feet, Mitch dragged him out of the house, onto the brick patio. As he pulled the back door shut, he heard the doorbell ring inside. The police were at the front of the house.

Mitch took a moment to lock the door to delay their exposure to Anson and his lies, then he sprinted out of the back door, across the courtyard, along the side of the garage, and through the open back gate into the alleyway. He threw the Taser on the passenger's seat as he got behind the wheel. Key, switch, the roar of the engine.

In the storage pocket of the door was the pistol that belonged to one of Campbell's hired killers. Seven rounds remained in the magazine.

He wasn't going to pull a gun on the police. His only option was to get the hell out of there. He drove east, fully expecting that a squad car would suddenly appear across the end of the alleyway, thwarting him.

He turned right into the street. And at the next intersection, he turned left, heading east again.

This area of Corona del Mar, itself a part of Newport Beach, was called the Village. A grid of narrow streets, it could be sealed off with perhaps as few as three roadblocks. He needed to get beyond those choke points. Fast.

Taggart could describe the Honda. In minutes, they would have the licence-plate number from the Department of Motor Vehicles.

He arrived at a traffic signal on the Pacific Coast Highway. Red. Heavy traffic surged north and south on the divided highway. Mitch glanced at the rearview mirror. Some kind of truck approached, still a block away. The roof appeared to be outfitted with an array of emergency beacons, like those on a police vehicle, but the dappled shadows cast by the roadside trees made it difficult to identify.

Out on one of the northbound lanes of the Pacific Coast Highway, a police car passed, parting the traffic before it with emergency beacons but no siren.

Behind the Honda, the worrisome vehicle cruised to within half a block of Mitch's tail, at which point he could read the word AMBULANCE on the brow above the windshield. They were in no hurry. They must be off duty.

He exhaled a pent-up breath. The ambulance braked to a stop behind him, and his relief was short-lived when he wondered whether paramedics usually listened to a police scanner.

The traffic light changed to green. He crossed the southbound lanes and turned left, going north on the Coast Highway. He had travelled only a block when a siren shrilled behind him. This time, in the rearview mirror, there was a police car.

Only fools led cops on a chase. Defeated, Mitch steered towards the kerb. As he vacated the lane, the squad car shot past him and away.

Mitch watched until the cruiser left the highway two blocks ahead. It turned left into the Village. Evidently Taggart hadn't yet recovered his wits enough to give them a description of the Honda.

Mitch took a very deep breath. He took another. He wiped the back of his neck with one hand. He blotted his hands on his jeans.

He had assaulted a police officer. Easing back into the northbound traffic, he wondered if he had lost his mind.

AFTER HOLLY EXTRACTS the nail from the plank, she turns it over and over in her sore fingers, assessing whether or not it is as lethal as she imagined. Straight, more than three but less than four inches long, with a thick shank and a sharp point, it qualifies as a spike all right.

Although the spike probably won't show if tucked in a pocket of her jeans, she worries that she'll not be able to extract it quickly in a crisis. Her belt offers no possibilities, so she considers her sneakers. She can't carry the nail inside the shoe; it will rub and blister her foot. Maybe she can conceal it on the outside of the shoe.

She loosens the laces on her left sneaker, carefully tucks the nail between the tongue and one of the flaps, and reties the shoe. When she gets to her feet and walks a circle around the ringbolt to which she is tethered, she quickly discovers that the rigid nail is an impediment to a smoothly flexed step. She can't avoid limping.

Finally she pulls up her sweater and conceals the nail in her bra, between the cups, pressing the point through the elastic facing, thus pinning it in place. She has armed herself, although her preparations seem pathetic.

Discouraged, she lies on her back on the air mattress, her head raised on the pillow portion. Earlier, she slept fitfully. Her emotional exhaustion breeds physical fatigue, and she knows that she could sleep again, but she does not want to doze off. She lies with her eyes open, though this darkness is deeper than the one behind her eyelids..

Later, when she wakes, she is still in absolute darkness, but she knows she isn't alone.

She sits up with a start, the air mattress squeaking under her, the chain rattling against the floor between manacle and ringbolt.

'It's only me,' he assures her.

Holly's eyes strain at the blackness, but he remains invisible.

'I was watching you sleep.'

Judging his position by his voice is not easy.

'This is nice,' he says, 'being with you in the numinous dark.'

To her right. No more than three feet away.

'Are you afraid?' he asks.

'No,' she lies without hesitation.

'You would disappoint me if you were afraid. I believe you are arising into your full spirit, and one who is arising must be beyond fear.'

As he speaks, he seems to move behind her. She turns her head, listening intently.

'In El Valle, New Mexico, one night the snow came down as thick as ever it has anywhere.'

If she is correct, he has moved to her right side.

'The valley floor received six inches in four hours, and the land was eerie in the snowlight . . .'

Hairs quiver, flesh prickles on the back of her neck at the thought of him moving confidently in pitch-black conditions.

The gentle voice is in front of her now, and Holly chooses to believe that it has not moved, that it has always been in front of her.

He says, 'The storm was windless at ground level, but hard wind blew at higher elevations, because when the snow abated, most of the clouds were quickly torn into rags and flung away. Between the remaining clouds, the sky was black, festooned with ornate necklaces of stars.'

She can feel the nail between her breasts, warmed by her body heat.

His stories always lead somewhere, although Holly has learned to dread their destinations. His voice grows softer, and he is close now. He may be leaning towards her, his face but a foot from her face.

'Some last snow was falling. A few late flakes as big as silver dollars slowly glimmered to the ground, as if something magical were aflame high in the night, some glorious palace burning on the other side of Heaven.'

As long as he is kept talking, he will not kiss.

Holly says, 'It sounds so magnificent, so beautiful. I wish I'd been there.'

'*I* wish you'd been there,' he agrees.

She feels his warm breath upon her brow, upon her eyes. It has no scent. And then it is gone.

He says, 'Do you believe in signs, Holly Rafferty?'

'Yes.'

'Omens. Portents. Harbingers, storm petrels, black cats and broken mirrors, mysterious lights in the sky. Have you ever seen a sign, Holly Rafferty?'

'I don't think so.'

'Do you hope to see a sign?'

She knows what he wants her to say. 'Yes. I hope to see one.' Struggling to keep fear from her voice, she says, 'You've seen many signs, haven't you?'

'I've seen scores. I have the eye for them.'

'Please tell me about one.'

He is silent. His silence is a sharp and looming weight.

If at all possible, she must avoid disabusing him of the strange dark fantasy that appears to have him in its grip. He seems to believe that she will eventually decide that she must go to New Mexico with him and that she will 'be amazed'. As long as he continues in this belief, she might be able to find some advantage over him.

When his silence begins to seem ominously long, he says, 'This was just as summer became autumn that year, and everyone said the birds had left early, and wolves were seen where they had not been in a decade. Have you ever been to Eagle Nest, New Mexico?'

'No.'

'I was driving south from Eagle Nest, twenty miles east of Taos. These two college girls were across the highway, hitchhiking north. They were serious seekers, in their good hiking boots and backpacks, and confident.' He pauses, perhaps for drama, perhaps savouring the memory. 'I saw the sign. Hovering above their heads, a blackbird, its wings spread wide, riding effortlessly on a thermal, but moving precisely no faster or slower than the girls were walking. They were unaware of it.'

She regrets having elicited this story. She closes her eyes against the images that she fears he might describe.

'Do you know what the sign of the bird meant, Holly Rafferty?'

'Death,' she says, opening her eyes even though she can see nothing.

'Yes, exactly right. You *are* arising into full spirit. I saw the bird and believed that death was settling on the girls.'

'And . . . was it?'

'Winter came early that year. Many snows followed one another, and the cold was very hard. The spring thaw extended into summer, and when the snow melted, their bodies were found in late June, in a field near Arroyo Hondo. I recognised their pictures in the paper.'

Holly says a silent prayer for the families of the unknown girls.

'Who knows what happened to them?' he continues. 'We can imagine some of what they endured. But if we're seekers, we learn from everything, and grow. Perhaps any death involves moments of illuminating beauty and the potential for transcendence.'

He switches on his flashlight and is sitting immediately before her, cross-legged on the floor. He wears the ski mask in which only his beryl-blue eyes are visible.

'It's time to go,' he says. 'You will be ransomed for a million four hundred thousand and, when I have the money, then the time will have come for decision.'

The dollar figure stuns her. It might be a lie. Holly has lost all track of time, but she is confused and amazed by what his words imply. 'Is it already . . . midnight Wednesday?'

Within his mask, he smiles. 'Only a few minutes before one o'clock Tuesday afternoon. Your persuasive husband has encouraged his brother to come through with the money quicker than ever seemed possible.'

Rising to his feet, he gestures for her to rise, as well, and she obeys.

Behind her back, he binds her wrists together with a blue silk scarf. Stepping in front of her again, he tenderly smoothes her hair back from her forehead. His hands are as cold as they are pale and he stares continuously into her eyes in a spirit of challenge.

She dares not look away from him, and she closes her eyes only when he presses thick gauze pads to them. He binds the pads in place with a longer length of silk which he loops three times round her head and ties firmly at the back of her skull.

His hands brush her right ankle, and he unlocks the manacle, freeing her from the chain and the ringbolt.

He plays the flashlight over her blindfold, and she sees dim light penetrate the silk. Evidently satisfied by the job he's done, he lowers the light. 'When we've reached the ransom drop,' he promises, 'the scarves will come off. They're only to incapacitate you during transport. Now we go.'

He takes Holly by one arm, and she does not shrink from his repulsive touch, but moves with him across the room and through an open doorway.

Here are the steps again, up which they led her the previous day. He patiently guides her descent, but she cannot hold a railing and therefore places each foot tentatively.

From attic to first floor, to ground floor, and then into the garage, he encourages her: 'A landing now. Very good. Duck your head. And now to the left. Be careful here. And now a threshold.'

In the garage, she hears him open the door of a vehicle.

'This is the van that brought you here,' he says, and helps her through the rear entrance, into the cargo space. The carpeted floor smells as foul as she remembered it. 'Lie on your side.'

He exits, closes the door behind him. The driver's door opens, and he gets in behind the wheel. 'This is a two-seat van. The seats are open to the cargo area, which is why you hear me so clearly. You do hear me clearly?'

'Yes.'

He closes his door. 'On our trip here, there were men to sit with you, to make sure that you behaved. I'm alone now. So . . . somewhere along the way, if we stop at a red light and you think a scream will be heard, I'll have to deal with you more harshly than I would like. On the passenger's seat beside me is a pistol fitted with a silencer. The instant that you begin to scream, I'll pick up the pistol, turn round in my seat, and shoot you dead. Whether you're dead or alive, I'll collect the ransom. You see the way it is?'

'Yes. I won't scream.'

'Consider this. I could have gagged you, but I didn't. Why didn't I?'

'Because you know you can trust me,' she says.

'I *hope* that I can trust you. A gag is effective but extremely unpleasant. I didn't want an unpleasantness like that between us, Holly, in case . . . in *hope* of Gaudalupita.'

Her mind works to deceive more smoothly than she would have thought possible one day ago. In a voice solemn with respect, she recites for him details that suggest he has indeed cast a spell over her: 'Guadalupita, Rodarte, Rio Lucio, Penasco, where your life was changed . . .'

He is silent for a moment. Then: 'I'm sorry for the discomfort, Holly. It will be over soon, and then transcendence . . . if you want it.'

13

The architecture of the gun shop had been inspired by stores in countless Western movies. Vertical-clapboard walls, a hitching post, and a covered boardwalk the length of the long building, all raised the expectation that at any moment John Wayne might walk out of the front door.

Mitch sat in the Honda, in the parking lot, examining the pistol that he had brought back from Rancho Santa Fe. Several things that provided useful information for a guy who knew squat about handguns were engraved in the steel. Near the muzzle, in script, were the words *Super Tuned*. Further back on the slide the word CHAMPION looked as if it had been laser-incised in block letters, and *cal .45* was directly under it.

Mitch now knew that he needed .45-calibre ammunition. Seven rounds would probably be more than enough—gunfights dragged on only in movies whereas in real life, within four rounds, somebody was wounded or dead—but buying more ammunition was a psychological need. Additional ammo would make him feel better prepared.

On the other side of the slide, he found the word SPRINGFIELD. He took this to be the maker.

The word 'Champion' most likely referred to the model of the gun. He had a Springfield Champion .45 pistol. That sounded more likely than a Champion Springfield .45 pistol.

When he went into the shop, he hoped he would sound like he knew what he was talking about. After ejecting the magazine from the pistol, he extracted a cartridge. The casing identified it as *.45 acp*, but he didn't know what the letters meant.

He returned the cartridge to the magazine and put the magazine in a pocket of his jeans. He slid the pistol under the driver's seat.

From the glove box, he retrieved John Knox's wallet. Using the dead man's money pricked his conscience, but he had no choice. His own wallet had been taken from him in Julian Campbell's library. He took the entire $585 and returned the wallet to the glove box.

He got out, locked the car, and went into the gun shop. There were aisles and aisles of gun-related paraphernalia. At the long cashier's counter, he got help from a large man with a walrus moustache. His name tag identified him as Roland.

'A Springfield Champion,' Roland said. 'That's a stainless-steel version of a Colt Commander, isn't it?'

Mitch had no clue if it was or not. 'That's right. It's a sweet gun,' he said, hoping people actually talked that way. 'I want three extra magazines. For target shooting.'

Roland appeared not in the least suspicious. 'Did you go for Springfield's whole Super Tuned package?'

Remembering the words engraved near the muzzle, Mitch said, 'Yes. The whole package.'

'You didn't bring the gun? I'd feel better if I could see it.'

Incorrectly, Mitch had thought if he carried a pistol into the store, he'd look like a shoplifter or a stickup artist or something.

'I've got this.' He put the magazine on the counter.

'I'd rather have the gun, but let's see if we can work with this.'

Five minutes later, Mitch had paid for three magazines and a box of one hundred .45 acp cartridges.

As he was about to leave the shop, he looked through the glass door and saw a police cruiser in the parking lot, blocking his car. A cop stood at the driver's door, peering into the locked Honda.

ON HIS SECOND LOOK, Mitch realised that the driver's door of the cruiser wasn't emblazoned with the seal of a city but with the name—FIRST ENFORCEMENT—and ornate logo of a private-security firm. The uniformed man at the Honda must be a security guard, not a police officer.

Nevertheless, the Honda would be of interest to him if he knew an all-points bulletin had been put out for it.

The guard left his car athwart the Honda and approached the gun shop purposefully. He had most likely stopped to do some personal business and had lucked onto the Honda. Now he was psyched up for a citizen's arrest. A real cop would have called for back-up before coming into the store.

The parking lot wrapped the front and two sides of the building, and there were two entrances to the store. Mitch headed out through the side exit and hurried to the front of the store.

The security guard had gone inside. Mitch was alone. He sprinted to the Honda.

The First Enforcement car had him completely trapped. He would have to abandon the Honda. He unlocked the driver's door and retrieved the Springfield Champion .45 from under the seat.

He popped the trunk and snatched the white trash bag from the wheel well, then he put the pistol and the gun-shop purchases into the bag with the money, twisted the neck of the bag, closed the trunk and walked away.

He walked briskly across the road towards the side of the parking lot, where there was a low, concrete-block wall topped by a steel-safety barrier. He vaulted the barrier, landing on a property belonging to a fast-food franchise. Cautioning himself not to run like a fugitive, he passed a queue of vehicles waiting in line for takeout and rounded the back of the restaurant. Ahead lay a small shopping centre with six or eight stores. He slowed down, looking in the windows as he passed, just a guy out on an errand, with one point four million to spend.

As he came to the end of the block, a squad car went by on the main boulevard, emergency beacons flashing red-blue, heading in the direction of the gun shop. And immediately behind it sped another one.

Mitch picked up his pace and turned left on a small cross-street, away from the commercial zone. He reached a residential neighbourhood with single-family homes, most of them two storeys, and the occasional bungalow. The streets were lined with huge old podocarpus trees that cast a lot of shade. Most lawns were green, trimmed, shrubs well kept. Most of the vehicles parked on this residential street were SUVs. He slowed down, squinting through the passenger-door windows at the ignitions, hoping to spot a key. When the police didn't find him at the gun shop, within a few minutes, they could have half a dozen or more units cruising the area.

He had assaulted a police officer. They tended to put his kind at the top of their priority list.

When he glanced at his watch, he saw the time was 1:14. The exchange was set for 3:00, and now he didn't have wheels.

THE RIDE LASTS about fifteen minutes and Holly, bound and blindfolded, is too busy scheming to consider a scream.

This time, when her lunatic chauffeur stops, she hears him put the van in park and apply the hand brake. He gets out, leaving his door open.

In Rio Lucio, New Mexico, a saintly woman named Ermina Something lives in a blue and green or maybe blue and yellow stucco house. She is seventy-two. Holly is thinking about her captor's words.

He returns to the van and drives it forward about twenty feet, and then gets out again.

In Ermina Something's living room are maybe forty-two images of the Holy Mother . . .

This has given Holly an idea. The idea is scary. But it feels right.

When the killer returns to the van, Holly guesses that he has opened a gate to admit them to someplace, and then has closed it behind them. The van coasts forward, maybe sixty feet. Small stones crunch under the tyres.

He stops again and this time switches off the engine. 'We're here.'

'Good,' she says, for she is trying to play this not as a frightened hostage but a woman whose spirit is arising to its fullness.

He unlocks the back door and helps her out of the van.

The warm wind smells vaguely of wood smoke. Maybe canyons are afire far to the east. For the first time in more than twenty-four hours, she feels sun on her face. The sun feels so good she could cry.

Supporting her right arm, escorting her in an almost courtly fashion, he leads her across bare earth. When they stop, a strange muffled sound is repeated three times—*thup, thup, thup*—accompanied by splintering-wood and shrieking-metal noises.

'What's that?' she asks.

'I shot open the door.'

Now she knows what a pistol fitted with a silencer sounds like.

He conducts her across the threshold of the place into which he has shot his way. 'Not much further.'

The echoes of their slow footsteps give her a sense of cavernous spaces. 'It feels like a church.'

'In a way it is,' he says.

After halting her, the killer says, 'Wait here.' He lets go of her arm.

She smells plaster and sawdust and hears a sound that makes her heart sink: the rattle of a chain.

'One point four million dollars,' she says calculatedly. 'That buys a lot of seeking.'

'It buys a lot of everything,' he replies.

He touches her arm again, and she does not recoil. Around her left wrist, he wraps a chain and makes some kind of connection.

'When there's always a need to work,' she says, 'there's never really time to seek.'

'Work is a toad squatting on our lives,' he says, and she knows she has struck a chord with him.

He unties the scarf that binds her hands, and she thanks him.

When he removes her blindfold, she blinks, adjusting to the light, and discovers that she's in a house under construction. He has put on his ski mask again.

'This would have been the kitchen,' he says.

The space is enormous, maybe fifty feet by thirty feet, the ultimate for catering large parties. The limestone floor is adrift in dust. Finished drywall is in place, although no cabinets or appliances have been installed.

A metal pipe about two inches in diameter, perhaps a gas line, protrudes from low down in a wall. The other end of her chain has been padlocked to this pipe. The metal cap on the end of the pipe, almost a full inch wider than the pipe itself, prevents the chain from being slipped loose.

He has given her eight feet of links. She can sit, stand, and even move around a little.

'Where are we?' she wonders.

'The Turnbridge house.'

'Ah. But why? Do you have some connection with it?'

'I've been here a few times,' he says, 'though I've always made a more discreet entrance than shooting out the lock. Turnbridge draws me. He hasn't moved on. His spirit's still here.'

Turnbridge had been a dot-com billionaire. The company that he founded—and that made him rich—produced no product, but it had been on the cutting edge of advertising applications for the Internet. By the time *Forbes* estimated Turnbridge's net worth at $3 billion, he had bought nine homes on a dramatic Pacific-view bluff, side by side, by paying over $60 million each for them. He tore them down to make a single three-acre estate with few, if any, equals on the southern California coast.

A major architectural firm committed a team of thirty to the design of a three-level house encompassing 85,000 square feet, an interior-exterior waterfall, an underground shooting range, and an indoor ice-skating rink. Turnbridge spent whatever was required.

He had been as passionately committed to the company he had created as to the house he was building. He believed it would become one of the ten largest corporations in the world.

When his company's stock price fell, after the rapidly evolving Internet exposed flaws in his business model, he borrowed to buy more shares at market. The price fell further, and he leveraged more purchases. When the share price never recovered, the company imploded and Turnbridge was ruined. Construction of the house came to a halt. Pursued by creditors, investors, and an angry ex-wife, Turnbridge came home to his unfinished house, sat in a folding chair on the master-bedroom balcony, and with a 240-degree ocean view in sight, washed down an overdose of barbiturates with an icy bottle of Dom Perignon.

The three-acre coastal property had not sold after Turnbridge's death. To complete the project as specified in the plans, a buyer would need to spend fifty million.

As a would-be real-estate agent, Holly doesn't dream of getting the commission for the Turnbridge house. She will be content selling middle-class properties to people who are thrilled to have their own homes.

In fact, if she could trade her modest real-estate dream for a guarantee that she and Mitch would survive the ransom exchange, she would be content to remain a secretary. She is a good secretary and a good wife; she will try hard to be a good mom, too, and be happy with that.

But no such deal can be made; her fate remains in her own hands. She will have to act when the time comes for action.

Now she says, 'I've been thinking about Ermina in Rio Lucio.'

'Ermina Lavato.'

'Yes,' she says, as if she had not forgotten the surname. 'I can almost see the rooms of her house, each a different soothing colour. I don't know why I keep thinking of her.'

Within his mask, his beryl-blue eyes regard her with feverish intensity.

Closing her eyes, standing with her arms limp at her sides and with her face tilted towards the ceiling, she speaks in a murmur. 'I can see her bedroom walls covered with images of the Holy Mother.'

'Forty-two,' he says.

'And there are candles, aren't there?' she guesses.

'Yes. Votive candles.'

'It's a lovely room. She's happy there.'

'She's very poor,' he says, 'but happier than any rich man.'

Opening her eyes, Holly says, 'I've never been there, I've never met her. Why can't I get her and her house out of my mind?'

His silence begins to worry her. She is afraid that she has overacted.

Finally he says, 'Sometimes people who've never met can resonate with each other.'

If Holly reads him right, she has sparked more interest than suspicion.

'Strange,' she says, and drops the subject.

He says, 'I've got some preparations to make. I'm sorry for the chain. It won't be necessary much longer.'

After he has left the kitchen, she listens to his footsteps fading through vast hollow rooms.

The cold shakes seize her. She isn't able to get them under control, and the links of her chain sing against one another.

MITCH WAS SQUINTING through the windows of the vehicles parked at the kerb on the residential street. When the doors weren't locked, he opened them and leaned inside. If keys weren't in the ignition, they might be in a cup holder or tucked behind a sun visor. Each time that he didn't find keys in those places, he closed the door and moved on.

Born of desperation, his boldness surprised him. He hoped that these residents were not people with a sense of community, that they had not joined the Neighbourhood Watch programme. For laid-back southern California, a depressing percentage of them locked their parked cars . . .

When he had gone over two blocks, he saw an empty Lexus parked in a driveway, the engine idling, the driver's door open. The garage door also stood open. He cautiously approached, but no one was in the garage. The driver had apparently dashed back into the house.

Because the car faced the street, he slipped behind the wheel, dropped his trash bag on the passenger's seat, pulled the door shut and rolled out of the driveway, turning right, away from the boulevard.

At the corner, ignoring the stop sign, he turned right once more and went a third of a block before he heard a thin, shaky voice in the back seat say, 'What is your name, honey?'

A shrunken elderly man was slumped on the back seat. He wore Coke-bottle glasses, a hearing aid, and appeared to be a hundred years old.

'Oh, you're Debbie,' the old man said. 'Where are we going, Debbie?'

Crime led to more crime. Mitch himself had now become a kidnapper.

'Are we going to the pie store?' the old man enquired, a note of hope in his quavery voice. Maybe some Alzheimer's was happening here.

'Yes,' Mitch said, 'we're going to the pie store,' and he turned right again at the next corner.

'I like pie.'

'Everybody likes pie,' Mitch agreed.

If his heart had not been knocking hard enough to hurt, if his wife's life had not depended on his remaining free, if he had not expected to encounter roving police at any moment, he might have found this amusing. But it wasn't amusing; it was surreal.

'You aren't Debbie,' the old man said. 'I'm Norman, but you're not Debbie. Who are you?'

'I'm just a guy who made a mistake.'

Norman thought about that until Mitch turned right at the third corner, and then he said, 'You're gonna hurt me. That's what you're gonna do.'

The fear in the old man's voice inspired pity. 'No, no. Nobody is gonna hurt you.'

'You're gonna hurt me, you're a bad man.'

'No, I just made a mistake. I'm taking you right back home,' Mitch assured him.

'Where are we? This isn't home. We're nowhere near home.' The voice, suddenly gained volume and shrillness.

'Don't get yourself worked up. We're almost there.'

'You're a bad sonofabitch!'

At the fourth corner, Mitch turned right, onto the street where he'd stolen the car.

'You're a bad, bad sonofabitch!'

'Please, Norman. You're gonna give yourself a heart attack.'

He had hoped to be able to pull the car into the driveway and leave it where he'd found it. But a woman had come out of the house into the street. Fortysomething, slightly stout, she looked terrified. She must have thought that Norman had got behind the wheel.

'YOU'RE BAD, BAD, BAD . . . !'

Mitch stopped in the street near the woman, put the car in park, grabbed the trash bag and got out, leaving the door open behind him.

Forty something, slightly stout, she was an attractive woman with Rod Stewart hair that was streaked with blonde highlights. She wore a business suit and heels too high to be sensible for a trip to the pie store.

'Are you Debbie?' Mitch asked.

Bewildered, she said, 'Am I Debbie?'

Maybe there was no Debbie. Norman still shrieked in the car and Mitch said, 'I'm so sorry. Big mistake.'

He walked away from her and heard her say 'Grandpapa? Are you all right, Grandpapa?'

When he reached the stop sign, he turned and saw the woman leaning in the car, comforting the old man.

Mitch rounded the corner and hurried out of her line of sight.

A block later, as he reached the next corner, a horn blared behind him. The woman was pursuing him in the Lexus. He could see her through the windshield: one hand on the wheel, the other holding a cellphone. She was calling 911.

LEANING INTO the resistant wind, Mitch hurried along the sidewalk.

The determined driver in the Lexus stayed far enough back that she could hang a U-turn and elude him if he changed directions and sprinted towards her, but she maintained sight of him. He started to run and she accelerated to match his pace.

Evidently she intended to keep him located until the police arrived. Mitch admired her guts even though he wanted to shoot out her tyres.

The car horn blared, blared again, and then relentlessly. She hoped to alert her neighbours to the presence of a criminal in their midst.

Mitch left the sidewalk, crossed a yard, opened a gate and hurried round the side of a house, hoping he wouldn't find a pit bull in the back yard. The yard proved to be shallow, encircled by a seven-foot cedar fence with pointed staves. He didn't see a gate. After tying the twisted neck of the trash bag to his belt, he climbed into a coral tree, crossed the fence on a branch and dropped into an alley.

He passed through a vacant lot. As he was crossing the next street, a police car swept through the intersection. The shriek of its brakes told him that he had been seen.

Across a yard, over a fence, across an alley, through a gate, across another street, very fast now, the plastic bag slapping against his leg. He worried that it would split, spilling bricks of $100 bills.

The last line of houses backed up onto a small canyon. He scaled a wrought-iron fence and was at once at the top of a steep slope of loose soil. Gravity and sliding earth carried him down.

Like a surfer chasing along the face of a huge wave, he tried to stay upright, but his feet went out from under him, and he slid the last ten yards on his back, raising a wake of dust, then thrashed feet first through a sudden wall of tall grass and taller weeds.

He came to a stop under a canopy of branches. While he remained in the cover of the trees at the bottom of the canyon, no one could see him from the rim. So many branches of different trees interlaced that even the raging wind could not peel back the canopy and let the sunshine in. The light was green and watery. Shadows trembled, swayed like sea anemones.

Mitch untied the plastic trash bag from his belt. It had sustained a one-inch tear, but nothing seemed to have fallen out. He fashioned a loose temporary knot in the neck of the bag and carried it against his body, in the crook of his left arm. He walked alongside a shallow stream and a damp carpet of dead leaves cushioned his step.

Although the population of Orange County exceeded three million, the bottom of the canyon felt so remote that he might have been miles from civilisation. Until he heard the helicopter. He was surprised they were up in this wind.

Judging by sound alone, the chopper crossed the canyon directly over Mitch's head. It went north and circled the neighbourhood through which he'd made his run. They were searching for him from the air, but in the wrong place. They didn't know he'd descended into the canyon.

He kept moving—but then halted and cried out softly in surprise when Anson's phone rang. He pulled it from his pocket, relieved that he hadn't lost or damaged it.

'This is Mitch.'

Jimmy Null said, 'Are you feeling hopeful?'

'Yes. Let me talk to Holly.'

'You'll see her soon. I'm moving the meet from three to two o'clock.'

'You can't do that.'

'I just did it.'

'What time is it now?'

'One thirty,' Jimmy Null said.

'Hey, no, I can't make two o'clock.'

'Why not? Anson's place is only minutes from the Turnbridge house.'

'I'm not at Anson's place. Make it two thirty. I've got the money right here. A million four. I've got it with me.'

'Let me tell you something about the money.'

Mitch waited.

'I got money. There are things that mean more to me than money.'

Something was wrong. Mitch had felt it before, when talking to Holly. 'Listen,' he said. 'I've come so far, *we've* come so far, it's only right we finish this.'

'Two o'clock,' Null said. 'That's the new time. You aren't where you need to be at two sharp, it's over. No second chance.'

'All right.'

Jimmy Null terminated the call.

Mitch ran.

14

Chained to the gas pipe, Holly now knows what she must do, what she *will* do, and therefore she can pass her time only by worrying about all the ways things could go wrong or by marvelling at what she can see of the uncompleted mansion.

Thomas Turnbridge would have had one fantastic kitchen if he had lived. When all the equipment had been installed, a top-flight caterer with platoons of staff could have cooked and served a sit-down dinner for 600 on the terrace from here.

The creep returns. He has put on a grey windbreaker and a pair of thin, supple gloves.

She is sitting on the floor when he enters but she gets to her feet as he approaches her.

Violating her personal space, he stands as close to her as a man would just before taking her in his arms to dance. He places his right hand on her left shoulder and she is glad that it is gloved.

After a silence, he says, 'Mitch will be here in a little more than twenty minutes.'

Her heart races at this news, but her hope is tempered by fear.

'I'll go now to watch for him.' he tells her. 'He'll bring the money into this room—and then it will be time to decide.'

'In Espanola, your life will change again.'

'Profoundly,' he says. 'And perhaps not only my life.'

She closes her eyes and whispers, 'In Espanola, is there a woman with two white dogs, dogs that seem to vanish in the snow?'

'Is that what you see?'

'Dogs that seem to vanish in the snow.'

'I don't know. But if you see them, then I'm sure they must be in Espanola.'

'I see myself laughing with her, and the dogs so white.' She opens her eyes and meets his. 'You better go and watch for him.'

'Twenty minutes,' he promises, and leaves the kitchen.

Holly stands quite still for a moment, amazed by herself. White dogs, indeed. Where had that come from? She almost laughs now at his gullibility, but there is no humour in the fact that she has got inside his head deep enough to know what imagery will work with him.

The shakes seize her, and she sits down. Her hands are cold, and a chill traces every turn of her bowels. She reaches under her sweater, and extracts the nail from her bra. Although the nail is sharp, she wishes it were sharper. Using the head of the nail, she scratches industriously at the wall until she has produced a small pile of powdered plaster.

The time has come.

When Holly was a little girl, for a while she feared an array of night monsters born of a good imagination: in closet, under the bed, at the windows. Her grandmother, good Dorothy, had taught her a poem that, she claimed, would repel every monster. Years later, Holly learned that it was titled 'A Soldier—His Prayer'. It had been found on a slip of paper in a trench in Tunisia during the battle of El Agheila.

Quietly but aloud, she recites it now:

'Stay with me, God. The night is dark,
The night is cold: my little spark
Of courage dies. The night is long;
Be with me, God, and make me strong.'

She hesitates then, but only for a moment.

The time has come.

WITH SHOES CAKED with mud and wet leaves, clothes rumpled and dirty, a white trash bag cradled in his arms and pressed against his chest as if it were a precious baby, Mitch hurried along the shoulder of the highway.

No officer of the law, happening to drive past, would fail to give him special scrutiny. He had the look of a fugitive or a madman, or both.

Fifty yards ahead stood a combination service station and minimart.

He wondered if $10,000 cash would buy him a ride to the Turnbridge house. Probably not. A guy looking like a vagrant, waving around $10,000, wanting to buy a ride, would make the station manager nervous. He might call the cops.

Yet buying a ride seemed to be Mitch's only option, other than carjacking someone at gunpoint, which he would not do.

As he drew near the service station, a Cadillac Escalade angled off the highway and stopped at the outermost pumps. A tall blonde got out, clutching her bag, and strode into the minimart, leaving the driver's door open.

The two rows of pumps were both self-service. No attendants were in sight.

Mitch shambled up to the Escalade and peered through the open door. The keys were in the ignition. Leaning inside, he checked the back seat. No grandpapa, no child in a safety seat, no pit bull.

He climbed in behind the wheel, pulled the door shut, started the engine and drove onto the highway. Although he half expected people to run after him, waving their arms and shouting, the rearview mirror revealed no one.

He sped north a few hundred yards to a roundabout on the north–south highway and then headed south. When he passed the service station, no tall angry blonde had yet put in an appearance. He raced past.

By 1:56, he arrived in the neighbourhood where Turnbridge's folly stood incomplete. Out of sight of the mansion, he pulled in to the kerb.

Cursing its stubborn buttons, he stripped out of his shirt. Jimmy Null would most likely make him take it off anyway, to prove that he was not concealing a weapon. He had been told to come unarmed.

From the trash bag, he retrieved the box of .45 ammunition, and from a pocket of his jeans, he withdrew the original magazine for the Springfield Champion. He added three cartridges to the seven in the magazine.

A movie memory served him well. He pulled back the slide and inserted an eleventh round in the chamber.

The cartridges slipped in his sweaty, trembling fingers, so he had time to load only two of the three spare magazines. He stashed the box of ammo and the extra magazine under the driver's seat.

One minute to two o'clock.

He shoved the two loaded magazines in the pockets of his jeans, put the loaded pistol in the bag with the money, and drove to the Turnbridge place.

A long chain-link construction fence fitted with privacy panels of green plastic fabric separated the street from the big Turnbridge property. The gate was closed, draped with chain. It wasn't locked.

Mitch drove onto the property and parked with the back of the SUV facing the house. He got out and opened all five doors, hoping to express his desire to fulfill the terms of the agreement to the best of his ability.

He closed the construction gate and draped the chain in place once more.

Carrying the trash bag, he walked to a spot between the Escalade and the house, stopped, and waited. The day was warm, not hot, but the sun was hard. The light and the wind cut at his eyes.

Anson's cellphone rang.

He took the call. 'This is Mitch.'

Jimmy Null said, 'It's a minute past two. You're late.'

THE UNFINISHED HOUSE appeared as large as a hotel. Jimmy Null could have been watching Mitch from any of scores of windows.

'You were supposed to come in your Honda,' he said.

'It broke down.'

'Where'd you get the Escalade?'

'Stole it.'

'No shit. Park it parallel to the house, so I can see the front and back seats.'

Mitch did as told, leaving the doors of the vehicle open. He stepped away from the SUV and waited with the trash bag, the phone to his ear.

He wondered if Null would shoot him dead from a distance and come for the money. He wondered why he *wouldn't* do that.

'I'm disturbed you didn't come in the Honda.'

'I told you, it broke down.'

'A stolen car—the cops could have chased your ass here.'

'No one saw me take it.'

'Where'd you learn to hot-wire a car?'

'The keys were in the ignition.'

Null considered in silence. Then: 'Enter the house by the front door. Stay on the phone.'

Mitch saw that the door had been shot open. He went inside.

The entry hall was immense. Although no finish work had been done, even Julian Campbell would have been impressed.

After leaving Mitch to stew for a minute, Jimmy Null said, 'Pass through the colonnade into the living room directly ahead of you.'

Mitch went into the living room, where the west windows extended floor to ceiling. Even through dusty glass, the view was so stunning that he could understand why Turnbridge had wanted to die with it.

'All right. I'm here.'

'Turn left and cross the room,' Null directed. 'A wide doorway leads into a secondary drawing room. You'll see another wide doorway across from the one you're standing in, and a single door to your left.'

'Yes.'

'The single door leads to a hallway. The hall passes other rooms and leads to the kitchen. She's in the kitchen. But don't go near her.'

Moving across the drawing room towards the specified doorway, Mitch said, 'Why not?'

'Because I'm making the rules. You stop just inside the kitchen.'

The hallway seemed to recede from him the further he followed it, but he knew the telescoping effect had to be psychological. He was frantic to see Holly.

When Mitch entered the kitchen, he saw her at once, and his heart swelled. Everything that he had been through, every terrible thing that he had done, was in that instant all worth while.

BECAUSE THE CREEP arrives in the kitchen to stand beside her during the last of his phone conversation, Holly hears him give the final directions.

She holds her breath, listening for footsteps. When she hears Mitch approaching, hot tears threaten, but she blinks them back.

A moment later Mitch enters the room. He says her name so tenderly. Her husband.

She has been standing with her arms folded across her chest, her hands hidden under her armpits. Now she lowers her arms and stands with her hands fisted at her sides.

The creep, who has drawn a wicked-looking pistol, is intently focused on Mitch. 'Arms straight out like a bird.'

Mitch obeys, a white trash bag dangling from his right hand.

His clothes are filthy. His hair is windblown. His face has lost all colour. He is beautiful. Covering Mitch with the pistol, the killer says, 'Come slowly forward.'

As instructed, Mitch approaches, and the creep tells him to stop fifteen feet away. 'Put the bag on the floor and kneel in front of it. I want to see the money.'

Mitch lowers the bag to the dusty limestone and gets to his knees.

Holly doesn't like to see Mitch kneeling. This is the position that executioners instruct their victims to take before the *coup de grâce*.

She must act, but the time feels not quite right. Instinct tells her to wait, though waiting is so hard.

'Show me the money,' the killer says, and he has a two-hand grip on the pistol, finger tightened on the trigger.

Mitch opens the neck of the bag and withdraws a plastic-wrapped brick of cash. He tears off one end of the plastic, and riffles the $100 bills with his thumb.

'The bearer bonds?' the killer asks.

Mitch drops the cash into the sack.

The creep tenses, thrusting the pistol forward as Mitch reaches into the white bag again. Mitch produces a large envelope and extracts half a dozen official-looking certificates. He holds one out for the killer to read.

'All right. Put them back in the envelope.'

Mitch obeys, still on his knees.

'Mitch, if your wife had a chance for previously undreamed-of personal fulfilment, the opportunity for enlightenment, for *transcendence*, surely you would want her to follow that better destiny?'

Bewildered by this turn, Mitch does not know what to say, but Holly does. The time has come.

She says, 'I've been sent a sign, my future is New Mexico.'

Raising her hands from her sides, opening her fists, she reveals her bloody wounds.

An involuntary cry escapes Mitch. The killer glances at Holly, and seeing her stigmata is astonished and distracted for one critical moment.

Holly has stabbed herself and worked the wounds with brutal determination. The worst had been having to bite back every cry of pain.

At once, her palms had bled too much. She had packed them with powdered plaster to stop the bleeding. Then, with her hands fisted in her armpits, as Mitch entered the room, Holly had clawed the plugs of plaster from the wounds, opening them.

Now, with her left hand, she pulls down the neck of her sweater. The killer's gaze rises from her cleavage to her eyes. She slips her right hand between her breasts to grabs the nail, and fears not being able to hold it in her slippery fingers.

The killer glances at Mitch.

She grips the nail well enough now, reveals it and rams it into the killer's face, going for his eye, but instead pinning his mask to him, piercing the hollow of his cheek. Screaming, he reels back from her and his pistol fires wildly, bullets thudding into walls.

She sees Mitch rising and moving fast, with a gun of his own.

MITCH SHOUTED, '*Holly, move!*' and she was moving on the first syllable of *Holly*, separating herself from Jimmy Null as much as her chain allowed.

Point-blank, aiming abdomen, hitting chest, pulling down from the recoil, firing again, pulling down, firing, firing, he thought a couple of shots went wide, but saw three or four rounds tearing into the windbreaker, each roar so big, booming through the big house.

Null reeled backwards, off balance. His pistol seemed to be fully automatic. Bullets stitched a wall, part of the ceiling.

Because he now had only a one-hand grip on the weapon, and the recoil tore it from him, it flew. The gun hit the wall, clattered to the limestone.

Driven backwards by the impact of the .45s, rocked on his heels, Null staggered, dropped on his side, rolled onto his face.

When the echoes of the echoes of the gunfire fading, Mitch could hear Jimmy Null's ragged wheezing. He wasn't proud of what he did next. In fact he almost didn't do it, but he knew that 'almost' would buy no dispensation when the time came to reckon for the way he had lived his life.

He stepped over the wheezing man and shot him twice in the back. He had expended all eleven rounds in the pistol.

Having crouched defensively during the gunfire, Holly rose to meet Mitch as he turned to her.

'Anyone else?' he asked.

'Just him, just him.' She threw her arms round him. He had never before been held so tight, or with such sweet ferocity.

'Your hands,' he murmured.

'They're OK, you're alive, they're OK.'

He kissed every part of her face. Her mouth, her eyes, her brow, her eyes again, salty now with tears, her mouth.

The room stank of gunfire, a dead man lay on the floor, Holly was bleeding, and Mitch's legs felt weak. He wanted fresh air, the brisk wind, sunshine to kiss her in. 'Let's get out of here.'

'The chain. He has the key.'

Crouching beside the body, Mitch withdrew a spare magazine from a pocket of his jeans. He ejected the spent clip, replaced it with the fresh.

Pressing the muzzle against the back of the kidnapper's head, just in case, he searched the side pockets of the windbreaker with his free hand until he found the key.

The chain fell away from her wrist as the dropped padlock rapped the limestone floor.

'Your hands,' he said, 'your beautiful hands.'

The sight of her blood pierced him, and he thought of the staged scene in their kitchen, the bloody hand prints, but this was worse, so much worse to see her bleeding.

'What happened to your hands?'

'New Mexico. I'll explain. Let's get out of here.'

He snatched the bag of ransom off the floor. She started towards a doorway, but he led her to the entrance off the hall, which was the only route he knew. They walked with her right arm round his shoulders and his left arm round her waist, past empty rooms. The hall was long and when they reached the drawing room they could not help looking towards the vast, dust-filmed view.

As they stepped through to the living room, an engine roared to life elsewhere in the house. The racket rattled through every room and chattered off the high ceilings, making it impossible to determine where it originated.

'Motorcycle,' she said.

'Bulletproof,' Mitch said. 'A vest under the windbreaker.'

The impact of the slugs, especially the two in the back, jarring the spine, must have knocked Jimmy Null briefly unconscious. He had not intended to leave in the van that he'd driven here. Having stashed a motorcycle near the kitchen, perhaps in the breakfast room, he'd been prepared to flee—if things went wrong—through any wing of the house, any door.

As the clatter of the engine swelled, Mitch knew that Jimmy was not intent on fleeing. It wasn't the ransom that drew him, either. Whatever had happened between him and Holly—New Mexico and two white dogs and bloody stigmata—all *that* drew him, and he was drawn, too, by the humiliation of the nail in the face. For the nail, he wanted Holly dead.

Logic suggested that he was at their backs and would come from the drawing room.

Mitch hurried Holly across the enormous living room, towards the equally huge entry hall and the front door beyond.

Logic failed. They had crossed less than half the room when Jimmy Null shot out of somewhere on a Kawasaki, bulleting along the colonnade that separated them from the drawing room.

Mitch drew Holly back as Null steered between columns into the living room. He made a wide turn out there and came straight at them, gaining speed, wild with rage.

Shoving Holly behind him, Mitch raised the Champion in both hands and opened fire.

Aiming chest this time, hoping for head. Fifty feet and closing, thunder crashing off walls. First shot high, pull it down, second, *pull it down,* thirty feet and closing, third shot. *PULL IT DOWN!* The fourth turned off Jimmy Null's brain so abruptly, his hands sprang away from the handlebars.

The dead man stopped, the cycle did not, rearing on its back wheel, screaming forward until it toppled, tumbled towards them, past them, hit one of the big windows, and shattered through, gone.

Be sure. Evil has cockroach endurance, Mitch thought to himself. Be sure, be sure. The Champion in both hands, he approached the dead man. No hurry now, circle him. Take nothing for granted.

Mitch peeled up the mask to see the face, but it wasn't a face any more.

They were done.

IN THE SUMMER that Anthony is three years old, they celebrate Mitch's thirty-second birthday with a back-yard party.

Big Green owns three trucks now, and there are five employees besides Iggy Barnes. They all come with their wives and kids, and Iggy brings a woman named Madelaine.

Holly has made good friends—as she always does—at the real-estate agency where she is second in sales so far this year.

Although Dorothy followed Anthony by just twelve months, they have not moved to a bigger house. Holly was raised here; this house is her history. Besides, already they have made quite a history here together.

Detective Taggart comes with his wife, Jennifer, and their two daughters. He brings the day's newspaper, wondering if Mitch has seen the story: Julian Campbell, between conviction and appeal, throat slit in prison—a contract hit suspected.

Although Anson is in a different prison, it will give him something to ponder as his attorneys work to stave off his own lethal injection.

Mitch's youngest sister, Portia, comes to the party all the way from Birmingham, Alabama, with her husband Frank and their five children. Megan and Connie remain distant in more than one sense, but Mitch and Portia have grown close, and he entertains hope of finding a way to gather his other two sisters to him, in time.

On this birthday evening, they eat a feast at tables on the patio and lawn, and Anthony sits proudly on his special chair. Mitch built it for him to a design sketched by Holly, and she painted it a cheerful red.

After dinner, there is a portable dance floor on the lawn, and the band is not as woofy as the one at their wedding. No tambourines and no accordion.

Later, much later, when the band has departed and all the guests are gone, when Anthony and Dorothy are sound asleep on the back-porch swing-seat, Mitch asks Holly to dance to the music of a radio, now that they have the entire floor to themselves. He holds her close but not too tight. As they dance, husband and wife, she puts a hand to his face, as though after all this time she is still amazed that he brought her home to him. He kisses the scar in the palm of her hand, and then the scar in the other. Under a great canopy of stars, in the moonlight, she is so lovely that words fail him. She is as mysterious as she is lovely, an eternal depth in her eyes, but she is no more mysterious than the stars and the moon and all things on the earth.

DEAN KOONTZ

Born: Pennsylvania, July 9, 1945
First job: tutor to underprivileged children
Fiction works currently in print: 55

RD: You're quite a workaholic when it comes to writing, putting in very long hours and painstakingly reworking each page before you're happy with it. Does that perfectionism show itself in any other areas of your life?

DK: Like any human being, I am incapable of perfection in anything. But in clothes, I favour pressed jeans with a crease, and classic Hawaiian shirts. To feel fresh, I change shirts three times a day. If you look in my sock drawer, however, chaos reigns.

RD: Gerda, your wife, has been your lifelong sweetheart. Can you give any tips on how to achieve a long and happy marriage?

DK: Marry someone with your sense of humour. I have an appreciation for the absurd, and Gerda has a sharp eye for the preposterous, so we laugh a lot. Because I can sometimes be singularly preposterous, she has more laughs than I do. Our rare arguments never last more than moments because the recognition of our foolishness reduces us quickly to giggles.

RD: What qualities should any husband aim to bring to a marriage?

DK: Cherish her as a child of God. If you truly married for love, then it was not merely her looks or personality that enchanted you, but her unique soul. If you remember that the essence of her is sacred, you will treat her with respect and have a sense of awe at the destiny that brought you together.

RD: You've spoken of your belief in an individual's power to overcome any kind of hardship or setback, and this optimism is always reflected in your books. Do you feel equally optimistic about mankind's future?

DK: I have seen evil win in the short run but never in the long run. Political passion (a poor substitute for personal responsibility), combined with utopian thinking (which gave us mass murderers like Hitler and Stalin), will do more damage, but I have confidence that a lot of good people will refuse to run with the panicked herd.

RD: Your dog, Trixie [pictured right], seems as close to you as a member of your own family. Can you tell our readers a bit more about why you admire the canine race, and Trixie in particular?

DK: Dogs have beauty without vanity, strength without arrogance, unconscious grace, and are without envy. They give unconditional love. When they see us in our underwear, they do not laugh. Trixie, a golden retriever, was once a service dog for a young disabled woman who lost both legs. Then Trixie needed elbow surgery and had to retire. She came to us when she was three, eight years ago. She is calm, sweet, dignified yet something of a clown. We love her as if she were a child.

RD: Your home in California must be quite amazing. Can you tell us about any of the comforts or luxuries that you particularly enjoy?

DK: We have a large pool in which we enjoy playing with Trixie, who has webbed feet and is a terrific swimmer. I have an arcade with old pinball machines and early video games like Ms Pac Man, which Trixie finds boring. Our library exceeds 50,000 volumes. We built a home theatre that seats twenty-two, and no sooner was it finished than the film industry stopped making movies we wanted to see.

RD: Is there anywhere else in America—or the world—that you'd like to live?

DK: Newport Beach, California, to which we moved fifteen years ago, is the first place that Gerda and I have ever felt at home. I feel deeper rooted here than the 100-year-old oak in our backyard.

RD: Have you ever visited the UK and what did you think of it?

DK: Because I work long hours and seldom fly, we've not been to the UK, though it is the one place I regret not having visited. It is the home of the mother tongue, after all, and my life is language. We do intend to come . . .

RD: On a lighter note, what three things would you have to take along with you to a desert island for a prolonged stay?

DK: Gerda, Trixie, and all 50,000 books in our library.

RD: And, finally, if you could invite four famous people, dead or alive, to dine with you, who would you chose?

DK: Albert Einstein because he believed in science not scientism. T. S. Eliot because I find his language beautiful and condensed, dense with meaning, yet so accessible. C.S. Lewis because I am in awe of the rigorous logic he brought to philosophical and spiritual matters. Cary Grant because I agree with the film historian David Thomson that he was the most natural performer and the finest actor in the history of the screen.

STEPHEN BOOTH

SCARED TO LIVE

On the very same night that the Peak District village of Foxlow is disturbed by a house fire, reports reach DS Diane Fry and DC Ben Cooper of the shocking murder of an elderly woman in a house close by. Can the two crimes be linked? As the search for answers takes their enquiries beyond Derbyshire to the other side of Europe, the detectives are faced with a startling revelation.

1

Sunday, October 23

Even on the night she died, Rose Shepherd couldn't sleep. By the early hours of the morning, her bed was like a battleground—hot, violent, chaotic. Beneath her, the sheet was twisted into painful knots, the pillow hard and unyielding. Lack of sleep made her head ache, and her body had grown stiff with discomfort.

But sleeplessness was familiar to Miss Shepherd. She often spent the hours of darkness waiting for the first bird to sing, watching for the greyness of dawn, when she knew there'd be people moving about in the village. There might be the sound of a van in the street as someone headed off for an early shift at the quarry, or the rumble of a tractor in the field behind the house. She didn't feel so completely alone then.

For Rose Shepherd, this was the world. A distant noise from beyond her electronic gates, a half-heard voice, a snatched moment of indirect contact. Her life had become so confined that she seemed to be living in a small, dark box. The tiniest crack of light was like a glimpse of God.

At two o'clock, she got up to fetch herself a glass of water. She stood in the middle of the bedroom while she drank it, allowing her toes to curl deep into the sheepskin rug, clutching at the comfort of its softness.

As always, her mind had been running over the events of the day. It was as if she had a video player in her head, showing the same scenes over and over again. If they weren't from the day just past, they were from previous days—some of them years before, in a different part of her life. The scenes played themselves out, and paused to allow her to fret about whether she could have done things differently. Then they began again, stalking backwards and forwards in her consciousness like restless feral animals.

But Rose was glad that she'd been out the previous day. No journey was without its risks, even if it was only the three miles into the village of Matlock Bath. Despite a diversion to the shopping village, she'd arrived too early, and had time to kill once she'd parked the Volvo.

Matlock Bath had been busy, as she ought to have known it would be. At first, she'd been disturbed by the number of people on North Parade, and nervous of the motorcyclists in their leathers, clustered by their bikes eating fish and chips out of paper wrappings.

She could smell those fish and chips, even now. The odour was so powerful that for a moment she had no idea where she was. Time and place began to blur, a street in a Derbyshire tourist village merging into an image of a deserted roadside with the smell of gunfire in the air, then whirling back to her bedroom. Feeling giddy, Rose sat down in a chair by the window.

No, no, she was wrong. It was a bad mistake she'd made yesterday. But she hadn't been able to avoid it. There was no other way out.

Rose breathed deeply, trying to control the dizziness. For a moment, it had been just as if those motorcyclists had entered her bedroom. She could hear the creak of their black leathers, the thud of their heavy boots.

The bikers had been irrelevant, though. Waiting in Matlock Bath, Rose's first impressions had been the steepness of the hills above her, the denseness of the trees, the roofs of houses perched among them in apparently impossible places. Soon a sense of her vulnerability had become too strong, and she had to get off the street, to find somewhere she could feel safer.

So Rose had paid her money to enter the aquarium, and for a while she'd watched children feeding carp in the thermal pool, knowing it was dangerous. But perhaps people were too wrapped up in their own interests to notice her nervousness.

She thought about taking some more of her herbal tablets. But she knew they wouldn't make any difference. Not now.

Her doctor knew about her anxiety and insomnia problems. She'd gone to him out of desperation, breaking her own rules. But he hadn't been able to help her. He'd never understood why she wouldn't continue taking the sleeping pills he gave her. He couldn't possibly have known that she was even more frightened of never waking up than of not being able to sleep.

Rose had always known she'd be killed. Well, it felt like always. She expected to meet her death that way because of the way she'd led her life. It was a question of when it would happen, and how.

She lived every day in fear of a phone call, a knock on the door, the smashing of glass in the middle of the night. Every time she left the house, she expected not to return. Whenever she looked through the window, she was surprised not to see dark figures in the garden, watching her house. For a long time now, she'd considered it more difficult to live than to die.

Rose smoothed out her sheets, turned over her pillows and went back to bed. Ten minutes later, she was hovering on the edge of consciousness when a black Mitsubishi Shogun with tinted windows stopped outside her gate.

LEAVING THROUGH the back door of a cottage on the corner of Pinfold Lane, Darren Turnbull saw the black car as it drew away from Bain House. He stepped back into the shadows, wishing that Stella wouldn't insist on having the security light. He had to walk through its glare to reach the lane by the church. Stella sometimes talked of him leaving her house like a thief in the night. With that bloody light, he was more like an actor stepping onto a stage.

Darren watched the vehicle coming back towards him from the corner. He was slightly puzzled by its speed. Most drivers would whizz through a place like Foxlow in seconds at this time, when there was no one around.

It was some kind of four-wheel-drive job. A big one, probably Japanese. Darren liked black cars and this one had tinted windows, too. That was cool. He could barely distinguish the outline of a driver as the car passed under a streetlamp near the phone box.

Finally, the car had gone, and Darren began to make his way to the back gate. His blue Astra was parked under the trees on Church Walk. No street-lamps here, just the old church and its graveyard somewhere in the darkness. Darren shuddered. He'd been scared silly of these places when he was a kid, and even now they gave him the creeps. Why Stella had decided to move here when she got divorced, he had no idea. It wouldn't suit him at all.

He grinned to himself as he got into his Astra. A visit to Stella was always worth while, he had to admit. As long as no one found out, of course—especially Fiona. She'd murder him for sure.

Darren shivered again as he drove out onto the street. But this time it was nothing to do with his superstitions. Foxlow suddenly felt very cold.

A FEW MINUTES LATER, the Shogun had turned at the top of High Street and was being driven fast down Butcher's Hill. Its headlights were on full beam, and anyone coming in the opposite direction would be too dazzled to see the vehicle's model or colour, let alone its driver. In a burst of sodium light, it would be gone as soon as it appeared.

When it reached the bottom of the hill, the Shogun slowed to a halt. It idled for a moment in the road, with its front windows half open. Then the driver rammed his foot on the accelerator, and the car surged off the road through an open gateway to the right. With its four-wheel drive engaged, the vehicle growled towards the top corner of the field, where it turned and coasted along the back gardens of the houses in Pinfold Lane.

Finally, the headlights died and the Shogun rolled in darkness. There was silence for a moment, then the whirr of a window lowering, the creak of seat leather as a body shifted position, the slow, careful scrape of metal, and then a final click. From a position behind the driver's seat came a green glow and a faint electronic beeping.

A hundred yards away, in Rose Shepherd's house, the clock was softly chiming three as the bedside phone began to ring.

2

Monday, October 24

Detective Sergeant Diane Fry pushed at the half-open door and stepped carefully past the yellow tape. In the hallway, she had to squeeze past a child's bike, and almost tripped over two bulging bin liners full of clothes, ready to go to the charity shop. The smell in the house was overpowering, despite a cold draught blowing in from the broken windows.

'Home, sweet home,' said a voice behind her. Detective Constable Gavin Murfin leaned on the front door, forcing it back against the bin liners with an ominous creak of hinges and a popping of plastic.

'I hope you remembered to wipe your feet, Diane,' he said. 'We wouldn't want to ruin the decor.'

Fry felt her shoulders stiffen. 'Shut up for a bit, Gavin, will you?' The moment she'd entered this house in Darwin Street, her skin had begun to feel prickly, the nerve endings screaming in sympathy with the dead.

Murfin sniffed, and rustled the empty sweet wrappers in his pocket. Fry did her best to ignore him. Everyone dealt with these things in their own way, of course. Murfin's instinct was to retreat behind a flippant façade. For Fry, the urge was to focus on the small details that could so easily be missed.

The first thing she needed to know was how much evidence had been interfered with. She could see at a glance that someone had disturbed the opened post on the hall table, where it lay in a pool of dirty water. She poked at the envelopes with a finger. One of them seemed to be a packet of photographs back from the printers, and another was a BT phone bill.

Surrounded by the remains of a family's day-to-day existence, Fry paused for a moment, listening to the slow drip of water from a ceiling. Her eyes drifted across the muddy carpet to the walls, scratched and gouged by passing equipment—hose reels, breathing apparatus, stretchers.

'Ugh. The *Marie Celeste*, with extra charcoal.'

Fry lacked the energy to answer Murfin this time. It was too early in the morning, and she was too depressed at having been on call when this came in. Derbyshire's E Division didn't catch an incident like this more than once every ten years. Of course, Edendale had house fires like anywhere else, but it was bad luck when someone died in one. Today was unlucky all round.

Fry tried to tune down her senses as she followed the stepping plates towards the tape that marked the inner cordon. At the foot of the stairs she turned right into the sitting room. Judging by what the neighbours reported, the occupants of 32 Darwin Street had been taken by surprise. Six weeks ago, Lindsay Mullen had ordered a new carpet for her lounge. It had a deep, thick pile, and it was a shade of cream Lindsay had always wanted, but her husband insisted wasn't practical. It would show up the dirt, he'd said. It was a shameful waste of money.

Royal Wilton in camomile, that was it. According to the uniforms who'd taken initial statements, the lady in the house to the left had heard the entire argument as Brian Mullen left for work one morning.

The carpet was black now, and trampled with charred debris. Dozens of boot prints had sunk into two inches of filthy sludge.

The problem was, the bottom edge of the door into the kitchen had sealed so tightly against the new Wilton that there was no gap for air to get through. If only a few wisps of it had seeped into the kitchen, they might have reached the smoke alarm, and the outcome could have been different.

'They never stood a bloody chance, did they?' said Murfin.

Fry glanced at him. His flippancy was gone, and he was sweating a little despite the draught stirring the curtains behind him.

'They say it's better to die of smoke inhalation than burn to death, anyway,' she said, though she didn't expect it to help.

She looked away from Murfin before he could distract her concentration. This room had been packed with plastics, too—TV, video recorder, racks of CDs and DVDs, boxes full of children's toys under a shelf in the corner.

Most of the toys were just a molten mess, multicoloured pools of lava that had run onto the carpet and congealed in the spray from the firemen's hoses. There were recognisable shapes here and there—the twisted controls of a PlayStation console, the burnt edge of a Monopoly game. The head and one arm of a Barbie doll waved from a skin-toned puddle. Something scorched and wooden gazed accusingly at her from blackened eyes.

Of course, the untreated polyurethane foam in the furniture had been the real problem. If Lindsay Mullen had spent her money replacing the cheap sofa instead of the carpet, her children might still be alive.

When she walked through to the kitchen, Fry found it almost pristine, apart from a few muddy footprints on the vinyl flooring. From the condition of the teak-effect units and the white painted walls, she would never have guessed there had been a fire at all.

'Do you want to have a look upstairs?' called Murfin, without enthusiasm.

'Yes, in a minute.'

Fry took a last look at the kitchen, with its silent smoke alarm. She noticed that the cooker was new, too. A Smeg dual-fuel with air-cooling system. A thousand pounds or so, she guessed. Money wasn't all that short in the Mullen household, after all.

She went back through the sitting room and joined Murfin at the foot of the stairs. She wasn't sure that she needed to visit the bedrooms. If a crime had been committed, the evidence would be found here on the ground floor. But Murfin was hauling himself up the stairs; Fry had no choice but to follow.

In a way, the bedrooms weren't quite so bad. It was clear that the flames hadn't reached here, though the furniture was covered by a layer of soot. The covers of the beds had been pulled back, revealing clean, unmarked sheets. The first room she saw might simply have been waiting for Lindsay Mullen to come home and clean up the mess. Apart from the markers where her body had lain when she collapsed from smoke inhalation, of course.

'Next room, Gavin,' she said.

'That's the kids' bedroom.'

'I know that.'

Jack and Liam Mullen had died without leaving their beds, according to the incident reports. They must have woken up choking, and died calling for their mum. The house would have been so full of smoke by then that the boys could never have made it to the stairs, let alone through the flames in the hall. Still, their bedroom wasn't a pleasant place to be. Murfin, a family man with children of his own, wouldn't even come inside the door.

Of course, the vast majority of house fires were tragic accidents. Faulty wiring, a fag down the back of the sofa, clothes left too near an electric heater. But sudden deaths went automatically to CID, as firefighters on the scene had other priorities than looking for a cause. Fry would only have further involvement if there was evidence of suspicious circumstances.

She heard a rustle and a cough, and turned to find a uniformed PC standing at the bottom of the stairs. He held his helmet in one hand as he wiped the sweat from his forehead with the other.

'DS Fry?' he said. 'I thought you ought to know straight away—'

'What is it?'

'We've been talking to the neighbours again. We ought to have found out earlier, but you know what it's like: everyone is in shock when a thing like this happens. The lady next door says it's only just occurred to her—'

'Out with it, for heaven's sake.'

He turned the brim of his helmet in his fingers. 'Well, it seems there were three children living at this address. A daughter, as well as the two boys.'

Fry glanced back at the closed door at the end of the landing, a third bedroom she hadn't entered. But the firefighters must have checked it, surely?

'The daughter could be away from home,' she said. 'Staying over with friends for the night or something. What age is she?'

The officer swallowed. 'About eighteen months old.'

Fry bit her lip. Her eyes were drawn past the PC to the two bin liners near the front door. One of the bags had split when Murfin pushed the door against it, and the skirt of a blue Baby Gap denim dress protruded from the rip.

'Where's the husband now?' she asked.

'Edendale General,' said the PC. 'He suffered minor burns and smoke inhalation trying to get into the house.'

'Did you say "trying to get in"?'

'Yes. He wasn't at home when the fire started. Didn't they tell you?'

'There seem to be a lot of things that no one's telling me,' said Fry. 'Has everyone around here taken a vow of silence, or what?'

Postman Bernie Wilding was already late with his deliveries in Foxlow that morning when he remembered the package for Rose Shepherd. That was unusual in itself—Miss Shepherd rarely got more than bank statements and junk mail. Most days, there was nothing in his van for her at all.

He did a three-point turn at the end of Pinfold Lane and drew up to the wrought-iron gates of Bain House. He lowered the window and reached out to press the button on the intercom, but got no answering voice. That was odd, too. Folk in the village said that Miss Shepherd never went anywhere, that she was a bit of a hermit, shut up alone here in this big house. And she'd never been out before when he'd called with a package. But he supposed even a hermit must do her shopping some time, visit the doctor or the dentist. Well, it was nothing to do with him, anyway.

Bernie scribbled a message on one of his cards, and was about to push it into the letterbox mounted on one of the gates. But when he opened the flap, he saw that a furniture store leaflet was still in there, along with a free newspaper delivered over the weekend. And that definitely wasn't like Miss Shepherd. She always emptied the letterbox—a sensible thing to do, otherwise it gave the impression there was no one at home.

Uncertain what to do, Bernie peered through the gates at the house. The curtains were drawn at the front, even on the ground floor. You wouldn't leave the curtains drawn during the day, unless you were sick, would you?

Bernie liked to think of himself as an old-fashioned rural postman, who knew his patch and the people he delivered to. He'd heard many stories about a postman being the first to raise the alarm when someone was ill or dead and even the neighbours hadn't noticed. It had never happened to him, not in fifteen years with the Royal Mail, but you never knew, did you?

The ten o'clock news bulletin was starting on Radio Two. Bernie knew he ought to get on—he'd already lost enough time this morning, with having so many special deliveries to make, and getting stuck behind a tractor, which overtook him every time he stopped. Miss Shepherd was probably out doing her shopping in Matlock. She'd just forgotten to empty the post from her box for once.

Bernie pushed his card through the flap, then reversed his van into the road and headed back through Foxlow.

DETECTIVE CONSTABLE Ben Cooper opened his fridge door, then closed it again quickly when he caught the smell. Another thirty seconds of breathing that in, and he'd lose his appetite for breakfast.

'Well, do you want me to call in and see the solicitor again tomorrow morning?' he said into his mobile phone. 'I can manage that, if you like, Matt. But I'm not sure it'll do any good.'

'He wants a kick up the pants, that's what'll do him some good. Maybe I ought to go in and see him myself. What do you reckon? I'll go straight into his office when I've finished the muck-spreading tomorrow.'

Cooper smiled at the thought of his brother bursting into the offices of Ballard and Price, his overalls covered in slurry.

'It wouldn't help, you know.'

Matt sighed in frustration. 'Bloody pen-pushers and bureaucrats. They seem to spend their time making life difficult for everyone else.'

'I suppose Mr Ballard has a job to do, like the rest of us.'

'Oh, yeah. He takes a lot longer about it, that's all.'

Cooper ran a finger round the fridge door, checking the rubber seal for gaps. 'I don't know what else I can do. You're the executor, Matt.'

'I hadn't forgotten.'

Of course, he knew what was bothering his brother. Probate on their mother's will was taking so long that he was starting to get worried about the future of Bridge End Farm. If money had to be found from the estate, the only way it could happen would be if assets were sold off.

Cooper left the fridge alone and crossed the kitchen, dodging the cat, which was sitting looking at him expectantly. 'Besides,' he said, 'don't forget how much Mr Ballard charges for his time.'

'You're right, Ben. Just a phone call then, I suppose.'

'At least it'll keep the subject fresh in his mind.'

There was silence for a few moments. The Cooper brothers had always been comfortable with silence, but today it felt awkward and wrong.

'Is there something else, Matt?'

'Yeah . . .'

Ben felt his stomach tighten. There surely couldn't be more bad news already. 'What is it? Something wrong with one of the girls?'

'No, they're fine,' said Matt. 'Well, I think so.'

'You're not making much sense, Matt.'

'Look, Ben, I've made an appointment to talk to Dr Joyce. And if necessary, I'll ask to see the specialist who treated Mum.'

'Why? We know what happened to her—it was a series of strokes. It happens all the time in people of her age.'

'I don't mean the strokes. I mean the other problem.'

The family had rarely referred to Isabel Cooper's condition by name. For a long time, it had been 'Mum's problem'. Towards the end, before she died in Edendale District General from a brain haemorrhage, it became 'the other problem'. Now, it seemed to Ben, there was no point in not spelling it out.

'Oh, the schizophrenia. I don't understand, Matt. What do you want to find out that we don't already know?'

'I can't talk to you about it on the phone—it's too complicated. Can you come over some time? I've got a lot of stuff to show you.'

'Well, all right. What if I call at the farm tonight when I come off duty?'

'That'll do.'

'See you, then.'

Cooper put out a bowl of cat food and placed it in the conservatory. Then he went back to the fridge, took a deep breath and eased open the door. He scooped out some rotten tomatoes, a liquefied lettuce, half a carton of sour milk, and a wedge of Stilton with its blue veins blossoming into a furry carpet. They all went into a plastic bin liner, which he tied up. He closed the fridge, put the bag near the back door, then put on his jacket and left the flat. For once, even the smell of the morning traffic was like a breath of fresh air.

He was unsettled by his conversation with Matt. He hoped his brother wasn't having to cope with too many worries at once. There were certainly some decisions to be made about the future of Bridge End, though. The new farming support payments favoured the more productive farms in the valleys, and an upland farmer's income could be halved unless he changed his ways. The suckler herd might have to go, for a start—grazing cattle were becoming as economically unviable as sheep.

On his way through the market square, Cooper pulled out his mobile and chose a number from his phone book. His call was answered straight away.

'Hi, it's me. How are you this morning?'

She sounded pleased to hear from him, and the sound of her voice alone made him feel better.

'Oh, I'm fine, too,' he said. 'I just wanted to find out how you were.'

He listened to her talk for a while, and it put a smile on his face as he walked towards E Division's offices in West Street.

EDENDALE DISTRICT GENERAL was on the northern edge of town, and even at this time of the morning it would take fifteen minutes to get there from Darwin Street, Diane Fry reckoned as she stood by her car.

'We should have made sure we had complete information before we came out,' she said, when Murfin came off the radio to the control room.

Murfin looked aggrieved. '*You* wanted to get the job out of the way as soon as possible. Turn it over to the coroner, that's what *you* said.'

'OK, Gavin, thanks.' Fry didn't like her words being quoted back to her, especially when she'd been wrong. 'It's a bit irritating, that's all.'

'Is that why you made me look in that last bedroom?'

She sighed. 'It had to be done, Gavin. You aren't here just to wreck the place and make stupid jokes. There was nothing in the bedroom, anyway.'

'You didn't know that at the time.'

'Right. How come the hospital staff have more information than we do? So the youngest child wasn't even at home. It shouldn't have needed a call to the ward sister to find out she was with her grandparents.'

Murfin was silent as he watched her get into her car. 'You know I've got kids of my own, don't you?' he said quietly, before she closed the door.

Fry bit her lip, caught out by a moment of tricky human emotion when she hadn't expected it. 'Sorry, Gavin.'

But he didn't seem to have heard her as he walked away. And by the time she caught up with him later, he was back to his old self.

BRIAN MULLEN was in a side room off one of the newer wards, with a PC on duty outside the door. Mullen was in his early thirties, sandy-haired, with a faintly pink complexion, as if his skin had been freshly scrubbed. His hands were bandaged, but otherwise he looked quite fit and healthy.

He was also sedated and deeply asleep.

'Naturally, he was in a very distressed condition when he was admitted,' said the ward sister. 'Apart from his physical injuries.'

'But otherwise he'll be well enough to be interviewed later?' asked Fry.

'You'll have to get permission from the doctor.'

Fry nodded. 'I need to know as soon as he's fit to answer questions, Sister.'

'Well, I hope we have less trouble with the patient when he wakes up. He almost injured one of my nurses when we had to sedate him earlier.'

Fry had been about to leave the ward, but she stopped halfway through the swing doors. 'What do you mean, you *had* to sedate him?'

'He was completely wild, shouting that he couldn't stay here, he had to get out. He was in a dreadful state.'

'He must have wanted to go back to his house. He knew his family were trapped in the fire.'

'Probably you're right . . .' The sister hesitated, sounding doubtful. 'I suppose it's not my place to say this, but that wasn't the way it seemed. If you'd asked me at the time, I would have said he was frightened.'

'Frightened?' Fry glanced at Brian Mullen, lying motionless in his bed. 'Well, whatever it was, he'll have forgotten it when he wakes up, won't he?'

'Not necessarily. It's his brain and body that are sedated. Deep-rooted fears are in the subconscious. And the subconscious never sleeps.'

COMING UP BEHIND the tractor again, Bernie Wilding had to slow down on the road between Foxlow and Bonsall. But the tractor driver pulled into a lay-by to let him pass, and the postman saw that it was Neville Cross, who owned Yew Tree Farm. His land ran right up to Rose Shepherd's garden.

Bernie slowed to a halt alongside the tractor and tapped his horn to get the farmer's attention.

'Morning,' said Cross.

'Just thought I'd mention—I couldn't get any answer at Bain House earlier. You know, Miss Shepherd's place? I wondered if you'd seen her about.'

'Can't say I have. We don't see her in the village much.'

'No, I know. I thought it was a bit funny, though. Her post was still in the box from yesterday, too.'

The farmer nodded. 'I'll keep an eye out.'

'Thanks a lot.'

Bernie waved and drove off, watching the tractor pull into the road again as soon as he'd passed. He'd probably get behind it again when he reached Bonsall, he thought gloomily.

LINDSAY MULLEN'S PARENTS lived in a large bungalow on the hillside above Darley Dale, a couple of miles north of Matlock.

'I like this sort of garden. No plants,' Murfin said as they walked past a Rover on the driveway to the front door.

And he was right, Fry noted. The garden seemed to be mostly gravel and stone flags. There was a birdbath, a sundial, a statue of an angel and dozens of terracotta pots that didn't contain very much. So much furniture, too—a patio set on the terrace under a green parasol, a wooden bench in the shade of an arbour, and a barbecue on timber decking at a lower level. On either side of the front door were solar lights shaped like Edwardian gas lamps.

A few minutes later, the two police officers were sitting in a conservatory with Lindsay's father, Henry Lowther.

'Sorry to bring you in here,' he said, 'but Luanne is asleep, and we don't want to disturb her. It's stressful enough for the child, poor thing.'

'Luanne is your youngest grandchild, sir?'

'Yes.'

'How did she come to be here with you last night?'

'We've been looking after her for a few days. Luanne hasn't been sleeping through the night, you see. Poor Lindsay wasn't getting much rest, so we offered to give her a break for a bit.'

'I see. And are you coping all right yourselves?'

'We're fine,' said Lowther. 'Luanne needs us, and it's best to have something to concentrate on. You know what I mean . . .'

Lindsay Mullen's parents seemed to be quiet people—no hysterics or outbursts of anger. But Fry had hardly caught a glimpse of Mrs Lowther before she disappeared, clearly on the verge of tears.

'My wife, Moira, isn't up to talking about it yet,' said her husband. 'I hope you understand.'

'Yes, of course. I'm sorry to have to bother you with questions, sir.'

'It's something you have to do.'

It was much too warm for Fry in the conservatory and she wondered whether Mr Lowther would notice if she surreptitiously turned down the thermostat on the radiator. But he was watching her expectantly.

'Could you tell me when you first heard about the fire, sir?'

'Yes. Brian phoned to tell us. That's our son-in-law.'

'What time was that?'

'I'm not sure. It was in the early hours of the morning. I was too shocked to check the time. He said he was phoning from the hospital—I remember that. At first, I thought it was him that had been in an accident. I couldn't understand what he was trying to tell me. I suppose I was still half asleep.'

The conservatory was probably so warm because it was full of plants—fuchsia, tree ferns, bougainvillea. Fry might be ignorant of what grew in the countryside, but she was familiar with house plants. During a spell with a foster family who'd run a small plant nursery in Halesowen, her job had been to write out the labels for the pots—and God help her if she got one wrong.

'How did Brian describe what had happened?' she asked.

'Well, he said he'd arrived home and found the house on fire. I gather he'd been out for the evening. Brian was very distressed, you know—understandably. And he'd suffered some injuries trying to get into the house. In the circumstances I'm surprised he had the presence of mind to call us at all. But I'm glad he did. It would have been worse, I think, to have been told by someone else. If anything could be worse than this.'

Mr Lowther was officially described in the forms as a managing director. In Fry's experience, most managing directors looked as though they'd eaten too many corporate lunches and Rotary Club dinners. But Lowther didn't. He had kept his leanness. Regular squash, or business not so good?

'That was all Brian could tell me, really. He said that the house was on fire. And that he thought Lindsay and the children were still in there.'

'What did you do?'

'We went up there, of course—to Darwin Street. But the fire was all over by the time we arrived. They wouldn't let us go into the house. So then we went to the hospital, but Brian was sedated. We sat around for hours before someone came and told us that Lindsay and the boys hadn't survived. It was horrible. It seemed as though we were almost the last to know.'

'It can feel like that sometimes. But people have their jobs to do.'

'I know. But it doesn't make it any better. Do you have any idea how the fire started?'

'Not yet. We think the seat of the fire was downstairs in the sitting room, but we need to examine the house more closely before we can be sure.'

'It must have been faulty wiring or something, I suppose,' he said.

'They'll find out what went wrong, won't they?'

Fry turned, surprised to see Mrs Lowther standing in the doorway, her eyes dried, her voice almost steady, as if she'd made a great effort to bring herself under control.

'We don't know yet whether it was an accident,' she said.

But Lowther shook his head. 'No, no. It can't have been arson,' he said. 'There's no one who could have had any reason to start that fire deliberately. Lindsay would never upset anybody. And as for Jack and Liam—'

He stopped, as if unable to express the impossibility in the case of his grandsons. His wife caught a surge of his emotion and began to cry again.

'What about Brian?' asked Fry.

'He wasn't even at home,' said Lowther.

Fry watched him, trying to detect an accusatory note in his voice. But perhaps it hadn't occurred to the Lowthers yet that their son-in-law ought to have been at home to protect his family, even if it meant he'd have died in the fire too. It would come later, that anger, the readiness to find someone to blame.

'Nevertheless, do you think there might be anybody he could have got on the wrong side of? Someone who might want to take revenge on him?'

'What could he have done to anybody to make them commit an evil act like that?' said Mrs Lowther, between sniffs. 'It doesn't make sense.'

Her husband nodded. 'Besides, Brian doesn't mix with people who'd do that sort of thing. He's a dispatch manager in a distribution centre.'

On the corner table was a set of photographs in silver frames. Smiling faces, boyish grins, a baby balanced on someone's knee—the Lowthers' grandchildren. Fry could see that Jack and Liam were fair-haired, with the pale look of their father, but the baby, Luanne, was much darker. The biggest frame contained an entire family group—Brian and Lindsay with all three children, their youngest child held proudly out front, taking centre stage.

Fry felt an urge to pick up the photos and look at them more closely, but she was afraid it would distract the Lowthers. Instead, she looked down at her notebook. 'I presume you know your daughter's house quite well?'

'Yes, of course,' said Mrs Lowther. 'We go there often. We were with them when they moved in. I helped Lindsay choose some of the furniture.'

Hearing that, Fry knew she'd have to pick her words carefully, or she was likely to lose Moira Lowther altogether. The untreated polyurethane foam wasn't her fault, but guilt knew no logic.

'First of all, the smoke alarm. They had one in the kitchen.'

'Yes, it was installed as soon as they moved in. Brian insisted on it.'

'Who advised them where to put it?'

'Advised them? I don't think anyone did. The kitchen was the obvious place. It's where accidents are most likely to happen.'

'I see.'

Of course, in one way the kitchen *was* the obvious place for a smoke alarm. But if Brian Mullen had bothered to read the manufacturer's instructions he would have seen a different recommendation. If he'd taken any notice of it, he might have kept his family alive.

'Lindsay was proud of her kitchen,' said Mrs Lowther. 'It's not six months since she had new units put in. It was immaculate.'

'Yes, I've seen it,' said Fry. 'I wonder, during the past few weeks, did Lindsay or Brian mention anyone hanging around near their house, or someone suspicious coming to the door?'

'No, not at all.'

Before much longer, Fry had exhausted her questions. She was glad to get out of the conservatory and away from the plants.

'What sort of business do you run, sir?' she asked as they walked back through the house.

'I own a very successful export company. We deal mostly in machine tools, which we sell all around the world.'

Not a wholesale florist's, then. She'd just wondered. There were plants everywhere. It was like the hothouse at Kew in here.

'Oh, you have a visitor,' she said when they reached the front door.

A man was coming up the path. He paused to smile sadly at the stone angel. He looked to be in his mid-twenties, smooth faced and wearing an overcoat. Fry wondered if he was a journalist.

'Oh, it's John,' said Mr Lowther. 'Our son.'

'Does he live here?'

'No, he has his own apartment, in Matlock. Poor John, he's very upset—he and Lindsay were so close.'

John Lowther looked at Fry and Murfin curiously as they met on the porch step.

'These people are the police, John,' said his father. 'They're here about Lindsay and the boys.'

'We were close. Did they tell you?'

'Your parents? Yes, they did.'

'I'm shut up completely.'

'I'm sorry?'

But John Lowther was looking at Gavin Murfin. 'I like your tie.'

Murfin looked aghast at getting a compliment. 'Er, thanks.'

'Are you all right, Mr Lowther?' Fry asked. 'I know it must be a very difficult time for you.'

His eyes travelled back towards her, but failed to focus. 'Pardon?'

'Have you thought of seeing your doctor?'

The young man laughed. 'I don't see my doctor, because he's not here.'

He went into the house, where his mother greeted him with a sob and a hug. Fry and Murfin walked back to the car. For a few moments, neither of them spoke. Then Fry started the engine and drove off.

'He seems a bit of a teacake,' said Murfin.

'You mean John Lowther? He was a bit odd, I suppose.'

'Two sandwiches short of a picnic, more like.'

Fry sighed. 'Is it getting near lunchtime by any chance?'

'Well, now you mention it—'

'All right, all right.' Fry knew when to give in to necessity. She couldn't understand the way Murfin lived to eat, instead of the other way round.

Sometimes she thought that most people had life upside-down, or back to front. Take the Lowthers, for instance—they had a garden full of furniture, and a house full of plants. Something wrong there, surely?

IN FOXLOW, a police patrol arrived outside the gates of Bain House at about a quarter past one that afternoon. PC Andy Myers pressed the intercom button on the gatepost a few times, but got no response.

'So what do we do?' asked his partner.

'One of us has to get his arse over these gates. There should be a release on the other side. Mind the spikes Phil. They look lethal.'

'Oh, thanks a lot. Don't strain yourself, will you?'

'I'm the driver. I have to stay with the car.'

His partner struggled over the gates, grumbling as he tried to avoid impaling his hand on a spike. Finally, his boots crunched down onto gravel and he found the button to open the gates.

'The bloke who phoned in says there's a bedroom window open round the back somewhere, and a light on,' said Myers.

'Why didn't *he* climb over the bloody gate, then?'

The two officers went up to the front door and knocked. They still got no reply. Myers began to walk round the side of the house.

'Yes, I can see the open window,' he called. 'Think we ought to go in?'

'I don't like that open window. There's a burglar alarm—you can see the box up there on the wall. And security lights, too. She's not some careless householder who'd leave her property insecure.'

'I'll call in and let Control know what we're doing.'

WHEN FRY AND MURFIN arrived back in Darwin Street, a man was standing in the garden of number 34. He seemed to have appointed himself some kind of supervisor, checking that everyone did their job properly. He was squinting through the viewfinder of a small digital camera at a SOCO in a scene suit carrying two bulging plastic bags towards a van.

'Hoping to sell some photos to the press, sir?' asked Fry.

He glowered at her. 'These are for my own records. I'm in Neighbourhood Watch. This'll come up at the next meeting, you can bet. I was right here from the start, you know. In fact, it was me that rang 999.'

'Would you be Mr Wade?'

'That's me: Keith Wade.'

He was so bundled up in sweaters that it was impossible to judge his shape. He was sweating a little, but whether from heat or exertion she couldn't tell.

'Did you take any photographs during the fire, sir?' she asked.

''Course I did. Look—'

He turned the camera round and held it up to her. A picture appeared on the LED screen. It was very dark—almost black, but for the faint outline of a roof against a dull, reddish glow.

'Are they all like that?'

'I followed the progress of the fire, and recorded how quickly the emergency services arrived.'

'We'd like copies of any shots you took during the fire.'

Wade looked pleased, then his face fell. 'I haven't got a colour printer.'

'Have you got Internet access? You can email them to us.'

'Yes, I can do that.'

Fry gave him her card, and he fingered it happily.

'Is it usual, sending a detective to a fire?'

'When there are fatalities, yes.'

'Fatalities, right. The two kids were killed, weren't they? Never stood a chance, they reckon.'

'And their mother, of course.'

He nodded. 'Tragic. I knew Lindsay and Brian pretty well.'

Wade's house was so close to the Mullens' that the smoke had stained his walls, too, and someone had trampled a flowerbed on their way to the fire.

'Mr Wade, has anyone been around in the last few weeks asking questions about the Mullens?' Fry asked.

'Asking questions? No, there hasn't been anyone.'

'Think carefully, please. It might have been someone who appeared perfectly innocent at the time. A market researcher calling at the door, then dropping in a casual question about your next-door neighbours?'

'No, I'd remember that.'

'What about your wife? She might remember someone.'

'I'm divorced,' he said.

'OK. Tell me what made you first notice the fire.'

'Well, I think I smelled the smoke. It must have been strong enough to wake me up. At first, I reckoned it must be someone's bonfire that had been set alight. Kids do that around here, you know—they think it's fun to see the fire engines arrive. But when I got out of bed, I saw a funny light on the bedroom curtains. It was sort of flickering, like someone was watching a huge TV screen outside. Do you know what I mean?'

'So what did you do?'

'I put some clothes on, went outside to have a look, then made the emergency call.'

Yes, and that sweater was probably the first thing he'd put on. It looked as though he'd been wearing it for months. The thing was brown and shaggy, with little threads of wool springing out everywhere.

'Did you see anyone outside at that time, Mr Wade?'

'No, not a soul. But I wasn't looking at the street, just at the fire. It had broken the sitting-room window, and there were flames going up the wall.'

'Were there any cars going by when you first saw the fire?'

'Not that I noticed,' he said. 'Just a minute.'

He raised his camera to his face and focused on something past Fry. She turned to see a liveried police car pull up outside number 32.

'Mr Wade, did you make any attempt to get into your neighbour's house when you saw the fire? Or were you too busy taking photographs?'

He looked hurt. 'Of course I did. After I'd made the call, I ran back out and went over the fence to their house. But there were already flames coming out of the windows, and I couldn't see a thing for the smoke.'

'You must have seen Brian Mullen arrive home later.'

He shoved the camera away in a pocket. 'Yes, poor bugger. He was going out of his mind. Is Brian all right, do you know?'

'His injuries are only minor.'

'That's something, anyway.'

Even out here, the smell of smoke and charring was very strong. Mr Wade himself seemed to reek of it. If he'd stood here wearing that same sweater while the fire was burning, it was probably impregnated with the smell.

'Are you normally at home during the day, Mr Wade?' Fry asked.

'Sometimes I work late shifts. I make deliveries for the supermarkets.'

'I see.'

'I ought to be in bed now. But I couldn't sleep with all this excitement.'

Fry looked across at number 32. The SOCOs had erected a crime-scene tent over the doorway, so it was impossible to see inside the house now, except for a vague shape moving past a blackened window now and then. The victims' bodies had long since been removed, and the firefighters had gone.

'Yes. Riveting, isn't it?'

THE CORPSE LAY at an awkward angle, half on a rug by the bed. It had been a nice sheepskin rug once, soft and white—until it soaked up most of Rose Shepherd's blood. Now it was stained dark red and caked into stiff clumps.

PC Myers raised a hand to the light switch, but remembered the light was already on. His partner stood in the doorway, tugging at his radio.

'What do you think she's done to herself?'

'Can't tell,' said Myers. 'She's dead, though.'

'Back off, then. Don't touch her.'

But Myers was crouching closer to the body, and he could see the circular hole punched neatly through the cotton of her nightdress, near her heart.

'Bloody hell, Phil,' he said. 'The old bird's been shot.'

3

Foxlow was one of those villages that looked as though nothing ever happened, but where the worst things often did, thought Ben Cooper as he pulled up outside Bain House. Not much traffic during the day, and no one out on the street. The residents were all at work, or in their gardens, or shut away in their front rooms, wondering what all the activity was outside.

The area was already swarming with personnel and vehicles. When Cooper reported to the RV point, he was amazed to see officers from the Firearms Support Unit patrolling the outer cordon with automatic weapons cradled across their bulletproof vests. That could mean only one thing.

Cooper's DI, Paul Hitchens, was crossing the garden with the crime-scene manager, Wayne Abbott. Hitchens was dressed in a dark suit and tie, keeping up his image as one of the smartest detectives in E Division. Abbott was wearing his shapeless pale blue crime-scene coverall.

Waiting patiently for them at the incident control unit was the divisional head of CID, Detective Chief Inspector Oliver Kessen. Until potential forensic evidence had been preserved and recorded, the scene was Wayne Abbott's domain, and everyone had to wait for his permission to enter.

It was somehow reassuring to see Kessen at a crime scene, though it indicated the seriousness of the incident. The DCI was always the still centre at the heart of events that might otherwise descend into chaos.

Cooper joined the fringes of the group, hoping for more information. The details he had so far were scanty. A woman found dead in her home, possible signs of an intruder.

The DCI was finishing a call on his mobile. 'Definitely a shooting?' he said finally, turning his gaze on Abbott, who was peeling off his gloves.

'Absolutely. At least three shots were fired, I'd say.'

'Why would you say that, Wayne?'

'You can see for yourself. Let's do a walkthrough.'

The DI was signalling. Cooper fell in step alongside him as they headed towards the house.

'The victim's name is Rose Ann Shepherd. Unmarried, so far as we can tell. It appears she lived completely alone—no other family members, and no staff. She's been resident in the village for about ten months.'

'Who found her?' asked Cooper, pulling out his notebook.

'Well, a neighbouring farmer raised the alarm, but it was actually the postman who first noticed something wrong—his name's Bernie Wilding. Mr Wilding could see that the victim hadn't emptied her letterbox.'

'So she's been dead since yesterday?'

'At least.'

They followed the path marked out for them to climb the stairs and reach the master bedroom. The victim's body still lay where PC Myers had found it, half on and half off the bloodstained rug, twisted at an unnatural angle.

'So,' said Kessen. 'Three shots, you said?'

Abbott stood over the body. 'Well, two shots hit the victim. The medical examiner says either one might have been enough to kill her. The third bullet embedded itself in the bedroom wall, up near the ceiling. See it?'

'Yes.'

'We'll be able to give you an idea of the weapon once the bullets have been recovered.'

'Time of death?' asked Kessen, without much sign of optimism.

'Between thirty and forty hours ago, according to the ME. Rigor mortis was almost gone when he examined the victim.'

'My God, forty hours?'

'At the maximum.'

Hitchens looked at his watch. 'That would put the earliest time of the incident at nine p.m. Saturday. And the latest at seven a.m. Sunday.'

Kessen sighed. 'Point of entry, Wayne?' he asked.

'On the face of it, the open window looks like the way the assailant got in. But it wasn't forced and there are no tool marks on the frame. We lifted several latents, though. I should get results on those within the hour.'

'The first officers to arrive had to smash a window to get in, which set off the alarms,' said Hitchens. 'They were going like crazy when I got here.'

'Our officers set off the alarms? They weren't activated by the assailant?'

'No, sir.'

Kessen walked out onto the landing and looked down the stairs. A SOCO was crouched over something in the hallway.

'What have you got there?'

'A video intercom system.' The SOCO picked up the handset. 'When someone presses the button at the gate, a tiny camera in the unit on the gatepost shows their image on the screen here.'

Cooper looked down at the body again as the exchanges went backwards and forwards around him. He knew nothing about Rose Shepherd, but he was sure she'd have hated anyone to see her like this. Her grey hair was dishevelled and fell in loose strands across her face. Her mouth had fallen open, and a trail of saliva had dried on her lips.

Kessen walked back to the bedroom and looked out onto the garden. 'There's quite a bit of money tied up here, isn't there?' he said.

Hitchens nodded. 'A few hundred pounds for that intercom unit alone, I'd say. Probably double that for the installation of the gates.'

'The victim must have really needed to know who was calling on her.'

'We've got house-to-house under way. But so far, everyone we've talked to is in agreement on one thing: Miss Shepherd never got any visitors. Apart from the postman—and even he didn't get past the gates.'

'Well, we just haven't talked to the right people, yet,' said Kessen.

'Why?'

'You're a property owner, Paul. Think of all the folk who come to your address. The refuse men to empty your wheelie bin, the tanker driver to deliver your central-heating fuel, the man who reads your electricity meter? No one can build a moat round their property and keep everyone out these days.'

'Rose Shepherd does seem to have been a very solitary person, though. She didn't mix with the neighbours, by all accounts. No one in Pinfold Lane knows who her next of kin could be. We found an address book but the entries seem to be all routine stuff—doctor, dentist, a local garage.'

'There must be something here to give us names. A diary, letters . . .? Try a phone bill. See what numbers she called most often.'

'Yes, sir.'

'How long had she lived here? Do we know that?'

'The neighbours say about a year,' said Hitchens. 'She moved in on her own, with no sign of a husband or anything.'

'You know, this is a large house for one woman living on her own.'

'She doesn't seem to have employed anyone, even a gardener or cleaner.'

Kessen brushed at a cobweb. 'It looks as though it could have done with the attention of a cleaner now and then.' He turned to Abbott. 'What about security? We know she had an intruder alarm.'

'A top-of-the-range monitored system, too. She wanted to be sure that there would be a police response if she had an intruder. We can check with the monitoring centre whether she ever had any alerts.'

'Doors and windows?'

'Five-lever mortise deadlocks, and hinge bolts.' Abbott tapped the fanlight.

'Laminated glass—almost impossible to break in the normal way.'

'She seems to have had good advice on security.'

'The one thing we've found in here is her passport,' said Hitchens.

'A UK passport?'

'Yes. Issued May 2000. Rose Ann Shepherd, British citizen, born 1944 in London . . .' He flicked through the pages. 'It looks almost unused. No stamps.' He turned to the back page. 'No next of kin.'

'No one she wanted informed in the event of an accident?'

'I guess not.'

In her passport photograph, Miss Shepherd was smartly turned out. Her hair was a darker shade of grey, swept back in a businesslike manner to match a white blouse, discreet ear studs and a hint of make-up. She had sharp blue eyes and a direct gaze, with the faintest of smiles at the camera.

Hitchens took a call on his mobile. 'OK, that's great. Thanks.' He turned to Kessen. 'A Vauxhall Astra was seen in the village in the early hours of Sunday morning. It doesn't belong to any of the residents, so far as we can tell. One witness is sure she's seen it in the village before, late at night.'

'Any details?'

'Light blue, seen under the streetlight near the phone box. No reg, but it probably started with an X, so it wasn't a new model.'

'You know, we need the media to come on board early in this one, Paul. We've got to get appeals out to locate the driver of that Astra, and anyone who had contact with Rose Shepherd in the last forty-eight hours. No—the last two weeks. God, I don't know—any contact with her, full stop.'

Cooper looked up, surprised to hear the DCI getting rattled in public.

But he could see what was bothering Kessen. The first twenty-four hours were the vital period after any murder. If you didn't have a strong lead within that time, you were destined for a long drawn-out inquiry—and the odds were against bringing the case to a successful conclusion. This murder might be forty hours old already, and there wasn't a lead in sight.

'There's absolutely no sign of an intruder,' said Kessen. 'Apart from this open window, which shows no traces of having been forced. Right, Wayne?'

Abbott had his phone to his ear. 'And no fingerprints either,' he said. 'I just got an update. The only prints we found on the window are a match for the victim's—and they were on the inside.'

'And every other window in the house is locked tight. Why not this one?'

'Perhaps someone used it to get *out* of the house,' said Hitchens.

'We're on the first floor. Did he clamber down the drainpipe?'

'Probably.' Hitchens looked out of the window. 'Actually, there isn't a drainpipe within reach. It's just a blank wall . . . He must have jumped.'

'In that case, Paul, you'll be looking for a suspect who ran away with two broken legs and a cracked spine.'

Hitchens sighed. 'So what's the alternative?'

Kessen joined him at the window. 'There's one possibility. That there never was an intruder in this house. The victim was shot from outside.'

Hitchens stared. 'From the garden?'

'No—the angle is wrong. The shots must have come from the field.'

'But the window—why was it open?'

'It's pretty clear, isn't it?' said Kessen. 'The victim opened the bedroom window herself. And someone waiting in the field shot her.'

'Jesus,' said Hitchens.

Kessen turned and addressed the room in general. 'Close off that road up there, and get the SOCOs into the field. That's where our gunman was.'

'YEARS AGO, I did a round out Leek way,' said Bernie Wilding, when Cooper found him sitting in his red mail van, waiting to give a statement. 'I saw those wallabies out there about as often as I saw Miss Shepherd in Foxlow.'

'The wallabies? Did you really see them?' Cooper asked, smiling.

'Only as an odd shape in the distance once or twice. I was never quite sure whether I was looking at a wallaby or a hare, really. But I always told everybody I'd seen the wallabies. Well, you do, don't you?'

'Yes, I would too.'

It was one of Cooper's regrets that he'd never seen a wallaby. No one who lived or worked in the Peak District doubted they existed. Plenty of drivers had seen them, and a few had run one over at night. The original animals had escaped from a zoo during the Second World War, and bred on the moors.

'Too late now, I reckon,' said Wilding.

'So they say. Too many people and dogs invading their habitat.'

'Oh, aye. People have killed them off, when the bad winters couldn't.'

Cooper thought he'd probably passed the test, proved his credentials as a local. 'What about Miss Shepherd?' he asked. 'You saw her often enough and at close enough range to recognise her, didn't you?'

Wilding screwed up his face thoughtfully. 'You know, the few times I did catch a glimpse of her, she always seemed to be wearing a headscarf, or something that hid her face. I could never be entirely sure it was her.'

'So you don't think you'd be able to identify her, Mr Wilding?'

'Not for certain. Sorry.'

'You spoke to her, though, didn't you? What did she sound like?'

'Well, I reckon she had a bit of an accent,' said Wilding. 'But I didn't speak to her often, and it was mostly through that intercom thing on the gate. I wouldn't recognise my own mother speaking through one of those.'

'Did you ever see anyone else coming or going from Bain House?'

'No, never.'

'And these gates were always closed, as far as you know?'

'Always. She kept everyone out, including me.'

'One last thing,' said Cooper. 'What did you bring for her this morning?'

'Oh, the package. It was a bit too big to get in the letterbox.' He handed over a small parcel about nine inches long. 'Miss Shepherd never got much mail. I hope it was nothing to do with what happened to her.'

'Well, it was the reason she was found today, instead of in a week's time.'

BY THE TIME Diane Fry arrived in Foxlow, there was no room for anyone to park anywhere near Bain House, and she had to leave her Peugeot on the road and walk to the RV point. Cooper saw her near the gates as he was clearing the way for Bernie Wilding to get his van out.

'Can you bring me up to speed, Ben?' she asked.

'Sure. I've made notes.'

As they walked towards the house, Cooper ran through the details. Fry found nothing to fault him on. He thought he'd done pretty well, considering he hadn't been at the scene very long.

They found Hitchens and Kessen at the edge of the field backing onto the garden. Wayne Abbott was walking across the field towards them, his boots crunching through the ridges of ploughed soil.

'I was always taught to go around the edge of a field so as not to damage the crop,' Abbott said. 'But I'm making an exception today, because the edge of the field is exactly where your tyre marks are.'

'The tyre marks of what?'

'A black car possibly, but a dark colour certainly.'

Kessen looked surprised. 'Why do you say that?'

'Well, I'm betting if they drove openly across this field they were hoping that residents living nearby would think they were out lamping.'

'Lamping?'

'That's when people go out into the countryside to shoot animals at night. Lampers use a bright light to dazzle their quarry.'

'Yes, I know about that—rabbits and suchlike.'

'Well, not just rabbits. Badgers, deer, sheep—you name it. The thing is, if local people thought somebody was out lamping that night, they probably wouldn't have bothered dialling 999, even when they heard shots.'

'I understand that. But the colour of the vehicle . . .?'

'Well, you wouldn't go lamping in a white car, would you? You want your target to focus on the light, not on the paintwork of your bonnet.'

'Nothing else, apart from the tyre marks?'

'Not that we can see.' Abbott shook his head. 'We'd have a better chance of coming up with something from a closed scene, like the bedroom. But a ploughed field? And two days after the incident? Better pray for a miracle.'

Kessen stared at the house. 'I wonder what the shooter did to get Rose Shepherd's attention, to get her to the window.'

'A phone call, I reckon,' said Hitchens. 'It'd be easy enough to phone her on a mobile from the car.'

'Yes. But what did he say to get her to come to the window? What *could* he have said that would make her walk straight into his sights?'

WHILE ABBOTT organised a detailed search of the field, Cooper took the chance to report what the postman Bernie Wilding had told him about never seeing Miss Shepherd's face clearly.

'I could understand it if she'd been physically disfigured,' said Hitchens. 'That would explain why she didn't want people to see her. But she wasn't.'

'What about motive?' asked Fry. 'Do you think someone in the village might have had a grudge against her?'

'How could they, if she didn't have contact with anyone in the village?'

'Well, I don't know. Maybe that's *why* she didn't have contact with anyone. We don't know anything about her. Where do we start?'

'There's one place we can start,' said Kessen. 'We need a list of individuals in the locality with firearms certificates. What about this farmer?'

'Neville Cross?' said Hitchens sceptically. 'He owns the land at the back of Bain House. But his farmhouse is way down there, two fields away.'

'He'll have a firearms certificate. Most farmers do. And no one would question Mr Cross driving over his own land, even at night. Perhaps no one would question him taking his rifle with him, either.'

'We don't know that he has a rifle,' insisted the DI.

'He's also the man who reported the open window at the back of the house,' Kessen continued. 'Thereby ensuring that he was involved in the investigation as a witness. You know the typical behaviour, Paul.'

'He was alerted by the postman that something might be wrong. That's why he took a look.'

'That doesn't mean he wouldn't have done it anyway, sooner or later.'

'What if he doesn't admit to having a gun?'

'We could ask him to cooperate with a gunshot residue test. At least we'd know if he'd fired a gun recently.'

Wayne Abbott shook his head. 'Sorry, it's too long since the shots were fired. A GSR test has to be done within the first few hours to get meaningful results. After forty-eight hours, the killer will have washed and wiped his hands enough to have removed all detectable traces.'

'A trace metal test to determine whether he's held a firearm?'

'Has to be within twenty-four hours.'

Kessen cursed quietly. 'Twenty-four hours is useless to us. Useless.'

The DI pointed at his two detectives. 'We've done the initial house-to-house, but the immediate neighbours will have to be interviewed properly. They must know something about Rose Shepherd. Take one of them each.'

'Right, sir.'

'A woman with no family and no friends,' said Hitchens bitterly. 'How can we reconstruct the life of someone like that?'

'She must have had at least one enemy,' said Fry. 'That's a start.'

'It's some kind of relationship, anyway.'

'Of course it is,' said Kessen. 'She was close enough to someone for that person to hate her enough to kill her. There's a history between them.'

'But Rose Shepherd seems to be a woman without a history.'

'That just means that she had a past she was trying very hard to hide.'

Fry touched Cooper's arm. 'Ben, have you got your car here?'

'Sure.'

'Give me a lift down the road, then. I had to leave mine miles away.'

'No problem.'

As they walked back to his car, Cooper stopped to take a last look at Bain House. Abbott's lamping theory was an interesting one. When a rabbit was caught in the lamper's beam, it was mesmerised by the light and seemed to forget to run away. Cooper had seen it happen.

For a moment, he thought about Rose Shepherd, shot down at her bedroom window. She must have been an easy target in a sniper's sights, silhouetted against the light. It was impossible not to picture her frozen to the spot, waiting for the bullet to strike.

'NICE BARN CONVERSION,' said Cooper as he pulled up. 'Somebody's done a good job of it. Probably worth a bit of money, wouldn't you say?'

Diane Fry nodded. 'More than I'll ever see.'

She got out of the car and walked across the gravel as Cooper drove away. Actually, it was more than a barn conversion. A range of farm buildings, including a tractor shed converted into garages and workshops, formed three and a half sides of a square, facing a central courtyard. The door of one garage stood open, and the nose of a blue BMW was visible.

According to information from the control room, these neighbours were called Ridgeway, Martin and April. Fry took a small detour before crossing the courtyard to their house, and looked in through the windows of one of the outbuildings. Games room. A gym. And a sauna. Very nice.

The Ridgeways themselves could have stepped straight out of *Derbyshire Life*. They had perfected the country look: corduroy, cashmere and tweed. Fry wasn't at all surprised when she discovered they both came from Luton.

Martin Ridgeway, who wore the corduroy, invited Fry inside, and led her into a dining room with six spindle chairs round a polished table.

'We noticed all the activity, of course,' he said. 'And a young constable called about an hour ago to ask us if we noticed anything suspicious in the early hours of Sunday morning.'

'And did you notice anything, sir?'

'No,' said Ridgeway. 'We're members of Neighbourhood Watch, you know. But our coordinator says the police won't give him any information. Has there been another robbery?'

'We're conducting enquiries into a suspicious death, sir.'

'Good heavens! I suppose we ought to have guessed it was something more high-profile, to justify all this activity. Who is it that's died?'

'Miss Rose Shepherd, at Bain House.'

'Oh,' said Ridgeway, sounding distinctly noncommittal.

'What do you know about Rose Shepherd, sir?' she asked.

'Was she foreign?' Ridgeway said vaguely. 'We heard a rumour in the village that she was foreign.'

'Not so far as we're aware. Did you never speak to her yourself?'

'No. Why would I?'

'Well, she lived right next door.'

He shook his head. 'It's not as if these are semidetached properties. I don't know anything about her.'

Sliding doors stood open to the garden, because it was still warm enough for that, even in late October. Fry could see a woman outside.

'Is that your wife? Could I ask her?'

'If you like.'

April Ridgeway was wearing the cashmere, with a waxed cotton body warmer and gardening gloves. When asked, she gave a similar story to her husband's. She had never spoken to the occupant of Bain House. There might have been some talk about Miss Shepherd in the village, but she made a point of not listening to gossip.

'How long have you lived in Foxlow?'

'Nine months.'

'So Miss Shepherd was already living at Bain House when you moved in.'

'I suppose so.'

'You're interested in wildlife, Mrs Ridgeway?' asked Fry, watching her tighten some wire netting on a bird table.

'Very much so. We both are, aren't we, Martin?'

'It's one of the reasons we came to live here, in the national park,' agreed her husband. He stood back and inspected his wife's handiwork. 'That netting is to stop the grey squirrels,' he said.

Fry frowned, struggling to understand why wildlife enthusiasts would put food out in their garden and then try to stop wild animals eating it.

'Our only regret was that we couldn't go somewhere that still has red squirrels. Reds have been wiped out in Derbyshire, you know.'

Fry didn't know, and didn't really care. 'Have you been aware of anybody lamping in this area?' she asked.

'Lamping?'

'You know what that is, sir?'

'Oh, we know what that is, all right. If we knew about anything like that going on, we'd report it straight away. But what has that got to do with this suspicious death you're investigating? Was the lady killed by poachers?'

'I'm afraid we just don't know.'

He took her ignorance as confirmation of his own fears. 'That's another problem our native wildlife is facing, you know. Animals are the first victims when society starts to fall apart. Look at all those stories of illegal immigrants stealing swans and butchering sheep in the fields.'

When Fry remained silent, Ridgeway gestured at the bird table and continued, 'We sometimes think of grey squirrels as the immigrants of the animal world. They're nothing but vermin, after all—rats with furry tails.'

Fry felt the anger rising, but she'd promised herself to be more tolerant of people she dealt with. She consulted her notebook, partly to cover her irritation, and partly to remind herself of the questions she needed to ask.

'Have either of you noticed a blue Vauxhall Astra in the village recently? No? A vehicle of any kind, acting suspiciously?'

'No.'

'Any vehicles at all visiting Bain House?'

'We can't see the entrance to the house from here, so we wouldn't know.'

'And did you hear anything unusual on Saturday night, or in the early hours of Sunday morning?'

'Our double glazing is very good. We don't hear much noise at night.'

'One final question, sir—do you possess a firearm of any description?'

Ridgeway hesitated. 'I do have an air rifle, but it's less than twelve foot pounds so I don't need a licence for it.'

'What do you use an air rifle for? No, don't tell me—let me guess. You use it for shooting squirrels.'

'Also crows, rooks and magpies, which steal songbirds' eggs. They're all classed as pests, so it's lawful to shoot them on private property.'

'I can understand that. But what's the problem with squirrels?'

'The invasion of grey squirrels has driven our native reds into remote sanctuaries, protected forests in Wales or Scotland.' Ridgeway took a step towards her and lowered his voice. 'Our kind of people are just like those red squirrels. We're being driven out by the vermin.'

'I think I'm finished here,' said Fry.

As she was shown out, she wondered why the Ridgeways had bothered joining Neighbourhood Watch if they knew nothing about their neighbours and couldn't even see the adjoining properties. But she supposed there was only one reason—they thought it would provide protection for themselves.

ROSE SHEPHERD's other neighbours were Edward and Frances Birtland. Their address was a bungalow, with a long drive leading off Pinfold Lane. It had been built after the introduction of national park planning regulations, so there were no red brick terraces and plaster porticos here, as in some of the fifties developments. This place was stone clad and mullioned, designed to blend in with its surroundings, but Cooper thought it looked as though it had been plonked down with no regard for the natural contours of the land.

'Yes?' The grey-haired woman who answered his knock peered cautiously past a security chain.

He showed his ID. 'Mrs Birtland? DC Cooper, Edendale CID.'

'Is it about the murder?'

'Oh, I see someone's been talking. Was it the officer who called earlier?'

'No, but word gets around.'

Cooper smiled. He was pleased to hear that, for once. 'May I come in?'

'Of course.' She took the chain off and let him into the bungalow. 'Would you like a cup of tea, Mr Cooper?'

'No, thank you, Mrs Birtland. I won't be keeping you long.'

Being called 'Mr Cooper' made him smile even more. That really was a rarity in this job.

Mrs Birtland led him into a back room. 'Ted, we've got a visitor,' she said.

Edward Birtland didn't get up when Cooper entered. He was seated in a well-used armchair by a stone fireplace, a fragile man of about seventy. He held out a hand politely, and Cooper shook it.

'So,' he said, 'how did you hear someone had been killed?'

Mrs Birtland chuckled. 'It was Bernie. Our postman knows everybody.'

'Of course he does. Now, the question I've come to ask you is how well you knew Rose Shepherd.'

'We didn't know her at all. She hadn't been in the village long.'

'About ten months,' said Cooper. 'Are you Foxlow people yourselves?'

'Of course,' said Mrs Birtland. 'We've lived here all our lives. We had a house on the High Street when we were married. We bought this little bit of land when Ted retired, and had the bungalow built. It took all the money we'd ever have—though we didn't know it at the time.'

Cooper glanced at Mr Birtland, who smiled sadly.

'I thought I had a good pension put away,' he said, 'with the company I worked for. But it didn't turn out that way. Once we'd paid for the bungalow, there was nothing left. So we just have our old-age pensions to live on.'

'The only way we could live any better is by selling up,' said his wife. 'And we could never do that.'

'Can you think of anyone who'd have known Miss Shepherd better?'

Mrs Birtland shook her head. 'No, not really.'

'Have you tried the Ridgeways on the other side?' said her husband.

'One of my colleagues is talking to them. Do you think they might have known Miss Shepherd well, then?'

'We couldn't say.'

The Birtlands glanced at each other. Then Mr Birtland said, 'They moved here about the same time as Miss Shepherd. We didn't know where any of them came from. Being located at this end of Pinfold Lane, we've started to feel as though we've been cut off from the rest of the village by incomers.'

'I see.'

Birtland looked at him expectantly. 'You haven't asked us yet whether we heard anything,' he said.

'It was the next question, sir.'

'Ah, good. Well, we've been thinking about it since we heard that Miss Shepherd had been killed. Was she shot?'

Cooper leaned forward. 'Did you hear shots on Saturday night?'

'Well, that answers my question,' said Birtland with a chuckle. 'We think maybe we did.'

'What time would that have been?'

Birtland patted his wife's hand. 'We disagree on that, I'm afraid.'

'Ted thinks it was about two o'clock in the morning, but I think it was more like three,' she said. 'I don't sleep too well sometimes, and I'm often starting to come awake by then.'

'But you didn't look at the clock to make sure?'

'No, we didn't. We didn't take much notice, you see. We often hear people shooting around here. I don't think Ted even woke up. If he did hear the shooting, he must have gone straight back to sleep, that's all I can say.'

Birtland laughed. 'I don't suppose that's much use to you.'

'Could you say how many shots you heard?' asked Cooper.

'Two or three,' said Mrs Birtland.

'Or four,' said her husband.

Cooper sighed. 'Thank you.'

'We would have come forward anyway when we heard somebody had been killed, you know. But we were told you'd be calling today.'

'That's all right.'

Frances Birtland accompanied Cooper to his car. 'I'm sorry we couldn't be of more help,' she said.

'Don't worry. But if you do happen to remember anything more about Miss Shepherd, or about any visitors she had—'

'Yes, of course, we'll let you know.'

COOPER PICKED FRY UP about a hundred yards down the road from the Ridgeways' barn conversion, on the corner of the High Street.

'Any luck?' he said when she got into the car.

'They didn't hear anything. Their double glazing is too good. You?'

'The Birtlands might have noticed the shots. But they've been here all their lives, and they're used to hearing people shooting rabbits.'

They pulled in through the gates of Bain House and parked behind a van.

'The Ridgeways think that Rose Shepherd was a foreigner,' said Fry.

'That's funny. The Birtlands think the Ridgeways are foreigners.'

Fry snorted. 'They're from Luton.'

'Exactly.'

They found the DI inside the house and Cooper told him what he'd learned from the Birtlands.

'Between two and three a.m.?' said Hitchens. 'That's the best they can do?'

'Sorry.'

'Well, it falls in the middle of our time scale, so it helps a bit, I suppose.'

'We're no closer to filling in details of Miss Shepherd's background, though,' said Fry.

Hitchens shook his head. 'Not much nearer. Although the owners of the village shop think Rose Shepherd's accent might have been Irish.'

'Do they? Her passport says she was British. Born in London.' Fry laughed. 'Irish is foreign enough for folk round here, I suppose.'

'Oh, we found a laptop—in the bottom drawer of the victim's wardrobe.'

'Well, that's good news,' said Fry. 'Has it been checked out yet?'

'We haven't had time to go through the files, but Miss Shepherd definitely had Internet access.'

'Any interesting email correspondence?'

'Nothing obvious. But it looks as though she might have joined some online groups, because there were different aliases and screen names. It seems Rose Shepherd had a social life, of a kind. But it was all online.'

'By the way, I've got the package that the postman was trying to deliver,' said Cooper. 'It isn't all that big, but it's heavy for its size.'

'Open it up. But be careful.'

When the packaging came off, they were looking at three books from an Internet bookseller. Maeve Binchy, Danielle Steele, Josephine Cox.

'Does that give us any clues?' asked Hitchens.

'The only surprise is that she ordered three books at once, since it meant they wouldn't go into her letterbox,' said Fry.

'Maybe they were on special offer,' said the DI, answering his phone.

Fry waited for a quiet moment, then approached him between calls.

'Sir, I need to review the house fire inquiry. You know, the triple death?'

'Not now, Diane. Unless you have evidence of malicious intent. Do you?'

'No, sir. Not yet.'

'Come back to me when you do, then.'

Fry bit her lip. She obviously wasn't going to get a look-in on the Rose Shepherd inquiry. But she had an inquiry of her own that she could make a mark with—if she could find the time to work it properly. The Darwin Street fire may be low priority, but there were ways round that problem.

She went outside and found Gavin Murfin eating a pork pie out of a paper bag. He'd got into the habit of bringing food with him if he thought he was going to be away from civilisation for a few hours.

'Ah, Gavin, you're not doing very much,' she said, taking hold of his arm and steering him towards her car.

'Well, actually—'

'Good. You're with me. But if you drop bits of that pie in my car, you know what'll happen. And it won't be pretty.'

As Fry negotiated the lines of vehicles in Pinfold Lane, she saw Ben Cooper standing in the gateway of Bain House. He'd stopped to speak to one of the SOCOs, Liz Petty. Fry watched them as she changed gear. She saw Petty push back her dark hair and confine it in a clip behind her head. Her cheeks looked slightly pink as she laughed at something Cooper was saying, and Fry wondered vaguely whether they were sleeping together.

'They make a grand couple, don't they?' said Murfin, as if answering her thought.

AFTER DROPPING Gavin Murfin off at West Street with his instructions, Fry drove straight back to Darwin Street. Things were happening here, at least. All the appropriate people were gathering, including the fire service's divisional officer and his investigation team.

The fire service had taken possession of the scene. They'd brought in their own dog team from Alfreton, and a chocolate brown labrador bitch called Fudge, wearing blue protective boots and a reflective harness, was now being deployed in the ground-floor rooms of the Mullen house.

To the dog, it was all a game. There'd be a chicken-flavoured Schmacko when it found what it was looking for. But a dog could locate flammable liquids faster than any conventional equipment. Lucky animal, Fry thought, not having to worry about what these humans had been up to in the house.

Fry's mobile rang. It was Murfin, his voice sounding slightly muffled. If he wasn't actually eating, he was salivating at the thought of his next snack.

'I called the hospital. They say Brian Mullen is awake and he'll be fit to be interviewed in the morning. Want me to come along with you?'

'Er . . . no thanks, Gavin. There'll be plenty for you to do on the Shepherd inquiry.'

'OK. I don't like hospitals anyway.'

As she ended the call, Fry saw the fire service dog padding across the debris in its blue boots, wagging its tail. Was it Schmacko time already?

'So what's the result? Did the dog find anything?'

'Yes. She identified accelerant in two locations in the sitting room,' said the handler. 'I've marked them for further investigation.'

'Great job. Thanks.'

Fry reached for her phone. Traces of accelerant were evidence of malicious intent. Fudge had just upped the stakes in this inquiry.

BELOW THE HILL, most of the fields at Bridge End Farm were still good grazing land. But much use that was to anybody now.

According to Matt, he would soon be a glorified park keeper instead of a farmer. Without headage payments, there was no way he could raise sheep. In future, all lamb bought in Britain would come from New Zealand. It would happen the same way it did with Brazilian beef and Danish pig meat, he said. Countryside Stewardship schemes were all very well, but Matt was baffled that the country didn't see any value in an ability to feed itself.

Ben drew his car into the yard in front of the farmhouse, trying to imagine the place empty and deserted, cleared of its animals.

'Bad do about that shooting in Foxlow,' said Matt, after greeting his brother in front of the house. 'It was Neville Cross who found the body, wasn't it?'

'Well, not quite. But he made the call. So the farmers' grapevine has been busy, has it?'

'Something like that.'

Matt removed his boots and stripped off his overalls in the porch.

'Come into the office, Ben. There's something I want to show you.'

The farm office was cramped and untidy. It was the aspect of the farm that Matt paid least attention to, because it meant being indoors. 'I'm a stockman, not a filing clerk,' Matt would say. But deep down, he probably knew that this failing was the reason he was doomed. These days, farmers had to be business managers and entrepreneurs if they wanted to survive.

Matt eased himself onto the office chair in front of the computer. 'I've been looking at the Internet,' he said.

'Blimey, at this rate you'll be catching up with the twenty-first century.'

Matt scowled. 'Most of it is a load of crap.'

'Yes. You have to learn to filter out the rubbish to find the useful stuff.'

Ben perched on the arm of a deep armchair. The chair itself was occupied by an aged border collie called Meg, who didn't even bother opening an eye. She was there by right, and wasn't moving for anybody.

Matt booted up and frowned at the screen as he waited to enter his password. 'I want to show you an article I found about schizophrenia,' said Matt. 'Well, to be more exact, about its heritability.'

For a moment, Ben was thrown by the word 'heritability'. It was an expression he was accustomed to hearing from Matt, but strictly in relation to livestock breeding. Genetics played a big part in breeding animals for desirable characteristics. But schizophrenia? It didn't make sense.

'What on earth are you trying to tell me, Matt?'

'It was something I heard one of the nursing home staff say, before Mum died. It hadn't occurred to me before, and nobody had ever mentioned the possibility, but apparently schizophrenia is hereditary.'

'What?'

'Ben, it's for the sake of the girls as much as anything. I need to know what the odds are of schizophrenia being inherited. Will you read it?'

Almost against his will, Ben ran his eyes over the text on the screen.

It has been verified that schizophrenia runs in a family. People with a close relative suffering from schizophrenia have an increased chance of developing the disease.

He straightened up. 'Why are you doing this, Matt. What's the point?'

'*What's the point?* It says that members of families vulnerable to schizophrenia can carry the genes for it, while not being schizophrenic themselves. They're called "presumed obligate carriers".'

'Matt, you don't know anything about this stuff.'

'I'm trying to find out. Look, there's a bit of research here that found that, in each generation, more family members were hospitalised with the condition at an earlier age, and with increasing severity.'

'And your conclusion, Doctor . . .?'

Matt turned to face his brother. 'My conclusion is, I reckon my kids could be eight times more likely than average to have schizophrenia.'

Ben shook his head. 'It's still a small chance, Matt. We were told that one in every hundred people suffers from schizophrenia. Even taking heredity into account, that's only a maximum risk of, what . . . eight per cent?'

'It's a bit less than our risk, admittedly.'

'Ours?'

'Yours and mine, little brother. The children or siblings of schizophrenics can have as high as a thirteen per cent chance of developing the disease.'

Ben sat back down on the arm of the chair. Meg groaned and looked up at him accusingly with one tired eye. She was a dog who liked peace.

'You know, I'm wondering now if Grandma had schizophrenic tendencies,' Matt went on. 'She had some strange habits—remember? But everyone in the family used to talk about her as if she was only a bit eccentric.'

'I do remember her being rather odd, but that doesn't mean a thing. It certainly doesn't mean you'll pass something on to the girls.'

'You know, sometimes I'm stopped cold by the thought that one of the girls could grow up to be like Mum. But schizophrenia is only about seventy per cent inherited; thirty per cent is due to environmental factors. So if we knew what other things influence people, we might be able to create a different environment, so the genetic switch wouldn't be flipped.'

'Matt, you're making far too much of this. Your girls are perfectly OK.'

Ben's attention was caught by a movement outside. The window looked out onto the narrow front garden and the farmyard beyond. His youngest niece, Josie, was sitting on the wall. He tapped on the window so that she looked up, and he waved. She giggled, waved back, then blew him a kiss.

'There is absolutely nothing wrong with Josie,' Ben said. 'Or Amy, for that matter.'

'Time will tell, I suppose,' said Matt. 'But I have to find out the facts. It was me who made the decision to have children. Well, me and Kate.'

'Have you talked to Kate about this?'

Matt ran a hand across his face. 'I need to know what to tell her first.'

'When you were looking up all this information on the Internet, did you come across any advice? What do they say you should do?'

'Talk to a psychiatrist.'

'And that's what you're going to do, right?'

Matt sighed. 'According to some of these websites, there isn't much chance of research having practical applications within five years—when it would be useful to me. Or useful to you, Ben.'

'I'm not planning on having kids any time soon.'

'What about that girlfriend of yours?'

'Liz? We're just . . . Well, we're just going out together, that's all.'

Matt gave him a sceptical glance. 'Be that as it may. In the end, you'll have to face the fact that a child of yours may be vulnerable to schizophrenia.'

'That's one thing I'm *not* going to worry about,' said Ben firmly.

A few minutes later, he left his brother in the office and went out into the passage that ran through the centre of the house. When he was a child, the passage and stairs had been cold, gloomy places. Now things were very different. There were deep-pile fitted carpets on the floor, the walls were painted white, and there were mirrors to catch the light.

Reluctantly, Ben turned and looked up the stairs. At the top, he could see the first door on the landing, the one that had been his mother's bedroom. After the death of his father, she had gradually deteriorated until the family could no longer hide from each other the fact that she was mentally ill.

Isabel Cooper had been diagnosed with chronic schizophrenia, and finally the incidents had become unbearably distressing. Ben shuddered at the memory. He never wanted to witness anything like that, ever again.

4

Tuesday, October 25

An incident room had been opened up in Edendale for the Rose Shepherd inquiry. Watching the staff arriving at E Division headquarters, Cooper deduced that the HOLMES system was being activated. He recognised an allocator he'd worked with previously.

With no obvious lines of enquiry, the HOLMES computer indexes would be vital in sniffing out correlations as information came in. One tiny detail could send the investigation in a new direction.

'The victim was killed with a semiautomatic weapon, at least three shots fired in rapid succession,' said DI Hitchens, opening the briefing. 'We know it wasn't a bolt-action rifle. The second shot had to have followed the first rapidly to strike the victim before she fell.'

'What about the third shot?' one of the officers asked.

'If we follow a rough trajectory from the impact to where the killer's vehicle was positioned in the field, we see that the third shot passed through the window at about the same height and the same angle as the others. So it was probably fired after she'd started to fall. That's why it missed.'

The DI paused, but there were no questions, so he continued: 'We've got preliminary reports from the teams on house-to-house. We're looking for a blue Vauxhall Astra that was seen in Foxlow in the early hours of Sunday morning, about the time of the shooting.'

'Just one sighting?'

'No, two. The Astra was seen driving into the village about eleven thirty, and leaving at about three a.m. It's possible some neighbours heard shots between two a.m. and three, but we can't narrow it down any further.'

Another hand went up. 'What about the gun, sir?'

'Well, we don't have the weapon yet,' said Hitchens. 'But we do have some bullets. Unfortunately, the heat generated by firing a gun destroys any DNA. It's sometimes worth having a look at the casings, though.'

'But there aren't any casings.'

'Yes, there are. We just don't know where.'

At one time, Cooper would have stayed at the back of the room during these briefings. He'd never really had the confidence to contribute his ideas in front of a crowd of people, most of them more experienced than he was. But today he found himself near the front, where Hitchens could see him. The DI knew he'd been a member of the force's competition shooting team for several years, so he wasn't surprised when Hitchens cocked an eye towards him.

'Anything you want to contribute at this stage, DC Cooper?'

He straightened up, noticing all the eyes suddenly turned towards him.

'If we're looking at the possibility of a professional hit, I can tell you that snipers are trained to pick up their brass,' he said. 'That would explain why there are no casings. A trained person reconnoitres the site and selects a place that gives him cover and an escape route. Then he takes his shot. But normally only one—the sniper's motto is "one shot, one kill".'

'But this killer took three shots.'

'To me, that doesn't sound like a real professional.'

'There was no sign of any casings in the field, so we presume our killer stayed long enough to pick them up.'

'Well . . . at night, in a ploughed field, that would be quite tricky. You'd be lucky to find one, let alone all three.'

'True,' agreed Hitchens, looking at him with interest.

Cooper leaned back for a moment and imagined himself sitting at the wheel of a car at night, in a ploughed field, with the driver's window open and three bullet casings lying on the ground somewhere outside the vehicle.

'Not just tricky,' he said. 'It would mean the killer getting out of the car and leaving footprints in the soil. But there were no footprints in the area where the shots were fired from, just tyre marks.'

'Maybe the casings fell close enough for the gunman to lean out of the door and pick them up without leaving the vehicle,' Hitchens suggested.

'No, that won't work. It was a high-powered rifle. The casings would have been ejected at speed.'

'What, then?'

'The casings must have been ejected *inside* the car.'

'Is that possible? If he was firing a rifle from the driver's seat?'

'The car was facing northwards, up the field, wasn't it? With the back fence of Bain House on the driver's side?'

'Yes.'

'Then, no,' said Cooper. 'I don't think it is possible. Whoever fired the rifle would have had to be in the passenger seat.'

There was a sudden buzz of interest. Cooper felt himself flushing—not with embarrassment, but excitement. He was sure he'd got this right.

'We'll have to get this checked out properly,' said Hitchens.

But Cooper mimed holding and pointing a rifle. 'With the window down, you'd want to rest the barrel of your weapon on the door for stability while you were aiming. That means the stock and the chamber would be well inside the vehicle, so your casings would eject against the back of the seat.'

'He was shooting from the passenger seat?'

'No, it would have to be from the back seat,' said Cooper.

'Wait a minute. This would suggest two perpetrators, right?'

'One to drive and one to shoot. It's the only way.'

'It makes sense,' said DCI Kessen, speaking for the first time. 'They went into the field, did the job and drove straight out again. No hanging around climbing over seats or packing a weapon away. Having a separate driver would cut down tremendously on the time they were exposed.'

'OK. That was useful, Ben. Thanks.' Hitchens looked at his file, indicating that he wanted to move the discussion on.

Cooper glanced across at Fry. She nodded and almost smiled.

'The good news is that we've had some calls from the public in response to photos of Rose Shepherd in the media this morning,' said Hitchens. 'So her passport photograph wasn't too out of date. Most interestingly, we've got a couple of potential sightings in Matlock Bath on Saturday afternoon.'

The DI brought up a map of the area for everyone to see. 'Matlock Bath is no more than three miles from Foxlow—on the A6, just south of Matlock itself. It's a popular tourist spot, even at this time of year, so it would have been busy on Saturday afternoon. But she must have stood out somehow for members of the public to remember her.'

'There's no CCTV in Matlock Bath, is there?'

'No. This isn't Glossop we're talking about. They don't expect major crime on the street. There will be some limited CCTV systems on commercial premises, but nothing on the street.'

'There's a webcam,' said Cooper.

'A what?'

'A webcam. You can go on the Internet and see a view of Matlock Bath promenade. I think they have it running pretty much every day.'

'Who operates it, Cooper?' asked Kessen, leaning forward in his chair.

'I think it's a photographic museum.'

'All right. Let's check it out.'

Hitchens waited to see if the DCI had finished. 'Next thing,' he said. 'We've had the victim's phone records checked, and we now know that a call was made to Miss Shepherd's home number at three o'clock on Sunday morning. The call lasted only twelve seconds. As you might have guessed, the caller used an unregistered pay-as-you-go mobile. No account, no address.'

'Pay-as-you-go phones,' said someone gloomily. 'The biggest gift that was ever made to drug dealers.'

'And paedophiles. And terrorists.'

'Now for the victim's background,' Hitchens continued. 'Rose Shepherd went to extraordinary lengths to protect her privacy. She left almost nothing of a personal nature to give us an angle on her life. However, we've had time since yesterday to go through her bank statements.'

'Anything interesting?'

'Nothing out of the ordinary. All the evidence points to Miss Shepherd being a model citizen, paying her bills on time, being no trouble to anyone.'

'Much too perfect to be true.'

'Perfect citizens vote, don't they? Is she on the electoral register?'

'No. And she's not in the phone book either,' said Hitchens. 'All we've got is her passport, her bank statements and utility bills. The other strange thing is that there are no obvious personal contacts. There *is* an entry on a blank page in her address book, though. Just three digits: 359.'

'A dialling code, perhaps,' offered Kessen.

'Well, we checked it out. The Highbury area of north London comes closest—0207 359.'

'What about the 0359 code? Where's that?'

'Nowhere. It's a BT code allocated for future network expansion.'

'Could it be a country code?' said Cooper. 'Where's the directory?'

'On the shelf.'

He picked up the directory and leafed through the back pages. 'They don't list international codes by number, but by country, in alphabetical order. Hold on . . . Well, that didn't take long: 359 is the code for Bulgaria.'

'Oh, great. There's a job for someone to follow up. Any volunteers?'

There was a ripple of laughter round the room as the atmosphere eased and officers recognised the end of the briefing approaching.

'Finally, the IT team are giving the laptop a going-over,' said Hitchens. 'If Rose Shepherd had information stored somewhere, it might be online. There are plenty of sites offering free web storage space.'

'Protected by a password, of course. We have to hope we strike lucky.'

'Basically, the victim's story seems to be this: she kept herself hidden away in Bain House for the best part of a year, then for some reason decided to have an afternoon out in Matlock Bath. We're working on the theory that she was seen there by someone who followed her home to find out where she lived. Somehow, they also obtained her ex-directory phone number. Then they wasted no time in eliminating her.'

'She must really have upset someone in the past.'

'Absolutely,' said Kessen. 'If we can establish why Rose Shepherd was in hiding, it should give us a lead on her killer. At the moment, she's something of an enigma. But that was all her own doing. In making it difficult for anyone to find her, she also made it harder for us to identify her murderer.'

FLOWERS HAD STARTED to arrive outside the house at Darwin Street, Fry noted. Floral tributes to Lindsay Mullen and the two children. They came from relatives, friends and neighbours, and even from people who'd never known them. Communal grief had become fashionable, even in Edendale.

Next door, Keith Wade was complaining to a uniformed constable that he'd had to park his car at the end of the road because of the outer cordon. Fry saw that he was still wearing the same sweater. It must smell like a badger by now. No wonder Mr Wade lived alone.

The fire investigator from the Forensic Science Service had arrived and was setting out his equipment in the Mullens' sitting room when she found him.

'Glad you could make it,' she said. 'DS Fry.'

He was a small, middle-aged man whose white paper suit emphasised his pear-shaped body. When he spoke, he revealed a Scottish accent.

'Quinton Downie,' he said, taking off a glove to shake hands.

'Do you have all the background information you need?'

'All you can give me, apparently.' Downie began unpacking what looked like a series of forms. 'By the way,' he said, 'I examined the outside of the building before I came in. Did you know there's unsooted broken glass in the vicinity of a side window?'

'What?'

'A broken side window. I wondered if your people had noticed it.'

'A lot of these windows are broken,' said Fry. 'That's the result of heat from the fire, surely?'

Downie looked up and smiled. 'If that were the case, the glass would be sooted on the interior surface. It isn't, which implies it must have been broken either in the early stages of the fire—or before it started.'

'You mean a point of entry?'

'Could be. You might want to get that window examined for fingerprints before the evidence is compromised any further.'

Fry glared at the back of his head as he continued to lay out his equipment. At that moment, her phone rang.

It was the sergeant in charge of the search team. 'I thought you'd want to know straight away, we've found an empty lighter-fluid can. It's butane, but quite an unusual brand, I believe. It looks like someone found a use for a hundred millilitres of Swan Extra Refined recently.'

'Where did you find it? How near the house?'

'It had been chucked in a wheelie bin a hundred yards down the street. The householder says no one at that address smokes, and she insists it wasn't there on Sunday when she last put some rubbish out.'

'You've got it bagged properly?'

'You bet.'

'Thanks.' Fry ended the call and turned back to Downie. 'Show me this side window,' she said.

He stood up. Together, they made their way out of the house and into a side passage. Brian Mullen's red Citroën still stood on the drive.

'OK,' sighed Downie. 'We have plumes of soot deposited on the exterior wall by smoke from the window. But the broken glass on the ground beneath the window is unsooted, indicating that the fire didn't touch this glass.'

'Yes, I see.'

'Even from here, I can see tool marks on the window frame,' said Downie. 'Did the firefighters obtain entry this way?'

'They didn't. They came in through the doors.'

'Right.' Downie turned to look at her. 'Pity about the shoe impressions.'

'What shoe impressions?'

'Precisely.'

Fry looked at the ground where they were standing. It was a muddy mess, covered in crushed vegetation and trampled by size ten boots.

'Shit.'

Downie shrugged. 'Think yourself lucky to get this much. The site of any fire is a challenge to the principles of crime-scene management.'

Fry felt herself getting angry. 'Three people died in this fire. The evidence mustn't be compromised.'

'I can assure you, Sergeant Fry, everything will be done by the book. By the way, the usual advice is not to fit a smoke alarm in the kitchen. Cooking fumes set it off too easily. For a two-storey house, the bottom of the stairs is the best location, with a second one on the landing as an extra precaution.'

'I'll be sure to let Mr Mullen know,' said Fry.

'Who?'

'The householder. The husband of the dead woman, the father of the two dead children. He's in hospital right now, but I'm sure he'll be pleased to know that he installed the smoke alarm in the wrong place.'

LIKE SO MANY RESORTS, Matlock Bath was biker heaven. Even today, motorbikes were parked against the kerb on South Parade, polished and gleaming. Most of the bikers on the pavement seemed to be well past their youth, though. Their leathers bulged in the wrong places, and when they took off their helmets their hair was grey and straggly, or missing altogether.

'Hell's Granddads,' said Gavin Murfin as they drove past. 'They don't do the ton any more, they just park up for a cup of tea and a fairy cake.'

'And to show off their bikes to each other, by the looks of it,' Cooper added.

'That's it, Ben. Nothing too strenuous at their age.'

But the statistics told a different story, and it wasn't funny. Last year, two bikers had lost their lives in one day on roads in the Matlock area. One of the victims had been in his forties, the other in his fifties.

'So where are these people who think they saw the shooting victim on Saturday?' said Murfin, yawning extravagantly.

'Rose Shepherd was seen at the Riber Tea Rooms on South Parade, and the Aquarium on North Parade. Oh, and the Masson Mill shopping village, a bit further down the road.'

'We'd better split up, I suppose.'

'It'll be a lot quicker, Gavin.'

Although it seemed to form one continuous promenade along the west bank of the River Derwent, Matlock Bath's main street was split into two halves: North Parade and South Parade. In the middle were a couple of three-storey stone villas that had somehow escaped being converted into commercial premises. Cooper parked his Toyota on the roadside in front of a shop called the Biker's Gearbox. Then he and Murfin took a parade each.

Cooper had drawn North Parade, and had to walk back the way they'd come. There had to be a dozen cafés and fish restaurants in this length of road alone, and the smell of fish and chips hung over the promenade like a haze, even though it was a weekday and out of season.

He passed the photograph museum, which was called Life in a Lens, and noticed that a Victorian tea room had been opened on the ground floor. He'd have to call and ask about the webcam later.

The aquarium's window display was of a deep-sea diver and treasure chest, but the ground floor was taken up by an amusement arcade. He asked at the pay booth for the member of staff he wanted, and was directed up the stairs.

'He'll be with you in a minute.'

At the top of the stairs, he waited by the original petrifying well. This was what the first visitors to Matlock Bath had come to see—ordinary items apparently turning to stone. Thermal water still ran down a channel through the building, gurgling ominously somewhere beneath his feet. The objects he could make out under their layer of calcium included teapots, a bird's cage, a telephone and a deer's skull, complete with antlers.

Suddenly, a man was standing beside him. 'You've come to see me?'

'Yes, if you called the police in response to our appeals.' Cooper fumbled for his ID, but the man didn't even look at it.

'I'm a bit busy, so you'll have to keep up with me while I'm working. I have to check all the safety precautions and signs while it's quiet.'

'All right. But before we go any further, is this the woman you remember seeing here on Saturday?'

The man glanced at the photograph. 'Yes, that's her. It's the same photo that was in the papers, isn't it?'

'Yes, I'm just making sure. The reproduction is sometimes a bit poor.'

In the aquarium, red-eared terrapins basked on a concrete beach under halogen spot lamps. There were vegetarian piranhas and South American snakeheads that swam with their long bodies hanging in graceful curves.

'She came in on Saturday afternoon, about two fifteen. Didn't stop here for long. She had a quick walk round, then stood by the thermal pool.'

'What made you notice her?'

'Well, it's not often we have people coming in on their own. A woman of sixty or so? She seemed harmless, but you never know.'

'So what did she do?'

'Pretty much what you did—stopped at the petrifying well, then came through here and looked at the fish. She liked the terrapins, as I recall.'

He opened a door, and they walked out of the heat of the aquarium onto a cool, tiled walkway beside an outdoor pool.

'This was the original baths, you know. The Victorians thought the water cured rheumatism. The pool is still fed by the thermal spring.'

Cooper looked over the side of the pool. It was full of colourful Japanese fish and fat mirror carp.

'The lady stood here for a bit watching the children feed the fish.'

'Did she speak to anyone?'

'No, she was just watching.'

Cooper waited while the man checked a side door. Despite the temperature of the water, it was much cooler out here, because the pool was open to the sky. Looking up, Cooper noticed a camera mounted on the wall, focused on the feeding station. There was a plop as one of the larger fish surfaced.

'Before you ask, there wasn't anyone else in here,' the man said. 'Did you think the lady might have come in the aquarium to meet someone?'

'It was a possibility. Was she carrying anything when she came in?'

'Come to think of it, yes. A carrier bag of some kind.'

Cooper followed the man back down the stairs. 'And did she still have the bag when she went out?'

'I can't recall.'

'And that was it?'

'Yes, that was it. Then she left.'

'Did you notice anything unusual about her manner?'

'No. I got the impression she was killing time. In fact, I'd have said she came in to get out of the rain—except it wasn't raining that day.'

'How was she dressed?'

'I dunno. A jacket of some kind. And slacks. Black, I think. Trousers, you know, not jeans. She wasn't scruffy.'

'Oh? Did you get the impression she'd dressed up a bit to come out?'

'Well, she'd made an effort, definitely.'

'But not to come here? She was just killing time, right?'

'She wasn't looking for anyone in here. She hardly seemed to notice other people. A self-contained sort of person, if you know what I mean?'

'Yes, I know what you mean. Thank you for your time.'

As he left, Cooper noticed that a view from the camera in the thermal bath was projected onto a screen over the entrance. On a busier day, you could watch from the street as children fed the fish or threw coins into the water. In fact, if he'd been standing here at the right time on Saturday afternoon, he would probably have seen Rose Shepherd.

BRIAN MULLEN'S HANDS were still bandaged, and he fumbled a bit taking off the radio headphones when he saw his visitor coming. From the look on his face, Fry thought he was going to leap out of bed and make a run for it. The ward sister had said yesterday that he'd been so frightened he'd fought against being kept in hospital. But what was he frightened of?

'How are you getting on, Mr Mullen?' she asked, pulling a chair up to the side of his bed.

'Oh, not too bad,' he said warily. 'You're the police, are you?'

'Yes, sir.'

'Everyone's been very good to me. A vicar came round. And there was a counsellor, to see if I needed help.'

Now the pinkness in his cheeks had subsided, Mullen's narrow, angular face looked very pale. His voice sounded hoarse from the effects of smoke inhalation, and he reached for a glass of water standing on the bedside cabinet, holding the glass carefully between the tips of his fingers.

'I hope the hospital have managed to keep the press away, sir,' said Fry.

'The press? I never even thought about them.' Mullen looked suddenly panicked. 'You've got to tell the doctors. I have to go home.'

'You're much better here for now, sir. You'll be able to leave when you're fit. Meanwhile, we need to talk about what happened at your house.'

Mullen lay back on his pillows. 'Oh God, I suppose it's necessary.'

'If we're going to find out what happened, it is.'

'Tell me something, though—is Luanne all right?'

'Your daughter, sir? Yes. She's with your in-laws. There's no need to worry about her. Why shouldn't she be safe?'

'I don't know. She's only eighteen months old.'

Fry watched his bandaged hands twitching, his eyes roving anxiously around the room. She was puzzled by his reactions. But Brian Mullen was a victim, a bereaved relative. Protocol called for politeness and consideration.

'Your daughter wasn't in the house at the time of the fire, was she?'

'No. Henry and Moira had been looking after her for a few days, to give us a bit of respite. Luanne wasn't sleeping, you see. She was having us out of bed every couple of hours.'

'Did your wife take anything to help her sleep, Mr Mullen?'

'Yes, I think she might have done. A couple of pills, maybe.'

'Any idea what she took?'

He shook his head, and Fry decided to leave it for a while. She could easily get the information from Lindsay's GP.

'As for you, I believe you'd been out for the evening?'

'I won't ever be able to forgive myself for that. I should have been there with my family. I could have saved them, couldn't I?'

'Probably not, Mr Mullen. You could have ended up a fatality yourself.'

'It would have been better if I had died with them. To have survived seems . . . well, it seems like a punishment somehow.'

Fry nodded cautiously. Statements like this always sounded false to her. She couldn't help thinking that Brian Mullen had been rehearsing the phrases in his head for maximum effect.

'Who were you out with that night, sir?'

'Just some mates.'

'Anyone in particular?'

'Oh, my mate from work, Jed—Jed Skinner.'

'And you arrived home at about one thirty a.m. Is that right?'

'Yes, I paid the taxi driver at the corner of Darwin Street, and I didn't realise what was happening at first. I saw the flashing lights from the fire engines. There was so much smoke.'

'When did you realise it was your own house on fire?'

'Not until I was almost there. Things looked so different with the lights and the smoke, and the hoses running across the road. I was thinking, "Some poor bugger's got a real problem there," and wondering who it was. It didn't seem possible that it was *my* house they were all looking at.'

'I suppose you weren't thinking too clearly at the time, either.'

'What do you mean?'

'Well, I expect you'd had a few drinks, hadn't you, Mr Mullen?'

The look on his face changed then. His colour went a deeper pink, his mouth twisted into a less relaxed shape. Fry tried her hardest to read his expression as guilt, but it looked more like petulance.

'Yeah, a few.'

'Which club had you been in, by the way?'

'The Broken Wheel.'

'All right. So when you finally realised it was your house on fire . . .?'

'I looked around for Lindsay and the boys, obviously. There was a crowd of people gawping. I couldn't see my family anywhere.'

'So you ran into the house?'

'Yes . . .' He hesitated. 'No, not straight away. I saw my neighbour, Keith Wade. I asked him where Lindsay was. He said he hadn't seen her, or the boys either. Well, I knew from the look on his face . . .'

'Knew what?'

'That they were still in there.'

As Brian Mullen reached the next part of his story, a physical reaction was evident in the tightening of his mouth, the half-closed eyes, the sheen of sweat that appeared on his brow. Fear, yes—and a memory of pain, too.

But he had been burned by the fire, of course, and his breathing had been affected by smoke inhalation, evident in the hoarseness of his voice, and perhaps in a peculiar inability to vary the pitch of his speech. That might be why his words sounded almost mechanical and insincere. Just might be.

'The firemen took no notice of me at first,' he said. 'They were too busy getting kitted out. They seemed to be doing everything so slowly. My house was burning, and my kids were in there, but these blokes were fiddling with masks and oxygen tanks. So I went in.' Mullen stared at her defensively. 'I knew where Lindsay and the boys would be. So it made sense.'

'Perhaps at the time it did,' conceded Fry.

He bridled at her tone. 'I couldn't stand there and do nothing.'

'So how far did you get?'

'Only to the stairs.'

'Tell me about it, please.'

Mullen winced at the memory. 'I ran in and got maybe half a dozen steps up the stairs. But then the smoke was so thick that I suddenly didn't know which way I was going. It was in my eyes and in my throat, and I was trying to hold my breath, but I couldn't. I started to feel dizzy. I wanted to carry on, I really did. But I only managed one more step.'

'And then the firefighters caught up with you and pulled you out?'

'Yes, that's right.'

Fry pointed at his hands. 'What did you burn yourself on, Mr Mullen?'

He looked at the bandages and frowned. 'I'm not sure. It must have been the banister rail. That would have been the only thing I touched.'

'With both hands?'

He shrugged. 'I suppose so.'

She let him think about that for a moment. 'You didn't go into any of the rooms downstairs? The sitting room, for example?'

'No. I knew my family would be upstairs, in the bedrooms.'

'Could your wife have been waiting up for you to come home?'

'No, she never did that.'

'You see, the sitting room is where the fire is believed to have started. It must have been obvious that the smoke was coming from there.'

'So?'

'Well, perhaps your instinct might have been to try to put the fire out.'

'It didn't go through my mind,' said Mullen. 'I can't understand why you're asking me these questions.'

'It's for purposes of elimination, Mr Mullen. It will help us to establish the cause of the fire.'

'What? Are you saying it was started deliberately?'

'It's a possibility we have to leave open. That's why it's important to establish your movements. If we find evidence of someone entering that room during the night of the fire, we'll know it wasn't you, won't we?'

Fry smiled at him, but he didn't look reassured.

'Don't worry about it now,' she said. 'You have a lot to think about. Let us know if we can be of any assistance. They've offered you counselling . . .?'

'Yes, all of that stuff,' said Mullen impatiently.

'And you do have some family in the area to support you?'

'There's Lindsay's parents. My dad is in Ireland. He hasn't been well himself, so he might not make it over.'

'Is there no one else locally?'

Mullen shook his head. 'There's only John.'

'John?'

'John Lowther. My brother-in-law. But Henry and Moira say he's devastated about Lindsay.'

Fry stood up. 'Well, take care, sir. We'll keep you informed.'

Mullen looked up at her, anxious now that she was leaving. 'I tested that smoke alarm regularly, you know. It was working all right.'

'Yes, well don't worry about that now.'

Mullen sank back onto his pillow, exhausted. Fry began to move quietly away, but his voice stopped her.

'We promised Luanne we'd take her to see the illuminations in Matlock Bath,' he said hoarsely. 'You know, with the parade of boats, and the fireworks? We were going to take all the kids there at half term, for a treat. It would have been Luanne's first time. We won't be taking them now, will we?'

Fry hesitated in the doorway. 'No, sir. I'm sorry.'

She walked out of the ward, trying to make sense of Brian Mullen. At times, the emotions underlying his responses had been too complicated to pin down. But one thing she was sure of. The idea that the fire might have been set deliberately had come as no surprise to him at all.

IN MATLOCK BATH, houses seemed to climb on top of each other in their haste to escape the valley floor. Above them were the two Victorian pleasure grounds on Masson Hill—the Heights of Jacob, the Heights of Abraham. Their slopes were occupied by modern leisure parks now, the shapes of fairy-tale castles poking up among the trees. From a base station near the railway line, strings of white cable cars carried visitors up to the attractions. Cooper could see the grey stone tower on the summit, a flag fluttering in the breeze.

Drawing a blank at the two B&Bs to the left of the aquarium, he walked a bit further up North Parade, where he found another amusement centre and a shop selling handmade chocolates, both of which were closed.

Across the road was the Jubilee Bridge—wooden planks and iron girders, with an old gas lamp on a central arch. It led across the river to a bandstand and the remains of a switchback railway.

Cooper remembered that the Life in a Lens museum stood on the other side of the aquarium. He took the chance to call in. The staff were very helpful. They agreed to send him the webcam footage for Saturday afternoon.

When he came out, a school party was queuing to enter the mining museum further down the road. There were two cameras on the outside wall nearby, but they were focused on the entrance to Brody's nightclub. When he was a teenager, Brody's had been known as 'The Pav', because it was on the upper floor of the Pavilion, above the mining museum.

But where the heck was Gavin Murfin? Cooper stood by his Toyota for a while, looking up and down the street. He supposed it had been a mistake to let Murfin take the interview with the waitress at the tea rooms. With the smell of fish and chips on the promenade he'd be giddy with hunger by now.

Finally, Cooper pulled out his phone and called Murfin's number. The ringing tone seemed to be echoed by a tune playing nearby. He turned and saw Murfin coming out of the ice-cream parlour, eating a choc ice. And waving.

'OK, I did the waitress at the Riber Tea Rooms,' said Murfin, when Cooper reached him. 'Nice lass, name of Tina. Get this—she reckons she saw Rose Shepherd talking to two other people in the café on Saturday afternoon.'

'Wow, you got more than I did,' said Cooper. 'What time was this?'

'Around two thirty, she thinks.'

'That must have been after Miss Shepherd came out of the aquarium.'

'Tina says the other two, a man and a woman, had come in earlier. The Shepherd woman came in about a quarter of an hour later on her own. She ordered a coffee, looked around, then went and sat at the couple's table.'

'Did she seem to know them?'

'That's what Tina's not sure about. There were no empty tables, so Shepherd would have had to sit with someone, and she chose those two.'

'Right. We don't know why, though?'

'Maybe because they looked the most harmless. All Tina can say is that when she took the coffee to the table, the three of them weren't talking and the atmosphere seemed cool. But they did chat a bit later on. The couple left the café first, and Miss Shepherd went out right after them.'

Cooper unlocked the car. 'Well, it's something at least, Gavin,' he said. 'She must have come down into Matlock Bath for a reason.'

'Oh, and I did a couple of shops,' said Murfin.

'Yes, the ice-cream parlour. I saw that.'

Murfin groaned theatrically. 'You know, you're getting as bad as Miss.'

'Get in the car, Gavin. We've got to call at Masson Mill.'

MASSON HAD BEEN the world's oldest working textile mill until production stopped fifteen years ago. Here, in the Derwent Valley, was where industrial history had changed. It had all started for Sir Richard Arkwright at Cromford Mill, just downstream. But Masson was his great flagship.

This mill had been designed to impress. The central bay was decorated with half-moons of glass between Venetian-style windows. Above the windows, Arkwright's name was spelt out on the brickwork in proud capital letters, and on the top of the bay stood a shuttered cupola.

One of the later extensions to the mill had been converted into a multi-storey car park. Cooper parked on the roof near a side entrance to the shopping village. Over the wall, he could see the weir, built to take advantage of an outcrop of rock on the opposite bank of the river. The water ran into a goyt, the fast-flowing channel that had driven the mill's waterwheels.

'What are we looking for here, Ben?'

'Eva Hooper. She runs a retail unit on the road level.'

Murfin opened the door into the shops. There were four open-plan retail levels, accessed from a central staircase. Each floor was divided into areas selling discount designer clothes, furniture, food, golf equipment. On the lowest level was a restaurant, lined with windows overlooking the river.

'Gavin, why don't you find the offices and ask about CCTV footage? There's a camera over the main entrance.'

'All right.'

Cooper followed the signs for the working textile museum. Perhaps it had been part of Miss Shepherd's afternoon out, before her visit to the aquarium. He left the shopping area and passed through an echoey room over uneven wooden floors that creaked and shifted underfoot.

He found a man taking money on a flight of stairs that led down into the spinning and weaving sheds.

'Were you working on Saturday?' he asked.

'In the afternoon.'

'Do you remember this woman coming in?'

The man looked at Cooper's photograph. 'No, sorry.'

In the rooms below, two enormous machines rattled away unattended, and stacks of shuttles sat in alcoves along the walls, below shelves full of old tools and equipment. Cooper could smell lubricating oil and hear the chug of the looms, leather belts spinning over wheels in the glass-roofed sheds. Signs pointed towards a distant doorway—the bobbin room.

Cooper turned back. 'Thanks for your time,' he said.

In a distant corner of the shopping village, he found Eva Hooper. Her unit sold prints of Peak District landscapes, postcards, ethnic gifts, pottery, leatherwork, gemstones—anything that tourists might be interested in.

'I think she was here,' she said. 'It was Saturday, so we were busy.'

'Yes, I understand,' he said. 'Did she buy anything?'

'I'm not sure. You could ask my assistant, but she's not here today. She works for me part-time when I'm busy.'

'What's her name?'

'Frances—we call her Fran.'

Cooper paused with his pen poised over his notebook. He'd spoken to a Frances very recently. 'Frances what?'

'Birtland. She lives a couple of miles away, in Foxlow.'

FRY WAS SATISFIED that she'd done everything she could to prevent any further loss of evidence from the house at Darwin Street. The examination had been thorough and the experts had even agreed on where the fire started.

One of the SOCOs assigned to Darwin Street was Liz Petty, who was unpacking a holdall full of stepping plates in the hallway. 'Watch where you're walking,' she said, without looking round.

'Yes, all right.'

Petty looked up then. 'Oh. Hi, Diane. How are you doing?'

'Fine.'

'Making progress on the inquiry?'

'Yes, thanks.'

'There'll be some publicity on this one, I suppose. There was a TV news van outside earlier. I don't know what they were filming.'

'They can film what they like. There's nothing for them to see.'

Fry found Quinton Downie in the sitting room, packing his equipment away. He looked satisfied with his efforts, reminding her of the fire service dog, the chocolate labrador. He was almost wagging his tail.

'Liquid accelerants are volatile, so it's good that we collected debris samples early,' he told her. 'Arsonists tend to use petrol, which has a low flashpoint but rather a narrow flammability range—it stops burning when the oxygen level is reduced. Hydrogen and acetylene are far more dangerous.'

'The accelerant in this case could be a butane-based lighter fluid.'

'The flashpoint of butane is about the same as petrol, well below ambient temperature.' Downie looked around the sitting room. 'In a closed room, there normally isn't sufficient ventilation for unlimited burning. If it had been airtight, the fire might have gone out. But there was a little bit of ventilation. You're lucky we're not looking at radiation-induced flashover.'

'OK, but here the victims died upstairs,' said Fry. 'Smoke inhalation. I can't understand why they never even made it to the stairs.'

Downie smiled. 'Look, it goes like this . . .' He demonstrated by closing his eyes and clutching his throat. 'You've taken a breath and you can't open your eyes because as soon as you do they water. You take another breath and the irritants hit the back of your throat. You retch and take an even deeper breath—it's a natural, involuntary reaction. It fills your lungs with toxic fumes. That disorientates you, makes you dizzy, and puts you down on the floor. While you're incapacitated, the toxicity takes over.'

To Fry's amazement, he lay down on the floor and demonstrated what it was like to be dead. She'd never seen anybody look less dead in her life.

'We used to say you had seven minutes to get out of a burning building. Now, with all the materials inside them, it's more like three minutes.'

'And that's why we advise people to install smoke alarms.'

'Ah, yes. The smoke alarm. Pity about that.'

'It was functioning, wasn't it? Mr Mullen says he tested it regularly.'

'No doubt he did. But, like most people, all he was doing was pressing the button. That just proves that the sound works and the batteries aren't dead. It doesn't tell you whether the detector is functioning.'

'What are you saying?'

'I took a look at the smoke alarm earlier. I'm guessing the family had building work done in the kitchen at some time.'

'Yes, they had new units put in about six months ago.'

'There you go, then. There was a thin layer of cement and plaster particles, with a couple of layers of dust. You're supposed to vacuum around the detector regularly to prevent the build-up of dust. I'm sorry for the chap, and all that. But facts are facts.'

'What about where the fire started?'

'Now, that's interesting,' said Downie. 'The point of origin would normally be near the area of greatest damage. But it appears to me that the fire was started by applying flame to a quantity of papers adjacent to this chair here, right among these toys.'

'But the other chair seems to have suffered most damage.'

'It's rather deceptive at first glance, isn't it? It's the nature of the upholstery that makes the difference.'

'Do you mean polyurethane foam?'

'All three items of furniture contain polyurethane foam padding. But the chair this side of the room is upholstered with a thick cotton weave. The cover charred and pyrolised, but the weave didn't fall away, so it provided some retardation of heat release.' He moved across the room. 'The settee, on the other hand, was covered in a partly synthetic fabric, probably polycotton. And this, I'm afraid, was a cheaply upholstered armchair, with what was probably a wholly thermoplastic cover over polyurethane foam, without any inter-lining. The cover melted and fell away to expose the foam to the fire. Hence the greater damage.'

'I think I see,' said Fry, surprised to realise that she actually did.

'Excellent,' said Downie. 'Well, that's my theory for now. I'll test some remaining fabric from the three items. But the carpet is probably going to be most helpful. Carpet absorbs accelerant well, and retains residue longer.'

Petty had moved into the sitting room and was concentrating her attention on a heavily damaged area of carpet.

'Is this where the accelerant was used?' Fry asked.

'We think so. It's one of the sites identified by the dog.'

Petty photographed the burn pattern before cutting into the carpet. She rolled up a sample with the foam backing on the inside and eased it vertically into a container.

Fry watched her for a moment, then left the house.

IN THE CID ROOM at West Street, Murfin was reading the witness appeal press release for the Foxlow shooting, with Cooper looking over his shoulder.

> Detectives are appealing for witnesses after the murder of a woman in Foxlow on Sunday. Miss Rose Shepherd, sixty-one, was killed by two shots from a high-powered rifle, fired from a field behind her house in Pinfold Lane during the early hours of the morning. Miss Shepherd had lived in the village for the past ten months, and police have yet to establish a motive for her killing.
>
> Meanwhile, officers are keen to talk to witnesses who might have seen anyone suspicious in the area during the last few days. They would particularly like to trace the owner of a blue Vauxhall Astra saloon which was seen in Foxlow around the time of the murder.
>
> The driver of the car is described as a white male, aged around thirty-five years old, about five feet ten inches tall and of medium build. He was wearing a black Parker style coat with the hood up.
>
> Anyone with information is asked to contact Edendale CID, or call the Crimestoppers line in confidence.

'A Parker style coat?' said Murfin. 'Will that be from the same people who make pens?'

'Oh God,' said Cooper. 'That's embarrassing.'

'They mean "parka", don't they? Even I know that.'

Murfin folded the press release up and tried to create wings so that he could throw it across the room. 'Now, we'll have a load of old biddies going round looking for coats that say Parker on the label. I don't think "parka" is even a brand name, is it?'

'No, it's an Inuit word. It means a coat made from a fur pelt.'

'Well, I can see you read books, Ben. Our local pub has a quiz on Tuesday nights. Fancy going in for it some time? You can win a keg of beer.'

'I don't think so, Gavin. Thanks.'

'Oh, I forgot. You've got better things to do in the evenings these days. Not allowed in the pub with your mates any more?'

'You've got it all wrong.'

To change the subject, Cooper asked Murfin if he'd heard about the fire service dog and its identification of accelerant at the Darwin Street house.

'I'm not a big fan of dogs,' said Murfin. 'Cats need less work.'

'I've seen that dog in action at previous incidents,' said Cooper. 'She has a great time when she's working. Absolutely loves it.'

'Well, I have to admit, the bitch did a good job at Darwin Street.'

Cooper caught a movement from the corner of his eye, and saw Diane Fry frozen in the doorway. She was staring at Murfin.

'Hi, Diane,' he said. 'We were just talking about the fire service dog.'

Fry unfroze slowly. 'Oh, yes. That bitch.' She moved into the room, waving a copy of the press release. 'Have you seen this? It's ridiculous.'

'Yes, we know,' said Murfin. 'We spotted it straight away.'

'Somebody should speak to Media Relations. This sort of thing makes us look stupid. I mean, what use is an appeal for information when they leave our phone number off?'

Murfin looked at the press release again. 'Oh,' he said. 'So they did.'

'The DI says we have a meeting tomorrow to review progress.'

'Another review? We never seem to do anything else.'

'It's better than wasting time and effort rushing off in the wrong direction,' said Fry. 'Regular reviews ensure the most effective use of resources.'

Cooper glanced at her. She was sounding more like a manager every day.

STELLA SEARLE looked away from the TV set in her bedroom towards the shower, where she could hear water running. Darren had bought her the TV. He'd do anything to keep her happy, except the one thing she really wanted.

'Daz!' she called. 'Darren!'

'What's up? I'm having a shower, darling.'

'Come out here. There's something on the telly you've got to see.'

'It'll wait. I won't be a minute.'

'No—now,' she said, using the tone of voice she knew he'd recognise.

'Oh, bloody hell.'

The water stopped, and after a moment he padded out into the bedroom with a towel wrapped round his middle. 'What is it, Stell?'

She looked back at the screen, but the newsreader had moved on to another item. 'They were just doing a bit about the woman who got shot in the village the other night.'

'Oh, that. Yeah, I heard about it.' He turned and began to head back towards the shower, clutching at the towel to keep it in place.

'They said the police were looking for witnesses,' she said. 'And they're looking for a car that someone saw in the village that night. A blue Vauxhall Astra. That's your car, isn't it?'

Darren hesitated with his hand on the shower door. 'What else did it say?'

'They particularly wanted to speak to the bloke with the blue Astra—a man in a parka, about thirty-five years old.'

Darren didn't reply. She glanced at him, and saw that he'd gone pale.

'Maybe the police think you might have seen something important. Did you see anything, Darren?'

Darren was silent for longer than she thought was natural.

'Did you, Darren?'

'No,' he said finally. But he didn't sound too sure.

Stella touched his chest, then flinched away at the coldness of it.

'No,' he said again. 'I didn't see anything.'

'Was there anybody about in the village when you left that night?'

He grabbed her arm then, and for the first time Stella felt a chill of fear.

'Get it into your head right now,' he said. 'I didn't see anything that night. Got it, Stell? I didn't see a bloody thing.'

5

Wednesday, October 26

Cooper was examining the yellow, square-sided can of Swan lighter fluid. 'Do we have a chance of tracing the shop it was bought from?' he asked Fry.

'Yes, if we had the manpower,' she said. 'You can buy the hundred millilitre can for about three pounds, but it isn't stocked everywhere. Anyway, we got an initial report faxed through from Downie's lab this morning. The chromatogram points to a common hydrocarbon fuel, n-butane.'

'Lighter fluid, then.'

'Specifically, butane lighter fluid. The positive samples were from carpet in the Mullens' sitting room, and from the toy box in the corner near the video. Not much accelerant used—but it wouldn't have needed a lot.'

'It could have been an accidental spillage, couldn't it?' Cooper asked.

'Have you tried accidentally spilling lighter fluid, Ben?'

'I don't even smoke. I never have.'

'Well, it comes in an aerosol can like this one, with a pressure valve that fits into the lighter. To spill it, you'd have to prise the top off the can.'

'Even so, Diane, one of the Mullens' kids could have done that.'

'Maybe. So which of the Mullens was a smoker—Brian or Lindsay?'

'I don't know.'

'The answer is, neither. And the only can of lighter fluid that's turned up is this one, which was found in a wheelie bin down the road. If this is the right one, then it wasn't put there by accident.'

Fry had called a meeting of her team. She'd managed to borrow DC Cooper from the Shepherd inquiry. Murfin was finishing a phone call.

'Right,' she said when he'd put the receiver down. 'We need to chase up forensics from the fire scene—particularly that sitting room. Brian Mullen swears that he never went in there that night. If we find any evidence of his presence in the room after the fire started, then he's lying.'

'Right.'

'Somebody will have to interview this Jed Skinner. That should happen before it occurs to Mullen to contact him so they get their story straight.'

'I'll do that, if you like,' said Cooper.

'No, let Gavin go. Mullen's story is that he came home from the Broken Wheel in a taxi, which dropped him off at the end of the street. I want you to find the taxi driver and confirm when and where he picked Mullen up and dropped him off. Then I'd like to know what happened to Skinner. Did the driver see him outside the club? Did he and Mullen share a taxi, even? We also need to talk again to the next-door neighbour, Keith Wade.'

'OK.'

'But first, I want you to come with me to the hospital.'

'OH, YOU'RE BACK,' said Brian Mullen when they entered his room.

'Sorry to bother you again, sir,' said Fry. 'This is my colleague, DC Cooper. We have a few more questions, to help us clarify what happened the night your family died. Is that all right, sir?'

He lay back wearily. 'I suppose so. As long as I can get out of here.'

Fry opened her notebook. 'You told me that you arrived home at about one thirty after your taxi dropped you off at the corner of Darwin Street. You saw the fire, but didn't realise it was your own house until you were closer.'

'That's right.'

'Who did you say you were out with, by the way?'

'One of my mates, Jed Skinner. I work with him.'

'Just one mate, was it? Just you and Jed out for the night?'

'Yes, like I said.'

Fry looked at her notebook. 'You told me you were "out with mates". That's "mates", plural.'

'Well, I might have said that. We were in the pub first off—the Forester's Arms. I'm a regular there, so I *was* with lots of mates then.'

'But only Jed at the Broken Wheel?'

'Like I said.'

'You went there alone, the two of you? And then you left together?'

'Yes.'

'And that was just after one. So the next person you spoke to must have been the taxi driver. And then there was your neighbour, Mr Wade. Shortly after that, you ran into the house, then the firefighters pulled you back out.'

'I've told you all this. For God's sake—' Mullen controlled his burst of anger, then raised his still bandaged hands, as if presenting the evidence.

Fry gave Cooper a look that told him to take over for a while.

'Do you smoke, sir?' asked Cooper.

'No.'

'What about your wife? I'm sorry to ask—'

'No, Lindsay didn't smoke either. I can see what you're driving at, but we both agreed not to smoke a long time ago, for the sake of the kids.'

'I see. What about other members of your family?'

'John smokes. But he knows not to when he's in our house . . .'

Cooper consulted his notes. 'That's John Lowther? Your brother-in-law?'

'Yes.'

Fry noticed a nurse hovering in the background. 'We'll let you rest now, Mr Mullen. You've had a terrible ordeal, and we appreciate your cooperation.'

'It's OK. Obviously, I want to help. I mean, it was my wife and kids who got killed in that fire. If some bastard—'

Fry stood up. 'I understand. Well, until we speak again, Mr Mullen, I'd like you to see if you can remember who else you spoke to that night at the Forester's Arms and at the Broken Wheel.'

'*What?*'

'Well, think about it, sir. The fire might have been started by someone who knew that you'd be out of the house at the time. Someone who'd seen you partying at the Broken Wheel, perhaps.'

Mullen nodded. 'So you're not letting go of this idea that the fire was started deliberately?'

'No, we're not,' said Fry. 'Is there some reason you think we should?'

'I just don't see how it's possible.'

'Well, we'll know that better when we get the forensic results.'

His shoulders sagged at the mention of forensics. Sometimes, the word seemed to carry a symbolic power, as if it was a scientific magic that human beings were helpless to challenge. And perhaps that was right. Forensic evidence could kick-start a process that was impossible to stop until the criminal justice juggernaut had crushed everyone in its way.

'Leave me alone,' he said. 'Leave us alone. Someone has got to look after Luanne.'

'I THOUGHT YOU were a bit rough on Mr Mullen,' said Cooper as they left the hospital and walked to the car park.

'Yes, I was. And wouldn't you have expected him to complain more?'

'But then you'd be saying he protested too much—a sure sign of guilt.'

Fry laughed. 'Look, you know the husband is by far the likeliest candidate in a case like this. We have to look at him thoroughly.'

'You've given him a chance to work out his story now, though. You warned him you were going to ask for the names of other people he saw that night. Shouldn't we have asked him right there and then?'

'My guess is he'd have said he couldn't remember. If I'd pushed him, he'd have got all stressed, and a doctor would have come and kicked us out.'

'So . . .?'

'So this way, I've given him time to think about it while he's recovering from his injuries. And if I've judged him right, the longer he has to think about it, the more anxious he'll get. Then he'll start trying to think up something to give us when we come back. That's where he'll go wrong.'

'Diane, I wouldn't have believed it possible, but I think you're getting more devious than ever.'

'Thank you.'

'You really think these tactics will work on Brian Mullen?'

'Yes. Don't you?'

'Only if he's guilty.'

COOPER HAD TO RING the bell of Keith Wade's house for several minutes before there was a thumping on the stairs in the hallway and the door opened. Wade glared at Cooper, then recognised Fry standing behind him.

'What's happened?' he said. 'What's the panic?'

He was unshaven and bleary-eyed, dressed in track-suit bottoms and a T-shirt that looked as though it had just been thrown on.

'Sorry, did we wake you up, sir?' said Fry.

'Yes, I told you—I do late shifts.'

'We won't keep you long. This is my colleague, DC Cooper.'

Wade glanced up and down the street. 'You'd better come in a minute.'

His house was pretty much what she'd expected. Stale smells of cooking and body odour, mingling with cigarette smoke. He had to move piles of newspapers off chairs to let them sit down.

'Yes, of course I remember Brian arriving that night,' said Wade when she prompted him. 'How is he, by the way?'

'Physically fine. We hope he'll be discharged today.'

'Great. He's a brave bloke, you know.'

'Did you see how he arrived?'

'No. He was only a couple of houses away by the time I saw him. There was too much else going on, you know. He looked pretty dazed.'

'What did he say?'

Wade frowned. 'I can't remember exactly. But he wanted to know if Lindsay and the kids were still in the house. When I said I thought they were, he went sort of berserk and ran off.'

'And that's when he tried to get into the house?'

'He *did* get in. The firemen had broken the door down by then. Brian ran past them and was in the house before they could stop him. Brave, like I said. I feel really sorry for him, you know. We've always been good friends. As for little Jack and Liam, they were nice lads. It's such a shame.'

For the second time, Wade seemed to have forgotten that Lindsay Mullen had died in the fire, too. There had to be a reason for the oversight.

'How had Brian and Lindsay been getting on recently?' asked Fry.

'Sorry?'

'You knew them well, and you live right next door. You must have been aware of any problems in their marriage. Domestic arguments tend to get a bit loud, and you're only a few feet away.'

Wade shifted uneasily. 'I don't want to say. It wouldn't be right.'

'In these circumstances, it's not right to keep anything back,' said Fry.

Wade looked at her, then at Cooper. 'OK, I have heard a few rows from next door,' he said. 'But it's normal, isn't it? God knows, I had enough bust-ups with Pat before she left.'

'Did the Mullens' arguments happen recently?' asked Cooper.

'Well, there'd been more of them recently. Come to think of it, I reckon I heard them arguing on Sunday night.'

'The night of the fire?'

'Yes, it must have been before Brian went out. I recall he slammed the front door a bit hard as he left.'

Before they left his house, Fry reminded Wade of his promise to email the photos from his digital camera. 'If you prefer, we could borrow the camera now and return it when we've downloaded the pictures?'

'No, no—I'll do it,' said Wade. 'I've been a bit busy, that's all. But I'll get around to it, I promise.'

THE CONFERENCE ROOM was packed for the briefing, with many officers pulled in from elsewhere to beef up the inquiry teams. Cooper saw Diane Fry come in and sit on the front row, not looking at anyone around her.

'First of all, we've had no luck tracing the Vauxhall Astra,' said Hitchens when the briefing got under way. 'Besides, it appears the Astra was never in the field behind the victim's house anyway.'

A scatter of groans and mutterings followed this announcement.

'Forensics tell us the tracks were made by something bigger than an Astra. More weight, wider tyres. And four-wheel drive.'

'We don't have any reports of a vehicle like that, do we?' said someone.

'What sort of tyres?' added another voice.

'We'll get a match on the tread soon,' put in Wayne Abbott, the crime-scene manager.

'Back to the drawing board, then.'

Hitchens was trying not to let his shoulders slump. 'We're starting to get a picture of the victim's movements on the afternoon before she died. We're concentrating on two people that Rose Shepherd met in Matlock Bath. The descriptions from the waitress who served them are vague, but we'll ask her to have a go at some e-fits, and there'll be more appeals in the media. Those two could be the only people who had contact with Miss Shepherd that day.'

He turned to the board, where photographs of the dead woman were displayed. 'Meanwhile, the victim herself remains a mystery. She had little contact with people in Foxlow, and we've found almost nothing that could lead us to anyone who knew her. That's got to be deliberate. We located a diary, but it's only one of those little appointment diaries. We're checking all the entries in her address book. There's always a possibility that some of them are coded in some way. Most of all, we need to trace anyone who ever dealt with Miss Shepherd, particularly if they ever visited Bain House.'

'We're not likely to find a Christmas card list, I suppose?'

'No such luck. Judging by her phone records, Miss Shepherd didn't have many friends. But there are a couple of puzzlers . . .'

Hitchens paused, perhaps for dramatic effect.

'Firstly, the victim's phone records for the past three weeks show two calls to the same public phone box, which turns out to be in a rural location in Bonsall Dale. Obviously, if you're going to phone someone in an isolated call box, it would have to be by prior arrangement.'

There was a bit of fidgeting around the room, but no one could suggest a reason why Rose Shepherd should have been ringing a call box.

'Does 359 figure in the number of the call box?' asked Cooper.

'Good question. The answer is no,' said Hitchens. 'Secondly, there are a couple of diary entries that refer to someone with the initials SN. There was an entry in her address book too, but it had been crossed out.'

'If we can still read the number . . .'

'It's another unregistered pay-as-you-go mobile.'

'This woman is unnatural.'

'Well, let's not get downhearted. We do have a couple of possibilities. Number one, there's the victim's GP. He's away at the moment, but he might have some information for us. Number two, there's her solicitor. According to Windsor and Ellis, the estate agents that handled the house sale, Miss Shepherd paid cash, and the address she gave was a hotel in London. They said it was a very straightforward transaction. She came up to Derbyshire only once, for the viewing, and signed all the papers at her solicitor's.'

'And they've given us the solicitor's details?'

'Yes, that will be prioritised today. And we're still getting calls from the public in response to the media appeals. Almost everything we've got so far has been third hand and uncorroborated, unfortunately. Nevertheless, I've asked the incident-room staff to collate the information.'

'What are we left with?'

'Well, the consensus in Foxlow is that Rose Shepherd was a retired headmistress who had worked in Scotland but came here to live after she inherited money from a relative. Some say her father, others an uncle.'

'That explains the purchase of Bain House, but not her secretiveness.'

'There's more: the word in the village is that she kept her valuables in the house, in some kind of secret stash, and that she was terrified the house might be burgled. There have been a number of break-ins in this area.'

'Yes, that's right.'

'The last titbit is that Rose Shepherd is said to have a boyfriend back in Scotland. She called him Douglas or Dougie, and he lives near Glasgow.'

'Has Dougie ever been seen in Foxlow?' asked Kessen.

'Not so far as we know.'

'Damn it. This means we're going to have to ask for assistance from Strathclyde Police. If they can track down a Rose Shepherd who was a headmistress in their area, it might lead us to Dougie.'

'There's more. The really good news is that we've found someone locally who had direct contact with Miss Shepherd.'

'Hallelujah.'

'It's a chap by the name of Eric Grice, a handyman who did occasional work at Bain House.'

'Perhaps he can tell us why she hardly ever left the house.'

'One suggestion is that she might have been suffering from agoraphobia. An irrational fear of open spaces.'

'But she went into Matlock Bath, didn't she?' said Cooper.

'Yes, and nobody reported her being in any distress. We've spoken to her GP's surgery, and she only ever consulted her doctor for insomnia. She seemed to be in good health otherwise, although they don't have access to her previous records. She told them she'd been living abroad . . .' Hitchens paused. 'Besides, whatever Rose Shepherd was afraid of, it wasn't an irrational fear. The bullets that killed her were real enough.'

'Do we have an update on the bullets?' asked Kessen.

'Well, they've gone to the lab,' said Abbott. 'The firearms examiner should be able to give us the make, model and calibre of the weapon, with a bit of luck.'

'Can't we run the bullets through the ballistics data base?'

'You mean IBIS? Well, we could—but you can only get an identification of a firearm if it's been found somewhere and test-fired in the lab. This weapon is still out there, being used. It won't be recorded in the data base.'

'But if the same firearm was used in an earlier incident where the bullets were found, could we establish a link?'

'Perhaps. Provided those details are on the data base.'

'Ask them to try, then,' said Kessen.

'If you say so.'

'What about the post-mortem report, Paul?'

'Pretty much what we expected,' Hitchens replied. 'One bullet entered near the victim's left eye and ricocheted around the brain for a bit before lodging behind the right ear. The other penetrated her left lung and was removed from a site close to her spine. A high-powered rifle can do a lot of damage.'

He pinned some photographs on the board. From the location of the bullet near the spine, ripples had spread out like a stone dropped in a pond, tearing flesh and crushing soft tissue.

'So far, we can't put anyone else at the scene,' Hitchens continued. 'In fact, we don't even have anyone to perform an official ID until her GP returns. Right now, the nearest thing to a next of kin is her part-time handyman.'

AFTER THE BRIEFING, Fry went with Hitchens to DCI Kessen's office to report her progress on the Darwin Street fire inquiry.

'As soon as he's well enough, I want to take the husband back to the scene,' she said, after she'd brought her senior officers up to speed.

'Why?'

'For a start, I want to see how he reacts. His response to the deaths of his wife and children has been a bit difficult to judge so far, but that could be the sedatives. Also, I haven't told him any details of how the fire started. I'd like to see if he lets slip something he shouldn't know. Or if he's innocent, he might be able to point us to some item that doesn't belong in the house, which might indicate an intruder or a visitor that we don't know about.'

'So you fancy the husband for this one, Diane?'

'Yes, sir. The neighbours say there had been problems in the marriage. And Mr Mullen's alibi for the time the fire started relies entirely on his best friend, Jed Skinner. Murfin went to see him and he confirms Mullen's story to the letter, but I think I might be able to break that alibi down without too much trouble. I need to do it before Mr Mullen is discharged from hospital, though, so they can't get together and tighten up their story.'

Kessen looked at her report. 'If Mullen *is* telling the truth, there must be someone who can substantiate his alibi—the taxi driver, for instance.'

'Admittedly, we haven't traced the driver yet. But even if we do, there was plenty of time for Mr Mullen to start the fire, get clear of the area and catch a taxi back again, arriving when the blaze had taken hold. Then he could do his tragic hero act in full view of the neighbours. Not to mention the firefighters, who were bound to hold him back, so he wouldn't have to be too much of a hero.'

'OK, it's possible. But what about motive?'

'If the marriage was in trouble, it might have come to a head recently. For example, if Mrs Mullen had told him she was filing for divorce, he might have been upset about her taking the children away.'

Kessen nodded. 'The dog in the manger mentality: "If I can't have the children, you're not having them either."'

'Yes, sir. There's one interesting fact from the fire investigator. He says the fire wasn't started in any of the logical places for a random arson attack. It began where the children's toys were stored in the sitting room. Apparently, accelerant was poured over them. That makes the attack seem very personal.'

'And it was carried out by someone with access to the house.'

'Yes. I'm not convinced by the side window being forced. There are no signs of entry inside the room. It's a kitchen window, and I'd expect to find marks on the window ledge or the work surfaces, but there's nothing.'

'Footwear impressions outside?'

Fry shook her head. 'Not after the firefighters had done their bit.'

The DCI looked thoughtful for a moment, then made a decision. 'OK. It sounds as though you've done all the right things, Diane. We'll review the inquiry again as soon as you've got some forensic reports. And let's hope your feeling about the husband is correct. If we have to eliminate him, it opens up a whole different ball game. A triple murder with no suspects is the last thing we need right now.'

ERIC GRICE laid down his electric drill and blew stone dust off the wall. As he wiped a film of sweat from his forehead with the back of his hand, he left a small streak of dust on his temple.

'And I suppose you're flummoxed,' he said.

'Flummoxed?' repeated Hitchens. 'That's an interesting word, Mr Grice. People usually say the police are baffled.'

'Aye. But flummoxed is worse.'

Hitchens didn't smile. People like Eric Grice rarely amused him. 'We've been asking around for a while for someone who had any contact with Miss Shepherd. It would have helped us if you'd come forward earlier.'

'I don't live in the village. I live in Matlock,' said Grice. 'My sister lives here, but she's on her holidays this week. Jersey. Late autumn break.'

'You know, it seems odd that so few people knew anything about Rose Shepherd when she was part of the village for the past year,' Cooper said.

'Well, she might as well have been living in a separate universe from the rest of us. That's the impression she gave whenever I saw her, anyway.'

'Did you see her often? Everyone else says she didn't go out much.'

'She sent for me to come round whenever she needed some odd jobs doing. She tended to save them up, though—enough jobs for me to do in one visit, like. She put up with a dripping tap or a few tiles off the roof for a while, I reckon, because she preferred it to having someone in her house.'

'You had the impression she didn't like you being there?'

Grice fingered a set of Rawlplugs, assessing the size of the hole he'd made in the wall. Then he snapped one off. 'I was only ever there on tolerance. It was like she had to grit her teeth before she even opened the door to me.'

'How many times did you go there?'

'I don't know. Five or six, I suppose. The last time was three weeks ago, to clear the guttering and sweep up dead leaves.'

'Mr Grice, did Rose Shepherd ever talk to you while you were at her house? Did she tell you anything about herself?'

'No, not her. Not a thing.'

'Any little detail that she might have let slip could be useful to us. Why don't you give it some thought—?'

'I don't need to,' said Grice. 'She never talked to me. She pointed out the jobs that wanted doing, then left me to it. Went up to her bedroom or something. I thought it was a bit odd at first. The second time I went up to see her, I tried to make conversation. Only to ask whether she wanted me to fix the loose corner of a carpet while I was there. But she got cross at that and told me she'd get somebody else in if I wanted to ask questions instead of doing the job. After that, I didn't even dare ask for a cup of tea.'

'I assume she paid well.'

'Aye. You do what the customer wants when they're paying over the odds.'

Hitchens was studying him carefully. 'I can't believe you didn't see anything in all the time you were in Bain House, Mr Grice. From what you've just said, you were practically unsupervised. Weren't you curious?'

'A bit. But I couldn't snoop about the place. I didn't want her to turn up suddenly and catch me at it. I'd have been out of a job definitely then.'

'Even so, you're an observant man, I'm sure. It would be hard not to notice anything. And the smallest thing might be significant.'

'OK, I'll give it some thought.'

'By the way, we'll need to take your fingerprints.'

'Why?'

'For elimination purposes. Since you visited Bain House several times, your prints will be there. If we know which are yours, we can discount them.'

'Oh, I see. All right.'

They left Grice to his work on the wall and returned to the station.

'So, what did you make of this handyman?' Hitchens asked. 'Do you think he was telling the truth?'

'Of course not. I bet he was all over that house like a rash. There must have been all kinds of things he noticed.'

'He's just not ready to tell us yet, right?'

'But he will,' said Cooper.

BRIAN MULLEN hesitated for a long time outside the front door of number 32. Fry gave him space. She reminded herself that it was the first time he'd seen his home since the fire.

'Take your time, sir.'

'I'm all right.'

Mullen seemed to regard her consideration as a spur to action. He stepped forward into the house via the approach path, through the plastic tape marking the crime scene. He almost stumbled in the hallway, as if he was suddenly lost and didn't know which doorway to turn into.

Fry wondered if he even recognised the place as his own home. There was almost nothing left of the original decor. Many familiar items would have been removed during the forensic examination. Instead, there were dozens of colourful crime-scene flags and disposable photo markers.

'There were some toys and other items near the source of the fire,' Fry said. 'Could you identify them for us, sir?'

She showed him the photographs and the exact locations where the items had been found. They included the melted Barbie doll and the remains of the PlayStation console. Then there was the blackened Monopoly board, with the red and green blobs that had once been hotels and houses.

She knew this would be painful for him. But Mullen did as he was asked, fingering the photos as if they were mementos of a holiday he vaguely remembered. He stood in the middle of the room, balancing uneasily on the stepping plates because he'd been told not to stand on the carpet.

'I've never seen this thing before,' he said, tapping one of the photographs with a finger. 'It looks like a kangaroo.'

Fry took it from him and checked the scene inventory. 'It was logged in as a wooden dinosaur, damaged by the fire.'

'It doesn't belong here.'

'Are you sure?'

Mullen shook his head. 'No, the kids didn't have anything like that. They were more into PlayStations and video games. Well, Luanne had her baby toys, too. But wooden dinosaurs? No.'

'So where did it come from?'

'I couldn't tell you.'

'Who else might be in the habit of buying toys for your children?'

'Their grandparents, of course. Or my brother-in-law, John. He might have picked the thing up somewhere, I suppose.'

Fry put the photos back in the file. The toy wasn't important, really. Many fathers would be vague about what their children played with.

'Let's leave that for a moment then, sir. Just walk into the hallway, would you? And mind where you tread. Stick to the stepping plates.'

Offering up a small piece of information seemed to have given Mullen confidence. At least he was doing something positive.

'What do you want to know now,' he asked.

'Were the doors downstairs normally left closed at night, Mr Mullen?'

'Yes. Why?'

'I was wondering who left the door open from the sitting room into the hall,' she said. 'If the fire had been contained in there a bit longer, the alarm might have been raised soon enough for lives to be saved.'

Mullen said nothing for a moment, but stood gazing at the stairs. 'Well, Lindsay might have left that one open,' he said at last. 'She sometimes did, if I was out. She knew I'd close it when I came home. Only I didn't . . .'

'I know. I'm sorry if this distresses you, sir.'

'I tested the smoke alarm every month,' said Mullen, with some difficulty.

'Did you realise that pressing the button only tests the sound of the alarm and the battery, not whether the detector itself is functioning?'

Mullen looked paler than ever. 'No, I didn't know that.'

Fry watched him, but felt no nearer to getting inside his mind. 'One last thing,' she said. 'Were you aware of anyone hanging around the house in the days before the fire? Anyone asking questions about you and your family?'

'No, nothing like that,' said Mullen.

'Right. I'll give you a lift to Darley Dale,' said Fry. 'That's where you want to go, isn't it?'

'Yes. I'll be staying with my parents-in-law until I'm sorted out.'

When she'd got him in the car, Fry let him sit quietly until they were out of Edendale and heading towards the A6.

'Tell me about the arguments you'd been having with your wife,' she said.

'What arguments?' said Mullen.

'According to your neighbours, there'd been several rows between the two of you in recent weeks.'

He shook his head. 'We had a row about the new carpet, that's all. I didn't think it was the most practical thing with three kids in the house. And I didn't like the idea of Henry buying things for us all the time, either. I told Lindsay I could support my own family without his help.'

'Yes?'

'But she could never say no to Daddy when he wanted to give her something. So it wasn't much of an argument. But we never had rows, as a rule.'

'That's not what I heard.'

'Well, you've got it wrong.'

They entered Bakewell, and Fry had to concentrate as she negotiated the narrow streets and the busy roundabout in the middle of town. She was able to relax again as they approached the entrance to Haddon Hall. But there were only a few miles left now.

'You told me earlier that Lindsay and her brother were very close,' she said. 'How do you get on with John Lowther?'

'Fine. Just fine.'

'Not even a hint of jealousy, perhaps? If John bought presents for your children, it would be natural for a bit of resentment to creep in.'

'Any resentment wasn't on my side,' said Mullen.

'Ah. So your brother-in-law begrudged someone coming between him and his sister? I can see how that might cause friction in the household.'

'You've got it wrong. And whoever told you that has got it wrong, too.'

And that was the last thing she got out of him. Mullen remained silent and sullen all the way to Darley Dale. Finally she dropped him off outside the Lowthers' gate, and he thanked her ungraciously.

Fry watched as Moira Lowther came out of the bungalow and hugged him. That was just like Mrs Lowther. Very keen on hugging people.

LATER, AT HER DESK, Fry read the pathologist's report on the Mullen family, which described how the hot gases had damaged the lining of the airways and lungs of the three victims. How damage to the lungs had precipitated pulmonary oedema, and inhalation of carbon particles blocked the air passages with mucus. Any burns on the victims were apparently post-mortem.

Finally, she put the report aside. Forensics would have to give her something to build a case on. It was difficult not to get impatient, though, when Brian Mullen was out of hospital and walking around.

Fry picked up the phone and called Wayne Abbott. 'Wayne, did you find any fingerprints in the sitting room?'

'The only ones we could retrieve came from members of the family. We were lucky to get what we did, considering the fire and smoke damage.'

'Did you lift any from the wooden toy—the dinosaur?'

'I'm afraid not. It was too badly charred.'

'And the lighter fluid can?'

'That's gone to the lab at Wetherby. They're giving it the works.'

'Is that our best hope, Wayne?'

'Right now, yes. Unless you can produce a likely suspect.'

'Thanks.'

She finished the call, but her phone rang again immediately. It was pretty much a one-way conversation: 'Great, OK . . . I see. Yes, sir, right away.'

Cooper was hovering at her desk when she finished. 'What's up?'

'The DCI wants us in for a meeting, right now. Remember the mysterious "SN" mentioned in Rose Shepherd's diary? There's only one name in her papers with matching initials: Simon Nichols.'

'THE INCIDENT ROOM are checking all the usual intelligence for clues as to who this Simon Nichols is,' Kessen told them. 'There's also a team going through all other sources: phone directory, electoral roll, DVLC . . . We should get results soon. Meanwhile, does anybody have any thoughts?'

'Whoever killed Rose Shepherd didn't enter the house, so far as we can tell,' said Hitchens. 'So we can conclude that he wasn't worried about there being any evidence in the house that would lead us to him. If he was a hired professional, there'd be no direct connection between him and his victim.'

'That's logical,' said Kessen. 'But what we need is a motive to narrow the field a bit. Any suggestions? I suppose we can discount robbery, since there was no attempt to enter the house.'

'Money could still be a motive,' said Hitchens. 'If there's a will—'

'There doesn't seem to be one in the house, and the firm of solicitors who handled the house purchase say they have no knowledge of one.'

Fry smiled. 'If someone out there planned this murder in order to inherit Rose Shepherd's money, they'll come forward eventually, won't they?'

'Eventually? That won't do. We need to show progress on this inquiry pretty quickly,' snapped Kessen. 'What other motives might we consider?'

'Jealousy? Revenge?' suggested Fry.

'Jealousy requires some kind of close personal relationship,' said

Hitchens. 'Miss Shepherd doesn't seem to have had any of those.'

'What about this Eric Grice? The handyman? I wonder if there was more to his relationship with Miss Shepherd than a bit of odd-jobbing.'

'Well, they were both unmarried, so that shouldn't have been a problem.'

'Judging by her obsession with keeping herself to herself, she would probably have rejected any attempts at intimacy,' said Fry. 'For all we know of Grice, he might not be the type to take that calmly.'

'But if he crossed the line, Miss Shepherd would have kicked him out, surely. Yet she let him keep coming to the house, didn't she?'

'Did she? How do we know that?'

'Only from Grice himself,' admitted Cooper.

'When does he say he was last at Bain House?'

'Three weeks ago, to clear the guttering and sweep up dead leaves.'

'Well, we know for a fact that he had contact with Rose Shepherd, which puts him in a very small minority for now,' said Hitchens. 'And he must have known which room she slept in. What sort of vehicle does he drive?'

'He has an old Land Rover that he carries his tools around in.'

'Four-wheel drive?'

'Of course. But Grice says he was always restricted to certain parts of the house. It sounded convincing,' said Cooper.

'Maybe,' said Fry. 'But Miss Shepherd isn't available to confirm that.'

'Right,' said Kessen. 'Let's take a closer look at Mr Grice. Get a detailed account of his last visit to Rose Shepherd. And check whether the tyres on his Land Rover are a match for the tracks from the field.'

Before he could move on, the phone rang, and Hitchens took the call. A smile came over his face. 'It seems Mr Grice's fingerprints were found in two of the bedrooms at Bain House,' he told them, 'including the one where the victim slept. So if he says he was never in those rooms, he's lying.'

Kessen looked around the group. 'DS Fry. I know you've got a lot on, but perhaps you'd like to have a go at our Mr Grice this time.'

'With pleasure.'

'AND WHO THE HECK are you?' said Eric Grice, winding the orange cord round the handle of his power drill.

'Detective Sergeant Fry.'

'Oh, aye? I don't have anything more to tell, you know.'

'Well, let's see, shall we? Mr Grice, you've given us a list of the rooms you visited in Bain House. Are you sure you haven't left any rooms out?'

'No, it's right,' he said. 'A lot of the work I did was on the outside, like.'

'In that case, Mr Grice, how do you explain the fact that we recovered your fingerprints from two of the bedrooms?'

'The bedrooms?'

'The master bedroom, where Rose Shepherd slept, and the second bedroom, just along the landing, where she kept her desk.'

'I don't know anything about that.'

'You never did any jobs for her in those rooms?'

He shook his head. 'She wouldn't have wanted me going in her bedrooms. Like I told you, the house was out of bounds, except for when I had to be somewhere to get a job done. I never even went upstairs to use the bathroom. She had a downstairs cloakroom, you know.'

'I don't think you understand, Mr Grice. I'm telling you that we found your fingerprints in two of the bedrooms at Bain House. Are you still denying that you went into those rooms?'

'Well, like I said—'

'What were you doing in Miss Shepherd's bedroom?' Fry demanded, leaning across the table and startling him in midsentence. 'And before you answer, Mr Grice, think about this: a murdered woman's body was found in one of those bedrooms, and you're the only person whose presence there we can prove. If you don't have an explanation, how do you think that's going to look when we charge you and prove to a court that you're lying?'

Grice blinked. 'It was my sister, Beryl,' he said, avoiding Fry's gaze.

'What was?'

'There's always been a lot of talk in the village about Miss Shepherd, you know. Nobody knew anything about her, but that didn't stop them talking.'

'In other words, it was all speculation?'

'Well, yes. There were a lot of half-baked stories, none of them true. Beryl kept on and on about it. She knew I was the only person who Miss Shepherd let into Bain House, so she kept pestering me. She wanted to show off to her pals in the village that she knew all the stuff they didn't.'

'The inside information.'

'Yes, that's it. I thought it was a lot of daft nonsense, but she wouldn't let up. So next time I was in Bain House, I took a chance to have a bit of a nosy about. Just to find a bit of something to keep Beryl quiet, that's all.'

'So you managed to get into the bedrooms?'

'Yes. Only for a quick look round. To see if she had any dead bodies or mad relatives hidden away in there, you know.' He gave her a tentative smile.

'How did you get into the bedrooms without Miss Shepherd noticing?'

'I was mending a leak in the kitchen, and I told her I had to turn off the water at the stopcock in the bathroom. She didn't know any better.'

'Where was Miss Shepherd while you were nosing around the bedrooms?'

'She was downstairs, in her sitting room.'

'And did you find anything interesting to tell your sister?'

'Not really. Well, nothing at all, as a matter of fact. It was boring.' He shrugged his shoulders. 'So I had to make some stuff up.'

'Hold on—you made things up about Miss Shepherd to tell your sister?'

'Well, yes. Otherwise she would have kept pestering me.'

'And your sister spread this false information around Foxlow?'

'That was the general idea. I didn't think there'd be any harm in it. None of the stuff was ever likely to get back to Miss Shepherd herself, because she didn't talk to anyone in the village. So it was harmless.'

Fry caught her breath. 'So what false information did you make up?'

'I can't remember now. It was just what came to mind.'

'Let me have a guess, then. Did you tell your sister Miss Shepherd was a retired teacher from Scotland?'

'Yes, I think so. I couldn't really tell—'

'And, Mr Grice, this is very important—did you tell your sister that Rose Shepherd had a friend called Dougie in Glasgow?'

Eric Grice nodded slowly, but said nothing.

Fry sat back. 'Well, sir, for a man who thought he wasn't doing any harm, you've certainly wasted a lot of people's time.'

'GOD DAMN THE MAN,' said DI Hitchens. 'I could cheerfully strangle him with his own drill cord.'

'At least he's talking now,' said Fry. 'I've got someone taking a statement from him, and we'll speak to his sister, too, to see if their accounts tally.'

'Meanwhile, it's back to square one in our picture of Rose Shepherd.' He looked at the board, scrubbed off some of the details and studied what was left. 'So what verifiable facts do we have? She's a British passport holder, born in London, 1944. And we've got her physical details—height, weight, hair colour. She moved to Foxlow ten months ago from London. She had plenty of funds, because Bain House wasn't cheap, and she was a cash buyer.'

Hitchens tilted his head on one side to look at the photograph of the victim from a different angle. It didn't seem to tell him anything new.

'Have we talked to everyone in her address book?' asked Fry.

'Almost everyone. The odd thing is that her book only dates from the day she moved into Bain House. Apart from the solicitor and the estate agent, nobody we've spoken to had any contact with her before then.'

'Did any of these individuals detect an accent?'

'Only those who were offered a leading question by the officer interviewing them. If they were asked if Miss Shepherd had a Scottish accent, they agreed she might have done. Otherwise, they had no suggestions to offer.'

'Grice has a lot to answer for,' muttered Fry.

'I don't think it made much difference. They couldn't agree on her age or appearance or manner either. You'd hardly think they'd met the same person.'

'Did we get anything from her contacts list?'

'Well, her dentist can tell us that Rose Shepherd had a few previous fillings. He ID'd her too, from the dental records. Her GP prescribed her Nitrazepam for her sleeping problems. And the garage can tell us what the emissions were like on her Volvo. Pick the bones out of that, if you can.'

'Why did she have trouble sleeping, I wonder?'

'Who can say?' Hitchens opened the file. 'One thing we did find in the house was the receipt for her car. It was bought from a Volvo dealer in Chesterfield a few days after she moved in. The receipt gives the recorded mileage at the time of sale, and we checked it against the current reading. She did about three hundred miles. The proverbial careful lady owner.'

'My God, she hardly went anywhere,' said Fry.

'She had no one to visit, did she?'

6

Thursday, October 27

Early the next morning, an officer from the incident room entered DCI Kessen's office at West Street, and placed several files on the desk. Watched by Hitchens and Cooper, Kessen thumbed through the files.

'Looks as though we've got the first hits from our Nichols trawl,' he said.

'Any Simons?' asked Hitchens.

'Oh, yes. Three. One of them lives in Ashbourne, and he's ten years old.'

'Damn it.'

'The second is eighty-five years old and he's in a residential care home in Alfreton, but he could have some connection with Rose Shepherd.'

'We need to spread the net wider, don't we?'

Kessen nodded. 'Unfortunately, these seem to be the only leads we have at the moment. Do you want to allocate them in the CID room, Paul?'

'Is there one for me?' asked Cooper.

'Yes, I saved this one for you specially, Ben. This Nichols lives on a farm. The address we have is Lea Farm, near Uppertown—wherever that is.'

'I know Uppertown. It's near Bonsall.'

'Bonsall?' said Hitchens. 'Just a minute—'

'Yes, Rose Shepherd made calls to a phone box in that area, didn't she?'

Hitchens smiled as he handed Cooper the file. 'Off you go, then. There's no time to waste.'

WHEN FRY ARRIVED at West Street, she found Kessen and Hitchens in the DCI's office, frowning over a document written in a language she didn't recognise. She leaned over the desk and looked closer. No—it was the alphabet she didn't recognise. Some kind of Cyrillic script?

'Morning, Diane. Take a look,' said Hitchens. 'This could be a whole new angle on the Shepherd inquiry.'

Fry picked a photograph from the file. It showed the rear view of a red Ford Escort with a foreign registration number and a shattered back window.

She raised an eyebrow at Kessen, and he took the photo from her. 'OK. A year ago, there was a double murder in a city in northern Bulgaria—a place called Pleven. This car was found by the roadside outside the city. The bodies of two people were in it—Dimitar Iliev, aged forty-three, and Piya Yotova, forty. Both died of bullet wounds.'

'What has this got to do with Rose Shepherd?' asked Fry.

'We're not sure yet. But it could have something to do with Simon Nichols. We got a hit on the name from Europol. They're building up a lot of intelligence on cross-border organised crime these days. According to their database, Simon Nichols is an alias for a Bulgarian criminal called Simcho Nikolov. They're sending the complete file on him ASAP.'

Fry tapped the photograph. 'He's a suspect for this shooting in Pleven?'

'He was a known associate of Yotova's, and he disappeared about the time of the shooting. The Bulgarian police have been looking for him.'

'So he could be a professional hit man,' said Hitchens.

'It looks that way,' said Kessen. He studied Fry. 'Europol have arranged for an English-speaking officer to liaise with us from Pleven, Diane. He'll be calling this morning. And I want you to deal with him.'

Fry was aghast. 'With respect, sir, I've got more important things to do than become involved in international liaison—especially on the basis of such a tenuous connection.'

'Not quite so tenuous,' said Kessen calmly. 'DC Cooper is following up a potential lead to Simon Nichols in the exact area where Rose Shepherd made calls to a public phone box. And don't forget that the victim had the international code for Bulgaria in her address book—the magic 359.'

STILL FUMING, Fry went back to her desk. Bulgaria. Bastion of Communism during the Cold War era. What else did she know about it? Nothing. She was trying to picture what a Bulgarian might look like when her phone rang.

'Hello, DS Fry.'

'*Alo*. My name is Sergeant Georgi Kotsev. I'm calling from Pleven Police Department, on behalf of the Bulgarian Ministry of the Interior.'

Fry tried to mask her sigh. 'Oh, Sergeant Kotsev. Hello. Thank you for sparing the time to talk to us.'

'It's a pleasure to cooperate with our colleagues in the UK.'

His voice was deep and only slightly accented. It didn't fit the Slavic stereotype that had been lurking at the back of Fry's mind—some hatchet-faced villain out of a James Bond film. Kotsev sounded smooth and articulate.

'I have your fax about the two shooting victims in Pleven,' said Fry. 'I wonder if you have any further information?'

'We know that they were both shot with an assault rifle, probably a Kalashnikov AK47.'

'Are AK47s commonly available in Bulgaria?'

Kotsev laughed. 'If you know the right people, of course. We manufacture a great many Kalashnikovs in Bulgaria. The US government bought thousands of them for use in Iraq. They operate better than the American M-16 in dusty conditions. Kalashnikovs travel well, like our wine.'

Fry could have listened to him talk for a while, his voice was so interesting. She guessed he'd be one of those people who were terribly disappointing when you met them in person, because their faces didn't match the picture their voices conjured up. Probably he *was* hatched-faced after all.

'Any idea of a motive for these killings?' she asked.

'Certainly. People want money. Sometimes they see a way of filling their pockets and getting away with it.' She could almost hear Kotsev shrug. 'And then they get drawn into events. They mix with the wrong people.'

'So Dimitar Iliev was involved in organised crime, is that right?'

'We believe so. But he was a small player who became greedy, we think.'

'Tell me what you know about Simcho Nikolov.'

'Nikolov is aged fifty-five, an army veteran. He was a companion of Iliev's for many years—they served together as soldiers, but fell on bad times after release from the army and turned to crime. For a long time, they were protected from prosecution by their connection with powerful criminal bosses.'

'But their luck ran out,' said Fry.

'Iliev's did, at least. We've had no news of Simcho Nikolov.'

'Well, could you keep us updated?'

'I'll fax you if we have new developments. Would that be suitable?'

'Yes, excellent.'

Kotsev paused. She thought she heard him drinking, and imagined a cup of decent coffee in his hand. Did they have good coffee in Bulgaria?

'And what about you, Sergeant Fry?' he said. 'What is your situation?'

'One of my colleagues is following up a possible lead to Nikolov. In fact, he's on his way to the address right now. I'll keep you informed.'

There was silence at the other end of the phone for a moment. The line to Pleven was so good that she could hear Kotsev breathing, and even the faint buzz of background conversation, and a door closing somewhere.

'If you would like someone to travel to England, to assist in your investigation, it can be arranged,' he said at last. 'Cooperation with our EU colleagues is encouraged at the highest level.'

'Well, I don't think that will be necessary, but I'll pass on your offer.'

'It's been a pleasure to liaise with you, Sergeant Fry. I hope we'll speak again soon.'

'Goodbye, then.'

'*Ciao*.'

Fry put the phone down. *Ciao*?

Then she noticed Murfin making frantic gestures at her with his phone.

'What is it, Gavin?'

'I've got that waitress on the phone—the one from Matlock Bath. She came in to do the photofits yesterday. I think you'd better speak to her.'

'OK, put her on.'

Murfin transferred the call, and Fry picked up.

'Good morning, Tina. I understand you have some new information for us. What is it? Have you remembered something?'

'Well, I've just seen something really. That woman I saw on Saturday—it's the one who's in the papers. The one who was killed.'

Fry was disappointed. 'Yes, Rose Shepherd. We know that, Tina. It's the other two people we're trying to identify.'

'No, no. That's what I'm trying to tell you. She's right here in the paper. I mean the woman Miss Shepherd met at the tea rooms. It's her.'

'Who's in the paper, Tina? I don't understand.'

Tina took a deep breath, and spoke more slowly. 'I'm looking at her photograph right now, Sergeant. She's the woman who was killed in the house fire in Edendale. Lindsay Mullen.'

THE FARM WHERE Simon Nichols worked lay on the plateau to the west of Masson Hill. After leaving Bonsall, where the road became single track, Cooper had to pass through Uppertown, then follow a couple of B roads before abandoning tarmac altogether for a route the maps would call 'unclassified', one of the old miners' roads that led to disused lead workings.

Despite what he'd told the DI, Cooper didn't know the area that well. He had to stop to consult his OS map, and try to interpret the spider's web of black and green lines that crammed the spaces between the B roads. To his left he could see the curious bumps in the landscape that indicated the covered shafts and overgrown spoil heaps of a long-abandoned mine. But he had no idea whether it was Low Mine, Whitelow Mine, or Beans and Bacon Mine. Or one of half a dozen other sites marked simply *Mine (disused)*.

Finally he found himself driving down a stony track, looking for a farmhouse that had been promised by a worn sign half a mile back. But before he found Lea Farm, he came across a farmer repairing a fence.

'Good morning, sir. DC Cooper, Edendale Police. I'm looking for a Mr Simon Nichols.'

'Simon? He's not here. He'll probably be holed up in his caravan, down at the bottom of the big field there.'

'Do you own this farm, sir?'

'Yes, the name's Finney. Michael Finney.'

'So you employ Mr Nichols?'

The farmer grunted as he unloaded posts from his pick-up. 'I suppose so.'

'When did you last see him?'

'Not for a few days, as a matter of fact.'

'Is that normal? I mean, if he's supposed to be employed here.'

Finney straightened his cap and turned to look at Cooper. 'Well, the thing about Simon is, he tends to drink quite a lot. Sometimes he goes on a bender and stays away for a couple of days. He turns up eventually. And he's a good worker, when he's sober. That's why I keep him on.'

'Can I take a look at the caravan?'

The farmer shrugged. 'If you like. I'll take you.'

The caravan stood in a corner of a field, almost hidden by a copse of trees. Cooper had to park his Toyota in a gateway and walk into the field.

'Keep him well out of the way, don't you, Mr Finney?'

'Simon prefers it down here. He likes to keep himself to himself.'

The nearer he came to the caravan, the more Cooper became aware of the silence in this corner of the field. Apart from the rustling of rooks in the trees, there was no sound or movement, no sign of life. He stopped and looked around. The field was enclosed by two walls that snaked across the landscape until they crested a rise. Halfway up the slope, a section of wall had fallen. This land hadn't been used to contain livestock for a while.

'I don't suppose Mr Nichols has a car, sir?'

'A car? No. I give him a lift into town now and then,' said Finney. 'Otherwise, he gets around on that.' The farmer pointed to a decrepit old motorbike propped against one end of the caravan.

Cooper knocked on the caravan door. 'Mr Nichols? Are you in there?' He knocked again, a metallic clanging as if he was hitting a big tin can. A big, empty tin can. 'Anyone home?'

'He might be asleep,' said Finney.

Faded orange curtains were drawn across the windows. Pressing his face close to the glass, Cooper could see a small slice of the interior through a narrow gap where the curtains didn't meet. He saw the edge of a folding wooden table, a scatter of papers, and two beer cans.

'Mr Finney, the occupant appears to be absent. Do I have your permission to enter this caravan?'

'Eh? Well, I suppose so. It won't be very nice in there, you know. Old Simon, he isn't the cleanest of folk.'

'It doesn't matter.'

Cooper tried the handle. It turned with a faint scrape of metal. He gave the door a yank, and it screeched as it was forced open.

The two men froze for a moment, suddenly reluctant to take a step closer. A fat bluebottle zigzagged slowly past them, too bloated to escape.

Finney drew in a sharp breath, as if he'd been punched in the stomach. His involuntary cry of disgust sent a flock of rooks clattering into the air. Then the farmer made a choking, gurgling sound and staggered towards the wall. He hadn't reached it before he doubled over and vomited.

Standing in the doorway of the caravan, Cooper covered his mouth and nose with a hand as he watched a pool of dark, sticky liquid hover on the edge of the step before trickling towards the ground. He swallowed hard as he fought a surge of nausea, and looked into the caravan.

Mr Finney had been right about one thing. It wasn't very nice in there.

'SHE MUST HAVE BEEN a stranger,' said Brian Mullen. 'I can't think who else this person would have been.'

Mullen was in the conservatory at the Lowthers' house in Darley Dale. His father-in-law sat near him, perhaps for moral support. Occasionally, Mullen glanced into the house, where his mother-in-law was keeping Luanne entertained. Fry didn't have much interest in babies, but this one seemed reasonably civilised and quiet.

'Did your wife mention meeting her, sir?' Fry asked.

'No. I knew she'd been out on Saturday, of course. Lindsay left me with the children for a couple of hours. Said she wanted to do some shopping.'

'Which shops did she go to?'

'I don't know. She wouldn't have told me that.'

'And she didn't say anything afterwards?'

Mullen appeared to consider it. 'Come to think of it, Lindsay did say she'd chatted to a couple of strangers in a café. I've no idea who they were.'

'Did she mention any names?'

'No. She probably didn't ask them their names, if it was just a casual conversation. I expect they just talked about the weather.' He looked at Fry. 'Do you think these people might have been responsible for the fire?'

'We don't know, sir. But if it occurs to you who your wife might have been meeting, or any details she let slip, please inform us straight away.'

'All right. Of course.'

Fry stood up to go. She hadn't achieved anything by the visit. In fact, she wondered if she'd just given Brian Mullen a get-out for the arson. Mysterious strangers didn't fit into her scenario.

'I PRESUME HE LIVED on his own,' said Hitchens, standing well clear of the caravan. A crime-scene tent was being erected over it.

'Yes, I think it would be safe to say that, sir.'

'What else have we got, Ben?'

Cooper flicked open his notebook. 'He's known as Simon Nichols, he's aged about fifty-five, and he'd lived here for eight months. The caravan belongs to the farmer, who doesn't seem to have asked many questions.'

'I hope he didn't pay too much rent. I've never seen such a dump.'

'I gather it was in exchange for his work on the farm. Free accommodation and probably less than the minimum wage.'

'And this is Nikolov?'

'Well, Nichols certainly wasn't his real name. Mr Finney never asked him about his nationality, but guessed he might be Polish. Nichols didn't speak much English, only what he needed to get by.'

'I bet "beer" was a word he knew,' said Hitchens.

'Yeah. And there's hardly any food in the caravan. Just cans of beer and half a bottle of vodka. He looks ill, too.'

'Dead people usually do,' said Hitchens.

'Not always.'

The DI ran a hand across his forehead. 'No, you're right, Ben.'

Cooper looked around the field. There were lots of gaps in the dry-stone walls, easy enough for anyone to get in or out of the area without having to come down the track or past the farmhouse.

'If the farmer can be believed, Simon Nichols lived a quiet, reclusive life and was hardly seen in daylight, except when he was working.'

'Great,' said Hitchens. 'He's already starting to sound like Rose Shepherd.'

'So KESSEN WAS RIGHT about not being able to cut yourself off completely,' Fry said later, when she had Cooper and Murfin together in the CID room.

'Miss Shepherd, you mean?' said Cooper.

'Of course. She not only had the postman, the meter reader and God knows who else coming by the house, but she was forced to have Eric Grice in to do a few odd jobs. And then she met Lindsay Mullen in Matlock Bath.'

'But do you think that was entirely by chance, Diane?' asked Cooper. 'Or could there have been some connection between them?'

'Maybe she wanted to give Lindsay something?' said Murfin.

'Why, Gavin?'

'Miss Shepherd seems to have known that she was in danger. What if she had an item in her possession that she didn't want anyone to get hold of? Why not pass it on to someone unconnected? A stranger, in fact.'

Fry began to move restlessly around the office. 'If she did that, she was sealing Lindsay Mullen's fate,' she said. 'It looks as though Rose Shepherd was already being watched when she went into Matlock Bath that day. And whoever was watching her must have followed Lindsay home.'

'Why would Miss Shepherd pick on Lindsay to talk to?'

'Why pick on anybody? For heaven's sake, who buttonholes complete strangers in cafés and engages them in conversation?'

'Rose Shepherd had cut herself off for so long, perhaps she just wanted a few minutes of ordinary conversation, even with a complete stranger,' said Cooper. 'You know what it's like. When you've got something preying on your mind and you find someone easy to talk to, it all comes spilling out.'

'Really?'

'Oh, well—maybe not you, Diane.'

'Thanks,' she said, and meant it.

'But it works that way with a lot of people. I think Rose Shepherd was so scared of giving away clues about herself that talking to people was too much of a risk. So she normally avoided it.'

Fry began to pace the room again. 'OK. So what was she hiding?'

'I don't know,' said Cooper. 'And it's difficult to see a connection between the fire and the shooting. And how does Simon Nichols fit in? The pathologist reckoned he'd been dead a couple of days. But if he didn't die until Tuesday, I suppose he could have been involved in both incidents.'

'Maybe Lindsay Mullen was in the wrong place at the wrong time, and got a good look at Nichols, or whoever was watching Rose Shepherd. So he took her out before she could give anyone a description.'

Cooper nodded. 'Before she could even know that Miss Shepherd had been killed. The body wasn't discovered until Monday afternoon.'

'Somebody wasn't taking any chances, were they?' said Murfin.

Fry stared at the ceiling for a few moments. 'Well, we know that Rose Shepherd had connections with a Bulgarian criminal, who's also been found dead. We don't have any more information on Nikolov until we get PM results and the intelligence files from Sofia.'

'You almost make that sound like a good thing, Diane.'

She looked at Cooper. 'Well, it means I can focus on the Darwin Street fire for a while. Unrelated, or not.'

A FEW MINUTES later, Fry finished reading the post-mortem reports on the Mullen family for the second time.

She picked up the phone and rang Wayne Abbott.

'Wayne, you know you said the fingerprints in the house at Darwin Street all belonged to members of the family?'

'Yes?'

'Which members of the family did you mean specifically?'

'Hold on . . .' She heard the rustling of paper. 'Here we go. Well, as you might expect, there were prints from the householders everywhere—that's Mr Brian Mullen and Mrs Lindsay Mullen. And the children, of course.'

'OK.'

'And we lifted a couple of prints belonging to the grandmother, Mrs Moira Lowther, in the kitchen. None from her husband, though.'

'Anyone else on the list?'

'Yes, the dead woman's brother, Mr John Lowther.'

'Where were his prints?'

'Oh, kitchen, bathroom, sitting room. Some of his were on the children's toys that we salvaged. I expect he used to spend some time playing uncle with the kids, don't you think?'

'Yes,' said Fry. 'That's probably it.'

THE ENGAGED SIGN was showing on the door of Interview Room One. Inside, John Lowther seemed to be sweating. Damp patches had appeared under his armpits, and his glasses were slipping on his nose. He looked like a man caught performing some shameful act. Yet all he was doing was sitting in a police interview room, waiting for the questions.

With Cooper sitting in to observe, Fry began by asking Lowther to confirm his name, age and address.

'I gather your address is an apartment, sir?'

'Yes, it's a new development in Matlock. They converted an old will, I mean mile. It's rather nice.'

'I see. Do you own the apartment, Mr Lowther?'

'It's a nine-hundred-and-ninety-nine-year lease. With nine hundred and ninety-seven years left to run. Less two years, you see. But it's no loss.'

Fry frowned. 'Right. And you're an actuary by profession?'

'—confession? Yes, I have very intensive experience in the field. I worked in Leeds for three years. But I left that job a year ago.'

'So you're not employed at the moment?'

He smiled. 'There's not so much work for actuaries around these ports.'

'I see.'

Fry could hear herself saying 'I see' too much, a clear indication to anyone listening that she hardly understood a thing Lowther was saying.

Suddenly, Lowther seemed to stare past her at something on the wall.

'Is there a dog here somewhere?'

Fry looked at Cooper to see how he was reacting, but he was quite still, watching carefully. She paused to gather her thoughts before her next question, but Lowther wouldn't allow a pause.

'One of my neighbours has a dog. A cross-bred Alsatian. Long-haired, shaggy—you know? All the time I've lived in the apartment, I've never heard it bark. Not even when the bin men come in through the back gate.'

'Mr Lowther, when did you last see your sister?'

'Oh, Lindsay? Last week. It could have been the week before.'

'Did you visit the house in Darwin Street on that occasion?'

He hesitated, contorting his mouth as if trying to work around some words that he couldn't pronounce. 'I can't remember.'

'Surely you can remember where you last saw your sister.'

Lowther stared in her direction. She noticed that the focus of his eyes was shifting back and forth, as though she wasn't really there to him.

'I can't remember. Did I say that already?'

Fry made a show of moving her notes on the table, to make sure she had John Lowther's full attention. 'I know you were very close to your sister, sir. But what sort of relationship do you have with your brother-in-law, Brian Mullen? Would you say there was some resentment between you?'

But Lowther barely seemed to have heard her. He made that chewing movement with his mouth again. Fry decided he wasn't trying to pronounce the words, but to suck them back before they reached the air.

Then, astonishingly, he smiled at her. It was a charming smile, friendly. *What a nice conversation we're having*, his expression seemed to say.

'Is there another question?'

Fry sighed. 'Yes. Mr Lowther, have you ever seen this before?'

She showed him a photograph of the wooden dinosaur.

'Tyrannosaurus.'

'Have you seen it before?'

'No. Is it from abroad?'

'We don't know.'

'Some people go abroad, hunting for whores. No, for babies.'

'What?'

'I'm sorry, I get confused sometimes. I'm not sure what you're asking me. Is it time to leave?'

'Do you want to leave, sir? You're only here voluntarily, so you can leave whenever you want. But we only want to ask you some questions. We're trying to find out how your sister and her children died.'

'What are they saying?' said Lowther.

Again, he seemed to be looking at something behind her. Or perhaps not looking at something, but listening.

'Are you all right, sir?' she asked.

'You don't have to believe what people are saying, you know.'

'What have people been saying to you, sir? Have you been hearing rumours? Please share any information you have.'

Lowther tilted his head. A bead of sweat formed at his temple. 'I've got exceptional hearing, I'm told. I can hear the people in the next room now.'

Fry tried for a while longer, probing for information about his feelings towards Brian Mullen, and about the last time he'd visited the Mullens' house. But the conversation kept veering off, and she didn't know how to bring it back under control.

When the interview was finally over, they watched John Lowther leave. Then Fry walked back and checked Interview Room Two.

'There wasn't anyone in the next room,' she said.

'So what was he hearing?' asked Cooper. 'Something outside?'

Fry shook her head. 'Let's face it, John Lowther is unbalanced.'

'Hang on, Diane. He could be faking it. All that stuff was verbal. It was like a smoke screen. He didn't actually answer any of your questions.'

'Well,' said Fry. 'I'll get his background looked into, anyway.'

Listening to the interview tapes afterwards, Cooper realised that he had heard this kind of erratic language before. It brought back unpleasant memories. Still, he knew that not every verbal quirk was a sign of mental illness.

Fry watched Cooper put on his jacket, ready to leave.

'Are you in Matlock Bath later this afternoon, Ben?'

'Yes. I've got to go back to the shopping village.'

'Do me a favour—keep an eye out for somewhere you might buy a wooden dinosaur.'

Cooper stopped. 'What? Oh, the photo that you showed Lowther.'

'I want to find out where this came from. Brian Mullen tells me he's never seen it before. If it was a gift for one of the Mullen children, it might have been from a recent visitor to the house.'

Cooper studied the photo closely, then handed it back. 'OK, I'll check it out. Oh, I nearly forgot—there was a message from Sergeant Kotsev.'

'Oh? What does he say?'

'He says his flight from Sofia lands at Manchester Airport at twenty to five.'

'What? He's coming *here*? Why weren't we told? Does he mean *today*?'

'I suppose so. Do you want to hear the rest of the message?'

'No, but you'd better give it me anyway.'

'Well, he sends his respects to Sergeant Fry. And he wonders if you'd be free to pick him up from the airport.'

COOPER DECIDED to drive down through Cromford to reach Matlock Bath. He joined the A6 a little beyond the village pond. After the tightly clustered cottages of Cromford, Masson Mill looked enormous. Its back wall overlooked the river, the long ranks of mullioned windows staring out across the rushing water like blank eyes.

Inside the shopping village, Frances Birtland had just arrived.

'My neighbour?' she said as she took off her coat. 'Rose Shepherd?'

'You don't remember your neighbour coming in on Saturday?'

'No. How embarrassing. I suppose I didn't recognise her.'

'Your colleague Mrs Hooper recognised her photograph in the papers.'

Mrs Birtland shook her head. 'I don't read the papers very much. They're always so depressing, aren't they?'

A customer was hovering behind him, and Cooper stood back for a moment, taking the opportunity to check out the wooden toys on the central display units. He'd completely missed them last time he was here.

Cooper picked one up. It wasn't a dinosaur, but the wood and the style of carving looked the same as the toy that Fry had shown him.

Frances Birtland was smiling at him, hoping for a sale.

'Where are these from?' he asked her.

'Eva has them imported direct from Bulgaria. Traditionally crafted and ecologically friendly. I think they're lovely, don't you?'

'Is there a dinosaur in the range?'

'Yes, but I'm afraid we sold the last one.'

BEFORE SHE LEFT West Street, Fry knocked on the door of the DI's office. She found Hitchens staring at a passport in a clear plastic wallet on his desk.

'Is that Rose Shepherd's passport?' she asked.

'Yes. The HOLMES team checked the passport number. It seems that no such passport was ever issued by the UK authorities. Rose Shepherd's passport is a forgery. A very good one—but still a forgery.'

'But that means—'

Hitchens swivelled his chair to face her. 'Yes, Diane. It means we have absolutely no idea who she really was.'

AT MANCHESTER TERMINAL ONE, Fry stood in front of WHSmith, waiting for Sergeant Kotsev to emerge from baggage reclaim into the arrivals hall. She recalled Cooper's comments as she'd left the office. 'How will you recognise him?' he'd asked. 'He won't be in uniform, surely.'

'Well, he's six foot two inches tall, with black hair, dark brown eyes and a neatly trimmed moustache.'

'How do you know that? Did it just come up in conversation?'

'Yes.'

But, in fact, the description had been in an email Fry had discovered in her inbox immediately after receiving the phone message. The Bulgarian was already in the air by then.

So when Georgi Kotsev appeared, Fry recognised him straight away. He was definitely tall and dark. He had good bone structure and a slight tan. A recent holiday in a Black Sea resort, perhaps? He wore a black leather jacket, quite new, though probably a cut-price copy of a designer label. Fry thought he'd have looked pretty good in a well-cut suit, too. His hair was black, trimmed short, but combed back to reveal a hint of waviness.

He also looked vaguely angry as he came down the ramp. But his expression cleared quickly when Fry introduced herself.

'Welcome to England, Sergeant.'

Kotsev smiled and shook her hand formally. '*Blagodarya*. Thank you.'

'If you'll follow me, I've got a car waiting.'

All the way from Edendale to the airport, she'd been worrying about the prospect of making stilted conversation with a stranger. But there'd been no need to worry. He began to talk without any prompting.

'I came by Lufthansa,' he said, as he followed her to the short-stay car park. 'The German airline, you know it? Only four hours and fifty-five minutes, including one stop at Frankfurt. Very quick, very efficient. A British Airways flight is two hours longer—and yet more expensive.'

'You know, your English is very good, Sergeant Kotsev.'

'Ah, *merci*. Thank you. And German aircraft have three inches more leg room. Did you know? That is important, too. For me, at least.'

'You're an admirer of German efficiency, then?'

'We have to give them credit for what they achieve,' he said.

Her Peugeot was fortunately close to the entrance. She was anxious to get in the car and be under way. 'Wasn't Bulgaria invaded by the Germans during the last war?' she said as she opened the boot for his suitcase.

The question had come out of her mouth before it even occurred to her she might sound like a character out of *Fawlty Towers*. That was the danger of small talk. The pressure to say something led to stupid comments.

Kotsev shook his head vigorously as he loaded his case into the car. 'No, no—we were on their side. It was the Russians who invaded us.'

'Really?'

'Sadly, there is some ignorance here about our history.'

Fry thought of the people Kotsev might meet back at Edendale. 'I can't promise you anything else.'

She exited the car park and negotiated her way out of the airport. Once they were back on the motorway, the silence began to feel uncomfortable.

'So where did you learn to speak English so well, Sergeant Kotsev?'

'Ah, I attended a good school in our capital, Sofia, and later at university. Regrettably, there are still very few police officers in my country who speak English well. That will have to change when we enter the European Union.'

'Still, it must be irritating to have us all coming to your country and expecting you to speak to us in English.'

'Ah, but ours is an unimportant little language.' He said it without sarcasm or bitterness, as if he actually meant it.

'Well, it's true that Bulgarian wasn't offered as a course option when I was a student,' she said.

Her visitor seemed to take in everything they passed on the journey. He'd pushed the passenger seat as far back as it would go to accommodate his long legs, and Fry was conscious of the fact that he could watch her from that angle without her knowing it. She stood the uncertainty for as long as she could, then she turned to meet his eyes. Kotsev had been right about how brown they were. They made her think of dark chocolate.

'So you are a graduate, Sergeant Fry?' said Kotsev. 'Police officers should have a good education, if we are to have the respect of the people. Myself, I attended the Sofia University Saint Kliment Ohridski.'

'I was at the University of Central England in Birmingham. We called it UCE. As a comedian said once, it isn't named after its initials, but the grades you need to get in.'

He regarded her quizzically, perhaps not fully understanding what she'd said, but recognising the self-deprecating tone. Fry immediately felt embarrassed. What had made her say that about her old university? UCE had given her exactly what she needed—a route to escape into a different world, where opportunities were available for the grasping.

'It's kind of you to escort me,' said Kotsev. 'You must be very busy, I'm sure. A shooting inquiry for you to pursue. Connections to organised crime. Worrying complications for a small police department.'

'Yes, it *is* a bit hectic.'

He fell silent until they were out of Glossop and travelling southwards along the ridge through Hayfield and past Chapel-en-le-Frith.

'So what sort of place is Pleven?' she said, trying to sound interested.

'Pleven is in the agricultural region of Miziya in the north of Bulgaria. It's surrounded by limestone hills. You might feel at home if you visited there.'

'Might I? Why?'

'Those are limestone quarries I can see ahead of us, if I'm not mistaken.'

'Oh. Probably.'

'So the hills are very much like these. But the city of Pleven has a population of a hundred and forty-three thousand persons. Not like this.'

'That's all right, I'm used to big cities. I don't really belong in this area.'

'I see. Myself, I'm a city person too—though I was born in a rural district. My family moved to Sofia, where I received my education. Later, as a police officer, I was assigned by the ministry to Pleven.'

'And you developed an expertise in organised crime?'

'Yes, indeed. I have been working recently in cooperation with the Organised Crime Groups Unit at Europol. We have had some great successes. Two years ago, we broke a major crime network that was spreading counterfeit euro notes into Western Europe. Four illegal print facilities were closed.'

Fry didn't speak. She was too busy suppressing a surge of envy. This guy was from some place in Eastern Europe that she'd never heard of, yet he was enjoying an exciting career, while she was stuck in this backwater.

She put her foot down on the straight stretch of road over the plateau towards Edendale. 'Not far now,' she said.

Kotsev nodded amicably. 'You know, when Bulgaria joins the EU, I would be interested in transferring to Europol in The Hague. Do you know The Hague? It's a good city. Very pleasant. Very civilised.'

Fry turned to look at him, to see if he was laughing at her. But she met his eyes, and she could tell that he wasn't.

FRY DELIVERED KOTSEV to the new Holiday Inn off Edendale's relief road and made sure he managed to get checked in all right.

'I hope you'll be comfortable here,' she said when he'd collected his room key. 'Our divisional commander has asked if you'll take part in a briefing in the morning. Will that be all right?'

'*Dobre*. That's OK. Thank you for everything, Sergeant Fry.'

'That's all right. Good night.'

'*Ciao*.'

He picked up his bag to go to his room, but instead of leaving through the revolving doors Fry found herself hesitating.

Kotsev smiled at her politely. 'Was there something else?'

'Well, I was just going to say . . . The thing is, I know what it's like arriving in a strange place where you don't know anyone. Eating meals alone is the worst thing, isn't it?'

'I will ask for room service and watch television while I eat,' he said.

'Oh.'

'Unless you were about to suggest a better idea?'

Fry took the cue. 'I'd be happy to take you to dinner tonight and show you a bit of Edendale. Well, it's preferable to sitting on your own, isn't it?'

Kotsev bowed slightly. 'A great deal better. I would be delighted.'

She let out the breath that she hadn't realised she was holding until then. 'I'll pick you up here at about seven thirty, then.'

'Seven thirty. Excellent. Goodbye for now.'

He insisted on shaking hands again. Then Fry watched him walk to the lift and press the button. He glanced back while he waited, and Fry was surprised to find herself still standing there like an idiot. She waved self-consciously. But he was already turning to enter the lift.

'*Ciao*,' she said quietly, as the doors closed behind him.

COOPER TOOK his brother's call that evening just as he was settling down to watch a good film with a bottle of beer in his hand and the cat on his knee.

'Ben, it says here that older fathers are more liable to have kids with schizophrenia. If you're between forty-five and forty-nine, you're twice as likely to have a child with the illness as a man of twenty-five.'

'Matt, you were still in your twenties when you had the girls.'

'Yes, well. Did you know schizophrenia starts to affect most people in their late teens or early twenties? In their *teens*, Ben.'

'Considering the average teenager, I wonder how they can tell.'

Matt had taken a breath to continue, but came to an abrupt halt. 'It's not funny, Ben. I can tell you're not in the right frame of mind at the moment. You must have had a bad day, or something.'

'As a matter of fact, it wasn't such a bad day—until now.'

He didn't really mean that, but there was almost a set script between them when they got to this stage. This was the way their arguments always went.

'Right. Sorry to have bothered you, I'm sure. I suppose you won't want me to share any information I find out when I talk to Dr Joyce tomorrow?'

'You'll suit yourself, Matt. It doesn't matter what I say.'

There was a muttered swear word, then silence. His brother had gone.

Ben found his eyes focusing on the framed photograph above the fireplace. And there was Sergeant Joe Cooper, his father, gazing out from his place in the second row, among all those other solemn-faced police officers lined up in their best uniforms.

It was odd, really. He'd spent so much time thinking that his life had been dictated and overshadowed by the legacy of Joe Cooper that he hadn't seriously considered what he might have inherited from his mother's side, or which of her chromosomes he'd been allocated during conception. Her hair colouring, yes. The eyes, maybe. But what else was lurking in his DNA that he risked passing on to future generations?

Then Ben laughed to himself. All of this anxiety presumed he would ever get married or find a permanent partner. He didn't have any such intentions at the moment, and maybe that was for the best. He'd hate to be in Matt's position, discovering the possibilities when it was already too late.

GEORGI KOTSEV leaned across the table at Caesar's restaurant and raised his glass. 'We say *Nazdrave*.'

'Cheers.'

'Yes. Cheers.'

'Is the wine all right?' asked Fry. 'There isn't much choice of places to eat in Edendale.'

'*Losho nyama*. No problem.'

Inexplicably, she'd felt the need to give Sergeant Kotsev a good impression of Edendale. As if it mattered, to him or her. They were both strangers passing through, except that Kotsev would be gone a bit sooner.

He looked at the menu. 'Could you recommend anything?'

'The confit of duck is excellent,' she said, since it was the only thing she'd ever eaten here.

'I think I will try a steak,' he said.

Fry wondered if he'd read her ignorance so effortlessly.

'What would you normally drink in Bulgaria?'

'Our national drink is *rakia*—grape brandy. Or wine. People of this country are acquainted with Bulgarian red wine?'

'Yes, of course.'

'Our white wine is also delicious. But Bulgarian folklore presents a lot of songs about red wine and only one about white, which goes: "Oh, white wine, why are you not red?"'

Fry laughed. 'You said you were born in a village. So your parents were country people, Sergeant Kotsev?'

'Please. Call me Georgi.'

'I'm Diane.'

'Yes, I know.'

Kotsev's brown eyes were rather sad when you looked closely. The dark hairs on his wrist curled over the band of a gold watch, and his shirt cuffs were white and crisp. His clothes surely hadn't come out of his suitcase like that, she thought, picturing him ironing his shirts in his hotel room.

'You know, my family in the past were mostly shepherds and goat chasers,' he said. 'Peasants, in other words. Sometimes men would come to our village from the city. If they wore long leather coats and had moustaches, we knew they were from the police or from the Party. One word from them could have changed our lives. It's difficult for you to understand the way we lived.'

Kotsev's English wasn't quite perfect, after all. She detected a tendency to pronounce the past tense of certain verbs as if there was an extra syllable. Liv-*ed*. Chang-*ed*. She put it down to a lack of opportunity to practise conversation with native English speakers, and found it rather appealing.

'Was this near Pleven?' she asked.

'No, in the far south, near the border with Greece. A remote region of Bulgaria.' He put down the menu. 'Have you chosen?'

'Yes, I think so.'

Kotsev looked at the waiter across the restaurant. That was all he seemed to do, yet the man was instantly at their table to take their order.

'But it's good to know a little of your family history,' he said a few minutes later. 'My grandfather worked in a macaroni factory. Sadly, my mother died when I was very young. I don't remember much of her. Only a green scarf with glittering threads woven through it. And I remember she had beautiful teeth. As white as Greek cheese, my father used to say.

'As for my father,' he continued. 'The memory from my childhood is a smell—a Soviet aftershave, which I think was called *Tachanka*.' He smiled. 'And you, Diane? What of your parents?'

'My parents?' said Fry. 'Like you, I remember almost nothing of them.'

'Nothing?'

'Almost nothing.'

Kotsev waited patiently, then seemed to realise that she wasn't going to say any more. When the waiter returned, they ate quietly for a few moments. Fry supposed she ought to ask him what he thought of the food. But food didn't interest her much as a topic of conversation.

'What exactly is your role in Pleven now, Georgi?'

'Oh, you wish to talk business?' he said.

'I'd like to know how you think you could help our present inquiry. Can you fill me in on some background?'

He nodded. 'Well, a lot of events have been happening in my country, because of the EU. Our government has been given conditions to meet before we will be allowed to join. "Clean up your act," they say. One of the things the EU does not like is our organised crime, our Mafia.'

'Is organised crime such a big problem in Bulgaria?'

'A big problem?' Kotsev laughed. 'You might say that. There are certain people who have become very rich running crime in my country. They rule their kingdoms by violence—punishment beatings, shootings, and they are very ruthless men. The *mutras*, we call them. Clever and cruel killers.'

'*Mutras*?'

'In Bulgarian, *mutra* means "ugly face". If you saw these people, you'd understand. Many of them were out-of-work bodybuilders or wrestlers. After the Change—you know, the events of 1989—they made a name for themselves by offering security to businesses—for a monthly fee, you understand. Owners who refused to pay fell victim to repeated robberies. You would call it the protection racket. Now *mutra* daddies drive around in armed convoys, and until now they have been untouchable.'

'Why untouchable, Georgi?'

Kotsev tapped his nose. 'Connections. It is said that some of our highest government officials owe their positions to an association with these gangsters. And now they're in a difficult position. Our government wants to join the European Union. The EU says we must get rid of our Mafia, and if we don't make progress it will delay our entry. A very big problem.'

'I see.'

'But, ah!' said Kotsev, throwing out a hand. 'Not such a problem, after all. Suddenly we have a miracle! And now, things are going our way.'

'A miracle?'

'In the past two years some of the most powerful Mafia bosses have been eliminated. One of them is shot leaving a casino after celebrating a victory by his football team. Another is gunned down with his bodyguards outside a bar. Sometimes an entire family is murdered. Each killing appears to have been carried out by an expert shot. The official theory concerns a war between rival gangs, who have employed hit men to do their dirty work.'

'That sounds feasible.' Fry knew that his silence invited another question. 'But that was the *official* theory. What's the unofficial one?'

Kotsev smiled. 'We have a highly efficient secret service in Bulgaria, the Durzhavna Sigurnost. Their usefulness did not disappear with Communism.'

'I'm not sure what you're saying, Georgi.'

'Some of these people have a talent for convenient assassinations. What more efficient way could there be to remove annoying criminals and avoid a trial, where embarrassing facts about government officials might emerge? A few extra *stotinki* in the pockets of a Durzhavna Sigurnost operative. Boom, boom. Problem solved. Now it's, "See, Mr EU Commissioner, we don't have the nasty Mafia any more. Now you can let us into your club."'

Fry put down her fork. 'That's incredible,' she said.

Kotsev's eyes crinkled as he held up a forkful of steak. 'To you, perhaps.'

'Even so, Georgi—'

He laughed. 'Yes, you're right. Even so. Like you, I do not believe our beloved secret service was involved in the killing of Dimitar Iliev.

'Who was it, then?' she asked. 'Simcho Nikolov?'

'Well, these killings were probably carried out by a local person, a paid assassin. Someone like Simcho Nikolov, perhaps. But it's possible they were ordered by a major Bulgarian crime boss, one of the remaining Mafia. A very powerful man, particularly now that some of his leading rivals have been . . . eliminated. A man with friends in high places.'

Fry fought a brief internal battle between her own ambition and what she knew to be the proper protocol. Finally, she sighed. 'It sounds like this is really a matter for Special Branch or MI5.'

'THIS IS PRETTY, but I still prefer cities,' said Kotsev, as they walked by the river after dinner. 'At ten o'clock at night in Sofia, the streets would be full, even though it's a Thursday. People would be selling sunflower seeds or salted sweetcorn. They would be buying books from fold-up tables. There would be loud music from stalls dealing in pirated CDs. A few counterfeit Rolex watches or Levi jeans, perhaps. Beggars and street artists, pickpockets and prostitutes. It would be like a party. Here, there is nothing.'

Fry studied him, wondering whether he was joking. It was difficult to tell sometimes. Then, when he saw her staring, Kotsev laughed.

'You like living in Sofia?' she asked.

'In some ways,' he said softly.

They had arrived at the point where water poured over a weir and the river formed little wooded islands populated by sleeping birds. Even at this time of the evening there were people by the river, enjoying an oasis of peace under the shadow of St Mark's Church.

'We have our tourist attractions in Pleven, also,' Kotsev said, pausing to admire the reflection of the illuminated church spire in the water.

'Really?'

'Oh, yes. If you ever visit our city, you must see our famous Pleven Panorama—the largest structure of its kind in the world.'

'Wonderful,' she said, though she wasn't sure she knew what a panorama was. She'd always thought it was one of those views of the countryside from the top of a hill that Ben Cooper loved so much. But that didn't sound like what Georgi was talking about.

'The Pleven Panorama tells a great story. The tragic destiny of our people, their dramatic fight, the compassion in the hearts of our Russian brothers. Within the Panorama, the spectator sees a charge of the Turkish cavalry, burning fires in the city, the Russians attacking a Turkish fortification. This attraction causes a great deal of interest in our city.'

'As you said, we don't know much about Bulgarian history here.'

'No, of course.' Kotsev began to walk on again, but Fry stopped him.

'Georgi, who should we be looking for? If Simcho Nikolov came, then who else is here?'

He laughed. 'You could start with seven thousand Bulgarian entrepreneurs.'

'You've lost me.'

'You don't recall?' said Kotsev. 'A few years ago, your government introduced a so-called visa fast-track system to encourage entrepreneurs from Eastern Europe to come to the UK and set up business. At that time there was an organised fraud in operation. One person submitted seventy identical business plans to support visa applications from Bulgarian individuals. They made a mockery of your entry controls.'

The breeze was turning cool down by the river. Fry shivered a little, wishing she'd brought something warmer to put on. 'So you're saying that pretty much anybody could have come into this country?'

Kotsev shrugged. 'If they could afford it. But it was expensive. Fraudulent papers might cost up to three thousand pounds—about the same amount of money that many British people were spending at that time on buying up cheap holiday homes in my country. Would you consider that irony, Diane?'

'Yes, that's irony, Georgi.'

Their feet echoed on the bridge. Fry suddenly felt reluctant to leave the darkness and the quietness of the river. She stopped halfway across the bridge and leaned on the parapet. Kotsev came to stand next to her, sharing that mysterious attraction to water.

'There must have been risks, though,' she said.

'Any risks were worth taking. You try to get a hundred individuals into the country and succeed only with forty? You've still made a hundred thousand pounds. That's a great many *stotinki* for a Bulgarian.'

Kotsev smiled then, his eyes crinkling again. 'You appreciate, there is a lot of information I do not have myself. But I'm sharing with you what I know—because I think we understand each other.'

Any answer would have felt awkward, so a silence developed. For a few seconds, it was just the two of them, surrounded by darkness, gazing into the water. Their hands were so close on the rail that they were almost touching.

Then a young couple appeared on the opposite bank and began walking across the bridge. Kotsev moved back from the parapet, brushing against her as he turned, and Fry caught a whiff of his scent when he touched her. She inhaled instinctively, trying to read some elusive meaning in a smell.

'*Kalina Tet-a-tet*,' he said quietly. 'It's Russian.'

Fry met his gaze, wondering how he'd known what she was thinking.

7

Friday, October 28

Fry was early for the briefing next morning. The room filled up around her, but she let the increasing level of noise wash over her.

The divisional commander, Chief Superintendent Jepson, had made an appearance to greet Sergeant Kotsev. They shook hands.

'I've emailed Captain Pirinski to thank him for loaning your services, Sergeant. It's so useful to have your experience in the field of cross-border organised crime.'

'Thank you, sir. I'm pleased to help.'

When he took the floor, Kotsev turned out to be an excellent speaker. He'd obviously had practice at presentations, and his almost perfect English and smart appearance commanded attention, even from this jaded bunch.

'First a little background,' he said. 'Your colleague Sergeant Fry assures me that not all of you are experts on Bulgarian history.'

Behind him, the chief superintendent chuckled.

'In the last fifteen years, organised crime has thrived in Bulgaria, its influence reaching all parts of our society. Sadly, the state apparatus has been too weak to deal with this problem. Too corrupt also, you might say. But no longer. Now, anti-corruption is a byword in our ministries.'

Kotsev spoke for a few minutes more, outlining the issues he'd explained to Fry the previous night, but in less detail.

When Kotsev paused, a hand went up. 'What about the couple who were killed in their car? Were they involved in organised crime?'

'Yes, we believe so. But there are also ethnic problems in Bulgaria, and Piya Yotova was a Romani woman. We do not know for certain who pulled the trigger in this case.'

'And Simon Nichols? How was he connected?'

'Simcho Nikolov? From our intelligence sources we know he was a major participant in counterfeiting operations. That was his area of expertise.'

'Counterfeiting operations? Would that include passports?'

'Yes. The counterfeiters' main area of business is forging euro banknotes. However, in the United Kingdom operatives are more likely to employ their skills in the production of false identity documents.'

There was a moment of silence when Kotsev had finished. Hitchens stood up to take over.

'It might be worth mentioning a bit of news at this point,' he said. 'The firearms examiners have identified the weapon that killed Rose Shepherd, and it turns out to be a fairly unusual item. This took some research on the lab's part, so I think we owe them a favour. They say it's a Romanian military sniper rifle, the Pusca Semiautomata cu Luneta, or PSL.' He paused briefly. 'As for Simon Nichols, we haven't yet received the full post-mortem report, but so far there is no evidence that his death was due to anything but natural causes, or an accident.'

'So he probably isn't a victim? In that case . . .?'

'Yes,' said Hitchens. 'We should be regarding him as a suspect for the Rose Shepherd killing. We need to find some way of establishing his movements in the last few days before he died.'

After the briefing, Diane Fry walked with Hitchens and Cooper to the DI's office, while Kotsev talked to DCI Kessen. The plastic wallet on Hitchens's desk was now labelled as evidence examined by the documents section at the forensics laboratory.

But Fry wasn't thinking about the Shepherd inquiry. Or about Georgi Kotsev. She was thinking about Europol.

She'd been aware of Europol, of course, as one of the organisations spawned by the integration of EU countries. But it had never occurred to her until now that it was a possible career move. As soon as she had the opportunity, she'd check their website.

'The passport has been confirmed as a forgery,' said Hitchens, interrupting her thoughts. 'Likewise Rose Shepherd's driving licence. With those two items, you can build an identity for yourself in no time.'

'What about her DNA and fingerprints?' said Fry.

'We're running them through the data base.'

'She's not your typical terrorist suspect, is she?'

'True. But she'd need the right contacts to change her identity so effectively. Nikolov looks most likely. When we discover her real identity, we'll find the motive for her murder. There must be something she did in the past that she was trying to conceal.'

Fry glanced at Cooper. He was nodding, but looked doubtful.

'Did I tell you?' he said suddenly. 'I think I might have found where the wooden dinosaur came from.'

During the briefing, Gavin Murfin had seemed fascinated by Kotsev's shoes. He'd sat with his eyes directed downwards, as if he'd been hypnotised.

'What do you think of him, Gavin?' asked Fry.

'His shoes are very shiny. Very military-looking. I bet he feels more at home in uniform.'

'All part of his professional manner, wouldn't you say?'

Murfin sniffed. 'By the way, West Yorkshire Police have no record of John Lowther. But I tracked down a former colleague from the building society where he worked. Apparently, the word around the office was that after Lowther left the company he was in hospital for quite some time.'

'What for?'

'Nobody ever knew. There was some speculation about a mystery illness. In those circumstances, people tend to assume cancer.'

'See if you can find out what was wrong with him, will you?'

Murfin hesitated. 'Diane, surely we could ask Lowther's parents? They must know about his hospital stay.'

'Yes, I'm going to ask them,' said Fry. 'But I don't trust them to tell me the truth. I want to make sure I have an independent account.'

'I can't promise anything. There's such a lot on right now.'

'OK, Gavin. Just try, will you?'

Fry seemed to have heard herself saying that far too often recently. Was she obsessing too much over irrelevant details?

'Where's your Bulgarian?' asked Murfin.

'Out somewhere with Kessen. When he comes back, I'm taking him down to Foxlow. He wants to see Rose Shepherd's house.'

Murfin answered the phone and held it out to Fry.

'Speak of the devil,' he said. 'It's Boris.'

Fry took the phone. 'Hi, Georgi.'

'Diane, I need to talk to you about the assassination of Rosica Savova.'

'The assassination of who?'

'The woman you know as Rose Shepherd.'

AS SHE STOOD in the sitting room at Bain House, Fry thought of the heaps of flowers and cards piling up outside the Mullens' house in Darwin Street, and the tributes in the local papers from people who'd known them, the poems from children at the school Jack had attended. There was none of that for Rose Shepherd. No one had left flowers at her gate.

'So who was Rose Shepherd really?' asked Fry.

'A woman by the name of Rosica Savova,' said Georgi Kotsev. 'She had a Bulgarian father, but her mother was Irish, from County Galway.'

'She could put on an Irish accent, if she felt like it?'

'It might have been natural. We don't know much about her history. But she had been working as an advisor for an adoption agency in Bulgaria for several years before she came here. We have an intelligence file on her, due to her association with Simcho Nikolov and Dimitar Iliev.'

'What crime was she involved in?'

'None that we know of,' said Kotsev. 'However, she was connected with the wrong people. That in itself causes us suspicion.' He admired the TV set and the stereo. 'What money did she have? You've examined her finances?'

'We've been through all her bank statements. Rose Shepherd had one current account and three savings accounts.'

'But not much cash in them, perhaps?'

'No, but—'

'It's not surprising. Rosica Savova must have lived in Bulgaria through the time of the 1996 bank collapse. That was when more than a third of our banks closed down, and much of our money simply disappeared. Everyone who lost their money then also lost their faith in banks. Have your people searched the house properly?'

'What do you mean by "properly"?' said Fry, bridling.

'Inside the walls, under the floorboards? The chimney?'

'Why would we do that?'

Kotsev turned slowly. 'To find her money.'

Fry took a call on her mobile. When she'd finished, she discovered Kotsev upstairs, tapping the walls of the main bedroom.

'Good news, Georgi. The blue Vauxhall Astra we're looking for was seen again in Foxlow last night. This time we got a registration number. The vehicle is registered to a Mr Darren Turnbull, of South Wingfield.'

'Is that nearby?'

'Not too far. But DI Hitchens is already on his way there.'

'Pity.' He tapped the wall again. 'It sounds hollow here. You should get your people back to examine the structure of the house.'

'Oh, I can't see how we'd justify ripping the house apart, Georgi.'

'You need Savova's personal information? Her private contacts? Where else would she keep them, but in her secret safe, with her money?'

'She used the Internet, Georgi. We think she might have stored information like that on the web. We just haven't found it yet.'

'The internet? *Gluposti*. Find her money, you find her heart and soul.'

Fry was thoughtful as they returned to the car and drove out of Foxlow.

'Georgi, what do you think of our methods so far?' she said.

'Very interesting. But your enquiries are in the wrong direction, Diane.'

'What do you mean?'

He waved a hand out of the window at the cottages they were passing. 'You are wasting your time with these slow-witted country people.'

'Hold on, I've got another call.'

This time, it was Hitchens himself. 'Where are you, Diane?'

'Just approaching Matlock.'

'Great. We're at Darren Turnbull's house in South Wingfield, but his wife says he's driven down into Matlock to go to the bank. His car should be parked by the railway station.'

'OK, leave it to us. We'll be there in a couple of minutes.'

A few minutes later, Fry coasted her Peugeot into the station car park at the bottom of Dale Road. They found the Astra almost immediately.

'OK, now we have to wait for him to come back.'

She parked where they had a clear view of the vehicle, and Kotsev eased his legs with a sigh. 'If I had seen Rosica Savova's assassin, perhaps I would not come forward and tell the police either.'

'Why, Georgi?'

'It could be dangerous,' said Kotsev. 'And in my experience, many people see things they keep quiet about, for their own safety.'

'Maybe.'

Suddenly he sat up straight. 'Is this the man?'

'Let's see which car he goes back to.'

A man was strolling along the line of vehicles. He was in his thirties, sandy-haired, wearing a black parka. He stopped, pulled a key from his pocket and approached the blue Vauxhall.

'Yes, that's him. Let's go.'

Turnbull looked up and saw them coming. He mouthed a curse, then turned and began to run towards the station.

Fry broke into a sprint, but Kotsev easily outpaced her.

'*Politsia!* Police!'

Catching up with Turnbull, Kotsev took hold of his arm and twisted it sharply behind his back, pushing his face into a wall. 'My friend, you shouldn't try to escape. You have to tell us what we want to know.'

Fry was frozen for a moment, shocked by Kotsev's action. 'Georgi!'

He looked at her, his eyes glinting, his jaw set.

'Sergeant Kotsev, you don't have jurisdiction here. This isn't Bulgaria.'

Slowly, he relaxed his grip on Turnbull's arm, but didn't let go completely. 'You do things a little differently, Sergeant Fry. But I know the methods that work with these people.'

'Let go of him,' hissed Fry.

Another moment passed. Finally, Kotsev stood back, and smiled.

'I apologise. I have no jurisdiction. This is your suspect.' He turned Turnbull gently away from the wall and dusted down his clothes. 'I apologise to you, too, my friend. I intended you no harm. I hope you feel well enough to be questioned by my colleague.'

Turnbull didn't look reassured. 'What the hell is this?'

'You *are* Mr Darren Turnbull?' said Fry.

'Yes, why?'

'Were you driving this car in the village of Foxlow on Saturday night?'

Turnbull's mouth dropped open. His brain still seemed to be working, but so slowly that no connection was being made with his vocal cords.

'Sir?'

'I can't tell you,' he said. 'I really can't. I'd be in big, big trouble.'

'Let's all go back to the station, then,' said Fry. 'And we'll talk about which sort of trouble you'd rather be in, Mr Turnbull.'

DARREN TURNBULL sat in Interview Room One. 'I suppose this is about the shooting, isn't it? The old lady who got shot in Foxlow.'

'Would you like to tell us something about that, Darren?' said Hitchens in his friendliest manner.

'I don't know anything about the bloody shooting,' said Turnbull, apparently missing the friendliness.

'Oh, really? So why did you mention it?'

Turnbull twisted his hands restlessly. 'I saw it on the telly,' he said, 'and read about it in the papers.'

Hitchens opened the file in front of him and made a show of reading the top page for a few moments, as if he was seeing it for the first time. He raised an eyebrow as he looked at Turnbull again.

'And having seen all those news reports, which all mentioned that we were appealing for the owner of a blue Vauxhall Astra to come forward, you nevertheless failed to contact us. Why was that?'

'I'm going to be in *big* trouble,' said Turnbull.

'Darren, you're being interviewed in connection with a murder inquiry. We have reason to believe that you were in the vicinity around the time the murder occurred, and yet you've failed to come forward voluntarily as a potential witness. Believe me, you're already in big trouble.'

Turnbull sighed deeply. 'I suppose I knew it would come to this in the end. I was visiting a friend in Foxlow. A girlfriend, all right?'

'Your girlfriend's name, please,' said Hitchens, with his pen poised.

'I can't tell you.'

Hitchens laid the file down. 'Let's get this straight, Darren. You're having an affair with a woman who lives in Foxlow, and you don't want your wife to know about it. Is that about right?'

'Yes,' said Turnbull grudgingly.

'OK, I understand that. But look at it this way, Darren. You're a potential witness in our inquiry. All we want is to ask you a few questions about anything you might have seen or heard that night. And we'll want to speak to your girlfriend to corroborate your story. And that will be it. Provided it all checks out, we'll thank you for helping us with our enquiries, and there won't be any need for us to speak to your wife.'

Turnbull nodded cautiously.

'On the other hand, if you continue to refuse to account fully for your movements that night, we'll be obliged to ask questions about your background and circumstances, find out who your associates are . . . Your wife would be the obvious place to start.'

'I hear what you're saying.' Turnbull hung his head.

Hitchens opened the file again and picked up his pen. 'Do you want to give me the name of your girlfriend now?'

'Stella Searle. She lives at Magpie Cottage, next to the churchyard.'

'What time did you arrive in Foxlow to visit Stella?'

'Oh, about half past eleven. I parked the car on a lane behind the churchyard. There are no lights there, but there's a back gate into Stell's garden.'

'Very handy. This Magpie Cottage—it would be right on the corner of Foxlow High Street and Pinfold Lane, am I right?'

'That's it.'

'So what time did you leave on Sunday morning?'

'It was close to three o'clock. I told my wife I was doing the late shift at the factory and that's when it ends, so I got home about the right time.'

'OK, now we get to the bit where you might be able to help us, Darren. Did you see or hear anything as you were leaving the cottage? I'm hoping you were alert enough to notice any activity, even after your visit.'

Turnbull lowered his voice. 'Yes, I did see something.'

'What did you see?'

'A black car. Big four-by-four. Japanese. Tinted windows. Smart motor.'

'Japanese? Did you recognise the make?'

'I'm not sure. Toyota, or Mitsubishi?'

Hitchens sighed. 'Did you happen to see the registration number?'

'No, sorry.'

'But you're sure of the colour? Even though it was dark?'

'I saw it pass under a streetlamp—the one by the phone box.'

'How many occupants?'

'One in the front, at least. I couldn't tell if there was anyone in the back because of the tinted windows. Sorry.'

'And this vehicle was heading in the direction of Bain House?'

'If that's the big house with the gates at the top of Pinfold Lane, it definitely went that way, then came back towards the High Street.'

'All right, Darren. We'll get someone to show you some photos, and we'll see if you can identify the make and model of the car you saw.'

'What? Can't I go yet?'

'Not yet.'

'I had no connection with that woman at all, you know,' he said. 'And I could put in a complaint about the foreign bloke. He hurt my arm. He's not supposed to do that, is he? I wasn't even under arrest.'

'If you want to make a formal complaint about the conduct of any police officers, speak to the custody sergeant and he'll give you a form to fill in.'

When they were alone in the corridor, Hitchens looked at Fry quizzically. 'Foreign bloke? Sergeant Kotsev?'

'He isn't quite used to our procedures yet,' said Fry.

'If Turnbull does put in a complaint—'

'I don't think he will,' said Fry. 'Do you? Too much chance of publicity.'

'No, you're right. But be careful.'

FRY WAS BROWSING the Europol website when Hitchens appeared and gestured to her. She followed him into the DCI's office.

'Looking at pictures of cars seems to have calmed Darren Turnbull down,' said Hitchens. 'He thinks it was probably a Mitsubishi Shogun he saw in Foxlow that night.'

'Excellent,' said Kessen.

'We've checked the incident logs, and nothing is missing locally, but South Yorkshire have a hit. On Saturday evening, a black Shogun was stolen from the car park of the Church of Free Worship in Totley. That's on the outskirts of Sheffield.'

'Even better.'

'Wait, there's more. Traffic already have a report of a Shogun abandoned under a disused railway bridge near Wirksworth. Burnt out, of course.'

'Our killers made a switch, then.'

'It looks like it, sir. DC Cooper's on his way there now to take a look.'

Kessen began to look a bit happier. 'Good work, Paul. But make sure any more stolen vehicles that are found get the once-over before they're returned to their owners. They could have made a second switch at some point. And pass that request to South Yorkshire, too.'

'Yes, sir.'

'So much for the famous village surveillance experts,' said Fry. 'They spotted Darren Turnbull's Astra twice, but they never saw the Shogun.'

Hitchens shrugged, then looked at her. 'What have you done with Sergeant Kotsev, by the way?'

'I've given him to Ben Cooper to look after for a while.'

THE SHOGUN had been abandoned under a bridge that was left over from a disused mineral line. It wasn't even a bridge any more, because the central section had been removed. But it had only crossed a farm track anyway. By the looks of the deep tread on the wheel tracks in the mud, the farmer had probably passed the Shogun several times without bothering to report it.

Someone had done a good job of torching the vehicle. It was difficult to tell what colour the paintwork had been, but a few unscorched streaks remained on the boot and the front wings. The interior, though, looked relatively undamaged.

Cooper refolded his map. 'There's not much we can get from the car until the SOCOs arrive,' he said. 'I'd like to take a look up this way, Georgi.'

Though Kotsev's stride was longer, he obviously wasn't used to walking over rough terrain, and definitely not uphill.

'Where are we going?' gasped Kotsev.

'Just to the top of this rise.'

A moment later, Cooper was standing at the top of the slope, letting the breeze cool his forehead. To the northeast, a dry-stone wall ran along the skyline, marking the road between Wirksworth and Middleton. He followed the wall a little further north—and there was the distinctive outline of a red phone box. He smiled. These old kiosks were such an integral part of the landscape that they were kept in the countryside as a conservation measure, as much as for emergency use.

Cooper took out his mobile phone and dialled a number.

Whenever he spoke to Liz Petty on the phone her voice always sounded so warm that it took him by surprise. He'd have to be careful not to make a nuisance of himself phoning her too often, just to hear her voice.

'There's something I wanted to ask you, Liz,' he said.

'Yes?'

'Do you think it would be possible to find out more about the weapon that fired the shots at Bain House, the PSL sniper rifle? I know the lab have pulled out the stops for us, but could you have a word with Wayne?'

'I'm not sure, Ben. What do you want to know?'

'Whether there are non-military versions of it.'

'OK,' said Petty. 'I'll see what we can find out.'

As Cooper ended the call, Kotsev arrived alongside him, breathing heavily and wiping sweat from his forehead.

'Georgi, how many people in Bulgaria have mobile phones?' asked Cooper.

Kotsev stared at him. 'Everybody, except for those who are too poor. And the very old, who don't understand them.'

'Yes, it's the same here. And even if you don't own a mobile, you have a phone in your house. Not many people are too poor or too old for that.'

'What are you saying?'

'Well, it's different, of course,' said Cooper, 'if you live in a caravan.'

If he could have seen over the next hill, he might have made out the red blob of another phone box in Bonsall Dale. That was the one Rose Shepherd had made two calls to in the past three weeks. According to the map, it was the nearest one to Lea Farm, where Simcho Nikolov had lived.

AS SOON AS COOPER walked back into the office at West Street, Fry slammed the phone down and glared at him.

'See, I took my attention off Brian Mullen. I let him know he was under suspicion, and then allowed him the chance to do a runner. I should have been completing the case against him by now so we could make an arrest. But I was distracted by the Rose Shepherd inquiry. How can anyone be expected to do two jobs at once, and do them properly?'

'What's happened, Diane?' Cooper asked.

'I need to talk to Brian Mullen again,' she said. 'He should be with his parents-in-law in Darley Dale, but they say they don't know where he is today. And he has Luanne with him.'

'That's bad news.'

'Bad news? It's a total disaster. I'm sending Gavin to speak to John Lowther, and to anyone else who might know where Mullen is.'

'Are you still fancying Mullen for the arson?'

'It happens, you know—some distraught dad decides to end it all, and take the family down with him.'

'But Brian Mullen didn't do that, did he? He was the one who survived.'

'Well, he could have chickened out at the last minute.'

Cooper shook his head. 'If that was the case, I'd expect him to be consumed with guilt right now. He'd be thinking he ought to have died with his family, blaming himself for his cowardice in not going through with it . . . '

Fry had stopped listening to him. She was staring at the photograph of the Mullen family—Lindsay and the two boys, with Brian holding baby Luanne. Three of them were dead, and two still survived.

A phrase she'd learned a long time ago in the playground was running through her head. *Three down, two to go.*

She looked more closely at the photograph of the Mullen family and held it up to the light from the window. She was studying the carefully wrapped bundle in Brian Mullen's arms. Luanne Mullen, aged about twelve months at the time the photo was taken. As she stared at the child's face, Fry suddenly realised how extraordinarily beautiful she was. Then she was struck by the contrast between Luanne and her father. He was fair-haired, angular and pale. Luanne had black hair—so black that it was startling in a child of her age. Her eyes were dark, too, like little pools of black ink.

And what about the mother? Well, there she was—blonde hair, showing light brown at the roots. And green eyes.

Three down, two to go. Fry could almost hear children's voices chanting it in the distance, their tone a mixture of triumph and challenge. It filled her with a sense of urgency, a conviction that an awful disaster could be taking place right under her nose while she was distracted by irrelevant detail.

'Ben,' she said, 'you know what? Right now, I bet Brian Mullen is thinking just one thing. That he ought to get on and finish the job.'

AS SOON AS SHE sat down in the Lowthers' conservatory, Fry lifted the photograph of Brian and Lindsay and their three children off the corner table. No pussyfooting around any more. She had told Cooper that she would do all the talking. 'Luanne is a very attractive child, Mrs Lowther,' she said.

'Yes, isn't she?'

'She doesn't look a bit like either of her parents, though. Her colouring is very dark.'

'It happens. There's no accounting for genes.'

'I know what you mean,' said Fry. 'But you can account for the genes in this case, can't you? Luanne is definitely your daughter's child?'

Henry Lowther remained impassive. Mrs Lowther fidgeted, reluctant to answer. But Fry was prepared to wait.

'No, she's adopted,' said Mrs Lowther at last.

'Ah, finally,' said Fry. 'And this adoption was how you came to know Rose Shepherd, am I right?'

'Yes, it's true.'

'And the meeting in Matlock Bath on Saturday? Whose idea was that?'

The Lowthers looked at each other. 'I suppose I suggested it to Lindsay,' said Henry. 'It was just a casual remark, really. "It would be nice to see Rose Shepherd again and say thank you, wouldn't it?" Something like that.'

'You're going to have to be more forthcoming with us, sir.'

Lowther got up from his chair and moved restlessly around the conservatory. 'You have to realise that they went through a difficult experience together,' he said. 'The adoption process in Bulgaria wasn't easy. It was a shock to arrive at that orphanage. We had never seen anything like it.'

'Tell us how it came about.'

'I have some business contacts in Bulgaria,' said Lowther. 'They came over here a few years ago to talk about forming trade links, and we made sure they had a good time while they were here, of course. They invited me over to Bulgaria for a little jaunt in return for our hospitality.'

'And did they show you a good time?'

'Oh, there was some vodka, and red wine. We explored the country a little.'

'Where did you go? Pleven?'

Lowther hesitated slightly. 'Dounav.'

'And Rose Shepherd?'

'I was put in touch with her through one of my business contacts. You can get hold of pretty much anything if you know the right people.'

'Was it you who suggested the adoption to your daughter?'

'I mentioned it as an option,' said Mr Lowther defensively. 'Lindsay was desperate for a girl. But after Liam's birth, the doctors told her and Brian they couldn't have any more children. Adoption is such a chancy process in this country. In any case, you can't get babies to adopt here any more. Once Lindsay heard about all those orphanages in Romania where babies needed parents, it was all we could do to stop her catching the next flight out. So we read up on it a bit—on the Internet, you know. And we found that Bulgaria was the place to go these days. So that's where we went.'

'You keep saying "we".'

'I couldn't let Lindsay go out there on her own.'

'No, but it might seem more natural for Brian to have gone with her.'

'Brian can't just take time off whenever he wants. But I can organise my time however I like, and I was ready and willing to go with her.'

'And Rose Shepherd helped you arrange an adoption?'

'She worked with the people at the orphanage.'

'Oh, of course. The orphanage.'

Lowther stopped pacing and stared out of the window at the traffic. His shoulders seemed to sag as he was forced to bring back the memories.

'It was in a small town about thirty miles from Pleven. When we found the place, it was a run-down building with peeling paint, full of chipped wooden cots and thin mattresses. It was awful. Lindsay nearly cried when she saw all the children in their cots, regardless of age. We discovered that they were expected to share clothes, and even toothbrushes. Food seemed to be in short supply, too. It was so depressing. Personally, I would have turned round and come home immediately. But then there was Zlatka . . .'

'Sorry? Did you say Zlatka?'

'Lindsay and Brian decided to call her Luanne, but her Bulgarian name was Zlatka Shishkov. She was so small and frail, with big eyes and dark, wispy hair. No one could have resisted her. Lindsay said afterwards that when she saw Zlatka for the first time she instantly felt a sort of gaping emptiness in her stomach fill up with love. She said that, in that moment, she became Zlatka's mother.'

Lowther stirred from the window. 'There were many bad times after that first occasion. Bulgarian adoptions require court approval—a notoriously slow process. Miss Shepherd was a great help, giving us advice all along the line, explaining all the bureaucracy. But at the first court hearing, the judge refused our application. He said there were minor problems in the paperwork. We had to hire a Bulgarian attorney to correct the errors.'

'And this was, what—twelve months ago?'

'Yes. Luanne was six months old when we brought her out of Bulgaria.'

Mrs Lowther smiled sadly. 'She's been slow to develop in a lot of ways. And she's very restless physically, isn't she, Henry?'

'She certainly is. And very emotional, too. Especially now.'

'So explain to me again how you came to meet with Rose Shepherd in Matlock Bath last weekend. How did you get in touch with her?'

'There was an email address—one of those free web-based accounts where you don't have to give any details of your identity to sign up.'

'I see. Well, we'd like that email address, please, sir.'

'I'll find it for you. You know, I don't think she can have checked her email very often. It took her some weeks to reply to my message.'

'You weren't aware that Miss Shepherd was living nearby?'

Lowther laughed. 'No, that was the amazing thing. I was stunned when she suggested meeting in Matlock Bath. Apparently she didn't travel very far once she got into that house at Foxlow.'

'She told you where she lived, then? Was that information in her email, or did she tell you when you met her in the Riber Tea Rooms?'

'Neither,' said Lowther. 'I read about the house in Foxlow in the papers, and then saw it on the TV news. As I said, I was stunned. To think Miss Shepherd lived only a few miles away from us.'

'Mr Lowther, why didn't you come forward and tell us you knew Rose Shepherd when you heard the news about her death?'

'Why? Good God, don't you think we've been a bit too busy with our own concerns?' Lowther's face reddened. 'Our lives have been turned upside-down. We've been backwards and forwards to the hospital and the mortuary, visiting Brian, identifying the bodies of our daughter and our grandchildren, fending off the press, doing our best to look after Luanne. Not to mention John. My wife has cried herself to sleep every night.'

'All right.'

Fry waited for him to calm down. Perhaps she'd been a bit unreasonable.

'Besides, nothing happened at our meeting,' said Lowther. 'Once we'd said what we'd gone to say, there was nothing else to talk about. After a while, Miss Shepherd gave Lindsay a gift for Luanne, then she left.'

'This gift, sir . . . Was it a wooden dinosaur?'

'A dinosaur? Yes. I believe so.'

That detail confirmed, Fry decided to try a different tack.

'What about a man called Simon Nichols? Did you have any dealings with him, Mr Lowther?'

'Nichols? No, the name means nothing to me. Who is he?'

'Someone else Rose Shepherd was in contact with.'

'Miss Shepherd never mentioned any names.'

Fry nodded, then changed the subject again. 'I don't really understand why Brian and Lindsay were so desperate to adopt,' she said.

Lowther shifted uncomfortably. 'Well, as I said . . . there was a problem. About three years ago, Brian had mumps. When you get them as an adult, it's a very serious condition. He became infertile.'

'Were you aware of any problems in your daughter's marriage?'

'Problems?'

'Had Lindsay and Brian been having arguments recently?'

'Most couples have disagreements,' said Lowther stiffly. 'As I said, we all went through a bad period during the adoption. But recently . . .?'

He looked at his wife, who seemed even more reluctant. 'If they had problems, then it was a personal matter between themselves,' she said.

'Mr and Mrs Lowther, where is your son-in-law?'

Neither of them answered her, and she began to get angry.

'And your granddaughter? She isn't here today. So where are they?'

The Lowthers looked at each other again.

'We don't know,' said Mrs Lowther.

Fry's mobile rang, and she saw from the display that the call was from Gavin Murfin. 'Excuse me a moment,' she said.

She stepped outside onto the terrace to take the call.

'Diane, you'll want to know this straight away,' said Murfin. 'I persuaded someone in West Yorkshire to make enquiries into John Lowther's spell there, and they just called back. Lowther was a psychiatric patient in Leeds for three months. That's why he had to leave his job.'

'Did you go to Matlock to speak to him?'

'I'm at his apartment now. But John's not home. And the neighbours say they haven't seen him since yesterday.'

'Oh, great,' said Fry. 'The Lowthers are really, really going to love me.'

WHEN MOIRA LOWTHER heard what Fry wanted to talk about now, she sat down unsteadily in one of the conservatory chairs.

'John is psychotic, not a psychopath,' she said. 'There's a big difference.'

'Yes, I'm sure.'

Her husband came and stood next to his wife, his jaw stiff with emotion.

'People don't understand that they're entirely different things,' said Mrs Lowther. 'Psychosis isn't characterised by a tendency to violence towards others. They're a risk to themselves, but no one else. Psychotics aren't manipulative either, the way psychopaths are. Our son is psychotic,' she repeated. 'Not a psychopath.'

'Yes, I understand.'

'Do you?'

'Actually, yes. I do. But tell me more about John's psychosis.'

'We will, if you like,' said Mrs Lowther. 'But you should talk to his specialist. Dr Sinclair can explain it a lot better than we can.'

JOHN LOWTHER'S HOME was a loft apartment on the fourth floor of a converted mill complex on The Cliff, high above Matlock Green, overlooking a conservation area. Despite the exposed roof timbers, the open-plan interior had a modern feel, all chrome and glass, and the tiny dining table set for two looked as if it belonged in an intimate corner of a fashionable restaurant.

'There's nothing of immediate interest,' said Murfin. 'But we did find a bottle of tablets on his bedside table. Orphenadrine.'

'Never heard of it. But you'd better check it out, Gavin.'

'OK, if you think so.'

Cooper walked in clutching a bottle of Buxton Spring water, as if he was taking a break at home in his own sitting room.

'So where do we go from here, Diane?' he said.

'I've no idea.'

'Have we got any clues at all?'

'No.'

Cooper tipped the last of the water into his mouth and tossed the empty bottle into a bin. 'We're really getting on top of this inquiry, then,' he said.

Fry didn't react. She listened to the silence of the apartment, well insulated and far enough from the main road to deaden the sounds of traffic.

'We've got to find out more about John Lowther's condition,' she said eventually. 'There's a job for you to do, Ben. I'll call ahead and get the interview cleared with his doctor.'

AN HOUR LATER, Dr Alexander Sinclair took off his white coat and put on a suit jacket, transforming himself from a clinical psychologist into a business executive. He sat down at his desk and put on his glasses.

'You appreciate this is very exceptional, Detective Constable,' he said. 'I'm only agreeing to this conversation on the understanding that I'm acting in the interests of my patient.'

'The circumstances are exceptional, too,' said Cooper. 'We wouldn't have asked for this information otherwise. We're extremely concerned for Mr Lowther's safety, and the safety of others he might come into contact with.'

'Very well. There are some specific details of this patient's history that I can't go into, but I can answer general questions.'

'Well, we already know that John Lowther spent three months in a psychiatric unit in Leeds. Was he sectioned?'

'No, he admitted himself, following a series of psychotic episodes.'

'What sort of episodes?'

'Auditory and visual hallucinations.' Sinclair looked down at the file. 'They were increasing in frequency and severity, so admitting himself to the unit was a sensible decision on his part. He had good insight at that point.'

'I'm not sure what you mean by insight, Doctor.'

'One feature of psychosis is that the affected individual doesn't recognise the bizarre nature of his own experiences. He might be unaware that his hallucinations are unrealistic. However, the level of insight can vary, and it can be quite good in some instances. This makes the psychotic experience even more terrifying. The sufferer knows, for example, that he shouldn't be seeing demons and angels, or hearing voices—but he sees and hears them nevertheless. And when a patient is aware that he's losing control of his own thoughts, it undermines the very concept of identity.'

'Yes, I see,' said Cooper. 'Can you tell me what John Lowther's hallucinations consisted of? Is it possible to say?'

'In general. He heard voices that commented on his behaviour, and told him to do certain things. That's why he admitted himself. He was frightened of what the voices might make him do, and he wanted us to stop them.'

'And did you?'

Sinclair hesitated. 'Mr Lowther was treated with antipsychotic drugs until the episodes receded, and then we adjusted his medication until he was stable enough to be discharged. Antipsychotic drugs work by changing the activity of chemicals that transmit messages in the brain. It's very important to take the medication regularly, and at the prescribed doses.'

'He'd have to be on antipsychotic drugs for some time, I imagine.'

'Yes. But his records do show that he was worried about the side effects. Mr Lowther complained that he put on weight. And he twitched a lot, which he found distressing. Also, he said the medication made him impotent.'

'He was very restless when we saw him last week.'

'Mr Lowther was prescribed Orphenadrine for the side effects, but he didn't like the idea of taking more tablets. So . . .' Sinclair hesitated again.

'You think he might have stopped taking his antipsychotic drugs?'

'It's possible. Mr Lowther said once or twice that the effects of the drugs were worse than a few harmless delusions. He thought he'd return to his old self if he stopped taking the medication. It's a common response.'

'Hold on a minute—"a few harmless delusions"?'

'That would be the way it seemed to him, at this particular stage. It is a normal function of the brain to filter out negative experiences. This applies to psychotic episodes as much as to anything else.'

Cooper nodded thoughtfully. 'So what happened when John Lowther was discharged from the unit? How was he being treated?'

'He returned to the community. He has family members in Derbyshire. It's normal practice to ensure that the family are fully aware of the importance of maintaining medication.'

'Who was supposed to do that? His parents?'

Dr Sinclair frowned at the file. 'According to his records, there's a sister.'

'She's dead.'

'Oh. Yes, your senior officer explained.'

'And I think she might have been rather preoccupied recently.'

'Mr Lowther must have been due for a review. Perhaps his GP . . . '

They looked at each other for a moment, conscious of the futility of trying to work out where and when the system had gone wrong.

'Basically, a dangerous psychotic was allowed out into society unsupervised,' said Cooper.

'John Lowther isn't dangerous unless he *has* stopped taking his medication. And even then, he's only a risk to himself.' Sinclair frowned. 'But the trauma of his sister's death might easily have disrupted his normal routine. I hope he hasn't gone beyond caring for himself.'

'Doctor, would Lowther's deteriorating condition be noticeable in the way he talks?'

'Yes, probably. Mr Lowther suffers from thought disorder, another symptom of psychosis. It can lead the patient to speak quickly and incessantly, or to switch topic in midsentence. He could eventually become incoherent, using inappropriate words or mispronouncing them.'

Cooper had been making notes. But his pen paused, and he looked up. 'Would you be willing to listen to a tape of an interview we conducted with Mr Lowther, and give us your opinion on it?'

'Certainly, if you think it would help.'

'How do you think he is likely to react in the present circumstances?'

'It's difficult to say. He'll be in a rather unpredictable state. But one thing I'm sure of: he must be a very frightened man.'

'Frightened of what?'

'Of himself, mostly. You see, if Mr Lowther is off the medication, his auditory hallucinations will return. At this stage, he should be lucid enough to understand what's going on and to be aware that it will get worse. He'll be facing the horror of what he might do at the urging of those voices, and the options he has left to prevent himself turning back into the evil monster he once considered himself to be.'

'And one option,' said Cooper, 'might be to end his own life?'

Sinclair nodded, then he seemed to slip from the script for a moment. 'I realise it's difficult to understand,' he said. 'Most of us know what it means to be afraid to die. But it's rare to meet someone who's scared to live.'

FRY BURST into the office anxious to know whether Cooper had returned from his visit to Dr Sinclair. But Murfin was taking a call as she walked through the door. His eyes were wide, and she watched him expectantly when he put the phone down.

'According to the authorities in Pleven, the Mullens' adoption application was never fully processed,' he said.

'What does that mean?'

'It means they didn't complete the adoption procedure. There were some legal problems, apparently, and their application was rejected by the court.'

'And what happened to Zlatka Shishkov?'

'They say they can't tell us that, for reasons of confidentiality. But one thing's for certain—she wasn't legally adopted by the Mullens.'

8

The bar of the Mulberry Tree in West Street was usually deserted once the lunchtime rush was over, and this afternoon there were only two customers—and one of them was there reluctantly.

For a moment, Georgi Kotsev smiled at Diane Fry and placed a strong, brown hand on the table between them, like an offering. He had left his glass of vodka untouched in front of him out of politeness, though she'd refused his offer of a drink.

'Baby smuggling,' he said. 'It's very regrettable.'

'Is that the word you'd use?'

'My English is not adequate, perhaps,' he said. 'But until the year 2004, baby selling wasn't a crime in Bulgaria. Even now, a woman who sells her baby has committed no offence. By law, she is regarded as a victim.'

'But what about the dealers? The middle men?'

'Yes, their activities are now a criminal offence, and if they're caught they go to prison.'

'Why would a mother sell her baby, Georgi?'

'Ah, babies are a valuable commodity. A mother might sell one to buy a house, or to feed the rest of her family for a little while.'

'It can't be so easy to smuggle babies out of the country, can it?'

'What? Bulgaria has five borders—Romania, Serbia, Macedonia, Greece,

Turkey—and all of them leaky, like a sieve.' Kotsev couldn't resist taking a sip of vodka. 'The main interest to us might be in the connection with the victims of the double shooting in Pleven. It seems they not only had a personal relationship, but they were also colleagues.'

'That's not unusual.'

'No. But guess where Dimitar Iliev and Piya Yotova worked.'

'An orphanage?' she said.

'You are almost correct. Iliev and Yotova were employed by an official organisation which places children in state orphanages.'

'So they had a lot of power in deciding the fate of those children? And would be in a position to falsify paperwork, take illegal payments—'

'Where money is involved, someone will become corrupt. But who can say whether it might not have been better to find a child a home, even if illegally, than let it stay in an orphanage for years on end?'

'Somehow, Georgi, I suspect these people aren't too scrupulous about checking where children are going to end up.'

Kotsev bowed his head slightly. 'Perhaps you're right. It's possible some of those orphans went to a bad fate.'

Fry felt suddenly exhausted. No matter how hard you tried to achieve some kind of justice, there were occasions when it was obvious you were wasting your time. Human nature would never change.

'So we're looking at a baby-selling ring, with at least four people involved. The two killed in Pleven, plus Rose Shepherd and Simon Nichols. Or, rather, Rosica Savova and Simcho Nikolov. Tell me, were Iliev and Yotova wealthy?'

'No, not all. They had an ordinary home in an apartment block in Pleven. They drove an aged Ford Escort, as you saw.'

'And Nikolov was pretty much destitute,' Fry said. 'So it appears that Savova made all the money from the enterprise.'

'*Da*. It would seem so.'

'Do you think there was a falling-out between them? Was it Nikolov that Rose Shepherd was afraid of? Did he come to Derbyshire looking for her?'

'I do not know, Diane.'

'Well, someone did. And the Mullens got innocently mixed up in this?'

'It depends what you mean by "innocently". They must have removed the baby from Bulgaria illegally.'

'True. But why would the Mullens' adoption have failed?'

'Who can tell? Adoption has become more difficult for foreigners since Bulgaria signed the Hague Treaty.'

'So they went for the illegal option. They must have been desperate.'

Kotsev nodded. 'Is there a photograph of this child?' he asked.

'Yes, here—'

He looked at the photo of Luanne for several minutes. Then he muttered under his breath something Fry didn't catch.

'She looks to me as though she might be a Roma,' said Fry.

Kotsev sighed deeply. 'Yes, you're right. I had a suspicion, but no more.'

'Suspicion?'

He waved a hand, as if he were swatting away a fly. 'It's possible this child belongs to one of our leading criminals, a very unpleasant gangster.'

'What do you mean "belongs to"?'

'They say he had a child, born to a young Romani woman. The woman ran away from him when the baby was born.'

'What happened to the woman? Is she dead?'

'People who upset *mutra* chiefs don't survive very long. But her body has never been found, that's all I can say.'

'And she sold the baby?'

'It is possible,' said Kotsev. 'Her concern might have been to save the child, to get her out of the way of danger. That is how it is with mothers, I understand. But fathers want their children, too. Sometimes very badly.'

'How would he have tracked her down here, to Derbyshire? Could his influence reach here so easily?'

'Yes. In fact, he might have preferred it. As I said, the country is changing. It's not so easy in Bulgaria for the *mutras* now.'

'Georgi, would a father really go so far to get his child back? Would he go to *any* lengths?'

Kotsev took a drink. 'I can't answer that question, Diane.'

Fry looked at him, wanting to ask him whether he was a father himself. But she was afraid it would sound too personal.

Kotsev shrugged. 'We might have expected the child to be taken—to be returned to her father. But that hasn't happened.'

'Not yet,' said Fry. 'It hasn't happened *yet*.'

'FEAR IS A VERY interesting emotion,' said Dr Sinclair. 'You can't be afraid retrospectively. You can only fear something that hasn't happened yet.'

Setting up the tape for him, Cooper paused before pressing the PLAY button. 'Scared to live,' he said. 'That's the way you described Mr Lowther's current state of mind.'

Sinclair nodded. 'Some individuals find life unbearable, every day a torment. They become convinced that dying is the only escape.'

Cooper couldn't think of an answer to that. He started the tape, and they listened to John Lowther's interview in silence for a few minutes.

'Yes, some people go abroad, hunting for whores. No—for babies.'

'What?'

'I'm sorry, I get confused sometimes.'

Cooper paused the tape. '*Babies* and *whores* sounds a very dubious association of ideas to me,' he said. 'I wondered if Lowther could be a paedophile.'

Sinclair shook his head vigorously. 'No, you don't understand how this works. What we're dealing with here is not an association of thoughts, but a dissociation. Mr Lowther's brain isn't making normal connections. He is probably saying words that *sound* like the ones he's thinking.'

'OK. Anything else?'

Cooper pressed the PLAY button again, and they listened to the rest of the interview. Sinclair jotted a few notes.

'Yes, in this interview, we can hear pressure of speech, where the patient speaks quickly and incessantly. Also derailment, or flight of ideas, when he switches topic, perhaps in response to an outside stimulus. There's also a degree of tangentiality, when he replies to questions in an oblique or irrelevant manner. To you, in your profession, that would probably sound evasive.'

Cooper nodded.

'He also reaches conclusions that don't follow logically, or his thoughts might have no conclusion at all. Sometimes the individual words are correct, but the way they're put together is wrong, resulting in what some clinicians call 'word salad'. Sounds rather than meanings govern the connection between words—a 'clang association'. He might also repeat a word over and over, or echo other people's speech.'

'That confusion in his speech was already evident a few days ago.'

'Really?' The psychiatrist frowned. 'Perhaps he had stopped taking the medication earlier than we thought.'

'Will this get worse?'

Sinclair gathered up his notes. 'Yes, as his condition deteriorates, he might become incoherent.' He closed the clasps on his briefcase with a click.

WHEN COOPER HAD briefed her on what he'd learned from Dr Sinclair, Fry thought about John Lowther's confusion of speech. He hadn't seemed to mix up his words when she'd seen him on Monday—not the way he had when he was interviewed. He'd been more vague and confused than anything else. Sinclair might be right. But perhaps there was another explanation.

Fry picked up the phone and called the pathologist who had carried out the post-mortem on the Mullens.

'What would be the effects on a person who'd suffered only slightly from smoke inhalation?' she asked.

'Mild hypoxia? Well, there might be effects on the voice. Coughing, hoarseness, stridor—that's a high-pitched sound, like croup.'

'Yes, but what about their behaviour?'

The pathologist hesitated. 'Well, this is just an informal opinion, but I'd say a person suffering from mild hypoxia would appear distracted, probably clumsy in speech and manner. Is that what you were thinking of, Sergeant?'

'Yes,' said Fry gratefully. 'That's exactly what I was thinking of.'

Ignoring the glances of Cooper and Murfin, she ended the call and immediately dialled the number of the bungalow in Darley Dale.

'Mrs Lowther, where would your son go? Where might he be heading?'

She could picture the Lowthers looking at each other, deciding what answer to give. Fry half expected the phone to be handed to the husband, but it was Moira who spoke.

'When John wants to be alone, he likes to go to the Heights of Abraham.'

HE'D FORGOTTEN the other voices. The voices that told him to do things. Somehow, he'd managed to put them out of his mind, until they started to come back. It was so strange, the way the brain could shut out things that it didn't want to know about, drawing curtains across the darkest corners, no matter how terrible the secrets that lay behind them.

John Lowther's hands trembled as he drove towards Matlock Bath. His palms felt slippery on the wheel, and the windows steamed up so badly that he had to turn the fan on full to clear them. For a moment, he considered letting the windscreen stay steamed up and driving blind, letting fate take its course. But in the next second, he knew the idea had come from one of his voices. His defensive measures were failing.

He parked near the old railway station at Matlock Bath and walked across the track to the cable car station. The whirr of motors and the creak of cables increased as a string of cars swung away, dipping and bobbing as they rose. Two strings passed each other high over the village, half hidden by the trees. He saw with relief that all the cars were empty. There wasn't much business for the Heights of Abraham at this time of year.

Arriving at the Treetops Centre, he headed for the narrow doorway that gave access to the base of the Prospect Tower. Built to take advantage of the views and provide work for the unemployed, the tower also contained a rare thing—a true spiral staircase. There was no central column, and the steps tapered sharply, so they were only wide enough to walk on if you stayed close to the outside wall and clung to the rail.

Finally, he stood at the top of the tower, with its 360-degree view. It was so misty today that it was like a steady drizzle falling on him. Spider's webs in the hawthorn bushes had collected the moisture and shone like silver handkerchiefs draped between the branches.

Lowther looked over the parapet. Matlock Bath was below him, with the A6 and the Derwent snaking their way from the north beneath the crags of High Tor. He could hear the traffic on the road below, the clank of machinery working somewhere, a flock of jackdaws on the hill. Then the cables whirred into life as another set of cars began their journey.

The cable cars stopped automatically near the top of their climb, to allow visitors to admire the view. He'd hung there himself on the way up, alone in his bubble high above the ground, where he'd imagined his cable car breaking loose and dropping towards the A6. The impact with the ground might stop the world whirling round his head, scare away the colours and shapes that crept closer to the corners of his vision like spiders in his brain.

He looked south towards Gulliver's Kingdom, with its towers and turrets and the screams of children riding the switchback. That was where most of the voices came from. The voices of children. They were difficult for him to ignore, and even harder to understand.

If he put twenty pence in the telescope, he might be able to see right into the theme park. He might make out the pirate ship on Bourbon Street, or the talking apple in the Palais Royale, or the Rio Grande Train Ride.

He didn't go to Gulliver's Kingdom any more. They'd asked him to stop going. They said he frightened the children. But there was nothing to be frightened of, was there? His hallucinations were under control now. He could spin them in his hand and watch the light play on them, turning on their sound for as long as he wanted to listen, then turning them off again.

It was good to give himself a little glimpse into that world, knowing he had the power to switch it off whenever he liked. Dr Sinclair had explained it was simply another way of seeing reality, and it was nothing to be frightened of. Well, as long as it was all under control, it was fine. And it was, right now. It was all under control.

BY THE STATION car park in Matlock Bath, a laurel hedge had dropped its big, poisonous black berries all over the path, where they'd been squashed by passing feet.

'We can go up on a cable car,' said Cooper. 'It's a lot quicker.'

'Oh, I don't think so.'

Cooper laughed. He'd bumped into Kotsev on the way out of the office at West Street, and the Bulgarian had somehow tagged along.

'It's fine, Georgi. You're not scared?'

'No, no. It's no problem.'

They climbed into one of the cars. It was big enough to hold six people, but it was a quiet day. The doors closed, and the cars rotated slowly before swinging out of the station They immediately began to climb steeply up the cable, soaring high over the river and the dwindling traffic on the A6. The sides of the car were clear acrylic plastic from ceiling to floor, so it was possible to look straight down at the ground, already hundreds of feet below.

'*Dyavol da go vzeme*. Oh, God.' Kotsev covered his eyes and gripped the edge of the seat tightly.

'Are you sure heights aren't a problem for you?'

'I'll be OK. OK, OK.' He peeped through his fingers. '*Mamka mu!*'

By the time they had reached the highest point above the valley, Kotsev was sweating and breathing deeply to calm himself. When the cars slowed down and hung stationary for a minute or two, high above the valley floor, he asked nervously, 'Are we broken? Do we need rescue?'

But then the wheels whirred again, and soon the cars were passing over the first gantry. From there, it was an easy coast in to the hilltop station.

'You can look now,' said Cooper.

Kotsev took his hand away. 'Yes, OK. It was a little too high.'

FRY FOUND Jed Skinner in the garage at the distribution centre outside Edendale, where he worked as a mechanic.

'Do you happen to know where your friend Brian Mullen is right now?' asked Fry, when they'd taken him into the supervisor's office.

'He's staying with his parents-in-law. They live at Darley Dale.'

'He's not there any more.'

'Oh?'

'When were you last in contact with him?'

'Yesterday. They wouldn't let me visit him while he was in hospital, but Brian rang me yesterday afternoon to say that he was out. He was pretty fed up, so I went over to Darley Dale to see him in the evening.'

'Did he say anything to you about leaving to stay somewhere else?'

'No, not a thing.'

'You live at Lowbridge, don't you, Mr Skinner?'

'Yes, but you won't find Brian there. He could have stayed with me, if he'd asked, but he didn't ask. Phone my wife if you don't believe me.'

'We might do that,' said Fry.

Skinner gazed out of the window of the office at a truck being backed out. 'Has Brian got the baby with him? Luanne?' he asked.

'We believe so, sir.'

'Shit. I hope you find them.'

'So do we.' Fry paused. 'Speaking of Luanne, we know about the adoption. Brian's father-in-law explained to us that Brian and Lindsay couldn't have any more children, because Brian was infertile after a bout of mumps.'

'Mumps?' said Skinner. 'Is that what he told you?'

'Yes. He said the illness caused physical damage that made Brian infertile.'

'Well, it's not what Brian told me at the time. He said it was an STD. I can't remember the exact name . . . something with "clam" in it.'

'Do you mean chlamydia?'

'Yes, that's it. Chlamydia was what caused the damage. If you get it too often, it causes scarring and blocks the—you know, the passage.'

Fry stared at him, her mind adjusting to a series of new possibilities. 'Mr Skinner, were you aware of any problems in the Mullens' marriage?'

'Problems? Why should there be?'

'Well, for a start, I presume Lindsay knew about the chlamydia? That would make quite a difference to their relationship, I think.'

The idea seemed to strike Skinner for the first time. 'You think she might have blamed Brian for the fact that they couldn't have another child?'

'Well, yes,' said Fry. 'And there are other things that might have upset her, too—like where her husband picked up an STD in the first place.'

'Hey, you're right. I imagine there were a few words exchanged.'

'But Brian never mentioned anything like that to you?'

'There were times when he was a bit pissed off, and I reckoned he might have had problems at home. But we never talked about things like that.'

Fry cursed as she left Jed Skinner and got back in the car. Male friends, what a waste of time. With a frown, Fry turned to her notes from the interviews with Brian Mullen, seeking the smallest clue. After a few minutes, she took out her mobile and called Cooper.

WHEN HIS PHONE rang, Cooper was standing by the lid of a shaft into the hillside that had been sealed by a steel grille. A bush rustled, and a small, grey shape slipped along a branch, stopping to pull off the berries.

'Ben, what are these illuminations that Brian Mullen mentioned?'

'Illuminations?'

'I'm sure he said they were in Matlock Bath.'

'Oh, yes. When people talk about the illuminations in Matlock Bath, they usually mean the parade of boats.'

'Boats?'

'They create designs out of lights and mount them on rowing boats. Then they parade up the river—when it's dark, of course. So what you see isn't the boat but something like, say . . . an illuminated London bus floating on the water. There's other stuff, too—fireworks, entertainment.'

'OK. So when does this happen?'

'September and October, but only at weekends. They call them Venetian Nights. It always attracts big crowds. Why, what are you thinking?'

'Brian Mullen. When I interviewed him in hospital, he said that he and Lindsay had promised to take Luanne and the other children to see the illuminations in Matlock Bath. It was supposed to be a special treat.'

'Yes, but surely he'd have more sense than to . . .'

Cooper stopped speaking, and Fry laughed. 'Everyone involved in this case seems to have gone headlong towards their fate with blinkers on. You'd think they were a lot of lemmings throwing themselves off a cliff.'

Then she was gone, and Cooper was listening to the faint hiss of his phone.

'Hey, here!'

Cooper spun round and found Georgi Kotsev running up the path with a Heights of Abraham employee in a high-visibility jacket.

'Have you got something?'

Kotsev pointed up the hill. 'He's at the tower.'

THE BURNT-OUT SHOGUN was in the garage, covered in a tarpaulin. Wayne Abbott greeted Fry and Hitchens with a clipboard in his hand.

'Yes, this is definitely the vehicle that was driven into the field at Foxlow. The tread pattern is an exact fit, and we matched soil from the tyres and wheel arches. Luckily, the interior escaped the worst effects of the fire, and we found traces of gunshot residue on the seat covers. What's more, we got some prints off the underside of the dashboard. They're in the system, too. Somebody's been in this car who has previous form.'

Hitchens took the print-out. 'Brilliant. Anyone we know?'

'Anthony Donnelly, aged thirty-seven, with an address in Swanwick. He has several convictions for theft from a vehicle and taking without consent, plus the usual extras—no insurance, driving while disqualified, et cetera.'

'Just an average car thief,' said Fry, feeling unreasonably disappointed.

'Mmm, maybe. The most recent charge on his record was in connection with an organised lorry-jacking scheme. Five or six people went down for it. But it seems Donnelly was acquitted.'

'So it could be that he's getting involved with more serious operators.'

'Driver for a hit man?' said Hitchens. 'Well, let's go and ask him.'

THE WHEELS AND CABLES were still humming and rattling, but it no longer seemed to be merely the whir of machinery, the hiss of high-tension steel passing through the air. The noises formed words, murmuring and chattering.

John Lowther looked down into the valley again. The fragile crystal of his mind had cracked. He could see the fragments lying on the ground, fading and turning brown, as if they were mere clay. Through the fracture in his consciousness, he heard a voice he recognised. In the past, this voice had forced him to do things that he had never wanted to do. And now it was back.

'*Johnny, you know what you have to do.*'

They would come for him soon. They would scent him out, sniffing the fear in his sweat. They would use dogs to listen for his voices when they became too loud. And one day the searchlights would catch him on the corner of a street, and the lights would probe deep into his mind and see what was there. And the whole world would know his evil.

COOPER COULD SEE John Lowther on the platform at the top of the stone tower. Even from this distance, he could tell that Lowther was trembling violently, and his eyes were fixed on the horizon, as if he were listening for some distant call. He seemed oblivious to the knot of people clustering round the base of the tower, staring up at him.

'He's been up there for some time now,' said the staff member. 'A visitor started to get uneasy about him. She said he was behaving oddly.'

'All right. Thank you,' said Cooper. 'Could you try and keep everyone clear of the tower. Well clear—back as far as the play area.'

The man turned pale. 'You don't think he might . . .?'

But Cooper put a hand on his shoulder. 'If you could just move these people back, sir.'

'Of course.'

Georgi Kotsev was examining the doorway to the tower. It was arched, like the entrance to a church, but so narrow that Kotsev looked as though he'd hardly be able to squeeze through it.

'A tricky location,' said Kotsev.

'It couldn't be worse.'

As he'd approached the tower, Cooper had called Control to report the situation. Help would be on the way, but it would take time.

'OK, let's go and talk to him.'

Standing close to the wall, Cooper took hold of the handrail and began to ascend. Mounting the spiral staircase was like walking up a twisted ribbon, or climbing a strand of DNA. You had to be careful, or you could fall right through the spiral and plummet to the base of the tower.

When he saw daylight from the platform, Cooper stopped and turned to his companion. 'Georgi, you'd better stay back out of sight. We don't want to frighten him too much.'

'*Dobre*. I'll be right here, behind you.'

Slowly now, Cooper eased himself the last few feet onto the platform. John Lowther was standing nearby, his hands resting on the parapet.

'Mr Lowther, do you remember me? Detective Constable Cooper.'

Lowther seemed to become aware of him for the first time. He tried to back away, but he was already pressed hard against the parapet and could only scrape slowly round the platform until he was on the eastern side, with the Heights of Abraham behind him.

'Just take it easy, sir. There's nothing to worry about.'

Cooper felt ridiculous as soon as he said it. He could see from the expression on Lowther's face that the man had plenty to worry about. It was all there in his eyes and in the twist of his mouth. Fear, verging on panic.

'You're quite safe, Mr Lowther. I'm here to help you.' Trying to inject a calmness into his voice that he didn't feel himself, Cooper spread his hands in a reassuring gesture.

'Is there a dog here somewhere?' said Lowther.

Cooper smiled then. Bizarrely, it sounded like progress. 'You recognise me, don't you, sir? I'm DC Cooper. We talked yesterday. I was with a colleague, and you told us about your neighbour's Alsatian.'

'Tyrannosaurus,' said Lowther.

'And we showed you a wooden dinosaur, that's right.'

'You don't have to believe what they're saying.'

A gust of wind brought the sound of children's voices up the valley from Gulliver's Kingdom. Laughter and screams. Kids hurtling over the switchback, plunging into the log flume, their mouths open, their clothes flying.

Lowther inclined his head. 'They're there,' he said. 'Not far away now.'

Cooper concentrated on the other man, tensed for a sudden movement. 'There's nothing to worry about, sir,' he repeated. 'All we need to do is get you down from here and take you to see a doctor. They can stop the voices, John. You know they can. They've done it before.'

'You don't understand,' said Lowther, shaking with agitation. 'Mum said you understood, but you don't. When people talk to me now it's like a different kind of language. It's too much to hold in my mind at once. I can't understand what they say. I have to try to figure it out from people's faces. But their faces always say something different from their voices.'

'Mr Lowther, please calm down and stop talking for a minute.'

'I have to keep talking, to drown out the voices.'

'We'll get you some treatment, to make the voices go away.'

'They'll never go away—not completely . . .' He seemed to be listening to something. Whatever it was terrified him. 'It's Lindsay's voice,' he shouted. 'Lindsay and the children. I heard them scream. I'll always hear them scream.'

'Look—'

What happened next, Cooper wasn't quite sure. He'd been trying to concentrate on what John Lowther was saying, to hold the man's attention and keep him talking. But something had spooked him. Lowther jerked backwards against the parapet as if he'd been shoved in the chest.

Then he was going over, and Cooper was diving forward to grab hold of him. He found only clothes to clutch at, smooth material that slipped through his fingers. He felt Lowther's weight shifting inexorably outwards as gravity seized him and dragged him over the edge.

'Georgi! Help me, quick!'

Kotsev came thumping up the steps, gasping as he reached the top.

'*Dyavol da go vzeme!* Oh hell!'

Cooper felt his muscles scream against the effort of holding on to Lowther's coat, but before Kotsev could reach over the parapet to help, Lowther had slipped out of Cooper's hands. His arms and legs flailed in the air, and his body bounced once off the tower as he fell.

It was only in the final second that John Lowther's screams joined those of the children that he could hear. A second of screaming, and then the impact. And all the voices were silenced for ever.

At the first sign of a police car in his street in Swanwick, Anthony Donnelly had legged it. A sign of experience, that, having the car facing the right direction, ready to go. Without the helicopter, he might have got clean away. But they saw his Mercedes come off the motorway at junction 24 and take the fourth exit at the roundabout. Then it turned into the Travelodge, and parked. Fifteen minutes later, their suspect was in custody.

'So you don't want to tell us about Rose Shepherd,' said Hitchens, watching Tony Donnelly now across the interview-room table.

'I've got nothing to say.'

They'd been trying for a long time, struggling through the kind of interview that made Fry think of banging her head repeatedly against a wall.

Donnelly and the duty solicitor stared back at the detectives across the table. They had an air of being two visitors at a zoo, wondering when these strange creatures were going to do something more interesting.

'What about Lindsay Mullen, then?' said Hitchens.

Donnelly hesitated slightly before he answered. 'No comment.'

'Where did you first see Mrs Mullen?'

'No comment.'

Fry could see Hitchens gathering his thoughts before the next question. Like her, he'd seen the brief expression of incomprehension that had passed across Donnelly's face when Lindsay Mullen's name had been mentioned.

'You saw Lindsay Mullen meet Rose Shepherd at the Riber Tea Rooms in Matlock Bath, didn't you?' said Hitchens.

'No comment.'

But the answer came more quickly this time, more confidently. Donnelly knew who they were talking about again.

'It was Rose Shepherd you were looking for, wasn't it?' said Hitchens. 'And you stumbled on Lindsay Mullen at the same time. How convenient for you. What would you have done otherwise? Break into Miss Shepherd's house and interrogate her until she gave you the information?'

Donnelly glared at his solicitor. 'What's this shit?' he said.

'Detective Inspector Hitchens, could you clarify what my client is accused of? We don't understand this line of questioning.'

'We're enquiring into the murder of Miss Rose Shepherd, who was shot and killed in Foxlow in the early hours of Sunday morning. We're also investigating the deaths of Mrs Lindsay Mullen and her two children, who died in a fire at their home in Edendale on the following night. And we'd like to know from your client the names of his associates in these offences.'

There was a long silence. When Donnelly responded, it was with a smirk that might have got him a punch in the mouth at one time, before interview rooms were equipped with video cameras.

'No comment,' he said.

FRY FETCHED TWO COFFEES into the DI's office. 'What's the plan, sir?'

Hitchens was spinning his swivel chair from side to side, making it squeal at the end of each turn. It was a habit he had when he was stressed.

'I'll let Donnelly stew for a while, then I'll have another go at him later.'

'He'd never heard Lindsay Mullen's name before,' said Fry. 'I could tell from his face when you asked him about her.'

Hitchens took a sip of coffee. 'I'm inclined to agree with you,' he said. 'It was almost the only time we got a genuine reaction out of him. He was surprised. And then he thought it was funny. It suggests there were more people involved than we first thought.'

Fry sat down, balancing her own cup on her knee. 'What do you mean?'

'If Donnelly doesn't know anything about Lindsay Mullen, it means the Darwin Street job must have been given to someone else. Separate teams, neither team knowing what job the other is doing. There'd be much less chance of them implicating each other that way.'

'So who was in the second team? Nikolov?'

'I don't see how. There's no indication that he left the farm during the last couple of days before he died. More likely, he picked up a newspaper or turned on the radio and heard about Rose Shepherd's killing. Then he drank himself to death.'

'He followed her to Derbyshire, then followed her into death?'

Hitchens blinked a little. 'Well, Nikolov was no hit man.'

'Who, then? They can't have expected to identify the Mullens so soon after finding Rose Shepherd. They'd have to recruit someone at short notice.'

'A local villain, dragged off the street for a one-off job?'

'Maybe. But one thing is for sure, we have no evidence to charge Tony Donnelly in connection with the Mullen killings.'

'No, none at all. But he's not going anywhere, since we have his prints from the Shogun. So we can worry about that later.'

'The case against him for Rose Shepherd will be tight enough, won't it?'

'If forensics come through,' said Hitchens. 'With luck, we'll get a DNA match from the car, gunshot residue from his clothes. There'll be something, don't worry. We'll build a tight enough case.'

Fry still hesitated. 'I wouldn't want the Mullens to get forgotten in all the excitement. In a way, the arson was a far worse crime.'

The DI nodded. 'They won't get forgotten, Diane. Why don't you get on with that line of enquiry now? The Intelligence Unit ought to be able to suggest a few names you'd go to if you wanted a nice house fire in a hurry.'

There was one other subject they weren't mentioning. It had all been gone through already, and it would be thrashed out again before long.

'And the Lowthers?'

'They're coming in tomorrow,' said Hitchens. 'And I'm not looking forward to it one bit.'

'Ben Cooper has gone home, by the way,' said Fry, though the DI hadn't asked her.

Hitchens looked hurt, as if she'd accused him of not caring about his officers. 'Yes, I know. But he seemed OK, don't you think?'

'As far as I could tell. But it was a hell of a thing to happen. Ben did his best. John Lowther was always going to do it, one way or another.'

'But knowing Ben . . .' said Hitchens.

'He'll be blaming himself. Right.'

AT HOME THAT NIGHT, Cooper went through his routine—feeding the cat, taking a shower, checking the fridge, remembering he had no food in the flat. That was the great thing about routines—you didn't need to think. You could switch off the brain and freewheel.

Then he switched on his computer. The evening's crop of email included a series of George W. Bush jokes, sent by a friend. Cooper was sure he'd seen most of them already, but he read them anyway, because it stopped him rerunning the images and sounds from a couple of hours before—the terrified expression on a face falling through air, a sickening crunch, a voice suddenly cut off. And the awful silence that followed.

The phone rang. It was his brother.

'Hi, Matt.'

It was Friday, the day of Matt's appointment with their GP, and he had known his brother would call this evening.

'You had the appointment with Dr Joyce today, right?'

'Yes, I did.'

'Was it any use?' asked Ben.

'Well, actually—yes.'

'What did he tell you?'

'Nothing. He just listened. That's all I needed, really—somebody to listen. I felt a lot better afterwards.'

'Well, that's good.'

Ben reflected that it was perhaps what he'd refused to do himself, to listen. He hadn't wanted to hear what Matt was saying.

'You know, I think I was getting worked up about this business over Mum's problem so that I didn't have to worry about the farm,' said Matt. 'Anyway, I thought you'd want to know. Was I right to call?'

'Yes, you were right, Matt. Thanks. I'll see you at the weekend, probably.'

A moment of silence again. 'Are you OK, Ben?'

'Yes, I'm fine.'

9
Saturday, October 29

When the Lowthers arrived at West Street the next day, Fry showed them into the DI's office, where they sat in an uncomfortable silence. Fry sat to one side, out of the Lowthers' immediate view. But it was her that Moira Lowther was looking at when she spoke.

'I told you John wasn't a danger to anyone but himself. He was psychotic, not a psychopath. I told you, but you didn't listen.'

Fry didn't know how to answer her. According to Cooper, Dr Sinclair had said the same thing. And it seemed they had both been right.

'Our officers did their best to save your son's life,' said Hitchens with a placatory gesture. 'It was a very difficult situation.'

'You were pursuing him.'

'No, Mrs Lowther.'

'*She* was.'

The jerk of the head was insulting, but Fry stayed calm.

'DS Fry wasn't at the scene when the incident happened,' said Hitchens.

'What about the officers who *were* there? Why can't we speak to them?'

'There'll be a full inquiry into the circumstances, I assure you.'

Fry and Hitchens exchanged glances. The inquiry wouldn't be comfortable, and these things often left a sour taste, but it all had to be done properly.

'We'll keep you to that promise,' said Mrs Lowther.

'Of course.'

Fry could still feel herself being glared at. 'We questioned John as part of the investigation into your daughter's death,' she said. 'We were trying to cover every possibility, that's all.'

'It's ridiculous. They were as close as a brother and sister could be.' Mrs Lowther choked on the last word. 'And now we've lost both of them.'

Fry looked at Hitchens for support. In a storm, you clutched at any straw.

'Mr and Mrs Lowther, I can't tell you how sorry we are,' he said. 'Believe me, if there's anything at all we can do—'

Henry Lowther had been sitting rigid and furious, his tension showing only in the throbbing of a small vein in his temple.

'Anything you can do?' he said, his voice an ominous whisper. 'Don't you think you've done enough to us already?'

COOPER COULDN'T HELP looking for the Lowthers' Rover in the visitors' car park that morning. Sure enough, they'd already arrived. The car was in front of the main entrance as he pulled up to the gates of the compound.

It was impossible to imagine how Henry and Moira Lowther would be feeling now. Cooper wondered if he ought to offer to talk to them, and whether it would do any good.

In the CID room, he found Gavin Murfin already at his desk. That was unusual in itself. Murfin never arrived at work before him.

'You know the Lowthers are here?' said Murfin when he saw Cooper.

'Yes, I do.'

'If I were you, Ben, I'd find a reason to get out of the office as soon as possible. The DI can deal with it.'

'Maybe.'

But Cooper took off his jacket and sat at his desk to see what he had to catch up with. There was nothing from Scenes of Crime, but there was a copy of the full post-mortem report on Simon Nichols, alias Simcho Nikolov, complete with a set of photographs. Cooper guessed that Nikolov hadn't been much prettier in life than he was in death. Not for the past few years, anyway. The marks left by the man's lifestyle were etched deep into his face.

Cooper had already spoken to the pathologist, whose conclusion was that Nikolov fell on his back, suffering a blow to the head on the way down. The bruise on his temple was the only physical injury. It wasn't enough to kill him, but it could have caused mild concussion. Exceptionally high levels of alcohol had been found in the bloodstream—enough to kill most people. The victim was also malnourished. But the cause of death was that, while he lay unconscious or in an alcoholic stupor, he choked on his own vomit.

Suddenly aware of someone standing at his desk, Cooper gave a start and looked up guiltily, not knowing who to expect. But it was Gavin Murfin.

'I brought you a cup of coffee,' he said. 'Since you're obviously not going to take my advice.'

'Thanks, Gavin.'

'No worries. You look as though you could use it.'

THE SQUEAK of the chair in the DI's office was really starting to get on Fry's nerves. Yet the noise seemed to give Hitchens some perverse pleasure.

'Do you have any evidence that Luanne Mullen is in imminent danger?' he asked, when she put her proposal to him after the Lowthers had left.

'Well, no.'

'What about Brian Mullen himself? A few days ago, you were convinced he was responsible for the fire. Can you substantiate a case against him?'

'No. But we should consider Georgi Kotsev's theory that Luanne Mullen's natural father is trying to get her back.'

'Yes, we'd have to take that seriously, if there was evidence,' said Hitchens. 'Is there evidence, Diane?'

'I can't produce any right now.'

'You see the problem. It's all supposition.'

'That might be true, sir. But the fact that Brian Mullen has gone AWOL with the surviving child looks very suspicious to me.'

'He's not legally obliged to keep us informed of his whereabouts. If he's taken the child for a trip somewhere, there's nothing we can do about it.'

'But I'm sure the Lowthers know where Brian is.'

'Have you asked them?'

'Of course. They just say their son-in-law is distressed and needs some time away from being hassled by us.'

Hitchens smiled. 'I suppose that could be true, too, couldn't it?'

Fry wasn't amused. 'I assure you, I don't hassle members of the public.'

'Of course not, Diane. But it's hardly surprising the family feel that way, is it? Let me tell you, I never want to experience as uncomfortable a half-hour as I spent with those two people this morning.'

'I'm certain Brian Mullen is going to turn up at the Matlock Bath illuminations tonight,' said Fry. 'As certain as I can be.'

'Why would he risk taking the child to Matlock Bath?'

'It was something he'd promised Luanne. But I'm also concerned that he's planning to do something rash and desperate. My feeling is that, unless we find him tonight, it could be too late.'

'It's not like you to base your reactions entirely on gut instinct, Diane. Have you got a personal problem with this case?'

'No, sir.'

Hitchens watched her, hoping she could give him some solid justification. But Fry stayed silent. The DI looked disappointed.

'Well, I'm sorry, but I can't authorise an operation to apprehend Mr Mullen at this event in Matlock Bath tonight. I've heard nothing to justify the use of resources, let alone the effect on the family. You could land us with an even bigger public relations disaster than we already have.'

BY FIVE O'CLOCK, all the car parks in Matlock Bath were full, and motorists were being directed to a park-and-ride facility at the rugby club a mile down the road. The pavements were packed with people queuing at the fish-and-chip shops or eating out of paper packages as they leaned over the railings to gaze at the river, throwing their last few chips to the ducks.

'I have to remind you that we're here unofficially,' said Fry. 'Strictly speaking, you're off duty.'

Cooper nodded. 'We understand that, Diane.'

Murfin shrugged. 'It means you can't tell me not to eat fish and chips while I'm working, right?'

'Right.' Fry looked at Kotsev. 'Georgi? There's no obligation on you to be here at all.'

'I wish to be part of the team.'

'Thanks, Georgi.'

'And I'm not to beat up any suspects, OK?'

Fry glanced at him, recognised that he was joking, and let it pass.

'I've told the inspector in charge of the uniformed operation that we're here, but he's far too busy to bother about us, anyway.'

'So what are we looking for exactly?' said Murfin.

'Brian Mullen. And, I hope, Luanne.'

Cooper coughed uneasily. 'Diane, if your theory about Brian Mullen is right, what will happen to the child? Will she be sent back to Bulgaria? Surely she wouldn't have to go back to her real father after all?'

But Fry's face was hard, giving nothing away. 'That won't be our decision to make. All we have to do is find them.'

'Let's get on with it, then, shall we?' he said.

Cooper couldn't help being sceptical about what Fry hoped to achieve tonight. A suspect loose among the crowds, strolling through Derwent Gardens with all these families? DI Hitchens had made the right decision, in Cooper's view. No responsible senior officer would authorise an attempt to carry out an arrest in these circumstances. The most they could do was keep Mullen under surveillance until he was in a location where the situation could be safely contained. And pray he didn't get away.

'Oh, and make sure you all stay in touch,' said Fry. 'That's what the radios are for.'

'Yes, how come you managed to get these radios and ear pieces issued, if we're here unofficially?' asked Murfin.

'Gavin, haven't you learned when not to ask questions?'

They started from the northern end of the village and separated, taking the riverside walk and the parade of shops in pairs. The village was getting packed. This was the last night of the illuminations, and the night would climax with a fireworks display from the top of High Tor.

Cooper knew he should be glad of something to do tonight. He needed to occupy his mind. Ever since the incident on the tower, he'd been asking himself the same question. Could he have done more to save John Lowther? If he'd acted differently, if he'd stayed back, if he'd made a grab for the man sooner . . . He supposed it would be for other people to judge him.

'This is more like home,' said Kotsev, watching the crowds.

'What?'

'A big party in the street. People having fun. Give me a few stalls selling sunflower seeds, and I would be happy.'

'You'll have to make do with fish and chips.'

Kotsev laughed. '*Mnogo vkusno*. Delicious.'

They walked slowly through the beer garden behind the Midland Hotel, overlooking the river. The illuminated boats were due to parade from New Bridge at the southern end of the village as far as the Pavilion, passing along the length of Derwent Gardens, which weren't yet open to the crowds. Clusters of people were gathered near the war memorial. Here, the shallow river was bordered by horse chestnuts, branches skimming the surface of the water. Disused, ivy-covered steps led down to the water's edge.

Cooper and Kotsev went to the car park on the corner of Temple Road, and walked along the rows of cars, looking in vain for Mullen's red Citroën.

'It looks as though the gardens are being opened up,' said Fry through Cooper's ear piece. 'The crowds are starting to move that way.'

'Well, at least they'll all be in one place. There are thousands of them. And they're still coming in. There's another busload arriving now.'

Cooper turned back to Kotsev. 'There are so many people,' he said. 'We'd better split up. You know what Brian Mullen looks like, Georgi?'

'I have the photograph. And there's the child with him—'

'Yes, probably.'

Cooper worked his way into the gardens, past the St John Ambulance, the Venetian Boat Builders Association and a stall for the Cats Protection League. A woman who looked like a gypsy pulled a scarf across her face and turned away from the light. A fortune teller, or perhaps a pickpocket. Well, it wasn't his business tonight.

It was dark now, and all the children were carrying rainbow spinners, yellow light sticks or flashing fish. One by one, they stopped and pointed at the illuminated butterflies and dragons in the trees.

Further on was the fairground. An old-fashioned ferris wheel, a mini waltzer, a set of dodgem cars and a train ride. Down at this end of the gardens, the mixture of smells was enough to make your head swim: diesel fumes from the generator running the dodgems, chemicals from a row of Portaloos, hot dogs and onions from a fast-food van.

'Even if they're here, there's no way we'll spot them in this crush.'

'Stay near the front of the crowd, Ben. He won't have Luanne at the back, if he wants her to see the boats.'

'OK.'

The strings of coloured lights were reflected and elongated in the water, and across the river the trees were lit by patches of brilliant colour—blue, green, red. Seven thirty came and went. By the time announcements over the PA system warned of the impending boat parade, people were already jostling for the best positions along both banks and on the new bridge.

'There are people standing three deep on the bridge. I don't know how it can take the weight.'

'That's nothing. They're about five deep this side of the river. It looks pretty much the same across the other side.'

The boats drifted out one at a time from the boat jetty until they were in the middle of the current. When they were midstream, each one lit up suddenly, to a cheer from the children on the bank. So the Empire State Building and the White House appeared all at once in the darkness, drifting above the water, glittering in multicoloured reflections. There was a miniature paddle steamer that floated in a pool of its own light, then a vintage car, a carousel, a biplane, a Viking longboat. As they came by, it was impossible to distinguish the boats from their reflections, red cascades bursting and rippling across the surface in the splash of oars.

'It's hopeless, Diane.'

'Keep trying.'

Cooper worked his way through the crowds on the bank. People were so tightly packed that it was impossible to walk normally. A light drizzle had begun to fall, adding a mist to the blur of coloured lights above the crowd.

Eventually, people began to drift out of the gardens again, and Cooper made his way back across the bridge. The crowds separated around him, music blasting his ears. He thought he caught a glimpse of the gypsy woman again, a blue scarf flashing briefly in the lights. When the band finished playing, the announcer started trying to persuade everyone to move across to the west bank of the river for the fireworks display.

An air of anticipation developed again as nine o'clock approached. Streams of people came back over the bridge to the gardens, or stood on the pavements outside the Pavilion, their faces turned up towards the rock face of High Tor. An expectant hush gradually developed.

Then the crowd was silenced by a terrific bang, which punched eardrums and stopped a few hearts, judging by the expressions on the faces around him. It was the maroon, the single loud report that signalled the start of the display. It was followed by flares, fountains and rockets, candles, brilliant white star bursts and red blossoms, exploding into sparks, bangs, crackles and whistles. Glittering, coloured fire hung over the tor.

'Hold on. Diane, I can see him.'

'Are you sure?'

'It's him and Luanne. They're right down the north end of the gardens, near where the boats are docking after the parade.'

'Can you get to them, Ben?'

'I'm on the wrong side of the river. The nearest crossing is the footbridge. I'll have to go back and cross over. Wait—he's moving.'

'Has he seen you, do you think?'

'I don't think so. I'm on the darkest part of the bank over here. But he's moving all right. God, he's started to run. He'll be on the road in a minute.'

'I'll get back to the car and drive down. Gavin, where are you?'

'By the ice-cream kiosk in the Pavilion car park.'

'Get to the road, and I'll pick you up.'

'I'm pretty sure there's no way out at the other end of the gardens,' said

Cooper. 'The nearest way out onto the road is by the netball court. I left my car at this end, Diane—opposite the church.'

'OK, we'll catch you up. Don't worry, he hasn't got a big start on us.'

But the police on traffic duty had closed off the entire stretch of road when the fireworks started, and Fry found lines of traffic were already backing up in both directions.

'Did Mullen get through?' asked Cooper when she told him.

'A CSO up here says a red Citroën went through like a bat out of hell just before they closed the road.'

'It's lucky I was on this side of the gardens. Georgi's with me now, and we're nearly at my car. Where do you suppose he's going?'

'He isn't going anywhere, as far as I'm concerned. His car will be stopped when it reaches Cromford. There are two officers posted at the junction, with manual control of the traffic lights.'

Kotsev followed Cooper into his Toyota. It bounced off the kerb and they accelerated down the empty roadway.

'He's definitely heading south, Diane?'

'Yes. There's nothing else that way, is there? No way he can dodge us?'

'There's just Masson Mill. It's only three hundred and fifty yards downstream from the gardens, but he can see the Cromford junction from there. If he sees the uniforms standing at the lights, he'll know what's going on.'

'Masson Mill? The shopping village?'

'That's it. He could turn into the car park at the mill. The walls are high enough for him to get out of sight there.'

They found Mullen's car on the forecourt in front of the main entrance. It was parked at an awkward angle between two other vehicles that had been left there when the CAR PARK FULL signs went up.

Cooper parked the Toyota across the Citroën's tail end to block it in. As they approached the vehicle on either side, he spoke into his radio.

'We've got Mullen's car, in the main entrance to the shopping village.'

'Who's in the car?'

Cooper peered in through the windows, though he'd already guessed the answer. 'No one, Diane. They've legged it.'

'Where could they have gone? The shopping village is closed.'

'They can't have gone far.'

Then Cooper saw an iron stairway leading down from the forecourt. At the bottom was a door into the second level of the car park, just below the road. The door was painted red and lit up like a beacon. And it was open.

'That's the obvious way, Georgi, wouldn't you say?'

'Let's go, then.'

'Hold on a minute.' Cooper fetched his torch from the back seat of the Toyota. It was a four-cell Maglite, weighing at least a couple of pounds. Not only would it give him a good light, but it was handy as a weapon, at a push.

He turned at the sound of a horn, and saw Fry's Peugeot approaching, and her window winding down.

'We'll come in from the other direction,' she called.

'There's a roof level up the ramp, Diane. You might start there.'

'OK.'

She put her car into gear again, but Cooper had put his hand on the door.

'How far are we going with this?' he said. 'I mean, Brian Mullen hasn't committed any crime that we know of.'

'He's running for a reason,' Fry said coolly, as the Peugeot pulled away.

Cooper and Kotsev clattered down the iron stairs and through the red door. The parking levels were already half empty. They shone their torches into the corners and along the sides of the entrance ramps.

They hadn't been there long when Cooper heard a voice in his ear.

'We're coming in now,' said Fry. 'These attendants haven't seen anyone in the last few minutes, but I'll leave them to keep watch. How many parking levels are there, Ben?'

'Three, I think.'

Cooper found a door by the stairs, which led into the main building.

'Hey, there's a door open here,' he said.

He and Kotsev entered the darkened mill and made their way slowly through the shopping floor, past counters and display units, racks of winter coats and free-standing shelves full of pottery. Cooper's torchlight reflected off mirrors everywhere, dazzling him with sudden bursts of glare.

When they came to the central stairs, Kotsev gestured enquiringly upwards, and Cooper nodded. He watched until Georgi reached the top of the first flight, then he moved on.

And it was better on his own, without the distraction of someone else's footsteps behind him. When he felt the floorboards shift and groan under his own feet, he knew he was near the wooden steps that led down to the museum at river level. He held his breath and listened. The faint creak of boards came from below him, somewhere near the bottom of the stairs.

The stairs led down to two doors, one opening into the spinning room and the other into the weaving shed. Some of the looms had been running last time he was here, and without the rattle of their bobbins and leather drive belts the place was much too quiet.

The smell of lubricating oil and leather seemed stronger in the dark. At this level, Cooper could hear a deep rumbling noise and feel a faint vibration through the floor. Common sense told him it must be the turbines running, probably supplying surplus power to the National Grid. But their rumble sounded more like the heart of the massive building, beating much too fast.

Cooper felt his own heart begin to thump faster, and his chest tightened. He froze to the spot, suddenly reluctant to go any further into the weaving shed. For a moment, the rows of looms blurred and distorted. They seemed to change shape, mutating into crouching beasts that lined a tunnel stretching away from him, beckoning him further into the darkness.

Cooper shook his head, trying to drive away the illusion. Then, at the far end of the weaving shed, he saw what his attention was being drawn to. His unsteady torchlight had picked out a shape on the floor. A bundle of rags, a pile of sacking? Anything was possible in this place. But Cooper knew it wasn't a bundle of rags, or a pile of sacking. It was a body.

He recognised the smell of blood.

Suddenly, his surroundings came back into normal focus, and his feet moved him forward again. Cautiously, Cooper edged round the machines until he was bending over the body and feeling for a pulse. Despite the blood spreading across the concrete floor, there were still signs of life.

There had been silence from his ear piece for several minutes, and Cooper knew he'd lost contact. He pulled out his mobile, praying there'd be a signal. He was in luck. First he called for an ambulance, then he rang Fry.

'Diane, I've found Brian Mullen. He's unconscious—he looks as though he's taken a bad blow to the head, and there's quite a bit of blood. But he's breathing all right. I've got an ambulance on its way.'

'And Luanne?'

'There's no sign of her, Diane. She's gone.'

There was silence on the other end of the phone for a moment. Cooper stared past the long rows of looms to a distant doorway. It had to lead out of the mill to the goyt, where the deep channels drew water from the river.

'OK, Ben, stay with Mullen until assistance comes. Is Georgi with you?'

'I think he's still upstairs. But, Diane—'

'Just don't do anything stupid.'

And then she was gone.

Cooper ran back to the stairs to shout for Georgi Kotsev, but was saved the trouble when Kotsev appeared at the top of the wooden steps.

Kotsev cursed quietly when he saw the body. 'And the child?'

'She's not here. Stay with him, will you, Georgi? Help is on the way.'

'Where are you going?'

'To find the child.'

They looked at each other for a moment. Kotsev seemed about to say something, but changed his mind. He nodded briefly.

'I understand.'

Cooper left him with Brian Mullen, and hurried down to the far end of the shed, tracking the sound of a closing door somewhere ahead. Above his head, a bridge crossed over the looms to the mill entrance at road level. Ahead of him, a cavernous space gradually revealed itself to be the boiler house. Four black, riveted monsters glinted in his torch beam.

He climbed back up the steps and paused for a moment, trying to decide between several doors and a series of smaller rooms. The door he chose turned out to be the bobbin room. One flick of his torch showed dozens of hessian sacks spilling bobbins onto the floor, wooden tubs full of bobbins, bobbins in drawers and hanging on the walls. Hundreds more of them were strung in bunches from the ceiling, rattling in the breeze blowing in from an open door. Cooper felt the chill striking through the doorway, and knew this had to be the passage that led outside to the goyt, and to the river.

He slipped through the door onto a wooden walkway over the water channel. The air was filled with the noise of the river. He could hear its rush and feel the vibrations of the current.

Cooper turned sharply to the left, not sure what he was reacting to. His senses were confused by the adjustment from the silent interior of the mill to the noise outside. A series of explosions reminded him that the fireworks display was still going on over the village. The cascade of coloured light helped him orientate himself. Beyond the goyt he could make out the bank of the river, and directly in front of him was an area of slippery concrete channels and sudden drops into black, lethal water.

Now that he was close to it, the roar of the weir almost drowned out the crack and scream of the fireworks. He thought he heard a shout, a woman's voice, but the words were incomprehensible. He was almost sure he saw a shadow flickering, and caught the rustle of a long skirt on concrete.

Then came the sudden sound of running footsteps. Cooper swung his torch, but he couldn't tell which direction the footsteps were coming from. The reflection of his Maglite off the dark water was too confusing.

He spun round too late and didn't see the black shape that came at him out of the night, or the fists that knocked him off balance. He teetered on the concrete edge, drawing a breath to cry out. His torch dropped from his hand and plunged into the goyt. A second later, Cooper was following it, falling towards the light as it spun down to the muddy depths.

It seemed a long time before the light stopped falling. Cooper closed his eyes against the shock and the roar of water in his ears. He panicked when he realised that he couldn't tell which way was up, and began to thrash his arms and legs. He seemed to hit something, or something hit him, he couldn't tell which. The cold was already striking through to his soaking skin.

He opened his eyes again, and saw that the light was receding now, drawing away from him into the gloom. He seemed to be trapped by some heavy, rusty object under the water. Just when he felt he couldn't hold his breath any longer, his head suddenly burst clear of the water and he gasped in a deep, ragged mouthful of air.

Dazed, Cooper realised that the collar of his jacket was being gripped by someone, and he was being dragged towards the side of the channel.

A deep voice laughed close to his ear.

'*Bezopasno li e pluvaneto tuk?* Are you sure it's safe to swim here?'

10

Sunday, October 30

While everyone else who was on duty had joined the search for Luanne Mullen, Fry was alone in the CID room at West Street, thinking of her conversation with Brian Mullen that morning. Same hospital, different ward. Mullen looked sicker and paler than ever.

'I always thought the adoption in Bulgaria was the wrong thing,' Mullen had said to her. 'I mean, I love Luanne to bits, and I wouldn't have parted with her once we'd got her. But I never thought it was right. It felt dodgy to me. I knew there'd be trouble. But Henry kept pushing and pushing, and Lindsay always went along with what he said.'

Mullen had lain back, exhausted. 'I've never been involved in anything illegal before. Never. I knew they'd catch up with us.'

'Who?'

'I don't know. But I was sure someone would come one day, to take

Luanne back. And once that Rose Shepherd turned up again, that was the last straw. But no one else could see it.'

'Is that what you were having arguments with Lindsay about?'

'No, we never had arguments, I told you. We disagreed about some things. But I was right, wasn't I? They did come. They've taken her back to Bulgaria, haven't they?'

'I really don't know, sir. I'm sorry. But we're doing our best to find her.'

It hadn't sounded convincing, even to Fry herself. The underwater search team was dragging the goyt at that moment.

'Can I ask you about something else, Mr Mullen?' she'd said.

'What?'

'Your next-door neighbour, Mr Wade.'

'Keith Wade? He's a good neighbour. He's always kept an eye on our house. Lindsay saw a lot of him during the day when he was on late shifts, and he always took an interest in the kids.'

'Mr Mullen, when you say Mr Wade kept an eye on your house, what exactly do you mean?'

'We gave him a spare key. So if we were away for the weekend, he could get in to deal with any emergencies.'

'He has a key to your house?'

'Yes, of course.'

Fry shook her head now at the memory of the conversation. As far as she was concerned, the question of who'd killed Lindsay Mullen and the two boys remained open. She still couldn't rule out Brian Mullen, but she was sure now that she'd been wrong about John Lowther.

Gradually, she found her thoughts focusing on Keith Wade. The perfect neighbour, the assiduous member of Neighbourhood Watch. The keen amateur photographer. The only person other than Brian Mullen who had been at the scene when the fire started.

Then another thought struck her. Brian Mullen had an alibi for the time of the fire—he'd been at the Broken Wheel with Jed Skinner until the early hours of the morning. That same fact had made it possible for Wade to get into the Mullens' house. If Brian hadn't been out late, the front door would have been bolted on the inside. But Lindsay had left the bolts off for her husband to come home. Wade could have known that, couldn't he?

Fry dialled a number. Ben Cooper was at home, recovering from his unexpected dip in the trapped waters of the Derwent.

'Ben,' she said, 'can I bounce something off you?'

'Yes, I'm fine. Thanks for asking, Diane.'

'Oh. Well, I can tell you're all right by the way you sound.'

Cooper sighed. 'What did you want to bounce off me?'

'Brian Mullen. You know that he denied the arguments with his wife?'

'Yes.'

'Whose word do we have that those arguments ever took place?'

Cooper considered the question for a moment. 'Well, the lady on one side of the Mullens heard the row about the carpet.'

'Which is the only one Brian admits to. And the rest?'

'We only have the other neighbour's word for those.'

'Keith Wade.'

'Yes, Wade. Why, Diane?'

'I'm thinking of getting Mr Wade in. Perhaps he wasn't such a good friend of the Mullens, after all.'

COOPER PUT the phone down thoughtfully. Neighbours had been a bit outside his experience until he moved to Welbeck Street. At Bridge End Farm, the nearest house had been several fields away.

'Who was that, Ben?'

'It was Diane Fry. They still haven't found the child,' he said. 'You know—Luanne Mullen.'

Liz looked up, her eyes suddenly full of concern. Her dark hair was loose today, curled round her ears in the way that he liked.

'It wasn't your fault if the child was snatched, Ben.'

'I didn't say it was.'

'No, but you were thinking it.'

Cooper raised his hands. 'It's a fair cop.'

Liz stood up and came towards him. When she was close, he could feel her warmth. In another moment, he'd be distracted completely from what had really been on his mind.

'Diane says there's a suspect in custody for the Rose Shepherd shooting,' he said. 'But it isn't going too well with him, from what I hear.'

Liz looked up at him, instinctively sharing the desire to see a satisfactory conclusion in a tragic case like the death of Miss Shepherd.

'Did I tell you about the gun, by the way?'

'The gun?' said Cooper.

'The gun you asked about, Ben. The Romanian PSL. I *did* tell you about the gun, didn't I?'

A DEFENDANT was always advised by his lawyers to smarten himself up when he appeared in court. Keith Wade had gone a step further—he'd smartened himself up for his interview at the police station.

'Mr Wade, thank you for coming in earlier to give us your fingerprints.'

'For elimination purposes, you said. Is that right?'

'Well, that was the idea.'

'What do you mean?'

'First of all, I want to take you back to last Sunday night again, when you first noticed the fire at your neighbour's house.'

He looked irritated. 'I think I've told you everything. Twice, probably.'

'How did you get into the house?'

'I don't remember.'

'Surely you do. You saw the smoke, made the 999 call, then . . .?'

'I opened their front door.'

'Do you mean you broke the door down? Surely it wasn't unlocked?'

Wade began to look sulky. 'Like I said, I knew Brian and Lindsay well. They leave me a key and I keep an eye on their house when they're away.'

'And you knew Brian was out that night, didn't you?'

'Well, yes. I always see him come and go.'

'Mr Wade, how did you get on with the boys? Jack and Liam?'

'Oh, them—'

'They were nice lads, you said.'

'Little bastards, that's what they were.'

'One was seven years old, and the other four, Mr Wade.'

He stared at her sullenly. 'I know that.'

'You're a smoker, aren't you, sir? It was obvious as soon as I walked through your door.'

'There's no law against it, is there?'

'Not in the privacy of your own home. But unfortunately, you took your matches and lighter fluid out of your house. You took them to your next-door neighbour's, didn't you?'

'Brian's a good bloke,' said Wade, leaning forward. 'I look out for him.'

'So why did you go into his house that night, pour lighter fluid in the sitting room and set fire to it? Why did you murder his wife and children?'

'What?'

'There's no point in denying it. We have your fingerprints from the can of lighter fluid that you used and left in a bin down the street.'

Wade shook his head. 'Brian's better off without them. Look at me—I'm a lot better off without my wife. Ought to have kicked her out sooner.'

'You mean you thought you were doing Brian Mullen a favour?'

'Well, you could put it like that. He was a brave bloke, but not that brave. I think that's why Brian went out so often, he couldn't face it.'

'So you stepped in. Watching out for your neighbour, Mr Wade? That's just great. Thank God we don't all have neighbours like you.'

'I don't want to talk any more.'

'You've said enough for now, Mr Wade.' Fry began to get up. 'You'll be charged later with the murder of Lindsay Mullen and her two sons.'

Wade looked at her with something like distaste. 'You know, I thought Lindsay would welcome a bit of company, with Brian being out,' he said. 'A bit of male company, like. But she was a bitch, like all the others. Brian is a lot better off without her.'

HITCHENS KEPT HIS CHAIR still for once, instead of making it squeal on its swivel. 'The SOCOs found Wade's digital camera,' he said. 'But all the photographs of the fire had been deleted from the memory card.'

'He must have been worried we'd find something incriminating,' said Fry.

'Like what?'

'He probably started taking photographs long before he made the 999 call. We'd have been able to see the time of each photograph on the memory card, and if we'd compare them to the time of his call, he'd have had some difficult questions to answer. So he deleted the whole lot.'

'You must have had him worried from the start, Diane.'

'He was an amateur. Look at how many mistakes he made.'

'Well, you always said the answer to the case would be close to home.'

'I didn't mean it like that,' said Fry. 'I was thinking about a member of the family. But I suppose your next-door neighbour is pretty close.'

Hitchens stood up from his chair. 'Let's go and see the DCI.'

In the DCI's office, they found that Kessen had just received the results of the latest actions from the incident room—a detailed assessment of Rose Shepherd's financial circumstances.

'Miss Shepherd had several savings accounts at different banks,' he said, 'but they were practically empty. And apart from interest, nothing has been added to any of the accounts as far back as we can go. Since the house purchase, the flow of money has been one way, into her current account, where it's been used to pay bills. With just her normal living expenses, she could have survived no more than another six months, I reckon.'

Fry took the print-out he offered her. 'She could have survived a few years longer if she'd flogged Bain House and bought a terraced property in the city somewhere. Or if she'd got a job.'

'Neither of those options would have seemed possible to Rose Shepherd,' said Kessen. 'She was too frightened of being tracked down.'

'Yes, of course.'

Kessen coughed. 'Are we finished here? We need all the manpower we can get at Matlock Bath. Don't forget we're still looking for the child.'

'What about Brian Mullen?' asked Fry. 'Should we interview him again? It does seem a bit tough on him, so soon after everything that's happened.'

'Leave it for now,' said Hitchens. 'I'll have another try at Donnelly first.'

'NO, LOOK,' said Donnelly a few minutes later. 'All I did was nick a car and torch it afterwards. No big deal.'

'You've done it before, Mr Donnelly, haven't you?'

'Well, yeah. When we were kids, we did it all the time round our way.'

'But you're not a kid any more.'

'No. Well, I *had* given it up. This was just a one-off. Did it as a favour. Someone wanted a car for a bit, that's all. A decent car, a four-by-four. I found the Shogun for him, and I did it as a favour.'

'Are you saying you didn't know what the vehicle was being used for?'

Donnelly chuckled. 'No, of course not. You don't ask questions like that.'

'We do.'

'Yeah, well . . .' He shrugged. 'I can't tell you, can I? No matter how long you keep me here, I can't tell you, because I don't know.'

'We don't need you to tell us that, Mr Donnelly. We already know. The car you stole was used to commit a murder. A shooting in Foxlow, in fact.'

'Eh? Well, I heard about that, but you can't . . . Well, you can't, that's all.'

'Mr Donnelly, unless you tell us who you did this favour for, you're our number one suspect right now.'

'For a murder? You've got to be joking.'

'Not at all, sir. I've never been more serious.'

Donnelly stared at him for a long moment, his eyes flickering anxiously as he worked out the odds. Either way, they didn't look good.

'He was good to me,' he said. 'He gave me a job when things started to go pear-shaped. I owed him a favour, that's all.'

'Who are you talking about, Mr Donnelly?'

Donnelly took a deep breath before committing himself. 'OK, I'll tell you.'

COOPER CAUGHT UP with Fry in the car park, between the security gate and the custody suite. A light drizzle was falling, and Fry seemed to want to get to her car quickly, but he stopped her.

'Ben? What the heck are you doing here? You're supposed to be at home recuperating.'

'I don't need to recuperate. I want to help. Are there any developments?'

He waited for the response he expected, wincing as he remembered what Liz had said to him when he put his jacket on to leave the flat. But, from Fry, it didn't come. She simply brought him up to date on Keith Wade, then told him about Rose Shepherd's dire financial circumstances.

'God, she must have been getting desperate,' said Cooper. 'There wasn't even anyone she could turn to for help or advice.'

Fry leaned against the side of a police van. 'You know, in those circumstances, I think you'd probably get to a point where you didn't care any more. Rose Shepherd was sixty-one—she was facing the prospect of another twenty or thirty years living like that, but with her isolation becoming more and more difficult to maintain day by day. Personally, I think Rose Shepherd might actually have welcomed her fate, when it came.'

Cooper stared at her, surprised by her sudden burst of empathy. Yet he wasn't at all sure about what she'd just said. He couldn't feel convinced that Rose Shepherd had welcomed death.

'Diane, there *is* another possibility she might have considered,' he said.

'What's that, Ben?'

'I wonder if she thought she'd found a lifeline. She might have made contact with someone she thought she could get money out of.'

'What?'

Cooper started his train of thought all over again. 'I asked about the rifle. You remember, the Romanian semi-automatic?'

'Yes.'

'Well, apart from the military sniper rifle, there's a sporting version of the PSL made for export, the Romak-3. It's a hunting rifle.'

Fry tilted her head to one side. 'What are you thinking, Ben?'

'I listened to the tapes of John Lowther's interviews,' he said. 'You remember his sentence referring to hunting? He said some people go "hunting for whores. No, for babies . . ."'

'Yes, I remember.'

'I wonder if that was an example of what Dr Sinclair called "clang associations", a confusion of words with similar sounds. I wonder if he actually meant some people go hunting *boars*. They still hunt them in parts of the world, you know. Bulgaria, for example.'

'So?'

'When Henry Lowther had that business trip to Bulgaria, it wasn't all vodka and red wine. His business contacts took him wild boar hunting.'

'How do you know that?'

'You asked him where he went and he mentioned Dounav. Well, I looked it up, and Dounav is a state game preserve in northern Bulgaria where they shoot deer, foxes and even the occasional wolf. But mostly wild boar.'

With the back of her hand, Fry wiped a bit of rain from her face, and her expression changed. 'And you'd use a hunting rifle for that, right?'

'Right.'

'OK, I'm with you, Ben. Let's see if we can check out Henry Lowther's financial status. I'd guess that bungalow at Darley Dale is probably worth less than Bain House. If Rose Shepherd was making an attempt to blackmail Mr Lowther, she might have seriously misjudged his ability to pay.'

RAIN SPATTERED on the glass roof of the Lowthers' conservatory and ran down the windows in long streaks. Inside, the atmosphere was humid, condensation forming on the leaves of the tree ferns. It almost made up for the icy stares from Henry and Moira Lowther, sitting together on their settee.

Fry gritted her teeth, steeling herself to resist the waves of resentment surging through the foliage.

'Luanne—she's still alive, surely?' said Mrs Lowther. 'The fact that you haven't found her yet . . . I mean, we *will* see her again, won't we?'

'I'm sorry, we can't say, Mrs Lowther. We're still looking.'

After that, the Lowthers just looked at her expectantly, offering nothing.

'I want to go back to what you told me about the adoption,' said Fry eventually. 'I understand the procedure for international adoptions can be rather complicated in Bulgaria.'

'You don't know the half of it,' Henry said, eager to talk now. 'The whole business is like some nightmare from a Kafka novel. We had to go to the ministry of justice and demonstrate that adoption would be in the child's best interests. You need declarations of consent from the child's natural parents—or the chief physician of the orphanage, in our case. Only when the minister gave his say-so could we apply to the regional court in Sofia.'

'A lot of documents required, were there, sir?'

'Documents? A whole bloody library of documents.'

Mrs Lowther was nodding in agreement. 'And they all had to be translated into Bulgarian, and certified by a notary public.'

Her husband took a breath. 'Yes, the process was far too complicated. It was an emotional and financial drain on the whole family.'

'Financial, sir?'

'Oh yes. With lawyer's fees and notary's fees, and the cost of travelling backwards and forwards to Sofia all the time, the expense was crippling.'

'But you didn't give up, did you?' said Fry. 'You found a way round the system, am I right?'

Lowther twisted in his chair to glance at his wife. They exchanged a look that carried too many meanings for Fry to interpret.

'Yes,' admitted Lowther finally. 'It was then—when we were all at our lowest ebb—that a miracle happened, as far as we were concerned. That was when we were contacted by Rose Shepherd.'

'So you weren't put in touch by a business contact, as you said earlier?'

'No, that wasn't quite true.'

'How did she first contact you?'

'She phoned the hotel we were staying at. Don't ask me how she knew about us. It was all a bit hush-hush—we had no way of getting in touch with her while we were there. We always had to wait for her to phone. She said she could arrange the necessary paperwork and deliver Zlatka directly to us. For a fee, of course. She told us she'd done it before for other foreign couples, and she even offered us testimonials.'

'And did she happen to mention that what she was offering was illegal?'

'No, certainly not. She led us to believe that it was entirely above board. She described herself as an international adoption agent.'

'A bit of fancy language makes all the difference, doesn't it?' said Fry.

Lowther looked at her accusingly, as if disappointed rather than offended by her sarcasm. 'She seemed like a godsend at the time, you know. Brian was the only one who had any doubts. But he only wanted whatever would make Lindsay happy. So he went along with it, despite his reservations.'

'Was it difficult getting Zlatka out of Bulgaria?'

'Not so far as I know. It was Miss Shepherd who brought the child out of the country. We travelled to Promahonas, just over the border in Greece, and she delivered Zlatka to us there. That was the arrangement.'

'Were you worried that Miss Shepherd wouldn't keep her part of it?'

He shook his head. 'We trusted her. She seemed a very genuine person.'

'And the money?'

'I paid for everything. I always helped Lindsay as much as I could, financially. For example, I helped buy some of the things for their house.'

'A Smeg dual-fuel cooker, for example?'

'Yes, that was something Lindsay particularly wanted. Brian would never have been able to afford it. But for some reason, he seemed to resent accepting my help. I only ever wanted to do the best for my little girl.'

'So how did the arrangement with Rose Shepherd work?'

'I paid half of her fee up front, and the remainder when she delivered the child. That was the agreement. It seemed very businesslike.'

'And who was the person you spoke to at the orphanage?'

'Her name was Piya. Piya Yotova. I hope she doesn't get into trouble over this. She was only trying to help.'

'Piya Yotova is dead. She was shot, along with a colleague, Dimitar Iliev.'

The Lowthers gaped at her in amazement.

Fry took advantage of their obvious shock. 'Mr Lowther, now that we've got the truth about the so-called adoption, would you like to tell me again how you came to meet up with Rose Shepherd last Saturday.'

'I told you, Lindsay wanted to say thank you. There was nothing wrong with that, was there? No matter how Miss Shepherd might have bent the rules in Bulgaria, you could see she genuinely wanted the best for Luanne.'

'And you got in touch with her by using the email address she'd given you in Bulgaria?'

'Yes, that's what I said,' agreed Lowther cautiously.

'Yet you've told me you had no way of getting in touch with her while you were there—that you always had to wait for her to phone you.'

He hesitated, and Fry knew she was on the right track.

'Actually, that's right,' he said. 'She gave me that email address when we saw her in Matlock Bath.'

'I see. And did she give you her phone number at the same time?'

'Well, yes. So we could keep in touch in the future, you know.'

Fry could tell by Henry Lowther's frozen expression that he had no idea whether he was saying the safe thing or not. If he denied having Rose Shepherd's number, would the police be able to prove he was lying?

'So the question remains, sir, how did you manage to get in contact with her before that meeting?'

'It was the other way round,' said Lowther. 'It was Miss Shepherd who got in touch with us. Perhaps you've worked that out.'

'Why on earth would she do that?'

Lowther had to think about that for a while. 'To be honest,' he said at last, 'I think Rose Shepherd was lonely. She knew no one in this country. I think she needed some kind of contact.'

'She risked a lot for a bit of conversation over a cup of tea, didn't she?' said Fry incredulously. 'I mean, she'd gone to a lot of trouble to give herself a new identity and made herself a recluse, all out of concern for her own safety. Why would she risk all that for an hour with you in Matlock Bath?'

Lowther remained silent. Fry looked at his wife instead, and saw that a worried expression had come over her face, a grey wash of despair.

'It was our fault she died, wasn't it?' she said.

'I'm sorry, Mrs Lowther? Would you repeat that?'

'The people she mixed with in Bulgaria, they must have come looking for her, to kill her. The same people who shot the couple in Bulgaria. And it was because of us that they found her.'

'Really? You think so?'

Lowther nodded at what his wife was saying, and sighed deeply. 'It all makes sense now,' he said. 'That's what happened, isn't it? It just goes to show what awful consequences the most innocent of intentions can have. I'm only glad that Lindsay never knew anything about all this.'

Fry felt a surge of revulsion at his sanctimonious expression. She could see him relaxing, smug in the belief that he'd get away with what he'd done.

'Actually, Mr Lowther,' she said, 'that's not the way *we* see it at all. And it isn't what your former employee, Tony Donnelly, says either.'

Lowther just stared at her, shaking his head slowly from side to side.

Fry leaned forward and spoke to him quietly, fixing her gaze on his.

'Nor was it the reason your son killed himself. Was it, Mr Lowther?'

And that was the bullet he was waiting for. Right between the eyes.

THE PHONE RANG on Fry's desk early on Monday morning.

'*Alo*. It's Georgi Kotsev.'

'Hi, Georgi. Will we see you today?'

'Diane, I'm sorry to tell you that my chief has recalled me. I would have liked to stay a little longer, but my duty is in Pleven now.'

'When do you leave?'

'There's a flight this morning, in three hours' time. Lufthansa.'

'Do you need a lift to the airport?'

'I have permission to obtain a taxi. My ministry is paying, so who can refuse? It will be here very soon.'

'I'm sorry we won't get a chance to say goodbye properly. It's been very interesting working with you.'

'*Blagodarya*. Thank you.'

'Did you hear that we've arrested Henry Lowther?'

'Yes, I heard.'

'We believe he murdered Miss Shepherd because she was attempting to blackmail him over the child. Unfortunately, Mr Lowther's export business was failing and he no longer had enough money to pay her off.'

'A bad choice of blackmail victim,' said Kotsev. 'What a pity.'

'Well, Lowther wasn't going to throw everything away that he'd done for his daughter. And when you've already been involved in one crime, it isn't a big step to the next one, is it?'

'No, that is true. And it will be a tight case, yes?'

'Yes. We found the gun when we searched the Lowthers' bungalow. And his son was driving the car. So we've cleared that up, Georgi. I'm sorry if it means you wasted your time here.'

'No, it was not a waste of time,' said Kotsev. 'Your theory is interesting. But it is a lot of *gluposti*. Bullshit.'

Fry was stunned into silence for a moment. 'You think we have it wrong?' Then she laughed. 'You have your own ideas. You want it to be connected to your Bulgarian Mafia. But, Georgi—'

'Where do you think the child is?' asked Kotsev.

'I don't know. Do you?'

'She was taken efficiently. She will be back home with her father soon.'

'Back home? Georgi, I hope not.'

'Could it not be for the best, Diane?' he asked tentatively.

'No, of course not. What do you mean?'

'No matter.'

Fry wanted to ask Kotsev more. She wanted to ask him lots of things. But there was a hint of distance in his voice that made her hold back.

'I will be pursuing my own enquiries in Pleven. Meanwhile, if I'm not available, you may speak to my colleague, Inspector Hristo Botev. You pronounce the "H" in the throat, almost as if it was a "C".'

'It sounds a bit Welsh.'

'Yes, a bit Welsh. My friend Hristo is very celebrated in Bulgaria.'

Fry smiled at his exaggeration. She didn't imagine that police officers were any more celebrated in Bulgaria than they were in Derbyshire. For most people, they were a necessary evil, at best.

COOPER CAME into the office, and saw at once that something was disturbing Fry. 'What's up?' he said.

'That was Georgi Kotsev. He's going back to Bulgaria this morning.'

'Well, his interest in the case is over, I suppose.'

'Not really. We still don't know where Luanne Mullen is.'

'If she's not dead, she'll be out of the country by now. Sergeant Kotsev will be more use back in Bulgaria, if she's ever going to be found.'

'Yes, you're right.'

Cooper hesitated. 'It's a pity, though,' he said tentatively. 'There was something I wanted to ask Georgi.'

'Anything important?'

'It was something I remembered from the incident at Masson Mill. Just before I ended up in the water. It was a very brief impression I had, but I thought someone else was there by the river that night.'

'Obviously there was—the person who pushed you in.'

'No, someone else, further away. I had the impression—well, I wanted to ask Georgi Kotsev whether he'd seen a woman.'

'A woman?'

Reluctantly, Cooper tried to describe his half-memory. It was no more than a shadow flickering in the darkness, perhaps the rustle of a long skirt on concrete. He might have been describing a dream. Or he might have confused it with the earlier glimpse of a woman who looked like a fortune teller, her blue scarf flashing briefly in the lights in Derwent Gardens.

Fry shook her head. 'There was no woman by the river, Ben. Georgi would have mentioned it if he'd seen her.'

'Yes, I suppose so.'

Cooper looked at her closely. Her tone seemed to confirm what he'd been suspecting for a few days now. 'Did you like him, Diane?' he asked.

Fry looked away. 'It was a pleasure to work with him.'

'A refreshing change, then?'

'You said it.'

'Is he married, by the way?'

'I never asked him,' said Fry. 'Why are you interested, all of a sudden?'

'No reason.' Cooper looked across to see what Fry was doing, and peered curiously at some stapled sheets of paper on her desk.

'What's this?'

'An application form.'

'Oh, I see. For Europol.'

'That's right.'

Cooper picked up the form and flicked through it, wondering why she'd left it where he was certain to see it. He stopped at the qualifications section.

'How many languages do you speak, Diane?' he asked.

'Languages? Are you kidding?'

'It says here candidates must be fluent in at least two languages of the European Union, including English.'

'Oh, damnation.'

Cooper saw that she was genuinely taken aback. 'You'll have to do some studying if you want to get into Europol. Which language do you fancy?'

'I don't have time to learn languages.'

He couldn't quite interpret the look that Fry gave him.

'Are you all right now, Ben?' she continued. 'You're not still bothered by John Lowther's death?' Maybe she just wanted to change the subject, or maybe she really was concerned for him.

Cooper was about to say no, he wasn't, when he realised there were thoughts just below the surface that he hadn't told anybody about until now.

'He'd already stopped taking his medication, hadn't he?' he said.

'Yes, some weeks ago. Lindsay became completely absorbed with the baby. She forgot about her brother's needs, or maybe she thought he was well enough to cope on his own. But he wasn't—he began to slip.'

'I bet he knew there was something wrong. But once his thoughts became too disordered, he wouldn't know why, or what the problem was.'

Fry sniffed. 'More likely he couldn't live with the knowledge that his father had involved him in a murder.'

'Yes, that as well. If he really understood what was happening.'

Cooper paused, considering his own comment. Because that wasn't what had been haunting John Lowther in those final moments, was it? His last words hadn't referred to Rose Shepherd, but to his sister and her children. *I heard them scream. I'll always hear them scream.* So those screams must have been inside John Lowther's head. Just one final illusion.

But not for the Mullens. Their desperation for a girl had brought terrible consequences for them. In a way, they had sacrificed two children for one.

'The Mullens did it all for the sake of that third child,' he said.

Fry nodded. 'And the child wasn't even theirs.'

'Not in a biological sense. But in a way, Luanne was the child they'd put the biggest investment into—time, effort and expense. Perhaps love, too.'

'Do parents think like that?' asked Fry. 'I'd have thought their own children would be the most important to them. Their own flesh and blood.'

But she sounded uncertain, as if it was a subject she wasn't qualified to speak on. Cooper remembered the few details she'd once told him about her childhood in the Black Country, when she'd been taken away from her parents and fostered. He wasn't sure what had happened to Diane's real parents. Maybe one day he'd ask—if he ever felt he knew her well enough.

'No, Diane, I'm not sure it always works like that,' he said, though he didn't really feel any better qualified.

'There's still no sign of Luanne Mullen. She's disappeared completely.'

'If you ask me, Georgi's right and she's back with her father.'

'If that's the case, it would all have been for nothing. We'd all have failed—me, you, Georgi Kotsev. What a waste of time.'

'Let's hope we hear something from Georgi, then,' said Cooper.

And, as he watched Fry's face, he thought that was one sentiment she probably agreed with.

'You know, there was a question someone asked right at the beginning, when we were in Rose Shepherd's house after the shooting,' said Cooper. 'No one had any idea how to answer it then.'

'What question was that?'

'What Miss Shepherd's killer could possibly have said to her on the phone that would make her go to the window and walk into his sights.'

'There's no way we'll ever know that, unless Henry Lowther tells us.'

'Well . . .' said Cooper, 'if Miss Shepherd was in such desperate financial circumstances that she'd decided to blackmail Henry Lowther, there *is* one sentence that might have made her do exactly that.'

'What?'

'*Rose, I've brought you your money.*'

THREE DAYS LATER, Diane Fry received a letter in the morning mail at West Street. It carried a Bulgarian stamp depicting a yellow butterfly, and the address was written in tiny, precise black letters.

Inside the envelope, she found a postcard and a colour photograph. Was that all? It seemed very disappointing. Holding the postcard by the edges, she looked at the front. The picture was a detail from the Pleven Panorama, depicting some epic battle that had liberated Bulgaria from Turkish rule.

The foreground was real. Brown mud, abandoned weapons, a makeshift trench with a dropped water bottle, an empty ammunition box. But the scene beyond was false. The exhausted soldiers were walking through an imaginary landscape, the dead bodies and the drifting smoke were painted in. Reality and illusion had been cleverly merged, and the line where they joined was almost imperceptible.

She flipped the card over and read the message:

Honoured Sergeant Fry,

It was my privilege to work with you in this recent investigation. I will remember it always, because it will be my last. My chief has been pleased to accept my resignation from the service.

As you read this communication, I will no longer be in Bulgaria. So where will I go now? That is uncertain. Perhaps I will move to your Derbyshire? As I told you, your beautiful hills resemble those around my home in Miziya. I hope you know you are very lucky!

Please give my regards to your colleagues. And my apologies to your Constable Cooper. Tell him, sometimes a man can see too much.

Ah, but you asked me a question once. You asked me would a father really go so far to get his child back? Would he go to any lengths necessary? I did not answer you then. This was because I knew what should be done, but I felt certain you would say I was wrong. You are a good professional. You have my admiration.

So now I will tell you the answer. Would a father go to any lengths necessary to get his child back? The answer is 'yes'. The answer is that I already did. May forgiveness be with God.

Dovijdane,
Georgi Kotsev

Cooper put his head round the door, and Fry hastily slid the postcard under the papers on her desk.

'I'm sorry to tell you this, Diane,' he said, 'but I phoned the Interior Ministry in Pleven and asked for this colleague of Georgi Kotsev's. The name he gave you was Hristo Botev, right?'

'Yes. What did Botev say?'

'He wasn't there. He hasn't been there for quite a long time.'

'Oh.' Fry looked at him curiously. 'He's retired, perhaps?'

'You might say that. When I eventually got someone on the phone who spoke English, he made me repeat who I wanted, then burst out laughing. In fact, he seemed to be sharing the hilarity round the office.'

'Did Georgi play a joke on us?'

'A pretty pointless joke. When he could pull himself together, the officer explained that Hristo Botev was a Bulgarian revolutionary martyr, who died fighting the Turkish Empire in the nineteenth century. It seems Hristo was a cross between Robin Hood and Winston Churchill.'

Fry could hardly bring herself to speak. 'OK. Thanks, Ben.'

'It must just be the Bulgarian sense of humour. Pity, though—I still want to ask him whether he saw a woman by the river that night.'

'There *was* no woman,' she said automatically.

When Cooper had gone, Fry put the postcard back and finally forced herself to look at the photograph.

The photo told her everything she needed to know. It showed two people standing in front of a wide, circular tower. She wouldn't have recognised the building, but for the postcard. The Pleven Panorama.

Georgi Kotsev was in full uniform, with his silver badge pinned to his breast pocket. And very smart he looked, too. The blue tunic and epaulettes suited him even better than a leather jacket. Below his service cap, Kotsev was smiling, a smile that had become familiar to Fry in the few days that she'd known him. It made her heart turn over.

But here, the reason for Georgi's smile seemed to be the woman standing next to him. She was very striking, black-haired and dark-eyed, wearing a blue scarf and a red silk blouse. She was no taller than Georgi's shoulder, and he had his arm round her waist. She was like a dark rose in his hand.

But that wasn't all. Not by a long way.

There were actually three people in this photograph. And here was when reality and illusion seemed to merge again for Fry. Who was to say that anyone's perception of reality was the right one, or ever had been? It was an impossible question.

But one thing she was sure of. Sergeant Kotsev was a professional, all right. The woman beside him had the distinctive look of a Roma. And the child in her arms was the most beautiful baby that Fry had ever seen.

STEPHEN BOOTH

Born: Blackpool, June 30, 1952
Home: Nottinghamshire
Website: www.stephen-booth.com

RD: You started young, writing your first novel at the age of twelve and editing the school magazine. Were you proud of those early achievements?

SB: I started even earlier than that. I was writing my own stories almost as soon as I could read. Yes, I was proud of what I produced, but it was a long time before people around me stopped calling it 'scribbling', so I kept it pretty much to myself. It's surprising how much freedom there was on that school magazine—decency was preserved, but politics and satire were allowed.

RD: You grew up in Blackpool—do you have any particular memories from those years?

SB: The town was always so crowded in the summer that we couldn't get near the attractions as children—in fact, there were some weeks when we were warned it was far too dangerous to go near the promenade. Then, in winter, when it was quiet, everything closed down. Very frustrating!

RD: After university, you did teacher training. Was it what you expected?

SB: No! I did my teaching practice in a large comprehensive school, and it was quite a shock to discover that there were children involved! Teaching requires a special talent and I didn't have it. In the end, I couldn't imagine spending one more day there, so I left. Teaching was only ever a fallback option because I couldn't get a job on a newspaper immediately after I graduated.

RD: What kind of journalism were you involved in and did you enjoy it?

SB: I enjoyed my time in newspapers tremendously. I started out as a rugby union reporter in Cheshire in the seventies. At that time all the national papers had production centres in Manchester and I also worked some night shifts on the *Guardian*, and as a 'down table' sports sub on the *Daily Express*, filling in for regular staff during holidays, etc. The *Guardian* never let me handle anything more important than the weather. I was in charge of letting readers know what the temperature was in Tokyo yesterday!

RD: What made you decide to get a smallholding?

SB: When I got a job in west Yorkshire, my wife Lesley and I moved to a village near

Holmfirth—*Last of the Summer Wine* country. Self-sufficiency was all the rage at the time, and we made friends with some people who kept goats in their garden. A year or two later, we moved house so that we had enough land on which to keep our own.

RD: Can you tell us a bit about Toggenburgs, your favourite breed of goat?

SB: They're a dairy breed from the Swiss Alps that were imported in the 1890s. Only a handful have been bred 'pure' in this country. They are very attractive, hugely productive compared to cows, and have great personalities—friendly, quirky and individual. I like animals with a sense of humour, and Toggs definitely have one!

RD: Do you visit Derbyshire a lot?

SB: As often as I can. In one way, I'd like to live there because I love the area. But from a writer's point of view, a bit of distance is very useful because I see the area afresh with every visit, and I notice new things. I spend a lot of time finding the right locations for each book.

RD: What inspired the Bulgarian element in *Scared to Live*?

SB: I'd been reading about Europol, the European equivalent of Interpol, and I was amazed by the extent of the organised crime they're trying to tackle. Much of it originates in the former Communist countries of eastern Europe and, because there are no internal borders, there is nothing to stop criminal gangs operating in any EU country now. They already have their tentacles here—yes, even in Derbyshire.

MATLOCK BATH

Stephen Booth chooses to set all his novels in Derbyshire's picturesque Peak District. The latest, *Scared to Live*,takes place in and around Matlock Bath, a town enclosed dramatically by the towering cliffs of a limestone gorge carved by the River Derwent. Originally made famous in Victorian times by its thermal springs, Matlock Bath still attracts huge numbers of visitors. Sights and local attractions include Richard Arkwright's Masson Mills, built in 1783, the Illuminations and Venetian Nights that take place on the Derwent every autumn, and a cable car ride to the Heights of Abraham above the town.

ORBIT

JOHN J. NANCE

Moments after Intrepid *starts orbiting the Earth a freak accident damages the craft, leaving space tourist Kip Dawson alone and trapped.*

Communications are out and he has no way of repairing the spacecraft.

While Kip tries to find a way of saving himself he is watched anxiously by millions on Earth—a very ordinary man caught in a very extraordinary situation.

1

Five miles south of Mojave, California
May 16, 9.23 p.m. Pacific Time

For Kip Dawson, the risks associated with being shot into space in a few hours are finally beginning to seem real.

Am I really going to do this? he thinks, braking the car hard, foot shaking, as he casts his eyes up through the windshield to take in the stark blackness of his destination. This last evening on earth—the very eve of his windfall trip into space—feels too surreal to grasp emotionally. He's sure of only one thing: at long last, it's scaring as much as exciting him.

He pulls to the side of the highway and climbs out to stare into deep space. He's oblivious to the sharp chill of the desert night. The deep velvet black of the cloudless night sky entrances him, and he hasn't seen the Milky Way so startlingly clear since he was little.

He feels like a child as he contemplates the vastness of it all. Provided there's no explosion on the way up, he'll be there in a few hours, encapsulated in a tiny, fragile craft, closer—if only incrementally—to all those stars.

There is no productivity in stargazing, the dutiful part of his mind is grousing, but he suppresses the urge to leave. He hears the song of a night-bird somewhere distant. A moment earlier a coyote had made its presence known, and he hears it call again, the howl almost mystical.

How small we are, he thinks, as he stands beneath the staggering scope of a billion suns strewn at least 10,000 light-years across from horizon to horizon, trying to embrace it; even the largest of his personal problems seem trivial by contrast.

His cellphone rings again, the third time in an hour, but he tunes it out, thinking instead about the details of the American Space Adventures space school he's attended for the previous two weeks and the awe he still feels when he sees the famous *Apollo 8* picture of the Earth rising over the lunar landscape. Everything in perspective. It's the way he's been told every NASA astronaut feels when the sound and fury and adrenaline of reaching orbit subsides and it's finally time to be weightless and breathe and look outside.

He recalls the video of sunrise from space, the colours progressing through the rainbow to the sudden explosion of light over the rim of the planet, all proceeding at seventeen times the speed of dawn on the Earth's surface.

In some recess of his mind he's been keeping track of the number of times his cellphone has rung, and the newest burst is one time too many. His spirits sag. Angrily he punches the phone on, unsurprised to hear his wife's strained voice on the other end. The humbling, exhilarating mood is evaporating around him, leaving only a duty to resume feeling guilty. He wonders if they're going to pick up at the same point in the argument.

'Sharon? Are you OK?'

There's a long sigh. He imagines her sitting in the dark den of her father's opulent home in North Houston where she's fled with their children.

'I may never be OK again, Kip. But that's not why I called. I just wanted to wish you well. And . . . I'm sorry about the argument earlier.'

For just a moment he feels relieved. 'I'm sorry, too. I really wish you could understand all this, but you do know I'll be back tomorrow afternoon, right? As soon as I get down, I'm going to fly directly to Houston, to you and the girls, and we can fly back to Tucson together . . .'

'You make it sound so routine. No, Kip. Even if you survive this madness, don't come here. Just go on back to Tucson. I'm too upset to talk for a while. We're going to stay here until I decide what to do.'

He keeps his voice gentle, though he wants to yell. 'Sharon, keep in mind that this is probably the only time I've felt the need to . . . not honour your wishes on something big.'

'Yeah, other than your so-called career.'

He bites his tongue and lets the sting subside. 'Honey, you've been asking me to throw away the dream of a lifetime, winning a trip into space.'

She makes a noise that sounds like a snort. 'Look, Kip. I only called to say I hope this thing is all you expect it to be, because the price you're paying is immense.'

'Sharon—'

'Let me finish. I wanted to say that I hope you make it back alive, Kip. You've always belittled my premonitions. I want you to come back alive, regardless of what happens to us, but I don't expect you to. So I have to face the fact that this is probably our goodbye in this life.'

'Sharon, that's nuts. I respect your premonitions, but they're not always right, and ASA does these trips twice a week. Over a hundred and fifty so far and no one's even been scratched.' He says the words knowing the facts won't change her mind, but he has to keep trying.

'I've loved you, Kip. I really have.'

'And I do love you, Sharon. Not past tense, but now.'

Silence and a small sob answer his words, followed by the rattle of a receiver searching for the cradle.

He lets himself slump back against the side of the car in thought, working hard to overrule the guilt-fuelled impulse to give in, call her back, cancel the trip and drive all night and all day straight through to Houston.

That would be the Kip thing to do, he thinks. The way he's always responded. Must repair everything. Must atone for the sin of taking her away from Houston and not following her plan for his professional life.

He's suddenly back two months before in his den in Tucson, the memory of the late-evening phone call from American Space Adventures still crystalline, a lovely female voice on the other end asking a few identifying questions before getting to the point. 'And, Mr Dawson, you did enter an Internet-based contest with American Space Adventures to win one of four seats on one of our spacecraft into low Earth orbit, correct?'

'Yes. It's always been a dream of mine, to fly in space.'

'Sir, I'm calling because you've won the trip.'

It's hard to remember exactly how much he whooped and smiled and jumped around in the moments afterwards, before explaining the happy call to Sharon. Carly and Carrie, their five-year-old twins, came running in to see what all the noise was about, followed by thirteen-year-old Julie, his daughter from his first marriage. Sharon shooed them back to bed without explanation before turning to Kip, and he was stunned at the look of horror on her face, her eyes hardening as she forbade him to go.

'Excuse me?' he said, still smiling. 'What did you say?'

'I said you're not going! I have this gut feeling and it's really strong, Kip. I don't want to be a widow.'

Within minutes it became an argument spanning the house, and then it turned somehow to encompass everything wrong with him and a marriage he'd refused to see as imperilled.

'All you think about is yourself!' she wailed. 'You're never here for me and the girls and now you want to go kill yourself in *space*? Then go!'

'I'm never here? For God's sake, I don't even play golf any more. What time do I take away from you?'

'All you do is work! The girls are suffering.'

'Name one school function I've missed.'

'Even when you're there, you're thinking about business.'

'Sharon, I sell pharmaceuticals. I'm a regional sales rep for a huge drug manufacturer. What's there to think about?'

'You could have been in the oil business, but no! You had to go be a peon for Vectra Pharmaceuticals and work your rear off for no recognition, no advancement, and no time for us.'

'Of course. I didn't go to work for your father. That's always it, isn't it? I don't measure up because I went out to get a job on my own.'

'Stupidest decision you ever made.'

Except marrying you! he thought, careful not to let his face show it. The thought shocked him, somehow defiling the very walls of the den he had shared with Lucy before her fatal accident. But that was long ago, before Sharon came along and caught him on the rebound. Before he caught himself growing numb.

It ended as usual with her storming off to bed alone. But, for once, this time he didn't follow her like the usual whipped puppy, begging to be forgiven. He made the decision that, for perhaps only the second time in his adult life, Kip Dawson was going to stay the course and cling to his dream.

KIP'S THOUGHTS RETURN to night in the high California desert, and he checks his watch, grimacing at the late hour. The cellphone rings yet again and he answers without looking at the screen, letting his voice convey his weariness with the game she's playing.

But the voice on the other end is different. 'Mr Dawson, Jack Railey at ASA. We couldn't find you in your room, so I thought I'd phone you.'

Kip chuckles. 'Is this a bed check? Am I in trouble?'

'No, sir. But we have a problem. Could we come talk to you about it?'

'What problem, exactly?'

'I'd rather not go into it over the phone. We do have some options, but I need to speak with you about them in detail.'

A kaleidoscope of possibilities, few good, flash across Kip's mind, depressing him. 'I'm just a few miles away. Where can I find *you*?'

He listens to the brief description of Railey's office location before promising to be there in fifteen minutes, his voice heavy with concern.

Mojave, California
May 16, 9.49 p.m. Pacific Time

As Kip approaches the airfield, the tails of nearly fifty mothballed airliners rise from the desert like a ghostly fleet of square riggers. The buildings of the Mojave International Aerospace Port come into view as well, the ramp awash with artificial orange light. He spots the specially outfitted Lockheed 1011 that ASA uses as a mothership to launch its spacecraft, the old jumbo jet sparking an unexpected stab of anxiety—as if finding it parked on the ground means that neither he, nor it, will be flying in the morning after all.

It isn't hard to figure out, he decides. Something technical has gone wrong, the launch has been cancelled, and now they want to give him his options for rescheduling. He's not sure whether disappointment or embarrassment will be worse. He can depend on one negative at least: rescheduling will give Sharon that much more time to complete her campaign to wear down his fragile resolve.

It always seemed too good to be true anyway, winning this trip.

ASA's headquarters are housed in a glass-sided six-storey building and finding Railey's office is simple. He's not surprised to see Richard DiFazio, owner of ASA, at the conference table. DiFazio gets up to shake Kip's hand.

'I didn't expect to see you again this evening, after the party,' Kip says, recalling the founder's appearance at their prelaunch celebration in a local restaurant. DiFazio had lingered through dessert to talk with one of Kip's flightmates, Tommy Altavilla, an extremely wealthy Seattle industrialist and raconteur who kept them laughing for hours.

'Kip, just after you left, Tommy had a heart attack.'

'Oh no! Is he all right?' The smiling faces of Tommy and Anna Altavilla are vivid in his mind.

'He will be. It was a relatively mild attack, but he's been airlifted to Cedars-Sinai in LA, and Anna, of course, went with him.'

'I'm sorry to hear this.'

'I know it. I mean, our first concern is Tommy's welfare, but after that we've got to address the empty seats on the flight, and it just got more complicated an hour ago when Tariq, your other fellow passenger, got a call from Riyadh to get back there fast. He couldn't tell us why.'

Tommy and Anna Altavilla and Tariq, a Saudi royal, each paid half a million dollars. Yet the Altavillas in particular welcomed their contest-winning freeloader as a full partner, and Kip will miss sharing this with them.

'Three empty seats,' he says. 'I see the problem. So when can I reschedule?'

'Well . . . that's why we wanted to talk to you, Kip. This trip is already unique because we have a small commercial payload scheduled—essentially an industrial, scientific experiment we're being well paid for—and we've made the decision to launch with or without passengers. So, if you're still up for it, you'll have the craft and your pilot, Bill Campbell, all to yourself—which means you'll get much more window time.'

His hesitation, if any, is measured in nanoseconds. 'Hell, yes, I'm up for it!'

DiFazio gets to his feet with a tired smile. 'Great! That helps us, too, you know, not having to displace a paying passenger later.' A worried look crosses DiFazio's face as he realises the implications of the phrase 'paying passenger' in front of a contest winner. 'I apologise for that reference, Kip. You're an honoured guest, and I didn't mean . . .'

'No problem. I'm glad it works out. This is, after all, a business.'

'I appreciate that,' DiFazio replies. 'We're all very glad you won the contest, and I've got to tell you on behalf of all of our folks that you've been a delight to have with us during training.' He starts to turn away, then turns back. 'Kip, I agree completely with Diana Ross, by the way, that given your enthusiasm for private space flight, we need to talk later about involving you in some of our advertising.'

'Can't wait.'

He walks back to the plush ASA guest quarters and his assigned suite. DiFazio's mention of ASA's publicity director has sparked a warm memory of the first time he saw Diana Ross.

He was a nonswimmer in deep water at a big ASA reception in New York, and she was the lifeguard—though he hadn't known it at first. The ballroom at the Waldorf that evening was full of polished, elegant women who made him feel like a stammering sophomore. One young woman in particular caught his curiosity as she glided effortlessly between conversations, greeting friends, her smile warm, her persona inviting. Her long, black hair framed a flawless, oval face, her eyes amazingly blue and unforgettably large, and he was shocked when she turned and smiled at him. Even across the room he averted his eyes for a moment from this long-legged beauty, but when he looked back he let himself notice an abundance of cleavage framed by an expensive, gold-trimmed gown and matching heels—the trappings of a confident woman.

Suddenly, she headed across the room straight for him, and he sidled closer to an enormous floral arrangement as if to hide while a flurry of prohibited thoughts flitted through his head.

'Why, Mr Dawson,' she said with an endearing smile, 'is that you in the potted plant?'

There was no way of knowing that she was an officer of ASA assigned to mentor him through the preflight publicity process, and discovering that had been a small letdown.

'I'm Diana Ross, ASA's director of publicity, and, yes, I've heard every possible joke about my name, and no, I don't sing.'

'Glad to meet you, Diana.'

She immediately turned to the business of asking him to sit for several TV interviews. 'The thing is, I'm in trouble here and I need your help. This soiree . . . this reception . . . is my idea. Oh, of course the primary purpose was to welcome you as the winner, but this party is really to get the media excited again so they can get the rest of the country excited. *But* . . . all we've been able to draw are two local TV camera crews and one reporter. Pathetic. I could generate that with a bake sale in Des Moines.'

'I'm sorry to hear that.'

She shrugged. 'We didn't expect private space flight to become quite so *routine* quite so soon. But here's the thing. I really need to have you participate in a couple of on-camera interviews with the two crews who were kind enough to straggle in. It'll be painless, I promise. Just be yourself and tell them what it was like to win, and how you feel about going into space.' She cocks her head, her eyes on his. 'So, how *do* you feel?'

'I'm excited,' he replied. But Sharon's angst was uppermost in his mind, muting his reaction.

'Excited, huh? Could have fooled me.'

Kip remembers laughing in mild embarrassment. It felt slightly disturbing, as if she could read too much, and there was an instant attraction beyond the physical, especially when he felt her businesslike façade falter as well. 'They'll ask me that? If I'm excited?' Kip had countered.

She seemed distracted for a moment as she studied his eyes. Then she said, 'They'll ask you that and more silly questions.' She deepened her voice: 'So, how does it feel to be going into outer space?'

'Outer—'

'Of course, we fly in low Earth orbit,' she said. 'Many local reporters don't know the difference between low Earth orbit and so-called "outer space".'

'Even my *cat* knows the difference,' he replied.

She laughed. 'Tomorrow morning, however,' she said with pride, 'you'll be on *Good Morning America,* and those folks know all about this stuff.'

His jaw dropped. There hadn't been any mention of national TV.

'Isn't that great?' she continued. 'My one big success in this campaign.'

But his pained expression was undisguised. Sharon Dawson never missed *GMA* and made no secret of being in love with the host, and she would see Kip talking about the very thing that had sent *her* into orbit.

He tried to find a way out. 'Diana, I don't think you want me on national TV. I'm kind of a private person.'

'Nonsense. Oh, by the way,' she said without missing a beat, 'I was sorry to hear that your wife couldn't be with us tonight. Forgive my prying, but is she worried about your flight?'

'You might say that,' Kip responded, irritated that she'd got it out of him.

'Can I help, in terms of providing information, to make her feel better?'

He looked away, trying not to send the ungracious message that he'd like to run. He forced his eyes back to hers before she got any closer to the truth. 'Diana, I'd prefer to stay in the background. I'd rather not do that show.'

'Please don't make me beg! I might have to buy you dinner, and I'm already over budget.'

The thrill he felt at that moment had nothing to do with national television and it surprised him, making him blush. It was the radical thought of dining with her. But he covered his embarrassment—and his interest—with a laugh.

Minutes later Diana guided him to an anteroom where she greeted a young woman reporter while a bored cameraman pinned on a microphone and positioned Kip just so. At last the cameraman indicated to the reporter that she could fire the first question.

'So, Mr Dawson. How does it feel to be going into outer space?'

KIP'S THOUGHTS RETURN to the ASA suite, his eyes on the clock. It's almost 11 p.m. but, even though he's tired, sleeping is going to be difficult. For some reason his mind has locked on Diana and his conversations with her in the weeks after New York, as well as the dinner they had—a delightful evening for just the two of them that felt dangerously close to a date. It ended with a proper handshake back in Mojave, but not before they'd discovered how much they had in common, and he was thrilled to hear her say his enthusiasm for what ASA was doing was so infectious she was thinking of making him their 'poster boy'. The publicity didn't matter to him as much as the chance to work with her. If there had been a mutual attraction in New York, the dinner endorsed it, and each subsequent verbal spat with

Sharon in the weeks that followed breathed more life into the reality that there were other women out there who might like him just as he was.

Kip sighs as he places his cellphone by the bed, surprised to find a message symbol blinking. He checks the call list and feels an instant loss at finding a Colorado Springs area code and his oldest child's phone number at the Air Force Academy.

Jerrod almost never calls, and to miss one of those rare moments hurts. Especially now. His son has always wanted to fly, and perhaps be an astronaut. But never in his wildest thoughts has Kip expected to beat Jerrod into space.

He retrieves the voicemail, expecting words of support. But Jerrod's message is angry and hurt, and it hits Kip like an unexpected punch.

'Dad, I'm having to talk to your goddamn voicemail again. Julie called in tears tonight, Dad, and said you were going ahead with that space flight and that Sharon says you're going to die, and that you haven't paid any attention to their worries. They're all torn up down there. My sister says you aren't listening to anyone. I'm tired of you thinking about no one but you, Dad, and . . . if anything happens to you, you'll be leaving an awful mess behind. I don't want my sister crying! Call me before you take off. I'm really mad at you! Julie doesn't deserve to be treated like this. Neither do the twins.'

Kip hears the catch in his son's voice, but the words are clear enough. There's been hardly a moment since his first wife's death that Jerrod hasn't been mad at him. And that doesn't make the hurt easier to bear.

He punches up his son's phone at the academy and it rings through to voicemail, but he's too stunned to leave anything but a cursory message.

Kip folds his cellphone, taking his time so he won't have to react too quickly to the renewed doubts that Jerrod's words have shoved back in his heart.

He should lie down, he thinks. He's running out of night.

FIFTY FEET DOWN the hallway, Diana Ross stands and debates with herself yet again. Kip Dawson has been back from the meeting less than fifteen minutes. For some reason, the thought of his going into orbit alone with Bill Campbell is unsettling, and she can't think why—other than the unusual nature of having only one passenger aboard, or maybe the gear collapse on ASA's other spacecraft several weeks back.

She poises her hand to knock. Is this business or is this personal? She's not sure. Maybe some of both: protecting her 'investment' in him as a potential spokesman and, at the same time, maybe scratching an itch?

Not that he's under her skin or anything. If she wanted companionship or marriage, she wouldn't be thinking about a married guy from Tucson.

Yet there's something about him.

She knocks gently and waits before knocking again. Minutes elapse before he opens the door just inches, and she smiles to see him leaning at an angle so she can't see what state of dress he's in.

'Kip! Sorry to bother you so late . . .'

'Diana! Hello. This is a pleasant surprise . . . I think. Is anything wrong?'

'No, no. I just . . . wanted to wish you a good flight, and maybe give you some pointers on what to expect.' *How lame!* she thinks, knowing the ground school has already covered far more than anything she could tell him.

He opens the door wider and motions her in and she enters, amused that he's holding a death grip on his bathrobe. He carefully reties it before closing the door awkwardly. She heads for the couch and sits.

'I was just about ready to dive into bed . . .'

She feels off-balance, as if someone of greater maturity is going to burst through the door and demand to know why she's invaded this married customer's bedroom in the middle of the night before his big flight.

She sees his look of panic, the expression transmitting that he's attracted to her and worried about having her alone in the room when he's naked beneath his bathrobe. The message is so clear she has to suppress a laugh.

'What I want to urge you to do is think about the fantastic sights you're going to see through the eyes of a poet, which I think you may be.'

'I've never written poetry, Diana,' he says, looking like he's failed to prepare for a test.

'No, I don't mean as in writing poetry, but as in looking at things as if through the eyes of someone who can appreciate the ethereal, the beautiful aspects, the emotional impact, and then put it into words.'

'That's a tall order for a mere salesmen of pills. But I'll try.'

Their eyes are locked for a few intimate moments, and she sees the sparkle of panic mixed with interest again as he looks away, as if embarrassed.

She gets to her feet suddenly. 'Well, I've got to let you get . . . ah . . .'

'Sleep. Yeah, I'm pretty tired.'

She looks at his eyes again, a smoky aquamarine colour. She realises that she's holding his arm, to steady either herself or him, she's not sure which.

He smiles.

She cocks her head unconsciously, forcing herself to release his arm. 'Well . . . I'd better go,' she says.

'I appreciate your coming by.'

'Thanks for letting me in.' She pulls herself away from his eyes and opens the door, hesitating as she turns. 'See ya. Have a ball up there tomorrow.'

And she's in the hallway, walking with careful dignity to the outer door. There's a bench just outside and she sits on it for a moment, wondering what just happened. That moment of eye contact had transmitted something between them, something exhilarating, and she gets back to her feet with a smile she can't completely explain, wholly unaware that she's left behind a deeply confused male, who's also smiling inexplicably.

2

Mojave International Aerospace Port, Mojave, California
May 17, 6.40 a.m. Pacific Time

Kip knows it isn't so, but the interior of the spaceship named *Intrepid* appears to have shrunk. He sat in this very seat just last week in the hangar, with Anna Altavilla on his left and Tommy Altavilla and Tariq in the back row. He didn't think that on the day of his actual flight it was going to feel like being crammed into an oil drum with windows.

Can this thing really fly? He's having serious doubts. It seems as flimsy as a toy, moving in all directions at once whenever either of them moves an arm.

He tries scooting his rear around in the seat he's been strapped to, but real sideways movement is all but impossible, and with Bill Campbell—his pilot/astronaut companion—already belted into the command seat in front of him, Kip can barely even lean forward.

The other three seats are gone, removed to reduce weight, which should make it look roomier but doesn't. He can smell plastic and cleaning chemicals and the evaporating remnants of his own cologne.

He looks to the right, checking his window alignment, aware that his eyes are squarely in the middle of the small, thick sandwich of glass and plastic that will have to protect him from the vacuum of space and the incredible speeds at the peak of their flight. He feels determined to see it through, despite the gut-level scream from his body and mind that no way could any human survive space flight in such a tiny, flimsy, *puny* craft.

But Bill Campbell has logged thirty-nine successful missions, he reminds himself. That means no unsuccessful ones. Yet.

'So how're you doing, Kip?' Bill is asking, grinning as he glances over his right shoulder at his only passenger.

'Just fine.'

'Yeah, right. You look green around the gills. Relax.'

'No, no! I'm . . . fine. Really.'

'It feels like a science fair project when you first strap in, doesn't it?'

'It just seemed bigger and more substantial the other day in the hangar.'

'It was. Something happened on orbit and it came back like this.'

For a few embarrassing seconds Kip is actually processing the statement. He catches on and winces. 'Oh, jeez, OK.'

'You'll be fine. This is an amazingly good piece of engineering. Best I've ever flown. Say, Kip. Did you tell me back in class you were a licensed pilot?'

Kip laughs at the aeronautical gulf between them. 'No, unfortunately. I've taken glider lessons and soloed, so I know basic stick and rudder, but I never quite got time to finish my licence.'

'Just wondered how much to explain and that tells me. Relax for a few, or you might even want to take a brief nap. I just heard Mission Control say we're delayed fifteen minutes.'

'A problem?'

'Yeah, one of the mothership pilots forgot his lunch.'

'Another joke?'

'Yes, Kip,' Campbell chuckles. 'Boy, you need to get loose, buddy. It's all OK. They just need a bit more fuelling time.'

As Campbell returns to his preflight duties, Kip lets himself think back through two weeks of ground school, wondering what he's already forgotten.

It was amazing how efficient the ASA ground school was in prepping people like Kip. American Space Adventures had accomplished the impossible in less than five years, they were told, and they had no intention of being shy about telling their story.

The company's chief astronaut, George Andrews, opened the first day. America's Space Prize, he explained, was created after the first private suborbital flight won the $10 million Ansari X Prize in 2004. Pioneering aerospace designer Burt Rutan had teamed with Microsoft billionaire Paul Allen to pull it off, using an air-launched craft called *SpaceShipOne*, built by Rutan's company Scaled Composites, and carried aloft by a mothership from the same Mojave airport. Once it had sunk in that private space flight was a fledgling reality, another, larger prize was announced. Bigelow Aerospace—a start-up company with big dreams to operate inflatable space stations as hotels—would need a way to get customers to and from their orbiting hotels. To win their $50 million prize, a privately funded company had no more than five and a half years to figure out how to build, with no government money, a private spacecraft that could fly at least five people into a 250-mile-high altitude for a minimum of two orbits, and do it a second time within thirty days.

ASA won the prize nearly a year ahead of schedule with a winged, double-tailed craft that looked like an overfed version of *SpaceShipOne,* and within six months were in full commercial operation.

'Our machine is a bit of a miracle,' Andrews told them. 'We couldn't just fire it up to sixty-five miles and let it glide back to Earth like Burt Rutan did with *SpaceShipOne.* We had to figure out how to carry enough fuel to get it to at least two hundred and fifty miles up, *then* accelerate it to seventeen thousand miles per hour orbital velocity, *then* lose all that build-up of energy without constructing a battleship of heat tiles like NASA's shuttle or running the risk of incinerating ourselves like *Columbia* if something went wrong. And we had to build in enough life-support and back-up systems for staying in space long enough to dock with one of Bigelow's orbiting hotels.'

The key, they discovered, was to air-drop the ship from a Lockheed 1011 jumbo jet, then use a very large load of rocket propellant to blast up to speed and altitude, and the same propellant to blast back to zero velocity before descending.

'That meant we needed a far more efficient fuel system and a lot of fuel, and thanks to thinking way, way out of any known box, we did it.'

'How about the dangers of all that fuel?' one of the class asked.

Andrews laughed. 'Nowhere near as scary as sitting on top of a virtual bomb, which is what the space shuttle does on every launch. I mean, is it risky? Of course. This isn't an airline flight. That's why we've got a half-day of release forms and informed-consent instruments our lawyers require you to sign. But don't forget, I—or one of our other astronauts—will be up there, too, and, just like you, we all have families to come back to.'

Some of us do, Kip remembers thinking sadly.

'OK, Kip. We're starting the checklists now,' Bill Campbell says, pulling Kip back to the present.

There is a point, Bill has already explained to him, when a professional pilot submerges a large part of his conscious will into his procedures and checklists. Kip watches that moment arrive, as Campbell runs through the complicated predeparture checks without a flicker of emotion.

Kip, however, is the wide-eyed amateur. For him, every motion, every noise, every radioed response between Mission Control and Campbell is just below the threshold of startling.

One of the pilots in the mothership has triggered his radio. '*Intrepid*, *Deliverance.* Comm check all channels and lock.'

Deliverance is the name of the highly modified Lockheed 1011 that engulfs them, the carrier aircraft from which they will hang until the four mechanical releases are triggered open at 60,000 feet.

'Roger, *Deliverance*. Checks in progress, showing nominal and green all channels. Telemetry initiation confirmed, all checks cycled and complete.'

'Roger.'

Kip has his own headset, and his microphone is set up so that when he speaks Bill can hear him—as can the support technicians on the ground. But he dearly wants to remain quiet, not wishing to interfere in any way with Bill's sequence or run any risks of helping something go wrong.

The checks are suddenly over, and he hears the sound of *Deliverance*'s huge high-bypass jet engines starting up.

It's amazing, Kip thinks, how fast this kind of private space flight has become so reliable and so routine. Crank the engines, fly to altitude, drop *Intrepid*, which does its thing at 310 nautical miles above the Earth, then comes home after making $2 million. Clockwork.

He feels the 1011 start taxiing. *Intrepid* is suddenly bobbling back and forth on its four attachment points. He looks out of the side window and back behind them, seeing enormous tyres rolling slowly.

Bill switches the air-traffic controller channels into Kip's headset.

'*Deliverance*, Mojave Tower. You are cleared for takeoff Runway Three-Zero. Winds are two nine zero at six, gusting twelve.'

So now it really begins! Kip thinks, still not believing where he is.

'Roger. *Deliverance* is cleared for takeoff, and we're rolling.'

Reluctantly, it seems, the aircraft–spacecraft combination rolls down the runway, gaining speed slowly, every bump and uneven section of the concrete surface magnified by the time it's transmitted through the attachment points to *Intrepid*. Kip feels his eyeballs wobbling with each jolt.

They work their way steadily up to 160 knots, then *Deliverance*'s captain eases back on the yoke, and the huge Lockheed wings cant up into the wind, producing, at last, more lift than there is weight to be lifted.

Suddenly, they are airborne, the washboard bouncing and yawing gone, the craft swaying gently on its attachment points as the ground drops away.

The spacecraft lurches as the landing gear retracts, then thuds into place somewhere behind them, and the gear doors close. The pilots are reducing the engine power now, setting up for a forty-minute climb to altitude.

Bill Campbell turns around to check on his passenger. 'Still with me?'

'You bet.'

'OK, not much to do for the next half-hour now as we gain altitude. But once we're dropped, things are going to happen fast and heavy.'

Kip nods and gives him a thumbs-up, but Bill continues.

'*Deliverance* will stabilise our flight level four-three-zero—forty-three thousand feet—and turn onto the launch heading. We'll get final clearance from Mission Control, and *Deliverance* will light her booster rockets and pull up to a twenty-two-degree climb angle. She'll push over at flight level six-one-zero as the rockets burn out, and she'll hold there for just long enough to drop us. You saw those guys get aboard in pressure suits, right?'

'Yes, I did.'

'That's because we can't pressurise a huge 1011 safely enough to guarantee they won't have their bodies exposed to blood-boiling pressure altitudes. As we taught you in class, we don't need to wear space suits inside *Intrepid* since this capsule is triple-redundant and self-sealing.'

'But you've got yours aboard, right?'

'Sure. It's compressed flat and stored, in case some impossible event means I need to float outside and repair something. But don't worry, it's aboard.'

'Good.'

'Where was I? Oh yeah. We'll confirm our clearance as we're dropping away, light our motor and we're off.'

'Hey, Bill,' Kip ventures. 'Is it really routine for you? This sequence?'

The curtain of professionalism parts for just a second as a large smile covers the man's face. 'It's Christmas morning every time, Kip. My dream comes true every launch.'

Kip nods as Bill turns back to the panel. 'I'm glad to hear that. I don't think I'd want to fly with someone who wasn't as excited as I am.'

The half-hour evaporates and Kip hears Bill once again running through a checklist, the same basic countdown he listened to from Cape Canaveral on so many launches.

'Two, one, ignition.'

The pilot's voice from the 1011's flight deck is utterly unemotional. 'Thrust nominal, commencing pitch-up and countdown.'

More numbers counting backwards. More lighted numerals and readouts changing on the liquid-crystal displays in front of Bill Campbell. Kip struggles to keep his eyes on what he knows is the altimeter, one of the few displays he can read. It shows them now climbing through 50,000 feet. He thinks the attitude indicator is showing a pitch-up of twenty-two degrees, but it feels like forty. *Intrepid* is shaking back and forth and sideways and he wonders if there's any way the real launch will feel as startling.

'Release minus two minutes, mark.'

There's a host of voices in his ears making sure everyone and everything is ready, their calm almost unnerving. Then there are thirty seconds left and the big aircraft is pushing its nose down to level as it slows, the altitude topping out at 61,000 feet, where the 1011 was never designed to be. Kip knows about the tiny window of time to launch. If something hiccups, they have no more than twelve seconds to fix it before scrubbing the launch.

He almost misses it, the call is so routine. The drop clearance—his clearance to fly to space—is issued from Mission Control, the count now less than ten seconds. Kip finds himself mouthing the descending numbers.

'Hang on, old buddy,' Bill says. 'It's about to get interesting.'

'Three, two, one, release.'

Kip thinks he's feeling time dilate. Nothing seems to be happening.

Wait, nothing *is* happening! They're still attached!

He looks at Bill, who is busy triggering his transmitter.

'We have negative release, *Deliverance.* Select prime back-up and confirm.'

'Shit!' is the singular response from above, as another voice intones 'Eight seconds in the window.'

'Primary back-up selected. Counting two, one, release.'

Something shoves them around, or so Kip thinks, but they're still merely a mechanical appendage of the 1011.

'Selecting secondary,' one of the pilots says, a trace of stress in his voice.

'Three seconds to abort,' another intones.

'Pressurising.'

'Two, one, release, dammit!'

This time the whole world changes. With whooshing sounds, a pneumatic back-up system forces the jaws of the four primary hooks open in slightly staggered fashion. In an instant, Kip's stomach has declared itself in free fall. His fingers dig a death grip into the armrests of his seat as he watches Campbell's right hand holding the primary ignition control.

'*Intrepid* away,' Campbell says.

'*Deliverance* in pitch mode,' is the response, the 1011 sharply turning and slowing to get out of the way.

Aren't we going to ignite our engine? Kip's mind is screaming.

'Cleared for ignition,' says someone somewhere on the ground, and suddenly ignite is exactly what the rocket does—the engine kicking the living hell out of his back as Kip hangs on and wonders how Bill Campbell can even react, let alone casually look up and back as he checks his controls.

'Ignition confirmed.'

'Cleared to climb, *Intrepid.* Godspeed.'

'Roger.'

They're being propelled forward with incredible force and speed, and suddenly they're also pitching up, on their own.

Soon they're almost vertical. Kip can see the little black dot in the attitude indicator coming into the centre of Bill's target, and while he knows it's only three-and-a-half g's he's feeling, it seems infinite.

Nothing in the ride up on the 1011 even remotely prepared him for the shuddering and bouncing of the little craft as it streaks straight up.

'Passing Mach 2, one hundred thousand feet.'

'Copy,' says the voice on the ground.

Mach 2, Kip thinks. *That's . . . about twelve hundred miles per hour!*

He can feel his heart racing, almost pounding out of his chest, his head locked forward by the ground-school caution that if he turns his head to look out of the window, he'll never be able to turn it back.

But in his peripheral vision, he can already see the Earth's curvature.

'My . . . God!' is all he can manage as he moves his eyes as far right as possible to take in the sight.

'So far,' Bill explains, 'I've been flying the controls like a plane. When we get higher, we'll have only the reaction-control jets to keep us pointed in the right direction. OK, passing one hundred and fifty thousand feet, and Mach 3.'

Kip knows that's about as fast as they're going to go before pitchover, before they're so far above the denser air molecules of the atmosphere that increasing speed won't cause frictional heating problems.

'Two hundred thousand feet, Mach 3.2,' Bill intones, adding a postscript. 'We're technically not in space yet, Kip.'

It sure looks like space to me, Kip thinks, keeping his eyes on the horizon as the g-forces decrease. He wants to yell, 'Whee-oooh!', but it would be undignified and might startle the pilot. Not a good idea, he decides.

The Earth's surface curves away like a huge ball now, even though they are just passing the so-called threshold of space, around sixty-five miles. The steady force in his back begins to lessen as Bill pulls the throttle to half thrust, using the ship's immense momentum in the absence of most air resistance to partially coast, partially thrust, up to the 300-mile point.

Five minutes go by slowly, but on the other end of it Kip feels Bill pushing the craft over, using the control jets now, throttling up as soon as he hits the right attitude, the g-forces reasserting themselves as the nose continues to drop slowly in relation to the horizon.

'Now the speeds get really industrial strength,' Bill is saying. They pass through 4,000 miles per hour, then 6,000, then 8,000 and 10,000, the digits incredibly difficult to accept. Faster than a speeding bullet. Far faster.

The gravity he feels now isn't gravity at all, but the acceleration of the engine as it thrusts *Intrepid* through the airless void towards 17,400 miles per hour. His mind replays every *Star Trek* clip he can recall of the Starship *Enterprise* streaking towards the speed of light. This feels like that looked.

'Stand by for a bit of a shock,' Bill calls.

'What? Is there a problem?' Kip's reply is sharp, instantly concerned.

Campbell laughs. 'No, no. It's just time to throw it into neutral.' He pulls the throttle back and cuts the rocket motor, the sudden loss of thrust and acceleration leaving Kip feeling like he's falling again, but forwards this time.

'We're weightless,' Bill announces. 'And congratulations, man.' He's reaching back now to shake Kip's hand. 'You have officially arrived on orbit above our planet.'

'We're here?' Kip turns to stare out of his side window.

'We sure are. We're almost welded up here in an orbit so stable it might not decay for maybe sixty years, give or take a few sunspots.'

Kip falls into awed silence, his hands still death-gripping the armrests, his stomach still confused about which way is up. At long last he lets himself breathe. *Sixty years,* he thinks, missing the reference to the sunspots.

It takes a few seconds for Kip to find his voice. 'For this moment at least,' he says, 'I feel like the luckiest guy in the world.'

Washington, DC
May 17, 8 a.m. Pacific Time/11 a.m. Eastern Time

Geoff Shear, the administrator of the National Aeronautics and Space Administration, sits in the back seat of his chauffeured government car, which is taking him back to NASA Headquarters from the Hart Senate Office Building. In a hearing room there, minutes earlier, he told the Senate

Subcommittee on Space that he was not going to stop turning to the media to complain about Congress every time it cuts down the space programme.

Shear loves being the head of NASA, but he hates like hell having to deal with the worst of the hypocrites on the Hill—senators and congressmen who convince the public that they support the space programme while behind closed doors try to emasculate it.

Still, he wonders how much longer he can continue presenting mediocre NASA programmes as grand 'accomplishments'. He can't be the only one who sees that the world's preeminent space agency is dying. NASA's record over the past decade is wimpy at best: no return to the moon, a man-in-a-can excuse for an international space station that is still an expensive façade, the space shuttle replacement programme in deep and probably terminal trouble, and a growing, dangerous feeling on the part of the American public that private corporations can do space better and cheaper than the government.

And then there's Richard DiFazio's ASA and DiFazio's personal campaign to undermine NASA at every turn. The fact that DiFazio is probably right about privatising space is immaterial. It's Shear's mission to keep NASA funded, alive and relevant in the public eye, regardless. But there are times he wishes the job of NASA administrator brought with it a licence to kill. No question who'd be first on his list. In too many ways, winning the private versus public battle has become his personal war.

Shear pulls out a sheaf of briefing papers he has yet to study, recognising the top one immediately as the one thing he does not want to see.

He's known for weeks that if *Newsweek* decides to disregard the warnings from NASA's friends and run a particularly hated article as a cover piece, the damage will be cruel. And here it is, as bad as he expected.

CAN NASA COMPETE WITH PRIVATE SPACE FLIGHT COMPANIES?

He scans the four pages of verbiage, then sits and thinks in silence. And what he's thinking is disturbing. The whole nightmarish subject is out of his control, but there it is, still in his head, the same image that dawned like a revelation while he was fly-fishing in Colorado just two weeks ago.

What if, he'd thought then, *one of their slapped-together, back-yard, two-bit excuses for a spacecraft goes down?* What if American Space Adventures —what a stupid name for a supposedly professional organisation—has an accident and loses one of their only two pretend-a-shuttles? The world would have graphic confirmation that the extreme dangers of space flight simply *must* be left to the might and wisdom of the US government.

Standing in the middle of that peaceful stream, he'd let an attack of conscience bring him up short, a moment of uncertainty, the horror of someone actually learning his terrible thoughts. My God, of *course* he didn't really want anyone to die just to convince Congress to fund NASA!

But he had no control over a private spacecraft. If one goes down, he'll need to be ready, he'll need the right things to say, with the right statistics to cite. Maybe he should even recommend that Congress put stringent restrictions on anyone but NASA attempting space flight?

No. That would anger the President. The White House is too committed to the free market. If the worst happens, Geoff concludes, as his headquarters slides into view, NASA will simply be there in sorrow to sympathise, and then soldier on for all mankind.

310 miles above the Atlantic Ocean
May 17, 8.32 a.m. Pacific Time

A sharp, almost metallic *plink* echoes through the interior of the spacecraft.

Kip doesn't want to tear himself away from the view through his window, but the sound is too loud to ignore, and he feels a pressure fluctuation in the cabin. He begins to turn his head forward, realising at the same moment that something wet has sprayed the back of his neck.

'Bill, what was that?'

Campbell is facing forward, but not answering. Kip can see the astronaut's headset askew, his hands floating up in front of him.

What on Earth?

'Bill?'

Still no answer. Kip leans towards him. There is a spot, almost like a hole, in the back of the pilot's seat towards the top, and there's a reddish mist floating around in the zero-g atmosphere of the cabin. He feels his stomach twisting up as he looks behind and sees a splatter of red on the aft bulkhead, along with what has to be another hole.

Kip begins clawing at his harness to release it so he can lean forward. The seat harness mechanism gives way and he launches himself too fast, floating over Campbell's right shoulder, twisting like the zero-g amateur he is, his back coming to rest against the instrument panel with a soft thud, his eyes fixating on his companion's blank expression.

Bill's eyes are open wide and fully dilated, and in the middle of his forehead is a small, red-tinged hole.

'Oh, *God!*' Kip gasps as he claws for something to hold on to, aware he may be kicking dangerously sensitive controls. He grabs hold of something with his left hand and shakes Bill with his right, praying for a response.

But there is none. The astronaut looks gone, a lot of blood leaking from the exit wound in the back of his head. He's beyond hope. What Kip felt on the back of his own neck is apparently Bill's blood.

Kip feels himself recoil in pure panic, as if he's preparing to run.

Oh my God! Oh God! What happened?

He already knows the answer. Something—a tiny space rock, a piece of space junk—smashed into and through *Intrepid* at an incredibly high speed and passed like a bullet through Bill's cranium, killing him instantly.

Keeping a small hit from exploding the craft or leaking out all the air was, they were told in training, a major engineering challenge. That was the very reason the spacecraft was built with self-sealing walls. But he never took the threat seriously. No one has ever been killed by a space rock, especially not inside a warm capsule. Have they? What are the chances?

Kip floats himself back towards his seat, shaking with confusion.

This simply can't be happening!

He grabs the mouthpiece on his headset and begins calling for help, before recalling that he has to press a button to transmit outside the spacecraft. He scrambles around the side of his armrest and finds it, then calls again.

'Mission Control . . . ah, *Intrepid.* Emergency! Mayday! *Mayday, Mayday, Mayday!* I have a big problem!'

What a pitiful understatement, he thinks, as he waits for the response.

'Mission Control . . . ASA Mojave . . . *somebody* . . . please come in!'

Between checking to make sure he's really pushing the transmit button and boosting the volume control to hear the response that isn't coming, a small lifetime passes.

He looks out of the window, recognising the Arabian desert moving by smartly beneath, realising he's as isolated now as if he were sitting in some trackless sand dune 310 miles below. No, he isn't working the radios wrongly. The radios just aren't working. *So now what?*

The luckiest guy in the world! he recalls thinking, mocking his own words of minutes before. From a lifelong dream to the worst nightmare in record time. The irony is almost funny.

He vaguely remembers something from the two weeks' training. Something about emergencies. About going to the laminated checklist.

Yes! Get the checklist! But which one? He can't recall any checklist labelled IN CASE YOUR ASTRONAUT/PILOT IS KILLED BY A SPACE ROCK!

The checklists and detailed procedures, they'd been taught, are contained in the master computer screen in front of the pilot. But there are physical versions—laminated duplicates—stored in a side compartment and Kip launches his body in that direction, coming in too fast again and thudding into the side wall. He works the latch and yanks out the bound stack of pages, riffling through them far too rapidly, his thoughts near hysterical.

Calm down! he tells himself, the command having little effect. Somewhere in these pages is a solution. He can feel it. But *where?*

He finds procedures for dealing with loss of oxygen pressure, failures of this or that instrument, and flight-control-system problems, and he finally seizes on one dealing with radio failure, ripping the pages back and forth as he tries to focus and deal with the information a step at a time.

No, dammit! Not the right one!

More page turning. He's aware that Saudi Arabia has slipped away and he's approaching the Indian subcontinent, flying over the Persian Gulf. Geography has always been a love, but there's no time now to do anything but take note. Whatever he has to do to get help . . .

For the first time since whatever object it was smashed through his world, Kip stops himself. His hands are still shaking, his heart racing, but his thoughts turn to a very obvious reality. There *is* no help! Even if he gets the radios working, physically no one can come up here and bring him home, because it's been made very clear that none of the governmental space agencies will lift a finger for a private space adventure.

Even NASA will ignore him.

No, he decides, he knows what he's got to look for now. If he can't re-establish contact with the ground, then it's up to him to do the same things Bill would do—throw the same switches he would throw—drop them out of orbit at the appointed time. And there has to be at least *some* time to figure it out. They haven't even completed one orbit. They were supposed to come down after four orbits. A bit less than six hours from now.

He's breathing so rapidly that he wonders if he'll deplete all the oxygen.

But Bill isn't breathing at all any more, so he's got double whatever they'd have had together. In any event there should be enough for six hours.

Also, he thinks, the electrical circuits are still on. The panel's still functioning. Lights and a heater are keeping him warm.

He looks forward, searching for the point of entry, and finds it at last, just below the command window frame. Whatever it was blew out through the back wall and into the equipment bay behind them, where it either stopped or left the spacecraft. And the automatic layer of sticky sealant has obviously worked. He can hear no hissing, no obvious loss of air pressure.

He worries for a moment about any other unseen, undetected damage back there, where the engine and fuel tanks are located. But if there was damage to the fuel, wouldn't he be dead now? Wouldn't there at least be flashing red alerts all over the liquid-crystal displays? They show nothing. He finds the fuel status indicators and manages to read that, as predicted, half the fuel remains and is safe a few feet behind him.

Once again he starts pawing through the checklists, selecting the ones on communication failure and reading carefully down each category, checking circuit breakers when he can find them and changing settings, each time expecting to hear the comforting voice of the controller back in Mojave.

But the headset remains silent.

He's ignoring the floating remnants of Bill's blood that he hasn't been able to mop up with tissues—just as he's forcing himself not to think about having to cover the astronaut's leaking head with a thin silver Mylar blanket before pulling his body out of the command chair. What was Bill Campbell is now a macabre hooded form tied to the back wall of the small cabin while the capsule's only living occupant sits in front of the panel searching desperately for a way to talk to the planet below.

And with Sri Lanka and the east coast of India sliding by beneath him, Kip finally exhales and sits back in the assaulted command chair, letting the checklists float in front of him as he struggles through the cobwebs of his panic and pulls the last curtain of denial aside.

Dear God, I am alone up here. And I've got five hours to learn how to get myself back.

ASA Mission Control, Mojave International Aerospace Port, Mojave, California
May 17, 8.53 a.m. Pacific Time

The whine of jet engines filters into the stunned silence of the sound-insulated control room. Outside on the ramp, the Lockheed 1011 named *Deliverance* is returning to her parking spot. Video and audio feeds carry what's happening inside the room, but the TV images are going only to the Internet and a bank of digital recorders, since no news organisations have requested them. With few exceptions, the world is neither watching nor listening.

Here, the response to what at first seemed a momentary communications glitch has become disordered, adrift, the assembled professionals milling around like a troop of actors who've run off the end of their script. They stand and look back and forth, consulting their monitors and each other for answers to questions they're having trouble even phrasing. Ultimately, all eyes migrate to one man.

Arleigh Kerr stands at the flight director's console, searching the faces of the eighteen men and women arrayed before him. A veteran of the same sort of control room at NASA in Houston, his angular features are well known in space-flight circles. Kerr is working hard now to find a way to stay the calm leader, the man with the answers.

Intrepid achieved exactly the orbit planned for it, and they all know exactly where the ship is at the moment. What they don't know is why virtually every communications circuit in the ship has failed simultaneously.

It's like someone yanked a plug from the wall up there, Kerr thinks to himself, embarrassed at the simplicity of the simile.

'Arleigh, we're cued up on the rerun of the last thirty seconds of telemetry,' one of his engineers is saying in his ear. 'Watch parameters forty-eight and ninety-six. I've highlighted them. Forty-eight is capsule atmospheric pressure. Ninety-six is internal structure vibration monitor.'

The graphed lines crawl across the screen in front of him in routine manner until one second before the communication link ends.

'See that? Pressure drop at the same moment we've got a loud vibration.'

'I see it,' he says. 'But what does it mean?'

'We think we may have lost a pressure seal. Explosively. Pressure drop, vibration—probably a loud noise—then nothing.'

'But why no radios? Why no telemetry?' Kerr asks. 'Even if we've lost Bill and his passenger, they don't need to be . . . alive . . . for the telemetry to keep working.'

'The other possibility, Arleigh, is that we collided with something.'

The thought has haunted him.

'Collided with *what*? We did all the usual NORAD checks before launch and we're online for any space junk updates. There's nothing out there.'

'That they know about,' the engineer corrects.

Feeling defeated, Kerr turns to Ian McIver, another NASA veteran. 'See if you can get one of NASA's high-powered cameras to look at him during the Australian transit. Let's see if we can confirm *Intrepid* is intact.'

'Arleigh, you *are* going to bring in Mr DiFazio, aren't you?'

Kerr nods, the act of alerting the company's chairman a painful call he made less than ten minutes ago. 'He's out of bed and on the way.'

No point in discussing *Intrepid*'s inability to take itself out of orbit automatically. From the first they've taught their passengers in ground school how to do the deorbiting job themselves in the event an astronaut dies, but it was complicated and never supposed to be necessary, since all the commands can be sent by remote and *Intrepid* can even be flown down to a safe landing remotely. That was their ace in the hole, but it depended on the communications links working. The idea that they could all go down at once is one nightmare they'd never fully faced.

Kerr picks up the phone and punches in the cell number of ASA's chairman and CEO, who is racing north from Lancaster in his car.

'Any change, Arleigh?' Richard DiFazio asks.

'No, sir. We have zero communication, no ability to remote-control, and no knowledge of whether either of our two people up there is even alive.'

'Keep the lid on this. I'm ten minutes out.'

'We do need to ask NASA for help. I . . . already gave the order to do so.'

'Oh, God! That will go straight to Geoff Shear.'

'Sir . . .'

'I know, I know. It's OK. Do what you have to do.'

NASA HQ, Washington, DC
May 17, 9.10 a.m. Pacific Time/12.10 p.m. Eastern Time

When the administrator of NASA calls an emergency meeting of his senior staff with outlying members suddenly yanked from their offices and piped in by videoconference, the entire neural network of NASA begins to vibrate.

That pleases Geoff Shear.

He enters the conference room next to his office and sits surveying the faces around the table and those on screen from Houston and the Cape.

'So ASA wants us to look at their spacecraft,' he begins. 'Why? Are they in trouble?' Shear is working to keep his expression serious and concerned.

One of the managers at Johnson Space Center in Houston answers. 'Yes, sir. They've lost all their communications.'

'Have we visually looked at them?'

Heads nod and there's a sudden switch on one of the screens to a video of the spacecraft in flight, a fuzzy, indistinct image shot with an incredibly long lens from a ground station in Western Australia.

Shear leans forward. 'So what am I seeing?' he asks.

'The craft appears intact. Most likely she's still pressurised and survivable. We don't see any visible damage, but . . . there's this.'

'Who's speaking?'

'Ed Rogers from Houston.'

The picture changes to what appears to be a digital radar display.

'This is from NORAD's array, just after ASA's ship reached orbit. I'm going to go frame by frame here, because we have just two radar hits on what appears to be a very small object approaching very, very rapidly from in front of the craft, then one single radar hit of it on the back side, in a slightly different trajectory. At the same point, on the visual image, there's a small burst of light that might indicate ejected debris aft of the capsule. We think they got nailed by something NORAD wasn't tracking.'

'And that's where the radios went?'

'Sir, it apparently passed through the equipment bay of their ship, and God knows what damage it did, but knocking out virtually all their communications and their propulsion, control and, eventually, even life support would not be an outlandish expectation.'

'Geoff, John Kent in Houston.' The voice of NASA's chief astronaut, a former Air Force colonel, is not a welcome intrusion.

'Yeah, John.'

'We have *Endeavour* in the vehicle-assembly building at the Cape and I can work up an emergency mission plan within an hour if you'd like.'

'Why, John?'

'If someone's alive up there, we can't just sit on our hands, can we?'

Geoff gets to his feet, his well-honed ability to put subordinates in their place virtually second nature. 'Thanks, everyone,' he says on the way out of the room, answering the question by default. Besides, he thinks darkly, Kent knows damn well what the policy is on rescuing privateers in space.

Aboard *Intrepid*
May 17, 9.16 a.m. Pacific Time

So Sharon was right after all.

Kip thinks of little else. The idea that he might somehow remember how to blast himself back out of orbit and find a way to land seems beyond hopeless. He looks at the pile of checklists in his lap, having read over several trying to get a mental image of the long litany of technical duties that he'll have to perform at the right moment in the right way to direct the rocket motor in precisely the right direction to lose all that speed they gained.

He sighs, shaking his head at the image of himself getting tangled up in what switch to hit next. Even if, somehow, he gets it all right and everything works, he'll then pop out in the lower troposphere and have an on-the-job learning experience trying to dead-stick an engineless spacecraft down to a runway somewhere without colliding with something hard and unforgiving.

No, Sharon is going to be right, he decides. *Most likely I'm going to die.*

He looks at his watch, then at the Earthscape passing below. He's in darkness now somewhere over the Pacific.

Wait a minute, dammit! he thinks, responding to a small wave of anger that punches at him. *What am I doing? Giving up without a fight?*

He takes a deep, if ragged, breath and forces himself to sit up.

OK, so what do we do first?

He starts through the checklists of steps again, determined this time to figure out and practise exactly what needs to be done.

He decides to try the retrofire sequence at the end of the second orbit. *So what if it's hard? I have to try.*

The reward is survival. Possible survival.

After all, he reasons, *they wouldn't have taught this stuff in ground school back in Mojave if they didn't think a passenger could handle it.*

The first sequence will be to turn the ship round, pointing the engine nozzles in the direction he's travelling. There may be an automatic system to do just that, he figures, since it's referenced in the verbiage of the checklist. But then how to initiate the manoeuvre on the panel? He imagines he may also have to use the control stick, the fighter-pilot-style, video-game-type hand control mounted on the right edge of the armrest.

He stares harder at the forward panel, determined to find the appropriate switches and learn how to use them, and slowly, very slowly, some of the nomenclature begins to make sense.

Johnson Space Center, Houston, Texas
May 17, 9.40 a.m. Pacific Time/11.40 a.m. Central Time

John Kent sits at his desk and rubs his closed eyes, wondering what else he can say to the wife of his longtime buddy Bill Campbell.

'Katie, it is entirely possible that Bill's OK and working hard to get them down, and just hasn't been able to cure the communications blackout.'

'I know,' is the barely controlled response from the Campbell home somewhere near Lancaster, California. 'I've always known the risks.'

'Look . . . I've got all our people monitoring everything, and I'm . . . do not repeat this, OK? . . . but I'm working on a rescue plan if, for some reason, we need to go up there and bring them back.'

The silence is long and telling. Katie Campbell knows well her husband's heartburn over NASA's official position regarding private space flight. And she knows John Kent doesn't run NASA.

'Thanks, John.'

'You hang in there and have faith.'

The call ends and he lunges from his chair, swinging open his office door and sticking his head into the outer office where a half-dozen other astronauts and engineers are waiting.

'Everybody come on in here. None of this leaves this room, but we've got to plan a rescue, just in case.'

3

Aboard *Intrepid*
May 17, 9.56 a.m. Pacific Time

There is a magnificent planet to admire just outside his window, and Kip forces himself to look up and take note of it. He remembers standing beneath the star field last night, wishing he was up here. Now he wishes he was back on that deserted road looking up.

But whatever happens, he made it to space, and saw its incredible beauty. *In other words*, he thinks, *it is worth it, whatever happens.*

He brings his eyes back to the checklist. *Intrepid* is programmed to fly automatically, and was set to keep its length parallel to the planet below, the nose in the direction of flight. He's read the messages on the computer screen to make sure that it's all working as advertised.

According to the checklists, just prior to firing the engine to slow down, the astronaut is supposed to feed the computer a new set of coordinates, three numbers that Kip has already written down. When those numbers are safely locked in the tiny silicon brain, the machine will automatically fire the reaction jets in just the right sequence to turn their tail end around almost 180 degrees and get the ship in the correct position to fire the engine backwards.

Kip looks at his watch. Thirty minutes to the turnaround manoeuvre, which he's decided to do during the second orbit. If *Intrepid* was programmed to turn itself automatically on the fourth orbit, he wouldn't be messing with it. But—if he's read everything correctly—the commands have to be manually typed in or the ship will never turn around. And only if the rocket motor is firing almost precisely against the direction of flight will they be able to slow down and essentially drop out of the sky.

He feels momentarily frozen. Part of him wants to stay for the full four orbits, but another part clamours to know whether or not he's going to survive this. *Maybe we should do it now*, he thinks. *After all, the automatic system can hold us in that backward position for a half-hour as easily as it can keep us flying forwards.*

He realises that he keeps using the pronouns 'us' and 'we' in every thought of what he should do and what's happening. Bill is dead. No other living being is aboard, yet he can't bring himself to shift to 'I' and 'me'.

Not yet.

His hand hovers over the small keyboard and he pulls back, deciding to wait for the right moment. Twenty-nine more minutes. He can do that.

He takes a deep breath, the first in perhaps the past hour. The air tastes a bit stale and processed. He thinks about the class ASA gave on the oxygen system and how the ingenious little devices behind him scrub the air of carbon dioxide, adding small amounts of oxygen as necessary to maintain the right balance. And he remembers someone saying the system can keep five people going for thirty hours before the CO_2 scrubbers become saturated and fail. With one person, he guesses, that means much longer. Still, the sooner he gets the hell out of this hostile environment, the better.

His left ear itches and he reaches up, surprised to encounter the earpiece from his headset, still inserted in his ear. He takes the whole apparatus off and scratches his ear liberally. That's what's been missing, he thinks. Other than Bill's companionship and guidance. All the way up he had a host of other voices in his ear, and now they're gone and it feels, well, lonely.

All that beauty just outside the canopy bubble and side windows and who can he tell? Not that most people haven't seen hundreds of spectacular pictures from space, but this is what *his* eyes are seeing, and it feels barren. A reporter without a paper. A TV correspondent without a mike.

He wishes he could show Jerrod what he's seeing, or at least describe it. Even Carly and Carrie, their little blonde heads bouncing with smiles and giggles, would love his word pictures, as would Julie—even with her eye-rolling teenage sophistication.

Funny, he thinks, how running back to them excitedly with some new experience, even as a salesman, was always a joy. It's as if his delight in pretty sunsets, a fun movie, a wild thunderstorm glimpsed across a purple desert, none of it became enjoyable until he could make it come alive for *them*. He was the camera for his family, the collector of vicarious joys.

And he realises with a start that he really doesn't know how to just drink it in for himself. That feels sad. Especially now, when 'himself' is all he has.

I should take some notes on this, Kip thinks, wondering why they never discussed a notepad. There are a few sheets of notepaper in the side pocket of his flight suit by his ankle, but he'd really like a big, thick notebook.

His eyes follow the curvature of the forward panel to one side, where a small laptop computer nestles in a rack. He'd completely forgotten about that. A back-up, Bill had explained, for the main computer and keyboard. It's connected to the Internet and he'd been told, along with the others, that they would be able to email their families from orbit if they wanted to. But surely now the computer connection will be useless.

He unclips the laptop and opens it, surprised to find a common-or-garden Dell, which spins into life just like millions of its counterparts below. He waits until the desktop screen is stable, then clicks on the Internet Explorer icon, not unsurprised when it comes up showing no connection.

He looks around, well aware there's nothing more to be done until it's time to fire the main engine to leave orbit. His eyes return to the laptop, and he feels the urge to communicate, even if it's only with a hard drive.

The little machine is powered by *Intrepid*'s circuits, not just its own battery, and there is a word-processor program loaded, all of which means he can use it as a notepad. He positions the laptop in the middle of his lap and feels it promptly float up and away from him.

He looks around, letting his brain work on the weightlessness problem until the long Velcro straps in a side compartment come to mind. He rummages around and pulls out one long enough to cinch the laptop to his lap.

Feeling almost clever, he brings up the Word program and sits for a few seconds trying to figure out a message that's suddenly appeared asking if he wants to authorise a continuous download feed.

Download what? He shrugs, aware that it doesn't make any difference anyway, since nothing he types will leave the hard drive.

OK, so I click on the 'yes' box and make it go away.

The dialogue box disappears and he opens a blank page and starts to type, stalling almost immediately.

Log entry—middle of Orbit Two.

Log entry? He chides himself. *What am I, Captain Kirk? Maybe a more personal approach. A glimpse of humanity.*

I have less than twenty minutes before trying to turn the ship around, and I'm scared to death.

Yeah, that's more like it. But I need some description if this is going to be for the kids.

The view outside is amazing, and if I wasn't so anxious to be sure I can get home, I'd want to stay as long as the oxygen lasts. It's hard to describe, Jerrod, Julie, Carly and Carrie, how deep black the background of space is and how magnificent the Earth is as it revolves below me. All those pictures we've watched from orbit can't really prepare you for what it's like in person. Worth a lifetime! Of course, I'm going to make it back to tell you all this in person, but I thought you might like to 'hear' about it in words as it's happening. Your dad in space!

He sits back and rereads, taking care to save the page before checking his watch and continuing. Five more minutes. But this feels good, and someday they'll love it. Or maybe his grandkids will.

ASA Mission Control, Mojave, California
May 17, 10.05 a.m. Pacific Time

Arleigh Kerr stands at the end of the small table in the conference room of Mission Control, a freshly emptied bottle of water in his hand. His gaze is fixed on his boss. There are only the two of them in the room.

'We need to get *Venture* ready to go up,' DiFazio is saying, referring to the only other spacecraft ASA has, the ship now sitting with a damaged landing gear in one of the hangars. 'If I have to send her up in less than perfect shape to get them back, I'll do it. No one else is going to help us.'

'Richard, I'm sorry to tell you, but we have no rescue capability. *Venture* is down for a month or more.'

'What?' DiFazio is almost out of his chair, his bushy eyebrows knitting together in a combination of pain and alarm. 'A *month*?'

Kerr's sigh is heartfelt. 'I just got the word from our maintenance chief. The right wing spar is cracked in addition to the gear problem. If we try to fly her, we could lose her going up or coming down. Complete wing loss.'

'Can't we rush the repair?'

'You're the composites expert, Richard. With cure times, they tell me, the best they could do is ten days. Something about rebonding that spar.'

'Oh my God! Without *Venture*, we can't even . . . we *couldn't* even keep to our schedule if this . . .'

'I guess the only good news is that we've only got the one passenger.'

DiFazio is shaking his head in pain. 'So, what options do we have?'

'We don't have a lot, Richard. You know NASA isn't going to help. Some other country? The Russians? The Japanese? I haven't called them. But it would cost more money than our entire capitalisation to buy a *Soyuz* launch from the Russians, for instance, even if they could get one together in time. And that raises another major question. Is anyone even alive up there?'

DiFazio looks staggered. 'We . . . we don't know?'

'We don't know anything, except that the ship is still on orbit and appears to be pressurised. But zero communication, zero telemetry, no indication that *Intrepid* is doing anything more than automatically holding its pitch and roll position, and . . . and, we're just guessing.'

DiFazio is shaking his head again, eyes on the floor. He takes a deep breath before looking up. 'Sorry, Arleigh. I wasn't ready for this, I guess.'

'Hell, neither am I! No one's ever taken even a major nonfatal hit up there before. Why us? Why now?'

'You know this could kill us. I don't mean to discount those two lives, but this could put us out of business.'

'Richard, you know how risky this so-called business is. The forces involved, the explosive power, the number of life-support things that can go wrong. I mean, we're vastly more reliable than the shuttle could ever be, but we've all deluded ourselves.'

'We haven't lost them yet. At least, we don't know, right?'

'True, but a word of warning, OK? I mean, I'm only your flight director, but when this blows into the public eye, we'd better not be heard kvetching about the financial losses.'

'Of course not. I've got Diana inbound right now. We'll put together a quick strategy.'

'It's gonna leak, Richard.'

'I know it.'

'And I don't have a clue what to say or do . . . other than wait and watch. We're trying the radios constantly, but if we see the capsule turn around in position for retrofire, then we know for certain someone's alive up there and following the checklists and we've got a chance.'

'Has someone called Campbell's wife?'

'Yeah, I have. It was brutal. She's tough, but she's scared to death.'

'And . . . our passenger?'

'We're holding off for another hour or so before we call Dawson's wife.'

'Don't wait too long. Don't let her hear it from the media.'

'No. No, we won't.'

'So what *are* you waiting for?'

'The end of Orbit Two. If Bill's alive and functional, I figure he'll want to get the hell out of there as soon as possible. When he passes through the window for second orbit return, that's when I'd expect something to happen.'

'How much longer?'

'Twenty-three minutes from now. At least that's the end of the window. Otherwise, he overshoots California, or worse.'

'But we still have two more orbits before it has to come down, right?'

'They could go longer. We figure they could keep breathing up there for roughly three days, or a bit less, before the CO_2 scrubbers saturate.'

Kerr gets to his feet, leaving DiFazio still seated.

'I'd better get back in there. I've been whipping everybody into a thinking frenzy to see if we've missed anything.'

DiFazio nods, waving him away. He picks up the phone, his eyes on the far wall, then replaces it slowly in its cradle.

Not yet, he thinks. *Not just yet.*

Aboard *Intrepid*
May 17, 10.20 a.m. Pacific Time

It's time.

Kip puts the laptop on standby mode and reinserts it in its holder before gathering the checklists and positioning himself in Bill's seat. A confusing feeling of excitement comes over him, a small rush before the sprint, he figures, his mind relieved finally to be at the threshold of action.

He runs back through the planned steps and reviews the three coordinates he must enter. *Intrepid* has to turn around 180 degrees to fly backwards, and the pitch and roll read-outs on the attitude indicator must be precisely right before he can fire the engine. With care, he punches in the three numbers on the master keyboard and triple-checks that he's got them right. His finger hovers shakily over the EXECUTE button for several seconds, then he forces his finger down, hearing a small click.

The screen changes, registering the fact that the new coordinates have been accepted, and suddenly there's a small box proclaiming that the automatic realignment manoeuvre has begun.

Thank God!

He holds his breath, wondering how it is that the small reaction jets on

Intrepid can be firing so gently that he can't even feel them. It's almost as if nothing is happening, despite the announcement on the screen.

He looks at the attitude indicator, willing it to move, but it's steady. He punches the EXECUTE button again, but still no movement.

OK, I forgot something, he decides. *What did I miss?* He runs back through the checklist. One by one he re-enters the coordinates.

Intrepid continues flying straight ahead. No pitch. No yaw. No roll.

No change.

Kip checks his watch. Eight minutes remain before the time for retrofire. If the automated system won't work, all he has left is the manual control.

But he's clicked the manual control button on that joystick before, in training. And he promptly lost control so badly they had to stop the spinning simulator. All of the instructors and fellow students were laughing when he climbed out, and the follow-up session wasn't much better.

He stares at the joystick. *I'm not touching that!* he thinks. *I'm only on Orbit Two. I've got time to figure this out. I don't have to force it right now.*

The logic of waiting is impeccable, but it's no match for his massive urge to get home *now!*

And without thinking he succumbs, adjusting his hand over the joystick and consciously punching the red button on top that reverts the spacecraft to manual attitude control.

Nothing much happens. There's a little drift now to the left, just a few degrees, and maybe a bit of roll, but he's not sure.

OK, time to try it.

He knows the controls are sensitive. The trick will be moving in only one axis at a time, and he reviews the basics without moving his hand.

Push forward to pitch forward, pull to pitch up. Twist left to yaw left, right to yaw right. Nudge the entire stick left to roll left, nudge it right to roll right. OK, which way?

He decides to yaw right a full 180 degrees, putting the tail into the line of flight. Then he can fine-tune it to exactly the right numbers.

Slowly, carefully, he rotates the stick to the right, a millimetre at a time it seems, until he suddenly feels and hears the hiss of the reaction jets yawing him in the right direction.

He releases the rotational pressure on the control stick, impressed at how smoothly *Intrepid* has begun to rotate to the right around its centre of gravity. Completing a full reversal, he twists the control back to the left until he fires another small burst to stop the turn.

But it's a bit too much, and the turn now reverses, very slowly at first.

He tries a tiny burst back to the right, but it, too, is overdone. Once more he's passing through the 180-degree point and continuing on around, this time beginning to pitch up.

He pushes the stick forward for a small corrective burst and tries to arrest the yaw at the same time, and suddenly he's turning back left slightly, pitching down, and beginning a left roll, all at the same time. The memory of what happened in the simulator returns like a nightmare, as *Intrepid* begins to tumble, slowly at first, then faster, the Earth beginning to gyrate and roll in front of his eyes.

Somehow he manages a glance at his watch. Four minutes left before he has to be rock-steady for retrofire.

Mojave International Aerospace Port, Mojave, California May 17, 10.53 a.m. Pacific Time

Diana Ross races through the front door of ASA's building. Sleep was difficult after returning home from her trip to see Kip. But she had every intention of being on the tarmac as they taxied out. Instead, she overslept.

Her cellphone is ringing and she curses quietly as she yanks it to her face, hearing a familiar name from the small list of aerospace reporters. She comes to a halt in the corridor and holds the cellphone back for a moment, staring at it as if she's discovered a pipe bomb in her hand.

So now it begins, she thinks. She always thought she had ice water in her veins. Now she's going to be tested.

'This is Diana Ross, ASA's PR director,' she announces sweetly, as if it was a routine day in the office.

DiFazio has emerged from Mission Control down the corridor and is walking towards her. She waves him to be quiet. He joins her silently, listening to her end of the conversation as she tries to convince the reporter in the calmest of tones that nothing in ASA's world is amiss other than a nasty communications glitch.

'Really?' is the sceptical reply. 'Then why am I looking at a live picture of your Mission Control and seeing absolutely no data streaming down from the spacecraft on any screen?'

'That's what a comms glitch sometimes entails. We're working on it.'

'I have a source who tells me it's far more serious than that.'

'Really? Could your source call us? We'd sure like to know what he knows.'

The reporter sighs. 'Look, I understand you're in damage-control mode and probably you don't know yourselves what's happening, but let me at least get some vitals on who's up there.'

'I'm just getting to work and I need some coffee,' Diana says. 'Give me your number and twenty minutes and I'll get back to you.'

The agreement is reluctant, but she ends the call and looks at Richard, taking in for the first time the depth of worry on his face.

'Richard? How bad is it?'

'We don't know anything new yet, but we're praying that Bill is OK and getting ready to retrofire in a few minutes. We're coming up on the end of the second orbit.'

DiFazio launches into a quick and tense briefing, then they move back inside Mission Control. Diana has long understood the risks of making a business out of space flight. But they've been doing it for almost a year now, week after week, without fail. It simply *can't* end badly, she thinks.

At the flight director's console she sees Arleigh Kerr, a receiver pulled to his ear. He speaks quickly and turns towards the rear, motioning to the boss.

'*What*, Arleigh?' DiFazio snaps.

'OK, Richard. NASA is pulling in a live long-lens picture, and it shows *Intrepid* is tumbling. He may be out of control.'

'Jesus.'

They all know the rest of the equation. A tumbling spacecraft can't fire its rocket motor and drop out of orbit.

'How long to the retrofire window?' DiFazio asks.

'One minute. They're watching.' Kerr raises the receiver back to his ear.

All eyes turn to the flight director as the seconds tick away.

Aboard *Intrepid*
May 17, 10.56 a.m. Pacific Time

The centrifugal forces have begun to pull Kip in opposite directions, but they aren't half as bad as the increasing frequency of alternating light and dark pulsing through the main windscreen.

He wills his hand off the joystick and realises that he's been clutching it. He works his fingers back and forth until they feel flexible again. There was something one of the astronauts told him in the simulator a week ago. Something to do with control sticks. What the hell was it?

Fingertips! That was it. He said that instructors could calm down pilots who were having trouble with formation flight by teaching them to fly with their fingertips to avoid overcontrol.

Kip moves his hand back towards the joystick, this time placing only the ends of his fingers on the top of it and moving them to fire the control jets in just one axis against the tumbling. He hears the jets hiss and feels the reaction, and for the first time the gyrations begin to slow. He does it again, tentatively, letting as much as a minute elapse between each burst, and finally daring to hope he might actually succeed.

He glances at the clock, hoping for a few more minutes before retrofire, but it's already too late. Firing the rocket now—even if he was in position and ready—would bring him down somewhere far to the east of Mojave. No, he decides, he's stuck for at least another orbit, another ninety minutes.

And with that realisation, some of his panic leaks away.

He tries a tentative burst to the left to stop the right-hand roll, and the frequency of the Earth's appearance in the side windows begins to slow.

One axis at a time he works at it, trying hard to keep the bursts very brief. After many long minutes he realises he's finally in the right attitude, flying right side up, tail first, and steady.

Kip punches at the computer screen to try to re-engage the automatic attitude controller, not believing it at first when the small box on the screen suddenly glows green. The coordinate readings are all within a few degrees of what he's supposed to have for retrofire.

Damn, I did it!

He checks the time. A little more than an hour to the next window, and this time he'll be ready.

He finds himself looking at the transmit button connected to his headset, wishing he could tell someone below of his success. He was spinning into oblivion, but he kept his cool, remembered the training, and he did it!

ASA Mission Control, Mojave, California
May 17, 11.01 a.m. Pacific Time

Arleigh Kerr suddenly raises the phone handset over his head like a trophy, his voice booming. '*Yes!* He's stabilised! The craft is apparently in position for retrofire. He's missed this window, but he's under control and alive!'

There are shouts and applause throughout the control room.

'No cigars yet, people,' Kerr says. 'But Bill's obviously on duty up there, so let's prepare for a deorbit in eighty minutes.'

It takes a few minutes for Diana Ross to remind the flight director and the CEO that the story is already leaking and she needs direction. The three of them step into the glassed-in conference room.

'This will sound very cold, but it's my job,' Diana says. 'We have an incredible opportunity here.'

'For what?' Kerr asks, indignant. 'What the hell does that mean?'

'It means that our future as a company depends on how we handle whatever occurs next,' she says. 'Good or bad. If we show strength, authority and perfect honesty, we will build an invaluable trust in the public mind. If we hide any fact, however small, sidestep questions, or appear confused . . .'

'Any appearance of weakness, in other words,' DiFazio adds.

'Exactly. Vulnerability breeds lasting distrust and even contempt.'

'I'm not a damned actor, Diana,' Kerr snaps.

'No, you're not, Arleigh. You're a steel-willed professional who knows private space flight will succeed. All I'm saying is, be careful to show that true face to whoever's watching. And they'll be watching from here on.'

Johnson Space Center, Houston, Texas
May 17, 11.20 a.m. Pacific Time/1.20 p.m. Central Time

'Talk to me.'

As John Kent walks through the door of the teleconferencing suite, that is greeting enough for his old friend and senior manager at Kennedy Space Center, Griggs Hopewell. In Kent's world, there is no need for verbal niceties when there's an urgent mission to accomplish.

'Good to see you, too, John,' Hopewell drawls. 'OK, let's get to it. We can make it happen, but we'll need twenty-six hours a day for four days and a blowtorch to everyone's behind.'

'*Endeavour* is ready, then? Enough to roll out to the pad?'

'Not as ready as I'd like, but yes. So who's going to fly, if this impossible mission comes about?'

'Paradies, White and Malone. What do you need to pull this off, Griggs?'

'How about authorisation for starters? You're talking tens of millions in prep expense. Shear is dead set against it and we're essentially in a mutiny here even talking about it on company time.'

'Look, I don't have a green light yet, but I'll get it.'

'From *Shear*? A guy who has an industrial-strength hatred for DiFazio? John, he *wants* DiFazio and anyone dumb enough to fly with him to bite it.'

'True, but he doesn't make policy; the White House does. Besides, ten minutes ago ASA's craft stabilised and aligned for retrofire. He may get down on his own. This is just a feasibility exercise.'

'John, Bill's a friend of mine, too. I also want him back safe.'

'Not the point. He comes down on his own or we go up to get him. Shear will be shamed into doing it by public pressure if nothing else. Keep your fingers crossed and get a playbook together for me, Griggs. Please.'

'Whoa, did I hear John Kent say *please*? That's a first. OK, I'll slam a plan together, but if Shear gets wind of this, neither of us will be holding NASA IDs past tomorrow morning.'

Aboard *Intrepid*, End of Orbit Three
May 17, 12.30 p.m. Pacific Time

The countdown ends in silence.

Kip's eyes dart around the checklist and back to the screen as he sits in disbelief. He's been prepared for retrofire for over an hour and never considered that the engine might have other ideas.

He's heard the engine fire before. He knows what it sounds like, feels like. When *Intrepid* was dropped by the mothership so many hours ago, the rocket engine roared and shook. The only roaring now is in Kip's head.

He punches the manual firing button again, just to make sure he hasn't been too timid. It clicks. Nothing changes.

Only seconds have elapsed since the programmed firing point. There's still time to fire, he thinks. *There must be a safety. Something else I need to throw!* Obviously he's done something wrong, something that can be fixed.

The checklist items begin to blur, but he forces his eyes to take them in item by item, expecting an 'Aha!' moment of recognition, the easy answer. So he's a bit late. So he comes down in Las Vegas instead of Mojave. What the hell. Just get the damn thing to fire!

But still the engine remains silent, and even though it's only the end of Orbit Three, Kip feels himself losing control. He begins flipping switches at random, snarling at the display and flailing, each wild action propelling him left or right in the zero gravity, restrained only by the seat belt.

With one final burst of frustration he hurls the checklist behind him, sickeningly aware of what it's hit as it thuds into the dead astronaut's body. '*Shit!*' he yells, his fists pounding the armrests of the command chair.

But he's hurtling away from the retrofire point at the speed of 25,500 feet per second, and the engine is still quiet as a tomb.

His anger subsides and in its place flows a cold and heavy fear, worse than anything he's experienced. No brakes, no parachute, no skyhook, no lifeline. No rescue of any sort if the engine won't fire.

Until a few minutes ago, his major concern was to find a way to pilot an unpowered gliding spacecraft with stubby wings to a safe landing somewhere flat and solid. Now even a crash landing sounds OK, as long as he gets out of orbit. The view of the Earth below suddenly seems an exquisite form of torture—home being dangled in front of him, but out of reach.

Oh my God, he thinks, swallowing hard. *What the hell am I going to do now? I can't just sit here and wait to die.*

He opens the relief port—a small funnel-shaped urinal dumping to the vacuum of space—and drains his bladder, before retightening the straps connecting him to the command chair.

He remembers the spacecraft simulator back in Mojave. The door in and out is on the rear cabin wall of the simulator, and at any time they could just turn the doorknob and walk out of the box into the hangar to safety.

He struggles against the seat belt to turn around, gripping the back of the chair, his focus snapping to the unbroken surface of the back wall.

There is, of course, no door.

Panic crashes over him like an emotional tsunami. He feels tears on his face as the images before him begin to compress into a tunnel, and then to a single point of light, just before everything goes dark.

ASA Mission Control, Mojave, California
May 17, 12.45 p.m. Pacific Time

Richard DiFazio quietly returns to the conference room and lifts a receiver, punching in the number he'd considered calling earlier, an international number he guards carefully. The male voice answers in Russian and switches adroitly to English with a cheery greeting, which changes to a serious tone at the news of *Intrepid*'s dilemma.

'And, of course, it will be a balmy day in the Bering Strait before our good friend Geoffrey is willing to help, no?'

'You've got that right. But you've got a resupply mission to the International Space Station coming up in two weeks, correct?'

'What you're thinking is not possible without money, Richard, and maybe not even then. Can your people last for eight days?'

'No.'

'Then you're asking the impossible, regardless of money. Launching inside of eight days from now would be suicide.'

'They're damaged up there, Vasily. Our astronaut . . . you've met him, by the way . . . Bill Campbell.'

'Yes, I have, but it doesn't change the reality of what we can do.'

'They were hit by something, they've lost all comms, and apparently he can't get the engine to light to kick him out of orbit.'

There's a long stretch of silence and the two wait each other out, Vasily giving in first. 'I already knew of this, Richard. Our people have been monitoring, too. But even if we could get there, you have no docking collars, no compatible hatches, and only one space suit. We can't tow him back home.'

'We have an airlock. We can stuff a spare suit inside the lock.'

'Perhaps. But it takes eight days, Richard. I'm sorry.'

Aboard *Intrepid*
May 17, 12.45 p.m. Pacific Time

Consciousness returns slowly. Dreamlike, fuzzy images of an upside-down cabin slowly coalesce until Kip realises he's floating in zero gravity around the ceiling, upside-down in relation to the cabin floor.

He reaches out and grasps the back of the command chair, working his body into it again and clipping the seat belt back on. He feels foolish and exhausted. He's never blacked out before. They explained that the cabin pressure in orbit would be the equivalent of a 10,000-foot altitude and that too much physical exertion would net light-headedness. That must have been it.

Kip looks at the clock. He's only been out a short time and nearly eighty minutes remain to the next retrofire point—the end of Orbit Four. He shivers, unwilling to believe he's hit the wall with no more options, and equally unwilling to delude himself that there are some. His anger returns, but this time there's no energy left for hitting or throwing or yelling. He sits, doing a slow burn, his mind still ricocheting off a dozen possible solutions, each one of which evaporates into little more than wishful thinking.

And suddenly there is nothing left but reality, and it feels like a black hole in his soul, sucking all that remains of him into another dimension.

And the guilt! The overwhelming, crushing guilt that he's done exactly what Sharon tried to prevent. He's killed his children's father, her husband.

He buries his head in his hands, and rocks back and forth until he's stunned enough and tired enough to escape into the blessed release of a numbed sleep.

The *Washington Post*, Washington, DC
May 17, 2.30 p.m. Pacific Time/5.30 p.m. Eastern Time

As the aerospace reporter for the *Washington Post* punches off the latest call from ASA, her instincts are on high alert. ASA is sidestepping key questions, and she's travelled the arc from passing interest in a rumour of trouble to a belief that the occupants of ASA's spacecraft are in danger.

What does she have? Two people aboard that craft, no telemetry and no communication. NASA saw them with a very long lens still in stable orbit.

So what's really wrong? Is communications loss the extent of it, like Ross wants me to think? When did they launch?

She dives back into the Internet and checks the launch time listed on ASA's website. And a quote from Richard DiFazio: 'Each flight is planned for four orbits of approximately ninety minutes each. We deorbit at the end of the fourth circuit after six hours.'

She checks her note on the time they dropped the spacecraft from the mothership: 8 a.m. Pacific Time.

And it's 2.30 p.m. out there now. That's over six hours.

My God, they're stuck up there!

The White House, Washington, DC
May 17, 2.45 p.m. Pacific Time/5.45 p.m. Eastern Time

Even after three terms in the US Senate and countless visits to the White House, Mitch Lipensky still feels the rush of history and power as he walks through the hallways of the Oval Office to the waiting President.

He greets the President like the old friend he is, and they settle down on opposite sides of the coffee table. There are only so many strings even a senior senator can pull for an immediate audience; this one has been triggered by a disturbing call from a man in Houston he considers an American hero.

'NORAD is telling me the pilot may be hurt or dead, Mitch. That whoever was on the controls was more likely to be an amateur with a steep learning curve—in other words the passenger. Is that what you have?' The President's voice is tinged with the Virginia accent of his youth.

'Yes, sir. I have the same report. But the important thing, to my mind, is that someone is alive up there with a few days of air left, and he apparently can't fire his engine and get out of orbit.'

'So no self-rescue. But is this something we have the ability to do?'

'We don't know, Mr President, because our esteemed NASA administrator has rejected even the most rudimentary attempt to find out. Are we going to let a bureaucrat like Geoff Shear reject a rescue only because it involves someone shot into space by a mere American corporation and not our mighty government? Dammit, Mr President, he's out of control.'

'Mitch, he's defending our ability to carry anyone into space. How long have we been operating with only two shuttles? Six years?'

The senator chuckles with a knowing smile. 'He's already called you, hasn't he?'

The President is smiling back, almost embarrassed. 'You know Geoff. But he's not an evil force, Mitch. He's got a point.'

'You going to let him cloud the bigger picture?'

The President looks at his shoes before shaking his head. 'Of course not. But Mitch, if we lose a shuttle in this, can you steer the Senate to adopt the replacement bill at long last?'

'No guarantees, but we can probably do it.'

The President slaps his thigh and stands, holding his hand out for Mitch to shake. 'I'll issue the order to get a rescue mission ready if possible. But Shear may resign, Mitch.'

'And, Mr President, your point would be what?'

They both laugh as the senator takes his leave.

The President picks up the phone. Within a minute the requested voice comes on the line.

'Geoff? This is your leader. What the hell are you doing upsetting senior citizens like Mitch Lipensky?'

ASA Mission Control, Mojave, California
May 17, 3.05 p.m. Pacific Time

The very sound of Vasily's voice on the other end of the surprise phone call is comforting, buoying Richard DiFazio's spirits.

'There is a chance, Richard. I did not realise we were as far along in our preparations as we are.'

'How soon could you launch?'

'This is the space station resupply mission, you understand. We would have room for two, and only to transport them to the station. From there, one of the escape capsules would have to be used to return. We don't have enough seats to do our mission and return two of your people.'

'One may be badly hurt, or worse. We may have only one alive.'

'If only one, we can bring him back after the resupply rendezvous.'

'How soon?'

'Five days.'

'Oh jeez, Vasily, they'll be dead by then.'

'Not if they're careful. There are conservation steps, even with CO_2 scrubbers. And if there's only one alive, you have twice the time, no?'

Silence while DiFazio grapples with that possibility.

'And . . . there is one thing, Richard. I'm sorry, but in the new Russia we still count every rouble, and this is a substantial change.'

'How much, Vasily?'

'Twenty-five million.'

DiFazio feels his blood pressure rising. Out of the question. Unless . . .

'Can't we get that lower? We don't have that kind of money.'

'One of your backers, Butch Davidson, certainly does. He makes more than that every week in interest, I think. Is good idea, true?'

Why he's hearing the word 'OK' coming from his mouth is a mystery. DiFazio knows Davidson's true penny-pinching nature, which contrasts so gratingly with his publicly magnanimous reputation. The thought of approaching him for such a sum scares him.

'I have two million I can wire you as a down payment,' he tells Vasily.

'OK. We will extend you credit, my friend. But the money comes due whatever happens up there. Success or failure, you agree?'

'Yes. Five days, right?'

'Yes. I shall email you the bank-account information within the hour. And then we begin.'

ASA Offices, Mojave, California
May 17, 5.03 p.m. Pacific Time

It was inevitable, Diana Ross thinks, and in some ways she's surprised it took this long. *Intrepid* has been gone for almost ten hours. The six flat-panel TV screens arrayed along the wall at the end of her desk are one by one posting their versions of the same basic message: 'A private spacecraft launched this morning has lost communication and may be in trouble.'

Two secretaries are handling the rising tide of media enquiries, and she's staying out of contact to think and write a statement for DiFazio.

The tie line from Mission Control rings.

'Diana? Richard. You called?'

She briefs him on the approaching media storm. 'I'm working on a statement,' she adds. 'You *are* going to be our face, right?'

'No. I want you to be the face.'

'Not a good idea, Richard. They look at me as a PR person.'

The sigh she hears from the other end worries her. He's a good man and a good leader, but in the last six hours he's been all but falling apart.

'Whatever you think, Diana,' he says. 'When do you want me over there?'

'Within the hour, if you can. Any changes?'

'No.' His reply is a bit too curt. She knows something new has happened. 'Who got the story first?' he adds.

'The *Washington Post.* Oh, Richard . . . someone did talk to Kip Dawson's wife, right?'

'Arleigh did.'

'Anything else I . . . need to know?'

More silence. Telling, pregnant silence.

'Are we going to get them back, Richard?'

Beneath the façade she's struggling to maintain, she feels like a frightened little girl watching the twisting trails of a shattered *Challenger* against the blue of her mind's eye.

Aboard *Intrepid*
May 17, 5.44 p.m. Pacific Time

There are sixteen sunsets per day in low Earth orbit, and at first Kip has no idea which one he's looking at. He glances at his watch, startled at how late it is back in California. He was supposed to be drinking champagne right now at a postflight party.

In sleep there were dreams he almost recalls, confused, kaleidoscopic, but dreams of his kids and meadows and for some reason a fast convertible. But he's pretty sure what he's perceiving now is reality, and it sucks.

A small wave of buzzing dizziness passes over him and he realises it has nothing to do with the zero gravity and his inner ear and vestibular balance system. It's his mind working overtime to reject this reality.

So how long do I have? Kip wonders. He paws through the checklists until he locates a chart with the number of people aboard plotted against the capability of the CO_2 scrubbers.

One person, five days. So that's it. In five days I'll sit here and keel over from CO_2 poisoning. Probably not an unpleasant death.

At least, he figures, without communication he won't have to listen to Sharon say, 'I told you so.' But the forced joke falls flat.

He thinks about how eager he was to take this flight, and how right Sharon was to worry, and how much he misses his kids. The twins, Carly and Carrie, are barely five. Kip knows they'll remember their father mostly from family videos and snapshots. He will easily be replaced, as long as Sharon can find an appropriately obedient male to dominate.

Julie, however, is thirteen, and losing her dad will be devastating. She's bonded with Sharon, but never lost the effects of her mother's sudden death.

Thank God, Jerrod is on his own now. But he'll miss his dad the most, mainly because of the unfinished business between them, and the anger he's never been able to defuse.

Some of Bill Campbell's words return, something he said just before dying about their orbit being so stable they could stay up here for sixty years.

My God, Kip thinks, *Jerrod will be almost eighty before this spacecraft falls into the atmosphere. How awful to know that your dead father is flying overhead every ninety minutes your entire life.*

Or maybe it won't happen that way. There'll be no rescue flight. They made that clear. But surely some spacecraft will eventually be assigned to come open the hatch and see what happened.

Or maybe he should just save everyone the trouble and, when the air is all but unbreathable, just shoot himself out of the airlock with Bill's body. The two of them would hardly be a flash in the sky on re-entry . . . or would they just be floating alongside *Intrepid* for decades?

Strange, he thinks, *that even death should be so meticulously planned.*

He pushes the images of Sharon and his children out of his mind for now. The need to decide his own fate is far too strong, and he finds himself facing it with an unexpected equanimity.

Do I have any chance at all? Is there anything I can do?

He already knows the answer. He's punched every button, read and reread the checklists ad nauseam, and it's inescapable that the projectile that killed Bill also took out the engine, or at least the ability to fire it.

No, face it, kiddo. We're dead in five days. Period.

So, he wonders, how does one spend five remaining days on—or in his case, high above—the Earth? Not that the choices aren't severely limited, but his mind is sharp, even if saddened and stressed and panicked.

He remembers the notes he was starting to write in the laptop. *But no one's going to read it . . . for at least a bunch of years. Maybe even sixty.*

But surely someone will eventually find and download and study everything he puts on that hard drive. So maybe he should write a narrative and copyright it to his kids and grandkids. It could bring some money.

Who knows? he thinks. *They pay ridiculous sums to read the stories of the seriously disgraced. Why not a dead dad from half a century before?*

He remembers a fantasy he's nurtured his entire life in which he owns a beautiful wooden-hulled sailing ship. He sees himself every evening repairing to his small walnut-trimmed captain's office, opening a big bound notebook and writing in a clear and ornate hand beautifully phrased passages about the day, his feelings, the state of the ship, and his life. How wonderful that would be. Like being his own Greek chorus.

Kip looks around, finding sudden similarities between where he is and that mythical ship's office. There's no big bound notebook, but there *is* a laptop aboard.

And there will be an audience someday.

The word 'epitaph' comes to mind.

United States Air Force Academy, Colorado Springs, Colorado
May 17, 6.33 p.m. Pacific Time/7.33 p.m. Mountain Time

Cadet Jerrod Dawson has never been summoned to the commandant's office before, let alone in the middle of the evening and immediately on return from a field trip. He has already saluted and reported to a major and a lieutenant colonel in the room, and is waiting for an explanation when one of the academy chaplains comes through the door.

'Sir, may I ask what this is about?' Jerrod can feel his stomach contracting in fear. He has purposely avoided watching or reading any news reports during the day, not wanting even to seem to be endorsing his father's self-indulgent flight. But now . . .

'Sit down, please,' the colonel directs.

Jerrod sinks into the nearest chair. 'Is this about my dad?'

The glances among the three confirm that much.

'You are aware your father was participating in a civilian space flight today, correct?'

'Yes, sir. Please tell me. Has something happened?'

'We don't know if he's all right or not, but we got a call from your mother.'

'My mother's dead, sir. That would be my stepmother.'

'Right. Well, let me tell you in as much detail as we have it.'

National Air and Space Museum, Washington, DC
May 17, 8.05 p.m. Pacific Time/11.05 p.m. Eastern Time

It's late evening in the Beltway, past 11 p.m., and the black-tie reception and dinner, attended at the last minute by the head of NASA, is winding down. The guests are taking their leave, the men looking sharp in their tuxedos, their wives and girlfriends mostly stunning in their evening gowns.

Geoff Shear is uninterested in both the pomp and purpose. His own purpose for being there is waiting just ahead in an alcove.

She turns, elegant but appropriately conservative, her last-minute invitation the result of a puzzling request to the museum. Her apparent mid-level position with the Agency would hardly put her in the same league as the mainstream crowd.

'Dorothy. Thanks for responding at the last minute.'

She smiles. 'Mr Administrator. What can I do for you, sir?'

He motions her into a side room. 'I have a mission for you, Dorothy. I've been ordered by the President to do everything NASA can to mount a rescue launch for ASA's apparently stranded spacecraft. You know this?'

'More or less.'

'OK. A presidential order is an order, but NASA cannot afford suddenly to throw caution to the wind. I need you to get down to the Cape. Should you ever be asked by some damned congressional committee, then these are my formal orders: you're there to coordinate and ensure safety for the Agency. You were asked to go down there by your supervisor.'

'I understand. I know how you feel about these private efforts. This launch attempt must not take place if there is too much risk, and I might just discover that there's far too much risk . . . the type the boys down south just didn't see at first.'

He's nodding, admiringly. 'I'm glad you see it that way. As you well know, I can't trust anyone at the Cape.'

'There's one thing I want.'

'Go ahead.'

'I've enjoyed being your fix-it agent, so to speak, especially after eight years in covert ops for the company. At least no one's been shooting at me here. But I'm ready to come in out of the cold, as the old reference goes. That desk you promised me?'

'You really want to fly a desk?'

'Can we make this my last assignment?'

'Why not. Although I'll need your help recruiting someone new. If you don't have your own eyes and ears, an administrator can never know what's really happening in the trenches. You've done that well, Dorothy.'

'Deal, then? Last assignment?'

'Deal.'

'You want reports back from me?'

'No. We need plausible deniability at all turns. In fact, there'll be no record of your having been here at this party tonight.'

'I figured. In that case, I should evaporate,' she says, placing her empty wineglass on a nearby ledge and leaving without another word.

4

Aboard *Intrepid*
May 18, 8.45 a.m. Pacific Time

Waking again from sleep, Kip is shaken by the realisation that more than a day has elapsed since launch.

The laptop has been opened and closed several times, but the words he wants to type seem stuck in his heart. Yet once again he pulls the weightless machine to him, secures it to his lap and stares at the keyboard.

A strange message pops up, asking his approval for some sort of connection, and he answers yes without thinking, then can't get it back.

What was that? he wonders. The connection utility shows the computer connected to nothing, no networks, no modems, no other humans.

He calls up a word-processing window and begins anew.

Anyone out there?

Of course not. At least not in my lifetime, which will be short. But let's pretend you are there, whatever year it is when you finally read these words.

For the record, I suppose I should yell Mayday, Mayday, Mayday! I'm a passenger on the private spaceship *Intrepid*, which launched from Mojave, California, and we were hit by some sort of small object, which came right through the cabin and right through my pilot's head, killing him instantly. No one can hear me on the radios, and apparently I have only four days of air left.

And this isn't fun any more.

I probably had more days of air than five at first, but I used it the first day panicking, crying, raging and generally acting like an idiot. But it's OK now. I know there's no chance of rescue or survival, and no magic solutions derived by teams of sweating scientists below in the eleventh hour. This won't be *Apollo 13*.

When I won this private space flight, they warned me that, if anything happened, neither NASA nor any other country's space programme was going to attempt to save me. I accepted the risk. But now . . . here I sit, knowing I have four days left to say something to a mute disc drive, and the worst part is I can't even say goodbye to my family and friends, even though I'm passing over their heads every hour and a half.

What's wrong, by the way, is that because of the thing that hit us, the retro rocket won't fire. So I'm stuck in a stable orbit and sick with guilt over the fact that my wife, Sharon, begged me not to take this risk. I expect my son, Jerrod, will never forgive me either, since he already continues to blame me for his mother's death, and my little girls will never have the chance to hear directly from me why this all happened.

Then he considers addressing his words to Diana, and the thought surprises him. For the tiniest moment, the idea of her feels like a focal point, an inspiration, a reason to struggle hard to come back.

And just as quickly that sparkle of thought evaporates.

At my ripe old age of forty-four, I'm that worst of all white Anglo males, the middle-aged dad with a midlife crisis, and I've been feeling for a long time like I've wasted the last twenty years, or at least that I went down the wrong road somehow.

No, no, no, he thinks. *I'm not going to sit up here and whine in print.*

He pauses, aware of a vague pain in his stomach, at first not recognising the symptoms of simple hunger. There's a selection of protein bars and other packaged food in a side compartment that he's already raided, and he pulls one of the bars out and wolfs it down with a water chaser from his squeeze bottle. Food is one of his lowest priorities.

He's distracted by the sun disappearing over the horizon again, the amazing beauty of the rapid change from ruddy red to deep purple and inky, star-studded black. He wonders whether, when it's all over and he's . . . wherever . . . beauty like this can still be perceived. Maybe it's even prettier there. Wherever 'there' is.

Heaven. He has his own definition, probably born of too little intimacy in the last few years.

In his early days he'd occasionally fallen in love so deep he couldn't eat or think for weeks. There was, for instance, Linda Hammel, and he smiles at the warm memory, wondering where she is. He has never discussed her with anyone. His folks would have been scandalised, and her father would have killed him. But now . . .

He looks at the keyboard, suddenly excited at the prospect of reliving those moments, even if only through a dreamy window of words.

All right, let's begin unconventionally. I've got to start somewhere, and both I and whoever I mention will have been long dead by the time you, my reader, find these words, so I think I'll tell you about my happiest times, my teen years, and my first real love.

Kalgoorlie-Boulder, Western Australia
May 18, 8.55 a.m. Pacific Time/11.55 p.m. Western Standard Time

Satisfied that his parents have quieted down at long last, Alastair Wood slides out of bed and quietly pads across the cold floor of his room. He pulls on a thick robe before sitting at his desk and firing up his most prized possession—a computer with a flat-screen monitor and the high-speed Internet connection that was his main gift for his just-celebrated twelfth birthday.

The sleepy look and deep circles under his eyes he carries to school these days are worth it for the midnight hours he usually spends at the keyboard. While so many of his school chums have their heads buried in video games, he's touring the world real time every night. And it *is* the whole world that pours into his personal portal, filled with information on just about anything he would ever want to know.

His father will never understand, and he's tired of being called a geek whenever he's discovered hunched over the keyboard at some ungodly hour.

The operating system completes its start-up routine, and there's a parcel of emails from friends, including one with a link he's never seen before, some sort of Internet router service. He clicks on the address. A long list of active email accounts parades by, and he selects a few at random, but they yield only a stream of ones and zeros.

Right! A challenge!

He selects a translation program and tries it with no effect, then pulls in another, and on the third try someone's real-time transmission is crawling across his screen, some girl complaining about a feckless boyfriend.

Boring. He pulls back a level and scrolls down to the very bottom, finding a message in progress without a coherent address.

Hmmm. Let's look at this private, personal communiqué.

He triggers the translation program again, and the words assemble themselves in English, the transmission apparently still in progress and scrolling across his screen.

> . . . record, I suppose I should yell Mayday, Mayday, Mayday! I'm a passenger on the private spaceship *Intrepid*, which launched from Mojave, California, and we were hit by some sort of small object, which came right through the cabin and right through my pilot's head, killing him instantly. No one can hear me on the radios, and apparently I only have four days of air left.
>
> And this isn't fun any more.

Alastair sits back, scratching his head. The syntax and tone don't match any of the hackers he knows who might try to pull such a stunt, but then he can hardly know all the tricksters on the planet. Someone, however, is trying a sophisticated scam, and he triggers a save program to record whatever comes and sits back to watch what the trickster will try next.

Private spaceship. Yeah, sure.

Just to be certain, he calls up the Google search engine and throws the words 'private spaceship' and 'Intrepid' into the search box.

Among the 16,000 hits that come back are several from the official website of American Space Adventures. Alastair selects one of them and sits forward slowly as he reads about the launch one day before—the name of the craft: *Intrepid*.

What the hell? A smile spreads across his face. *Buggers almost got me!* Whoever the hacker is pulling the stunt, he's cleverly used the right names.

Can't fool me! he thinks, watching the evolving message once again. After ten minutes, he decides, he'll run the whole thing through a matching program and see where in reality it came from.

FORTY-FIVE MINUTES later, Alastair's attention is still on the screen. He's about to send an alert to thirty-three of his email friends, around Australia and the world. Especially Becky Nigel, the only girl he really likes, who keeps in touch despite moving back to the UK.

> Hey, mates! I've stumbled on a really cool scam artist trying to wind me up. He sez he's stranded in a private spaceship. The bloke's creative, I'll give him that. Thought you might want to have a look. It's coming in a continuous scroll so you have to record it yourself. I'm sending the first stuff I captured.

He includes the web address and switches the screen back over to the evolving message from Kip.

> . . . growing up in my ideal family. At least I thought they were ideal, and I loved my folks, both of whom are gone now. Dad was an executive with a big mining company and an upright, reliable, serious and dedicated father, who defined life as a series of challenges a man met with responsibility for those who depended on him. But I guess when he was programmed as a child, someone forgot to include the concept of fun.

The symbol for new email pops up in the corner of Alastair's screen and he opens a window to read it while still watching the evolving narrative.

From: Becky
Hey, blockhead! Guess what? There is a private spacecraft in trouble right now on orbit, and there are two men aboard, an astronaut named Bill and a passenger named Kip Dawson. Don't you ever watch the telly? You're too cynical, you know that? Ever consider this might be real?

Before he can send a reply, a host of other emails start snapping in from his friends, all apparently tuning in and reacting to the strange narrative.

If this is real, he thinks, *the guy says no one can hear him on the radios. Do the space officials know about this?*

He sits back, uncertain, as if he's just witnessed a serious crime or a terrible accident and he has to be the one to alert the authorities.

He wonders how upset his dad would be if he tapped on their bedroom door now and asked for help. Maybe he can handle it himself, but he's getting a really creepy feeling.

ASA Headquarters, Mojave, California
May 18, 10.20 a.m. Pacific Time

Richard DiFazio's cellphone rings and he keys it on.

'So, my friend, NASA has decided to get the shuttle ready to go up and do what you've retained us to do.'

'They'll never make it in time, Vasily. At least, I don't think they will.'

'We don't think so either, but you know what happens when NASA has a blowtorch to their ass. They usually move fast.'

'But . . . you're still going to try, right?'

'Of course. But things have changed. Now it has become a political matter and a matter of Russian honour.'

'Excuse me?'

'Our president has become involved, and when he discovered that NASA was going to try and probably fail, and that we were getting ready to do this for you for a price, he directed us to cancel the charge and be the ones to pluck your people back as a humanitarian gesture.' There is a pause, then laughter. 'Your deposit is already being wired back to you. We are on schedule now.'

'Thank you, Vasily!'

'Oh, one other thing. The Japanese Space Agency's Hiragawa just called me. He said the Chinese are about to make a similar decision to help.'

'You're kidding?'

'No. It may get crowded up there.'

Aboard *Marine One* en route from the White House to Andrews Air Force Base
May 18, 10.30 a.m. Pacific Time/1.30 p.m. Eastern Time

Ronald Porter, Chief of Staff, hands the President a one-page summary of an intelligence report less than an hour old.

'Our buddies in Moscow have decided to ride to the rescue.'

'A special launch?'

'Actually, they're moving up a scheduled ISS resupply mission.'

'Don't they know we're going to send the shuttle?'

'They don't believe we can.'

'Well, hell, Ron, get someone on the phone to set them straight. Have Shear make the call.'

'Their president is determined to be the white knight. I talked to Shear. He heartily advises that we cancel our effort.'

'I'm sure he does. I had to order him to get cracking.'

'He has a solid point. We have only two shuttles left, and when you push something on an emergency basis, you cut corners, take additional risks.'

The President sits back in thought as the *Marine One* pilots begin the descent to Andrews. Suddenly, he's forward again, in Ron's face. 'There's a principle here, Ron, and in my view it's worth the risk. One, we protect our own, civilian or government. Two, we may have only two shuttles left, but we don't have to plead for help because we're afraid to use them. Three, this goes to the heart of American trust of and pride in our capabilities, and in NASA.'

'So, we fly?'

He's nodding. 'Damn right we fly. Unless there's a solid, no-foolin' safety concern beyond the routine.'

Kalgoorlie-Boulder, Western Australia
May 18, 10.50 a.m. Pacific Time/May 19, 1.50 a.m. Western Standard Time

The connection to the web address carrying the alleged transmission from space has apparently frozen, and Alastair thinks he knows why. His own mailbox has been overloaded by emails from addresses he doesn't recognise.

He pulls up another screen and calls up a bulletin board he's found, a site for people nuts about space travel. Sure enough, the message from the man calling himself Kip is there, too, and still actively scrolling!

Another excited message from Becky has made it to an alternative mailbox, and he opens it quickly.

Your stranded spaceman's transmission is exploding. Someone's retransmitting it everywhere and I've already seen it on eight sites. And Ali-boy, I think the poor guy IS really up there and is really, REALLY screwed! And the story he's telling is so amazingly rad.

Alastair checks the time, amazed to find it's two in the morning. He feels like he just sat down. Whatever all this is, he decides, it is way more than he can handle now. But there is one thing he hasn't done yet that just has to be accomplished. He checks the email address of the company in California that launched the spacecraft, and writes as simple a message as he can.

Dear American Space Adventures,

I don't know if it's real or not, but there's a guy saying he's a passenger in your spaceship *Intrepid* and he's sending a continuous letter into the Internet, and I'm forwarding the website address. It's frozen up on me, but I'm sending a file with my record of the first part of what came in.

If there really is a problem, I hope everything turns out OK.

Your friend, Alastair Wood

Kalgoorlie-Boulder, Western Australia

Jeez, what would it feel like to be up there all alone? he wonders, knowing that some of the words he first read might hold the answer to that.

Maybe he should reread them. But first he decides to look at his jammed-up mailbox. He opens the latest message, not believing the address: ABC, the Australian Broadcasting Corporation, his national network.

Dear Sir or Madam,

We have been forwarded a copy of an email you sent to several friends last night with a web address that apparently is the only live transmission from a stranded space tourist on an American craft in orbit. If this is true, and you are the one who somehow found it, we would very much appreciate the opportunity to interview you. Won't you please call us at our toll-free number in Sydney? Wherever you are in Australia, we can send a camera crew to you.

James Haggas, Executive Producer

The number is at the bottom, and Alastair sits there staring at it, wondering what to do and remembering that this thing started by his hacking into a private transmission. Not terribly legal.

I should get on the telly and tell the whole bloody world? I don't think so!

Suddenly, the urge to shut down the computer and hide overwhelms him.

Can they find me through an unregistered email address? he wonders, his stomach contracting with worry. *Dad will kill me.*

He snaps off the desk light and dives under the covers. The bedcovers always feel like the best defence against a world gone mad.

ASA Mission Control, Mojave, California
May 18, 1.18 p.m. Pacific Time

For the previous agonising day and a half, Arleigh Kerr has had to deal with the reality that without communications a flight director has virtually nothing to direct. Two of the staff have kept Mission Control operating, but it's felt like a deathwatch.

And now, from the most unlikely quarter, contact?

Kerr stands at his console, waiting for the room to fill, as his people rush back in, all wearing cautious expressions. When the room is back up to strength, Kerr leans down to his computer keyboard, then glances up at the largest of the screens before them, waiting for the text to appear.

'What's this, Arleigh?' the flight dynamics controller asks.

'It's coming in through an obscure site on the Internet, one of the servers we've used for email. We would have never seen it except someone way out in the boonies of Australia emailed us a half hour ago.'

'But what *is* it?'

'We think,' Kerr says, 'that it's our passenger, Kip Dawson, trying to communicate. But apparently he doesn't know anyone's reading. I've got a lot more, and if this is truly him, it tells what happened yesterday.'

Kerr highlights the first portion about the impact and Bill Campbell's demise and lets it sink in.

'I want everyone to read everything he's written. I don't know what we can learn that can help him, since we can't talk back, but I want you to scour every line for facts that might help us get him down.'

'How is this being transmitted, exactly?' the woman in charge of capsule communication asks.

Kerr shrugs and looks around the room. 'Anyone?'

One of the engineers stands up. 'We put a very small transmitter package on there to handle the volume of downlinked photo files so the passengers could reach their loved ones by Internet if they wanted. It uses the same antenna array as the S-band transmitter. But it's powered separately.'

'We can *send* as well as receive?' Kerr asks, excitement building.

'No. Unfortunately, we only set it up for downloads.'

'But . . . how did he trigger it?'

The engineer shrugs. 'I don't know, unless one of the autoconnect features on that laptop kicked it in. Wait a minute. Arleigh, are you familiar with what they used to call "spyware"?'

'No.'

'Programs that record each keystroke in an endless string and store it in some nondescript little file. Our programmers may have put one of those in the computers on *Intrepid* as a kind of digital recorder. If, somehow, the output of that keystroke recorder got routed to that individual transmitter, it would explain why we're only getting what he types when he types it.'

'Somebody get the programmers who worked on this thing and find out, OK?' Kerr instructs.

'Are we relaying this to NASA?' the engineer asks.

A commanding feminine voice fills the room from behind, and Kerr turns to find a startled-looking Diana Ross standing in the entrance.

'Arleigh? Everyone? It's not just NASA getting this. Thanks to a sharp reporter at the *Washington Post,* what we're apparently doing . . . our server, I mean . . . is relaying this to the world. Most of the media have picked up on it, and they're breaking in everywhere with it. All the cable news networks. I haven't read everything that's come down yet, but . . . the poor guy thinks he's dying and I guess he's writing about his life. Very private stuff.'

There's a slight glistening in the corners of Diana's eyes and Kerr realises she's tearing up as she turns to go.

A stunned silence prevails in Mission Control as one by one the controllers read what's been written so far, then tune in to the live feed.

You know, I never knew it could be so much fun to describe moments like that one in the back seat, on that mountainside. We were lucky, Linda and me. I loved her as well as *made* love to her.

I truly considered Linda an accomplishment. I don't mean a notch-on-the-bedpost, I mean the fact that I made her feel good. I cared for her that summer, and she became a part of my life, however briefly, and I a part of hers.

Kalgoorlie-Boulder, Western Australia
May 18, 3.58 p.m. Pacific Time/May 19, 6.58 a.m. Western Standard Time

Daylight is streaming into the room as Alastair wakes up, startled by the sound of heavy footsteps on the stairs. He can hear a television on somewhere in the house. The door opens and his dad walks in.

'Alastair, wake up!'

'I'm awake, Dad. What's happening?'

'I've been watching the news, son, and there's something on now you're going to want to hear. There's the most amazing message coming down through the Internet from a guy stranded in orbit on a private American spacecraft, and they wouldn't have found it if some hacker right out here in Western Australia hadn't broken into someone's computer.'

'R-really?'

'Yes. He's a bit of a hero and they're looking for him. He may get a twist in his knickers for the hacking, but overall he's got a thankyou coming. Come downstairs and see this. Could be someone you know.'

Denver International Airport, Colorado
May 18, 4.20 p.m. Pacific Time/5.20 p.m. Mountain Time

The copy of *USA Today* in Jerrod Dawson's lap with the headline about his father's perilous situation has numbed him, leaving him awash with guilt as he waits for his Houston-bound flight to board.

Why he's going to Houston isn't clear, and even as they were granting the emergency leave and helping arrange a military fare, he felt reluctant about going there at all, except to see his sister and two half-sisters. The thought of Sharon in the role of his mother is infuriating. He can barely be civil to her. While he likes her father, Big Mike, he couldn't believe it when he found out that Sharon had left his dad and run back to her own daddy in Houston.

And, of course, there's the small matter of Sharon never liking him. He loathes her for what she's done to his father, roping him into having two more children. As if they hadn't already been a family.

Not that he doesn't blame his dad, too. But it's his dad he needs to talk to. And he can't because he's 310 miles above the planet and stuck there.

Jerrod fights back unbidden tears.

Johnson Space Center, Houston, Texas
May 18, 5 p.m. Pacific Time/7 p.m. Central Time

'Ever hear of someone named Dorothy Sheehan?'

Griggs Hopewell's voice is too recognisable for John Kent to need an introduction, and the calls between them have been accelerating all day.

'Should I, Griggs? Who is she?'

'Well, she's from headquarters, as far as I can tell. But I'm wondering just exactly what she's been sent down here to do.'

'I don't recognise the name, but is she causing problems?'

'Twice today I've had safety stops declared out of the blue by people who would normally never pull the emergency brake, and she's the only new kid in town.'

'I'm not following. Are you connecting dots between her and headquarters' safety concerns, or are you just being your usual paranoid self?'

'I'm just suspicious of who she is and what she's doing here.'

'What's her security clearance?'

'Total. She can go sit in the cockpit and honk the horn if she wants.'

'Shouldn't be hard to find out who she works for.'

'I already checked. She's a low-level safety-compliance officer a long way down the food chain from our esteemed admini-shredder.'

'So, aside from that, any other show stoppers yet?'

'No. So far as we know at this moment, we will be able to get our bird off the pad in three days. We'll set the launch window formally in a few hours.'

'Our guys should already be there.'

'Your three T-38s arrived two hours ago. My only big worry, John, is that someone's waiting in the weeds to pull a safety stop at the very last second, and we'll lose the window. The long range on the weather is not encouraging.'

'By the way, Griggs, you are aware of what's happening with that live transmission from the ASA craft?'

'Yeah, but I haven't seen it. What's the guy up there talking about?'

'Personal stuff. Every woman in the place is glued to CNN. All the news outlets are broadcasting it live by now, and I've got a few of our number watching in case he says anything that could help us.'

'John, find out more about Dorothy for me, will you? She worries me.'

George Bush Houston Intercontinental Airport, Texas
May 18, 5.53 p.m. Pacific Time/7.53 p.m. Central Time

As Jerrod leaves the plane, he realises that he hasn't enough cash for a cab ride. He calls Big Mike's house for a pick-up. Fortunately, Mike himself answers and volunteers to send someone.

There's an electronic billboard with a news crawl mounted over the concourse, and he wonders why it's stopping so many passengers in their tracks.

A familiar arrangement of letters catches his attention and he, too, stops, wondering why the name Jerrod Dawson is moving across in front of him.

He turns to a tired-looking man in a business suit next to him.

'What's going on? What is that?'

'That's a message coming down from that poor guy trapped in space. He's got an angry young son in the Air Force Academy and he's talking about how much his son's rejection and anger have hurt him.'

Jerrod stands stunned and immobile as the man looks at him.

'Say, you're from the academy, too. You know this Jerrod Dawson?'

Jerrod's eyes are transfixed on the moving words.

What I wouldn't give to be able to hug my boy again without the barrier of that anger. What I wouldn't give to have my little boy back, my first-born. I've prayed myself dry that one day he'd realise that his mother's accident was not my doing, that I couldn't save her, and that I wasn't rejecting her memory by remarrying. Now, of course, any hope of that grace dies with me in, what, five days.

The businessman next to him is trying again.

'I was asking if you knew his son, Jerrod Dawson? Hey, are you all right?'

Jerrod is sinking to his knees, sobbing, and he can't do anything to stop himself—or hide the name tag that the man is now reading as he leans down to take the distraught young cadet by the shoulders and try to help.

'Oh my God in heaven! You *are* Jerrod Dawson!'

Aboard *Intrepid*

May 18, 5.50 p.m. Pacific Time

The cereal bars are beginning to get tiresome, and Kip wonders if there isn't at least one freeze-dried version of a real meal for his last. It's one of the few thoughts he hasn't entered in the computer. So little time, so much to say.

I had no idea I was so . . . so verbose.

The pause to munch another bar and drain more water has brought him back to the present. He has to live here for a few more days, but the hours he's just spent wandering through his past have been therapeutic. He's been jumping around from good memory to better, whole hours spent ignoring the inevitability of CO_2 scrubber saturation. But for the time it's taken him to eat something and use the relief tube again, reality has claimed him, and he feels the almost desperate need to start typing again.

Kip looks up, taking note of another brilliant sunset, realising how few are left. Better to tackle his adult life. Not just the good parts . . . but how he got to age forty-four with such feelings of worthlessness.

No, not worthlessness, he corrects himself. *Hopelessness. Apathy.*

He takes one more squirt of water, stows the bottle and resumes.

I didn't have to get married at twenty-two, but it just seemed that Lucy was the logical one to marry. We enjoyed each other's company in a passive sort of way, plus we both wanted two-point-three children and two cars in the garage and the great Middle-American lifestyle. In other words, we agreed to marry our middle-aged selves at twenty-two. How pathetic it seems now, not that I didn't love her and grow to love her more, because I did. But that we did the practical thing and decided that waiting to fall in love with someone was a silly waste of time, because, undoubtedly, you'd eventually fall out of love, and then what do you have? So, we just bypassed the passion and fast-forwarded to rocking on the front porch.

And life? It took one look, rolled its eyes and moved on, leaving us there.

Jerrod and Julie would hate to hear me say this about their mother, but the truth does sometimes hurt. She was a wonderful mom (despite battling the depression she tried valiantly to hide). But neither of my kids grew up witnessing parents with the kind of passion for life I see all around me now . . . guys and gals who, despite being married or just together, love being spontaneous and can still hold decent jobs and professions. Lucy and I were incapable of just doing something on the spur of the moment. And yet, isn't that where life gets fun? When it's not so meticulously planned? Why didn't someone tell me?

A sudden beeping courses through the spacecraft, bringing Kip's attention to the front panel. Lacking the experience to scan the complicated array of instruments and see an anomalous indication instantly, his eyes dart back and forth looking for a blinking light.

The beeping continues unabated. Kip, trying to zero in on the source of the sound, slowly works past the echoes around him and finds himself laughing almost uncontrollably for a few seconds.

He reaches out and cancels the alarm he set himself on a sophisticated little clock on the forward panel and looks up in time to catch the next sunrise before turning back to the keyboard.

Here I sit, 310 miles and an impenetrable distance above my planet, and it's literally like pulling the lens back and getting a broader view. My God, it makes me want to yell at everyone down there: Don't waste time feeling bad about being an imperfect human. Acknowledge your mistakes, correct them and go on, but take the risk of enjoying what you've got, and be brave enough to change what doesn't work.

And if I truly did have a bullhorn loud enough to be heard down there, I'd say one more thing, loud and clear: Tell your kids how much you love them and how proud you are of them, and spend as much time with them as you possibly can. You see, I'll never have another chance to tell my son and my daughters how much their dad loves them. But all those moms and dads down there still do. What a gift.

5

Kalgoorlie-Boulder, Western Australia May 19, 7.45 a.m. Pacific Time/10.45 p.m. Western Standard Time

The chances of remaining anonymous being slim to none, Alastair forces himself to head downstairs in search of his father. It was hard enough to feign innocence this morning before school. The live narrative from space is now a worldwide story, and, according to his father, the local search for the hacker who started it will be successful. 'The police will force the Internet provider involved to divulge the owner's name,' he said. 'They may want to thank him, but they'll probably prosecute, too.'

Tonight, a round of pleading emails from the Australian network has pushed him past the tipping point, convincing him to confess now, rather than after a public discovery as they haul him to the nearest jail.

He walks down the hallway to the living room, practising his opening line. *Dad, there's something I have to tell you.* No. *Dad, I need to tell you something important.* Dammit, no. *Dad, I have a confession to make.*

The TV is still on, of course. He could hear it from his room. And his father is in the same spot he was an hour ago, on the couch, concentrating lest he miss reading a word. He is holding what looks like a handkerchief.

The man stuck in orbit—Kip—is talking about his son in the Air Force Academy again. Alastair doesn't understand why the son is so angry, but the father's remorse touches even Alastair's tough father.

'Dad?' he says, tentatively.

There's no response.

'Dad?'

This time he sees his father's broad-shouldered form jump slightly.

'Yes, son?' All Alastair can see is the back of his head.

'I . . . have something to tell you, Dad.'

'Right. Go ahead.'

Weird, Alastair thinks. *Why isn't he turning around to look me in the eye like he always does?*

'Dad, that kid they're looking for? The one who found the transmission?'

'Yes?'

'I . . . should have told you before . . .'

His father is turning around now and Alastair can see his father's eyes are red-rimmed, his face damp, as if he's been crying.

'Should have told me what, son? You know who the fellow is?'

'Yes.'

'Well, tell me.'

He swallows. 'It was me, Dad. I did it. I'm so sorry! I know I promised I'd never hack into anything again, but I—'

His sentence is interrupted by the frightening speed of his father's six-foot frame rising from the chair and covering the distance between them. Alastair flinches, totally unprepared to be scooped up in a bear hug.

'Dad? Are you OK?' Alastair asks after a few seconds of pure shock, straining to breathe.

His father nods at first instead of speaking, which is strange. When he finds his voice it's a strained, reedy version of it. 'I'm so sorry, Alastair.'

Confusion crackles through Alastair's brain, the words making no sense. His father should be angry, stern, red-faced, and working his way to some sort of punishment. Some yelling wouldn't scare him half as much as this.

Yet he's standing here almost holding me off the ground and crying.

'Dad, I don't understand.'

'It's hard to explain, son.'

'Could . . . could you try?'

'I just want to hug you for a second, OK?'

'Sure, Dad.'

'I've kind of taken things for granted, son. I've been hard on you, even when you've done such a good job in school. I tell you when I'm upset with you, but I haven't told you enough when I've been pleased.'

'You're *pleased*?'

His father is nodding, smiling, his big, wet face looking like some benevolent alien rather than his strict dad. He thinks about asking, *Who are you and what have you done with my father?* but he's too shocked to be funny.

'I've let myself get too busy to be there for all your games and plays and things. And we haven't gone walkabout for a year.'

'You've been to almost everything, Dad, and I know you're busy.'

'So was the poor fellow you discovered, Alastair. He was very busy, and there he sits in orbit, dying, can't tell his kid how proud he is of him, and how much . . .' The sentence trails off, incomplete.

'Dad . . .'

'And about the hacking. Did you tell the authorities what you found when you found it?'

'Yes, I emailed the space company in California and they thanked me.'

'Then I couldn't be prouder of you.'

The bear hug starts again, along with words he can't recall ever hearing.

'I love you, son!'

Alastair can feel him shaking slightly, and he pats his father's shoulder.

'That's OK, Dad. Really. I love you, too.'

Pad 39B, Kennedy Space Center, Florida
May 19, 8.25 a.m. Pacific Time/11.25 a.m. Eastern Time

The Deputy Space Shuttle Programme Manager stands on an upper gantry bridge and adjusts his grip on the railing. It would be useful to look over the side to the base of the launch pad some 150 feet below to see whether Jerry Curtis had stepped into the elevator yet, but Griggs Hopewell is not about to try it. What happens to his head with such a view is a nightmare he's smart enough not to revisit. Even after three decades at the Cape, no one knows he's a hopeless acrophobic, and he intends to keep it that way.

Predictably, Curtis—the Director of Safety and Mission Assurance—was anything but pleased about being called out to the top of the launch complex. Though Hopewell tries to keep the volatile manager's feathers unruffled, there are times he has to pull rank, and this is one of them.

Hopewell takes a deep breath.

'Where the hell is that insubordinate bastard?' he growls to himself. The delay is wearing thin, even though he'll never tire of standing beside the monstrous form of the shuttle, especially when it's poised, ready for launch, as it is now.

There's still a chance they can make the launch window, but it shrinks with each new delay. After a cut cable, a safety stop, two personnel complaints about overtime and the latest dust-up over the fuelling schedule, he's beginning to detect sabotage in the air, and Curtis seems to be rubber-stamping even the flimsiest concerns as genuine safety problems.

The elevator is rising now, and Hopewell readjusts his grip and waits.

The cage door opens and disgorges Curtis, who appears spoiling for a fight, yet smart enough not to start one.

'OK, Griggs, I'm here. What?'

'Jerry, I called you up here to answer a very simple question.'

'Yeah?'

'You want to launch this thing on time?'

'What? Of course!'

'You understand the go order comes from the President of these here United States, right? And he's the ultimate boss?'

'What are you saying? That I'm doing something to frustrate this launch? Have you forgotten the basics of system safety?'

'We had a cut cable this morning. How'd it get cut?'

'I don't know. I've got an investigation going. It doesn't look like anything but a mistake.'

'I'm getting a work-to-rule headache out here, too, with those two clowns filing their complaint last night.'

'It's handled.'

'Yeah, but why now, Jerry? Someone ask them to complain, perhaps?'

'I don't like your implication, Griggs.'

'Well, I don't like delays unless they are truly safety-related, and if you or any of your people—including that little gal from DC—'

'Dorothy? She's just doing routine safety audits.'

'Right. And I've got beachfront property in Phoenix for sale. If anyone starts using artificial safety reasons to delay this launch, Shear won't be able to save the culprit from professional oblivion, you included.'

'Are we done here?'

'I hope so. I just want to make sure you understand. A presidential order means a national priority. If it's really a safety issue, I'm with you. If it's artificial, I'll strap your ass on one of these rocket blasters and launch it myself.'

North Houston, Texas
May 19, 1.55 p.m. Pacific Time/3.55 p.m. Central Time

Jerrod enters the smoky den tentatively, like his invitation might have expired. He's spent most of the day with Julie, watching his father's story and words. Even Sharon was decent to him, and he feels beaten down enough to appreciate that, putting his discomfort around her on hold so as to support his dad with his attention and his remorse.

'Sir?' he asks, seeing Mike Summers's form in a recliner.

Big Mike gets to his feet. 'Jerrod. Come over here.'

'You want to talk to me?'

'I sure do. Come sit down. Would you like something to drink?'

'Maybe a beer. Thanks.'

Mike gets a couple of bottles from a small refrigerator and hands one to Jerrod before motioning him down and returning to his chair. Jerrod twists off the top and settles onto a small couch opposite.

'You been watching all day?' Mike asks. 'Your dad's writings?'

Jerrod nods, noticing the large stack of printed pages by Mike's chair.

'I ditched going to my office today and printed up a record of everything he's said so far . . . and I read it, and son, I gotta ask you something, man to man. All right with you?'

'Yes, sir.'

'I'm pretty direct, Jerrod, so I'm just going to say this. Now, just what the hell are you so angry about?'

'I . . . with all due respect, sir . . .'

'Can the bull, mister! Just talk to me. Why are you so damned furious at him? For marrying my daughter?'

'No, I mean . . . no.'

'Another pile of manure! Of course you are. And I know it's not because of who she is, but because he brought her in to replace your mom, right?'

Jerrod nods.

'OK, and some of that's natural. But why are you so mad at your old man that you've . . . stomped his heart flat? Huh? What'd he do to deserve that?'

Tears are welling up now and Jerrod is trying to hide them, as well as his anger at being cornered. 'I was wrong, I guess. I should have forgiven him.'

'For what?'

'For . . . you wouldn't understand.'

'No, I would, and I want to hear you say it. Does it have anything to do with your mom's fatal accident?'

'I'd rather not—'

'You think he set that up somehow?'

'Of course not.'

'We both know she was sick that day and had no business driving. She told you she had the flu, right?'

'He made her drive! OK? My sister was waiting at her school for hours for Dad to pick her up, but he couldn't break away, so he leaves Mom to do it, knowing full well she was too sick.' The words are a snarl.

Mike eggs Jerrod on. 'That's all bull, son!'

Jerrod is on his feet, his eyes aflame. 'No, it isn't! You don't know anything about it. You weren't there, and I was!'

'I don't have to have been there. I know what you're saying is bull. Your mama had no business driving that day. She killed herself.'

'No!' Jerrod's eyes are closed, his arms in the air, fists clenched, his body shaking, as he tries to avoid punching his stepgrandfather. He doesn't hear Big Mike rise from his chair to suddenly grab him by the shoulders.

'It's OK, Jerrod. Those are the things I wanted to hear you say.'

Jerrod looks stunned and Mike continues, nose to nose.

'I wasn't there, but there's a lot more to the story you never knew, and your dad never told you, and it's time you heard the truth.'

'What?' Jerrod's voice is subdued, suspicious.

'Come here and sit.' Mike guides him back down and scoots his own chair closer. 'I know you heard the crash, Jerrod. I know you ran to the end of the block, saw her car in flames, and ran the rest of the way to the wreck. I know you burned yourself trying to get her out, and that you watched her burn to death. I can't erase . . . no one can erase those terrible images. But, son, your mama was taking several drugs from several different doctors, none of whom knew about the others. Two of them should never have been taken together, because one of the dangerous side effects is hallucinating.'

'Hallucinating? Like . . . like on LSD?'

'Or worse. Or maybe just seeing things that weren't there, or not seeing things that were. Like a stoplight. Like the one she ran through.'

'I didn't know this.'

'I know you didn't. And your dad wrongly believed that, if he told you, you'd be even angrier with him for slandering your mom.'

Jerrod searches Mike's face for any sign that he's being lied to.

'But here's the rest of the story. That day, Julie had already been picked up safely at your dad's direction by a family friend, but he couldn't get your mom to accept that. She was paranoid and thought he was lying, and despite the fact that she had been warned not to drive, she did it anyway.'

'I remember Dad called, but she said it was to tell her he wasn't coming for Julie.'

'Yes, that's right. He wasn't coming because she was already picked up.'

'He told me some of those things, but I never believed him. I asked my mother once weeks before if she was taking something because she seemed so out of it, but she said no and I believed her. And . . . and that day, I only heard her side of the conversation.'

'In fact, when she sounded so strange on the phone he left work and screamed towards home. It's fortunate you didn't lose both of them that day.'

'How do you know all this, sir?'

'Your dad sat right here one night a few years back and told me the whole story. He felt so guilty that he didn't see it coming, didn't know about her doubled prescriptions. See, guys like him and you and me, we get this idea that if anything happens on our watch, it's our fault, regardless. Especially where women are involved, 'cause, see, we're supposed to protect them.'

Jerrod buries his head in his hands. 'Oh God, I never gave him a chance, and now . . .'

'OK. Look, I think they'll get him down from there. I have a lot of hope for that, and you should, too. But there's something else. What's really been going on with you, Jerrod, is that you keep blaming yourself even more than him. You think deep down that if you'd been faster, stronger, smarter, or what-the-hell-ever, you could have pulled her out of that car before the fire killed her. You know why I know that? 'Cause you're a male, and that's the way we think. Especially about our moms. Son, I *saw* the pictures, OK? She was trapped. There was nothing you could have done!'

'I could have pulled her out of the window.'

Mike sighs deeply, considering whether to push on. 'Jerrod, she had been completely impaled on the steering column after the wheel broke off. Run through, all the way to her backbone.'

'I . . . saw her look at me . . . Her mouth moved . . . She was screaming . . .'

The only grandfather he's ever known moves to sit alongside him, putting a big arm round the boy and pulling him into a hug, hanging on as the tears finally flow.

Aboard *Intrepid*
May 19, 4.15 p.m. Pacific Time

The so-called terminator—the line of demarcation between night and day—is crawling across the middle of the United States again, but Kip has to check his watch and think to realise that it's been two days since he should have returned to Earth. He figures he has two more days before breathing begins to get difficult.

He knows that his dead pilot is about to become a problem, despite being sealed in plastic as well as Kip could manage. A body in room temperature for two days has already gone through rigor mortis, and Kip fears that soon he'll be inhaling the odour of decomposition. Earlier, he stopped writing for a half-hour to search out Bill's pressure suit, wondering if perhaps putting him in it and sealing everything wouldn't be the best course of action. But he's convinced he's waited too long.

Besides, he might decide to go for a space walk and just end it out there as his own satellite.

But for now the air remains OK and the pull to get back to the keyboard is great. He isn't happy with the way his life looks so far, and he's hoping it will get better, rounding the corner of the last ten years. It seems so ordinary, and he's caught himself wanting to lapse into fiction a few times, spice up a few things here and there.

But the fact that it is, or was, his life forces him to stay honest about the details, even some that he would never have spoken about on Earth.

There's an incident a few years back that still bothers me to the point of losing sleep, something I did nothing about in order to save my job. I didn't find out until too late, and when I discovered the corporate leaders knew about it, I was convinced they would can me if I said anything. I just stowed the evidence away quietly and sat on it like a coward. I'll never know how many people, if any, have been injured or maybe even killed. But a corporation that knowingly ships a bad, completely inactivated lot of a major antibiotic just to avoid the costs of a recall has to be committing a criminal act.

Kip stops, wondering whether to risk putting down the details, knowing they could put several executives of the American branch of the company in prison. But who will care twenty or fifty or whatever years from now? And if by some miracle he does get rescued, he can quietly delete it.

Ah, what the hell. No one's reading this but me anyway.

I think I want to tell you in detail exactly what happened, and how I found out.

The White House, Washington, DC
May 19, 4.18 p.m. Pacific Time/7.18 p.m. Eastern Time

Ron Porter strolls to the desk just outside the Oval Office still occupied by the President's secretary. She waves him in.

He expects to find the President behind his desk, but instead sees him in front of the TV, quietly reading the latest words from Kip Dawson.

Porter, too, has been caught in that distraction all day, cancelling any productive work as he watched the words on his computer screen.

'Pretty amazing, huh, Ron? Just one guy, but I can't quite stop reading him. And . . . frankly, he's making a lot of sense on some things.'

'Mr President, two items. First, the Chinese have just let it be known that they're going to launch on Saturday to go get him regardless of our plans to launch *Endeavour* Saturday around noon, and the Russians plan to launch Saturday at the same time. On top of that, the Japanese Space Agency says they're preparing an emergency launch for Friday.'

'This is ridiculous. What are they going to do if they all make it up there? Draw straws? Has Shear tried to discourage them?'

'No. He's *en*couraging them. The Russians in particular. He says it's because *Endeavour* may not be ready, even though they're already on the extended countdown.'

'Call Shear at home, will you, and tell him now's the time to pare this down to one reasonable back-up launch. I know he can't control those folks but he can beg and wheedle. And the second item?'

'Nothing we can do about it, but we just celebrated a completely unexpected, undeclared national holiday. Actually, more like international.'

'What are you talking about, Ron?'

'Our business community is reporting massive absenteeism and the retail sector is reporting plummeting sales. Everyone's staying home to read what Dawson is writing. Estimates suggest that over two-thirds of our people are actively watching this, and probably close to a billion worldwide.'

'Good heavens.' The President is drawn back to his own TV screen, Dawson's words snagging his attention. 'Wait, I want to read this.'

I have to admit I feel guilty about this, too. So much so that if I were able to survive and return, one of my first acts would be to go to the nearest US Attorney and give him a copy of everything I just wrote. And the sad part is that, now that I go back through it, I realise I do know where the evidence is . . . where the bodies are buried, so to speak. Right there in my filing cabinet in my den under the 2004 tab. The folder with the red exclamation point on it and a rubber band round it. By the time anyone reads this, I'm sure everything in that cabinet will have been long since burned or buried in some landfill. But I know in my heart that there had to be at least a few patients out there who died or had a terrible time because the good old reliable Vectra penicillin they'd bought from us wasn't working. Someone needs to be prosecuted for this.

'Did you see that, Ron? Vectra knowingly sold bad penicillin?'

'Yes, sir. We should act on this, don't you think?'

The President is nodding. 'Let's get those records he mentions protected.'

'FBI?'

'Yes. Quickly.' He turns back to the TV, quietly addressing the unseen writer as Porter hurries from the Oval.

'So, what other bombshells do you have for us, Kip?'

Kennedy Space Center, Florida
May 19, 5.57 p.m. Pacific Time/8.57 p.m. Eastern Time

John Kent has lost count of how many night-time approaches he's made to the KSC runway in one of NASA's T-38s. Touchdown and aerobraking are followed by a rapid taxi to the ramp where an unmarked NASA car is waiting. He joins Griggs Hopewell in the front of the car.

'Why am I here, Griggs?'

'I need your help, John. We've got a presidential directive to launch and a soft sabotage operation being run by our dear administrator to prevent us from launching. I don't know why Shear is silly enough to believe he can send an operative into my space centre and not be found out.'

'The woman you told me about?'

'Miss Dorothy Sheehan. I've had one of my guys watching her, and where Sheehan shows, nothing goes. She's not red-tagging anything herself, but throwing her HQ weight around so that anything she points to someone gets excited about. All day today it's been one crisis after another, not one of them legitimate. I've warned Curtis, because I think he's in cahoots, but I don't have enough evidence to go over Geoff's head to the White House.'

'And the bottom line is?'

'We're not going to make this window, John, if this crap continues.'

'He's been against this from the start. Anything involving DiFazio—'

'But we don't want another *Challenger*, John. And since you is my bona fide partner in crime, I want to review everything they've fingered so far and have you take a long look at the overall plan.'

'Look over your shoulder?'

'Exactly. I'm afraid of pushing too hard.'

Hyatt Regency Hotel, Los Angeles, California
May 19, 8.30 p.m. Pacific Time

In a plush Los Angeles hotel room, with a mini-bar Scotch in her hand,

Diana Ross settles into an easy chair, thinking over the day's events. The TV is on. Kip's last-typed words still hang along the bottom of the screen, the end of a surprisingly introspective tale of his second marriage and how the progressive withdrawal of sexual interest by Sharon Summers Dawson affected him slowly, insidiously. He wrote about his frustration and his attempts to ignore it. He talked about trying to tell himself it was OK, that he could survive semi-celibacy as Sharon became sexually colder.

But she's been wholly unprepared to read that Kip fantasised about her while in training in Mojave—a revelation written with her name clearly attached that's led to an instant phone explosion and morning-show bookings for tomorrow. She's gone through a series of rapid responses from shock to embarrassment to anger to a growing, deep sense of connection.

So I affected him that much!

For several hours she's been worried that he'll say more, take his fantasy into the literary bedroom or something equally tawdry. When he described the feelings their one dinner together had sparked in his love-starved head—thoughts that maybe he should consider ending his marriage and looking for someone like her to love—it was not a welcome accolade. Half the planet has now been invited to think of her as a virtual pin-up girl, if not a potential homewrecker.

How on earth am I going to live this down? she wonders. At the same time she feels guilty that she's irritated over his words when the man has less than forty-eight hours of air left and has absolutely no intention of embarrassing her. And in the end, she decides to deal with the morning-show interviews by laughing it off. After all, she's done nothing to encourage him, and these are only the private musings of a dying man.

Nevertheless, questions keep echoing in her head. *Why now? Why me?*

She knows the answer, but she's been avoiding it: she's in his head.

And now, somehow, he's in hers.

Aboard *Intrepid*
May 19, 8.40 p.m. Pacific Time

Waking from each nap is becoming more and more confusing.

Somehow Kip has developed the ability to fall almost immediately into REM sleep, something he could never do on Earth. But coming out of REM is a slightly wrenching experience, the dreams left behind so real and visceral that each time he has to think carefully about what is and isn't real.

But then the full reality of his situation returns.

This time the dream was all about sex and he hates to leave it. Of everything in this life, he thinks he'll miss sex the most.

If that's how I measure my existence, I was already near death.

The thought makes him chuckle and he considers writing something really steamy, just to show his future reader who he really is, lusty Kip Dawson, a lover devoted to the female of the species who didn't get much practice.

He poises his fingers over the keyboard, visualising Diana Ross. Of course, he could substitute any pretty female in such a narrative, but if he's going to fantasise in writing it should be Diana, whom he can see so clearly.

But then he feels a twinge of puritanical alarm, and chivalrous concern for Diana. Even if his words aren't found until she's a much older woman, such X-rated musings could embarrass her, and he would never want that.

He laughs again at how different the mental wiring is between male and female, and how abysmally unaware most women are of the simplicity of the male mind on the subject of sex.

Think driving force of life! Think the most beautiful element of life. Think I'd rather die without it.

He's had no hope of getting that through to Sharon.

Oh, great! he chuckles. *I find the true meaning of life with less than two days of it left. Impeccable timing!*

He can see a lot of things more clearly now, having chronicled his entire life and come to the conclusion that at best he would give it a C minus.

Then again, what sense does it make to spend the remaining hours whining and crying and carrying on? Nothing will change as a result, except that he'll lose the chance to add to his narrative. Besides, death will be a new beginning. He believes that, doesn't he?

Kip feels a shudder ripple through him, a primal fear of what's on the other side of that one-way door he's facing. He forces his mind back to his narrative. It's safer there, like a warm and familiar room with four walls and window shades he can pull against reality. *Intrepid* itself has begun to feel a little like that, and for two days he's been able to stay uniquely focused, living his life over again.

He has only two more days. But he also has the keyboard in front of him and a hard drive that doesn't know the difference between the real life he's been writing about and the life he wishes he'd had.

Virtual reality, virtual life. What is it they say in Hollywood? Do a rewrite? Good. I'll rewrite my life the way it should have been.

The idea begins to take hold, bringing a faint smile.

Maybe I'll earn a PhD. Perhaps a Nobel Prize for some discovery in one of the sciences, after a short but stellar career as a navy carrier pilot.

Suddenly, he's paging back through what has become a massive document, looking for the place where he first began to regret the way things were going. He finds the spot around page forty and begins highlighting everything afterwards, page after page of his life the way it was. His finger is over the delete button now as he thinks about all he's written, two days of electronic scribbling for forty-plus years of an unfinished, imperfect life. He pushes firmly, hearing the click, as over a hundred pages disappear.

Time to start over.

Los Angeles, California
May 20, 3.10 a.m. Pacific Time/6.10 a.m. Eastern Time

The limo headed for ABC's local studios and the West Coast *Good Morning America* set will be ready in ten minutes, but Diana Ross is having trouble tearing herself away from her laptop with its web connections. Every major radio host is shifting from backgrounders and interviews with Kip's friends aired the day before, to open debates about sex and wifely duties and professional obligations versus time with your kids. Newspapers across the nation have special columns on the President's order for NASA to launch a rescue mission, and details about an FBI raid in Tucson that netted a Vectra regional executive trying to steal the very evidence Kip Dawson revealed from space. The *New York Times* has an entire transcript of Dawson's words as a special section, as do the *Wall Street Journal* and *USA Today*. Instant books have been announced by a host of publishers.

Diana looks down at her coffee cup suddenly as if it's betrayed her. She's drained the contents without realising it.

An instant message from Richard DiFazio pops up.

'You up?'

'Yes. The morning shows are at 7 a.m. Eastern.'

'Did you see the latest, Diana? About his divorce?'

'His what?'

'I just caught it on TV. He's writing up his divorce filing. It just started.'

Aboard *Intrepid*
May 20, 3.12 a.m. Pacific Time

Kip pauses, wondering why lawyers have to use such convoluted words to say the simplest of things. Drafting his own divorce filing has been relatively easy so far, though he's sure that it would disgust any lawyer.

Once more he rereads the words, wondering if Sharon will even be alive by the time anyone actually sees what he's composed.

To the Pima County Superior Court, Arizona:

Comes now Kip Dawson in the matter of the request for dissolution of the marriage of Kip Dawson and Sharon Summers Dawson. Due to irreconcilable differences, Kip Dawson hereby requests the court to dissolve the marriage between the petitioner and the respondent. All Petitioner's personal property and all of Petitioner's share of the marital community property are hereby transferred to Respondent with Petitioner's blessing, inclusive of bank accounts, savings accounts and all real or personal property of whatever kind wherever situated. Petitioner shall retain only his automobile, his father's wicker chair, his filing cabinet and the contents thereof, and one half of his retirement account. Petitioner requests the immediate grant of this petition. Signed electronically and certified correct in the physical absence of any living notary at this location, I hereto affix my signature, Kip Dawson.

He adds the date and sits back, wondering if he should finalise the divorce before going out with anyone on a fantasy date in his new, recreated life.

Yeah. It would be unseemly otherwise without a final decree.

Pima County Superior Court, Arizona. In the matter of Dawson versus Dawson, Petitioner's petition is granted in full as petitioned. By order of the court.

There! Now I'm truly free to start over.

OK, now for the *real* story of my life. I was born to a branch of the Rockefeller family and filthy rich from the word go.

He stops, appalled by the flippant nature of the words against the truly serious intent. He backspaces to erase the sentence. This may be fun, but it's deadly serious fun, if there is such a thing.

So, how do I want to have it start? How do I want to begin my ideal life?

Strange, he thinks. It should be so easy to figure out.

ASA Mission Control, Mojave, California
May 20, 4.55 p.m. Pacific Time

Arleigh Kerr replaces the receiver as Richard DiFazio comes back into the nearly deserted control room.

'Any news?' Kerr asks, aware that the final urgent meeting between their director of maintenance and the chairman was scheduled for an hour before.

'It's final. We can't fly. I saw all the reasons up close and personal and he's right. We'd probably lose our second ship. How about you?'

'The Japanese have scrubbed their launch, pulled the plug.'

'And Beijing?'

'Still scheduled for a liftoff tomorrow morning, three hours before the Russians, and four before the shuttle.'

'Two down, three to go.'

'He's got a fighting chance. Three launches are good odds.'

'You're sure the scrubbers will hold?'

Kerr looks at him long and hard. 'No. I'm not sure. But death by CO_2 isn't instant. If someone can get him out of that airlock before he's too far gone, he could make it. We've briefed all of them.'

'And if you were to bet?' DiFazio asks.

'I wouldn't. Not on this.'

Kennedy Space Center, Florida
May 20, 5.05 p.m. Pacific Time/8.05 p.m. Eastern Time

There are times, Griggs Hopewell thinks, when he can almost recapture that old feeling of NASA invulnerability, those heady days when there was nothing they couldn't do.

It is night again at the Cape, the night before the launch. Hopewell stands in the heavy night air, swatting at an occasional mosquito as he looks at the shuttle lit up so spectacularly a mile away. The morning he knows will be a challenge. He's aware that Miss Dorothy from DC has not given up, and thwarting her will take a masterful effort.

On schedule his cellphone rings and he answers. 'Yes?'

'OK, we've got what we came for.'

'Anything overt?'

'Not yet. If she's got a specific plan, it's buried in what we found, but there are some very interesting names in the data base on her laptop.'

'I'll meet you in ten minutes as planned.'

Aboard *Intrepid*
May 20, 6 p.m. Pacific Time

Kip sniffs the air again. Yes, it is there. Faint, but there, and where there is some smelly evidence of the process of decomposition, there will be more.

He's stopped typing, aware that his fanciful life story rewrite has wobbled too far afield. It's not even a good fantasy, and it feels so narcissistic. No, he decides, he should be writing about something else, maybe how he wishes the world was, rather than how rich or famous he'd like to be.

Well, not famous. That's never turned him on, though now he supposes he'll be a tiny footnote in space history: 'First contest-winning space tourist dies in orbit.'

With the odour, he can't get Bill out of his mind. He's read about the hatch and the airlock now, and knows what he didn't understand before. This isn't like a Hollywood movie where the hero can pull a handle and blow anything in the airlock into space. Someone live has to be inside the airlock to work the outer door. Since there isn't room for two of them in the lock, that means getting into Campbell's space suit, completely depressurising the ship, opening both doors and floating Bill out. He's tried to calculate how many hours of air would be lost, but he can't find the formula. At least he'd have the air pack on the suit, but when that ran out, he might have nothing.

So, I sit here and die with a stench, or just die faster in clean air. Wonderful choice.

So far it isn't that bad, though, he thinks. He has just over twenty-four hours anyway, according to his best calculation. So perhaps it won't matter.

To be on the safe side, he carefully hauls the sealed space-suit pack out of the side locker along with the helmet and opens it up, spreading it out and trying to remember the steps they'd been taught on what to don first.

Just in case, he thinks, putting the suit aside. *Just in case.*

He returns to the keyboard, and for minutes he sits quietly, thinking about the idealised 'life' he's constructed in words. Bianca, his Brazilian wife who never was, not only couldn't wait for him to come home, she was the woman who was at his side in everything, personal and professional, as loving and as caring for him as he was for her.

> I think so many men forget, or maybe never know, the basics of how a woman's mind works, the simple desire to be loved, cherished and not taken for granted. Expressions of love, tenderness, caring, attention and appreciation are things we men want, so why do we forget that women do, too?

He stops, thinking about Sharon, recognising that the failures were not all hers, that he could have done so much better.

Too bad I'll never have the chance to put what I've learned into action.

He leans into the keyboard again.

Anyway, with Bianca, I had never even imagined that kind of relationship, where you just long to be with each other.

OK, look . . . I have a confession to make, future reader. There was no Bianca. It's all my confused dream, my ideal, of what I would have liked my life to be like. I erased the real one because I wanted something better and more exciting, something filled with accomplishment, except for my kids, whom I love. My real kids. Jerrod, my first-born, Julie, and my twins, Carly and Carrie. I miss them more than anything else about my life. All of them.

True, I did make myself a well-known artist. I could have decided to make myself a king or a Bill Gates billionaire—someone else rich and spectacular. But I've come to the conclusion that, whoever I decide to be, I'm still me, regardless of the money, the trappings and all the education in the world. I think who we are remains the same, and I think inside each one of us is a little child who won't tell the adult in us what's wrong. And very often that little child is still very upset over something that happened so far back he can't recall the details, only the hurt. So in this 'new' life of mine, I think what I tried to palm off on you had everything to do with that little boy in me and what he's upset about, not Sharon, or even Lucy's loss.

When I was born, Dad was forty-one. So many years later, here he was an infirm eighty-something, couldn't take care of himself, and Mom was gone, so I had to act. I found a good retirement facility; I knew he hated it, but he went quietly and I sold the house. I was very efficient and took a month off to get everything done. I thought he'd appreciate that—the efficiency. And once I'd made sure everything was OK, I said goodbye. With a handshake, the way he always dealt with me. I was just south in Tucson and I intended to come by at least every month. But something always came up, and when I'd try to call too late at night, I'd get a small lecture from the night nurse. I used it as a licence to stop calling. So life slipped by and one night, when I was lamenting the lack of open expressions of love in my family, I decided to go see him and tell him I loved him, words that had never been spoken between us. I was going to take the time because I could never seem to find the right moment to call, and because he was getting very old and frail. I started looking for the right opportunity—which really means that I started making excuses why I didn't have the time. I was still playing that game when word came that he'd died. Alone. Just up the road.

Every time this spacecraft soars over Phoenix I think about him. All those years, and I could never just call and say, 'Hey, Dad, you know what? You don't have to say anything, but I love you.'

Terra-Net Corporation, North American Network Control Center, Pittsburgh, Pennsylvania
May 20, 7.45 p.m. Pacific Time/10.45 p.m. Eastern Time

The unique three-dimensional display in the middle of the circular command centre is beginning to change, but only one technician sees it: the indication that perhaps as many as a million people more than normal suddenly picked up their phones for a long-distance call.

The technician flails his right hand for the attention of the shift supervisor, whose eyes also go to the display. Both men stand in puzzled silence as a third checks with another major telephonic network, discovering the same sudden jump in activity worldwide.

A young woman with pulled back hair and thick glasses leaves her position several tiers back and comes up quietly behind the supervisor, a laptop computer in her hands.

'I know what's causing this. I just called my mother, too.'

''Scuse me?' the supervisor says. 'Everyone's calling your mother?'

'No. Everyone's calling someone they should have called long ago. It's Kip Dawson, and what he just said.'

6

Kennedy Space Center, Florida
May 21, 5 a.m. Pacific Time/8 a.m. Eastern Time

Once the ENTER key is pressed, she knows there will be no going back. Dorothy Sheehan thinks over the steps again, restraining herself from sending the benign bit of computer code into the system until she's certain that all bases are covered. The entire assignment has been an exhilarating contest of wills, a shadow fight between Griggs Hopewell and herself, but she's thinking ahead to the good life to follow, with the promised office job and real weekends to herself.

OK. Here goes.

She waits for the tiny string of code to add itself to the appropriate program, and gets the return message before logging off and shutting down. If it works as planned, the minute alteration will disrupt things just long enough to scrub the launch, the code alteration then disappearing.

Dorothy carefully wipes off the keyboard and anything she's touched before moving to the door of the empty office, one she selected some days before on learning that the normal occupant was out of town.

She thinks back to the close call last night when she almost walked right in on whomever Hopewell had sent to search her laptop. There was nothing to find, of course, and she hadn't planned to use it for a mainframe insertion, anyway. Much too risky.

Dorothy chuckles at the thought of the people waiting right now to catch her computer's numeric signature entering the mainframe. They'll be waiting in vain, of course, but their trap was cleverly laid.

She checks her watch—8.12 a.m. Eastern Time. The slightly delayed Chinese launch should be happening right now. She knows Shear will be calling the President for permission to scrub the second someone else achieves orbit, and if so, the little adjustment she made may never even make an appearance before it evaporates.

The possibility that Hopewell and company might somehow defeat her, or worse, catch her in the act, is unfortunately part of the game.

But all my bases are covered, Dorothy thinks. *Besides, I'm not forcing anyone to make a no-go launch decision. I'm just helping them with their rationale, and saving the nation one hell of a lot of money in the process.*

Aboard *Intrepid*
May 21, 6.03 a.m. Pacific Time

For perhaps the first time since his voyage began, Kip wakes up without falling. He rubs his eyes, aware he's getting comfortable with his weightlessness, this feeling of floating. Then he's jarred back to reality.

Oh my God, this is day five, isn't it?

He closes his eyes, trying to fight back hysteria. The fifth day is no longer an inestimable series of sunrises and sunsets in the future. It's today. Sometime in the next twenty-four hours it ends. And so does he.

I'm going to die today, Kip tells himself, but the words in his head aren't believable enough, so he speaks them out loud: 'I'm going to die today.'

I thought I was resigned to this. I thought I was ready.

But if so, why are his hands shaking? He's known for four days he wasn't going to make it, but facing it now overwhelms him.

He forces a deep breath, suddenly remembering he should sample the air first. But either the odour from Bill's remains has abated or he's become used to it. He thinks he can last the day now without a space walk. After all, he thinks, a space walk would be a very dangerous thing to try.

Wait a minute! Dangerous? He's actually embarrassed. *So what if it's dangerous? I could play with matches today, run with scissors, insult a serial killer, or rat on the Mafia with complete impunity!*

At least he's coaxed a chuckle out of himself.

He's read that death-row inmates, no matter how brazen and sociopathic, lose their bravado just before execution, and he sees why. It's not hypothetical any more. Leaving this life and this body is about to be his new reality.

What happens, he wonders, when the scrubbers saturate? Will he suddenly feel light-headed? Will he keel over? Or will it be long and agonising?

He catches sight of the unfolded emergency space suit and wonders why the idea of putting it on and going outside is tugging at him. Should he do it to die out there? Would it be any easier?

No, something else, some reason that he almost recalls from a dream and can't put his finger on.

The tool kit, that's it!

The suit has a small tool kit like nothing he's seen before. They showed the components in ground school but he barely paid attention. Now he turns and pulls the suit to him, searching for the correct pocket and pulling out the silver-plated kit.

That is what I remember! he thinks, finding a pair of wire clippers and three colours of electrical tape along with several wire nuts. The thought about a space walk wasn't for hurrying his demise, it was all about trying to repair whatever had been screwed up by the object that hit them.

He can visualise himself wiggling into the suit, figuring out how to pressurise it, stuffing himself in the tight little airlock and floating outside. Maybe another meteor will get him, fast and painlessly. And he'd be doing all that struggling to play in-flight mechanic?

The thought is exhausting, and he decides not to decide yet. After all, there's much more to write before he's ready to think about trying. And it would be a lot more comfortable to stay inside and slip away slowly.

But as he turns back to the keyboard, there it is, that misguided feeling of hope, a glimmer that there could be some way out he hadn't considered.

NASA HQ, Washington, DC
May 21, 6.10 a.m. Pacific Time/9.10 a.m. Eastern Time

The fact that it's ten minutes past nine and his phone hasn't rung can't be good. Geoff Shear opens the tiny instrument and finds the symbol that confirms the ringer is set to on. It is.

The Chinese *Long March* missile boosting their crew capsule into low Earth orbit should have cycled through first- and second-stage cut-out by now and their astronaut—all by himself in a three-person craft—should be approaching orbital velocity.

The cellphone suddenly corks off. Shear flips it open again.

'Yes?'

'This is Jake at the National Reconnaissance Office. The Chinese scrubbed, Geoff. There was a major fuel leak early this morning, and they couldn't resolve it.'

'Shit! How are the Russians doing?'

'Still on countdown for liftoff noon our time. I'll call you back, as things progress at Baikonaur.'

Launch Control, Kennedy Space Center, Florida
May 21, 8.44 a.m. Pacific Time/11.44 a.m. Eastern Time

'Out of limits means out of limits, Griggs!' The launch director is standing now, hands on hips, the computer screen showing the excessive temperature readings displayed on his master console.

'Stand by, Cully. Do *not* declare a hold yet.'

'Look at the count, Griggs! How long do you need?'

Griggs Hopewell has a receiver to his ear and a prepositioned computer team on the other end, physically stationed at a hastily constructed war room one building away.

'Two minutes.'

'You've got forty seconds.'

Cully Jones shakes his head and turns back to the screen, the temperature indication climbing in a tank that could explode if it were to heat up another twenty-five degrees. A high reading can't be written off as just another artificial computer-generated anomaly. Safety demands belief in your gauges, until you have solid, almost irrefutable evidence they're lying.

This does not feel right. The series of bad readings and interrupted communications that have marked the last ten minutes are either evidence of a serious, systemic computer glitch—as Griggs insists without much evidence—or a launch sliding towards disaster.

Hopewell turns back to him. 'OK! Cully, check it now. We're reading raw pick-up data and bypassing the distribution processor that's been causing so many bad readings.'

The display blinks and the temperature drops thirty critical degrees.

'That's real? I can trust it?' Jones snarls.

'You bet. This is just more of the nonsense we've been fighting all morning. The basic distribution processing program is apparently corrupted.'

Another engineer is in his ear on the intercom, and Jones closes his eyes to concentrate on what he's saying.

'I have a complete data dropout on the solid rocket blasters. Total.'

'Stand by!' Once more Cully Jones turns to Hopewell, who is still hanging on to the phone to his emergency computer team. '*Griggs?*'

'I heard, dammit! Hang on.'

'I'm declaring a hold.'

The countdown is descending through T minus sixteen minutes, the tension in the control room increasing exponentially.

Aboard *Intrepid*
May 21, 8.44 a.m. Pacific Time

Kip leans into the keyboard once more.

Having now solved all of mankind's problems (the doomed passenger says, facetiously), it's time to turn my attention to some of my own. The challenge is how and when I should pull the plug, or should I just plan to slip off to 'sleep'.

The other thing that has me fibrillating is an embarrassment: If I had a boat that sprang a leak, wouldn't I at least *try* to plug the leak? Of course. But I've sat here for days waiting for Godot, assuming that nothing more can be done, even though deep down I've known all along it's not true. There is one more overt, physical thing I can do, or at least try.

I'm going to wiggle into Bill's space suit and see if there's anything I can repair outside. What are the chances? Below zero. Yes, I'm somewhat mechanically inclined and I can wire up a mean set of speaker wires. But not high-tech messes caused by high-speed objects hitting spacecraft.

Still, what's the worse case? I die outside instead of inside, but better with my boots on . . . space boots though they may be.

You know, I'm feeling a little punchy. I wonder if the CO_2 build-up has already begun? I feel looser. Or maybe just relieved we're getting close to the end. Relieved and scared out of my mind. That, I think, is the real reason I'm going to go outside and play with the vacuum. I need something to do besides sit here and wait for the inevitable.

I hope you understand—whoever you are and whenever in the distant future you read this—just thinking of another human absorbing all this verbiage has given me a form of companionship. I thank you for that! I thank you for sitting through my grumbling and crying and pontificating.

If any of my kids are still alive when this is found, please see that they get the separate letters I've written to all four individually. And if Sharon is still alive, just this: I'm sorry. I wish things could have been better for us as a couple.

And there is one last overall message I guess I want to leave.

I want for all of you a future in which every human has firmly in his or her mind the scene the three *Apollo 8* astronauts saw back in 1968 when this tiny, beautiful blue marble we live on rose over the edge of the moon as they raced along the far side—an almost iridescent oasis of beauty in an endless, star-speckled sea of black nothingness—and they realised they were looking at spaceship Earth, their home. Suddenly, wars and borders and conflicts based on economics and theories seemed utterly stupid, and while in reality we're a long way from being a species that universally shares that startling view, we must—you must—keep moving in that direction.

That goal of harmony and love that a man from Galilee tried to teach us so long ago is still the goal we should strive for, regardless of what labels we put on the message. 'Us' seems a strange concept, since I'm leaving. But I was a part of spaceship Earth and the human family, a pioneering species that is still relatively blind to a profound truth that's so hard to see when you're working hard and paying bills and raising kids: We are all so very connected! Even me, here, waiting to die in space. I'm connected to everyone down there, and . . . you know, it's amazing. . . . as soon as I type these words I feel the warmth of uncounted prayers and a sea of goodwill and good wishes, as if the entire population of the planet was somehow telepathically saying, 'Everything's OK. Regardless of what happens, it's OK.' I know that no one down there can discern a single thought of mine, but since I've been up here I haven't felt as enfolded as I do at this moment. Now, though, I have to try some self-help, so that I will know I didn't just sit here and ignore options, no matter how impossible they may be. So, if I don't get to write another word, thank you. I left this life as calmly as I could. Not bravely, just calmly. And you know, after everything is said and done, I have been very, very fortunate.

Kip sits back and rereads the last few lines, hoping to feel a rush of satisfaction. But the only closure is that now he can't wait any longer.

The space suit is floating behind the command chair as he unstraps and moves into position to use the breadth of the small cabin for the struggle. Bill was at least ten or fifteen pounds lighter and a little shorter.

He finds it surprisingly easy in zero gravity to pull the legs and arms in place, hauling a bit to get his head in and up through the metal helmet collar. He can feel the fabric of the shoulders pressing down firmly because of the difference in their height.

Item by item, gloves, boots, zippers, interlocks and air packs, he assembles the space suit until all that remains are the helmet and pressurising.

Once the helmet is in place, the white inner hood pulled over his head, he finds the appropriate lock. The control panel on his left arm is already glowing with a small LED annunciator, and he pushes the button to power it up and pressurise, hearing the tiny fans come alive. As the oxygen mix floods the suit and the arms and legs go semirigid, he checks the clock on the forward panel. Twenty-five minutes have elapsed.

Not bad for a rank amateur, Kip thinks, checking that the tool kit is secured inside the Velcroed pocket before floating to the airlock.

Even for a small, naked man slicked up with grease, the airlock would be a challenge. For a moderately sized man in a pressurised space suit, it's like folding himself into a post-office box, and at first Kip all but gives up.

This damn thing must be here for show only! Kip thinks after trying first an arm, then a leg, then his head through the inner door, and finding that either the service pack with the air supply and batteries or some other appendage catches on the door sill each time. He feels an urgency propelling his struggle and cautions himself to slow down. A ripped suit or damaged service pack will doom the entire effort.

OK, then, let's go back to headfirst.

He rotates himself around until he's floating on his back and slowly guides his head and shoulders and torso inside, curling forward as he carefully pulls in his legs, folding them just enough to let the boots clear.

Like crawling into a front-loading washing machine, he thinks.

He pulls the inner plug-type door closed and works the locking mechanism until a small green light illuminates on a panel he can barely see.

There are several switches to be thrown before the pressure dump valve will motor open, and he goes through the sequence carefully. When he's down to the last button push, Kip takes a deep breath, remembering almost too late to unfold the nylon tether strap and hook it into the metal loop within the lock. He assumes the outer door is supposed to remain open while he's outside. Nothing else would make sense.

The button pushes easily and he takes another deep breath, as if the air in his suit was going to be sucked out as well. The pressure gauge begins dropping towards zero, but nothing changes in the suit except the sudden increase in the rigidity of the arms and legs.

An orange zero-pressure light illuminates on the panel, and then a green light on the latch mechanism. Kip begins rotating the wheel to remove the latches, surprised at how easily the door swings open into the void.

ASA HQ, Mojave, California
May 21, 8.51 a.m. Pacific Time

Like a gathering of pallbearers, Diana thinks as she glances at the stricken faces of those standing outside Richard DiFazio's office, eyes downcast at the latest message from Kip.

'We've thought through everything we know, boss,' Arleigh Kerr begins. 'Using a laser to blink Morse code at him was about the last, most desperate suggestion. But there's no way to tell him no fewer than two spacecraft are trying to get off their pads to reach him.'

'He's going to die trying to space-walk, right?' DiFazio asks.

'We teach all of them the basics for a space walk. If he can't get the suit on and tested to a green-light status, he probably won't try it.'

'But if he does?'

'There's no way this guy can fix a spacecraft, and he doesn't have a hand thruster, so if he forgets to connect his tether, he'll . . . just float away. Or he'll tear his suit and die trying.'

'Or he'll just spend his final hour outside on purpose,' DiFazio adds, speaking their collective thoughts. 'I know I probably would.'

'Well, the view's going to be better out there,' Kerr agrees.

'So, bottom line, there's no chance for him outside, and even if he succeeds in not floating off, there's no way he can fix the ship. Right?'

'We don't have any idea what it would take to repair the ship, but the chances are slim to none. Anyway, if we figure an hour for him to get ready past the time he stopped typing, he should be heading for the airlock now. That means about one and a half hours and he'll either be dead or back inside and typing again.'

Aboard *Intrepid*
May 21, 9.06 a.m. Pacific Time

Kip floats out of the airlock head and shoulders first, checking to make sure the tether is tight before turning around and facing the surface of the Earth passing below without the constraint of *Intrepid*'s tiny windows.

Oh my God!

With almost a 180-degree view from his helmet, he's simply flying along, his own satellite, as part of Texas slides beneath him. Only the fans and the hiss of the air supply break the silence, and he turns starward, shocked by the moon hovering clear and bright above. For a long time he just stares, floating, flying, incredulous, and wishing he'd done this days before.

No point in going back inside, he figures. *What a way to leave! Thank you, God, for this chance!*

He can see the Gulf Coast below, along with Pensacola to the east. A line of thunderstorms is marching towards Atlanta to the north and he can see lightning flashing, noiselessly visible from space.

Nothing can prepare you for the magnificence of this! he thinks, wishing he still had the laptop in front of him and the ability to share this, too, with the distant future.

He knows the suit has approximately an hour and a half of air. So he'll have one and a half hours to take all this in and . . .

Whoa, I came out here to check the tyres, he recalls, pulling on the tether to rotate back towards *Intrepid*.

He sees no indication of meteor damage near the door, so he begins pulling himself upwards and over the top of the spacecraft. But there are no handholds, and suddenly he's floating up and away slowly with no choice but to pull on the tether, which starts him back towards the door.

Kip floats motionless beside the open hatch, while he figures out how to get to the other side. There is no handheld thruster to propel him, and no handholds on the fuselage, but he has a tether at least as long as the spacecraft, and the nose is only fifteen or so feet in front of the hatch.

Kip uses the open door as a launching pad for propelling himself along the fuselage towards the nose. He waits until he's just abeam of the tip of the nose before looping the tether over the top of the fuselage and round like a rodeo cowboy throwing a rope. With the line now going over the top from the door and coming back to him under the chin of the nose, he tightens his grip and pulls, letting his shoulder bounce off the left side of the nose. Carefully, keeping his speed slow and controlling his momentum, he comes round to the right side and finds what he's been looking for.

A hole approximately three inches wide of flared metal and fibreglass sits just next to where an inspection panel has been blown away, providing access inside. The cavity is just behind the point where the pressure bulkhead divides the livable capsule inside from the service areas behind. He carefully touches one of the edges, closing his fingers round it to stop his drift. There are wires visible just inside. He can see a major wiring bundle slit in half by whatever hit them as it exited the side at a shallow angle.

No wonder the engine wouldn't fire!

He stares at the damage, wondering whether to try for a closer look.

The small tool kit in the leg pocket of his suit contains a knife and electrical tape, both on tethers of their own. Overcoming the momentary urge to just give up and return inside, he begins assembling what he thinks he'll need as he floats to one side of the hole. He places the knife beside him and lets go, marvelling at how it just sits there in space, gyrating slightly with each tug of the tether, its own tiny little satellite.

The severed wiring is chaotic, but as he looks more closely, he can count perhaps twenty actual wires completely cut and others merely grazed.

OK, suppose I treat this like speaker wire? Is there colour coding? Yes! Look at that! Red, orange and green stripes go to whatever else has red, orange and green stripes. I'll probably run out of air before I can get them all, but what the hell.

He secures himself with his left hand, which is holding both the edge of the hole and the wire, and starts working inside the hole. With the knife blade he neatly scrapes away the insulation round the first cut wire, before finding the other end and doing the same. Twisting them together and taping off the result is incredibly awkward in the inflated gloves, and he worries about slicing open his suit on the jagged edge of the hole, but he keeps each movement under tight control and slowly works through each of the wires, going faster as he gets more familiar with the bulky gloves.

There is intense heat from the sun's unfiltered rays on his left side and he remembers to change position to keep from overwhelming the suit, which is getting warm inside.

The suit's control panel is showing twenty minutes of air left by the time he finishes splicing every wire for which he can locate a mate. He folds and replaces the knife and the tape, before pulling himself back over the top to the open airlock door, where he stops to make a critical decision.

It would be so much more meaningful to die out here, he thinks. *Just a button push to blow the suit. But, if I do, I'll never know if the repairs have changed anything. Is there any chance the radios could be working now and I could reach someone?*

And what if, somehow, he's reconnected the rocket?

No! Kip cautions himself. *No way the engine is going to light off. That would require a professional. The best I can hope for is that somehow I've bumped something the right way and restored space–ground communications. But as long as I'm floating here trolling for meteors, I'll never know.*

Five more minutes, he decides, drinking in the view as the terminator slips by below, just past the Red Sea, and he watches the glow from what he decides must be the Saudi Arabian desert city of Riyadh, sitting like a twinkling, grounded star against the darkness of the desert beyond.

He knows by now that the retrofire point—should he need it—is just under an hour away, which means that even if he decides to test the rocket motor, he'll have to wait for that window. Not that anything will happen.

But he does feel the tiniest glimmer of hope.

OK, he decides. *Let's get back in, and once I'm sure nothing's going to change, I'll come back out and end it here.*

Office of the Administrator, NASA HQ, Washington, DC
May 21, 9.06 a.m. Pacific Time/12.06 p.m. Eastern Time

The Russian rescue mission and the administrator of NASA go into motion at the same moment. In Russia the *Soyuz* spacecraft clears the Baikonaur launch pad while in the Beltway Geoff Shear is already speaking to the White House aide he's had holding for ten minutes.

'OK. Put him on. Quickly.'

Less than a minute goes by before the President picks up to hear that the Russians are under way.

'I urge you to let me scrub our launch, Mr President. It's unnecessary now.'

'How much time on our countdown, Geoff?'

'Coming up on eleven minutes, sir. We just came off the hold.'

'Geoff, I want our guys to do the job. You know that.'

'Yes, sir, but—'

'This is the sort of mission the shuttle was supposed to be able to do. Even if we have to compete with a parking lot full of spacecraft up there, I want Kip on our shuttle.'

'Mr President, we've pushed everybody down there very hard to accomplish this emergency mission so we can comply with your directives, and frankly there have been all sorts of technical problems, and even though we've gotten past most of them—'

'Are you telling me the launch is unsafe?'

'I . . . don't know for a fact that there's any inordinate danger, more than usual, but whenever you push hard like this, things can go wrong.'

'What's gone wrong?'

'Just a lot of computer problems and glitches and low readings. The countdown has been threatened over and over again. But it tells me—'

'But you can't say definitively that you're violating safety parameters?'

'No.'

'Very well, then. We launch, Geoff. And that's that. Get our guys up there and get Kip Dawson down safely. Clear enough?'

'Very well, Mr President. Keep your fingers crossed.'

Geoff hangs up and sits for less than a minute, weighing the dangers of triggering what he considers his own 'nuclear' option—his last chance to keep the shuttle grounded. Suddenly, he's pulling his cellphone from his pocket and punching up the screen to send a coded, numeric text message:

80086672876

One minute later his phone beeps and the return message appears with a simple 'OK.'

Kennedy Space Center, Florida
May 21, 9.08 a.m. Pacific Time/12.08 p.m. Eastern Time

Dorothy Sheehan stares at the cellphone display in disbelief, wondering if the number she's been given as a code matches what she's seeing.

She quickly checks and feels a shiver when the number matches.

If Shear had asked her to have a cyanide capsule embedded in a tooth against capture she wouldn't be more surprised. There's no time to return to the vacant office she was using. The launch will be safely scrubbed, but she'll be almost instantly traceable as the saboteur.

Why didn't I prepare for this? she thinks, knowing the answer. What she's already embedded can have no direct safety impact on the shuttle or the crew, but what Geoff Shear has just ordered could lead to a major computer shutdown just before liftoff, when the readings could confuse the launch crew.

The thought of just walking away and reporting there wasn't time crosses her mind, but her deal with Shear depends on success.

She glances at her watch. Just over six minutes remain. She powers up her laptop, then makes entries in the office computer, establishing a connection from inside to out through the laptop's air modem. The program she needs to load is a complicated string of computer code, and she checks the connection, moving through the office computer's now-breached firewall to the main NASA network, looping it through a server to confuse where it came from.

The code has to replicate over the course of at least a minute before inserting itself in the master program as a basic program patch. She takes a deep breath and hits the load button.

Launch Control, Kennedy Space Center, Florida
May 21, 9.13 a.m. Pacific Time/12.13 a.m. Eastern Time

'*Yes!*' Griggs Hopewell lowers the receiver and turns to the launch director, the report from his computer team still ringing victoriously in his ears. 'Caught her red-handed monkeying with the program, and my guys stopped the program patch she tried to install.'

Cully Jones is nodding appreciatively but his eyes are on the countdown clock now ticking under two minutes while he presses his headset closer to his ear and motions Hopewell to silence. 'What? Which one?'

Jones leans into his screen as he triggers a series of entries before answering the reporting engineer somewhere in the room.

'I see it. Has it been steady up to now?'

Hopewell punches into the same net and struggles his headset back on in time to hear the remainder of the response: '. . . no problem I can see before, but it's suddenly climbing into overpressure.'

'The read-out is hard-wired or telemetry?'

'That's telemetry, Cully. Fifty psi and still climbing. I have a corresponding temperature rise and a pressure warning on the relief valve.'

Hopewell flips through one of the manuals as fast as he can, conscious of the count reaching T minus one minute. A complicated transmission diagram opens before him, and he examines the circuit controlling the dangerous readings they're discussing before turning to Jones.

'Cully, the readings go through a computer processor. Not the same one, but equally vulnerable.'

'I thought your guys stopped the interference?'

'They did,' Hopewell says. 'But something must have slipped through.'

'We don't know that. We can't assume that. I have to call a hold.'

'Yes, we do know that!' Hopewell's voice is rising in intensity. They're out of time for this argument, but the launch window is too small for a hold. 'Cully, it's through the same basic switching equipment and equally vulnerable and this happens just suddenly? I don't think so.'

T minus fifty-eight seconds is flashing on the screen. Everyone in the room is aware that once the countdown reaches thirty seconds the debate is over. The launch can't be stopped.

'Systems, what's your recommendation?' Cully asks.

'It's out of limits. No fly.'

'Hold the count,' Cully orders.

'No, goddammit!'

Jones is turning now, his eyes flashing anger. 'Two words, Griggs. *Challenger* and *Columbia*. We stay conservative. You object?'

Hopewell stares at the resolve in Jones's face and shakes his head.

Cully triggers the interphone channel. 'The count is holding at T minus forty-two seconds. We have thirty seconds to decide to scrub or resume the countdown. Systems, where are we?'

The man turns from his console two rows away, his face reflecting genuine fear. 'Pressure is out of limits, temperature approaching out of limits, and I have a report from the gantry shelter of heavy venting. We need to get the crew out, now! This is real!'

'Then we're scrubbed!' Cully barks.

Launch control explodes into action as the practised team at the pad moves towards an emergency extraction of the two crew members while Cully Jones runs through the checklist to purge the dangerously overpressurised tank before the contents can explode.

Griggs Hopewell sits quietly, watching and listening, slightly stunned.

My God, this one was real, and I led myself into the assumption that Sheehan did it.

Office of the Administrator, NASA HQ, Washington, DC
May 21, 9.16 a.m. Pacific Time/12.16 p.m. Eastern Time

Word that the launch was scrubbed has given Geoff Shear a smug feeling of restored control. Somehow, he's going to have to do something really special for Dorothy Sheehan. She's succeeded against overwhelming odds.

His cellphone is vibrating in his pocket and he whips it out. It takes him a few seconds to realise that he's talking to Dorothy herself.

'Why are you calling?' he asks, puzzled. *She knows better.*

'I'm in trouble, sir. I think I've been discovered.'

'What did you say? I heard we scrubbed down there. Thanks for everything you were doing down there to keep us safe.'

Geoff's mind is racing. Any call could be monitored and Sheehan should know that, which means she's seriously frightened, and dangerous.

'Where are you calling from?' he asks.

'I'm outside, in my car, getting out of here. I . . . I guess I just need some coordination since my purpose here is done. All the safety checks and such.'

'Well, Dorothy, your assignment was clear. Double check to make certain we weren't pushing safety limits. Just come home.'

There's a telling hesitation. 'Well, sir,' she says, her tone hardening. 'I got this call and I responded as requested.'

Five seconds of silence pass before she speaks again, her voice this time low and serious. 'You're going to let me twist in the wind, aren't you?'

'What does that mean? Dorothy, if you've . . . done something improper, then you need to tell security about it. I have to go.'

He ends the call, erases the number from the display and punches the phone off, a small chill climbing his back. Sheehan was supposed to be rock-solid reliable, his own ex-CIA operative with steely nerves and endless resources. How could she crack? This is all containable, he tells himself. But that doesn't soothe him, and with the sixth-sense survival instincts of a high-level bureaucrat, he can already hear footsteps behind him.

Aboard *Soyuz*
May 21, 10.05 a.m. Pacific Time

Sergei Mikhailovich Petrov is not surprised to find himself precisely where he expected to be: on orbit, 310 miles above the planet and precisely 70 miles behind the private American spacecraft.

He glances at his companion, Cosmonaut Mikhail Rychkov, who is hunched over his computer display. 'Our closing rate is what?'

Mikhail replies without looking over. 'Forty metres per second.'

There will be a turnaround and a braking burst from their main engine necessary in forty-eight minutes, followed by the delicate task of carefully approaching the winged craft from beneath and slightly ahead. In the rushed preparations of the previous two days, the plan coalesced only as far as parking the *Soyuz* just above the private space plane and sending Mikhail out on a dangerous space walk with the spare pressure suit they plan to stuff into *Intrepid*'s airlock.

The right leg pocket of Mikhail's suit is brimming with black markers able to take the exposure to the vacuum of space. Using a white posterboard and a tethered cloth, he'll write instructions in English for Kip Dawson to read through the forward windscreen. At least, that's the plan. The back-up is equally risky, given the size of their space suits and the tiny airlock on *Intrepid*; Mikhail has substantial doubts whether he can fit inside if he has to go in to prepare Kip for the transfer.

Sergei has the high-powered binoculars out and is searching the void ahead, a smile forming on his face that Mikhail notices.

'You see him?'

'*Da!* And he's still flying backwards, facing us, which will make it easier, I think.'

ASA Mission Control, Mojave, California
May 21, 10.05 a.m. Pacific Time

Had a wayward buffalo wandered into and through the control room, the effect would have been much the same. The disbelieving looks on the faces of the control-room technicians accompany a stunned paralysis as their collective minds try to grasp the fact that every monitor, including the big-screen display, has burst back to life with information from *Intrepid*.

The first technician to get to his feet glances at the door, then back at the screen, wanting to call Arleigh Kerr in from his office but not wanting to look foolish if this is some sort of hallucination.

'What the hell is this?' someone else is asking.

'We must have accidentally triggered an old simulation run,' says the assistant flight director. 'Let's stop it and figure out how it got triggered.'

One of the occupants of the front tier of monitors stands up. 'But look at the time signature,' she says. 'The time and date stamp are current. Today. As in now. This is *Intrepid*'s live telemetry back online! *He did it!*'

Kennedy Space Center, Florida
May 21, 10.05 a.m. Pacific Time/1.05 p.m. Eastern Time

Griggs Hopewell sits heavily in his office chair, waiting for the confrontation with Dorothy Sheehan, feeling certifiably old. Despite the continued presence of the shuttle on the pad rather than on orbit, the system worked, but the net effect has been depressing. The past week has pushed his limits.

'Griggs? We've got Miss Sheehan here.'

He snaps to mentally. 'Everyone come on in.'

A sombre delegation files into the room and he sees that Dorothy Sheehan has been cuffed. The head of security for the space centre follows with one of his officers, trailed by Cully Jones and the head of the legal staff. Sheehan's glare is meant to melt steel, but the fear in her eyes is ruining her act.

'For God's sake, Nelson, take those cuffs off this lady. What's she going to do? Run out and steal the shuttle?'

'We did catch her trying to run out of the front gate, so to speak,' the security chief says while pulling out his cuff key and unlocking her.

'Have a seat, Miss Sheehan,' Hopewell says, motioning to the couch.

She complies, her eyes boring into his face.

'You're familiar,' he begins, 'with the old term "red-handed"?'

'Look, I don't know what you think you're doing—'

Hopewell raises his hand, stopping her. 'So, Miss Sheehan, would you care to tell us precisely why you were attempting to sabotage the launch of our little rocket out there?'

'I was doing no such thing!'

Hopewell shifts forward in his chair. 'Let's get one thing really straight, OK? We have you. We have the evidence to put you in a federal prison, probably for life, and the only thing you have to cling to right now is the hope that if you tell me who, what, where, when, how and why—including every conversation in exquisite detail you had with Mister Geoffrey in Washington leading up to your actions—I might decide it's the bigger fish who need frying. Nod your head if you understand, and let's cut the bull.'

'You want to deal?' she asks, triggering a broad grin from Hopewell.

'You have no idea how much,' he says. 'So you cut the cards, Ma'am.'

Her jaw clenches, and she fastens her eyes on his. 'If I'm allowed to walk,' she says through tightened lips, 'I'll give him to you in a sealed box.'

'You do that, Sheehan, you walk. You'll never set foot on a NASA installation again, but you won't have to limit the rest of your days to a cell.'

'Do we have a deal?'

'Well, if you can deliver, then yes. We have a deal.'

She nods. 'Right. So happens, I have tapes of just about everything Shear and I discussed. And because of where they were made, they're admissible.'

ASA Mission Control, Mojave, California
May 21, 10.10 a.m. Pacific Time

Diana Ross stands in silent shock at the back of the reactivated Mission Control room, recalling the story of Lazarus. If Kip can be brought back to Earth, there would be room for the word 'miraculous'.

Yet, if he doesn't re-enter *Intrepid* before an hour and a half are up, all the cosmonauts will be able to do is recover bodies.

News that the telemetry downlinks from *Intrepid* are working again took a few minutes to reach her office, and she figures it is some sort of overwrought misinformation. But there it is, the data streams moving across the screens as if nothing had ever been amiss—with the exception of voice communication, which has not been restored.

In the background she hears Mission Control's repeated attempts to hail *Intrepid*. But no answer from Kip, and no further typing.

'The external airlock door is showing open,' the assistant flight director reports. 'The inside door is still closed, inside atmosphere still breathable.'

'Dammit, he's got less than fifteen minutes of air left to get back in there,' Ashleigh Kerr is saying, as much to himself as to the control room.

Diana thinks back to the shock hours ago upon reading of his intent to leave the ship and the frustration she felt at not being able to scream at him to hang on, that help was coming. She focuses now on the numbers cascading down on one side of the screen while her mind reaches for him so many miles away. Daring to hope, just a little, was logical. But the startling reality is how much it impacts her. She knows fatigue is in charge now. If there's some uncontrolled, starry-eyed tendency to slide towards falling in love with him, it would be, she thinks, like falling in love with Elvis. And yet Kip to her has become as compelling as gravity.

The thought is interrupted by a shout from one of the console positions.

'Hey, everyone! *Intrepid*'s outer door just closed, and I'm getting a pressure drop inside!'

Aboard *Intrepid*
May 21, 10.12 a.m. Pacific Time

Strange, Kip thinks, how climbing back inside felt like spoiling a good stage exit. But he's agreed with himself to try the rocket one last time, on the chance it might make a difference. And now, sitting in front of the command panel, the thought hits him that if it fires he'll have an incredibly complicated flying machine to guide through the atmosphere, without the benefit of flight training. Not to mention figuring out how, and where, to land it. Succeeding in a space-walk repair, a deorbit burn and a re-entry, only to crash and die in a botched landing would be awful.

He's already flipping through the checklists, looking for one for emergency re-entry. *There!* He opens it, reading too quickly, having to force himself to slow down and reread it.

Someone down there, Kip thinks, decided to write the checklist so that a rank amateur could follow it. And even with a dozen glider flights and basic stick and rudder skills, and a couple of fixed-wing flights in a single-engine Cessna in his head, Kip has never felt so much like an amateur.

He checks the time. Twelve minutes to go. Just time enough to learn how to place the small bullet-shaped icon on the attitude indicator in the arms of the moving 'V' that is the flight director, the key to keeping the ship in the proper attitude on the way down.

He keeps looking for the information on how to punch an autopilot button and let the ship fly itself, but either it doesn't exist or he can't find it. He'll have to fly it manually and hope for the best. He realises that he's actually thinking of re-entry as a real possibility and getting way ahead of himself. After all, if the engine doesn't fire, the rest of it is academic.

KIP SITS in the command chair staring at the western edge of the planet, wondering why a bright blue light had been sparking intermittently on the horizon line. He turns to the beckoning laptop keyboard. But there are only four minutes remaining.

For some reason it feels good to speak out loud, after so many days of silent thoughts, at full volume. 'So, are we ready?'

He looks at the attitude indicator, noting the target dot nestling snugly where it should be in the 'V' for retrofire. Five minutes of rocket thrust at more than three g's of deceleration will be required to get home. If he's slow in firing, he'll drift eastwards, away from Mojave.

He pulls the laptop over suddenly, unable to resist.

OK, I have two more things to say. First, I've just been outside and tried to repair this little craft, and I have no idea whether I made any difference, but I'm going to try to fire the engine once more in a few minutes. Second, I have finally realised something that to me is very important: It turns out that I have never been Kip Dawson until now, until I was forced to be honest about my life. I am electing life on my own terms, and even if I have only a few minutes of it to enjoy, it feels wonderful. I get the point now.

Just under one minute left. Kip positions his hand on the sidestick controller, fanning his fingers and waiting as he forces from his mind the fatalistic 'reality' that the motor will not fire. Of course it'll fire. He'll simply *will* it to fire. All positive thoughts. Mind over matter.

He watches the second hand crawl below ten seconds, unable to resist the urge to voice his own countdown.

'Nine, eight, seven . . .'

The words seem to echo in the small cabin, something he hasn't noticed before. He's bracing for the thrust in his back.

'Two, one, and we have *ignition!*'

Kip's left index finger shoots towards the ignition sequence button and presses hard. He can feel the click of the switch.

And that's all.

For a moment he sits with his finger still depressing the switch, as if the engine is just thinking about it and may get around to firing in a few seconds. But the seconds move towards a minute as he pulls his finger back and presses the switch down again and again, not frantically, but with a determination to get his message across: *You are hereby commanded to fire!*

The engine, however, isn't complying, and instead of feeling great angst Kip feels strangely composed and calm.

He pulls his hand away, his mind moving steadily back over the checklist items needed to fire the engine. The checklist is in his lap, and he finds the right page and begins moving down the list, double-checking every switch, aware that more than a minute and a half have already passed and he'll commit himself to landing somewhere way east of Mojave if the engine fires.

'Ignition primary and secondary bus transfer switches should be off. They are. Ignition emergency disconnect relay one and two guarded on. Where are those? Oh yeah, they're positioned right.'

He stares at the switches. Small red plastic covers known as 'switch guards' cover each one to prevent a sleeve or wayward hand from accidentally flipping the tiny lever. *So are they off or on when closed?* he wonders, opening one of the guards to expose the metal toggle lever inside.

It's off. So when the guard is closed and down, the switch is off.

'Wait a minute.' He flips open both guards and moves the switches to the 'on' position, double checking the language in the checklist. 'For God's sake, don't tell me that's why the engine didn't fire four days ago!'

Were they open or closed then, those guards? He can't remember.

His breathing has accelerated and he can feel his heart pounding and his face reddening, more from embarrassment than anticipation. All this because he didn't follow the checklist four days back?

At least now, he figures, they're in the right position.

Once again his index finger stabs at the ignition switch.

Aboard *Soyuz*
May 21, 10.39 a.m. Pacific Time

'One thousand metres, closing at five per second,' Mikhail Rychkov intones in the calm voice of a man serenely on the razor edge of his technology.

Sergei Petrov nods, his eyes still focused on the just-received message from Baikonaur Mission Control that is wrinkling his features.

'You believe we should drop down in case he retrofires?' he asks, knowing the finite amount of fuel in the manoeuvring jets and estimating how much it will take to change orbit even that slightly.

'You've been watching with the binoculars, Sergei. Have you seen any movement? Any evidence that he's seen the laser I've been flashing?'

'*Nyet.* Nothing. But let me look again.'

Sergei plucks the instrument from where it's been floating by his face and focuses once more on the forward windows of the backward-flying American space plane. The image steadies and suddenly looms larger, as if he's triggered a zoom lens. He shakes his head in confusion.

'What am I . . .?'

'Sergei!' Mikhail is barking the words. 'He's coming! Coming at us!'

The mission commander grabs for the controls, recalling now the sight of a burst of *something* alongside the craft just as it started zooming in.

Sergei's hand reaches the firing control and jams their main engine to life, thrusting forward while canting the angle of firing downwards, but the oncoming vehicle is accelerating towards them.

A rapid calculation flashes through Mikhail's mind, pairing 500 metres with the steady acceleration of the ASA ship and yielding a catastrophic closing speed by the time it reaches them. But at last the two cosmonauts can feel their craft thrusting ahead of the oncoming space plane's trajectory.

It's too late to do more, and as the American spacecraft fills the forward window both men cringe in anticipation of a thunderous impact.

As if it were a holographic projection, as soon as *Intrepid* fills their eyes, it flashes past, missing their craft by a tiny margin they can only guess at, shooting through the empty space around them, no wake turbulence to rattle their craft, and nothing but the accelerated heartbeats in the *Soyuz* capsule to mark its passing.

Aboard *Intrepid*
May 21, 10.40 a.m. Pacific Time

Kip doesn't have a spare second to be confused.

No time to wonder about what flashed past the forward windscreen less than a minute after ignition. Maybe a satellite. Maybe nothing. Whatever it was, it seemed incredibly close, yet it whooshed past without a sound, like an illusion. It was a familiar shape somehow, but his attention is too focused on the forward panel to think it through.

Kip's right hand is working the sidestick controller constantly with small, intense movements, and there's a tiny flash of pride that he's already learned not to overcontrol. Three g's of thrust are pressing at his back and pulling at his face, but it's all as bearable as the ascent was four days ago.

He checks that he's aimed *Intrepid*'s nozzles in the right direction, and holds the ship steady with a massive force of will, playing a video game with life-or-death consequences in keeping the tiny dot in the 'V' on the attitude indicator. The nose slowly comes up, changing the rocket engine's thrust vector from all horizontal deceleration to a mix of vertical and horizontal, keeping gravity from yanking *Intrepid* too rapidly back towards Earth.

The engine should cut out, the checklist says, when he's at eighty degrees nose up, still flying backwards, at an altitude of ninety miles with almost no forward speed. He'll have less than a minute, when the fuel runs out and *Intrepid* begins to free-fall, to use the reaction thrusters to raise the tail and turn the space plane around. Then he'll be falling belly first, like some sort of man-made leaf, into the upper reaches of the atmosphere.

Three minutes elapse, feeling like ten. The nose-up angle is nearly thirty degrees now as he slowly arcs back towards the planet. The numbers on the screen indicating forward velocity are down below 8,000 miles per hour, the stars still visible outside the window.

So far, his control movements are steady, competent, even professional, and he can't figure why. He doesn't know nearly enough to do this. Yet here is his right hand, moving the stick with calm competence, as if he's a *real* astronaut.

Suddenly, the noise and thrust and shaking and moving numbers that are the cacophanous reality of this return to Earth begin to recede. He feels an unexpected tranquillity descend over him, validating that his hands really do have it under control and his mind is free to float. He's being enfolded by a peace he's never felt before, never imagined. It's a crystalline moment of aching, indescribable beauty, and tears come unbidden to his eyes.

They are, he realises, tears of appreciation for just *being*, and for the first time in his life he finds himself overflowing with a love of the moment and of life as it is—a love so deep, so complete, that even if it all ends within seconds, the contentment will have too much force not to live on.

Kip Dawson's mind returns to the reality of *Intrepid*'s cabin, the sounds rising in volume around him but altered now and somehow incapable of threatening him, even as his adrenaline flows like a flood-stage river.

He shakes his head against the g-forces. Engine cut-off is less than forty seconds away, the nose-up angle approaching sixty degrees. Forward speed is coming under 1,500 miles per hour, and still he's holding the dot in the 'V'.

He was four minutes late firing the engine, so the landing will be somewhere in eastern Arizona. He wonders if anyone at Mojave has a clue he's not still in his stable orbit. If he can't find an airport and ends up hurt or dead in the back country, he figures they won't find him for days or weeks.

Or maybe even years.

Engine shutdown catches Kip by surprise, kicking him forward. Again he's in zero gravity. He checks the descent speed: 260 feet per second. He sees the target dot on the attitude indicator blinking red as it moves down. He moves the sidestick controller to follow, startled when the Earth swims back into view. *Intrepid*'s nose changes pitch from near vertical through the horizontal and down to twenty degrees below the horizon. He wants to look at the surface below and try to figure out where he is, but his eyes have to stay riveted on the attitude indicator until he feels the ship stabilise.

The quietness of the engine is almost unnerving, and he remembers to consult the checklist Velcroed to his knee before reconfiguring the ship and raising the tail structure to keep down the speed of re-entry. He triggers a small hydraulic pump, and a tiny whine begins from somewhere aft. On the forward panel a series of push buttons light up that control the process of feathering the ship. He pushes them in sequence, and feels the change in the tail structure as it rises to a nearly eighty-degree upward deflection.

The altimeter shows they're descending through 400,000 feet. *Eighty miles*, Kip thinks, *the upper beginning of the atmosphere.* His gaze takes in the horizon once again as he uses the sidestick to bring the nose up, stopping at ten degrees down. The curvature of the Earth is still pronounced, the darkness of space beyond still stark and amazing.

He remembers to reposition the seat, leaning it back and tightening his seat and shoulder harnesses against the five-g peak deceleration to come.

Where am I? He cranes his neck to see better through the forward windscreen, looking for anything identifiable. The map display should be showing what he's over, but it has switched to some diagnostic screen and Kip punches the buttons round the perimeter, trying to get the map back.

He can see a line of snow-covered mountains far below, and one of them resembles Pikes Peak. But when he looks more closely, he realises that Colorado is much further north. He could twist the sidestick controller around and yaw left or right to see better, but he's afraid of disobeying the V on the attitude indicator.

A hint of slipstream noise is becoming more pronounced as he descends below 300,000 feet, no longer in space but still in the far upper reaches of the atmosphere. The speed is fairly steady now, just under Mach 3.

A red symbol has begun blinking urgently on the forward display and Kip leans forward to read it: WARNING: LEFT STRUT UP-LATCH NOT LOCKED.

He understands. The twin tail booms are in the up position, yet the left one is not locked, and the increasing pressure of the airflow is trying to force it down. If that happens, he'll start spinning and speeding up.

Kip pulls the other checklist to his lap and flips to the page covering major emergencies, amazed that he isn't frantic. He reads that the first step is to verify the hydraulic pump is still on. He looks at the panel. The switch is on. But the pressure is zero, indicating the pump has failed.

Slowly, as he looks at the horizon, *Intrepid* begins to rotate to the left.

There is a manual procedure, Kip sees. A cable can be pulled to secure the up-latch, and it's in a panel beneath his left leg. The g-forces are already building as Kip snaps off his seat and shoulder harnesses and dives forward, his left hand scrambling for the panel, his right hand holding the checklist. He finds the left boom T-handle and grabs it, then looks at the checklist.

'Ensure aerodynamic control automatic engagement has occurred.'

There is a lighted message on the screen. His eyes are blurry, his body straining forward against the g-forces, but he finally sees the words.

OK. Engaged.

'Pull nose up momentarily to twenty degrees high, then pull T-handle.'

He understands what has to happen. *Intrepid* is spinning to the left, and it will get worse as he pulls the nose up. But if he pulls on the T-handle at exactly the right moment . . .

There is no time to think about it. Kip grabs the stick and pulls it back, feeling an amazing increase in g-forces as the ship's belly becomes perpendicular to the relative airflow, slowing him. The spin becomes a blur, and he's having to pull almost to the stops to get twenty degrees nose high.

Now!

His body protests at the elephant of force that's just jumped on his back, crunching him down as he hears the boom clang into position. He yanks hard on the T-handle, pulling it out to the stop before the sickening feeling of a broken cable registers. *Intrepid* has transitioned back to slightly nose down, and the T-handle has come completely out with no resistance on the line.

Something on the forward panel has changed, though, and as he strains to look, the warning light is gone. He leans forward against what feels like five g's, and finally spots the locked indication.

Locked! God, I did it!

Kip forces his torso back into the command chair, and as he fumbles for the seat and shoulder harnesses he realises that the left spinning is stopping, the world outside slowing from a blur back to identifiable landscape.

The altimeter reads 190,000 feet. The curvature of the Earth is still pronounced, but the horizon is showing a distinct atmospheric glow. His entire body is hurting from the fight with the g-forces and he has to remind himself to look back at the checklist. The procedure is only half complete. If the hydraulic system can't lock a wayward tail boom, it can't unlock it and move it down, and, with the tail flipped up, *Intrepid* is uncontrollable.

The g-forces are slowly diminishing with his speed as Kip once again concentrates on the checklist. He's missed a section, he realises. He never checked to find the circuit breaker for the hydraulic pump.

Once more he leans forward, finding a panel compartment of circuit breakers. He forces himself to focus on the placards next to each breaker until he locates one that has, indeed, popped out.

Primary Tail Boom Hydraulic Pump. That's it!

He pushes the small button-type breaker in, feeling the click and hearing the tiny whine once more as the forward panel shows the pressure rising.

Thank God!

He's steady at last, facing generally south, altitude 102,000 feet, and he thinks he can make out the Rio Grande as it defines the Texas–Mexico border around El Paso, somewhere to the southwest.

The computer map is still not showing and he attacks that problem now in frustration, searching for the right button before the map suddenly swims into view on the screen, his position clearly indicated over New Mexico.

As soon as the tail is realigned he'll be a flyable glider with only one chance at landing. He can glide miles in any direction, but where should he go? He tries the checklist as he comes through 80,000 feet, but he can't find a section on how to get the map computer to display emergency landing sites.

The tail boom transition will be at 60,000 feet, and he strains to hear the tiny whine of the hydraulic pump against the roar of the airflow.

OK, let's see . . . I'll need to know where the landing gear switch is.

It's easy—a small recessed switch on the left side of the panel. But he knows there are no speed brakes or flaps, and *Intrepid*'s speed just before landing will be close to 200 miles per hour, its stubby wings providing lift only in the most cursory way.

The altitude is coming through 60,000 now, the ship buffeting slightly, and Kip goes back to the page on tail reconfiguration. He pushes the stick forward, watching the attitude indicator for the appointed twenty-degree nose-down attitude. *There. Twenty down.*

He pushes the buttons for boom release and retraction and hears the whine increase. The nose pitches down severely as the tail aligns and he can see the indicated air-speed rising and feel, and hear, the slipstream increase.

Two green lights flash on, indicating both tail booms are locked, and he pulls hard, feeling the g-forces climb until the nose is up, and he realises he's no longer riding a spacecraft, he's flying a high-speed, heavyweight glider, and probably headed in the wrong direction. He's still too high to make out a strip of concrete a mile or two long.

He looks back down at the screen, relieved to see airfields suddenly indicated, apparently in response to the tail reconfiguration. But it's showing no airfields within the purple arc that he assumes is his gliding range.

He banks left, startled at the responsiveness of the craft. He can barely see anything through the small windows with the seat pitched back, and he slides it upright again. Then he pulls the nose up more, diminishing the descent rate and the forward air speed as he shifts his eyes to the screen.

Roswell is sixty miles to the west, and it looks like it's the only available runway. The purple circle has increased in size, and he slows more now as he brings *Intrepid* around to a western heading, hoping to expand the range circle by slowing until it includes Roswell's airport.

And finally it does! Roswell is within gliding distance.

But at what speed? He's dropping through 40,000 feet with a forward air speed of 350 miles per hour. *Slow more.*

Squeezing his memory for every ounce of his limited flying experience, he brings the nose up more, to almost twenty-degrees nose-high, watching the rate of descent decrease as he trades air speed for maintaining altitude.

At 190 she's still controllable. He'll let her slow, he figures, until the nose drops suddenly and he's in a stall, then he'll simply recover like all airplanes recover. At least he's always assumed that's how it works.

At 160 she's mushy but still flying, nose high, and suddenly he realises the descent rate has started increasing again quickly to 4,000 feet per minute even with the nose up at almost thirty degrees above the horizon.

He's read about this sort of thing, a stall in a high-speed jet with the nose up, and he feels the cold possibility that he's gone too far.

Kip shoves the control stick forward, but nothing happens. The nose remains high, the air speed languishing at 160 knots. He's falling straight down with *Intrepid*'s belly nearly horizontal, and the descent rate is over 10,000 feet per minute as he comes through 30,000, feeling fear creep again into his gut. It seems incredible that he could snatch defeat from the jaws of victory by screwing up basic flight. How damned unfair that he could come this far and still die.

A kaleidoscope of images flashes through his mind until the tail appears clear and unmistakable as the solution. The hydraulic pump keeping the tail in a horizontal position for re-entry is still on!

With a stab at the appropriate button he ports the hydraulic pressure to unlock the twin boom tail and move it to the up position, poising his finger over the opposite control switch as he feels the aerodynamics changing.

Suddenly, *Intrepid* flops forward, nose down, and Kip punches the retract button, keeping forward pressure on the stick. He sees the two green locked lights illuminate before pulling g's to raise the nose and slow the air speed.

But now he's below 20,000, and a glance at the map tells the tale. The purple glide range circle has shrunk, and Roswell is out of reach.

There is, however, a new target coloured red just to the southwest: a short runway. If he runs off the end of the concrete at a slow speed, he might survive.

He knows now to keep *Intrepid* above 200 miles per hour. He banks to the right, bringing the ship to a southerly heading, the altitude now coming through 15,000, but the rate of descent only 3,000 per minute and holding.

He sees a few towns below, and he can see roads and a few rail lines. At 11,000 feet he can see evidence of wind below, plumes of dust, when he looks closely, indicating a strong west wind.

And he can see the purple circle retracting away from the airport he's trying to reach, the edge of the circle finally passing over it.

No more airports within the circle.

Kip feels his pulse rate climbing as he searches through *Intrepid*'s windows. Empty fields everywhere. A few railroad tracks and a small number of cultivated fields, but no runways, no airports, no ribbons of concrete.

Except for the highways.

He has no choice. There will be power lines and signs—not to mention cars and trucks going one heck of a lot slower than 200 miles per hour—but he's through 8,000 feet now with nowhere else to go.

He sees a two-lane highway running east and west and turns to the east, bringing *Intrepid* around steadily and overshooting slightly, then moving left a quarter mile until he's tracking straight down the highway below and coming through 4,000 feet. There's a small rain shower off to the south, and he can see a big truck moving towards him perhaps a mile distant.

Landing gear!

He checks the air speed, holding at 210, and flips the switch for the gear. He hears a whooshing noise and several *thunks* and three green lights appear on the upper right-hand panel.

Two thousand two hundred.

At 2,300 feet he sees the truck pass safely beneath him, but another one is coming at him, and he knows even *Intrepid*'s short wingspan is too wide to fit both of them on the same two-lane road at the same time.

He drops through 1,500 feet. The rate of descent is frightening. At more than 4,000 feet per minute, it's like he's just dropping at the roadway. A normal airplane touchdown is less than 200 feet per minute.

The truck is more distinct ahead, a tanker of some sort, the gleaming metal of his tank reflecting the afternoon sun, and coming towards him. No other vehicles that Kip can see, but now, like a parade of apparitions, several more big rigs rise from the undulating heat waves over the highway.

Kip's fingers are fanning themselves on the stick controller, his eyes taking in the road, the truck and the horizon before flitting quickly to the last items on the Before Landing checklist.

Gear down and locked, seats up . . . I think that's it.

Something to the right of the roadway a mile or more away ahead catches his attention, another road or something at perhaps a forty-five-degree angle. He locks his eyes back on the highway, wondering if the oncoming truck drivers have spotted him dropping from the sky. If so, there's no indication. The big rigs are getting closer by the second.

The angled ribbon of concrete to the right looms in his mind and he focuses on it as an alternative. Whatever it is, even from a mile out he can see that it's cracked and overgrown with weeds.

But the road ahead is impossible, and Kip makes the choice without another thought. He pulls on the stick gingerly, feeling the craft respond as he settles through 500 feet. The other road seems to end barely a mile or more in the distance, like it's merging into the desert, but at least the terrain on the other end is flat. He realises it is an old runway, maybe military, and there are a few buildings along the far end.

He pulls his aim point to the right. He's at 185 now, and doesn't dare get slower before being right over the threshold of the old runway. As he turns towards the end of the old runway he rolls right slightly, feeling *Intrepid* drop more as he stops the turn.

In an instant he's yanking *Intrepid* to the right, using the rudder to help skid towards the end of the concrete ribbon, holding his breath as the truck he'd been aiming at disappears behind him. The ship aligns with the runway and he snaps it back to wings level, yanking the nose up to stop the frightening rate of descent, trying to exchange speed for lift as the threshold of the cracked and broken concrete runway moves beneath him.

He feels the air speed bleed away, unsure how far off the surface he is, amazed when the main wheels squeal onto the surface.

Suddenly, it's like trying to control a kid's tricycle accelerated to a hundred miles per hour on a bucking surface. He plops the nose-wheel on the ground only to find himself rocking left and right. He works the control stick as he fights to stop overcontrolling the nose-wheel steering, the speed less than 100 miles per hour and slowing fast.

There's a partially collapsed hangar to the right ahead and a still intact building of some sort. As he slows to seventy he sees a weed-infested taxiway leading to a ramp where two Stearman biplanes are sitting.

He gauges the broad expanse of concrete in front of the building, and as his speed drops below forty he decides to risk hitting the brakes, pressing on the top of the pedals as he steers right, bringing *Intrepid* off the runway and coasting to a halt in front of the old brick structure, kicking up a cloud of dust and dirt in the process.

And the unbelievable fact that he is once again sitting static on the surface of the Earth, still alive, begins to sink in.

7

ASA Mission Control, Mojave, California
May 21, 10.59 a.m. Pacific Time

Arleigh is losing it, Richard DiFazio thinks, but who can blame him? The telemetry all the way down told of an excruciating series of near disasters—the wrong attitude, a near fatal problem with the tail boom, and the unmistakable signature of a stalled spacecraft dropping uncontrollably towards a spot in eastern New Mexico.

And then nothing. The data stream stopped.

There are phones to both of Arleigh Kerr's ears as he tries to get more information. With the world aware that *Intrepid* has boosted out of orbit and is re-entering with an untrained Kip Dawson at the controls, the guesswork on where the spacecraft will come down has launched scores of camera crews in planes and helicopters. The moment New Mexico seemed to be the end point, an airborne armada headed in from all points of the compass.

In the meantime, a worldwide television audience too large to measure has been watching long-distance images of *Intrepid* descending, in the most widely watched global cliffhanger since *Apollo 13*.

DiFazio glances at Diana Ross, who has been progressively destroying pencils. He knows better than to ask what she thinks. She thinks what he thinks—that it will be a miracle if Kip survives.

But it's already a miracle that he figured out how to guide *Intrepid* through re-entry.

A secretary has appeared at their side with word that a car is waiting to take them to DiFazio's jet, now fuelled and waiting a quarter of a mile away.

West of Gladiola, New Mexico
May 21, 11.04 a.m. Pacific Time/12.04 p.m. Mountain Time

The quiet is overwhelming. Behind the instrument panel, gyros are still spinning and fans still running, but once he snaps off the master switch, the sound of his own breathing is startlingly loud.

Kip looks round at the plastic bag that contains Bill Campbell's body.

'At least we got you home, Bill,' he says, as reverentially as he can. And suddenly his need to be out of the tiny cabin overwhelms him.

Kip works to open the inner hatch, glancing at the brick building through the window. The stuccoed walls of the old structure are crumbling, as if the building was melting slowly back into the desert along with the rest of what had to have been a Second World War Army Air Corps field.

Intrepid's inner door swings open easily, and Kip pulls the equalisation lever to dump any remaining air pressure in the cabin before swinging the outer door open. He's still wearing Bill's space suit, without the helmet, and the trip out through the hatchway is quick. His feet land on a dusty slab of broken concrete, and he works to regain his balance, walking shakily to the edge of the slab and onto the sandy ground. His legs feel weak, strangers to gravity, and he sinks to his knees to scoop up some of the earth and let it run through his fingers. Incredible feelings of relief and deliverance course through his body. He remains on his knees looking up in the sky and letting the unfiltered light fill his eyes as he takes a deep breath of the sweetest air he's ever tasted. There is springtime in the flavour of it, oxygen-rich and redolent of life. A stiff breeze is blowing and kicking up dust, but he gratefully breathes that in as well with a huge smile as he gets to his feet at last, aware of the approach of a vehicle somewhere behind.

He looks round as an old Ford pick-up rumbles to a halt, its stocky occupant getting out carefully, as if approaching a suspected crime scene. The man, who is wearing jeans and a flannel work shirt, waves as if embarrassed, a grin on his broad, squarish face as he gives the spacecraft a thorough looking over and walks close enough to offer his hand.

'Hope you don't mind me dropping in like this,' Kip says, his voice sounding strange and unused.

The fellow is probably younger than he, Kip realises, his face tanned and deeply creased as if he's spent a lifetime on the open range. But there are laugh lines as well and the etched evidence of an easy smile.

'I saw you headin' for the runway. Man, you were smokin'.'

'I know,' Kip says, shaking the man's hand.

'What were you doing, two hundred knots on final?'

'Close. I didn't see the runway until the last minute.'

'It's kinda overgrown all right. Sometimes at dusk I can't even find the damn thing. But you did good, man! Helluva landing.'

'Thanks.'

'You do know we don't have any services here, right?'

'Sorry?'

'We don't have any gas.'

Maybe it's a delayed reaction to the greatest stress he's ever known, but Kip suddenly feels light-headed, as if whatever the man just said has been completely garbled on the way to his ears.

'This . . . runs on a different type of fuel,' Kip says, feeling idiotic.

'I'm just kidding you, Mr Dawson.'

'You . . . know my name?'

'Hell, yes! Who doesn't? I'm Jim Waters, by the way.'

Kip looks round at the ship, as if it might have disappeared. But no, it's looming behind him with the incongruity of a pink elephant in a parlour.

'I should have landed in Mojave, California,' he says.

'I know. I'm really tickled you'd pick my little duster runway. Although there was a time it was a big military field.'

'Where am I, exactly?'

The smile broadens as Jim looks down momentarily, taking his time with the best straight line he's had in ages.

'Why, this is a planet called Earth, Kip.'

'No, no . . . I know this is New Mexico, but *where* in New Mexico?'

'Oh, a few miles to the west of the tiny town of Gladiola.'

'I really need to use your phone, Jim, if you have one. To let everyone know I made it down OK. They probably have no idea where I am.'

Jim is shaking his head. 'I don't think it's going to be necessary, Kip.'

'Why not?'

'Take a look.' Jim gestures to the northwest, towards Albuquerque.

Kip follows his gaze to where something undulates on the horizon. A small air force of helicopters rises into view, racing towards them, as Jim's cellphone starts ringing in his pocket.

Air Force Clinic, Holloman Air Force Base, New Mexico
May 21, 12.30 p.m. Pacific Time/1.30 p.m. Mountain Time

Somehow, Kip thinks, the reaction of everyone he's met so far is weird.

There was all the excessive handshaking the moment the Air Force crew members tumbled out of their helicopter to prepare him for transport to the nearby base. Even stranger, the base commander met him at the door minutes ago and ushered him into this private room, where a Colonel Billingsley, the chief of the hospital, was waiting for him.

Now the doctor motions him onto an examination table and checks his vital signs, the silver-grey hair suggesting a man in his late fifties.

'Doc, when did you hear I was coming down in New Mexico?'

'Oh, not until just before you landed. Breathe deeply for me.'

Kip complies, waiting out the multiple stops of the stethoscope around his back before speaking again. 'Everyone seems so . . . engaged with this. Has there been something on television about my coming out of orbit?'

There's a knowing laugh. 'You mean, about the space walk, and your decision to try the engine?'

'My . . . *decision*?' Kip sits staring at Billingsley not comprehending. 'How . . . how on earth could you know anything I said up there?'

Colonel Billingsley laughs. 'You're kidding, right? We may be out here in the wilds of New Mexico, but we have cable, so to speak. You wrote it up there and we read it down here.'

'Wait . . . you were able to read that comment down here somehow?'

The doctor sits down carefully on a metal stool, his eyes searching Kip's face. 'Kip, hasn't anyone told you yet?'

'Told me what?'

'For the last four days, everything you wrote up there on your laptop was sent streaming back real time to a single channel monitored here on Earth.'

'WHAT? The Air Force was able to read what I wrote? How?'

'My God, Kip,' the doctor says softly, 'I had no idea you didn't know. You see, every time you punched a key up there on your laptop, that letter appeared almost instantly on television screens and computer monitors all over this planet. Billions and billions of people have been reading everything you wrote *as* you wrote it.'

'Everyone's been reading . . . *everything*?'

'Yes. And thinking very hard about a lot of what you've had to say.'

'I was just writing for myself, and . . . and . . .'

'And whoever would find that hard drive fifty years from now. I know. That's what made it so incredible. We were watching the real-time thoughts of a doomed man grappling with his fate and his life. And, I might add, a guy who utterly refused to give up. That makes you heroic in my book.'

The blood drains from Kip's face as it begins to sink in. He tries to call up a memory of everything he wrote but it's impossible, given the stream-of-consciousness that flowed through the laptop. But what he does remember is enough to curl him into a foetal ball.

Oh, my God! Sharon! The way I talked about her, and about Jerrod, and sex and everything else to the whole world! How can I face anyone again?

'They broadcast everything?'

'Every word. And people were acting on it. For instance, you talked about your employer's misconduct with that bad batch of antibiotics, and federal indictments have already been issued.'

'Against me?'

He laughs. 'No, Kip. Against the guys in your company who did what they did. Hell, you're probably not even aware someone filed your divorce for you?'

'My . . . *divorce*?'

'You wrote out the papers up there and someone printed them out down here and raced to the nearest courthouse, I think in Tucson.'

He feels the room getting a bit fuzzy. 'Doc, I feel like I'm standing buck naked in front of the whole world. You know that dream everyone has where you're suddenly out in public without clothes?'

'Hey, man. One of the greatest things about what you wrote was the glaring truth about your own feelings.'

'But . . . I mean . . . how do I deal with this? What the hell do I do now?'

'You already know, Kip. You wrote the answer. You go out there with your head held high and live for yourself, knowing you're one of the few humans on the planet who's been truly honest with himself.'

'Yeah. Honest. Any chance the government would let me disappear into the witness protection programme?'

'You've got a booming voice now, Kip. Use it well. We're all listening.'

The White House, Washington, DC
June 2

Suddenly, Geoff Shear sees that what he's walked into is an ambush.

He should have been clued in, he thinks, by the others already assembled in the Oval Office. The FBI Director, the Attorney General and the White House Chief of Staff would not normally be expected to evaluate NASA's emergency scrub of a shuttle launch.

Nothing sinister had been reported by his sources in the last few days, but the fact that Dorothy Sheehan evaporated has been scratching at him.

Now the President has entered with little more than a glance at him, and stands behind his desk. Shear feels his blood running cold.

'Geoff, you recall what you personally promised me when I took office and chose to keep you on as head of the agency?'

'Yes, Mr President.'

'I told you that, above all else, I demand two things. Honesty in communicating any disagreements or distasteful information, and complete lockstep obedience when I've made a decision.'

'Yes, sir.'

'You've violated both. Jim? Hand him the evidence.'

The FBI Director leans over and plops a manila folder in Shear's lap.

'Evidence?' Geoff feels his stomach flip-flopping.

'Yes, Geoff. From the woman you sent to sabotage the rescue mission. When you've had a look at that folder, you'll understand why I have a decision to make. One, to prosecute you to the fullest extent of federal law in what will be a slam-dunk case, and put your ass in a federal prison; or two, have you resign immediately and preserve the illusion that we know what the hell we're doing in this office.'

'Mr President—'

'Geoff, you're busted. And you're going to twist in the wind for the next forty-eight hours while I decide what to do.'

The others are already following the President from the room as a secretary appears, quietly motioning a stunned Geoff Shear to an alternative exit.

Lawn Lake, Rocky Mountain National Park, Colorado
September 8

Jerrod Dawson smiles at the symmetry of the curve in his fishing line as it describes a lazy arc through the evening air.

He lets the hand-tied fly drift past the pool he's been aiming for, and looks back at the campsite. Dad is waving at him to come in, presumably to help cook the three rainbows they pulled from the lake last evening.

He pulls in the line and wades back to the bank.

Kip is kneeling over the campfire, smoke beginning to rise into the pristine blue-black of a perfect Colorado twilight. Jerrod thinks he's never seen his father as happy and content. But then again, before the last few months, he's never really seen his father at all.

He remembers that sudden flight from Houston to the military hospital at Holloman Air Force Base, and the shock of having his father rush through a door to hug him and apologise. How could that happen, he wondered. The man wearing his father's face seemed totally changed, offering his love, and no defence against the anger Jerrod had long displayed, and no longer felt.

THE LAST ORANGE streaks of slow-yielding sunlight flaring over the ridge line of the mountains to the west are giving way to a stunning canopy of stars in a moonless sky, and Kip wonders if he noticed such subtle gradations of colour before his space flight. He glances at Jerrod, revelling in the easy way they're now communicating. Jerrod puts down his plate and studies his father's face.

'Dad, what we talked about last night? The truth is, at first, I was too scared to read everything you wrote. But about day three, I read everything. Even the embarrassing stuff.'

'The things about you, you mean?'

'Naw. That . . . I needed to see that, Dad, to have any idea how much you were hurting, to understand how much I was nursing a blind anger.'

'Then, what was embarrassing?'

'The girl stuff about your dates in high school.' He laughs. 'Way more than we need to know. I hope you apologised to those poor women.'

'I've apologised to everyone. Including that Russian crew I nearly hit when I was blasting out of orbit. They went on the rest of their mission to the space station, but I think they had to shovel out their cockpit, so to speak.'

'I heard. One other thing I've been meaning to say to you, Dad. I mean, I think you know it, but I need to just say it.'

'Go ahead.'

'I want you to be happy. You should be dating. And I don't care if the divorce from Sharon is final or not.'

'It will be, in a month.'

'Well, I just wanted you to know. Dad, I've buried Mom. At last.'

Kip studies his son's eyes, stunned that another taboo subject has been softly opened. 'So . . . should I accept one of those marriage proposals I'm getting daily from desperate women all over the globe?'

Jerrod laughs. 'Yeah, at random, Dad. That would be real smart. Man, I can't believe those women. Who's answering them for you?'

'Diana Ross, I think. Or a secretary.'

'By the way, she likes you a lot. And I think she's cool, too.'

Kip nods. He's thinking about the awkward visit from Diana a few hours after his landing. The trip from obscure contest winner to perhaps the most famous living human on Earth scared the hell out of him, and it had been calming to hear her voice down the corridor and see her swing in the door and look so relieved, actually hugging him and hanging on. Kip marked it off to raw emotion and the intensity of the moment, but in the months since, she's become the scheduler for the media demands for his time, and their phone calls and meetings have grown constant.

'You going to write that book? Have they finalised the contract?'

'I have to. No, wrong answer. I *want* to. That and the fact that I need the money, now that I've quit selling pharmaceuticals.'

'So, what are you planning after that?'

'The same thing I want you to do, son. Something I didn't know how to do. I'm planning to appreciate every minute of this life.'

Grand Central Station, New York City
October 18

Kip finds a phone booth in the grand old railway station to reach her phone in California.

'So, what are you up to?'

Diana's laugh is like music, especially when she's feigning stress.

'Drowning, I am, in the process of setting up the next Internet contest.'

'How many this time?'

'Four winners.'

'And let me guess, this time ASA is guaranteeing at least four days of stark terror for each one while the world watches?'

'Well . . . I did take one of your ideas. They get their own laptop while on orbit and can type directly into their own website during the flight. Of course, we just can't guarantee a two-billion-strong audience like you got . . .'

'Lucky me.'

There is a moment of silence.

'You said in your text message you had something serious and professional to ask me?' Diana says.

'I do. But first I want to know when I'm going to see you again.'

'I get a lot of offers, too, Mr Dawson, thanks to everything you wrote about me.' She pauses. 'How about this evening?'

'Diana, I'm in New York.'

'I know. So am I.'

'*Really*? Where?'

'Turn around.'

The grin on her face as Kip realises she's standing right behind him is infectious, and he pulls her to him for a hug that becomes a tentative kiss.

'How did you . . .?'

'I followed you from the publisher's office. You know, jumped in a taxi and had fun saying, "Follow that cab!"'

'This is great.'

'But . . . ' she says, holding him back. 'I need to know what that important professional question is you were so hot for me to answer.'

'It's a serious one.'

'OK.'

'I mean, considering all I went through up there.'

'Uh-huh.'

'And because I've been your poster boy ever since.'

'You've done very well for us, Kip, especially considering the various ways we tried to kill you.'

'I'm glad you appreciate the danger I was in.'

'I do. *We* do. So, what's the question?'

He glances skyward, then back to her, eye to eye.

'When can I go up again?'

JOHN J. NANCE

Place of birth: Texas
Favourite author: James Michener
Website: www.johnjnance.com

John Nance has been called a renaissance man and, given the extent of his achievements and interests, it's easy to see why. He is a well-known broadcaster, internationally recognised air safety analyst, former airline pilot, lawyer and sought-after public speaker. In addition, although he is now retired from the Air Force, he still holds the position of lieutenant colonel in the USAF Reserve. Above all, Nance has made a name for himself in America as the author of chillingly realistic airline thrillers such as *Blackout* and *Skyhook*. Thirty years and 13,000 hours of flight time as a pilot, as well as his experiences as a decorated veteran of Vietnam and Operations Desert Storm and Desert Shield, lend his books an unequalled credibility, and readers love them partly because they can rely on Nance to intelligently explore very real, current issues.

His extensive experience has also been put to good use in his work as an aviation analyst on ABC News in the States and he is often called upon by the media to give an informed opinion. When the World Trade Center was attacked by terrorists in New York, for example, it was Nance who went on the Oprah show to discuss the aircraft-related issues raised by that terrible event.

His enthusiasm for the marvels of engineering produced by today's aircraft industry is contagious and he refers to flying as the greatest technological achievement in human history. 'I know some people would tend to say, "Now, wait a minute, our greatest achievement is cracking the atom or coming up with this advance or that advance," he remarks. 'But when you stop and consider the fact that within a hundred years we have gone from non-powered flight to making air transportation literally routine—basically buses with wings flying all over the world in which we carry millions and millions of passengers every year—it is virtually incredible. To me that is one of *the* greatest success stories.'

He also points out that, because of continual improvements to flight technology in the last few decades, it has become a very safe way to travel. 'There is no question that flying in a commercial environment is safer than taking any other form of transportation, including pretty much walking through your own house. More people are killed in bathtubs every year than in commercial crashes. Even if you tried to get into an airplane accident as a passenger, you would probably have to take flights for the next four thousand years before you would have a solid statistical chance of trouble.'

Having said all that, making airlines even safer is one of Nance's passions. He hasn't personally experienced very many crises while flying. One exception was when he was on a book tour in the States and an electrical fire sent smoke into the cockpit and one of the windshields shattered. 'I had to declare an emergency on an airplane for the first time in my life. It nearly killed us. If I hadn't had a lot of pilot time I could have blown my approach because of nerves. That's what happens to a lot of private pilots.' Luckily, Nance was able to make an emergency landing at a nearby airport.

It's great to hear from an expert that the next time you board a jet you should do so in total confidence. The editors of Select Editions would only advise their readers not to read a John J. Nance book while waiting for takeoff!

INTO THE GREAT BLUE YONDER

Space tourism seemed, for a long time, like a futuristic dream. Now, for a very few lucky and wealthy individuals, it has become reality. The first private individual to undertake the journey into space was American businessman Dennis Tito. In 2001, at a personal cost of $20 million, he travelled on board the Russian spacecraft *Soyuz* to the International Space Station, which orbits the Earth. Since then, two more men have joined the select band of space tourists.

Currently the race is underway to make space tourism cheaper and more accessible. Richard Branson's company Virgin Galactic is working towards sending space-craft carrying passengers into the suborbital area of the atmosphere—that's just below the point where the Earth's atmosphere ends and space begins, about 100 kilometres up.

Prices are expected to fall dramatically, and many people, including celebrities such as Morgan Freeman, William Shattner and Sigourney Weaver have already signed up for the experience.

UNDER ORDERS © Dick Francis, 2006
Published by Michael Joseph

THE HUSBAND © Dean Koontz 2006
Published by HarperCollins

SCARED TO LIVE © Stephen Booth 2006
Published by HarperColliins

ORBIT © 2006 by John J. Nance
Published by Simon & Schuster Inc, USA

The right to be identified as authors has been asserted by the following in accordance with sections 77 and 78 of the Copyright, Designs and Patents Act, 1988: Dick Francis, Dean Koontz, Stephen Booth, John J. Nance.

Illustrations and Photos:
Page 4: www.tonyyu.com.hk; page 5: Dean Koontz © Jerry Bauer; Stephen Booth © Julie Dawn Thomas; John J. Nance © Patricia Davenport.
Under Orders: 6–8: Illustrator: Claire Rankin; image: imagebank; page 149: RUS/JDP Reuters/Action Images.
The Husband: 150–2: image: stone+; pages 290–1 © Jerry Bauer.
Scared to Live: 292–4: images: iStock; page 454: © Julie Dawn Thomas; page 455: Matlock Bath: Robert Morris/Alamy.
Orbit: 456–8: illustrator: Curtis Phillips-Cozier; images: Taxi/imagebank; page 574 © Patricia Davenport; 575: Soyuz spacecraft: Action Press/Rex Features.
Dustjacket spine: imagebank.

Printed and bound by GGP Media GmbH, Pössneck, Germany

244/06